The Destiny Changer

Farley Dunn

THREE SKILLET

THE DESTINY CHANGER, Dunn, Farley L

First Edition

Beware the Angels, Book 1

 THREE SKILLET

www.ThreeSkilletPublishing.com

Cover design by Farley L Dunn

ISBN: 978-1-943189-12-0

Chapter 1

Ramiel, Herald of Hope

"Uriel!"

The call thundered across the blackness of deepest space, and there was no reply, and that was not as it should be. In the distance, Earth shone a blue and green jewel. A quarter moon shimmered like pale silk off to one side, and behind it stretched the enormity of the Universe, a backdrop of smooth velvet sprinkled with gems. On the opposite side, not quite twin suns glared with incandescent fury, one a familiar yellow, and the other shimmering with the white-hot of fusion resonance.

"Uriel!"

The call reverberated once again as Ramiel darkened in rage. Uriel would soon know his wrath. He would see to that. A flickering ball of brilliance appeared at his fingertips, and it pulsed with power, barely contained. His incorporeal hand shifted, and the ball of light crackled, shooting out tendrils of flaming violence for hundreds of miles, and that was as it should be.

Still, there was no response, and Ramiel's eyes flashed. The blazing light of the stars in the distance shuddered with his rage, and the icy chill of the cosmos withdrew from his presence, as if attempting to hide.

"Uriel!"

He called a third time, this time drawing enormous quantities of power from the vast engines of the Unity. The power channeled itself through the Seat, accompanied by a deep-throated hum. The chair blinked out of existence for a moment before reappearing, shifting just for an instant against the fabric of space and time. The sound of Ramiel's voice rang like a thousand thunderbolts throughout the emptiness, magnified by the Seat. Uriel must attend!

This time space directly in front of him bent, and with a violent cleaving of the blackness, a Place of Power exploded with an eruption of inconceivable energy. Then it faded and was gone. Uriel stood before Ramiel, even though to corporeal eyes, the blackness of space was as empty as it had been moments before.

Then a second flicker in the blackness punched a hole in the fabric of space. Uriel's ever-present familiar appeared at his side. The arrival of the familiar was a discordant and very bold note of defiance, and Ramiel read it as such.

"I have done nothing to warrant being cast out. Yet, here I stand at the Seat of Power, and Earth lies in the distance. Why do you do this to me?"

Ramiel laughed. "Be prepared to Traverse, Uriel. I know your truest failing. Once a traitor, always a traitor."

"A traitor, because I would return power to the Mind?" Uriel gave his own laugh of contempt. "I would attempt to do so again."

"The Mind is our slave now. He will never be free again." Ramiel's unseen fingers moved, and the ball of light quivered, darkening on one side as an opening appeared, and his knife-edged laughter rang out once again.

Uriel, Bearer of Destiny

"I will be cold, Ramiel. The Triune Mind is remembered warmth." He might earn a reprieve even yet, if he pretended to

6

be contrite.

"The Triune Mind has betrayed the brothers. You must accept that." Ramiel's words were bitterly harsh.

Brothers! Uriel remembered, as did everyone, awaking in the Unity's latest incarnation, and the horrific knowledge that all in the Unity had become male. Then the news was made worse, for at the sub-atomic level, the Unity and this dimension were incompatible. Only the polarity reversal caused by contact with matter from this dimension—atmospheric disharmony—allowed the brothers' incorporeal bodies to become corporeal. To maintain those bodies, energy consumption was prodigious. No brother on Earth could stay warm.

Uriel hated the cold so very much.

Behind Ramiel space bent and exploded violently. "Wings, Uriel!" Glowing brightly, the sign of great power, a new brother stood next to the Seat, and this brother pulsed with energy.

"Archangel!" Uriel rose, growing in stature. Gabriel, known as the Citadel of Justice and Power, had stood on the Triune Mind's side, as had Uriel. He also remembered that they were not allies. They had since taken different paths.

Even so, once . . . once.

For many eons they had been friends and more, or as much more as *brothers* could be. In other incarnations, as other genders, they had been even closer. The two were inexorably drawn together.

"Not now, Gabriel!" Ramiel's command split the blackness, leaving glittering remnants of icy anger in its wake.

"Yes, *now*—" Gabriel began, his presence growing against the background blanket of stars.

"Stop! I command you!" Ramiel's voice sent thunder rolling across the blackness. "The passage is already prepared for this one." Each time he spoke, the growing ball of light at his side quivered, responding to his every movement.

"A few moments for an old friend? They are mine to share." They stood outside the Unity, and the sense of time flowed the speed an Archangel wished, a day equaling a thousand years, and a thousand years a day, if the Archangel so desired.

7

At Ramiel's reluctant nod, Gabriel smiled and turned to Uriel. "Uriel, remember your Mandate. You must find each human's Destiny and lead each one forward, if you wish to be allowed to return." His words were warm and hopeful.

Uriel's response was not.

"All of them? Alone?" *At one time you would have chosen to follow me to that blue and green globe. No longer.* That burned deeply, and anger sapped his better judgment. "Take my place, *Archangel.* Or better yet, come with me!" His eyes softened just for a moment in hope as he looked into his old friend's eyes.

"I cannot, Uriel."

Uriel knew better. It had been done before.

"I once loved you, Brother," Gabriel continued more softly. "I would love you again, given the chance." He reached out in a token of repeated well-wishing. "Your wings. Remember your wings, Uriel."

Then, Ramiel's anger tore them apart.

Ramiel, Herald of Hope

"Enough!" Ramiel's patience was gone, and he laughed as Uriel fell to his knees. "You've had your say, Archangel. Your Triune Mind is no longer the supreme power here. Let me be about my business."

"Hope? You offer hope to Uriel? That is your assigned role, Ramiel, although the hope you give escapes me."

"I remember another Mandate also, one you would be wise to heed. I am also the one who will guide Uriel back to the Unity, if his sojourn on Earth is successful. For that reason, I expect to be treated with greater respect."

Gabriel's words lanced out in a white-hot torrent, "Stand aside, Brother! I will not ask again." Gabriel turned to Uriel. "Strength is mine to give. It is yours, old friend." A glistening *otherness* appeared in the space between them, quickly settling

8

around Uriel, and it seemed as if Uriel physically expanded against the barrenness of the surrounding blackness. Gabriel continued, "May you also find nourishment to fuel your undertakings upon Earth, and without delay."

Renewed anger consumed Ramiel, and his new-found levels of fury dimmed the radiance of the nearby sun. The Seat of Power was his, and not even Gabriel could deny him that. The Seat hummed with the massive power drain as Ramiel raised his hands above his head, and with a resounding reverberation, he clapped them together. The ball of light at his side shattered, the glittering shards lancing through the darkness. When finally it coalesced once again, only Ramiel and Gabriel were left looking over the two suns hanging above the glittering Earth. With a second clap of his hands, the ball of light streaked earthward, elongating into a thin pencil of white-hot energy.

"It hurts when the lightship comes to a stop," Gabriel mused.

"Why did you come, Gabriel?" Ramiel eased back into the Seat of Power. He glared at the Archangel. He dared not do more, though.

"Uriel is an old friend." Gabriel paused, reaching to touch the Seat of Power.

"Hands off," Ramiel snarled. "The Seat was once yours to occupy, but you lost this. Not everyone calls you Archangel anymore."

"Easy, Ramiel." Gabriel's tone was even, and his words were soft, but the steel was back. "The Seat might be mine no longer, yet my power is undiminished."

Ramiel's eyes narrowed. "Just stay away from it."

Then, in a shimmer of nothingness, the blackness of space bending once more in the oddest way, the chair was vacant, and Gabriel stood alone.

He smiled, and then he was also gone, the void twisting for a moment, leaving the surrounding space as it had been all along, empty and black, with only Earth, its single satellite, and the twin suns overhead to fill the darkness.

Uriel, Bearer of Destiny

In a flash of incandescence—lightning to any human who happened to be watching—Uriel's lightship detonated in an implosion of luminescence just after it hit the atmosphere, leaving him falling unsupported—backwards!—from the heavens directly toward Earth.

"Dear Unity above!" Uriel screamed his curse. "Trade places with me, Gabriel," he bellowed, but the words were torn from his lips even as he spoke.

Remember his wings? He needed to be fully corporeal to deploy. The chill of the approaching world meant his body was firming up as the disharmony of his native dimension resonated with the atmospheric particles of this one. Glancing down at his limbs, the familiar glow had begun. He also noticed the genitalia between his legs and remembered the need to cover those parts as quickly as he could find clothing. He clapped his hands briskly together, and in a tumultuous flash of billowing light, wide feathery wings appeared at his back.

Crying out with the enormous effort, he rotated his torso until he faced forward, and he threw his wings wide. Gravity grasped his sturdy frame, yanking him earthward, leaving his torso and legs angled toward the ground. The body he assumed in his corporeal form was not Gabriel's slender, streamlined sleekness. It was all muscular power, and right then, its heaviness punched through the sky. His wings wrestled with the buffeting atmosphere, their surfaces vibrating as the wind ripped past their exterior edges, and ever so slowly, his descent slowed.

It was good that it did, too. The ground had been arriving too quickly for comfort. He could see streetlights, and that concerned him. Once, a night landing would have been considered safe, the cover of darkness giving the brothers time to locate sufficiently concealing bodily coverings. Now, everything was electrified, brilliantly lit even at midnight, and compromises had to be made. Being freshly corporeal, he would not be able to fade fully. In the event people were in the vicinity, a cemetery or a church was a good option for concealment. He could wrap himself with his wings for some time, disguising himself as a stone statue until either the area was clear or his body reached Equilibrium, allowing him to fade from sight.

He was falling toward a brightly lighted convenience store. Cars were strewn about, one pulling into the fueling bay. As he began to beat his wings, slowing his descent even more, his eyes searched the scene for other options. A nearby park was darkened and available. He dismissed that possibility at once. It would surely have trees, and branches could hurt. Pain didn't interest him. Warmth did, and he was glad he could see no snow falling. He hoped he had come during summer, hot, hot, glorious summer. Landing freshly corporeal and unadorned in a snowstorm was not his favored method of verifying his value to the Unity of Being. He—and all the brothers—preferred the furnace blast of the midday sun.

His eyes caught the flickering of red off to the side, and he knew a rush of relief. Flames, the most desirable sort of warmth. The faint wail of sirens told him it must be a structure fire. His heart quickened at the prospect of unlimited heat. Plus, in the midst of all the confusion around a structure fire, who would notice one freshly corporeal being that was clearly and distinctly from out of this world?

Drawing close to the ever-brighter flames, he began to luxuriate in their perceived warmth. Shifting his weight, he saw a large fire truck squeal to a stop. It disgorged numerous men dressed in burly fire-fighting equipment, and a ladder began to extend toward a second-story window. Then, in a blazing cascade of sparks, one corner of the roof crashed in, and flames leaped toward the sky.

"Heat," he breathed expectantly. He aimed directly for the roar of the flames.

He slipped through feet first, his skin shifting in color, and glowing red in the midst of the inviting incandescence. Hitting the floor, he dropped into an easy crouch, looking around with a grin. What luck! The wood under his feet was still solid, and several walls were even intact. He was in a bedroom, it seemed, although the furniture was already charred to barely-recognizable contours. He must find another room. With the intensity of this fire, the flames would not provide a screen for long.

Hitting a charred door with his shoulder, he stumbled into a hallway, wincing at the very real pain in his side. Newly corporeal, he felt pain—as well as pleasure—more intensely than he would at any other time. As soon as he found clothes, food was his next goal. Once he had plenty of nourishment, such inconveniences as charred doors—and other physical barriers—would be things of the past. For now, though, doors, even charred ones, were meant to be used.

The smoke had blackened the walls, but out of the bedroom, the damage was less severe. Grasping the knob of a door across the hall, he heard the wail of a human child from the other side. Rescuing a human child would ensure the favor of the Unity of Being. When Ramiel viewed the Records, he would see that Uriel had done well, fulfilling his Destiny as expected. To return to the Unity, Ramiel held all the keys, and Ramiel unlocked all the doors. If there were truly a child to be saved, then Uriel must be the one to rise to the task.

There was a deeper level to his decision to help the child, though. What had Gabriel said? *Remember your Mandate.* Uriel was the Bearer of Destiny, and all humans had that, a Destiny. The saving of the child was as compelling as his need for warmth.

He hit the door again and again, determined to attempt rescue, despite shards of pain lancing through his shoulder. He flung his muscular frame against the wood with all his strength. With a thud, the door flew back against the wall, sending a shower of sparks from the adjoining surface into the room.

There, underneath a window, with the sash opened just enough to let a steady stream of clear air inside, was a baby's crib. Even so, the infant would not live for long, not if it didn't find escape from this house. He was the child's only chance.

Watch, Ramiel, he sent skyward. *This is my first good deed, and I've just arrived.*

Still, even to rescue a baby, a man must have clothing of a

sort, and he *would* appear to be a man as soon as his wings were gone. Stepping to the crib, he glanced at the infant inside. The baby squealed in delight. He brushed the child's face, the barest touch of its human flesh washing overpowering sensations over him. He also felt the building repulsion of the sub-atomic polarization fields that, like similar poles of hand-held magnets, would soon keep them from touching at all. The atomic structure of this universe excited his race's sub-atomic matrix, and like two magnets, it had proven impossible to tear the two dimensions apart. The closer to Equilibrium he became, the harder it would be to touch a human at all. The natural stabilization of his atomic structure would force the poles of his internal matrix to reverse directions, and Equilibrium would be complete.

So many times he had wished it weren't so.

He turned and hunted for clothing. He snatched at a pale, woven coverlet lying on a nearby chair and wrapped it around his hips, tucking it in securely at his waist. "Not quite modest," he grumbled, "but it'll have to do." Reaching inside the crib, he pulled the infant to his chest and brushed his face against its downy hair. A thrill ran down his spine. It was the taste of cinnamon, and also of frankincense and myrrh. All humans were like this . . . when he could touch them.

Yet, this infant must be protected, if he wanted to earn his passage back into the Unity. He flexed his powerful shoulder muscles, and in a great sweep of superheated air, his wings unfolded and wrapped themselves around his body, insulating both him and the infant from the flames. Uriel was instantly cold, but he felt the baby snuggle next to him, seeking the scant warmth of his nonhuman skin.

Flames were already licking into the baby's room, and as he stepped through the doorway into the hall, he paused in apprehension. His feet were standing in a hell that had not been there just moments before. At the end of the hall was a stair landing. He began to run that direction. He heard a flaming timber fall just behind him, then he leaped back as another crashed just where he had planned to place his foot. Hearing the sizzle of superheated moisture, he glanced up to see open sky above.

Water had begun to rain down over the house, but he accepted it as too little too late. He must make a break for it, exposure or not.

Leaping over the burning timber at his feet, he placed his feet on treads that were already aflame. He tucked his wings tightly as he bounded down the steps two at a time. He could see through the opening where the home's double doors had been broken down by the firefighters. Flames licked a wall just behind his head, and he paused to bask in its red, flickering embrace. At the same time, he could smell the coolness that rushed at him from the gap just ahead. He stroked the baby's skin, basking in the sensation of cinnamon and myrrh filling his pores.

Hearing shouts of alarm, he saw four firemen, burly with their full complement of gear, standing just outside and looking his way. One fireman fought with the end of a huge nozzle, directing it into the flames. The others helped him out, one carrying an ax in his hand.

He had waited too long, afraid to move quickly and decisively. Still, men were impressionable, and they would see what they must. With only a "Suggestion," he could take care of that.

Kneeling, he bowed his head to protect the small creature he held from the burning wall at his back. Flexing his shoulders, he let the great feathered wings that had provided life-giving insulation to the infant unveil themselves in a grand sweep of motion. With the brush of luminescent wingtips against the room's charred surfaces, glowing sparks burst from within the burned walls at his back and flashed through the air, forming glittering fireflies. For a moment he paused, his wings fully extended, still holding the babe in his arms, with his head bowed in a shielding gesture.

He could now dispense with his wings, becoming a man in appearance, blending in seamlessly with the humans before him. Placing the small bundle in his lap, he lifted his hands, palms raised, readying them to come together, so that he could hand the child to one of the human benefactors waiting just outside.

Fire Fighters, Engine No. 4

A hush fell on the four watching firemen. Beyond a doubt no one could survive inside that raging firestorm. The entire structure was engulfed, and it was falling down as they fought the flames for control. As they watched, the mysterious angel balanced a package on one knee, and with a clap of its hands and a great flash of rolling, blinding light, its wings were gone. Only a man remained. It was only when the man—or the angel, rather—stood that they could see what it held. It was a child, the very one they'd hoped to save and had already accepted as lost.

Then the angel, for they were convinced it could be nothing else, stepped forward, and with a nod, handed the infant to one of the firefighters. The angel smiled, its glowing aura clear against the red of the fiery furnace. To the men's amazement, before their very eyes, the man—the angel, rather—stepped back to the flames, shimmered for a moment, faded, and was gone.

Their responses were very different. Two of the men crossed themselves, a sheen of moisture appearing in their eyes. The man holding the hose fainted dead away, the nozzle flinging itself free and dancing an ecstatic two-step across the ground.

The man holding the baby looked at the child, unable to tear his eyes away. She was his goddaughter and great-niece, and he could tell the child's parents their baby was saved.

Uriel, Bearer of Destiny

"Pleased with yourself, Uriel?"

He glanced up, looking for the unseen voice, immediately angered. Yet, corporeal eyes would see corporeal flesh, for Uriel desired it so. He simply had to locate the speaker first.

"Maalik, is that you?" He spit the words, an accusation against the silence. He named a brother often called the

Guardian of Hell. At the ensuing silence, he considered, *If not Maalik, then who?*

"Israfel?" Uriel named a reprobate beyond all reprobates, and his insult sliced the air, a knife dividing the redness of the flames. That dark one's mission was to signal the end, and this destruction would be like him.

Rotating in a complete circle, opening his arms wide, he yelled, "Chayot HaKodesh! Show yourself! You who are known as the Holy Beast, are you afraid of being seen? Surely it is you, for who else would create such destruction and remain to exult in the aftermath?"

"Afraid? I have not run. Rather, I wish to be found." The words danced in mirth. A noise exploded to the side, and sparks and embers flew wildly as the staircase crashed to the floor. Laughter ensued, embodied in a ghostly wavering in the flames. "Come up, Uriel. Enjoy the warmth with your *brother*."

Uriel narrowed his eyes, and the form became more distinct. Then, he clapped his hands together violently. In a brilliant flash of roiling light, his majestic wings once again opened at his back. He knelt in a quick movement and thrust himself into the air, his wings launching him easily to the second floor landing. Another angry clap of his hands, and in a secondary flash of brilliance, the wings were gone.

"My unseen companion is my brother? One who will not show himself? I think not." Any *brother* of Uriel's would have saved the child and then made himself known.

"I give, *Brother*, and will hide no longer. Welcome to my display of magnificence." The distortion within the flames coalesced into a solid, wingless human form, and an arm swept wide, indicating all around them.

The words irritated Uriel, both for their taunting as well as the fact they had to be spoken aloud. One who was a brother and a friend would simply *think* the words, and they would be *known.*

The man turned and walked down the hallway towards the room where the baby had lain. Stepping over several fallen beams, more than one still ablaze, he paused at the bedroom door, turning to motion Uriel along.

"Come, friend Uriel."

Still spoken. He now recognized this brother. It *would* be Kafziel, the Emissary of Solitude and Tears. He knew this one, and too well. It had been a long time since he'd been a part of the Unity. This was no coincidence, Kafziel here in this place at this time.

Following Kafziel into the room, he paused, seeing the brother standing at the empty crib, the sides now aflame with heat and light. The small mattress smoked. He watched Kafziel reach a hand and rock the tortured bed.

"So, Kafziel." He took a step closer. "What?"

Kafziel turned his head to look directly at him. "The warmth." He inhaled a deep breath and released it in obvious pleasure. "Not since we Encapsulated the Triune Mind have I felt such warmth. See?" He pointed to the open window. "I saved the child for you. I knew you were coming."

Kafziel had tricked him into rescuing the child! He had known he would see it as an opportunity he could not resist. "Lucifer!" he spat, the use of the vile name intended as an invective of the worst sort. The memory of the brother once called the Illuminator of Light was a raw wound for many of the Unity. "I should have known as soon as I saw the flames. It was all too convenient."

"Lucifer?" Kafziel rubbed his hand down one charred wall. "You honor me, Uriel. Your friend, Lucifer, has not been seen for quite some time, although I have seemed to do quite well in his place. Has he perhaps gone *deeper?*"

Below ground, Uriel knew he meant. Those who remained long from the Unity required protection—as well as warmth. Both could be best found deep underneath the earth's crust.

Kafziel stepped away as a support on the crib finally burned through, and it collapsed to the floor. The mattress burst into flames as it came to rest, and one side of Kafziel's body brightened with the newly intense light.

"Kafziel," Uriel warned. "My patience grows thin."

"Ah!" Kafziel moaned in ecstasy as he extended an arm to a burning wall, running one hand through the flames. "Your mention of Lucifer brings to mind how he craves the heat even more than most. More than me, for sure, and I am always chilled." He stepped to stand against the window, the glass now blackened from the smoke. The spinning lights from the fire trucks flashed across the building. Something in another part of the house crashed through to the ground floor, and the building shifted under their feet. Firemen could be heard yelling to one another, that they were withdrawing from the fight, and concentrating on containment only.

"You have me here." Uriel crossed his arms. "Stop the charade. What do you want? If nothing more than to show me this, then I am gone."

"Come with me, unless you doubt yourself, Bearer of Destiny. You have one yourself, you know. Surely you can direct your own, even as you drive those around you." Kafziel turned to smirk at him. "You will find what I have to offer very interesting." Then he shimmered and stepped directly through the wall. A great flash of light through the blackened window followed by the beat of powerful wings told Uriel he was gone.

Uriel ran at the wall. With a flicker, he was through the plaster and brick; and tumbling into the open air, he clapped his hands sharply. The brilliant light of corporeal energy transference flashed around him, and his feathery appendages unfurled into the smoky air. With a flex of his torso, his wings bit into the night, and he was aloft.

"Interesting," Uriel spat under his breath. "I am not interested at all." His great expanse of wings pushed the air aside. He followed a trail only he could sense. The errant brother's flight had disrupted the corporeal structure of the air, tearing at the fabric of the surrounding atoms. He'd altered their internal bonds, and any brother could sense that. The atoms would eventually repair themselves, and the trail would be gone. For now, though, the night sky held a luminescent conduit of broken bread crumbs, and at the end, Uriel would find the fool for whom he searched.

"Interesting!" he spat once again. He had no interest in anything Kafziel had to show him. None at all.

Chapter 2

Gadreel, Deliverer of Destruction

Gadreel, the highest authority in the Unity, wielding a Mandate to show men the Blows of Death, and who had been the one sent to deceive Eve, the mother of all mankind, strode down a corridor. It was less a corridor than a set of spatial coordinates, an unoccupied area connecting two places with assigned functions.

One of those assigned functions was the Secondary Forces Chamber, not really a chamber in the literal sense, but a specific location in space where the Triune Mind was Encapsulated. At the opposite end of the "corridor" Gadreel searched for Chitar and Gupat, the Recorders of the Deeds of Man.

There was a reason Gadreel was Mandated to show men the Blows of Death. To deceive Eve, he had assumed a dimensional interface from a previous incarnation, a Ladon, a serpent-like dragon humans often mistook for snakes. It was a form he'd also used later with the Greeks, when in the Garden of the Hesperides, he was assigned to guard a tree of Golden Apples. He'd gloried in his duties on each occasion. Gadreel's anger, when it burned, burned hot.

"Chitar!" The name thundered in the blackness. "Gupat!"

Even louder, the second name rang out.

There was no response, and something else caught his attention. Far below on Earth, on the lush Florida peninsula, a great tower of flame punctuated the night. After some extended moments, the fire burned brighter and sharper, soon breaking free from the bonds of the blue and green world, and climbing into the blackness overhead. The object approached and passed directly through the empty space occupied by Gadreel and his very insubstantial corridor. Gadreel picked up the ones and zeros of human digital technology, as they dopplered past.

"Time on the clock is 21:10."

"Confirmed and marked. Any streaks up there?"

"Just that idiot you guys sent up here with me. Jim's moving his hands in front of the view port."

"That's interesting to know, Chet. You're going to like this. All lights green across the board. Good luck on your trip to Io."

Then it was gone. Gadreel dismissed the annoyance, bellowing, "Chitar!" The stars seemed to flicker under the onslaught of his anger.

In a violent flash of twisting space, Chitar appeared fully before him, meek and subservient.

"Gupat, attend!" The second name rang out, and from out of the void, space twisted once again, and Gupat also appeared, prostrate as he spoke his buttery soliloquies.

"Glorious and Holy Gadreel. How may we assist you?" Gupat cleared his throat.

Gadreel smiled. It was well that these two appeared contrite, for Chitar and Gupat had been devout followers of the Triune Mind who had found themselves on the losing side. Thankfully, their services were still needed, and for that reason, they had been kept around.

"I must review the Deeds of Man. You have recorded them faithfully?"

"Oh, most faithfully, Holy Gadreel." Incorporeal motions with incorporeal hands invited him to enter the Chamber of Deeds. As the three moved forward, the Forces holding the Chamber in place flexed, then gave. The Energy Nodes kept the Chamber eminently stable, though. None of the brothers

20

expected any less, for without the trustworthy Nodes, all accumulated Records would be lost. No information had ever been lost, so it followed that none ever would.

"I wish to observe a matter of importance." Gadreel stepped forward.

"Specifically?" Gupat grunted his question sourly. When Gadreel turned his way with a darkening expression, the brother cowered, rephrasing his request. "To which event do you refer, Eminent Gadreel? All the Events of Man have been faithfully recorded. Please state your most specific request."

"A recent conflagration. Very large. A child was saved." Pleased with Gupat's humility, Gadreel smiled.

"As you wish, Mighty Lord." Chitar chittered his pleasure. He reached a hand, and a disturbance appeared in the blackness. A series of scenes flashed rapidly across the disturbance, many of them filled with raging infernos. His hand moved back and forth, narrowing the visible choices, and eventually only three remained. He flipped between the three, and he turned to Gadreel with a bow.

Gupat stepped up. "We can narrow the choices further. What more can you tell us, Lord Gadreel? Or, do you wish to view all three?"

Gadreel watched the images. "Uriel was there," he offered.

Chitar's face beamed. He flicked the images, and then only one remained.

"Show it to me." Gadreel was eager to validate numerous suspicions. He could be certain if Uriel were in the image. Then there was the earthbound brother, a traitor if ever there was one. If Kafziel were involved, as he now suspected, then there was no end to the trouble that might be brewing, even if some claimed that a Watcher could cause no lasting harm.

If these Records showed what he expected, a new agenda would need to be set, and quickly.

Within Chitar's disturbance floating in the blackness, a scene of a burning house flickered into motion. At first the flames were small and could have perhaps been easily contained. Yet, they advanced through the structure rapidly, much more quickly than seemed possible. A man could be seen

21

running from the flames, while dragging a woman after him. She appeared to be fighting him, screaming and pointing back toward the house.

"Sound?" Gadreel motioned to the image. "I wish to hear the woman's complaints."

Chitar touched the image, and a frantic voice could be heard.

"Cristian! Angelina! She's in her crib at the top of the stairs. You must let me go to her."

"It's too late, Lucita. Would you both die?"

Gadreel motioned, and Chitar's hand silenced the voices. The flames continued to crawl over the house until something at the back corner caught his eye.

"There. Enlarge and replay." His finger pointed to the spot he wished to see.

The scene flickered in reverse, the shadows jumping oddly, and something withdrew from the house. In the image, the flames seemed suspiciously hungry.

Then, with the brush of Chitar's touch, the picture once again crawled forward, the scene jerking in an exaggerated slow-motion display. With feathered wings tucked at his back, an angel—a brother, obviously—appeared out of nowhere. Gadreel made a small motion, and Chitar's finger shifted. The image froze. Another shift of incorporeal digits, and the view of the head displayed before them rotated to reveal the face.

Gadreel spun away. The face was Uriel's. Kafziel, traitor, had conspired to draw the Bearer of Destiny to his side. It could be nothing else. Gadreel had not believed this was possible. Kafziel was merely a Watcher, never a Doer. He was the Emissary of Solitude and Tears, and alone, he had little power.

He could connive, though, and it seemed he had. That was the only possible conclusion to be gleaned from this data, and if Kafziel's hands were found directly manipulating these events, it was surely a bid to gain access to Uriel's power, claiming it as his own.

He turned back to Chitar and motioned for him to continue, to see Kafziel tumble through the wall of the burning home, his wings appearing in a brilliant discharge of corporeal disharmony energy transference. Gadreel's jaw tensed. There was no doubt at all, now.

Without further words, the space Gadreel occupied bent oddly, flickered, and he was gone. He didn't even express his gratitude to the two brothers who had been so very helpful in his quest.

From the expressions on their faces, they didn't mind one bit.

Uriel, Bearer of Destiny

Uriel's muscular frame was built for short, powerful bursts of speed, rather than the long strides of Kafziel's slender endurance machine, and he threw his strength arduously into each wingbeat, chasing a trail of corporeal atoms, shattered at Kafziel's passing, that led him along the path he must follow. As he forged ahead, the breadcrumbs grew brighter, and he grunted with satisfaction.

Then, with no warning, the trail was gone. Slowing in mid-flight, the momentum of his forward thrust forcing him to throw out his massive wings as a brake to bleed off speed, he hovered. He could only do this for a few moments, no matter how much he desired, for his torso would exhaust quickly.

"Curse you, Kafziel," he muttered. "To tire beyond my limits is to fall from the sky, and such a landing for a newly arrived brother? That which hurts, really hurts." He also knew pleasure in a newly minted body felt equally intense. Angels, and he laughed inwardly at the term, had to be careful.

Looking back at his own visible flight path, he located where the trail in the night sky became two, meaning they were surely nearing their destination. The *interesting* thing would be there, although Uriel didn't expect to find it so very interesting. No. He expected to lash out and make Kafziel pay.

"That's right," he called out violently. "In angel blood!" And his feathered appendages stroked the air equally violently. Then, with a tightening of his torso, he threw himself forward once again. The cold of the dark night wind rushed against his

23

face, and his words screamed his anger between each beat of his wings. "You will pay, Kafziel! You will bleed your unholy blood, you vile creature. I am freezing, wearing only a loin-cloth, and I could have been warm. Let's see how interesting it is when you shed your body's fluids before me!"

Interlude 1

Kafziel awaited Uriel's arrival. Little did the Bearer of Destiny know his desperation and that what he had to offer was very good, indeed. It was the satisfaction every brother of the Unity desired, and in fact had desired for the millennia they had been stranded in this dimension.

He offered Uriel his heart's desire: a female of their species.

When captured by this dimension, the brothers had become male—all male—and their bodies had mimicked the terrestrial lifeforms on this puny little world, down to the testosterone that drove them to madness. The brothers of the Unity were mad with need, and yet, they couldn't touch a one of the women on Earth.

Kafziel, devout deceiver that he was, had found a way. He had procured a mixed-blood woman, a human half-breed—a female "brother"—who was now at his disposal. He intended to offer her to Uriel as his gift.

He only wanted one small thing in exchange. Power. Uriel's power, not to put too fine a point on it. He wanted influence, the authority to act, to be a Doer instead of a Watcher. To achieve his goal, what greater power was there than that of the Bearer of Destiny? To have it in his grasp even for a moment . . . how glorious it would be!

He knew he would have to make his offering to Uriel carefully. Never companions, and more often than not at odds with one another, Uriel would cast his motives in a dark light. Kafziel was confident, though. He simply had to plant the idea in Uriel's head carefully; make the powerful brother think it was his own. Once Uriel was aware of Kafziel's offer, how could he resist? Eons of pent-up frustration were bottled up in his newly corporeal form, and he would not be able to pass this opportunity by.

Kafziel smiled, and it was not one of welcome. He had discovered a little-known ambiguity in this dimension's tenuous hold on the brothers' atomic structure, and after centuries of careful planning, he had exploited it for his own designs. The truth was that a brother could not touch a human except—and this was important—except for the first few minutes after becoming corporeal.

Now it was time to reap his rewards. Uriel would give anything for a human touch, and when Uriel was ready to trade, Kafziel would take everything he was willing to give, especially his Mandate of Destiny.

It was the ultimate prize, to hold the destiny of the human race in his hands. How wonderful it would be!

Chapter 3

Angioletta Bacciarelli, Daughter of Kafziel

Angioletta Bacciarelli struggled against sleep and against the darkness. Her face was aflame with heat. She fought the voices and memories that came to her.

"How lucky you are, my dear Angioletta. You are beautiful beyond compare."

No, she murmured, even as she slept. *I'm just me.* She didn't see what most people noticed about her. Her skin seemed to have an internal glow, as if freshly scrubbed and buffed to a clear luster. It was the skin of a cherub, and acquaintances felt warmed by her presence, calling her an angel in the most flattering terms. How lucky she was, they'd murmur when they thought she couldn't hear.

To Angioletta, she was just herself, and she didn't feel charmed at all. All her life she had craved heat, never able to satisfy her need for warmth. In the summers, she threw her windows wide and baked under an electric blanket. In winter, she wrapped in the warmest of thermal wear.

It was never enough, though.

Now, she was too warm, unbelievably, incessantly hot. She dreamed of the Sahara. She couldn't escape the blinding fire in the overhead sky. She could clearly make out two suns, one a furious yellow, and the second one white hot. It was double vision, surely, from dehydration. And yet, she saw that second sun sometimes, a voice in her dream suggested, didn't she? Angioletta thought she might have as a child, but the nuns hushed her each time she spoke of it. Soon, she had not mentioned it at all, and then her eyes began to avoid the sky. She hadn't wanted to see.

"You remember, though," the voice whispered, and she did.

The nuns had told her other things, also.

"Angiola, you must remember to never leave your toys about."

She didn't know then that her very existence was unknown to those who wielded the power within the familiar walls of her convent home. It was a home, too, if enormously huge and half empty. In those vast spaces, she had enjoyed half a hundred mothers. They had enjoyed her, too, loved her, and all were equal in her eyes. She bounced from one to another, oft times doing as a child does among parents, playing one off against another to get her way in some small matter.

The nuns, her mothers, delighted in this child who had been given to them by God. When they abandoned their families, many left behind much-loved brothers and sisters, nieces and nephews. They missed the joys a child could bring. Privately they shared that a child's presence didn't distract them from Christ. Rather, a child's simple trust showed them God's mercy toward his faithful. Surely they couldn't be faulted for loving this beautiful child, for she *was* beautiful, with a glow that made her seem ethereal. Angelic was the word many of the sisters preferred, although that term was used only in private. Angiola was as close as they dared.

"Quickly, Angiola! Into the cupboard. Not a sound."

She often had to hide. A finger would be pressed to her lips, and the door would enclose her in darkness. There was no fear, though, not from the closing of the door. It was never dark, and for a very good reason. The small girl carried her own light with her, the ethereal glow of her skin.

Once, working her fingers at the door, she peered out

through a narrow crack. A severe woman she didn't know came in, and she watched her laughing, playful mothers drop their heads and stand, silently waiting.

"Someone is eating too much of the convent's food." The sharp words were curt, a knife carving truth from a web of dishonesty. "A loaf of bread is missing from the kitchens."

Angioletta saw her mothers looking at one another, even as she placed her hand on her own pocket. She felt the remains of a loaf of bread there. Her heart beat fast, and she wanted to burst from the cupboard to show the woman it was not her mothers' fault.

The severe woman frowned, though, and it frightened the innocent child as the darkness never had. She would die rather than face this inquisitor. How her mothers put up with it, she didn't know.

When the doors were later opened, the nuns found their precious angel in tears. As they hugged her and asked her to explain the liquid eyes, she began to sob and just held out the remains of the bread. The nuns looked at each other, puzzled. Angioletta sniffled and whispered, "I will not eat any more of the mean lady's bread."

One especially pretty nun understood immediately, and she reached for the child, drawing her into an embrace, and whispering, "You can eat all the bread you wish, my sweet Angioletta."

Just as quickly, the other nuns pulled the child away, whispering, "You mustn't show a preference for the child, Sister Mary. She must never know."

It was that same Bride of Christ who came to her bedside the final night before she left her mothers' care forever. She was sixteen, and a foster home had been found for her just outside Naples. Her mothers had thrown her a farewell party—the mother superior was visiting church officials in Rome—and she was to be driven to the train in the morning. She lay in the dark, the angelic glow emanating from her skin, the same one she never thought of as special.

"My dear Angioletta—" The words from her mother stopped, broken, and unexpected sobs escaped into the night air.

"It will be all right, Mother." Still, she was puzzled. Up to that time, she had always been known as Angiola. Once before, and only once, someone had called her by that pet diminutive. "Why do you call me Angioletta?"

It was several moments before an answer came. Then, it was in a broken whisper, barely audible. "I have always loved you, Angioletta, even more than all your other mothers." The next words came out in a rush. "I'll never see you again, but there are things you must know. I have sworn not to speak to you of this, but I must. Do not question, as I have little time. Nearly seventeen years ago, an angel visited our convent." A short laugh punctuated the story. "Visited me. No one else, just me. He was beautiful, with the most glorious feathered wings, just like in all the pictures."

"An angel?" Angioletta was puzzled. "Why would he visit just you? Did he bring you a message?"

"He brought me you."

Angioletta had been told all her life that she was an angel, a gift from the angels, and as beautiful as an angel. She grasped the hand that touched her arm, enjoying its warmth, and suffered an epiphany. No child has fifty mothers.

"You are my original mother, aren't you?"

"Yes, my beautiful Angioletta. You must tell no one what I've told you." There was a hand pressed to the girl's face, and then the nun was gone.

Angioletta didn't see her natural mother the next morning, for it was one of the elderly nuns who came in early to wake her and drive her to the train station. She packed a loaf of bread and some cheese, and in moments they were gone.

From that day forward, the young woman was no longer Angiola. She became her mother's child, Angioletta, the messenger from an angel.

Interlude 2

The things Angioletta's mother didn't tell her daughter had been shared only once, many years before, and then spoken of only in whispers. She had tearfully shared with her fellow nuns how the angel had glowed in the darkness. He had embraced her, and his skin had been like ice yet tasted of vanilla. She had tried to warm him, and when she ran her hands across his bare back, there had been no wings to obstruct her touch, just the rippling muscles of a man. It was only later that she remembered that, for when she had wrapped her arms around him, her thoughts had been focused elsewhere.

The sisters had understood, accepting her tale when she had begun to swell with the child. After all, they were cloistered. There had been no opportunity, none at all, and at least a virgin birth hadn't been claimed, a second messiah. An angelic visitation had seemed very plausible, indeed.

The mother superior and the old monsignor were not known to be believers in modern-day miracles, though. Quite the opposite. As the old convent was large, as well as mostly unoccupied, the decision had been made to raise the child secretly, claiming her as the sisters' gift from God.

There was one other thing. None of the nuns had ever spoken of it aloud, but their belief in their sister's claims had less to do with their trust in her story, than the way the child's skin glowed as she lay in her crib. No normal child ever did that, so she must be a gift from the visiting angel, as their sister had described.

Thus she became Angiola, the angel from God.

Uriel, Bearer of Destiny

Uriel was not built of hollow bird bones, able to glide for hours. He was a jumbo jet, only able to soar because of his great expanse of wings. It took fuel, too, a lot.

Even in darkness, his approaching surroundings looked decrepit: abandoned vehicles, most heavily rusted; water towers on spindly legs, with faded and unreadable paint on the side; railroad tracks extending from a boarded up, chained entrance half-buried in the side of a hill; mounds of tailings scattered about. There was even an old rail car. It seemed to be the best-maintained object in the area, especially compared to several wooden buildings off to the side. One of the buildings had OFFICES still legible in faded letters on the front. The roof had fallen in, though.

Uriel smirked sourly as his feet gently touched the ground. "Not *interesting* at all, Kafziel. You bring me to an old mine? Already I am bored."

As his momentum carried him several steps forward, he raised his arms high and clapped his hands sharply. The space around him flashed into day-like brilliance, the corporeal disharmony energy transference briefly flooding the area. He sighed in relief, working the soreness in his shoulders.

"Kafziel," he called, turning in the small circle of subdued light his skin created. "You are here. I can feel it. Your passage through the night sang your way to me." He laughed, finishing his circle, *feeling* for the Emissary of Solitude and Tears. There was nothing. When an "angel" remained in corporeal form for too long, he began a gradual transformation from true, shifting out of phase with those around him, losing his ability to sense other brothers or communicate without words over long distances.

It was apparent that Kafziel had been here a very long time. It was further proof he was a fool.

"Welcome me, Kafziel." His words boldly rang out once more, shattering the darkness. "I have followed as you wished. Will you hide from me still?" Uriel taunted, "Are you only the Watcher of Solitude, Presider over the Deaths of Kings? Has your sojourn on Earth not encouraged you to action, good brother?"

His words achieved the desired effect.

"So, Wingless One." Kafziel's voice glittered with daggers of sharp-edged glass. Gone were the honey words from the burning house.

"I see my barbs have struck home." Uriel turned in his circle of light, and he laughed.

"Bring me your tired, your hungry. It is this society's motto." The words were still razor-edged, and sharp laughter accompanied them. "Are you tired, Uriel? Hungry? You've come a long way. Be nice to me, and I may feed you, even give you a place to rest. Would you like that, my friend? A place to ease your travails, to be at peace with the world?"

"Peace? I do not wish peace." Uriel flung his words at the hidden brother. "I wish my hands to be around your throat, you foul excuse for a brother."

"Before I feed you? Tsk, tsk. Do you know how to climb, Uriel?"

"Show yourself, Kafziel! Do you fear me?"

"Here, Brother."

Uriel watched a luminescent form, still winged, step from behind a rocky crag. Long arms rose above the brother's head. A handclap, a brilliant flash washing the surrounding rock into momentary day, and Kafziel was wingless. Uriel pointed along the tracks to the mine's boarded-up entrance. "The entrance is here, Watcher, if this broken down mine is your home. I presume you carry a key? It appears I am locked out."

"For one such as us? We are never locked out."

"Yet, I find such is the case." He walked over, shaking the door, snorting when dust flew from the joints. Kafziel's words held truth. Yet, to step through this solid surface would surely pull more from him than he could afford to give.

"The real entrance is up here, Doer. You will locate it easily enough." He turned, but before he disappeared, his voice rang out one more time. "You may feel free to dispose of the loincloth, Brother. You will find no humans to offend." Then, he was gone.

Uriel glanced down. He pulled his covering tighter, tucking it in at the waist, all the while muttering, "I will keep it, *Brother,* for it will remind me I do not do your bidding."

He cursed a few times as he climbed the path. He knew he was being teased along. He found a door and yanked it wide, surprised at the ease with which it moved. Then he noted the panel set into the wall just inside the opening. A series of small lights winked their green approval. One glowed an unhappy red. Several rusty barrels were scattered about, and along one wall was a pile of lumber. To the side, a wire cage was built against another wall. The metal was brown-crusted with age, and an old

32

control box was attached to the rock wall at its side. Everything was covered with a layer of heavy dust. The security system with its blinking lights might be new, but everything else in the old mine seemed to be as it was when abandoned a half-century or more before. The air was fresh, though, and warm, very warm. That felt better already.

After a moment, a repetitive clanking sound began. Then, a cage began to rise within the existing one, an old service elevator.

"I won't be caged, you know. I also wait to be interested. You promised." He strode forward and grabbed the cage's metal grid work, shaking it violently. "Watcher, I also grow lonely. Spare me! I thought the charade was over."

When the clanking stopped, he slid a metal door aside. Inside, he saw a panel with two large buttons, one with an arrow pointing up and the other down. Roughly, he reached a hand and slapped the down arrow, finding himself jostled when the metal cage jerked and began a downward descent. He luxuriated in the continually increasing warmth that surrounded the cage as it sank into darkness.

The cage clanked to a stop, and several overhead florescent bulbs flickered on, one at a time, the series of hesitant fixtures leading down a long corridor until the space they illuminated disappeared out of sight. At irregular intervals, there were wooden beams across the ceiling, held up by additional timbers. Not all of them looked especially safe. In several places, they appeared spaced to provide for doorways or corridors that led off to the side.

Closer were a number of wooden crates, and among them were two or three of the metal barrels he had seen up top. One of the wooden ones had the lid askew, and he flipped it aside. Foodstuffs! As he reached inside, a hand grabbed his arm, and he felt a body leaning against him. Snorting with irritation, he whipped around, only to find himself face-to-face with Kafziel. He slapped his hands on the brother's chest and forced him roughly away.

"Stand back, Kafziel, for you disgust me."

"What?" The Watcher held out one arm, motioning to the

open crate with a disarming smile. "I disgust you? I offer you food, Uriel."

"As you lean against me? Are you now flouting the Strictures, Watcher? Has being on this planet skewed your affections?" He laughed harshly, the hunger in his belly a torment.

"I always have such good form here on Earth." Kafziel smiled, and he ran a hand across a shoulder. It was covered with a silky, white shirt, and his body was sharply defined underneath. "Despite your doubts, I have touched the flesh of a woman."

"You have not changed. Do you have a new Mandate now, perhaps one fashioned as Teller of Lies?" Uriel snorted at the blatant falsehood. No one would believe it, for it was impossible.

"Come with me, my friend. All I ask of you is one day of your time. Let us visit. This night and tomorrow, give that to me, and the next night, you are free to go. Besides, I've still got my surprise to show you." Kafziel grabbed Uriel's arm, pulling him forward.

"Tell me of this human you've touched." Uriel pulled his arm free, a sneer on his face. "You hide underground because you are cold. You would have to be on a mountaintop to lie side by side with a female of this world. Even then, the touch of your flesh against hers would be a torment for her."

Kafziel laughed. "For me, also. Still, as long as we haven't reached Equilibrium, you'd be amazed at how close to a woman we can get." He leaned in to whisper conspiratorially, "That along with being on the top of a mountain makes it especially easy. I know. I've been there."

"And just what does that mean, Leviathan of Lies? You've been there?" If so, innumerable Strictures had been broken to do this, and repercussions from the Unity would be swift and severe.

"My poor, innocent brother." Kafziel laughed again. "Are you not a connoisseur of human manuscripts?"

"Why must you always bait me, Impostor? Just speak what you mean."

"There is an old holy book here on this world. Not everyone ascribes to it, but many do. In one place," and he put a hand to his chin as if in deep thought, "Genesis, I believe, the sixth chapter, it tells how the sons of God intermarried with the daughters of men and so on. Then the humans' god became displeased and forbade the practice for all time. Hmm. Now, tell, me, Uriel. Just what do you think that refers to?" He laughed again, very loudly. "Sounds like our Stricture from the Unity of Being to me, and wasn't that just like something the Triune Mind would do?" He grinned.

Uriel frowned. He knew the reference, and he shuddered. For Kafziel to have made the connection . . . still, the brother was a Watcher only. If the power of a Doer ever fell into his hands, then all creation had better watch out.

"You will have the day you ask of me, if it is to be a day of feasting. I must have food and have it now." Uriel felt himself weaken to Kafziel's proddings. He allowed himself there were two reasons. He wanted to know more of Kafziel's claims, but more importantly, he did truly need to replenish his body. For that, he would give almost anything Kafziel asked, although the troublesome brother might regret the asking later.

Kafziel grinned, murmuring, "Of course."

"Let's get to it. I am starving."

Kafziel laughed, reaching to clasp Uriel on the back as if in friendship. Uriel suspected it was anything but, but he had no strength to argue it now.

Chapter 4

Gadreel, Deliverer of Destruction

"We have an *Injustice* here, Gabriel." Growing impatient, Gadreel tried again, this time layering his words with sweetness. "Ramiel told me of your well-wishing for your old friend. Would you have Uriel suffer in his moment of distress?" By the time he finished, his words were a razor, slicing cruelly. "He will, without your help, and it will be so unfair. Come, Gabriel. Show yourself."

Twin ripples in the darkness caught his attention, the space twisting in that odd way of arriving brothers, and in an explosive convulsion, two unexpected comrades were with him. He laughed in derision when he saw them.

"I seek Gabriel, the Archangel of Justice and Power. I call him to stand before me, demanding his attendance, and who do I see instead?" He ridiculed his unwelcome guests. "The beginning and the end have come to join me. Asbeel, you who were Chief of the Brothers, and you!" He laughed harshly, his eyes turning and locking on the second brother. "Zadkiel, Envoy of Freedom, Benevolence, and Mercy. You who stayed Abraham's hand. The Triune Mind calls himself the Alpha and the Omega, the First and the Last, yet I have that standing here with me now, and the Triune Mind is still sequestered. It seems the Mind has become somewhat redundant. Useless. A pitiful shadow of his former glory."

"As you wish, Gadreel," the two murmured as one, even as they knelt together, each on one knee.

Asbeel coughed. "I was Second Chief, Great Gadreel. Sort of like," clearing his throat, "vice-president."

"What?" Gadreel bristled at the rebuke, and his anger detonated into the void. "Did I hear you speak to me, O Master of Arcane Earth Trivia?"

"I was only Second Chief of the Brothers . . . and Earth trivia is vastly interesting, Holy Lord. My apologies." The response was whispered.

"What do you disturb me with?" Of all the brothers, none thought more of status and position than Asbeel. Zadkiel was worse. He was a fool. These two had Mandates that would be of no use at all to his needs, one being that of Leadership, and the other of Kindness and Compassion.

"Io." Asbeel took a step backward, calling out in a carefully modulated voice, "O, Great One."

"Io?" Gadreel lashed out disdainfully. "Tell me of Io. What is your concern of this place?"

"You must know, Gadreel." Zadkiel spoke up. "We use Io."

"And how do we use Io, my good brothers? I seem to recall it is very cold there, and it has no atmosphere." Gadreel controlled his irritation by the barest margin. Zadkiel's Mandate was Compassion. Gadreel would rather see Asbeel's Leadership. He had been Second-in-Command of all the brothers. Had the Second lost his spine so quickly, and in only these few short millennia?

"Oh, but there is an atmosphere, Good Gadreel. Warmth, too. It is necessarily localized near the satellite's volcanic activity, but that's what makes the little moon so intriguing." Asbeel grinned.

"And this is why you've come to disturb me—"

"We go there for enjoyment, a number of the brothers do, anyway. It's sort of a . . . um . . . like a—" Zadkiel paused as if choosing just the right word.

"Like a vacation." Asbeel's enthusiastic answer completed his companion's stumbling explanation.

"A vacation?" Gadreel bellowed, his expression turning hard, and his self-control evaporating. "A *vacation?*"

"You know," Asbeel was now in full swing, and quite oblivious to Gadreel's outburst, "a break away from the usual things one does all the time. Are you not aware of Fantasy Island? 'The plane! The plane!'" Then he stopped, whispering contritely, "Zadkiel warned me to keep my arcane knowledge of Earth facts to myself, for surely Gadreel has no interest in such minutiae."

Gadreel lashed out, "Minutiae? I know what a vacation is, Asbeel. Do you think me a fool? 'The plane! The plane!' I cannot fathom what purpose there would be in visiting *Io* for a vacation. Is it possible you can enlighten me? Either of you?"

Both brothers now cowered. Zadkiel whispered once more, "For the challenge, Munificent Gadreel, to see whether we can guess the next volcano to erupt. They emit warmth—and a tenuous atmosphere for a time. We take on the barest of corporeal bodies for a short while and enjoy shifting from dimensional interface to dimensional interface, remembering all the forms we have taken before. The penalty for guessing incorrectly which vent is next to explode is to be very, very cold.

"But then, we never reach Equilibrium, so it draws little of our energy. It is quite safe. It is only a game."

"And this is a cause for disturbing my *duties?*" Gadreel needed his presence here to sound official. It was far from that, but no one except he and Gabriel needed to be aware of the real purpose.

"A human ship is approaching Io. What if it sees the brothers flitting in and out of the atmospheric pockets near the volcanoes?"

"Oh, you are fools!" Gadreel laughed at the absurdity of the two standing before him. The liftoff from earlier. One of the men had mentioned Io. "Make them see what you wish them to see. Have you spent so little time on Earth that you've forgotten how to do that?"

Zadkiel and Asbeel looked at each other for a moment before answering. "Equilibrium must be gained before a Suggestion can take hold."

Asbeel added, whispering, "There is not enough atmosphere for Equilibrium, Mighty Gadreel."

"Ghosts, Asbeel. They will see you as ghosts, record your images, and on Earth, a whole new entertainment genre will spring to life. I think you have nothing to worry about. Go play your vacation games on Io, and the humans will be no wiser. Soon they will fly home, their governments will realize they have spent far too much money for far too little information, and the little moon will be all yours once again."

"Still," Asbeel suggested. "They should be monitored. Their sensing equipment grows sophisticated. One day they may find us."

"Not today, Brother. Now tell me, have either of you seen Gabriel? I have called him, and he has not appeared."

"Recently?" Asbeel was cut off as Zadkiel jabbed him with an incorporeal elbow.

"Of course, recently." Gadreel caught the motion and felt his irritation flare. "Did you think I meant anytime in the previous thousand years? I know an evasion when I hear one."

"He spoke to us a short time ago." Zadkiel looked up meekly.

Asbeel blurted, "He had an errand to complete, one for the Triune Mind. He asked us to run interference until he could get here." He stopped, an expression of dismay on his face.

"So, that's the way it is." Gadreel's face darkened, and the stars around him seemed to dim. "Be gone, fools!"

Frightened space twisted just so, forming twin whirlpools of blackness, and he was alone again.

He whispered, "So, there is something going on between you and the Triune Mind, Gabriel. I intend to find out what. You will not free the Mind, no matter what you think. Your conniving will come to no good end, because I am stronger."

He raised his head to peer across the distance to the Unity, and he called once again in an imperative tone, "Gabriel!" For the moment he was satisfied. His message had gone out, and if

Gabriel had any sense, he would pay attention and attend.

Angioletta Bacciarelli, Daughter of Kafziel

Angioletta's hands grasped the bed linens, and they were damp. She fought the sleep that held her trapped. In that frightening state between reality and imagination, she dreamed hot and frightening dreams.

Her first realization of her difference had come in one of her university classes. For some reason now long forgotten, she had arrived at class unprepared for a major quiz. As she tossed in her dream, she remembered her panic as she pulled up her personal calendar. The date for the quiz was there in red, and she had somehow missed it. The professor called for the class's attention, standing with a stack of test booklets in her hand. Angioletta closed her eyes in desperation, whispering to herself, "Please, not today. Of all days, I cannot take this test today. Please, Professor Nonnigan."

Then, of all things, the professor cleared her throat and spoke brightly to the students, "Class, I do believe I will postpone the test until our next class meeting. A few extra days' preparation will certainly help us all." She frowned, as if surprised at herself, and then she shuffled through several thin books on her desk. Pulling one out, she smiled. "Have your notes out, and be prepared to keep up."

That was the first time.

Then, her dream shifted, and she stood by a road. It was night, and the sky was very dark. The air had been cold, but now, inexplicably, it was almost too warm for comfort, even for her in her dream. She realized she was encased in several layers of clothing.

A black car drove by very slowly, one with deeply tinted windows, and it frightened her. She looked up to the sky, wishing for a full moon, only to see a ghostly sun off to the side, one that gave no light at all. *"You cannot see a second sun, Angiola. Do not speak of such things, girl."* She looked away, the sweat on her brow bringing a chill.

Then, she was in the back seat of the car, and a man was at her side, one who glowed in the darkness as she did. He was very handsome, and it seemed as if she should know him: his face, it was as if she had seen it before; his brows; the shape of his chin; even the turn of his lips. She had seen that face already, in her own mirror, looking back at her.

"Father?" she whispered. Her question surprised even her.

He smiled, and it was beatific. He opened his mouth, and his spoken words were the melodious song of a choir of angels.

"Smart girl."

Obviously, he intended them to be comforting. Somehow, though, she didn't feel comforted at all. She felt she had just been caught in a trap, a very devious, very sticky web of a trap.

Asbeel, Second Chief of the Brothers

Space twisted, and with the barest of shimmers, Asbeel stood in the darkness that flowed between worlds. He was cold, but with the Triune Mind sequestered by the Rebellion, he never felt warm. Everyone was cold, although it was worse when he traveled outside the Unity.

He waited for a moment, looking over the green and blue world hanging just under his feet. White clouds swirled across its surface, and about a third of it was shadowed with night. In that darkness, bright clusters of lights showed the locations of cities, and it seemed warm and welcoming. An occasional flash of light suggested a meteor had hit the upper atmosphere, creating what the humans liked to call a shooting star.

In the darkness surrounding the globe, pinpricks of distant suns hung sharp and bright. None of them twinkled. Only those next to the surface of the planet blinked and faded through the thick atmosphere.

He glanced at the two suns, recognizing one for what it really was, the Unity of Being. That was where he wanted to go next. It was not in this dimension, not really. Rather, it was not *of* this dimension. It could only be seen by the incorporeal.

Then there was Earth. Exile. That's what the little planet

stood for. The worst penalty inflicted for the most heinous of crimes was banishment, and that was to the small world below.

It was not a place his people generally chose to be, if given other options. Asbeel knew he had no interest. His sole wish was to be placed once again as Second Chief of the Brothers. His Mandate was Leadership, and he was abysmal at anything else. At least he and Zadkiel had been of service to Gabriel even through the turmoil of the Rebellion. That would be a star in their crowns if the Triune Mind were ever returned to power . . . *when* the Mind returned to power

He felt space open and close at his side, and he turned to find Zadkiel beside him. "About time, fool! Did you get lost?"

"Fool? Who turned into a steady stream of information?"

"You are right. I am a fool." Asbeel's face dropped, and Zadkiel relented, smiling. After all, his Mandate was Benevolence and Mercy.

"We succeeded, all the same." Zadkiel grinned at his companion. "You and I did that, friend."

"We did? Are you sure?"

"That's what kept me. I took a detour to check in with Gabriel. He got his little errand completed."

"Do you think Gadreel will really take care of the humans on Io?" Asbeel smiled hopefully. He was glad to have helped out Gabriel, but the thing about Io was a real concern.

Zadkiel laughed. "I remember now why I treasure you as a friend. You are ever hopeful about the most arcane things. Still, no, Asbeel, I do not think he will."

"No?" He said the word with despair.

His friend looked at him and laughed once again. "We weren't there to get help with Io. You knew that."

"We weren't? I thought maybe the timing was to help Gabriel, but it is an important matter. Playing in the volcanoes is very entertaining. You and I had the best time ever when we were there last. I hope it wasn't our last time."

Zadkiel laughed once again. "Now, who is being the fool? Gadreel was right. The humans have been seeing ghosts on their own world for millennia. Why should they not also see them on Io?"

"I'm cold." Asbeel had lost interest. "Can we go back into the Unity now?" He looked longingly at the fusion orb hanging in the darkness.

Zadkiel grinned. Then the blackness around him twisted, and he was gone. Asbeel immediately focused his thoughts, his space twisted also, and with the barest of glimmers, he stood at his friend's side once again.

The scene the two entered was vastly different than the one they left behind. They found themselves inside the Unity. This was no set of empty spatial coordinates anchored by Energy Nodes. The Unity of Being contained the reality of their very different dimension Encapsulated within its walls. Within that space the surfaces were solid, the brothers were real, and the streets gleamed with golden light.

At one time the Triune Mind had resided in the center of the Unity, his Seat of Power shining brilliantly, giving warmth and energy to all the brothers. It had never been dark or cold. In a twist of empathy, the Mind had taken the small world just outside the Unity's boundaries as his own, personal charge, slowly giving up the quest to return the Unity to its proper dimension. Many of the brothers had wanted to go home. Anger had been stirred, and some had risen in revolt, trapping the Triune Mind, and muting his powers—as well as the energy he provided. The Unity had been moved nearer this world's sun, and it was now their only real source of warmth. It provided adequate light, but the heat was never sufficient.

Asbeel and Zadkiel wanted to go home, too, just not at the cost of keeping the Mind Encapsulated in Gadreel's Secondary Forces Chamber. They wished Gabriel success in freeing the one-time leader of the Unity.

Now, though, they had other things to attend to.

"Ready?" Zadkiel looked at his companion with expectation.

Asbeel understood perfectly. Over the eons, pent-up testosterone had caused much of the Unity's society to degrade. At times, it was downright dangerous. Shifting his weight, Asbeel bent his legs. Then, flinging his wings back, he leaped into the sky. His appendages were brilliantly white, and unlike the feathers the brothers manifested when in corporeal form, these glistened with light, shimmering in the glow that permeated everything around them.

In the Unity, he was virtually indistinguishable from Zadkiel—or any other brother. They both sported pale, golden skin, with matching hair billowing from their heads. Looks weren't how they told each other apart. Instead, each brother bled an essence signature. It was their "souls" that made them who they were, whether good or bad.

Inside the Unity, there was also no air to press against, and there was no gravity, not as it was known on Earth. The great wings were for maneuverability, for adjusting momentum, for shifting mass and controlling flight. Bending space while outside the Unity was certainly easier, but this was what the brothers were made for, and it was wonderful.

Some incarnations were inherently better than others.

Ashbeel turned, and he was pleased to see Zadkiel's wings opened at his back. He waved as his friend crouched and leaped, sending his mass forward, his momentum carrying him straight into the heavens alongside Asbeel.

They had a job to do.

Interlude 3

Asbeel and Zadkiel faced one enormous problem. There was no end to the Unity, not in the practical sense. They had never flown the entire diameter of its spherical shape, and even given the additional centuries they might possibly remain trapped in this dimension, it was doubtful they could. After all, it was every bit as large as the corporeal sun just outside its boundaries. It was a universe unto itself, the size of a million Earths, and there was no lack of space for the brothers to make their homes.

It was also the ship they had journeyed in since the beginnings of their travels, shifting from dimension to dimension, collecting information, storing it away, and living their lives in blissful prosperity. It had been perfect, that was until they had shifted that final time. Then, Earth had caught them, and they had been unable to find a way to free their ship.

Their ship was now a prison.

They had become stuck, incorporeal except within the boundaries of their massive, dimension-jumping ship. No matter the size of the prison, the bars of their incorporeality kept them locked up tight, invisible to corporeal eyes. It was only outside the ship, with the excitation of the brothers' sub-atomic matrix by the planetary atmosphere, that they enjoyed their temporary corporeal forms, ones that resembled the like poles of two magnets, repelling them from ever touching a human.

It had been done, though.

Just ask Kafziel. He *knew*—in the most Biblical sense—just how it felt, too, and he had the proof of his escapade sequestered deep in his mine. Plans had been made, and no important players had been overlooked, not Uriel, and especially not the daughter who had become Kafziel's unwitting playing card.

Chapter 5

Jim Morrison, USA *Rapide Explorer*

"So, Chet." Jim Morrison, one of the two astronauts aboard the *Rapide Explorer* and headed to Io, paused, checking a readout on the console mounted just above his head. His parents had been rock groupies, naming him after the famous singer. The best he could do was warble the birthday song, and not well, at that.

The spacecraft they were in was quite large, but most of the interior space was reserved for equipment. The human cargo had been deemed of secondary importance, or at least the two astronauts riding inside joked that way. Reaching to a display at his side, Jim touched one icon, and it brought up a table showing real-time mechanical attributes from all over the ship. Tapping one with his finger, he made a small adjustment, pleased to see the readout on the console change slightly. Another tap on the display, and it returned to its waiting bank of icons.

"Jim, you needed something?" Chet Lawry, Jim's partner, rested to one side of the cabin, a band around his waist holding him gently against the wall. He came from a wealthy family of academics who had seen him as a social experiment. Could anyone say steak sauce? Yeah, that was them. He sometimes opined that he was lucky to have turned out normal.

An electronic reader was in his hands. He had uploaded the latest novel from his favorite author. Even so, his expression remained neutral. The two men got along easily, a requirement for the extended time this mission was expected to cover, and he waited for a response. His novel wasn't going anywhere.

Jim wiped his hands on a CleanCloth, dropping it through the elastic opening of a refuse bin when he was done. Bodily oils could foul the equipment if allowed to build up, and the easiest way to prevent that was to clean the skin regularly. He laughed softly. "How many moons now?"

"Moons, Jim?" Chet chuckled. "I know how you tend to broach questions by roundabout paths. This probably isn't about moons at all."

Jim laughed, reminded how transparent he was. "Jupiter. We're going to Io. Then there's Europa, Ganymede, and Calisto, all discovered by Galileo. Plus the four large, regular moons, for eight total." He paused, reaching to touch a different readout, pursing his lips, then looking at Chet. He shook his head but didn't go on.

"Okay, Jim. Eight regular moons, prograde with circular orbits. Sure. We all know that." Chet pushed his reader to the wall, and a Velcro strip on the back held it there. After a moment, the display went blank, a small green light blinking at the bottom. If he left it alone long enough, even that would turn off. It was important to conserve power on the ship. Small measures meant there would be plenty of what they needed for everything they intended to do.

"They keep finding more, though. Oddballs. Retrograde or elliptical orbits. Little misshapen rocks. It seems the last one doesn't even have a defined orbit yet. So, is it sixty-three or sixty-four now?"

Chet laughed softly. "Does it matter?"

Jim moved to a window. There were several, two quite large. He absently wiped the one he was at with his sleeve, although it was perfectly clear. He took a deep breath and sighed, staring at the darkness. They were traveling at a greater speed than any man had moved before, and it was impossible to tell. The stars were frozen in space. The outside of their craft was far below zero, and their only external warmth emanated from the exhaust vent that bled their excess internal heat. They did generate a lot within the confines of their four walls.

"Gathering your thoughts, Jim?" Chet released the band around his waist, and he pushed off to float beside his friend. "Something going on?"

"All those moons. Ground-based telescopes, then the Hubble. Whatever that newest one is called. We're developing even better stuff now, and still, it seems we keep finding more."

"That's good. Technology gets better, and we get smarter. It is good, right?"

"Sure. Just, what else is out there that we're not seeing, only because our instruments aren't good enough? Gases, invisible particles floating around, life forms we can't even guess are there. Maybe there are forms of radiation out there that we can't even measure, and no telling what they're doing to us."

"Worried?" Chet slapped him on the shoulder and grinned. "Don't be. Either the evil radiation gets you, or it doesn't. You can't do anything about what you can't detect."

"Radon. Radon used to kill people because they couldn't detect it." He pushed off to the readout he'd adjusted minutes earlier. "I keep getting odd readings. Not far off, mind you, but just enough that they're not what they should be." He tapped the readout. "It's like we have an extra passenger or something."

"Inside?" Chet looked around the space. There were three other small areas in their part of the craft, but there was no room for a stowaway.

"I know it's silly, but it's like we have one outside, stealing our heat. At times the exhaust temperatures are just a fraction cooler than they should be, and other times it's as if our balance is slightly off. Attitude jets fire, and the ship isn't quite on target. Things like that." At Chet's look of concern, Jim waved his hand to salve his mind. "It's not enough to affect our mission in any way, but it's unexpected. That's all."

Chet nodded. "That's why they sent you, Jim. You have a

mind for details, and you'll keep this vessel in top form." He floated back to his reader, turning to wink at the other man. "By the time we get to Io, we'll be so used to all these little quirks that nothing'll surprise us. We'll go, ho-hum, is that all the little moon's got to offer? We should'a stayed home."

Jim's pensive mood finally dissipated, and he laughed. "Right, Chet. I wouldn't have stayed home for the world."

Just then the speakers in the cabin crackled, and a voice came through.

"Hey, guys. This is Houston calling. Brad here. Just wanted to see if ya'll are awake up there. Got an unusual reading on your heat signature, but then it leveled out. Get back to us on that.

"Also, Jim, Sara sends her love." A chuckle accompanied the words. "Says she'd send more than that, but it won't translate over the airwaves. The kids, too. She says they miss you already. We'll have some video for you later. It'll come in a package, and you'll have to crack it open. You'll like it, though. Jim, there's one Sara says is just for you. She made me promise I'd tell you not to let Chet see. Sorry, Chet.

"Oh, and Chet? You've got a second grade class down here says you promised them a lesson from space. Sally Ride Elementary, Ms. Walderson's class. Smile for the camera. Make us look good.

"We'll be waiting on your response. It'll be a while, so I'm going for coffee now. Take it easy, you guys.

"Houston, out."

The speakers went dead. Jim reached to his display, and he touched the *Save* icon. He brushed alongside one eye with his thumb, and it came away damp.

Chet saw, and he turned away to pull his reader from the wall.

Jim knew he had indeed given up the world to come on this little adventure: the world, his wife, and his three kids. Those decisions weren't always easy to live with. He would be okay, but he needed a little privacy for a while, and he was grateful for Chet's discretion. That was a small thing to do for a good friend.

49

As he watched his friend turn his eyes to his novel, soon engrossed once more, he rubbed his thumb alongside his other eye, and it came away damp as well.

Uriel, Bearer of Destiny

Uriel slapped Kafziel alongside the shoulder. He slapped hard, too, to make sure it hurt, to get his attention.

Kafziel stopped and turned. "Am I your whipping boy, now? What's gone wrong in your life that you have to take it out on me?" His eyes crinkled, though, the look telling of one who felt very much in charge of life, of one who could afford to be generous.

Uriel didn't smile in turn. He was certain there was something Kafziel wanted. He wasn't sure what, but it wouldn't be anything that pleased him, not with the Watcher involved. He would eventually know, but at this moment, other priorities ordered his time.

"I have told you I needed food. Have your corporeal ears forgotten how to listen? Perhaps another brother elsewhere will show more compassion." Uriel was in desperate need, too. This corporeal body consumed prodigious amounts of fuel. First rescuing the child, then the flight to this hidey-hole had used up reserves he didn't have to spare. He turned as if to leave, but a hand grabbed his arm, and a soft voice whispered into his ear.

"Nay, Brother. Stay with me. I will provide for you. Remember, you have promised me one day. Now take a deep breath. Surely you cannot miss what I have in store for you."

"Do you not listen?" Uriel shook the hand off his arm, growling his annoyance. He once again regretted following this *brother*, and would be gone now if he weren't so depleted.

Kafziel cuffed him on the back, laughing. "It is you who do not know how to listen. Breathe, Uriel. Through your corporeal nose. You will like what you smell."

He did as he was asked and was surprised to feel his stomach tighten and growl. "Meat? Truly, I will put aside my irritation for a meal. Take me there, Brother."

Kafziel pointed the way with his head, and he stepped forward. "There is a room down this corridor. It contains an old smelting forge." He turned and laughed. "This place was perfect. It even has an endless source of fuel for heat. It seems a deposit of natural gas was tapped within the mine, and it was piped directly to the forge. The fumes apparently began killing off the humans, and the mine was abandoned. So much the better for me."

They stepped through a doorway into a room that was wonderfully hot. It was a large space with rock walls, bearing a sooty, rock ceiling. Backed into one wall was an enormous forge for smelting metal, and it glowed red with warmth. A number of heavy iron tools of various sizes and shapes leaned against the rock at its side. Off to one side a living space was set up, with sofas, chairs, and even an enormous area rug. A large, veined mirror leaned against one wall, for Kafziel to preen, surely. There was no other reason for it that Uriel could see. Electric lamps perched on end tables, and they glowed brightly.

The smell of cooked meat permeated the space.

"I see lights. From where do you steal your electricity?" Uriel had seen it back in the tunnels, but here? This was indeed a home, of sorts, and it would use a lot. Kafziel was not the sort to pay for what he took.

"I am not a thief, Uriel. At least not in this. The natural gas powers a small generator, originally for the smelting operation. This room was filled with conveyer belts and bins. I scrapped it all, keeping only the machines I found useful. The forge keeps it nicely warm in here, no?"

"The food. You have a cook, too?" Somehow, knowing Kafziel, the idea hardly seemed beyond belief. There was certainly some slave toiling away in a dungeon-like cave.

"Ha! My *brother* does have a sense of humor, if somewhat warped. I desire my solitude, especially when it comes to humans. I prefer to stand behind the scenes and watch them cry their sorrowful tears—and die, too, of course. The kings, especially." He chortled with the irony of it all. "That is my Mandate, you must remember, to Preside over the Deaths of Kings. Yet, for all my time here on Earth, I am not allowed to help a one. Pity." He grinned, showing that the thought didn't seem especially distressing to him.

"You are cruel, Kafziel." Uriel frowned. "Still, I continue to sense meat. It is the only reason I still remain. What is it? As importantly, where is it?" He turned in the great space, looking. There was no food preparation area he could see, just a large table pressed up against one wall. Several heavily built chairs were sitting alongside with their backs against the rocky surface. "Or, is this a scavenger hunt? I find the food, and you let me consume it."

"Brother, come see my forge. You will find it most appealing." He walked that direction, motioning with one hand. As he moved, he quickly unbuttoned his shirt, stripping it from his body, and flinging it onto one of the chairs. "I never like wearing all the clothes this world requires. Only here, where it is warm, can I shed the obnoxious cloth. See, Uriel? This is my home, and it is quite comfortable. You could be at home here. I have food, warmth, and more surprises for you, also. Could you not be happy here?"

Uriel stepped to the shirt and snatched it from its place in the chair. Putting it to his nose, he inhaled sharply. "Smells like you, Kafziel. Like the flames from earlier, too. What fabric is this that it did not consume itself in the fire?" He knew his own wrap had only survived because he had kept it insulated with his wings. It had also traveled through the wall with him, but he didn't think of that as unusual. Anything that touched him was affected by his atmospheric disharmony. It became part of his being after a fashion, part of his "vortex," able to be carried with him whatever he did. Inanimate items did so, anyway. Animate items, flesh and blood, were not so easy. Those were the magnets, the opposite poles that could not be pressed together.

Still, that didn't keep the clothes from burning off the brothers' bodies should they step directly into flames.

"Nomex." Kafziel kicked his shoes off. They were obviously scorched, unlike the shirt.

"Nomex?" He had never heard of that, but then he didn't usually chase down structure fires just to bask in the flames.

"A substance similar to Kevlar. You have heard of Kevlar." Kafziel looked at him with a smirk on his face. "Surely!" When he nodded that he had, Kafziel continued, "It is a variety of the same stuff. Kevlar has strength. Nomex has other qualities, like fire resistance. It can be woven into anything. Firefighters use it in their suits, as do men who drive race cars. Nomex is very versatile, and for almost any situation." He looked at the charred leather on his shoes. "Except shoes. Good leather is the only solution there. I digress, as you are here for food, not a lecture on the finer points of maintaining proper decorum in the presence of prudish humans. And rightly so."

He reached to the side of the forge and pulled open a metal door. Inside, hanging on several metal hooks, were a number of small animals, dressed, their flesh golden brown. A deep pan of water, now only half full, sat underneath, steaming. The aroma spilled out into the room, and it made Uriel's stomach rumble.

"You did this, Kafziel? It smells excellent." Uriel leaned in, drawing in the smells as if he could consume them as he stood there.

A snort answered him. "No, Uriel. My *cook* did. Of course it was me." There was a certain element of pride in his words. He reached inside and grabbed one with his bare hand. He took it to the table and broke it open, the warmth making him sigh. He handed a section of roasted meat to Uriel.

Uriel bit into the steaming flesh, the taste swamping his brain with pleasurable sensations. He chewed for a moment, enjoying the heat as it slipped down his throat.

He also grunted his appreciation when Kafziel offered him a chair, and he sat at the table with the dismembered carcass in his hands. Then a jug of water appeared at his side. He nodded his thanks, grabbed it and chugged several swallows down. He had needed this, desperately, the food and the warmth.

He was also reminded of Kafziel's earlier words, and he couldn't get them out of his mind. *"You'd be amazed at how close to a woman we can get. I know. I've been there."* Been there? Been where, on top of a mountain? It would be unimaginably cold for a brother, but many of the brothers had been to the tops of the mountains on this puny world. Or, had he meant he'd been close to a woman? If so, what woman, and when? How? It had been forbidden in the Unity since being trapped in this dimension. No one would dare!

Kafziel was cunning, though, and that had him worried. He dreaded what he might find. He would be forced to deal with it, too, if he wanted Reunification with the Unity.

He grabbed another bone, one that had a good-size piece of meat still attached. Putting it to his mouth, he dug his teeth in. As he glanced up, he saw Kafziel standing at the end of the table watching him. His skin gleamed in the heat, his torso tight and muscular, and a smile graced his face. It was an exceedingly beautiful face, too, as were all those of the Unity. What stood out to Uriel wasn't his good looks. It was that the smile on his face wasn't a particularly nice smile, one intended for well wishing. It was one that made his blood run cold, and for some reason, the food he was eating didn't have quite the same flavor from that point on.

He needed fuel, though, so he continued to consume his meal. He had promised twenty-four hours, and he would deal with Kafziel when he had to deal with him. Now was the time for replenishment.

He grabbed the jug of water and took several more draughts, his eyes on Kafziel the entire time.

No, this didn't feel good at all. Not one little bit.

Chapter 6

Chief Mabry, Albuquerque Fire Department

"Get out of my office! You've been drinking too much, the lot of you!" Chief Mabry growled his disgruntlement, as he threw papers around on the top of his desk. They had been in a sort of order when he started, but obviously no longer.

He looked at the men standing in front of him. *Fools!*

"Chief, no. Not a drop." It was the man who'd fainted dead away, letting the water spray across the ground. He went by Sam, although Samuel Abrams was his full name.

"Sam." The chief leaned back in his chair and crossed his arms, all the time chewing one lip. He didn't like this at all. "Come, now. Angels in the fire? Right in the middle of a burning house?" He leaned forward quickly and slammed his hands on the desk, startling the men in his office. "There's no such thing as angels, and you know it, Sam." His face burned hot, and he felt the damp suggestion of sweat on his forehead.

Another man stepped up, a big redheaded man named Gunnar Eriksson. He twisted a baseball cap in his hands. His forehead and nose were charred brighter red than his hair.

"Chief, Sam's telling the truth. You'd a been there, and you'd know." All the men nodded vigorously. "Besides, Chief

Mabry, we were all on duty when the call came in. No beer in the fire hall, ever. Rules. We follow the rules, don't we, men?" Gunnar turned to the others behind him for encouragement.

"Fools!" A new headache started just behind the chief's eyes, and he felt a rock forming in his stomach. "Give me a break. *Angels?*"

"Only one, Chief Mabry." That was from Sam.

The chief stood, jerking erect more abruptly than he intended, his chair rolling suddenly and smoothly across the polished floor, finally crashing loudly into a set of gray file cabinets at his back. He stepped to the window and looked out, pulling at the blinds with one hand. He watched the goings on in the street for a short time, letting silence fill the room. A red car drove by, then a school bus. It was empty except for a driver. The sun was brilliant against a crystal blue sky. There was only one sun, too, but he thought nothing of that. He had never seen more than one sun above his head in his entire life.

Then, with a snap, he released the blinds and turned to his men with an incredulous expression on his face. "Angels?" Seeing Sam open his mouth to speak, he raised one hand to slow him down. "Okay, Sam. Only one angel. Still, you see my point." He shook his head and ran a hand through his hair, a puzzled grin on his face. "I mean, see it from my angle. Think how it sounds when you tell me a man wearing wings, full blown angel wings, strode out of that burning house and handed you, Alonso, an uninjured baby."

"My goddaughter, Chief Mabry." Alonso Silva smiled, stepping forward. "You should see her. Not a mark on her, boss."

Chief Mabry smiled. It was clear Alonso loved the child. "I've seen her, and I also noted there were no marks at all." In spite of that, disbelief washed across him each time he thought of it. An angel! He closed his eyes. "If this gets out . . ." He couldn't go on.

"Chief." A fourth man, Rodrigo Jimenez, normally reticent, spoke up. "We were the only ones who saw it. Sam had the hose—" The men chuckled as they glanced at each other. They had also seen Samuel drop the firehose, and pass out, as well.

"—and when the angel—" He dropped his eyes, his rising embarrassment shown in his deepening color. "—the man, rather, handed Alonso the baby, he just stepped back into the house and vanished, like he was never there."

"Vanished?" The chief's eyes popped open. My god! How bad was this going to get? At least these jokers hadn't said that to the press. "As in walked back into the fire, you mean. If so, we'll find his remains, perhaps that of a homeless person." He had a new, hopeful look on his face.

"No, Chief Mabry. Like vanished. He was there one minute, and the next he was just gone. Tell him, Gunnar." Rodrigo looked expectantly at his friend, for they were indeed friends. Coworkers, also, but like all men who worked dangerous jobs, they had long ago bonded as brothers.

"Faded, boss." Gunnar rolled his hat in his hand. "Just faded into nothing-like, smooth as a baby's bottom." He nodded at Alonso. "No offense to your goddaughter intended, Al." He called Alonso that sometimes when he was nervous, not that Alonso liked it. This time his friend let it slide.

"Still," Chief Mabry persisted, not willing to rescind his disbelief too easily. "One of the other stations, someone you didn't recognize. That must be who you saw. You weren't the only engine there."

"You don't get it." Samuel stepped forward. "Chief, we never even made it into the house, none of us. It was engulfed when the first engine arrived." He pulled Alonso to his side, putting his hand on the man's shoulder. "The first thing Alonso said was, 'Poor Lucita. How will I tell her we couldn't even make a try to save little Angelina?'"

"Then you crossed yourself, huh, Alonso? Remember? Your hand hit your helmet when you did." Gunnar grinned and poked the man's shoulder.

Chief Mabry sighed, sinking into his chair. He picked up a newspaper from his desk. It was from the previous day, so of course had nothing in it about the fire. He tossed it aside. "No one else saw?" His gaze flashed across the men standing before him, and his eyes dared them to say otherwise. "Good. Mum's, and keep it that way. No need to become a laughingstock." He paused, breathing hard for a moment, then he nodded to Alonso. "Glad the baby, Angelina, you say? is all right. Wouldn't have it any other way."

"Thank you," Alonso started, and then he choked up before he could say more.

Chief Mabry simply waved his hand, his eyes now gritty with emotion. "Just get out of here," and he swiveled his chair to hide his burning eyes. When the door had closed, and he knew he was alone, he slammed a fist into the arm of his chair.

"Angels! Dear Mother Mary, I hope this doesn't get out. I'll never be able to attend another Fourth picnic in peace ever again!"

Fire Fighters, Engine No. 4

Alonso whistled, grinning at his friend Rodrigo's antics. It had all started in the chief's office, and now Rodrigo was wound up like a top.

Rodrigo grabbed Gunnar's arm. "The second angel. Why didn't you tell of the second angel?"

Samuel froze in his tracks, a frown on his face. "Second angel? What do you mean, Rodrigo? No one told me about a second angel."

Gunnar grinned. "You were out cold, friend. Stay awake if you want to see all the angels."

"In the house?" Samuel, again, confused. "You telling me there was another angel?"

He had the right to be confused, too. He had, indeed, been passed out, and he had missed it all, all except the one angel walking from the burning building, glowing just like in the pictures on his grandmother's walls, giant feathered wings and everything. Of course, the wings had been gone by then, but it was the wings each man most remembered.

"No, my friend, not in the house." Alonso threw his arm across Samuel's shoulders, the small intimacy one of affection for a close friend who didn't quite get the full picture. It was the way Alonso's stepfather had always spoken to him when he really wanted his stepson's attention. Alonso had unconsciously picked up the endearing habit.

"Then where?" Samuel turned with a puzzled expression to find his friend's face just beside his. He jerked away a fraction, and then relaxed when he saw grins on his friends' faces. "This is a joke on ol' Sammy, right?" He glanced at the other men and smiled.

"They flew away," Alonso's voice whispered in his ear, "just like in a movie." He gestured with his hand, moving it out and up toward the sky. He chuckled. It was easier to make it a joke on Samuel than to accept it as truth. Easier for the moment, anyway. He'd deal with the reality of it later when he talked to Rosita and Lucita. They'd have to know the truth, no matter what the chief said.

"Sure." Rodrigo joined the game, his feet walking backwards to look into Alonso's and Sam's faces. "Like magic, they came through the house's wall, and big wings appeared." He put his hands together at the wrists and flapped them like wings, directly in front of Samuel's face. "Up into the sky, then they were gone." He laughed, slapping Gunnar on the shoulder. "Right, Gunnar?"

Gunnar's eyebrows pulled together, and he worked his mouth. He said nothing.

The other men shouldn't have found his hesitation surprising. After all, he was only one generation removed from the old country, and they had heard his Jewish grandfather speak of things no one believed, winged statues that moved when no one was looking, and miraculous rescues by angelic beings glowing with internal light. Then there was the story of the three Hebrew children thrown in the fiery furnace, kept safe by an angel from God.

"Gunnar, right?" Rodrigo laughed desperately.

Rodrigo was as on the mark in his desperation as Gunnar had been with his hesitation. He'd grown up with a picture of an angel on the wall above his bed, one very much like the picture Samuel remembered from his grandmother's house. It was uncannily like the one that had walked from the burning building, delivering the child into Alonso's waiting arms.

"Sure, Rodrigo." Gunnar gave a half grin, and he glanced at his coworker, but his eyes dropped away quickly. Then, his demeanor abruptly shifting, he barked out a rough laugh. His voice brightened, and his face lifted into an agreeable smile. "Sure, Rodrigo." The others turned to look at him as he continued. "The angels, my old grandfather's angels, they just flew away. Now, I'll have my own crazy stories to tell my grandchildren, and they won't believe me, either."

Gunnar's three friends clapped him on the back. The night had been dark, the flames had thrown confusing shadows, and they'd all been exhausted. Why, when Alonso had rushed inside to snatch his goddaughter from the jaws of death, it'd been the spray from Samuel's hose that had kept him safe while inside the burning structure.

An angel? They all laughed once again, the sounds of their voices as they walked down the street causing people around them to look their way and smile. They were obviously good friends who enjoyed each other's company very much, and for the four, something had clearly gone very well indeed.

Even Alonso laughed at his earlier need to tell Lucita and Rosita about an angel rescuing little Angelina. Why should he be modest, when it was he who'd braved the flames in spite of the protests from Gunnar and Rodrigo? He even remembered Sam grabbing the hose, yelling encouragement to him, that he would keep the flames at bay.

Now, baby Angelina was safe in her mother's arms. Alonso didn't have any smoke in his lungs, although he guessed he'd better have himself checked out later, just in case. After all, he'd been right there in the thick of the battle. He'd had to, to save his goddaughter.

And so, Uriel and Kafziel became no more than shadows, flickering images brought about by the shifting flames in a burning building. The four had been distraught that a life might be lost, and their desperation had caused them to see hope in a heavenly being, one with powers far greater than their own. The men of Engine No. 4 should have never doubted themselves. With years of experience in their ranks, the four firefighters had stepped up to the task, and a child's life had been saved.

Jeqon, Chief of the Fallen

"You be lookin' for ole Gabe? Whoo-be! That a good one."
Jeqon, Chief of the Fallen, laughed, his fingers dancing in the
ether. Without the golden skin and pale hair of the other
brothers, he stood out in the Unity like a sore thumb. His
uniqueness was fine with him, though. He liked to stand out. A
large chunk of something that appeared suspiciously like stone
hit the ground at his side. He jumped back and laughed, waving
off the falling object as nothing.

"That was close, don't you think?" Asbeel and Zadkiel had
come for help in finding Gabriel, and Jeqon was the man, if he
could be convinced to help. Asbeel's wings caught the surrounding light, sending off glittering sparkles. Their substance
was featherless and translucent, more dragonfly wings than the
feathered kind. Unlike on Earth, these wings could not be
dispensed with and brought back at will.

Just off Asbeel's shoulder, a light flickered, his familiar.

"Urgent! Smurgent!" Jeqon danced a little two-step, his
voice a musical singsong. "Gabriel be such a drag." He giggled
a silly little sound, and with an effort, he straightened his face.
He had a flickering light of his own. He reached and stroked it
absently. "So sorry. It just that Gabriel be all justice and power.
He love that Triune Mind. He love that Uriel, too." He caught
Zadkiel's eyes, and he winked, letting his amusement spread
across his face.

"So where is he?" Asbeel made a frustrated face.

"You be lookin' for Uriel? I know where he be." Jeqon
danced another quick jig, his dark wings opening to counter-
balance his fancy footwork.

"Not Uriel, Jeqon! Just tell us!" Still, Zadkiel kept his eyes
peeled for additional falling objects. There were sounds of yet
another brawl coming from the tower rising next to them. "Is it
safe here?"

"Safe as it be anywhere." Jeqon winked again, quite aware
how it made his gold tooth sparkle. "You called for him? He be

61

out there. If he want you to find him, he listen to you. If not, he blow you off."

Zadkiel snorted his frustration. "Tell us this instant, Jeqon. Where can we find Gabriel—"

Just then, a winged brother with yellow-red blood running down his face crashed into Zadkiel, knocking him down. With a rough apology, the brother crawled to his feet, and with a burst of muscular energy, leaped back into the air, returning to the fray far overhead.

Jeqon grinned and reached a hand to help Zadkiel stand. "You two been gone. You not know, then." He reached to his head, twirling one of his tightly woven, spiky stalks of hair.

Asbeel glanced to the golden brother at his side, and back to the dark-skinned one in front. "What don't we know?"

"Quiet, Ash," Zadkiel said, absently running his hand down the outside edge of one wing, frowning at one spot as if it might have been injured in the collision. "Let me handle the questions."

"No," Asbeel retorted. "What don't we know, Zadkiel? What? I don't get it."

"Tell me where you go, first. Then I tell you about Uriel," Jeqon teased.

Zadkiel smiled at Jeqon, explaining their absence. "We've been to Io, jumping the vents."

"Ah!" Jeqon flexed his fingers, making sure his disappointment was clear on his face. "Io. I been wanting to party there. You been, and none invited poor Jeqon. So unhappy, poor Jeqon." He made as if to wipe a tear from one eye. Then he laughed. "It be fun, you know, to jump the light fantastic?"

"Jeqon," Asbeel wailed. "Just tell us!"

Jeqon laughed. "Uriel be cast out some time ago. By Ramiel. Some say Uriel be in cahoots with the Mind. Me? I think he be just a party brother, like old Jeqon. He party too hard, and he be sent down below. You want Uriel, you look there." He snickered. "You freeze you buns off, if you go."

Zadkiel frowned. "Jeqon, you don't think Gabriel, um, went down with Uriel, do you?"

"Ole Gabe?" Jeqon crinkled one eye, not quite enough to be

a full-blown wink. "They be on opposite sides. No. He be here in the Unity. Somewhere."

"You know, then. Will you help us find him?" Asbeel looked hopeful.

Jeqon laughed. "Naw, man. Got me a party happenin' upstairs." He pointed to the top of a series of celestial towers. Faintly, loud music could be heard, and unexpectedly, one brother, pale and golden like Asbeel and Zadkiel, was flung from a balcony. He fell for a distance before recovering, then drunkenly began to heave his wings back and forth, carving an erratic path back to the same balcony. It looked like the same brother who had crashed into Zadkiel earlier.

"Jeqon! Shame on you!" Asbeel shook his head.

"They be havin' a good time, partyin' down the river. Whew, boy! I got to get me back up there." Jeqon's dark wings began to unfurl, and he felt their edges quiver in anticipation. He shifted them, and as he pumped his wings, giving one short brush against the light glowing all around them, he felt his feet rise into the sky. "Gotta go!"

Then, with increasing rapidity, his wings pumped, flinging his body forward in a repeated series of motions. His momentum built rapidly until he was surrounded by sky, the only black object in the Unity of Being. Finally, in a series of rapidly executed backthrusts, he slowed until he settled on the balcony, just where his party was in full swing.

His laughter rang shrilly in the ether.

Zadkiel, Envoy of Freedom, Benevolence, and Mercy

"What a waste of time!" Zadkiel thumped his knuckles against his forehead, mumbling to himself. "Think. Jeqon's chief accomplishment in the past few millennia has been what?"

"Oh, oh! I know!" Asbeel raised his hand excitedly. His familiar danced around him, jumping and sparkling, reflecting its master's emotions.

"You know what?" Zadkiel spat his words with irritation.

"'And it came to pass, when men began to multiply on the

face of the earth, and daughters were born unto them, that the sons of God saw the daughters of men that they were fair; and they took them wives of all which they chose.'" He stood proudly, a pleased expression on his face.

"So? And that means?" Zadkiel popped his friend on the shoulder.

Asbeel snorted, "Now who's stupid? That's real history, you know. I just quoted it from one of the humans' holy books. The Bible, I think they call it. Genesis 6, if I remember my history references correctly. That was all Jeqon's fault, you know. He took a party down there, and they had entirely too good a time. They got to *know* the women, in the Biblical sense, if you get my drift. The Triune Mind stepped in, and that's when that silly Stricture got made up."

"You mean, it was all Jeqon's fault." Zadkiel felt foolish. All this time, and he'd never made the connection.

"Oh, my! I can see it on your face. Jealous, now? I was Chief of the Brothers—"

"Second Chief," Zadkiel quickly corrected.

"Okay, Second Chief, but all the dirt came through me. I had to deliver that message directly to the Triune Mind. He was so angry, I thought he'd explode." His face fell. "Instead, he made that awful Stricture. Poor Gabriel. Uriel, too. Now, they can never be together until we escape this dimension, and that's why I was weak and helped sequester the Mind. Oh, I feel bad about that sometimes."

Zadkiel's mind was already leaping ahead, though, putting two and two together. Kafziel and certain stories he had discounted. Now, learning that Uriel was already on Earth.

If this were true, if Gadreel and Kafziel had teamed up somehow, it was a disaster. He turned to Asbeel. "Brother, we've got to find Gabriel, and now. Follow me." He flexed his torso, and his wings snapped outwards, beating against the sky, lifting him heavenward. He noticed a glowing disturbance at his side, and he nodded, satisfied. His own familiar had finally come to join him.

"How, Zadkiel? How can we find him?" Asbeel's wings expanded also as he called, and in a quick leap, he was just behind his friend, his own familiar following at his heels. He turned his head to look as a sharp, cracking sound ripped through the ether just behind him. With a racing heart, he twisted sideways just in time to avoid the falling railing from the balcony where Jeqon's party was in full swing. It was no consolation that there was no gravity in the Unity. The natural attraction between the objects that made up the great vessel could cause falling objects to impact with substantial force, anyway.

Those that were thrown hurt even worse.

"Come along, Ash!" Zadkiel motioned with an outstretched arm.

Asbeel cried with desperation, "Zadkiel? We can find Gabriel, can't we?"

Zadkiel didn't have an answer to that, because the Unity was very big, a million times the size of Earth. There were millions of places a brother could hide. All he knew was that they had to start looking, and if they didn't start now, the quest was already lost.

Rosita, Alonso's Wife

Rosita spoke softly, one hand on Lucita's arm. "I have the newspaper. Wait here." She stood, and taking a deep breath, stepped through the door into the brightness of the adjoining sun room.

It was the middle of the day outside, and usually she would have all the living room curtains pulled back. The sun would stream in, and the bright colors on the walls would create a lively and warm atmosphere. The room had a Western Mediterranean flair, the decorations ones often found in Spain, or perhaps in parts of the country of Mexico. It was a happy space, one made for family and parties.

Today, the living room curtains were drawn, and light from a lone lamp pooled over the wooden floor. The crucifixes and musical instruments on the walls hunkered in the dimness, their shadows long against the deep colors. The infant Angelina slept quietly on the sofa, and Lucita brushed strands of black hair from her cheek.

Rosita returned to the door, the paper in her hand, one of the deepest shadows falling across her face. She paused, letting out an exhausted sigh. The paper was a heavy weight on her heart.

"Rosita, you cannot be so serious." Lucita laughed. "Open the curtains, please. It's so dark in here."

"Do not ask me twice, not until you have seen this."

"As the baby is sleeping, I will not. Come sit, please."

She stepped into the room and sat in the chair beside the lamp. With care, she placed the newspaper in her lap. From within it, she withdrew a single sheaf of white paper. A picture was drawn on it.

"May I see it, Rosita?"

Rosita looked at the paper, then set it aside, her hand shaking. "This first, Lucita." She held out the newspaper. "The story of Angelina's rescue is here. My Alonso is mentioned. It says he rushed into the flames, saving little Angelina's life."

"So I've heard." She took the paper and opened to the story. "It's just like Uncle Alonso. Angelina will know the tale. She will hear of it every day. I'll make sure of that." She smiled, reaching to brush the little girl's face with her hand.

"Alonso went to the doctor, Lucita." Rosita glanced at the younger woman, then turned her eyes quickly. They were already moist, and she was afraid she would cry. "After the rescue, you must know. It is a thing all the firemen must do, to check for smoke in the lungs."

"He's fine, is he not? I didn't think about the smoke. Oh, I would feel terrible if Uncle Alonso suffered an injury. How our home could burn so quickly, I have no idea. Cristian and I have spoken of it, and it seems unnatural, somehow."

Rosita took a deep breath and brushed the hair from her face. "Your Uncle Alonso is fine. However, that night, I caught him with this. He drew it. When I asked him about it, he couldn't explain it. I can't either." She held up the paper, and the image on it caught the light. It was a drawing of an angel surrounded by flames, with great wings opened at its back. In its hands was a baby, clearly the one lying on the sofa at Lucita's side.

"This is beautiful. May I have it for the baby's new room when we get the house rebuilt? It depicts Uncle Alonso as an angel." Lucita glanced at her aunt, a smile on her face. "What, Rosita? I don't understand. You wish to keep this?"

"No. It is yours. It's just Alonso. It all happened as the papers say. Up here Alonso agrees." She tapped her forehead with her finger. Then she paused, and she felt her lip quivering. Her finger slowly reached to tap her chest. "Here he says it happened like in the picture he drew." She reached one finger to point at the angel Lucita held in her hand.

A single tear rolled down her cheek, as she forced a smile on her face. She didn't know what else to say, because Alonso never lied to her, and that meant he must be telling the truth this time, too.

That didn't necessarily make her feel the least bit better.

Lucita, Alonso's Niece

Lucita's heart was chilled at Rosita's words, and she reached and stroked her baby's cheek one more time. Cristian had spoken to Sam, to express his thanks in rescuing little Angelina. Sam had said the same thing. In his head, he knew he'd held the hose on Alonso, keeping the flames at bay as he rescued the baby. Yet, in his heart, he was convinced it had been an angel from God. He knew it, and no one would ever persuade him otherwise.

"My little angel," she whispered, and her hand reached to hold the baby's small one in her own. "Someone up there must care for you very much. They sent an angel to stand watch over you. We'll say a prayer of thanks every night so that we never forget."

And the drawing. It would go in Angelina's room, and with its reminder, no one would be allowed to forget the night that an angel from God had come from the heavens just to protect one little baby girl.

"Thank you for the drawing, Rosita. I'll always treasure it. Please give my love to Uncle Alonso." After a moment, she felt her heart lighten. "He was so sweet to draw this for me."

In that moment, that was just what had happened. Her Uncle Alonso had drawn a picture of an angel for his little great-niece, to let her know she would always be watched over and protected, no matter what happened around her. How simple it seemed!

Rosita stood, and she looked around the dark room.

"Why, Lucita! It seems I have forgotten to open the curtains. How unusual of me! I need some sun in here. How else will we all be happy?" She laughed, and she threw back the coverings from the windows, bathing the room in light. Baby Angelina fought against the sudden brightness, her nap disturbed, and she began to wail her dismay.

"Oh, look what we've done." Lucita's words were in baby talk, and she pulled a pacifier from her pocket.

"No, none of that." Rosita reached for the child. "She just needs a good hug, that's all. Now that she's awake, we can get to know each other better. Isn't that right, Angelina?" She reached and wiggled the little girl's nose, and the crying subsided.

Neither woman remembered the disquieting feelings that had surged through her heart just moments before.

Chapter 7

Uriel, Bearer of Destiny

"Are you paying attention, Kafziel? We have company." Uriel cocked one ear, listening, and he smiled in anticipation. A snuffling echoed in the rock-walled tunnels outside Kafziel's enormous, heated living chamber. He harbored no doubts about who drew near. It was his familiar, in corporeal form.

"Did you leave meat on any of these? Some may be needed for your friend." Kafziel laughed, and it sounded like camaraderie. "I suspect your familiar will be hungry."

"What do you know of a familiar's hunger?"

"I know of your familiars." Kafziel paused, the snuffling having grown louder, and he chuckled. "This one sounds very large. I'm unsure I have that much food on hand."

Uriel frowned. He didn't believe any claims of friendship that this brother might make. Something in the corridor fell, and there was a yelp.

"What, Uriel? Are you not pleased to see your familiar?" Kafziel chortled sourly. "Call him."

"He will come if I call, Kafziel." *And do as I command.* Uriel put one finger in his mouth and licked it clean, glancing at the other brother. "Do you trust him? If you remember my familiars, you know they are territorial to a one."

Kafziel hefted the meat and paused. "He? You know this? How?"

"He will be." It just *happened.* Uriel stood.

"Will he take a treat from my hand?" Kafziel laughed, lifting a bone and hefting it into the air.

"You might consider letting me be the one to feed him." Uriel turned to the pile of bones, hunting for another one with meat still attached. He picked at one in front of him, pulling a small sliver of tender meat off in his fingers. He held it to his lips and sucked it in. "Trust me. This familiar is male. Canine and very aggressive."

"And filled with fire," Kafziel joked.

"Go ahead. Invite him in. I want to meet him." He did, too. The familiars were the corporeal brothers' most trusted companions, and for that, Uriel sent up a quick thanks to Gabriel. Those without them were at a serious disadvantage. And filled with fire, as Kafziel suggested? He had been, on their last sojourn to Earth.

A mournful howl interrupted events, and Kafziel cocked his head to listen. "Dog?"

Uriel grinned. "Wolf. This familiar I'm looking forward to. Have that meat ready, Brother."

He let out a piercing whistle, knowing his familiar would take on the characteristics of whatever form it assumed, just as the brothers did. The brothers were simply able to focus their corporeal forms more precisely than the familiars. Still, human form gave human characteristics, and wolf form would give wolf characteristics. This animal would be hungry, taking food where it was found, and it would respond only to him. Anyone else had better step aside.

A gray, scruffy canine tore into the room, its lips pulled back, and its teeth showing. It was huge, for no Earth-wolf had ever grown to this size. Its head was low to the floor, and a warning growl emanated from its throat. It glanced at Uriel, then at the meat in Kafziel's hand. It moved toward the food, its jaws snapping with intent. Kafziel began backing away. Uriel laughed, pleased with the sudden shift of power.

"He's hungry. He won't be as patient as I was. I'd toss him that meat, if I were you." He stepped behind Kafziel. "*Now*, I suspect would be a good time." He clapped him on the shoulder, startling the other brother into dropping the meat in front of the animal. The wolf leaped on it, its front paws holding the bone steady, its jaws ripping into the tender flesh. Shaking its head from side to side, the meat tore lose, and the hungry animal snapped powerful jaws, catching it before it could strike the floor.

When Kafziel knelt to watch, the animal paused and snarled, snapping at him when he didn't move away quickly enough. Its eyes burned with a yellow intensity that was enough to unnerve even a wayward "angel."

"I need one of these," Kafziel muttered. He grinned as he glanced at Uriel. "On my side, though. Is it always like this?"

"He, Kafziel. And yes. In this form, he will be all wolf. After he finishes eating, then he'll calm." He walked closer, only to have the animal growl. The growl muted to a rumble as Uriel knelt at the animal's side. The wolf continued to chew and swallow as Uriel placed his hand behind its ears and worked sturdy fingers into the fur.

"Do you not fear the beast?" Kafziel, pretentious death monger that he was, shivered.

"Even I respect this." Uriel stood and stepped slowly away.

"A name? Do you give him a name, or is he just Wolfie?" With the animal settled and chewing quietly, some of Kafziel's arrogance seeped back into his voice.

"Malak." To Uriel it was a label to be proud of, unlike the similar Maalik, which, when spoken, whispered dark etchings of the one who was also called the Guardian of Hell. Soon, he knew, the connection with his familiar would be strong enough for their thoughts to meld on a simple level. Then the name would be even more applicable.

Kafziel chuckled. "Messenger. Why messenger?"

Uriel's mien changed, and with no advance notice, he called harshly, "Malak! Attend! Protect!" In a blur of motion, the gray animal dropped the remains of its meal, and it leaped straight for Kafziel. It landed no more than inches from his body, its exposed teeth poised just at his crotch. An ominous growl rumbled from its throat.

Kafziel hissed, "Uriel. Call the animal off." His words were low and measured.

"Get the *message*? He does whatever I command. That's why I call him Malak, no matter his incarnation. I want a message sent, and he delivers." Uriel laughed and let out a short whistle. The animal slowly backed away to stand at his side.

Kafziel reached to brush his hair from his face. He seemed surprised to find it damp. "Am I safe from your *messenger*, Uriel?"

"Safe, if you behave." He moved back to his seat. "Now I wish to know why I am here. You summoned me, but I know you, Emissary of Solitude. You have a reason for my presence, and it's not because you desire company. Ulterior motives suit you best. What is yours?"

Malak padded softly to his side and dropped to the floor. Each time Kafziel moved, a low growl emanated from the animal's throat.

"I have no motives." Kafziel's voice was smooth and placating.

"I do not believe this is all from the goodness of your heart." Any smoothness from Kafziel served only to convince him it was certain to be a lie beyond all lies.

"I am a brother. You are a brother." Kafziel smiled, and he seated himself at the table, his eyes trained on the animal on the floor. "I only wish to offer you a gift."

"A gift? More than just this food?" Uriel knocked a bone to the floor, where Malak snapped it up. The bone shattered between the wolf's teeth, and the crunching sounds told the strength of its bite. "Perhaps you will give me freedom from this hole in the ground that you have claimed as your den." His hunger satiated, his patience with this wayward brother slipped. He had no desire to retrieve it, either. Rather, he wished to be gone from Kafziel's presence, and with Malak at his side.

Kafziel laughed. "Oh, Uriel, much more than just this food." He casually pushed one of the bones, setting it rolling across the table. "I offer you food for the soul: cinnamon, myrrh, and frankincense."

"What food for my soul, conniver? I cannot survive on spices, no matter how appealing they are." He remembered the baby, though. Hours, half a day—a full day, now!—had slipped away here in this underground lair, and he still remembered the feel of its skin. Even so, that treat had come and gone. He had reached Equilibrium by now, and he would not be able to touch another human before returning to the Unity. What did cinnamon, myrrh, and frankincense count? They were nothing to him, must be nothing to him, no matter how his body demanded relief.

He placed his hand on the wolf's head, and its yellow eyes looked up at him, the animal's first glance away from Kafziel since Uriel's command to protect him. The familiars that followed the brothers to Earth were not outstandingly intelligent, no more than the native Earth species they mimicked. They were loyal, though, and already the telepathic link between the master and his familiar had begun to form. By the animal's response, there could be no doubt Malak sensed Uriel's sudden, intense longing, and just as easily, the wolf sensed when it was hidden away in a safe place in his mind. The animal turned a gray muzzle to look back at what it could see of Kafziel's lower body underneath the table.

Kafziel picked up a small gobbet of meat lying on the table, and he held it to his mouth, pausing for a moment when the familiar at Uriel's side lifted its head. Then slowly he pushed it inside, chewing, grinning to see the head drop once again. When he finished, he swallowed and chuckled.

"This is really good, you know that, Uriel?" He reached to find another morsel. "I see why Malak enjoyed it so. I have more hanging."

"I also noticed his enjoyment, and he has had enough for the time being. Get to the point, Kafziel. You have one, I suppose." Uriel drummed his fingers one time, unconsciously touching the top of the wolf's head to let it know the drumming meant nothing.

"Am I handsome, Uriel?" Kafziel smirked, suddenly playful. When Uriel frowned, he continued. "Seriously, look at me.

73

I have even features and wonderful hair." He shook his head, and his shoulder-length tresses caught the lamplight. They were thick and shiny.

"For what reason do you ask? This seems to me a trick question that can only have a wrong answer. Do you wish to trip me with your empty statements?" Stories had come back to the Unity, where they had been inserted into the Corporate Memory. Kafziel was known to use words to his own advantage, often twisting them to meanings of his own. There was a reason the humans on this world who called themselves Satanists sometimes worshiped him instead of the Lost One of Light.

"No tricks, Uriel."

Just lies. Uriel kept his accusation unspoken.

"Tell me, though, if I were a woman, would you desire me?" Kafziel smiled, and there was beauty in each movement of his face.

"I would desire any woman." Uriel laughed. This subject was a touchy one for most of the Unity. All the brothers in the Unity desired copulation, and none were given release. "There is none in the Unity who would say otherwise. To bastardize an earthly poem, 'How do I love thee? Let me count the eons.' Even you, Kafziel, would I take to my bed, if only you had the proper mechanical systems."

He would, too, the Strictures be damned. Still, male upon male . . . and Gabriel leaped into his thoughts. *Gabriel!* He was gutted with the memories. The Archangel and he were no longer on the same side, and it had been millennia since they had been mated as opposite genders. Perhaps one day again, but that would be a time far in the future. If only someone had the knowledge, the strength to break the hold this corporeal dimension had on them, then they could be together. Only the Triune Mind had a chance of success, and Uriel wasn't sure he could free the Mind, not alone, and certainly not here on Earth.

Release from this dimension would not be soon.

Kafziel stood, his torso bare and glistening in the light from the lamps. He turned to Uriel. "Look at me, Brother. I am an angel, worshipped on this world. I stand at the heads of kings, and I observe their deaths, duly recording each one for the Corporate Memory. Yet, I retain my form always, never aging, never weakening, and always beautiful." Without warning, he clapped his hands together, and in the flash of brilliance that roiled across the room, filling every space, giant, feathered wings spread from his shoulders. He drew air into his lungs, swelling his chest; and he stretched his wings as wide as they would go. As the feathered appendages moved upwards and out, the muscles across his torso and abdomen shifted with the massive weight, for the wings were heavy. These were no lightweight canary wings that the brothers wore.

"Pompous fool!" Uriel snorted his words. "You are as beautiful as you claim, but you have unused equipment between your legs, and it would surely get in the way. I do not desire you."

"Unused?" Kafziel let his wings drop, wrapping them around his body. After a moment, he kicked his pants from underneath his wings, landing them in the middle of the floor. "I grow tired of these human contrivances. In the Unity we never require these *coverings*."

"I told you, Kafziel, I am not interested." Uriel saw what had slid across the floor, and he snorted. Malak raised a furred head, and he reached a hand to calm his pet. "Even if the Strictures were not in place, I would not be interested. Only with Gabriel—" His eyes burned, and he turned his head away. The desire was strong because they had once loved each other as opposite genders. Affection was what connected them now . . . yet, love, too, for love transcended genders.

Kafziel laughed. "Uriel, you thought . . . that I . . . that you and I? Ha! You are a fool." He released his wings, opening them wide, and the perfection of his skin stretched from his face to his feet. The light was just dim enough his glow could be seen, and as he stood there, in his appearance, he was truly the Emissary of Solitude and Tears. He was beautiful either clothed or unclothed, for there was an exquisite perfection about his form. No one could doubt that.

Clapping his hands, the space brightened, and the wings were no more. He sighed. "I miss them when they're gone.

They are heavy in this gravity, though. I tire when I carry them too long."

"You don't need to tell me. I followed you all the way here." Uriel stood. "If you please, I will take your pants, though." He glanced at the other man for permission. "May I?" At a nod, he dropped his own wrappings, and he reached to the floor for the clothing. Deftly, he slipped the pants on. They fit rather more snugly than they had on Kafziel, cupping Uriel's every muscle. He was stockier, and it was to be expected.

"I do need to correct one small observation of yours, Uriel." Kafziel grinned, now at the heart of his game.

"Oh?" Uriel knelt at Malak's side, and when the animal rolled over, he began to vigorously rub the wolf's stomach. Without looking up, he continued, "What observation did I make that was incorrect?" *Handsome? Pompous fool?* He thought those observations were each beyond question, and he had made both. With which did Kafziel disagree?

"My *machinery,* as you so crudely put it, has not gone unused."

"Your hand does not count, Kafziel." Uriel laughed. At least he had found *something* to be entertaining while down here in this hole in the ground.

"I have a daughter, Uriel."

This time Uriel glanced up, and he narrowed his eyes in disdain. "Twist your words any shape you wish, *angel.* There is no daughter." He stood, and he motioned to the wolf. "Heel, Malak. We are being lied to now, and I know that old holy book. Liars burn in the Lake of Fire. Poor Kafziel must be really cold to want that punishment." The wolf was to its feet immediately, and its head felt for Uriel's hand.

"She's here, Uriel. She's real." A smirk of victory painted Kafziel's lips.

Uriel turned, and in the massive floor mirror, he caught a glimpse of himself next to Malak, with the wolf poised at his heels. In the golden light of the cave, they made a striking pair. Uriel was bulky, muscled in appearance, strong in body, indeed, and his hair was as full and dramatic as Kafziel's. His shoulders were broad, and his hands were huge. A gray wolf stood at his side, its scruffiness smoothed out with a good meal in its stomach. They were a pair to strike caution into others' hearts, to be feared and avoided by mortal men. It was for good reason that Uriel was the Bearer of Destiny, chosen to be stationed at the Triune Mind's Seat of Power, sent to warn Noah of an impending flood, the "angel" who brought earthquakes and other natural cataclysms to guide the destinies of men. He was also considered the wisest of the brothers to be stationed at the Triune Mind's Seat, for his brightness in the Unity was not merely of the physical kind, but of the spiritual kind, if the brothers had anything of the sort. It was more of an intellectual illumination, one that came of caring for the right.

And care, he did.

It had failed him when the Triune Mind had separated him from Gabriel, though. Love had turned to hate, and all Uriel had wanted was away from this crazy little world that held the Unity trapped.

There was one other thing. He had also wanted one other thing. Gabriel. That had not been within his grasp, either, and for that, the Triune Mind had paid.

"You hesitate, Uriel."

The words pricked at him. He didn't hesitate. He doubted. What Kafziel claimed must be false.

"You held the baby, Uriel."

He remembered. Cinnamon, frankincense, and myrrh. It was the smell, no, the *taste* of every human on this planet. It crept into the skin. It didn't have to be breathed in through the nose, or taken in through the mouth. It washed the skin with flavors that were too exquisite to be ignored, and it made him want to touch every human he came in contact with. Only . . . only, he couldn't touch a one, just that small infant in those first few moments before he had reached Equilibrium. Only in those moments had he been able to take the child in his hands and deliver it to one of the firemen. An hour later, and no such touch would have been possible. Still, cinnamon, frankincense, and myrrh. His heart surged in longing.

"I held a woman, Uriel."

Kafziel's words were proud, now, because they spoke truth.

77

Uriel could hear the difference. He studied the brother, appearing as a man, standing before him in his naked beauty. Any woman would desire him. His body was lean, and his muscles were long. His face was indeed beautiful.

Then, Kafziel smiled, and it contained the purity of something he rarely showed. Honesty. "Twenty-five years ago. I planned it out, Uriel. I found this old convent in Italy near Rome. It would be simpler, meaning I would have more time, I thought, if the place I chose was on a mountain." He was excited now. His pride in this one achievement was written all over him.

Uriel frowned, unconvinced. "Still, even on a mountain—less corporeal, I grant—while it might be possible, it would not be a pleasant experience for the human. It would also have been recorded in the Chamber of Deeds. No such knowledge is in the Corporate Memory." He had spent time browsing, and recently, too. He would have noticed such an affront.

Kafziel walked to Uriel, keeping on the side away from the wolf, and he placed a companionable arm across his shoulder. "You forget, Brother. We have the first few corporeal moments when the disharmony is still so in flux that we are, in reality, semi-corporeal."

Uriel remembered. He'd barely gotten his wings called up in time.

"Those who record the Deeds of Man cannot see us, yet." Kafziel grinned, gloating.

"And what benefit did that provide you? The Corporate Memory would have known your intent as soon as you integrated back into the Unity. You would have been prevented." In addition, each time Uriel rode the lightship—lightning, to humans—down from the Unity, he never had time to do more than get oriented. He was also usually angry, he had to admit, and that distracted him from doing more than getting his wings functioning.

Laughter preceded Kafziel's answer. "I didn't make it back into the Unity. I had *planned* this, Uriel. I needed to be away from Earth, to become incorporeal, then come right back down. I think I threw horrid insults at Ramiel, and he dropped me right back out of the Unity. It turned out perfectly, too. The lightning—" A portion of the brothers had taken to calling it that, too. "—left me just above the convent I had chosen."

Uriel was not convinced, though. "You were not disoriented? All I ever want when I first reach Earth is to find a source of warmth. You actually recognized this was the same convent?"

"The same. I was *focused,* Uriel. I had *planned* this, and it was going to be successful, too. It had to be, for my long term plans depended on it." He laughed. "It was indeed successful short term, also. I dropped in, did my angel thing, and oh, the taste of that woman's skin. Too bad I had to rush the deed. It wouldn't do to be halfway finished, only to reach Equilibrium, and–" He pressed his palms together, then flung them apart suddenly. "Slam, bam, thank you, ma'am. Sorry, it was fun, and I'm outta here." He laughed uproariously, and it was loud and self-absorbed. "Still, not too bad on my part. I left her a present, too."

Uriel's heart hammered in his chest; he knew what Kafziel insinuated. "There could not be a child. It is not possible." They were of two different races.

He also knew that while in this dimension, the brothers took on human characteristics. In that moment, he remembered Genesis 6. The human's holy book told more truth than the humans knew. By this time, he had stepped back to a chair, and he let himself be seated. His face was in a sweat.

"You are beginning to believe."

"A mixed-blood child. It cannot be." The cave blurred before him.

"Genesis 6, Uriel."

"What?" He glanced up, his eyes catching Kafziel's. "I remember Genesis 6." Dear Triune Mind, he remembered Genesis 6.

"I quoted it to you earlier. Do you recall?" Kafziel grinned. "The sons of God blah blah intermarried with the daughters of men and so on. That was us, Uriel. Don't tell me it's not possible. I've done it." He leaned forward and whispered intently, "She's here, my daughter, and you can touch her. A human woman you can hold in your arms."

Uriel's eyes narrowed. A woman that he could touch? Cinnamon, frankincense, and myrrh? He felt the heat build in his blood, unbidden, yet not at all unwanted. Oh, how he desired that! A woman at last, here, waiting on him.

There was nothing his body craved more.

Chapter 8

Gabriel, Citadel of Justice and Power

Gabriel sat on the tallest spire of the highest rampart in the Unity. One elbow was on his knee, and a lone finger rested alongside his lips. His back was bowed, and his half-opened wings occasionally shifted position behind him, maintaining his balance. His skin emanated the pale golden glow of all the brothers, his hair shimmering with light. On Earth they would say he was beautiful—*strikingly handsome,* for those in Western Culture—as were all the brothers in the Unity.

He wore nothing except his skin, as well as his wings, of course. When all were the same, the party-oriented Jeqon excepted, what was there to hide?

The black brother's very obvious differences were his own special penalty for a misdeed committed many years ago. In the aftermath of the Biblical Flood, unsure whether any of the daughters of men remained, he had made one more attempt to party, traveling with several of the brothers to Earth. Instead of crowded cities of willing humans, only Noah's daughters had been readily available. Then Noah's son Ham had joined in the festivities, and they had mistakenly let the party spill over into old Noah's tent. It had been unintentional, but there he was, drunk, and in the buff.

Later, Noah was none too pleased about the events, and he cursed his young progeny. Once the newly dark-skinned Hamites began to spread across the earth, Jeqon traipsed back to the Unity, feeling pleased to get off unscathed. He soon found the Triune Mind was a bit irritated, too, and he let Jeqon share Noah's, ahem, *blessing* to his younger son.

Now, to Jeqon, it no longer seemed a punishment. Rather, it was his calling card, one that spoke of his willingness to flout authority, to skirt the edge of propriety, to push the envelope, so to speak.

That very willingness to circumvent the mandates of leadership was why he was asked to carry Zadkiel and Asbeel's message to Gabriel. The Archangel was needed, and Gadreel and Uriel were somehow in the picture. Would sweet Gabriel be interested in the news? It was of the freshest quality.

Gabriel, he who had been First to the Triune Mind, First Chief of the Brothers—above Asbeel's rank of Second—and who had announced the birth of the Christ child, was in a funk. He knew he was in a funk, too, just as he knew it was an old-fashioned word that many humans would find hopelessly outdated. He didn't care. Things had not gone his way for many centuries, longer if he cared to count, and in spite of the off-handed concern he had shown Uriel, it had broken his heart to see him so roughly cast down to Earth. There was still love there, even if Uriel would not admit it.

For all that, a wide gulf had opened between them, that of support for the rightful leader of the Unity as opposed to whatever had driven Uriel to follow after Gadreel. It was a hard cross to bear.

"Jesus, I know your pain."

He laughed sourly. Gabriel was the one who had rolled the stone from the man's tomb, telling the women who had come by that the body was no longer inside. He wished someone would roll this stone from his shoulders. He'd just come from the Triune Mind. None of the Three Glorious Faces of the Triune Mind had been able to offer any reasonable hope for resolution of the current situation. Each had been quick to admit that giving up the search for a way back into the Unity's home dimension had been a grievous error, and yes, they readily accepted the blame for the Rebellion that had overthrown the natural order of the brotherhood. At any rate, even if they could free themselves, there was no guarantee that this dimension could be escaped.

At least light still permeated the Unity, even if the Mind couldn't be freed. It was not the brilliant warmth the Triune Mind had once flooded across the enormous vessel, but nothing could be done about that.

Gabriel took in the huge promontories, small in the distance, which thrust sharply into view, many with great buildings extending fancifully into the mists, touting towering turrets and arches weaving elaborately in the absence of gravity. Slender ribbons of golden walkways stretched from tower to distant tower, although they were rarely used for transit. They provided perches, more, dotted with small gathering spaces for viewing the vast beauties of the Unity's expanses. Wings were the preferred method of travel, whether to the ground below or between the tallest minarets.

His eyes scanned the distances, leaping from point to point. Eyes here were not like corporeal eyes, able to focus only at close range, but unable to make out detail at great distances. Across the reaches of the Unity, things were lost to view only from being blocked by intervening protuberances. A simple shift of the eye muscles, and distant items quickly sharpened into clarity, with even the smallest detail visible.

Somewhere out there Gadreel still called, and although he had kept it tuned out for a time, Gabriel knew he would have to answer eventually. The summons couldn't be good, not if the Deliverer of Destruction had become involved, not for Gabriel, and not for Uriel, either.

His eyes narrowed when he saw black smoke rising in the ether. Somewhere, a conflagration had begun to decimate another section of the once beautiful ship. Perhaps a bet had been placed—the brothers had grown accustomed to doing that, betting—and the loss of that wager had been unacceptable. Revenge had been exacted by destroying all within hundreds of

Earth-miles. Such irresponsibility had begun to occur more and more often with Gadreel in control.

Gabriel wasn't ready to move against him yet, for all the pieces of the puzzle weren't in place. He needed more time, if he was to be successful.

To the side of the darkening smoke, a number of golden brothers hung in the distance, their wings sparkling against the brilliant sky, too far to be seen by corporeal eyes, but quite clear to Gabriel. One turned, spinning faster and faster, becoming a blur against the brilliance. Then he stopped, his wings outstretched, and he let himself fall loosely from the sky. While there was no gravity in the Unity, there was a certain attraction between objects, and unstopped, he would hit the ground hard. Would he be injured? Not seriously, but Gabriel recognized the brother's actions for what they were, a game of daring, to spin fast enough to lose consciousness, hoping nearby friends would be quick enough to pull one's wings from the sky before reaching the ground. There had never been such stupidity in the Unity before the Triune Mind was Encapsulated.

Then, the other brothers broke formation and dived for their unconscious friend. Gabriel turned away, no longer interested. The fool would be rescued, although perhaps he deserved not to be.

He sighed, mentally dropping his privacy screen, and he grimaced at the sudden blaring that assaulted him. Everyone could hear it. It was Gadreel, still screaming his name.

Standing, he leaped, and his wings caught the sky. With several rapid beats, he rose in the ether far above any of the solid structures making up the Unity, and once he was far enough to feel truly alone, he slowed the thrusting of his wings to a bare whisper, gliding with security and confidence. At times he needed to be away from what his home had become. Destruction and stupidity had never run rampant through the Unity before. Now, it was more common than not, and conditions continued to deteriorate.

He paused for a moment, luxuriating in the peace he found in the skies of his home. Unlike on Earth where the feathery wings were heavy and cumbersome, here they were lightweight and as natural as being alive. It was glorious to fly when in the Unity. Why did any of the brothers remain down below by choice? He had no answer to that. Now, he had a call to respond to, and making Gadreel angry wouldn't help matters.

His wings stilled themselves for a moment, and he reached his hands above his head and clapped them together. Just for that fraction of a moment before his palms met, he glowed with the image all mankind carried of the heavenly angels. His trim body, slim and long, floated motionless in the brightness of the sky. His skin was the pale gold of an early summer tan. His hair was a mass of blond curls, tumbling to his shoulders. All around him, the glow that filled the ethereal skies of the Unity shimmered, as did Gabriel. Truly, no mortal, had he or she been able to access the Unity of Being, would have been able to overcome his or her awe to focus on the fact that there was no clothing on this "angel." His golden body hair blended so completely with his golden skin that he indeed seemed androg-ynous, a truly sexless heavenly being.

How mistaken they would be, for he was anything but.

As he winked out of existence, a smile grew on his face. There was a rebellion against the Rebellion, and he wondered if Gadreel knew. If not, he would soon enough. When the time came, Gabriel would see to it that he did.

Kafziel, Emissary of Solitude and Tears

"You believe me. I can tell. Your face tells me you want her." Kafziel was smug, and he tasted the tang of victory.

It was a monumental triumph, too, one twenty-five years in the making. He had found the girl—his daughter—brought her here, had no small hand in Uriel's casting out, and now had them together in one location. The sudden need on Uriel's face told him of the burgeoning desire erupting within his body. The earlier infant had been just the reminder the brother had needed to tip him over the precipice: the feel of cinnamon, frankincense, and myrrh against his skin. No brother could resist it. It drew them the same as a dark-weary moth to a beckoning flame, a mariner to the siren's call, or as surely as a teenage human girl in the first flush of womanhood drew the attentions of a lovesick human boy experiencing the initial longings of manhood.

That was to say, the feel of human skin against that of a brother was irresistible. He knew. A quarter Earth-century ago, he had lain with his human partner just for those short minutes when he hadn't yet been fully corporeal, and he had taken away a memory that haunted him still, one of spices he could never enjoy again. Each time he brushed his hand against his daughter's face, he remembered, and the longing was back as strongly as ever, all in that simple touch of spices, the final two spoken of in the holy book, in the story of the birth of the Christ child around whom this world had built a religion.

Poor humans, to be able to offer so much, and for the brothers not to be able to take any of it. *Rather*, considered Kafziel, *poor me,* for by any standard, he was the only one that counted.

Uriel, Bearer of Destiny

Uriel's eyes narrowed. "A woman, for the taking. This daughter of yours is human, you say?" He could hear the huskiness in his voice as he fought his desire, even as he could feel the heat rising in his body. His skin was overly warm within the air of the cavern, and he knew what coursed over him, flooding every nerve, every muscle, every thought with anticipation.

Kafziel, scoundrel that he had proved himself to be, was right. He did desire her.

His head spun with the possibility, and in that rush of sensation, he could no longer focus his thoughts. The last time he had been with his own amour, they had been in another dimension, wearing bodies of differing genders, four-legged ones with furred torsos and heads that could pass for human. In that incarnation, they had loved each other passionately. It had been so long now that he felt sometimes it had never happened.

86

These bodies, though, these corporeal bodies they took when on this planet, craved the touch of cinnamon, frankincense, and myrrh, and just the thought that it could be his this very day made his pulse race wildly underneath his skin.

"I brought her here just for you."

Uriel glanced up to see Kafziel immediately before him. He drew in a sharp breath, surprised he hadn't seen him approach. It was the need. He knew that.

The slender, golden brother knelt before him, his face filled with the appearance of concern and understanding. "She sleeps in the next room—"

"Here?" Uriel's interruption was abrupt and harsh. He felt concern flood his veins. It was his Mandate checking the need, filtering the lust that had nearly overtaken him. "She tolerates this heat?"

Kafziel took Uriel's hands in his. When Malak dropped a raised tail and growled warningly, Kafziel glanced down at the animal, then gently released Uriel's hands. "As do all brothers. She is one of us."

"Wings? She can call her wings? The glow of corporeal disharmony? She has that, surely, if she is one of us, as you say."

"Wings? I do not know, Brother. She is half-human, after all." Kafziel laughed, placing a curled fist on Uriel's clothed knee, then glancing at Malak. When the growl didn't reappear, he let his hand remain. "I have not told her the lineage that fathered her into existence, so of course I couldn't ask if she would please try to fly." He chuckled at his little joke. "No wings so far, but she definitely glows." He reached and tapped Uriel's bare chest with his knuckles. "Just like you and me."

A growl, low but distinct, caused him to pull his hand away.

"Her appearance? She must be beautiful if she is a brother, as you claim." Uriel softened Kafziel's beauty into that of a woman, and he saw her as she must be. His stomach wrenched with desire.

"As I am, Brother Uriel." Kafziel's words were those of an intimate, a concerned confidant, one who only has the best interests of a friend at heart. He oozed buttery comfort.

"As you are." Uriel spoke the words with narrowed eyes.

"You do still agree that I am very handsome?" Kafziel's eyes sparkled with his question, and his honey skin glowed.

"I need not answer that. You know how beautiful you are." At a look of mock protest on the other man's face, he laughed a short bark of humor. "You know what I say is the truth. You are not handsome. You are indeed beautiful, Kafziel. Our disagreements aside, I will admit that to anyone."

Kafziel dropped his head for a moment. He had a wide smile on his face when he looked up. "As I am beautiful, Uriel, my daughter is even more so."

Uriel stood, his eyes dancing about the interior of the mine. "Sleeping, you say. Where, Emissary?" He riveted him with a look, one of iron and rivets and manacles that could never be broken free. "I see no one besides us."

"Let me take you—" Kafziel motioned to a doorway, reaching out a hand as if to lead his brother.

Uriel's Mandate was strong, and forcing the fog of desire away, he was immediately awash with doubt. He saw Kafziel as he was: a liar and a conniving cheat. He narrowed his eyes, and hatred flew from them as lightning from the heavens. He barked, "Malak! Attend!" The wolf leaped to his side, Kafziel already the sworn enemy, his flesh there for the animal's fangs to taste.

Kafziel's hands flew up, and he backed a step, his eyes cutting to the yellow eyes at Uriel's side. "I speak truth, Brother. She is yours. My daughter. Her skin is as beautiful as golden flax; the touch of her flesh is as the spices of the Orient. I fathered her, and I gift her to you."

"Offer proof, if you would have me believe you."

"In back, Uriel. There are a series of chambers there. I have made use of more than one of these rooms." He laughed lightly, motioning around the great space.

"You said she sleeps, though. We have been here the better part of a day. It would not surprise me to know the sun has risen and set again while we have occupied ourselves within this space." Trust in Kafziel didn't flow easily. He had come through with the food, and Uriel had enjoyed the warmth. Be that as it may, there was something clearly devious about this. "Show her to me. I wish to speak with her."

A few moments earlier, he would have fallen upon any female offered to him, anything to satisfy his sudden need. Yet, there would be a price to pay for anything Kafziel offered, and Uriel would be wise not to forget that. He blinked to see the other brother standing at an opening in the wall, one just beside the superheated forge. He realized he hadn't seen him move. It was the need that still burned in his veins.

"Coming?" Kafziel smiled, and he turned toward the opening, motioning with one hand. His body caught the light, gleaming. The corridor just in front of him was filled with darkness, and silhouetted, his perfection seemed impossible. His shoulders flowed into a narrow waist, then dropped past his buttocks into long, muscular legs. He would have been a runner, if his body had belonged to a human athlete. As he stepped forward, he moved with grace, an ease of motion that defied description, one that made him seem to walk on air, even as his feet touched the soil. Indeed, without his wings, he still appeared the angel he was reputed to be.

Even so, Uriel knew him as the Emissary of Solitude, bringing only sorrow, and in that, he brought happiness to no one. He dared not hope this girl, this woman, this *daughter*, was all that Kafziel had promised, if she were here at all.

He crouched and forced his fingers into Malak's fur. He leaned to the animal and whispered, "Come with me, boy. Be safe. Be quiet. Help me if I call." Then he stood and walked forward. He glanced down, satisfied to see the trusted familiar at his heels. Striding to the door, he slipped into the darkness. Finding a long corridor, he picked up his pace, easily catching Kafziel. He clapped a hand on the wayward brother's shoulder to slow him, waiting until he came to a stop before removing his touch.

Kafziel turned to him, his expression warm and helpful. "Yes, my brother?"

"She sleeps, you said." Uriel took a deep breath and released it. Although his mind doubted Kafziel's honesty, his body had not released the totality of its need. It caused his breathing to come too quickly, and he suspected it clouded his judgment. "What have I not been told? Brothers do not sleep."

Kafziel dropped his head and chuckled. "I have told you the truth." He looked up, and his eyes were clear and honest in the way of an expression that had been practiced until it was perfect. "She is my daughter. She goes by Angioletta, although I believe her given name is Angiola. She sleeps, because all humans must."

"Italian. She is Italian, then." Uriel considered any implications that might entail. She might speak only her native tongue, although that would present no difficulties for a brother. All languages were his. Still, to know her origin was to know the person.

"I told you the convent was near Rome." Kafziel's words were easy, although measured. "She emigrated as a teen, and I located her in Los Angeles." He laughed, truly amused. "It was so appropriate. I lost track of her for many years, only to finally find her living in the City of the Angels. I should have looked there first."

"That's many miles from here. She chose to travel so far with you?" Uriel's doubts were not assuaged so easily, not over such an impossible thing.

Kafziel paused, and his face turned serious, for the first time hardening his features. "She did not want to come with me. My Suggestions to her . . . she fought them easily, overturned them as soon as she realized what I was doing. I couldn't have her run away, not with you coming for a visit, dear friend Uriel. As I said, she is asleep. She is also yours."

I couldn't have her run away. With those words, insight swept over Uriel, and he knew. This woman was drugged. Kidnapped and drugged, if Kafziel had acted as he normally did. He would want her still . . . well, his *body* would want her—*did* want her!—but he was not one to take advantage of a drugged human. He didn't want to admit, and would certainly have denied it were he asked, that just minutes ago, when he first heard Kafziel's offer, even drugged, he would have fallen on her with no hesitation. His body still cried for release, but his mind refused the thought of taking his pleasure at another's unoffered expense.

He shook his head to clear his thoughts, forcing his thinking away from that which had been denied him so long. "Gabriel," he whispered, "I was willing to betray you." He turned, prepared to exit this den of lies and be gone from the Watcher's foolishness.

"Uriel, surely you aren't leaving." Kafziel caught his arm, and he laughed. "Have I offended you? This way. My daughter waits."

He reached and pushed open a heavy wooden door. Inside, a portion of a room revealed itself. Appointed rather more luxuriously than the previous chamber, it glowed with a gentle radiance. A lamp was on a chairside table, and it burned gently, its warm light making the space seem inviting after the darkness of the corridor. The foot of a bed was visible.

"Come see, Uriel." Kafziel pulled on Uriel's muscular arm, inviting him in.

Uriel's disgust at Kafziel's crudity gripped him. With anger in his words, he forced his rebuke out. "To bed a slave? Is that it, Kafziel? I am aware your mating with her mother was surely no consensual act, no matter that she probably invited you into her bed. What lonely woman cloistered in a convent would not take a brother, an *angel* of your beauty, if you appeared to her unbidden in the middle of the night? The weakest of Suggestions would sway her mind." He reached to calm the wolf when he realized there was a constant growl coming from the animal's throat.

Kafziel laughed softly. "Still, she is my daughter, Uriel. I have stroked her skin. She is all you will want her to be."

Uriel choked out his response. "You have bedded her already, disgusting even the most depraved of the earthbound brothers?" He pictured Lucifer. The Lost One of Light was known to have done viler things.

"Hardly." Kafziel chuckled, although the sound was terse and condescending. "You cannot believe that of me. I stroked the skin on her face, only." He leaned in and whispered, "I saved her just for you. I've seen your expressions. I've watched your body. You want this woman. Step inside and see if she is

91

not as beautiful as I have said. Take her, Uriel. Treat her gently—or not. She is yours. If she survives your affections, then she belongs to you to share with your friends."

"You would not care if she dies?" Uriel was further infuriated, and he took a menacing step forward.

"If you wish otherwise, you may certainly leave. There are other brothers who have expressed interest." Kafziel paused, and his next word was whispered in an offhand manner, as if it didn't matter. "Lucifer."

"You would not." Uriel growled, and he heard it repeated in the animal at his side.

A laugh, one foreboding and malicious, was his answer.

"You are as vile as any I have ever known, but this is your daughter. You could not, not the Lost One of Light."

"I could, and I would. However, you see, I came to you first. You are the Bearer of Destiny. Perhaps it is this girl's Destiny to become yours. She was sired for this very purpose. If that isn't Destiny, then I don't know what is. After all, you are here."

"You reprobate." The words spat themselves out, and they spoke truth beyond any that had been broached so far.

"You misjudge me. I am no reprobate. I am the Emissary of Tears, and I watch over the deaths of kings. I have seen too much sorrow, and I have no more sympathy for suffering. You might know, I did turn down Samael. He was definitely interested. He offered to fight you for his chance at her. No, I told him. I was not interested in his offer. *He* was, though. If you don't want to avail yourself of my generosity . . . someone will." Kafziel shrugged, and in that moment, it revealed him as the callus and indifferent purveyor of depravity that he was. Gone was the brother with honey for words and oil in his manner.

Images ran through Uriel's mind of Samael, the Dispenser of Death, the Seducer, the one known to many as the Grim Reaper, and they were not attractive ones. He felt no doubt Kafziel was telling the truth now. This was the Emissary of Sorrow he knew, and it meant he couldn't simply walk away, not and leave this half-human to the mercy of a Unity filled with brothers who had not been able to bleed their building hormones for thousands of years. Their bodies were polluted with need, and one half-human woman would not be enough to satisfy them all.

Possibilities for her rescue tore through his head, and none of them seemed plausible. For her safety, he could not spirit her away himself. His body already fought with him, wanting desperately to take control of this situation, to taste this woman's skin; or perhaps he was simply paying attention to it again, and only by determination was his mind refusing. That struggle alone wracked his gut with turmoil.

Still, if he walked away . . . and in that moment, with a searing agony that tore his essence wide, he remembered, no, *knew* who he was. He couldn't walk away, for the same reason he hadn't been able to abandon the baby earlier. It was his Mandate, as well as his ticket back into the Unity. If he left her to Kafziel's devious devices, it would be found out. Yet, no matter how strongly he desired to rescue this woman, one he hadn't even seen yet, his body wanted her almost beyond control. He dared not risk that, no matter how he desired what was just through that door.

"Go in, Uriel. I see it in your tormented expression. You desire what I've offered. Step inside. You may take your wolf with you." Kafziel laughed, motioning with one hand.

"Your cost?" Uriel still needed time to think. "I know this is not something you wish to give away." His mind was near blind with his body's screaming need, and for a moment, he squeezed his lids tightly, trying to blink it away. "You mentioned a trade. A trade for what?"

He felt Malak rub against his leg, the wolf's fur rough even through the Nomex pants. The animal felt his unease, as well as his indecision. Uriel knew. Their minds had already begun to meld.

"Something you will not need for a while."

Uriel laughed, his blood crazy with sensation, his words growing heedless. "My wings? You have your own. Malak? He will not respond to you. I have nothing else, Kafziel. Not even my own clothes. What I wear is yours."

"Something simpler, Uriel." Kafziel stepped into the room, clearly in an attempt to draw Uriel after him. "Come. See my prize. See that she is as beautiful as I have promised. I should be allowed to sire more children. They would interbreed with the humans and improve the race."

Uriel did step forward, unable to stop his feet from moving. The bed exposed itself fully, and as he glanced at the form lying there, he saw the brother's words had been no boast.

"She is indeed beautiful, Kafziel."

She had the coloring of one of the brothers, golden with clarity of depth in her skin, and in the muted light, she glowed against the bed linens. Sweat threw a sheen across her face, and lying on top of the coverlet, her slender arms twitched sporadically.

"Step to her, Uriel. She dreams, and it is of you." Kafziel reached to her, brushing his hand down her cheek. He closed his eyes, with ecstasy written on his face. "Her mother felt this way. All those years ago, and I remember it exactly." Then he pulled his hand away and opened his eyes. He coughed and smiled wistfully; and abruptly he laughed, shaking his head and stepping away. "That was only my fingertips. When you lay with her, Uriel, and the sensations rush through your loins, you will know such bliss. It will be worth whatever price you are asked to pay. I will guarantee it. Remember, I've been there."

"With her mother." Uriel knew pounding in his temples, and in that moment he envied Kafziel.

Kafziel stepped to Uriel, one eye cautiously on the wolf, and he touched an arm. "Come, stroke her skin. Just once, Uriel." When Malak shifted position, keeping two yellow eyes trained on him, the brother released the arm, backing away, and indicated with his head, almost pleading. "Just one touch, Uriel. Then, if you wish to leave, you may go, no questions asked."

Uriel wanted to walk away, just to leave this girl with her father, and let the situation work itself out without him. Oh, how he wanted to do that! He also wanted to yell to the other man to exit the room, and he wanted to throw himself on this woman, no matter what the Unity might say. He clearly remembered the touch of the child's skin, and it had been the

94

taste of ecstasy. That brush of sensation . . . he could barely think of more than how his skin would feel pressed against hers.

He stepped forward to stand beside the bed, burning with the heat in the room. Or perhaps, he was willing to admit, it had become warm with the heat of his need. She lay there, her eyes twitching with some dream living itself out deep inside her thoughts. Not of him, he knew. Still. Perhaps. He reached, hesitantly at first, then abruptly he stroked her cheek. As his skin touched hers, he staggered with the inrush of sensation.

It was true; she was everything Kafziel claimed, and his brain clouded with desire. His heart pounded as his eyes watched one of her arms shift with his touch, and the glow against the cloth reminded him of the first time the Unity had slipped into this dimension.

They hadn't known then that they were already trapped, and the brothers had exulted in their new forms, the splendor of the Unity, the wings on their backs, and the soaring through the expansive ethereal skies. He and Gabriel had first noticed the glow when they'd found an enclosed space to simply sit and enjoy each other's company. The glow of their skin had been impossibly striking, their tall, pale-gold forms driving back the darkness. They had spoken of previous incarnations, of the dimensional interfaces they could assume during their time here, and in those moments, they had known their love for each other would never fail them.

It had, though. Uriel's love for Gabriel hadn't dissipated, but still, their love had failed them. Gabriel was not here with him, and this girl's skin was like liquid fire surging through his veins.

Still . . . still.

Uriel had been unable to cast away the love they'd once known. Gabriel had been his, and yet, in this moment, at this girl's side, he knew how alone he was. Gabriel and he had taken different sides in a protracted war, and now they were divided forever. Their love hadn't lasted.

He knew he could take this girl. Still, the pleasure would come to an end, an hour or two or twelve away. She hadn't offered herself to him, and for that reason, he could not expect more than just this one sensation-laden night of release from his pent-up need. Once his body was sated, he would be forced to allow her anger to drive him away.

He jerked his hand free. He needed to think, to clear his mind, to know what to do, and he could not do that with his skin against hers. It must be what he knew was right. He had a Mandate. He must lead this woman to her rightful Destiny, no matter what his body cried for him to do. He must return to the Unity, where he would find Gabriel. Their relationship had been broken, but broken things could be fixed. He was certain of that. He was also certain that if he took this half-human in his arms and satisfied his need for her, there would be no repairing his relationship with Gabriel ever again.

In a burst of anguish, fueled by a desperate lost love and a bodily need he could hardly contain, he yelled for Malak to *attend.*

"Protect!" came his next cry, and he was pleased to see the great gray canine snarl with sudden fury, leaping for Kafziel.

In that moment, coming to a decision he didn't even know he intended to make, convinced he could not leave this woman, he grabbed her in his arms, wrapping her in the surrounding bedclothes. With a cry of victory, he tore past a snarling mound of dog and man, hoping Malak did enough damage to allow him and his charge to make it to the surface. There would be no passing through solid walls with this half-human in his arms. He must go rapidly, too, because once out of the mine, without enough of a head start, Kafziel would be able to trace his trail.

As he exited the door, he yelled back through the opening, "Malak. Kill!"

A snarling cacophony of deadly wolf and startled brother chased Uriel down the corridor. As he ran, stopping to adjust the awkward package in his arms, his repeated jostling shifted the dead weight. She was a dead weight, too, but at least she was wrapped in the bedding. His skin wasn't touching hers. Now, if he could just get her to safety.

Safety? He wasn't sure that was possible. Where on this planet would this woman be safe? Once her secret was out, as

96

he suspected it already was, every brother who had been deemed an outcast from the Unity would be searching for her, wishing to make use of her.

As he slapped the controls on the lift, he looked at the face of the woman in his arms. He admitted that to himself. She was no girl. He could feel the difference through the bedding, and there was a difference. She was every bit as beautiful as Kafziel had claimed. More so, he thought. Oh, much more so.

The clanking of the arriving metal cage demanded his attention, and he stepped inside. With his elbow, he depressed the button displaying the up arrow. He knew his first moment of relief as the cage began to move.

He wished he wasn't forced to leave Malak behind. Still in all, he had confidence in the wolf. He had no doubt that Kafziel would come out on the losing end of the stick in any confrontation with Malak. If the animal survived, it would come to him. It would search him out, and they would be together once more.

After an interminable time, the cage reached the top, and with several loud clanks, the doors released themselves. Uriel hefted his load, and he stepped into the dusty passageway. He looked at the crates of food, and he wished he had a way to carry some with him. He couldn't, though. This woman was more important.

He also realized he couldn't don his wings and heft her through the air wrapped in these slippery linens. It would be risking a fall that would surely kill her.

Carrying her to the door, he shifted her awkwardly to one arm, and grabbing the handle, he flung it wide. Once outside, he set her carefully on the ground. Peeling away the bedding, he saw she was dressed in clothing that was, thankfully, a little more prim than what he'd expected to find. Perhaps it was her convent background, for linen sleepwear covered her from neck to ankles.

He glanced around. It was, as he had suspected earlier, growing dark again. He wished he could wait until the light was fully gone to fly, but they were out from civilization, so it was a risk he felt he could, no, *must* afford.

Standing, he clapped his hands together, and in a great flash of light, its brilliance billowing across the lonely rock outcroppings, he felt the weight of his wings across his torso. Flexing his muscled arms, he brought his enormous appendages to his sides, and he leaned to pick up the woman.

As he reached for her, he felt the brush of his skin against hers, and he staggered. A rush of spices flooded his senses, and with great effort, he pushed the feelings aside. Lifting her in his arms, he draped one of her bare limbs across his shoulder. He tensed as the scent of cinnamon, the perfume of myrrh, and the soothing of frankincense once again permeated his awareness. It also aroused his loins, but that he would ignore—he must!

"Oh, Gabriel," he whispered hoarsely to the heavens above, his words tearing themselves from his throat. This was not what he wanted. His heart cried for the one he'd loved for as long as he could remember. "Look what I've gotten myself into. It's you I need."

He paused, choking back his feelings, for the woman in his arms had not released her hold on him at all. He wanted both, for his heart was pulled in one direction, and his body in the other. He only hoped his heart was stronger.

Then, tensing his legs, he bent them into a crouch, and judging the extra hundred pounds he carried, he leaped, his great, feathered wings flinging themselves forward to catch the air. As the appendages at his back pumped, he held his charge tightly, one arm under her legs, and the other holding her upper body next to his. Her face rested in the crook of his neck, and one limp arm encircled his shoulders. It surprised him to discover that somehow the touch of her skin against his seemed to empower his wings rather than hinder him. He flew higher and stronger than he had when chasing Kafziel, and it didn't seem to tire him at all.

It didn't occur to him that extra levels of testosterone might do that to him. He felt he could fly all night, and the extra weight he carried in his arms was no more than a feather to him, easily carried aloft in the growing dusk.

Old Joel, Town Drunk

Uriel thought he would be unseen. He failed to consider that flying "angels" in the near darkness of a desert sky are only invisible if no one is watching.

In the gathering gloom of the evening, he had an observer as he carried Angioletta to safety, and Uriel's audience of one was very aware of him. Far below, two corporeal and very human, although quite bleary eyes watched it all.

Old Joel had hitched a ride west out of Phoenix. In spite of his good intentions, he just hadn't been able to stay on the wagon any longer. He sat in that trucker's cab, and finally he reached into the old backpack he lived out of, taking an occasional sip out of the brown bag he'd picked up at the convenience store back in the city. Pretty soon, the driver caught on. When Old Joel started singing brashly—and well off-key—he was unceremoniously dumped alongside the road, backpack, brown bag, and all.

He was pretty drunk, though, so Old Joel hadn't really minded too much. He just wandered off into the desert, looking for a cool spot to spend the night. When he heard the ruckus overhead, he looked up. He fell to his knees at the sight, because there, right over his head, glowing in the fading desert evening, was an honest-to-God angel, flying through the air, with real, honest-to-God wings. He was carrying a woman in his arms, just like in all the pictures he'd seen in the soup kitchen lines. God bless him, if she didn't glow, too.

Without a second thought, he reached in his backpack, and he pulled out that brown paper sack. He'd already emptied most of it, but he knew he didn't want any more. He pulled that bottle out and dashed it right against a rock, shattering it to where he couldn't drink another sip.

"Jesus," his old lips stuttered, his bristly chin quivering, "I'm goin' straight tonight. You done give me a sign. I'm a goin' back ta Phoenix, even if'n I have ta walk the whole way. Tomorra night, I'll be workin' the soup line, just like the good reveren' askt me to. I'm sorry, Jesus. You doan have ta tell me twice."

His old feet shuffled back to the highway, and he crossed the road to hold his thumb out. He was surprised when the very next car stopped to offer him a ride.

Kinky Kinkerson, Reporter

For the ensuing hour, Kinky Kinkerson, the driver of the car, listened to the old fool tell his story a hundred different ways, a crazy tale of being visited by an angel from God.

Later, after dropping Old Joel off at the mission, Kinky stopped at a local motel. Once inside, he flipped open his cell phone, and he dialed in a number. When it picked up, he chuckled into the line, "Remember that house that burned the other day, and that baby that was saved? What did your reporter overhear the firemen saying? Something about an angel with wings? Well, I have another one for you, this time just out of Phoenix. Yeah, you heard me right, a real, wing-wearing angel, right out of the pictures on my grandmother's kitchen wall."

Chapter 9

Gadreel, Deliverer of Destruction

Gadreel ran an invisible hand along the back of the equally invisible Seat of Power, admiring its beauty greedily. It told of the magnificence of his authority, of an uprising he had heralded, and one he had led successfully, too. After all, he was the Leader of the Rebellion, Rightful Replacement to the Triune Mind, the One Who Would Lead the Brothers Back to Their Home Dimension. That last title was rather cumbersome, but someone had called it out into that long-ago foray, and it had been a monkey on his back ever since. It amused him when it was used as a term of respect. He personally preferred Glorious One. No one ever called him that, though.

The Seat ... no matter the names he was called, the Seat symbolized his eternal power, for the Seat was rock solid, as it had been since it was removed from the Unity of Being. It would never be moved from this place, for the Energy Nodes located at various coordinates held in place those items that must be held in place.

He settled into the Seat of Power, feeling the Strength of the Ages as it bled into his being. The Seat was the pilot's chair from the ship, the vessel named Unity of Being, in which he and his brothers had repeatedly slipped through dimensional inter-space. The Triune Mind had been genetically formulated as the pilot, his three faces capable of three different and very necessary skills. With any one of them taken away, piloting the ship was impossible. It was for that reason he had been spared. Without the Mind, the original purpose for the journey was moot. Under the current circumstances, Gadreel mused that perhaps the journey was without further purpose, no matter what. The voyage had already covered so much time, eons of it stranded here in this corporeal dimension alone, that it was hard to remember just why they had started out in the first place.

There was another problem with the length of time they had been stranded here. Some had developed concerns about how long individual life could be sustained in the Unity without shifting to a new and different dimension. It was the shift between dimensions, and the reformation of their bodies, that gave them renewed life. They had already been here for thousands of this world's years. Was the increasing degradation of the Unity's social mores a signal of impending doom?

Now, though, more immediate matters weighed on Gadreel's mind. His was not that of Triune function, the Planner, the Rememberer, and the Executor. The Mind had been bred to run this society, and even he had failed. How could Gadreel do better?

Even so, arrogance steeled Gadreel's backbone. He would best the Mind. He must! He would garner all help that was available, and he would lead his people home, no matter what it took.

To complete that, right now he needed Gabriel. Double-crossing, troublemaker Kafziel was in cahoots with that fool, Uriel, and if Ramiel's words could be trusted, Uriel was working to return the Mind to power. It must not be allowed, and if he needed to coerce help from those who otherwise would refuse, he would do whatever it took. The Unity was his now, his to wrench free from this cursed place, no matter what or who he had to destroy to achieve that goal.

Sitting in the Seat, now removed from the Unity and anchored in this spot for the continued security of the Rebellion, he *called* once again for Gabriel, knowing that the seat would double the force of his command.

When his sending didn't return to him, he smiled. It seemed the Archangel had finally lowered his defenses. There was no doubt he knew of Gadreel's demand for his presence. He would come. He'd be a fool not to.

Besides, if he didn't, it would be time to pull out his final trump card, the Triune Mind's four Pets. They would surely make a mess of things down there on that pretty little globe, but what did Gadreel care? The important thing to remember was that Gabriel, carrying the Mandate of Justice and Power, would care very much, especially as Uriel was involved.

Rising from the Seat of Power, with his nonexistent arms crossed over his nonexistent chest, Gadreel assumed a stance of superiority. When his visitor arrived, he wanted Gabriel to be very aware who was in command, to acknowledge just who knew all the facts, and to kneel before the one whose will would be done. The Archangel would bow to Gadreel's request, for such acquiescence was Gadreel's alone to command.

The blackness in front of the Seat of Power bent, twisting into a Place of Power, slowly at first, then with an accelerating vehemence that was alarming. The stars beyond dimmed to blackness, the canvas of space becoming blank for a time, and the distant pinpoints of eternal suns only returning when Gabriel began to materialize in front of Gadreel. Just for a moment, Gadreel was satisfied, for Gabriel's command performance proved his subservience to the one who held the Seat of Power for his own.

Then, Gadreel's eyes were blinded by a brilliance that exploded into a concussive force, nearly bringing him to his knees.

Interlude 4

Of course, Gabriel didn't really materialize in that particular location in space, not in the physical sense, no more than the Seat of Power was actually to be found in that specific location among the celestial bodies. It was the Energy Nodes that determined what was there and what wasn't, that kept certain coordinates in the vastness between the worlds reserved for the perceived presence of the Seat of Power. It was the Energy Nodes that allowed Gadreel to stand with his arms crossed, and that permitted Gabriel's essence, his *soul,* to coalesce in that particular space and at that particular time, right in front of the one who had called him out of the Unity.

Gadreel had thought he would stand tall, his power dwarfing that of the recalcitrant Archangel, and that there would be a clear division of power. He had pictured his foe abased at his feet, with himself as the Victor, poised, commanding and proud in front of the Seat of Power, and shaming Gabriel into submission. He would then take the high road, telling the one-time First to the Triune Mind how the Unity needed his help down on Earth, that one of the brothers had been deceived into a betrayal that could endanger the very stability of power in the Unity. He would tell how the Four Horsemen had already been prepared, although he knew they certainly had not. It was only the Four Familiars of the Triune Mind. They would stir devastation enough. He would encourage Gabriel that only his intervention would keep their rampaging destruction at bay. Could he please travel to Earth and return Uriel safe and sound? What a great favor he would be providing to the Unity!

He got a surprise, for Gabriel's appearance was not quite what he expected. True, there was a clear division of power. Yet, once space bent, the stars flickered, and Gabriel burst onto the scene, it was not the usurper to the Seat of Power who stood tall in his dazzling display of authority. This was no meek Gabriel wishing only to offer a word of caution to a good friend, one who was being cast from the Unity to the punishing corporeality they knew as Earth, coyly stepping aside when frowned upon. This was no weakling willing to bite his tongue and remove his hand when told to absent himself from the Seat of Power. That Gabriel was a simulacrum to be pulled from Gabriel's bag of tricks when subservience would do the most good, only to be put aside when the good was accomplished.

Gadreel held no authority greater than Gabriel's own

Mandate of Justice and Power, and yet he had commanded the Archangel's appearance, for the one who was more powerful to come at his bidding. Gabriel didn't relent lightly, nor did he come in the best of humors.

In the blackness of space, grounded by the Energy Nodes that made his presence possible, Gabriel's blazing manifestation exploded into Gadreel's consciousness. Were corporeal eyes able to see into incorporeal dimensions, a vivid flash of energy would have throbbed into sudden existence, its power blinding. The backwash of corporeal photons as they were thrust aside would have crisped living flesh.

It was perhaps good that the two brothers were not really there, and only their incorporeal selves remained anchored by the Energy Nodes. For that reason, and that reason only, Earth and her moon still turned in their orbits, and the sun continued to pour forth its life-giving energy.

It was only by the grace of the brothers' incorporeality that human life didn't cease in that moment of Gabriel's transition from the Unity into Gadreel's presence.

Incorporeality, it seemed, had its good points, for the sake of humanity, at least.

Gadreel, Deliverer of Destruction

Gadreel shuddered under the onslaught of Gabriel's blinding flash of unearthly incandescence. Fear coursed through his incorporeal veins, although he refused to show it, no matter how terrified he felt, and he was indeed terrified.

So, he did the only thing he could. He trembled.

Gabriel was the First of the Brothers, the Citadel of Justice and Power, the Great Archangel, second only to the Most Loved of Brothers, Michael. It had been a long time since Gadreel had viewed Gabriel as he really was, the third most powerful brother in the Unity. He had forgotten, too, just how real power felt. It washed across him, it felt good, and it also ripped any semblance of self-worth from him.

Instinctively, he felt his knees start to give, his own

unconscious prostration to Gabriel as natural in the order of things as his own dominance had become over the other brothers in the Unity. Then, understanding what that would say about the respective power the two brothers claimed, he drew himself fully erect. He would not bow before this traitor to the Rebellion. The Rebellion had proven its worth. It had conquered the weak leadership that had led it astray, albeit by trickery and lies, and the Triune Mind had been Encapsulated. Even Lucifer had been called in to help out, claiming a desire for forgiveness, and pleading the chance to prove he had changed his ways. The Mind had so wanted to welcome the Lost One of Light back into the Unity, and in that moment of charity, his downfall had been ensured.

It had been a downfall, one of horrific scope, and the ramifications had been widespread and definitive. Darkness had fallen over the Unity, with the skies in the great vessel going black. The wrenching of the Seat of Power from its stanchions had sent shockwaves throughout the mighty edifice. The stabilizing action that passed for gravity in the Unity, that natural pull of objects toward other objects, was temporarily overridden, and brothers who were flying through the darkened ether experienced a total loss of control, their wings flinging them helplessly about, and forcing the brothers to veer wildly from side to side.

Even those who had rejoiced in their victory suffered as much as the rest, as the very fabric of the Unity was turned inside out. No one was spared. Only Gadreel's Mandate, that of Revelation, one of opening panicked eyes to what might yet be, gave the desperate Rebellion a sense of renewed success, of assured victory, even in that moment of terrible calamity. With Ramiel at his side, using his own Mandate of Hope, the two slowly pulled the Unity from the precipice of despair. A knowledgeable team was sent into the bowels of the mechanisms that drove the Unity to effect corrections, and soon the unpleasant consequences began to right themselves.

Now, though, millennia later, the Unity was supremely secure. The great fusion orb was carefully nestled near the corporeal sun that fed Earth's needs, and light, coupled with

106

warmth, once again flooded the vast space. There were no concerns the Rebellion had not addressed, and even the Triune Mind had been spared to serve as the pilot once again, although of course only when the solution to their dilemma had been discovered. Gadreel had the right to stand tall. His knee would never bend to a minion of the Mind, had no cause to kneel to anyone, even as it had for so many eons when in the presence of the Three-Fold One.

No, the Archangel would bow his own knee first.

As Gadreel drew himself up and stepped toward Gabriel, his arrogance certain upon his face, he watched with disbelief as the space on either side of the Archangel bent, and then each black core of twisted ebony exploded with power, the energy writhing in the blackness, unseen to all but incorporeal eyes. Gadreel involuntarily fell back, stumbling against the Seat of Power itself, his heart throbbing in his chest, or at least throbbing where his chest would be, if he actually had one.

Through the newly opened Places of Power stepped six accompanying brothers, their movements bold and assured, and they gathered on either side of Gabriel, placing themselves equidistant from each other. The sight was certainly impressive, even if the Archangel's look of surprise was comparable to the expression of astonishment Gadreel knew must be painted on his own face. After all, he had called only Gabriel, although after his sending from the chair, he knew most every brother in the Unity would certainly have heard.

The gathering throng was intimidating.

The two brothers on either side of Gabriel held flaming swords, for they were the twin Six-Winged Seraphim, Barakiel and Elemiah. They were magnificent beyond any that occupied the Unity. They had once guarded the entrance to Earth's original Garden of Eden, protecting the Unity's first ventures on Earth from the barbarism of the earliest humans. At Barakiel's side stood Hizkiel, Chief Aide to Gabriel when bearing his standard into battle. The presence of that brother alone set Gadreel's heart on edge. Was this to be war once again? At the one-time aide's side was Kasbeel, previously known as Biza, Orator of the Oath Shown to the Holy Ones. That was a tricky brother, for he had at one time tried unsuccessfully to get the True Name of the Triune Mind from Michael.

When his eyes skipped to Gabriel's other side, Gadreel's fortitude was truly shaken. His hand grabbed the arm of the Seat of Power, and his legs went weak, for there stood Raphael, the Healer, the One Who Signals the Judgment. Beside him was Jeremiel, who had once Presided over Souls Awaiting Resurrection, although many knew him as Raziel, the name he had been called when promoted to greater duties.

This was truly a gathering of more power than Gadreel had seen in one place in many an eon. If he were one to admit to fear, he would have found it crawling up his spine at that point. Instead, he allowed that the Seat of Power, although insubstantial and incorporeal, was uncomfortably sharp against his backbone. That was the reason his spine crawled. He had been taken by surprise because of so many brothers appearing at once, he had stumbled against the Seat, and the result was unwarranted discomfort, that was all.

He felt the sour taste of irritation rise inside. It galled him. "What is this, Gabriel?" Gadreel's voice lashed out with greater bravado than he felt. He stood, towering as best he could, his height coming from his perceived presence in the void rather than from actual inches. "I called for you, alone. You must bring others with you to intimidate your betters?"

Gadreel felt his resolve weakening. Raphael, Kasbeel, and even Hizkiel! He had not dared face those three together even during the Rebellion against the Triune Mind!

"They brought themselves, Gadreel, although I do not know how." Gabriel seemed inordinately pleased with his companions. "I welcome my friends to stand at my side."

Just then, a small fold twisted within the blackness, one very near Gabriel, and with a shimmer of nonexistent light, a seventh companion appeared.

Raphael called gently to it, "Go, little familiar. Your master awaits. You did your job well." His gentle manner illustrated the reason Raphael welcomed the human label of angel, for his Mandate dictated benevolence and concern, the essence of all things angelic.

The small disturbance sidled up next to Gabriel, where it seemed very content.

"So, you followed me, little one? Surely you didn't lead these others here all alone." One of Gabriel's nonexistent hands reached and stroked the small companion, for it was his second, his familiar. It had come to find him, for as with all familiars, it was known to love him and him alone.

"Your little one only helped, Gabriel." Another voice, deeper—although "deeper" was in the minds of the listeners only, because no voices really spoke in the blackness of the void in which they stood—came from the one known as Hizkiel. "Here." He tossed something to Gabriel, who caught it easily. It was an Energy Node, portable, now turned off.

Gabriel's eyes looked up, twinkling. "I see I now have supporters willing to reveal themselves. My little one left the Energy Nodes as markers. How clever!"

"This one, too. Catch, Gabriel."

Gadreel fumed as he watched Gabriel turn to Raphael, and he was even more irritated when he saw Raphael smiling. The Angel of Healing tossed a small item Gabriel's way.

Gadreel started forward. "I demand you give me—"

Gabriel laughed. "It's only another portable Energy Node. You needn't worry. It's not engaged." His words carried sharp barbs. "Thank you, Raphael."

"Your familiar tracked you, placing the Nodes for us. We were able to make it understand that we could not follow you without them." Raphael's eyes crinkled at the expression on Gabriel's face. "Once you were here, we simply slipped through after you."

Gabriel tossed the two items in his hands, catching them easily, then he laughed loudly. The surrounding space pulsated with his mirth, the very heavens flexing around him.

Gadreel saw Gabriel's laugh as an affront, and he was not amused at all. It told of Gabriel's resources, his power, and his confidence. His laugh suggested he had nothing to fear from Gadreel, that Gabriel knew the truth, that Gadreel's only power was in controlling the key to the Secondary Forces Chamber.

Surely Gabriel didn't think that information would become his.

Gabriel spoke, and his words rumbled across the blackness. "What do you need, black sheep? You called me, and most strongly. For a long time, too, as my brothers Zadkiel and Asbeel can attest. Though they have not come to this place with the others, they earlier ran interference, and for that, I am grateful." He glanced at those standing at his side, each offering their support to him.

Gadreel churned with fury. He dared not display weakness. He mustn't, and he didn't have to. He still had a trump card to play. With arrogance and condescension in his voice, he threw out his winning hand.

"Kafziel."

The word tumbled into the blackness, filled with superiority and detachment. Casually, Gadreel turned away, as if it were nothing.

It was now up to the others to consider Kafziel and how he had committed the heinous act of choosing a life on Earth rather than returning to the Unity. He was known to cavort with both Lucifer and Samael, the brother also known as Malach HaMavet, the Dispenser of Death.

Few were as reviled among the brothers as Kafziel.

"You have a reason for speaking that abhorrent name?" Gabriel's words growled from his throat, the sound a threat laced with barbs of barely contained fury. "It is an insult for the ears of a brother to even hear the name of that cast-out one."

Gadreel turned, unaccountably filled with a renewed sense of control. This situation would be his. He knew it, because Gabriel had revealed the strength of his hatred for the earthbound brother, one who was earthbound by his own twisted choice. How could Gabriel refuse the task he would set before him?

"You are aware that Uriel has ridden the light to the world below." Gadreel's words were soft and wistful, as if he wished such an act hadn't been so. He did wish that, but it was not for Gabriel's sake. He only lately suspected he might have been

110

made the fool, for he remembered no truly evil thing Uriel had done this particular time. It seemed more that Ramiel had claimed Uriel's involvement in a counter rebellion, and Gadreel had reacted very quickly, simply wanting the infidel banished.

Now, it all seemed rather more complicated, an unexpected and nefarious plan that had been set into motion by the very act of Uriel's banishment. It was much too convenient that Kafziel should happen to be there just when and where Uriel had landed.

Gabriel snorted with derision. "You know that I am fully aware of Uriel's plight. I was there to wish him farewell. Why do you sport with me? I am no sparring mate, Gadreel. Speak your piece, or let me go."

There was no "let" to it, although Gadreel would never admit as such. It was the same with the other six brothers at the Archangel's side. Remaining was no more than good manners, to keep from stirring up blood that had been darkened too many times already. The fact goaded Gadreel beyond all measure.

"Uriel is with Kafziel."

Gadreel spoke the announcement lightly, leaving it to hang in the air. He knew the information would rankle, and he wished it so. He must create enough animosity in Gabriel that he would throw aside all caution, rushing to the world below to protect his precious Uriel. Kafziel must be stopped, something only Gabriel could do, and urgency was paramount. If the earthbound brother managed to gain control of Uriel's Mandate of Destiny before Gabriel could rescue him, then disaster upon disaster might well ensue.

"Kafziel," Gabriel repeated, his voiced laced with shards of bitterness, sharper and more piercing than a two-edged sword. His face had darkened, and his pulsing power had taken an ominous tone. He had become frightful to behold.

Gadreel felt the palpable pleasure of victory. His simple statement, although only four words, had done exactly as he had intended. Now, just one more thing.

Gabriel had to be forced to act.

Gabriel, Citadel of Justice and Power

At the first news of Uriel's plight, Gabriel's heart had slowed in his incorporeal chest, or to be more precise, his sense of time had stilled itself abruptly. After all, he had no heart in his present state. He was no more than energy and electrons and matter that didn't belong in this dimension, stuck here only because of the sub-atomic Velcro that wouldn't turn his race loose. Electrons from his own impossibly diverse dimension had intermingled with other equally infinitesimal atomic particles, and weavings that were easily untangled within the same dimension had become inextricably locked.

A surge of anger toward the Emissary of Sorrow swept through Gabriel. How many royal personages had met their end with Kafziel in attendance? His worldview was skewed in favor of life's endings, of moving on, and of always searching for a new path, a new solution to any problem he faced. The individual cost was of no consequence to Kafziel. Gabriel knew that. He also knew Uriel would be vulnerable to such a person.

It had happened before, for Uriel to be misled. Uriel believed in others, took his Mandate seriously, far too seriously for Gabriel's way of thinking. After all, what good was a Mandate if the brother it was assigned to couldn't factor in his own judgment when the need arose? Uriel saw only the opportunity and never the deceit surrounding the opportunity.

Azrael's Holy Lance was one such example.

Out of misguided helpfulness, and at Azrael's nefarious Suggestion, Uriel had blessed the centurion's spear, imbuing it with a certain semi-sentience of its own, although it was rather more an ability to give confidence to a human's intents rather than true thought of its own. Still, the weak-minded centurion had followed through on Azrael's whispered Suggestion, and the holy man hanging limply on the bloodied cross, his breathing ragged and nearly gone, had given up his life when the spear had pierced his side. It was Uriel's gift that had made that possible.

It wasn't for no reason that numerous religions even now called it the Spear of Destiny. Uriel's Mandate of Destiny was what it really was, or at least residual effects of it. Uriel still refused to admit his actions had been a mistake, although two millennia of war centered on that one event in human history told the truth of the matter. The centurion should have broken the man's legs like the other two criminals at his side, and then the world would have gone on with far less trouble. Uriel's failing that day still mattered to the Unity, because that very event with the Spear had bled over into the Unity, causing much of Uriel's estrangement from the Triune Mind, and enforcing the rift that had grown between Gabriel and his most desired—although now estranged—companion.

A new level of understanding coalesced in Gabriel's mind. The Spear of Destiny. Azrael. Now Kafziel. It was happening again. With the darkness of space focusing his thoughts, his anger began to boil. Uriel's innate goodness was being maliciously twisted once more. No such deceitful trick, one such as had long ago been deviously foisted upon Uriel, driving an unforgotten wedge ever deeper into their relationship, could be allowed to be repeated. No heat-craving, cast-out brother who remained earthbound by choice had that right.

Gabriel swung his head, and the blackness of the heavens shifted, giving way before him. His eyes blazed with fury, and the stars dimmed against their brilliance. He looked at each of his companions in turn, searching for their support. Their fierce loyalty told him the truth. They had already joined him in whatever cause he took as his own. He would have fought the battle alone, but with his companions at his side, success was assured.

Kafziel was already defeated, and Uriel would be freed.

Interlude 5

The six at Gabriel's side believed in him unreservedly.

The twins, Barakiel and Elemiah, together with Hizkiel and Kasbeel, were his to command. Raphael, too, who, along with

Jeremiel, comprised two of the greatest of the brothers, believed in him wholeheartedly, for they could find no fault in the Citadel of Justice and Power. They, as one, trusted in Gabriel, and not just because they understood his righteous anger over Uriel's unprovoked subjugation. Each, for reasons that were his alone, placed himself in Gabriel's hands, whether for good or for evil, for none of them truly believed any wrongdoing could come of anything Gabriel did.

If, for some unknown reason, that was the direction he took them, then they would follow as a group, right into the depths of Lucifer's lair, if that's where he intended them to go.

The Seven, the Triune Mind's perfect number, carried the strength of the Unity in their collective grasp, and woe to any who would choose to step in their way.

Gadreel, Deliverer of Destruction

Gadreel noted the building storm with satisfaction. It was exactly the scenario he had written in his imaginings. Well, almost. He hadn't expected the Archangel's six companions, but they weren't totally unwelcome. Far from it if they joined Gabriel in the hunt for the wayward brother. Each had a skill that could benefit the chase, even Kasbeel, although Gadreel suspected he might be the weak link in the chain, seeing as how he had changed sides once before.

"What of Uriel and Kafziel?" Gabriel's voice thundered, interrupting Gadreel's brooding thoughts, and it was a great trumpeting in the blackness. "You say they are together, Gadreel, but with your deceitful tongue, you do not say what you mean. It was how you sequestered the Triune Mind, by trickery and lies. Only shadowy creations of fancy come from the mouth of one who requires deceit to usurp power that belongs to another."

Gadreel's laughter met Gabriel's thrust, and he parried in return. "Oh, I do say exactly what I mean, Archangel Gabriel." He knew that would rub a very old wound raw, for that very term of respect had once upset the status quo in the Unity, paving the way for the Rebellion. There were many "angels" and "Archangels," but when the Triune Mind had sent his Authorities down among humans to whisper Suggestions into their ears, by chance, or perhaps not so much by chance, creating the assemblage of passages many called the Bible, in all the words that were written, only one Archangel was named.

Indeed, Michael was the Prince of the Brothers, and his name had been heralded in the battle of the Rebellion—by the wrong side, of course, the losing side. Still, he was the Prince of the Brothers, having long ago assumed the mantle Lucifer had cast aside.

Yet, he had been usurped for eons by the less powerful Gabriel. Gabriel was the only Archangel described as such within those ancient holy pages. *Archangel* Gabriel. Even Archangel Michael was simply called Michael. It rankled among many in the Unity that the name of Gabriel was better recognized among humans.

It didn't matter that there was a valid reason Gabriel got all the glory in that old holy book. He was one who shone with a Glorious Light, one of intellect instead of just strength, outshining even the six-winged Seraphim. That had pleased the Triune Mind immensely, and he had frequently spoken of Gabriel as his greatest pleasure in all the Unity.

However pleased the Mind had been with Gabriel, the status quo had been cruelly upset, the Rebellion had flourished, and in the aftermath, the Mind had been Encapsulated. For Gadreel to name Gabriel as Archangel, especially in this circumstance, was to grind salt into that memory, to rile his fury to untold ends. It was to remind him that he had betrayed a friend—by omission if not by intent—and that he was about to let it happen again.

Gadreel, inordinately pleased, continued, "I have been to the Chamber of Deeds. Chitar and Gupat met me there, generously revealing the chronicle of your paramour's sojourn on the world at our feet." He laughed, smug in his success. He had Gabriel now. All the strength contained in the essence of just that one brother, and it was nothing against the simple twisting of a few words.

"They are there now, Chitar and Gupat?" The words rumbled through the blackness, as Gabriel's angry resolve lashed the heavens. "I wish to see such Records."

"No. They are currently performing other duties." Gadreel's lips barely moved, and he attempted to sound sincerely sorry, as if he would summon them back if he could. "They have returned to the Unity."

He paused, letting the silence brew before taking off on another topic, one filled with distraction. Gabriel's overly focused anger needed to be gently diffused for a time. Left too long, and it would become a volcanic eruption. Volcanoes burned and destroyed. Gadreel didn't want to be destroyed, not at this stage of the game.

"It was so much easier when all these . . . *necessities* were kept within the boundaries of the Unity." Gadreel motioned around him to the stabilized Energy Nodes that kept invisible machinery—unseen to human eyes, anyway—and other ancient engines secured within certain spatial coordinates, a sweep of one arm indicating the great corridors that connected the far-flung locations. "It is so inconvenient to traipse around this chilling void just to get my job done." He sounded petulant, as if it were Gabriel's fault—and the Triune Mind's by association.

"Not my doing, Gadreel." Gabriel didn't use the old terms of honor when speaking the brother's name. "You could have left these within the Unity. The removing to this location was your choice, not mine."

"Perhaps . . ." Gadreel sighed, pretending to be truly tired, uncaring whether those around him interpreted it as real regret or just exhaustion from one too many discussions on the matter. Those who knew him well might say it was just another layer within the pretense he foisted upon his listeners. "Just perhaps I could get Nabu and Lipika."

"Fools," rumbled a deep voice from behind Gabriel.

"They are . . . perhaps . . . not as skilled at drawing the

116

information out—" Gadreel remembered Chitar's incorporeal hands flipping through the scenes, eliminating with skill those that were not what he sought. "—but they are on duty even as we speak."

Gabriel snapped his fingers sharply, the action creating no audible sound, although something crackled through space, and his familiar was instantly at his side. The small companion had responded more to the intensity of its master's need rather than to any actual noise. Its energy winked on and off several times in an irregular pattern, felt rather than seen, but the series of winks, together with a certain telepathic link, provided a clear channel of communication with its master. After a quick moment, the space around the familiar bent, and the companion vanished.

Gadreel snorted, glad to see it gone. The small familiars irritated him, never mind that he'd once had one of his own and long ago wished it upon another. Its usefulness had been at a cost of his time, and that had been too great a price to pay. Now he wished to move matters along.

"Gabriel? Shall we attend the Chamber? You will see the proof of Uriel's defection to Kafziel's presence." Gadreel smiled sweetly. It was when he was crossed that the sweet would turn sour, and nettles would lace his syllables with prickles. For now, he wanted his words to simply invigorate.

"There is no need." The anguished words tore themselves from Gabriel's throat, lashing through the dark skies of the void, the spoken energies reaching out in a cascade of turbulent power, dancing across the dusty moon, and then after a moment, continuing across space to break upon the skies of Earth.

On that small, blue and green world, unexplained sparks flew from exposed, overhead power lines. Computers unexpectedly burned out their motherboards, and light bulbs exploded in their fixtures. Meteorologists at NOAH checked their charts for unexpected sunspot activity and were mystified to find none at all.

With the current flight to Io in progress, the information was immediately dispatched to NASA over shielded lines.

In the heavens, the battle of wills continued.

Gadreel knew he had made his point, for Gabriel had buckled just as he had intended. He could not stop now, though. With words of honey, he held his hand out to Gabriel, and he questioned in a sincere voice, "You do not believe me?"

Gadreel smiled, for he knew success was in his grasp.

Gabriel, Citadel of Justice and Power

The problem was that Gabriel did believe.

Gadreel was a lying sneak, but Gabriel also knew the Chamber of Deeds could not be altered or erased, and what went into the Chamber of Deeds eventually made it into the Corporate Mind. If Gadreel claimed it was there, it was. While Gupat and Chitar were not always the smartest of individuals, they could find anything that had been recorded on the face of Earth. Gadreel would not dare claim such a thing if it was not true, not and also offer to reveal it.

"I have sent my familiar on a small errand. Its return will tell me much. From you, though, I must know, what is Uriel's business with Kafziel? You say they are together, but you do not say where or why." *And I will twist your neck if you lie!* He left whose words unsaid. Gadreel would know of their truth soon enough, if he faltered in this.

"The Chamber, my brother." Gadreel's words were counciliatory, but the smirk in his tone was equally clear. "In your visit there, you can learn all I already know, both the where and the why."

"Speak their business to me!" Gabriel's anger lashed out, and even the Seat of Power shook under the assault.

Gadreel withdrew a full step, as if buffeted by a sudden wind. Even the six at Gabriel's back bowed their heads against such wrath, for to look upon the anger of the Warrior of the Triune Mind, the Mighty Archangel himself, was to tread on careless ground. Even the Seraphim's swords didn't burn so brightly as Gabriel's fury. Best it was to look away until the anger was spent.

Even still, Gadreel's haughtiness, cracked but not broken, forced his shoulders back. He barely choked out the words, "I do not know, Brother." His eyes dropped, for even he dared not look at the source of the dazzling power that surrounded him.

"You name me brother?" Gabriel's voice thundered his query. "You who turned the Unity upside down, who tore the Seat of Power from its stanchions, who cast the brotherhood's rightful leader into a prison from which even I cannot help him escape? How dare you call me *brother*!" His words tore at Gadreel, lashed at him in the name of the Unity, although deep inside, stirring the anger, his heart was rent with concern for Uriel. "Tell me of what you do not know, and I will discern what I must. Now speak to me of all you have been made aware."

Gadreel did, too, although what he had to say was less than he had let on he knew. It was enough, though, and indeed, more than he had learned from simply cajoling Gupat and Chitar. A home had been sparked into flames by Kafziel. Uriel had joined him there. Together they had navigated a great distance to Kafziel's home in an abandoned mine. The depth of the mine had hindered the recording of the conversations there, but it was known that Uriel had left abruptly, followed shortly by Kafziel. A third person had been involved, a female. The readings indicated the third person was a brother. It must be a human, for the person Uriel carried in his arms was clearly female.

"You lead me along falsehoods, Gadreel. Such is not possible, for the third person to be a brother and also a female. A female by definition must be human." Gabriel grew in stature, his blinding countenance crackling with anger, and the jagged diamonds now fully exposed. On distant Earth, a storm swirled into being, the disturbance in the upper atmosphere creating wind shears that brought up great swaths of Pacific moisture, forcing them directly over Eastern Asia. "Yet you claim this is recorded in the Chamber of Deeds. Do you have further proof?"

His earlier haughtiness crumbling around him in the face of Gabriel's rising anger, Gadreel's words trembled. "A scene on a desert road, one recorded very recently. A human, a man, walking alone in the darkness, looked up to see a brother Traversing the sky. It was Uriel, as sure as the Chamber shows truth. A female was held in his arms, and she glowed in the darkness, in the same manner as we all do while corporeal upon Earth." They also glowed to some degree in the Unity, but that was left unspoken.

Even with Gadreel's answer out and on the table, Gabriel's anger continued to flash in undiminished brilliance. His hand made a fist, and lightning flew from it, exploding in the distant depths of space. Energy crackled all around him.

Gadreel, with desperation written on his face, impulsively cried, "It is in the Records, Brother."

Behind Gabriel, one of the Seraphims' Swords of Power flashed in the blackness. Then, as quickly, the second Seraphim's Sword flashed. A Voice of Power rang out, "We bicker, and still Uriel must flee. Let us take to wing. He is our brother, and for that alone, we would provide assistance. For you, Gabriel, he is much more."

That was Barakiel, the One Who Signals the Coming Judgment. As his initial words were forceful and strong, his final words were barely more than a whisper, and Gabriel's heart was touched.

The Archangel turned. "Your twin? Speaks he, also?"

The second Sword drooped toward the ground, although there was no ground for it to hit. Its light undimmed, it was apparent the second Seraph had fallen to one knee in humble subservience.

"As my brother feels, this day so do I. To Earth, you must let us fly." The twin to Barakiel arose, his answer complete, for he was one of the Eight Who Guarded the Tree of Life. He would also assist a brother in distress.

"You others?" Gabriel's gaze swept the remaining four. In their eyes he found agreement. Satisfied, he twisted his head to lock eyes with the one who had drawn him nigh.

"Somehow, I feel your foul hand in this, Gadreel. If I determine it to be so, I will return to vent my anger upon you. For one I call a friend, I will do this. I will cast myself from the Unity, riding the plasma flares to Earth, and in the doing, I will become corporeal once again. I will rescue this friend," —one who was once much more than a friend— "from whatever dangers surround him. In the Name of the Triune Mind, it will be so."

Gadreel raised one hand, interjecting, "I am afraid it is too late for so simple a rescue. Uriel has surely succumbed to Kafziel's wiles. You must now rescue your friend from himself. Pursue him ruthlessly, Gabriel, or he will be lost to you forever."

Gabriel's face darkened, and in that moment, the light from the stars themselves seemed to dim. Then, a lightship pulsed into being, launching flaming shards of blood-infused liquid energy far into the blackness. With no further warning, space bent violently; and with an implosion of unimaginable power, he was gone.

The two Swords of Power pointed right at Gadreel, and their ominous intent was perfectly clear. Lightships flashed into existence at their sides, two first, searing in their hot cauldron of boiling anger. Then four more eruptions swept all darkness from the sky. The first two consumed the Seraphs in a catastrophic cataclysm of unleashed furor, and they were gone, also.

Without further ado, four other beings winked out of existence, carried by the lightships, and Gadreel was left alone in silence.

Gadreel, Deliverer of Destruction

It was with some relief that Gadreel watched the streaks of light heading toward that blue and green planet hanging in the darkness of space not too many millions of miles away. There would be a grand expanse of thunder and lightning this night, and there wouldn't be a cloud in the sky. Heat lightning, he believed it was called, although when the brothers riding the lightning emerged, they would be as cold as ice, no matter how warm the day or night at their determined location. It was always like that, now that the Triune Mind was Encapsulated. Notwithstanding, each of the brothers knew what to expect. They had better. They weren't getting back into the Unity without Uriel, and that was another one of Gadreel's trump cards. He held all the keys, or at least his pet minion Ramiel did, every single one.

NASA Mission Control, Houston

"Jim? Chet? Houston, here. It'll take several minutes for this to reach ya'll up there, but we thought it'd be wise to keep you informed. We've just registered a series of spikes in EMP waves. Don't know the cause, because there's nothing up there to make 'em.

"We're trying to determine if they could have resulted from sunspot activity reflecting off the Jovian cloud cover. Seems unlikely, but that's the only thing anywhere near. You might pull in your sensitives for six hours or so, just in case.

"We'll be expecting you to be in blackout for the next quarter day. Drop us a line before you hike up your skirts.

"Houston out."

Chapter 10

Interlude 6

With a snarl and a snap of powerful jaws, Malak tore into the flesh covering Kafziel's collarbone, exposing muscle and blood that was not quite red. After all, Kafziel's tissue was out of phase with this universe, only corporeal when exposed to Earth's atmospheric gases.

No humans knew that, of course. The color of "angel" blood had never become a matter of discussion on Earth. It was rare for one of the brothers to actually bleed while corporeal, and for that reason, few humans had observed their vital life fluids.

In addition, any injury that broke the skin stimulated the atmospheric disharmony that turned them from "spirit" into "flesh." The regeneration of "angel" wounds was voracious, healing almost before the injury was completed.

Only an injury of immense magnitude could cause a brother's death before the body could heal itself. Being crushed in an earthquake, the removal of one's head, or being impaled, especially in a vital organ such as the heart, was the most common way for a brother to meet his end. Being unable to access one's wings when the lightning deposited a brother at a great height in the atmosphere was rare, but it was one additional danger the brothers faced. That only happened under extreme disorientation, and the number of falling deaths due to wing malfunction could easily be counted on one hand, even after all these eons.

Death from wolf strike was another thing altogether.

Kafziel, Emissary of Solitude and Tears

The flayed flesh across Kafziel's shoulder hurt like the devil's own fire, to quote numerous outspoken humans, but the contest was evenly matched, and it wasn't likely to do more than inconvenience him. The same was true for Malak. The wolf's wounds, should the man be able to inflict any, would regenerate just as quickly as the man's.

Such regeneration didn't stop the pain brought about by the snarling and lunging beast that kept him pinned to the floor. Nearly a hundred pounds of spitting fur snapped and tore at exposed flesh, and Kafziel soon began to regret that he hadn't continued to wear clothing. His discarded layers of Kevlar might have afforded him some small protection.

Putting his arm out to ward off an attack to his thigh, the wolf's incisors clamped down on his open hand. Kafziel yelled in agony as pain lanced along his nervous system and directly into his brain, burning all thoughts of anything else from his mind.

By that time, his shoulder was nearly healed, but skin had been nipped from his chest to his ankles. He was well aware the flow of the milky-pink blood laced with oily yellow fluid would continue to weaken him, even as his body healed itself. He would need to feed from the remaining meat he had roasting in his forge before he brought up his wings to pursue Uriel.

None of that was in the forefront of his mind, though. It was all on the imbedded teeth and the violent shaking that consumed his arm, the mastication that originated in his hand and had set his brain aflame.

He beat at the wolf, attempting to force it to let him loose,

124

but the animal was quick. It held his hand firmly even as it danced away from his fist, its yellow eyes flashing demonic intent with each reflection they caught. By means of the food it had earlier consumed, this was no longer the scrawny animal that had first entered the underground chamber. Malak's fur now gleamed, and the creature's body was sleek and taut. The "familiar" had cause to give in to no one.

"Away from me, beast," Kafziel spat at it, having grown tired of both the attack as well as the smell of Uriel in the animal's touch. Drawing back a bare foot, he kicked at the creature's furred chest, hoping to provoke the wolf into at least backing away. He knew Uriel's intent; it was to allow his familiar to slow him down until all traces of his path faded from the sky, and he would not have it.

Malak did release the hand, and the gathered storm that was in its every movement expanded ominously, even as it withdrew several steps. The animal doubtless remembered Uriel's insistent directive, as much for the emotional telepathic missive as for the spoken word. *Kill.* The beast was certainly trying, although there was little chance it would be successful. However, terrorize, harass, and maim; the animal had done all and more, and it would continue to the death if possible, and if not, as closely as could be broached.

Kafziel had to move, and he leaped to his feet, his limbs bloodied, although his wounds were nearly healed. Just the same, he was drained, and his breath ripped from him in painful gasps. The quivering of muscles preached to him the necessity of refreshment. He must eat, and he must do so quickly. He must also fly, for Uriel had taken his prize. The game was not complete without success, and he would be the victor.

He grabbed a crooked iron bar from beside the forge, and he held it up for Malak's observation.

"See, wolf?" He panted for air, the simple words stealing his remaining vitality from him. His healing body continued to pull his strength, even as he stood. Food was now paramount, and to feed, the animal must be disabled.

"Come to me," he hissed. He let the iron bar fall in a wide loop, then swept it up again in an ominous arc of momentum, creating a dead zone separating him from the snarls and spitting growls. Seeing the animal drop into a crouch, he knew his final chance had arrived. The creature was preparing its death leap, and the death must not be his own.

Even before Malak vaulted from the floor, the heavy bar was in transit toward the heavens and back home again. The man swung his body in a twisting vortex of incredible speed, the iron death pulling at the far reaches of gravity, its centrifugal force screaming in a great whistle of air, demanding to be allowed to make its own path.

Just before the massive canine head reached Kafziel's torso, the crook at the end of the iron bar tore into Malak's skull. The sounds of the killing were the bar's own, but the yell of triumph was from the man's throat. The beast fell where it was hit, and the room was abruptly, eerily silent.

Kafziel glanced briefly at the killing stick in his hands, and with a snort of relief, he let it fall clatteringly to the ground. He dropped his hands to his thighs and stood for a time, bowed, as adrenalin pumped fading residues of compulsion through his veins. Then, with exhaustion, he fell to his knees.

Yes, angels—or brothers, to be exactingly accurate—had adrenalin, for when they had shifted into this dimension eons ago, they had taken on many of the mammalian attributes of this corporeal plane. Adrenalin, perspiration, anxiety—as well as desire—were theirs in abundance, and not until they left this place would those things be taken away.

For now, Kafziel thanked the Unity above for his adrenalin, or at least for not collapsing in total exhaustion as he gasped for breath. He hoped he had enough energy to step to the forge for food. The wolf at least lay still, although he doubted it was dead. It only needed to be injured badly enough to remain where it lay until he could be gone from this place. That satisfied his requirements.

He painfully put one foot forward and forced himself erect. With a groan that told of grossly tortured muscles, he stepped heavily toward the smoking chamber. Flinging it open, he threw himself into its warmth, the blood so recently leaked from inside his body crisping on his bare skin, the remnants flaking away in the heat. He reached for one of the food items—he had no idea what—hanging from a hook, pulling it roughly off. Dropping to the floor, he tore into it, letting the juices run down his chin onto the bare flesh covering his torso. In the red fury of the fiery furnace blazing around him, his skin glowed crimson, and meat's juices seemed to flow like blood.

Once sated, he leaned his head back for a moment to allow his strength to return. The flow of life back into his veins felt sensuously sweet, and the heat of the forge's furnace left him invigorated. He took several deep breaths, and finding himself renewed, he leaped to his feet, tearing from the chamber, his urgency restored.

Once in the middle of the room, he drew himself erect, his chest filled with pride. He once again saw himself as he was, and it was glorious. He was indeed the most beautiful of the brothers, and his plans were in place to gain everything he had ever desired.

"I am now a Doer, Gabriel." He called to one who could not hear him, one that he knew was not even on Earth. Nonetheless, the news would reach the Archangel. There were ways. "Did you see? I didn't stand by and watch as death passed me by. I reached out and took what I wished, and I will do so again. I am coming for you, Archangel."

His words were strong and full of bravado. They were also full of the intensity of adrenalin, even if they were meant in all sincerity. Still, it was the adrenalin, not truth, which gave his body the strength and courage it needed.

In that moment, he took advantage of both.

Not forgetting the need to gird his loins, yet the press of the moment forcing his decisions upon him, he grabbed at the coverlet Uriel had cast aside, holding it as it dangled from one hand. He glanced at the wall, for a moment intending to fling himself through its atomic matrix, the quicker to tear after Uriel and his stolen prize. Then he remembered the Bearer of Destiny's complaints about his earlier exhaustion, and his need to avoid the walls of the mine. There was much to do to retrieve his prize, and slipping through the tightly packed stone would drain him immensely.

"Damn you, Uriel!" Running toward the metal lift, he slammed his hand to start its cycle. "Great Mind, hurry!" He grabbed the metal door and shook it violently, wishing for the very first time that he had replaced this with a speedier model.

Then, looking down, he glimpsed the uncovered genitalia between his legs. As the lift worked its way downward, he took the time to wrap himself, tucking the coverlet at his hips with a deft touch. On his slender, golden body, the pale cloth seemed perfect, a heavenly wrapping especially for one of the angelic host. No one could have painted a more accurate image of one of Botticelli's angels, if he'd had one to model at his side.

In sharp contrast, once at the surface, the expression on Kafziel's face was not one Botticelli would have ever condoned on one of his ethereal beings. This angel's brows were furrowed, his face was flushed, and great heaving gulps of his vocal fury soaked the night. He sniffed and reached with a hand, feeling for the most tenuous of trails in the air.

Then, unexpectedly—for a man in such stages of disappointment—a smile crept across his face. A remnant of Uriel's passage had been found. Golden hands reached to the darkness overhead, and they threw themselves together. With a crisp slap of sound, the displacement of atmospheric disharmony flashed through the night air, peeling back the darkness, and Kafziel's feathered wings were instantly at his back. They pulled at his shoulders like great leeches, their weight causing him to stagger momentarily, his sense of balance not quite under his control. It was residual weakness from the wounds he had received down below, and impatient, he leaped in spite of it, taking to wing. He could not wait for additional strength; he must follow quickly, for the path was fading. Only with determination and the most sensitive of olfactory organs would this pursuit be successful.

The chill of flight in the open air quickly stripped the warmth from his body, and in the quiet of the night, a solitary wolf's howl echoed through the loneliness. It was a mournful sound, indeed, with no one else to hear.

Interlude 7

Kafziel should have paused and listened, for not only had he forgotten to close the smoker's door, the outside entrance had also slipped his mind. Any wolf that could make its way into the old, abandoned mine could surely make its way out again, and the great beast that was Malak was not just any wolf. This wolf had been given Kafziel as its prize, and that prize would be redeemed, one way or another.

Malak stood underneath the inky blanket of the chill night sky and howled for Uriel, but no answer came. Sniffing the air, it caught faint traces of its master, and in the same direction, it smelled another, one it had recently tasted. Satisfied it would not lose its way for the sake of a few more morsels of food, it turned back to the rock wall at its side. Although Kafziel had been in a desperate rush, forgetting safeguards he otherwise might have automatically locked into place, it wouldn't have mattered. Familiars were well adapted at phasing their molecular structures to slip between the atoms of otherwise solid-appearing objects. Malak could slip in and out at will, just as the brothers could, although at a cost. The act of shifting its molecular structure used precious internal resources, disastrous if the animal were ill or poorly fed, but with the remains of an antelope at its disposal, the wolf had all the food it needed. After feeding once again, sating itself completely, it would be off to rejoin its master.

Shifting its internal structure so that it was in phase with that of the rock, it shimmered slightly and slipped back inside to the warmth it had found within the old mine. It had located yet another haunch left in the warmth of the forge. The wolf was very hungry. Its recovery from the injury Kafziel had inflicted had taken much from it.

Soon the battle would be reengaged, for its directive had not been accomplished yet. Malak had been told to *kill,* and that's just what the wolf intended to do.

Angioletta Bacciarelli, Daughter of Kafziel

Light brushed the sky with softness born of the early morning. Flakes of snow caressed Angioletta's cheek, and she reached one gloved hand to brush them away. They pricked her skin with cold, although it didn't bother her overmuch. She had been so hot just moments before and was glad to be outdoors in the fresh air.

It was rather funny that she didn't remember stepping outside, then she let the oddity pass, determined to enjoy the brisk winter coolness. The day smelled fresh, and she breathed in deeply. There was a familiar aroma in the air, if she could just place it.

Looking behind her, she saw the convent that had been her home for her entire life. She pursed her lips. She never went outside. Never. Yet, it was so beautiful in the snow that she suddenly wondered why her mothers had never let her out to play under the open sky. Frozen frosting capped the stone turrets, the crenellated walls giving the massive structure the look of a medieval fortress. It loomed large as it wrapped the side of the mountain, and she realized she had never explored more than a small portion of the mammoth structure. By its battered and haphazard look, the old convent had been built in numerous sections, each one divided from its sister by stubby turrets, some rounded and some squared off, acting as markers along the walls.

Between two of the clunky stone towers was a great, recessed arch. Three doors were underneath, each one separated by a gas lantern, lighted against the falling snow, directing visiting traffic to the doors, inviting them to find refuge in the safe haven of God's House. Of course, the refuge could only be a temporary one, as this was a cloistered facility, and the only nuns who could interact with the public were those with a special dispensation to do so. That had not included many of Angioletta's mothers. Few of them had ever seen the outside of the facility since the day of their arrival, and none that she knew of had ever seen it as beautiful as it was today. It was truly a sight that took her breath away.

She closed her eyes and drew in another deep inhalation of crisp perfection. That smell again, so sweet, vanilla! She inhaled the sweetness of crushed vanilla bean in the air, and it was the scent of heaven.

She shook her head to clear snow from her eyelashes, and she pulled her coat tighter around her neck. The chilled air had felt good on her face earlier, but now, as if a coin had flipped from one side to another, it was suddenly much colder. As a little girl, she remembered nights like this in the convent, when storms raged just outside the walls, and the chill seeped through the walls, stalking the corridors, reaching into the small rooms, and taking the life from those who were too old or too infirm to fight any longer.

The wind became frighteningly brisk, toying violently with her hair, and reaching cold fingers into her clothing. She shivered, now freezing, yet somehow she felt safe, as if someone held her, protecting her from all harm. She'd felt that way with her mothers in the convent, loved, safe, even when she'd been cold. The feeling was the same now.

Yet, within the safety twisted an undercurrent of fear . . . of falling.

The wind grew stronger, and she gasped in concern. She turned to go back to the convent, only to realize she could find no footing on the ground underneath her feet. She was hardly warm any longer, either. No matter how she tugged her clothing around her, the fingers of the wind found their way inside. The snow whipped at her face, pushing at her, throwing her balance askew.

Feeling herself falling, she threw out her arms, struggling to regain her lost balance, only to feel the pressure of other arms that held her tightly, safely encompassing her once again, the smell of vanilla permeating the wind, filling her nostrils, and soaking through her being like a balm. She rested one hand against the side of her face, but it wasn't her face at all. It was her guardian angel, the arms of her imagined father from her mother's story, and he was protecting her from the fury of the storm.

She smiled, strangely at peace, wrapped in protecting arms that would never let her come to harm, arms that would hold her aloft above the morass of worldly woes that had so recently seemed to permeate her life. Even the blustery wind and the numbing cold could not take that away from her.

The world around her darkened once more, and with her thoughts delving into a vanilla garden of delights, Angioletta sank into herself and was gone.

Uriel, Bearer of Destiny

The scent of cinnamon, the perfume of myrrh, and the intensity of frankincense wracked Uriel's body. Dear Unity, he could barely think for the touch of this woman's skin against his own! At least she had quit struggling in his arms. He'd been afraid for a moment he would lose his hold on her.

As the wings at his back strained with their double load, thrashing the night air, he felt his body's resources telling him the extra weight he carried. He hadn't realized the extent of his rising exhaustion until his cargo had fought against him. Each time he'd readjusted his grip, he'd come near to being overcome with her feminine charms. Her legs were soft, her breasts were firm, and her hair brushed against his neck. She was as much a woman as any brother had ever been in any previous dimension or form.

Then, she had rested a hand against his chest and relaxed. It was as if she had decided to snuggle against him. When he had looked down, a smile had formed on her face, and her beauty took his breath away. Her skin glowed against his, her lips were full, and her eyelashes were long and thick. She was angelic in the way the word was used in the most flattering of human descriptions, and any brother in the Unity would desire her.

He certainly did.

Pushing his mind from that thought, he knew he'd better find a place to stop and hole up. If he became exhausted, he would no longer be able to resist her, and resist her he must, if he wanted to earn his way back into the Unity.

Sweeping his eyes across the landscape below, he searched for lights. Unlike his first night here, this was no city landscape. Kafziel had led him far into the desert, and there was little to choose from. This woman in his arms needed more than just a sheltering rock overhang for protection. She needed warmth and a bed to sleep off whatever drugs Kafziel had given her.

A moving light caught his eye, and he realized it wasn't just one, but a pair. A road ran just below him, twisting with the terrain. Signs reflected in the car's headlights, small ones flickering quickly as the car passed, then other larger ones, highway signs, illuminated for longer periods as the vehicle approached and drove on by. The road was a guide. Follow it, and he would find some sign of habitation, either a fueling station or perhaps rooms for the night.

He never considered having no funds with him to be a drawback. He had been fully corporeal for some time now, and it would be no problem to Suggest whatever he needed a human to believe. A cash register might come up short at the end of the day, or an accounting of clothing supplies might show an unexpected loss of inventory. Uriel would be long gone by then. Any memories of the sturdy man who had been so eloquently charming would absolve him from suspicion. Shopkeepers would look elsewhere for blame, placing it where they would, or choosing to let it go without the discrepancy being resolved.

It was a flicker of light far in the distance that brought relief to his tiring torso. A blue square with the number six centered in the middle anchored his attention, and he knew it for one of the humans' motels. There would be a convenience store nearby, for humans couldn't do one without the other. It would provide needed food. His body must be replenished, and Angioletta was certainly starving behind that smile. Her father would not have had the courtesy to feed her, not being the brother Uriel knew. His daughter had been nothing more than a bargaining chip to him.

Still, first things first. A bed in which for his charge to rest, then he would go in search of food.

Uriel's wings beat against the sky, the soft *whup* of each

stroke carrying easily across the desert landscape. When his passenger shifted, he placed a hand against one side of her face, pressing her head against his chest, holding her steady. The touch of her cinnamon skin again flooded his body with sensations of warmth, longing, and desire for things he could never experience in his current incarnation.

"Gabriel!"

The word jerked itself from his throat in a desperately choked cry, as he pressed his eyelids closed against the pain. The battle brewing in his body was one he only hoped he could win, and his eyes were gritty with desperation. He missed Gabriel, and yet, this woman drew him in like a moth to a flame. If he gave in to this overwhelming longing, then Gabriel would never take him back. Their chance for love would be dashed forever.

Realization flooded over him once again. His Archangel had deserted him, and for the first time, he admitted he had nothing to lose. He was glad for the wind against his cheeks, because it kept the moisture of his pain dried from his skin. He didn't want anyone to know the torment that ripped apart his heart.

It was the blare of a radio that diverted his attention, bringing him back to the moment. Opening his eyes, he felt the blood drain from his face.

"Great Mind, I have been a fool once again," he muttered, the words themselves a curse against his stupidity. His moment of self-pity had dangerously distracted him. The motel was directly ahead, and his only choice was to slow or crash. He beat his wings hard against the air in an attempt to drastically reduce his forward momentum, while at the same time scanning the area for the best spot for a less-than-disastrous landing. An expanse of flat roof spanned the top of the building, several cars huddled in a narrow strip of dark paving wrapping the structure, and off to one side, the blackened waters of an unlighted swimming pool glimmered in the depths of the night. Part of the roof had a low parapet around the edges, and it would provide some manner of protection from prying eyes. He didn't know if he had enough control to aim that precisely, though.

Then, there was the second problem. He still had too much forward momentum. He forced his wings to cup at his sides to create the greatest possible drag. It did no good. He hadn't calculated properly for the additional weight of the woman in his arms.

He cringed in dread at the impact he knew was to come. As the motel's roof swelled in his vision, he wrapped his wings around them both, and he turned to let them take the brunt of the damage, hoping they might offer some measure of protection. As his exposed appendage tore into the tar and gravel roofing, the rough surface bit into his wing, abrading the feathers like sandpaper on soap. Within moments, it had torn completely through, and his bare shoulder skidded unprotected along the rooftop. The stain of not-quite-red blood and shredded flesh, resembling the remains of ruined cottage cheese, left a smear on the roof of the motel. Before he came to rest, the violence of his landing twisted him, and the edges of his second wing also caught on the gravel, shredding still more feathers, and sending them cascading like a snowstorm down the path of destruction.

Once all was still, he lay gasping for breath. His shoulder pulsed with fiery pain, and one wing was in tatters. He groaned with a moment of self-pity, and wincing at the discomfort, he unwrapped his wings from the woman's body to check her condition. She might be on the roof of a motel, still out from the drugs she had been given, but she was at least uninjured. He was grateful as well as somewhat surprised he had managed that.

Sitting up, he reached to his shoulder, grimacing at the tortured tissue. Gravel was imbedded deeply in his flesh, and it would need to be picked out, either before he healed or after. His skin might repair itself astoundingly fast, but it wouldn't spit the gravel out just because he was too lazy to dig it from underneath the surface. Also, his wings were tattered, and they would heal slowly, if at all. To remove them and bring them back up again would be their only refreshing. To do so, he would have to eat soon. His body's repairs would drain his reserves immensely.

There was an occasional downside to the brothers' rapid healing here on this planet, and this was one of them.

He turned as Angioletta moaned at his side. He reached to her, pulling his hand back just before touching her skin. Despite his pain, his greatest desire was to brush the tips of his fingers against her flesh, but he didn't dare risk such a touch. It was difficult enough to be this close to her, but it would be even more difficult to break that contact once it was made.

He leaned back, frustration welling up inside him. He wanted her, and still his memory of Gabriel kept him from her. He dared not touch her again, not now on this roof. What he needed was to get her down and to a secure location. They would soon be followed. All he could do was attempt to gain enough time to lose his pursuers and to hide Angioletta away until he could figure out what to do.

A door slammed below. They'd been noticed, if not already seen. Below, he could see a powerful flashlight flickering across the blacktop, resting for a moment on one car, then on another, not yet finding anything amiss.

It would once it decided to look a little higher.

"These odious wings," he muttered. He was quite aware of the attention they would attract when he removed them, but it had to be done. He reached his hands to clap them together. The actual deed proved more difficult than he imagined, as a hundred pinpoints of pain shot through his upper torso, throwing him forward in excruciating agony.

"Dear Holy Triune Mind," he gasped, his eyes blinded with the biting stings of a hundred crazed insects, all determined to make this particular moment of his life a pure and living hell. In all his eons, he'd never known agony like this, not continuing bolts of it. Even here on Earth, the worst of pain was fleeting. The brothers' bodies healed, and the pain faded. This? It went on and on.

Still, the wings had to be gone. He'd missed the section of the roof with the parapet. This location was totally exposed to the parking lot below. The energy transference would attract entirely too much attention, but that could be explained away with a Suggestion or two, perhaps as a sparking power line or a flash of heat lightning.

At least when he required them again, his damaged wings would return to him fresh and whole. If only his body could be clapped away, to be returned in perfect, painless form.

He must find a way to do this.

Glancing into the parking lot, the flashlight was exploring farther afield. He wondered how long it would take it to turn to the roof.

Holding his damaged arm to his side, he twisted the palm upwards. His stomach churned, and he swallowed bile. If he were to die—a serious possibility, he'd begun to think—what would happen to this woman? The thought was too much to bear. He imagined Lucifer or Samael finding her here. The image spurred him on.

Reaching his good arm directly in front of him, he brought his hands together as sharply as he could manage. Brilliance briefly flared across the rooftop, and he was relieved to feel the weight of his wings gone from his back.

As expected, his actions didn't go unnoticed.

The flashlight whipped around to bounce along the top of the motel, flitting from side to side for a moment, a firefly not sure exactly where to land, until it caught him directly in the face. It jerked off for a moment as if in disbelief, then it found him again and stayed there.

Uriel put his hand to his eyes to shield them from the glare.

"Hey!" The voice was deep and angry. "Get off my roof, you danged idiot. What are you doing up there, anyway?"

The door from earlier slammed again, and a woman's voice joined the man's, causing the light to slip away for a moment.

"Nigel? You find what done that up on the roof? We got another pole cat up there?"

Uriel watched as the woman stepped beside the man and put a hand over her eyes, as if to block the sun, in spite of the fact that the parking lot was completely black except where there was artificial light.

Uriel's eyes adjusted to darkness faster than any human's, and he glanced from the man to the woman. She was older, and he appeared to be of early middle age with a tight beard and a tendency to a spare tire. She could have been his mother, but she wrapped her arm in his like there was more than just blood kinship there. The bearded man leaned over and kissed her on the forehead.

"Nah, Rikkianne," the man replied. "Just some fool kids again, stargazing on the roof. Should just call the cops." He began to search with the light again.

"No, Nigel. Not this time. I got to see who's stupid enough to get on that roof. It's hotter'n Hades up there, even after the sun goes down. What fool'd climb up there to stargaze?" She turned to see where Nigel's light flashed, and when her eyes found Uriel, she called out, "Hey! You one of them Saunders boys? I got your momma's number on my cell, if I need to call." She reached into her pocket and pulled out a red phone, as if any normal human would be able to see it with that flashlight in his eyes.

In that lifting of the phone, Uriel felt a glimpse of the woman bleed through her bravado. First he saw the woman's name on her phone display. Rikkianne Kristofferson. Then there was the barest whisper of something else seeping through her thoughts, a relation to a famous singer, she would brag, as if she were still younger and prettier, the way she sometimes remembered herself.

He smiled. Humans, so fragile, and still so vain, even lost in the fractured destinies they never managed to find.

The man controlled his thoughts better, was more structured, perhaps less braggadocios. Uriel got nothing there.

Uriel glanced down at the human he'd rescued, and his mind raced. He had a drugged woman at his side, his shoulder was excruciatingly painful to move, and he was on a motel roof. He needed help getting down. More precisely, he needed help getting Angioletta to a safe location. His choices were severely limited, and he made the only one he could.

He drew in a breath to call out but was interrupted before he could speak.

"Hey, you!" The words again came deep and loud. It was the man. Softer, Uriel heard, "Rikkianne, he don't seem to want to answer you."

138

"We'll see, Nigel," she murmured. Then, forcefully, "Bobby Dalton? That you? You better not be doing the nasty up there on my roof again. I got cameras up there now, you know."

"Cameras?" In that word, the man's name came through. Nigel Platis. He pictured his name on an unpaid work order, and there was doubt there.

That told Uriel much. There were no cameras.

"Really?" It was Nigel again, and the light wavered.

"Shush!" Rikkianne. Then, loudly, "Bobby, I tell your momma you got on them blue boxers again, and she'll know I seen you. I seen you that night out by the pool, and I know them boxers." She muttered more softly, "Seen what was in them boxers, too, and I don't want to never see that happening again."

By that time several others had come into the parking lot, probably the owners of the cars parked here and there. Several of them were in robes, and one or two were laughing at the accusations. Rikkianne didn't seem to notice, but Nigel nudged her, clearing his throat.

"Rikkianne. We got company."

She was on a roll, though, and loud again. "I don't care if they wanna listen. I don't want that going on up on my roof." Calling more loudly, "You need to grow out of that, you hear me? It give us a bad reputation. Bobby Dalton! You answer me, you hear?"

Uriel found that, in spite of his pain, he could smile at the woman's accusations. The boy was assuredly just in the first stages of manhood, if Uriel was any judge of human boys, and apparently very inventive as he dealt with his burgeoning physical urges.

Still, this was not about a boy named Bobby. This was about a woman named Angioletta.

He called to the couple, "I'm not Bobby. I'm sorry. I've fallen on your roof, and I may need help down. I seem to have injured my shoulder." That was the truth, too, and any part of the truth he could include in his plea for help would make the humans down below more responsive to his requests. "Nigel? Rikkianne? Please?" They were certain to be more open to him

139

if he used their names.

Rikkianne slapped Nigel's shoulder. "Heavens, Nigel. How's that man know my name? You know someone I don't?" Then, she turned on him, her focus immediately shifting. "Nigel, you fink." Her use of that belittling label revealed more about her age than she would have liked. "You been playing cards with a new bunch of your losers? That one of 'em? I bet it is. I should have your hide!"

He fired back with his own accusations. "Me? Maybe you been seeing the ice delivery man. He sure stayed a long time last week." Then, just as quickly, the barbed comments were gone, as if they were a regular part of the couple's tit-for-tat, and he laughed. "Nobody I know. Just give me a minute to find out who it is." He called to the roof, "You the ice delivery man?"

Rikkianne took over, calling up in a loud voice, "Naw, I think you're a card shark. You taking my Nigel's money? He cain't win no ways to Tuesday."

Uriel laughed despite the pain it brought. "No, I'm neither. I just need your help. My wife is here with me, and she won't wake up. Please, will you help me?" The wife part was *not* the truth, but not waking up? The statement would balance itself out in credibility.

He didn't enjoy bending the truth, and quite liberally, in his estimation. Still, to tell them she was a woman he'd stolen from her father's home, and while drugged? He didn't think so.

"A woman? Why didn't you say so? She still breathing?" Nigel immediately reached to his waist, not waiting for an answer, and unclipped some keys. He pointed with his flashlight to a shed on the other side of the parking lot and handed the keys to a youngish-looking man. "I got me a ladder in there. Go retrieve it."

Rikkianne didn't seem swayed so easily. She called up to the roof, "Hey! How'd you and your wife get up there, anyway? You said you fell. How'd you fall on our roof? There ain't nothing to fall *from*."

"Shush, baby. We'll find out when we get them down." Nigel grasped her arm, but she wouldn't be distracted.

"No! Bobby Dalton climbed up the planters by the entrance last time he was on the roof." Her voice was loud enough for everyone in the lot to hear. "When you called him out, he fell down from up there, leaving his jeans on the roof, them blue boxers all showing, you remember, but he fell *down*. How can someone fall *up* onto our roof?"

"Rikkianne, I'm sorry," Uriel intervened. "We did fall down onto your roof. Our plane was in trouble. I'm a pilot, you see, and we had to ditch all of a sudden. We hit your roof pretty hard. I'm all banged up." Another lie. It was at least in the ballpark. He did fly, and they did ditch.

"Your plane crashed?" A different voice, a boy's, one probably about the mysterious Bobby's age.

For a moment, Uriel wondered if they were the same.

"Where's it at?" A man's voice, similar to the boy's.

Probably this one's father. That meant the boy was not Bobby.

"Over the ridge." That was far-fetched, and it made Uriel wince. He began to concentrate on a Suggestion, hoping no one would think to go check. "We were the only two on board. I think the plane traveled a ways before it hit the dirt."

"I saw a bright flash." An older man's voice, for there was a palsied shaking as he spoke. "My wife made me come out and look. Was that it?"

"Me, too. I saw it." A young mother carrying a baby. "It lit up really bright. I think it was loud, too." The voice quavered as if not sure, then became more confident. "I'm certain of it. There was a flash and a loud sound. That would be right, because you always see the light first and hear the sound afterwards, like lightning during a thunderstorm."

"My wife, please." It was another Suggestion, and in it, she was injured, in dire need of medical attention. He hoped it was convincing.

Rikkianne slapped Nigel sharply on the shoulder, the Suggestion working its magic. "What's taking you so danged long, Nigel? That poor couple up there nearly dead from a plane crash, and you just standing here. Oh, you make me so mad sometimes."

141

Nigel turned to the young man just bringing up the ladder. "There. Lean it against the roof." Together they got it in place, and it was only moments before the two of them were up on the roof. Nigel expressed amazement at the distance the man had skated across the roof to have done no more than bung up his shoulder.

Uriel knew he didn't see it as it had first been. The ragged wound had healed over by that time, although it was still heavily dimpled and very sore. Nigel marveled, as did Rikkianne, at the lack of injuries on the woman, but they expressed profound relief in the mercy of God as they installed her in one of the motel's unused rooms.

Both Nigel and Rikkianne remarked on how Uriel refused any assistance in climbing down from the roof. That was strange, they whispered, as he could barely move his arm. Several times they thought he was going to fall. He never did, though, and Rikkianne whispered to Nigel that they could chalk up his odd behavior to being a bit addled over his wife not coming to. Some food? Sure, they'd said. There's a vending machine. We'll bring you something. A knife? We'll see what we can find.

That last request concerned the people in the parking lot at first, but soon it seemed as right as rain on a parched field, and their concerns slipped away from them, just like the ones over why Uriel would be piloting an aircraft with no shirt on.

Later that night, with food and drink on a small table just inside the door—for Uriel desperately needed to eat—Nigel and Rikkianne left the poor couple alone in their room, wishing them a quick recuperation from their horrid ordeal, certain there was nothing a good night of sleep wouldn't heal. Uriel had wished it that way, and the Suggestions of a brother were as good as gold where humans were involved.

He sat on the bed next to Angioletta for a time, her breathing even and easy, wishing she would wake, and hoping she didn't. He wanted to reach and touch her again, just to stroke her face, but he knew it would suck him in like a firestorm. If he allowed that, he didn't know how he'd find the strength to pull himself back. The longing was so strong, it overshadowed the hunger that had begun to drive him on the roof. Instead of heading for the table loaded with snacks, he jerked from the bed and went to stand in front of the mirror. This was going to be a long night, because he had repairs to do, and they weren't going to be fun.

He picked up the knife he'd requested Nigel find for him. It was a pocketknife, well used, with one broken blade. To its credit, there was a pointed tool that looked good for digging, and he'd told the man it would do just fine. When Nigel had asked what he needed it for, he said he hoped to hike out to the plane tomorrow and find his wallet. The man had nodded and said he understood. No man wanted to go out into the desert without at least some sort of protection.

It wasn't protection he needed, though. He required surgery, and no mortal man would be able to dig into his shoulder. It was something he'd have to do himself.

Carefully, with one hand, he eased Kafziel's pants from his legs and stood bare in front of the mirror. His one piece of clothing would have to be kept clean, because he'd need to wear it again.

He steeled his face as he reached toward the open knife. It was probably the least sterile operating instrument ever known to man, although that wasn't a big matter to a brother. No Earth diseases could attack Uriel's bodily systems. His defenses would slough them off like a duck landing on a frozen lake. It was the pain that had him worried, that and the weakness that would come from the loss of blood.

Stepping into the bathroom, he closed the door and flipped on the overhead heater, casting his pants on an open suitcase rack against the wall. He needed the room to be warm, at least, for he'd grow even colder as he began to cut himself.

He laid the knife on the toilet seat along with a washcloth and stepped into the tub. He shivered as his buttocks pressed against the porcelain surface, the chill of the cast iron tub like ice to his skin. Reaching for the knife, he closed his eyes for a moment, sending a mental plea for help to two people. One he was certain would never listen to his cry, and the second wasn't a person at all.

"Gabriel," he whispered, for he felt the link was stronger if spoken aloud. It had proved itself so numerous times with Malak. "I need to feel your friendship, old friend. I need it more than you know." He drew a ragged breath, wishing beyond hope for his fondly remembered companion to be at his side.

"Malak," his second call started. "Come find me, my familiar. You're good for my essence, and this would be easier with you nearby."

He folded the washcloth several times, carefully placing it in his mouth, and working his jaw to embed his teeth firmly into the fabric. Then, he reached with the knife and began to cut. Soon, not-quite-red blood began to run down the drain. Not yet halfway finished, his eyes blurred with the pain, and his hand shook as he felt for yet another stone. Determined, he again touched the point of the blade to his skin and pressed. His body writhed as his fingers pushed against his flesh, until the stone finally popped free, and then his hand went limp, leaving the knife to clatter to the bottom of the tub.

He'd hoped to remove them all, but his exertions had decimated his body's drained resources. He had forgotten to eat, and as his lightning-fast metabolism struggled to heal the wounds the battered tool made, all his reserves were quickly exhausted, and soon there was nothing left.

His head lolled to the side, and the washcloth fell from his mouth. His arms rested at his sides, and his hands lay in his lap, palms up as if in supplication, his self-inflicted shoulder wounds still seeping. His body didn't even have enough reserves to continue healing itself.

This brother who had put the welfare of a poor young woman above his own lay in the blood-soaked tub barely breathing, now unconscious, and completely unaware just how close he'd brought himself to a death that could soon be very real and very forever.

Wolf strike wasn't the only way for a brother to reach his end.

Chapter 11

Nigel Platis, Motel Manager

A bolt of lightning split the sky, crackling through the darkness with a brittle rumble. Its sudden brilliance illuminated half the desert, glittering off car windows and stock tanks, causing cattle to jerk their nodding heads heavenward. For that brief few seconds, it was noon at midnight, and there wasn't a cloud in the sky. Then it was quiet again, as if the night had never been broken.

Nigel squinted at the room's window, rubbing one eye, then he reached to the side of his old Naugahyde recliner, past the rip Bobby Dalton had put in the arm when they'd moved it into the motel room he and Rikkianne called home. It was taped over now.

Pushing the chair's wooden lever forward with his hand, he made to stand before he realized the footrest hadn't retracted. He jerked the lever and pushed on the footrest at the same time. "Dang thing's finally broke 'til it don't work at all," he muttered, standing.

"What's that, Nigel?" The water in the bath sink shut off, and Rikkianne stepped through the door. Her hair was twisted in small tufts of paper, clipped with equally small plastic-coated wires. Some sort of dark cream oozed from the bottoms, and by the smell, it was time to darken recalcitrant roots. They always stayed up together nights she did her roots. The smell was too awful to sleep, and anyway, someone had to be up in case a new guest showed up wanting a room. That's exactly what would happen if they both called it a day, and at four in the morning, too.

"Dang chair broke," he called louder, irritation coloring his words. He scratched at his overhang as he walked to the opened door, looking outside into the desert night. Several cars were scattered in the parking lot, and off to one side, a chain link fence wrapped around the end of the pool. The net was standing up next to the fence, the pole jutting high into the night sky. He really should go out and put it away, but no one would be swimming before daybreak. It'd be okay until then.

He absently worked his tongue in around his bottom teeth, pushing his lip outwards. His beard needed trimmed, and it irritated him. Still, that sky was what concerned him now. It was black as far as he could see, except for the stars twinkling in the sky.

"What you seeing, Nigel? Anything?" Rikkianne walked to stand behind him, one hand toying with the unnaturally dark tufts atop her head, frowning when she found one wire pulling loose. Expertly, she twisted it back into place, never missing a beat. "Something out there?"

There never was, the look on her face said, although there had been earlier. The crash landing on their roof and the couple in the room around the other side of the building now seemed perfectly normal to them, as if such events happened in their neck of the woods on a regular basis.

"Lightning, Rikkianne. Just out of the blue, and no clouds to be seen. What do you think of that, old woman?" He grinned, though, and he put his arm around her. He loved Rikkianne as much as he'd ever loved anyone, and he didn't care how her hair smelled. Well, not unless he was trying to sleep, but that's why they stayed up all night when she fought back against her roots.

"Heat lightning, you big baby." She teased him. "Besides, it was out of the black. Ain't no blue out there." She pinched his spare tire, but not hard.

They stood side-by-side, the late night winds brushing their skin with coolness after the desert heat of the day. A frog croaked down by where the well had a slight leak, the wild tangle of grassy weeds just large enough for it to find food to survive. Somewhere just beyond the parking lot, the breeze caught a yucca stalk, rattling the leaves one against another. It gave off a melancholy sound, one that spoke of the desert and the hardy souls who found life better here, folks like Nigel and Rikkianne. Over the years the desert had become theirs, and they knew its every nuance.

That was the reason it was with some measured surprise that they watched a distant bolt of lightning crackle down from the heavens. It was way out past Hinkle's Mound, almost too distant to see easily. A single bolt of bluish light, it seemed to lance straight from the heavens overhead, instead of sideways like most normal lightning. That sent a shiver up both Nigel's and Rikkianne's spines, although neither one mentioned it to the other. Why should they? It was just simple heat lightning.

Without any warning, just to the south, another bolt of bluish flame flung itself from the sky, screaming with the fury of the gods. This one was close enough that it set off several car alarms in the parking lot, and Rikkianne stumbled back six inches or so, catching herself and laughing.

"That one almost snatched us right out of this here doorway, Nigel." Her voice cracked with nervousness, though.

He pulled her tight. "Nah. Never even hit the ground. I watched it, saw it come all the way down. Pretty as a peach." He reached and kissed her head. "Near 'bout pretty as you."

A light flickered on in one of the motel rooms, then several more. A curtain was pulled back, then a door opened. The horn on one car beeped twice, and the wail of its alarm promptly ceased. Two other cars continued their intermittent honking until their lights flashed, and their cries of distress were stilled also.

"See, Rikkianne? All's quiet again. The desert always wins, no matter the mess Ma Nature throws at it."

147

At that moment, two more widely separated strands of lightning pierced the sky, reaching long fingers through the blackness. They were both there at the same time, although they weren't quite twins. One reached a wicked finger down first, the one closest, even if it was still a good distance away. Then, before it could finish stretching its muscles, another appeared out of nowhere, back toward Phoenix, very far away, perhaps even farther than the city itself. Still, they were both there at the same time, the closest one disappearing first, the Phoenix one remaining 'til last. The reports that followed were sharp and crisp, as if this lightning was too clean, too organized, something planned and released with intent, then as quickly removed back to the heavens. It was not at all like regular lightning, messy, bleeding off tendrils every which way, all the electricity to be wasted in the summer sky.

"Enough, Nigel." Rikkianne pulled back from the door. "This ain't the desert tonight, not the one I love. I want to close it off." When the man at her side didn't move fast enough for her, she pulled at his arm. "Now, Nigel."

He did close the door, reaching to his side to flip on the air conditioning unit. Although the night air had been cool in comparison to the heat that had blanketed them earlier in the day, closed up, the room would quickly grow stuffy. Besides, the electric was on the building's account, and that made it like free for the two employees who lived there.

While his hand was still on the controls, a sixth bolt of lightning beat against the night, rattling the very windows in the motel. Nigel jerked his hand back from the thermostat, quivering with the sudden rush of adrenalin that surged through his body. Another car alarm, lower and deeper, perhaps an SUV, cried its distress just outside the door, and almost as soon as it started, it honked twice and stopped, satisfied that all was right with the world.

He turned to see tears running down Rikkianne's face. He stepped to her and grabbed her in his arms. "Baby! I'm so sorry. I should'a knowed you'd be scared." His arms pulled her tight, one hand brushing the tightly wound tufts of hair on her head. "Ah, I'm mussing your hair."

"I don't care about my hair, Nigel. Lightning like that don't just happen in the desert, not in *our* desert. I don't know what it all means, and it just don't feel good, none at all."

Neither of them thought of the man who had been found strangely injured on the motel's roof just hours before, together with an unconscious woman at his side. Instead, as they stood there, their fear and their intimacy brought on a different kind of relief, one that would take them—Rikkianne, especially—far from the unusual circumstances tearing the night outside. In fact, for the next few hours, Nigel wouldn't even mind the smell of Rikkianne's hair.

He would have other, more intimate matters on his mind.

Interlude 8

Four wide paws padded silently along a path of dirt and wiry grasses, occasionally pausing in the darkness. Sensing something, they stopped. This pause was longer than most. Yellow eyes blinked, catching starlight that was barely there, the pupils glittering in the night. Moist nostrils twitched, then a furred muzzle lifted and turned, finding something in the dry air lying heavily across the desert, something only a wolf could possibly pick out of the myriad smells wafting in the gentle breeze. The muscular animal arched its back and pointed its snout to the sky, letting a low moan build in its throat. Within moments, it burst forth in a mournful wail, calling to the one it hoped to find.

The wolf searched for Uriel.

It also searched for Kafziel. The trail was there: traces of scent lingering in the breeze from the bodies that had passed in flight; small odorificants that continued to drift slowly to the ground. To pick up a path laid in the sky by a winged "angel" was rather more difficult than following a walking man's steps across the ground, but it could be done.

A streak of lightning crackled through the sky, its sharp report ricocheting across the desert, stirring the sparse life that had managed to nudge a toehold in this dusty environment.

Yellow eyes looked up, searching, understanding. There was no question what had just happened. To a brother, or to a familiar of a brother, natural lightning was just that, to be ignored or dismissed, inconsequential. In this case, the wolf was well aware it had seen no ordinary lightning. It had seen the arrival of a brother.

Malak padded forward once again, then as its legs picked up speed, the animal's long body stretched out, soon loping across the desert floor. As another, second flash lit the sandy terrain, revealing scrubby tufts of grass and the occasional towering saguaro, the wolf didn't even pause. It had no way of knowing just who was being cast from the Unity, but it was Uriel at the end of the trail it followed. Only finding Uriel mattered, and of course, afterward, finding Kafziel. Kafziel must die. Only a word from Uriel could change that command.

Four more lights flashed across the sky that night before it became dark once again, and still Malak ran, crossing the occasional lonely blacktop highway or leaping rusty wire fences. Inside its flexing canine chest, a massive wolf heart pumped life-giving oxygen throughout its body. What the animal sought was growing closer. It could smell it, for Uriel needed Malak, and the need was strong. Something up ahead had happened, something big, something that had flooded the air with scents screaming out the Bearer's presence. No matter that the animal was really a familiar from the Unity, a "second" to a brother, Malak was in all reality a wolf, and as a wolf, it could smell impending death in the air.

It would be Uriel's death, if help didn't arrive soon.

The muscles in the animal's legs picked up speed, drawing energy from where it could, pushing its massive head through the night. Its goal was within reach, somewhere out there, and the oversized wolf pressed forward into the darkness.

Its paws pounded the dirt as its focus remained narrowed to one thing.

Find Uriel.

Of course, it hadn't forgotten the second, and that was to kill Kafziel.

Kinky Kinkerson, Reporter

In a Phoenix parking lot, just across from a motel room with an open door, the newspaper reporter sat at a picnic table with a cigarette dangling from between two fingers. The streetlight directly across the road glowed with a pinkish color, providing just enough light to see, but not enough to wash out the spark of radiance from the end of the cigarette.

He put it to his lips and drew in sharply, the tip glowing brightly for a moment. He held a phone in his opposite hand, the display dark. His posture was one of well-practiced waiting, although the anticipation in his shoulders was clear. This was a man ready to take a call.

He thought of the "angel" the old drunk had seen, or at least thought he'd seen, and he smiled. Perhaps he shouldn't have called Albuquerque. It was just that after the firemen's story, then the old man's assurances in what he'd seen in the desert, the excitement had overtaken him.

He jumped as the phone in his hand sparked to life, and he touched the screen to answer it, not bothering to verify the caller. He'd answer no matter who called. His phone was his life.

"Kinkerson, here." He paused for a moment, then grinned. "That's right. You have the right guy. Kinky is what my people know me by. Is this Donovan?"

He glanced up as a streak of lightning danced to the west of his location. He watched it, waiting for a few moments, then steeled himself for the noise. It came sharp and loud, unusually crisp.

"Sorry," he spoke into the phone. "Summer storm somewhere. Did Julian tell you about the angel?" He chuckled, unsure whether this Donovan character would laugh him off or not, and wanting to have an out if he needed to laugh it off himself.

Then, not watching the sky, focused on his call, he jumped

151

when another bolt of lightning, distant, danced in the sky. Off to the south another hit, then three in a row, one east of the city. That one startled him most, for the report to crackle around him almost as soon as he saw it.

"Hold a minute, Donovan. Got some weather here. Let me step inside." He stood as he continued his conversation, feeling a twinge of pain in his back, one that bothered him when he sat hunched over for too long. "Yeah, it was this crazy old man. Picked him up on the side of the highway outside Phoenix. Listened to him go on for an hour on the drive in."

He paused for a moment, listening, then continued.

"Yeah, well, I'm in Phoenix, now. His name? Called himself Old Joel. His story reminded me of those firemen back in Albuquerque. You know the ones who rescued that little girl from that burning house the other day?" A pause. "Yeah, Chief Mabry's crew. Them. Anyway, there's no proof, but it could run as a special interest thing, two reports of angels in less than a week. Might sell some copy. What do you think?"

By that time, he was back inside his room, and he reached and closed the door. Outside, the parking lot was empty, with only a few scattered cars for decoration. The old picnic table hunkered silently, bathed in the pink light from the streetlight, all underneath a clear sky. Stars twinkled overhead. The night had healed the heat of the day, and a cool breeze caressed the motel.

What Kinky didn't realize was that he had just seen six more "angels," although he wouldn't have recognized their unusual mode of transportation, unusual for humans, anyway. The "lightning" had ferried them toward Earth, flicking them free short of the ground, trusting in their ability to fly their newly corporeal bodies to whatever safe destination they desired.

It was some time before Kinky's light went out, but he never reopened the door. Who knew what storm might be blowing up, and in the desert, they were often quick and deadly. He'd seen enough destruction in his job with the paper, and he knew not to tempt fate. Weather didn't make excuses for anyone, not even good old Reinhardt Kinkerson.

Angioletta Bacciarelli, Daughter of Kafziel

Angioletta swam upwards in darkness, her arms, her thoughts, her consciousness mired in thick honey. It had a sweetness to it, one tinged with the velvety softness of smooth vanilla. She had learned to love vanilla after she left her mothers' home. Her new family had celebrated holidays with eggnog, vanilla eggnog, and she had come to adore it. Now it seemed as if it were all around her, permeating the very air she breathed.

She knew it couldn't be so. Not vanilla. It was honey that had her mired. The thick sweetness surrounded her, and still, she struggled to the top, to get past the cloying stickiness engulfing her, drowning her, pulling her back down.

Doubling her efforts, she knew she must escape.

She awoke in a tall building, a penthouse, she was sure, for it was surrounded with walls of glass. Outside the sun was bright, and it glittered off the windows of neighboring tall buildings, although none reached so high as hers. The room was filled with people, and she realized she knew them all. They were the children in the middle school where she taught sixth and seventh grade. She enjoyed them, for she'd bonded with them in a way most teachers never did. Now they laughed as if at a party, although she didn't know whose.

Glancing out the windows she noticed an intersection in the street just outside the building, and she laughed when she saw several boats. The street was a wide canal, and the sidewalks were its borders. A race was starting, and she called to her students.

"Look! We're so lucky. A boat regatta's just beginning. Look down, students! Look down!"

The children ran toward the windows, pointing to their favorites, excited to be in this excellent apartment with its perfect view. Angioletta leaned in, putting her hand on a tall boy's shoulder, pointing to the boat she admired most. Its wake spread out behind a speedboat that was surely an old-style Mercury

Cougar, down to the gleaming chrome bumpers. She whispered to the boy that she wasn't an expert on old cars, but a neighbor in her home of Los Angeles had owned several. This one seemed to be an early model, one from the late sixties.

Somehow that seemed important to her, although she didn't know why. Then, as it gained steadily on the others, within minutes, her class began cheering it on.

As the race reached the intersection, and the boats began to turn, everyone ran to the adjoining wall to see more boats coming at them. One blonde girl, adorably petite, grabbed for a life jacket hanging on the wall. As will happen in dreams, Angioletta realized they were actually aboard a yacht sailing in the middle of the race. Their yacht reached the intersection where the other boats had turned, and without any sort of warning, they were following in the direction of the racing flotilla. Several of her students leaned out the windows to see the latest wave of racers speed around them. The yacht heeled to one side, causing shrieks of laughter from the girls as well as the boys.

One final car came flying down the watery road, an older notchback Mustang, and it was speeding through the water backwards, its taillights breaking the surface of the canal, although no one seemed to find that in any way unusual. Angioletta whispered to the tall boy that surely the driver was indeed, *must be*, facing the proper direction.

Then, with sickening clarity, the car skipped over the crest of another boat's wake, twisted into the air, and the hood and doors flew open. It careened wildly end over end like an awkwardly skipping rock. The boy's hand grabbed his teacher's. All the students gasped in astonishment at the horrific scene as it unfolded.

Angioletta jerked, and the unusual race was gone. She felt her heart pound. The race had been so real, and she had been there.

Slowly, the world beneath her eyelids brightened from black to a dim gray, and her breathing quickened. Her face was unusually warm, although that quickly faded. She realized it had been warm in her dream, but it wasn't warm any longer.

Her face was cool, too cool.

Shifting position, she was in a bed, and she smiled, understanding the reality of everything that had happened to her recently. None of it had been real, the man in the black car, the heat that had been more than she had ever desired, not even the guardian angel who had kept her from falling. Even the boat race through the city had simply been in her imagination, even if she might wish for the angel who had held her to be real. He had felt so good, had *smelled* so good. The vanilla! She smiled broader, remembering. Her angel had smelled of vanilla, and he had kept her from slipping away when her feet had found no purchase.

A sudden, sharp crack of noise shook the room, vibrating the window in its frame. Thunder! Her eyes flew open as brilliant light stretched probing fingers around a drawn curtain, just as quickly withdrawing and leaving the room in darkened peace. Her heart pounded in the aftermath's dim silence.

She glanced around. The ceiling was flat and white, and at one corner, a crack reached a tenuous finger toward a ceiling fan. It never occurred to her that she could see exceptionally well to be in a room that was bathed in near blackness. All people saw so well, didn't they?

The crack in the ceiling was an old one, she could tell. It carried a darker hue of white, as if air had seeped through the opening for quite some time, leaving a lingering residue of dust. A chair and a table were by a plain, metal door, tagged in the middle with a list of room prices. A tray on the table held numerous food items, mostly of the snack variety. Another bed, a match to her own, was to the side of hers, the spread neatly folded over the pillows. Underneath her hands, the linens were rough, clearly of a mediocre quality. The bedspread that stretched out around her was tinted a bilious green that matched the walls. It was still tucked under the pillow on the opposite side, but pulled loosely back where she lay, and roughly draped around her shoulders.

Throwing it aside, she glanced down, relieved to see she still wore the pajamas she last remembered donning. At least she thought she'd put them on. It seemed everything lately

155

carried an element of confusion, as if things around her weren't exactly what they seemed to be.

She shivered. She was cold, very cold. She also needed the bathroom.

Swinging her feet to the floor, she glanced at the various openings in the room. Across from the window was a recess, mirrored, with a wide counter. She could see a faucet rising above it, so that must be the sink. The bathroom would be to the side. Once she took care of her personal needs, she could begin to figure out just where she was, although she was surprised that she wasn't more concerned. For some reason she felt . . . *safe,* although that seemed odd to her. How could she feel safe in a strange motel room when she didn't remember how she got here?

She remembered vanilla and inhaled, trying to find it again. All she smelled was the acrid cleanliness of bleach and pine cleaner. She clung to the vanilla sharply etched in her mind. It was as sure as her memory of her mothers in the convent, or the glow that lit her skin each night in the dark. It just *was,* and it strangely calmed her and made her feel secure, *protected,* as if no harm could come to her in this room.

Standing and walking toward the bathroom, she stopped at the mirror. She saw herself just fine, although others might have only been able to see shadows. It had always been so. The shadows rarely dimmed Angioletta's sight, not truly. Perhaps it was the glow from her skin. She never considered it might be due to eyes that saw more than those around her, that her vision worked more efficiently than that of someone fully human. Of course not. She was fully human. Why would she think otherwise?

Glancing at her reflection, she smiled at her rumpled, windblown look. Running her fingers along her scalp, pushing them into her hair, and separating the tangles, she leaned her head back as she worked her hand through to her roots. Finally, she shook her head sharply side to side several times, inordinately pleased with the results. Perhaps with brighter lights she would have been less happy with how she looked, but in the dimness, with only the faintest glow from her skin, she felt she looked absolutely radiant. *Radiant.* Who else did she know who could make that claim?

She could tell. She was feeling better. Obviously.

Laughing out loud, satisfied with this odd moment in her life, she grabbed the handle to the bathroom door, and twisting, flung it wide.

What she saw inside caught her very much off guard, for lying in the brilliantly lit tub was a very naked man, one who was solidly built with a strikingly handsome face, and he displayed a masticated shoulder oozing copious amounts of not-quite-red blood. He was unconscious, and he hardly looked alive. Only the rise of his chest convinced her he was indeed not a corpse.

She backed up a step, instinctively glancing into the room for the phone, aware of the intense warmth inside the bathroom. It drew her, in spite of the injured man in the tub. However, the phone. She was certain there must be one. All motel rooms had phones.

Then, common sense kicked in, and she knew it was up to her to do something, and quickly, too. Otherwise, this poor soul might indeed meet his maker, and she would never get to know just who he was. She wasn't even qualified to give him his last rites.

Grabbing a towel, she looked up to the ceiling, realizing the heater was going full tilt. That was why she felt warm in this small space, and for that, she was grateful. She knelt by the tub, pressing the cloth gently to the destroyed shoulder, wondering just what could have done so much damage. It was butchered. Then she saw a gleam of metal in the tub, and reaching inside, she picked up a pocketknife with a pointed blade extended, immediately releasing it in horror to watch it clatter back inside. A washcloth lay at the man's side, and the bottom edge was wet with blood.

"Dear God," she whispered, looking in the man's face, wishing she could see into his eyes. "You did this to yourself? Why?" She lifted the towel from his shoulder, her eyes narrowing at the red already absorbed into the white terry, puzzled at the yellow tint she saw in it, as if it wasn't really blood at all. It must be, though. It was coming from this man's skin.

Pressing the towel gently against the skin once again, she saw multiple nodules running down his arm. She wondered for a moment if he had contracted some form of skin cancer or had a congenital defect.

Glancing around was when she noticed the numerous asphalt-covered stones scattered around the room. Gravel, she realized. Reaching to her side, she picked up one from the floor. It was road gravel, or perhaps the kind used to cover a flat roof. She had picked this very stuff from the tires on her car on more than one occasion.

She glanced back to the injured shoulder. Had this man been in an accident, or perhaps harassed—tortured!—by a road gang of thugs? Surely he hadn't been run over, or heaven forbid, dragged behind a car! She shuddered at the thought as she reached to press her hand against the flesh of his upper arm just where the lumps under the skin hadn't yet been broken free. As soon as her body touched his, her mind went blank, the crush of her senses overwhelming every thought in her head except one.

Vanilla!

He was the smell, the taste, the velvety smooth comfort—the *safety*—of her vanilla. It was this man she had dreamed of, and here he was, dying in this bathtub.

Her heart raced in her chest, even as she knew she must do something. Defeating her in its overwhelming intensity, just for that moment, she could only think of one thing.

Vanilla!

She couldn't remove her hand from his skin. He was the one who had made her feel so oddly safe. How could that be? Still, the taste was on his skin.

Vanilla!

Chapter 12

Raphael, Angel of Healing

The wind whipped past Raphael as he tumbled in the cold, thin air of Earth's upper atmosphere. For a moment he was disoriented, having *Traversed,* then segued directly into freefall. He was learning once again how torturous visiting this world could be as his body slowly coalesced into corporeal solidity.

It was well worth the price, no matter. He was here for Gabriel, both as a friend and as leader of the counter rebellion.

Despite his desire to help, just now his thoughts were all about the darkness surrounding him, the wind whistling past his face, and just why, in all the eons the Unity had been stranded here, they'd never managed to focus the *lightning*—he spat the word in his thoughts—to provide at least a semblance of accuracy in landing sites.

He knew the answer to that, though. Few brothers actually *chose* to come to this planet; they were normally cast out in disgrace, the great plasma flares flinging them away when the energy aura was pressed too hard. Few in the Unity cared if outcasts were flung accurately onto the surface of this world. The intent was to send them away, to cast them down—and let them earn their way back, if they were so inclined.

Some weren't.

Orienting himself, he took in the stars overhead, together with the moon he could just glimpse over the horizon. With barely a thought, he attuned his resonance with the planet's powerful magnetic field, and in doing so found the cardinal directions. Just to the *west* was a glowing carpet of jewels, the lights of a city. It was Phoenix, he thought. If so, he'd come down too far *east*, a good distance from his goal. No telling where the other six had appeared.

When a glow began to emanate from his skin, he knew it was time. He reached his hands above his head, his fingers long and sinuous, and clapped them together sharply. An aura of brilliance lit the night sky, and great feathered wings materialized at his back.

Unlike Uriel's near-disastrous entry into Earth's atmosphere, Raphael experienced little difficulty. He was no neophyte when it came to the use of his wings. After all, he was the Healer, as well as the One Who Signals the Coming Judgment, the event that was better known by the brothers as an upcoming shift through the dimensional interface to a new plane of existence, even if his Mandate had been rather useless of late. After all, the Coming Judgment—the much-desired signal that the Unity was freed from this corporeal prison in which they were trapped—could never come at all, if the Triune Mind wasn't freed.

It was the same with his Healing Touch. It was his specialty, although he rarely had cause to travel to these domains any longer. With this world's modern medicines, his healings had been few and far between of late.

Then the wind caught his newly-corporeal wings, and he immediately pulled his arms in front of him, tensing his torso with all his might. He was buffeted by the thickening atmosphere. His tousled white hair glittered with fireflies, the evidence of his healing Mandate, his wings doing the same, and with a quick snap of their feathered surfaces, he abruptly and securely halted his fall. With only the barest of effort, he remained poised nearly motionless in the dark sky.

He looked about the darkness, his wings in constant motion,

feeling completely at ease in the viscous, corporeal atmosphere. He could sense several of those who had stood with him at Gabriel's side. Having traveled to Earth together, they were in sync with each other and would remain so. What one thought, the others could hear, if they chose to listen.

He sent out a cry, "Kasbeel! Hizkiel! It is time for the Circle of Brothers to gather! Seraphim, hold your Swords aloft for all to see!" And then he waited.

He had no concerns about his cry being overheard by Kafziel—or Israfel, Maalik, or even the much-reviled Chayot HaKodesh. Not even Lucifer could listen in. After a certain amount of time on Earth, the corporeal form began to shift from true. It might be only the slightest amount, but it was just enough that the mental communication so prevalent in the Unity was lost. The frequencies resonated differently for disenfranchised brothers who resided for great lengths of time upon Earth.

Raphael first recognized the presence of Gabriel. When in sync, the brothers didn't have to announce their presence. The knowledge, the *image*, of who they were was just *there*.

"Archangel! I await the Gathering. We will be as one!"

"Raphael! Shortly, for we await Jeremiel."

It was Gabriel's call, and the image of the Archangel flooded Raphael's mind. To a lesser degree, Raphael also sensed his own image, the white hair that wildly refused to lie against his scalp, his long fingers that had so often offered healing to the hurting of this poor world, as well as the glittering fireflies that constantly surrounded him like a halo. Gabriel's calling resonated with images of the sender and the receiver, for both were in the Archangel's thoughts.

"The others are here?" Raphael felt his voice quiver with anticipation.

"Be of patience. Kasbeel has come through, as have you and Hizkiel. We will gather shortly." Gabriel's golden warmth filled the words.

Then two additional images washed Raphael's senses, and they were of the two brothers he had sensed at the onset. The first was Kasbeel, with his slender limbs and hair—dark, curly, and tousled—layered against skin the color of peaches and cream. The second had legs like tree trunks, with flesh the color of cinnamon, and hair of powdered black anthracite. It could be no other than Hizkiel.

"Mighty Archangel, command us," Kasbeel called, a sense of urgency in his words. The peaches and cream flooded through, also.

"Archangel, yes, for in days past, that was my title. Whether I am still mighty remains to be seen." Gabriel laughed.

Raphael felt more than heard Gabriel's laugh. He also sensed guilt interwoven into his words. He knew that *Rescuer* was the name Gabriel desired to be called. He had been at Uriel's side when he was banished, and he had made no effort to snatch him from Ramiel's clutches. None of this had to have happened.

A blinding flash, one exploding with the radiance of a white-hot star, shredded the darkness. The Seraph Twins, too brilliant to look upon, with their flaming Swords of Power raised in clasped hands, appeared in each of the brothers' minds.

Raphael laughed with exultation, and Gabriel did the same, for they knew of the destructive power the Seraphim commanded.

"Ah, Gabriel, it now seems we have two more," Raphael encouraged. "We will find the strength of ten thousand, and none shall stand before us. For is it not written in the Strictures that one shall put a thousand to flight, and two shall put ten thousand? How will Kafziel withstand seven of the most powerful brothers from the Unity?"

"Jeremiel will indeed provide strength. He is the One Who Once Presided over Souls Awaiting Resurrection, and he carries immense power. He will be most welcome." Gabriel's golden presence permeated the words. Unstated was the knowledge that if the first six brothers provided the combined strength of over ten thousand, Jeremiel's arrival would double their power to that of twenty thousand and more.

Then, thunder rumbled in the darkness, and the blue and red image of flames flooded Raphael's mind. It was one of the

162

Seraphim, and he prepared to speak.

Raphael paused to listen.

"Against any humans, we might easily prevail." The spoken phrase trembled with power. "However, against our earthbound brothers, we must not fail."

By the use of a couplet, it was sure to be Elemiah. His was the skill of rhyme, and it carried its own sort of authority, one to equal his Sword of Power, for it was a strength of speech that mesmerized, bringing the mighty unwittingly to their knees.

"Brothers?" Barakiel, the second of the Seraphim, upbraided his twin for the use of that familial term. The word crackled with brittleness, and the darkness filling the night trembled at the explosion of power in that one naming. "Dare these still call themselves brothers?"

Far across the desert floor, a new star flashed white with the brilliance of noon, and it burned with fury. All who had come to this world in Gabriel's support knew it for what it was: Barakiel's Sword of Power, for it flashed with his righteous indignation. If the Seraph had stood in his brothers' physical presence, the power of his Sword would have forced them to bow in submission.

Then, as quickly, the light in the desert dimmed.

Instead, now there was only sorrow, or perhaps Barakiel's regret for his momentary lack of self-control. His anger had flared, his Sword had been wielded, and now his theatrics shamed him.

"Brother Barakiel, to friends you stand near. It is not our rebuke you have to fear." Elemiah's song was soft and forgiving, and it soothed the minds of those who took it in, even as the power within the speaker's rhyme trembled to be released, rumbling thunder across the desert floor.

"My apologies." Barakiel words were filled with the gentleness of a summer breeze. "I am the Lightning of God," he used the Earth term for the Triune Mind, "and I wish to cast swaths of death upon all who defy him. With regrets, I do not wish to bring pain to my brothers."

This word for the brothers was one that indicated the closest of companions, ones for whom it was not too much to offer one's life.

"Be not submissive, Brother," Gabriel instructed, again using the intimate form of the word, "for your zeal for righteousness is the strength in your Sword." His golden visage was interwoven with his words, and the sending told of tenderness, as well as of a long and close companionship. "Take heart and know we are each of one accord. Brandish proudly the iron in your demeanor. We are here to save one of our own."

The words Gabriel used, *one of our own,* told of his bond with Uriel, and Raphael understood it as such. The nuance in the meaning meant one who was closer than the closest of brothers; one with whom many lifetimes of intimacy had been achieved. Such told the depth of Gabriel's love for the one he wished to rescue from Kafziel's clutches.

Without warning, a brilliant light, unequaled even by that of the Seraphim, filled the night sky, and it was the sudden, cracking snap of a whip. Lightning glared, and the brilliance that remained outshone the lightning that had brought it. It was there and gone, and with it came thundering reverberations of unleashed power.

The brothers already scattered across the desert bowed their heads and waited for the fury to pass, for it was indeed fury. An image interlaced with brooding power washed across their minds, and each brother knew their final companion had arrived.

"I am ready to battle!" The words were those of Jeremiel, and they carried the thunder of a thousand storms in their delivery. The very dust of the ground stirred as his power whipped across the desert floor. For eons he had presided over brotherly essences awaiting resurrection into the Unity, and his authority had been unimpeded. He knew how to twist the corporeal workings of this world to his bidding, and his strength would fill any void left by lesser brothers. His confidence was his assurance of that.

"We welcome you, Jeremiel," Raphael called, feeling the repeated pattern of other voices joining his own.

"I sense my brothers, and," Jeremiel paused, his next words softer, "I sense my brother."

His two-fold reference to his brothers was telling. The first was filled with the fortitude of the Bonding of Those with a Common Goal. The second was entangled with grief for one who had suffered mightily and might already be lost. The first told of great strength, and the second revealed a broken heart, for that was Jeremiel's Mandate, to find strength in brokenness.

"I had thought you delayed, Jeremiel, and now you are here. Welcome." Gabriel's golden glory permeated his words, threading itself throughout each syllable, and it warmed those who accepted its sending, even as they were still separated in the darkness of the Arizona night.

"My errands were essential. Still, I wished not to concern you. Before Traversing, I visited with Jeqon, and he offered his help, that which he can give."

His words told much. Jeqon had his finger on the pulse of all things that happened both in the Unity and on Earth. If anyone would know of Uriel's whereabouts on Earth, it would be the Unity's only Brother of Color.

"Gadreel has set his challenge, and we must be the ones to rise to it." Gabriel's presence was felt in the words, for it was he who spoke. "Our brother, Uriel, has been betrayed, and he believes himself to be following truth. Kafziel, known to this world as the Angel of Solitude, must be separated from his prey, and there can be no mercy."

Gabriel's words, although they were not really words at all, blasted across the night sky, roiling the dust of the earth, and shaking leaves from small bushes. Animals hunkered with fear in their dens. While the creatures of the desert didn't know that incorporeal beings turned corporeal hovered in the air above their peaceable kingdoms, and that a war among the "Heavenly Host" was brewing, they sensed the fear that comes with Spoken Words of Power. They were wise to be afraid, too, for the seven brothers in the skies above controlled a combined power that if unleashed could wreak havoc on this world.

Raphael heard yet more things in the Archangel's cry. This deed, the betrayal of Uriel, was the ultimate insult, and it would find no forgiveness from him. This betrayal was as close to Gabriel's heart as it could get.

"My wings beat the darkness with the furor of a wrong unrequited, and I wish for the Circle to gather." Jeremiel's words thundered out, the image of his brooding mien infusing his proclamation with power. "Barakiel, thrust your Sword high, and let your anger rage. We will see you, and we will gather. You will be our standard, and none will thwart our plans."

A vivid watercolor of concurrence washed the sky, and a new star—albeit temporary, being Barakiel's Sword—sundered the night. Its brilliantly glowing surface seemed a shape strangely less that of an old-fashioned sword and more of a cross hovering in the sky.

Raphael saw it and for some reason thought of a long-ago crucifixion. A man had died, for it was recorded in one of the humans' holy books. He had then risen again, and the course of the world had changed forever.

That had been the result of Raphael's healing Mandate.

He hoped no one died today. This world had enough troubles already.

Old Joel, Town Drunk

The light from Barakiel's Sword wouldn't have surprised any humans watching. Its outline, anyway. That same star shape had been repeated above more manger scenes than lines had ever been drawn in the shape of a pentagram, and besides, didn't the very air that provided life to Earth twist the light that traveled down from the stars in the heavens? It was that very twisting that caused the stars to twinkle in the depths of the night, at times giving them long, sparkling tails.

It wasn't mysterious at all.

One person did see it flash into life. Old Joel. Just like some few others in Phoenix—for several did eventually look up—he thought it was a bright, new star. Just as Jeremiel challenged Barakiel to raise his standard high, Old Joel stepped outside to search the night sky in the slim hope that the angel he'd seen earlier might have been something more than just the liquor. In

166

that moment, as the new star flashed into being, he felt hope as well as reassurance well up in his chest. His angel was coming again, and others would have to believe.

Then, nothing more happened, and he knew it was just a star.

As he turned to step inside, he heard a familiar sound, the brush of something beating at the air, a noise that he had heard not so long ago, as he had stood in the depths of the desert. Blotting out the stars directly overhead was a huge set of wings, and hanging underneath was the glowing form of a man.

Old Joel stood for a good length of time, for he quickly understood about the star. It was the Star of the East, although it was more to the northwest. Still, he supposed it must be east of somewhere. He had just seen an angel on wing, and it was following the star.

Surely a great event was happening out in the desert. The Messiah, the Christ child, had come over two thousand years ago, so he knew it couldn't be that. He also accepted that there were more things in Heaven and Earth than the Good Word had ever recorded, and he was certain this was one.

After all, he had witnessed a glowing angel out in the desert, and now another had flown right over the City of Phoenix. If this wasn't a night of miracles, he didn't know what was. There had been seven flashes of lightning in a clear sky, hadn't there, and hadn't he always been taught that seven was God's perfect number?

Old Joel shivered with anticipation, and it wasn't from the temperature in the air. He had goose bumps, for he knew the desert was a special place tonight. He also knew that inside his heart he would never be the same. He had heard from God twice, and that was more than any man in the world deserved, especially a drunk like him.

He chuckled as he headed back inside. An *ex*-drunk like him.

Just as he closed the door, a much smaller flash of lightning crackled through the sky. In any event, it was way out in the desert, and it went mostly unnoticed. There was something unusual about this flash of lightning, though, because as it

167

exploded and disappeared, leaving the night at peace once again, the scream of an oversized bald eagle split the night.

Interlude 9

This eagle was a familiar, come to join its master, and it had no trouble at all in sensing which way to head. It looked for a winged glow in the heavens, for there were seven, and the one that it sensed best was the one it needed to find.

Gabriel.

Kafziel, Emissary of Solitude and Tears

Kafziel, on wing and searching for Uriel, watched as the initial lightship vomited the first arriving brother into the upper atmosphere.

As the lightning tore along its path, the shifting energy exploded the surrounding molecules in the air, sending them violently cascading against one another in a roiling surf of sound. The lightning seemed to cry, *Earthbound brothers, those shifted out of true from the Unity, beware! Hide! Cry for the mountains to fall upon you to protect you from the fury of The One Who Comes! Those in flight, pain is your due, and none shall escape!*

Such was the reason many of the brothers on Earth hid deep within the bowels of the planet. The rock shielded them from the arrival of newly cast-out brothers. Kafziel, however, was in airborne pursuit of Uriel. He wasn't shielded at all.

The first blast of thunder rippled its energy through the skies, its time-distorted wave of molecules quite visible to one who was a Watcher. Kafziel watched it roll in, his own control of time more a manipulation of the way it was perceived instead of a real twisting of the passage of events, but it was a sort of control, nonetheless.

He had seen the arm of iridescent, blue lightning thrust its rider from the heavens, and he had steeled himself for the blast.

He was out of resonance with the Unity, had spent too many years on this puny planet, and the more he shifted out of phase, the greater the pain of each new brother's arrival.

It hit him in mid-wingbeat, the visible energy jarring against his corporeality, beginning at the tip of one feathered wing, shifting it to incorporeality just for a moment, the flesh becoming invisible, then sliding along the length of the wing until it reached his outstretched, more human-like extremities.

It was excruciating, crisping every cell in his body to fusion-fired ash.

His arm next felt the pain sweep past. Then it caught his knee and moved up toward his groin. It would be severest where his body contained the greatest concentration of nerve cells: the tips of his fingers; his mouth; his groin. He grimaced at the thought of that, but the expression was quickly replaced with something darker, for the wave moved rapidly. It was the sense of time distortion that made it seem to last forever.

The pain was molecules being torn apart and reassembled, the corporeal body formed by the atmospheric disharmony being ripped back into incorporeal form—just for a fraction of an instant—and then abruptly and crudely being thrown back together, the molecules in their new corporeal form shifted just a fraction out of position with the old. The body tried to copy the purer frequency of the brother entering the atmosphere, but it was impossible to hold the new, slightly different, purer resonance within the space it occupied.

The most severe pain in the process was the atoms within the molecules churning in torment as they struggled, no, *fought* to find their proper place in the universe once again. That place was only a fraction of a nanosecond's travel from where they had started, but to travel the trip was to drag superheated sand-stone over a raw wound.

Then, as the blast of thunder ripped through Kafziel's abdomen, he felt the torture of the ages as his groin was ripped from between his legs. In that barest fraction of a second, when his most precious bodily organ was brutally torn from him, dissolved into nothingness, and given back to him slightly out of phase, only to feel that raw wound sandpapered back onto his corporeal body, the feeling was more of a torment than he could bear.

Letting a scream from deep inside his throat tear the blackness around him, the very sky withdrawing from his agony, he reflexively wrapped his wings around himself for protection, only to realize the wave of blistering pain had already passed him by.

Falling like a stone, the air grasping at his feathered appendages, and gravity pulling him earthward, sending him tumbling, he thrust his wings wide, slowing himself until he could control his fall. He must search for Uriel's trail quickly, for the thunderous passage of a new brother's arrival would soon distort the path's remaining luminescence beyond sensing.

What he didn't expect was the second blast of yet another brother's arrival so soon after the first. If he had, he would have found shelter.

By the time Jeremiel, the final brother, crashed through the barrier, his newly corporeal body sending roiling waves of power across the desert landscape, Kafziel was no longer able to maintain his flight in the air. Too many times the pain had ripped his flesh, and he could barely think of anything other than his damaged nerve endings. He lay huddled against the severe cold of the desert floor, his hands cupped around his genitals, actually praying what fractured prayers he remembered to the Unity above for the pain to cease.

It did, finally, fading quickly once the seventh brother was completely corporeal. Within moments afterward, the pain was indeed gone, for it could not remain once the body had reentered its residual disharmonic phase. It was only the memory of the torment that remained, and the fear that it would soon return.

No more was the pain gone when there was something else entirely that took over Kafziel's attention. A battering rush of wings made him look up, and then a mighty screech filled the night sky. It was when long, razor-sharp talons bit into his shoulder that he knew the animal that had claimed him as its own.

He knew something else, too, for he could feel in the touch

170

of this creature the one who was its master. This raptor was an extension of Gabriel. He laughed at that, as much as he could with those talons piercing his flesh, for in that touch, he realized that the mighty Archangel Gabriel had come to lowly Earth to claim his own, to rescue his precious Uriel from the clutches of lust.

That was when the brilliance in Kafziel came into its own. As a Watcher, he had a long history of opportunities to do nothing but think and plan, and he had grown very good at it. His mind shifted with the necessity of his changed circumstances, and he knew what he would say, twisting the facts to his own ends when Gabriel came, for he knew he would come.

Uriel had somehow learned the secret of the old days, the time when Jeqon, he who had been a Chief of the Brothers, had spilled his merrymaking onto the surface of this world, provoking the brothers in their first hours of corporeality to take the daughters of men for their brides, foisting children upon them, and creating those who would later become the legended giants of this world.

None of their progeny still lived, of course, at least not as giants. In stature, they had been little taller than the full-blooded humans around them. Instead, they had been large in ability and strength, and for that reason they were seen as giants, larger than life. As with most exceptional abilities, those qualities had become diluted with succeeding generations.

Still, Gabriel would remember, he who had been the Triune Mind's right hand, now known as the mighty Citadel of Justice and Power. He would recall the turmoil that had raged throughout the Unity, as well as the singular proclamation by the Triune Mind that there would be no more marrying or giving in marriage—copulation, in a word—therefore protecting the sanctity of the daughters of this world.

That proclamation had eventually become a Stricture of the Unity, one that was obeyed faithfully, at least in practice, if not in intent. Now it had been broken, and by Uriel.

Kafziel was certain Gabriel would cast doubt on his scathing tirade as he maliciously maligned Uriel. That was the overriding beauty of the tale. It was all recorded in the Chamber of

171

Deeds, and anyone could observe Uriel running with the woman; fleeing from the proffered warmth of Kafziel's safety and security. Uriel wanted her for his own, had probably fathered her himself, and refused to share her with any of the brothers. He had told Kafziel so, and then he had run.

Even the eagle with its talons sunk deep into his flesh could not slacken Kafziel's renewed enthusiasm. This new shift in the tide of events had turned at just the right time, and all was going to produce success, indeed. Kafziel was creating changes. He had become a Doer, and that was very satisfying to his earthbound essence.

It was when the howl of a wolf, one that sounded not quite mortal, brushed the night sky that Kafziel's blood began to thicken. He blamed it on the cold, for he was chilled to the bone. Even so, it could just as easily have been the memory of the ferocity with which that very wolf had fought him back at the mine.

He didn't need more pain, not anytime soon. To him, the brothers' entry onto this corporeal plane had been torturous enough, even if his skin bore no scars.

Chapter 13

Interlude 10

A snarling spitfire crashed into Kafziel, barely avoiding the eagle ripping into his shoulder. Long canine claws extended at full reach tore into the feathered flesh that made up Kafziel's corporeal wings. A howl of satisfaction quickly shifted to a growl of remembered anger, and dripping teeth, ones just slightly longer, and slightly more deadly than those of a normal wolf, tore into his neck.

The eagle on Kafziel's shoulder went careening into the darkness, its own feathered wings catching the air easily and lifting it aloft. Still clinging to its talons, gobbets of flesh dripped yellow-red blood. The creature's mouth opened wide as it thrust heavenward, and an ear-splitting scream raked the sky.

These familiars knew what their masters knew, felt what their masters felt, and both familiars knew this brother, this out-of-phase misfit, was one who was reviled, and he was to be taken down. In addition, Malak had an even stronger reason for his attack. The wolf had been given a very specific order by Uriel.

Kill.

It was one the furred canine would do its best to carry out.

Kafziel, Emissary of Solitude and Tears

Kafziel let his pain roll from his throat, the wings at his back hindering his efforts to wrestle free. Having the eagle latched to his shoulder had been inconvenient, but at least it had simply rested once its claws had bitten into his flesh, holding itself in a stable position. It hadn't tried to rip his body in two. This wolf was another matter. It had already done its best to mutilate him back in the mine, and it had come entirely too close. Not only had Kafziel been at his strongest then, he had also been in his own element, able to call upon makeshift weapons that could even the score.

Then, ripping one arm from underneath the wolf's paw, feeling the muscle give way as the razor-edged claws sliced trenches in his flesh, he reached high overhead and slapped his two hands together. In that instant, blinding light illuminated the desert, seething in the blackness as mist across a darkened sea, and much of the wolf's hold evaporated. The animal grasped wildly for support, one set of claws raking down Kafziel's bare back, shedding flesh and blood along the way.

In that second of perceived freedom, long talons slashed Kafziel's face, the earsplitting cry of the raptor reminding the hated brother that the fight was not the wolf's alone.

Kafziel threw himself to the ground. He realized this could easily be about life, for he could die out here.

Before he could leap to his feet to run, he felt sudden and intense pressure directly on his head, pressing his face to the ground. In that moment of touch, he knew reinforcements had come, and not for his benefit, either. The two familiars must have been working in tandem to delay him until help could arrive. It wasn't Uriel, though. Nor Gabriel. The two familiars hadn't exulted in this reunion. When a familiar and its master were rejoined, the melding of their resonances bled through to those around them.

"Dear Unity! Get off my face!" Kafziel spat his words in a harsh and ugly bark of furor and rising contempt. When the

174

pressure intensified, he grabbed at the source, realizing it was a foot that kept him immobile. Clutching the attached ankle with both hands, he arched his body and twisted hard, putting all his strength into shifting the offending foot from its hold on his head.

The pressure was unrelenting.

He lay angry and spent, gasping. This wasn't fair! This must be one of the newly arrived brothers, one who had just come to this world. Something left him puzzled, though. Those who were freshly arrived usually came down ravenous, weak and near to starvation. This one had strength and to spare.

Then a bright light, one that contained brilliance beyond comprehension, flooded the desert, and with a reverberation that shook the very dust upon the ground, the source of the light slammed into the soil just inches from his face. The rest of the world disappeared in that blaze of light. The stars above were gone, the small creatures of the night were silenced, and only those involved in this battle of wills still existed.

"This is a world in need of care. However, where Kafziel resides, there is trouble enough to spare."

The pressure was suddenly gone from his face, and he rolled to his side, putting one hand to the ground for support. In those few moments pressed against the dirt, his wounds had already healed over, but he could feel the weakness. He wouldn't admit to it, though.

He glanced up at the brother standing over him, and as quickly he closed his eyes. The brother was aflame. The item piercing the ground at his side glowed with the intensity of this world's primary sun. The brilliance swelled outward in the shape of a flaming cross. It was from a sword, and not just any sword. It was one of the Swords of Power. It was within his reach, and Kafziel's heart pounded with desire. He'd like to get his hands on that. Doing so would prove even more difficult than claiming Uriel's Destiny, and as he was finding out, even with a quarter-century's planning, that wasn't going so well.

Then he remembered the rhyming pattern of speech the towering brother had used, and he threw his head back and moaned in despair. This was Elemiah, twin brother to Barakiel,

175

and this one would trap him with his melodious rhymes. In fact, he had probably done so with those few phrases already spoken, and Kafziel wouldn't even know. This was a disaster, for Uriel had to be found. Angioletta had to be found. She was his ticket to more power than he'd ever known, and she was, indeed, his. He had created her from his own loins, and he would not give up what rightfully belonged to him.

In spite of Kafziel's righteous anger, a yellow-eyed wolf panted at his right hand, and one very vicious bald eagle had landed at his left. Elemiah stood in front with his arms crossed, his erect form towering over the other three, his features blazing in the brilliance that had wiped away the desert night. The Seraph carried no gentle glow that would fade to nothing in the brightness of the morning sun. His was a six-winged, pulsing torrent of luminosity that ripped the sight from mortal eyes, causing those who approached to fall to the ground, covering their faces just to continue to exist.

Kafziel grasped at his only option. He would have to best this brother with words of oil and honey, making them sweet to the taste, and yet slick enough to go down without too much critical consideration.

"Elemiah, I have tried to do good and failed." He dropped his head as if dissolute at an attempted good deed slipped through his fingers and beyond his ability to complete. He let a ragged breath escape his chest, and one sob choked from his throat.

Elemiah laughed at the theatrics, the sound ringing in the desert silence, for even the insects had quieted themselves in the glory of his presence. The Sword of Power had that effect on beings of this world.

"I observed your foolishness from afar. Now it grows even more bizarre." With a slight shift of his torso, the great wings at his back opened a measure, and he seemed to grow.

"No, Great Elemiah—" Kafziel knew the Seraph's posturing was only for effect, but it worked. He was cowed.

"Do not pander to me, Kafziel, you who refuse to return to the Unity." Elemiah didn't complete his rhyme, as angry blades of light flashed from his eyes. The words of the unfinished couplet sliced like shards of ice, and the light that surrounded the brother grew brittle and sharp at the edges.

Still, Kafziel schemed. If he could channel that power to recapture his daughter, it would be worth the effort, no matter what it cost. He opened his mouth to reply, but the Seraph's hand lifted, and he found he could not speak.

He could groan, though, and he did so. Quietly, all the same. He didn't wish to antagonize this brother, not and lose his chance at reeling him in.

With the tone of an arrogance that came from unrivaled power, Elemiah continued his couplet, "From your evil deeds which you have wrought, do you think I will grant you immunity?"

Kafziel groveled, his eyes downcast to indicate subservience. He made a sound, testing, and found he could speak. "Only hear me out, Great Elemiah." He tried the title again, peering from under his arm, relieved to see the Seraph remain quiet. If he could just get him to listen, then his plan had a chance.

The glowing lips parted once more. "I listen only because I must, Kafziel. Yet, even now you are under my spell." The sound of his words reverberated with power. "Speak well, and let truth be your friend. Second chances will not be given again."

"You are kind, Elemiah." It was as he expected from this pompous brother. He might have power, what with that Sword, but he also thought much too highly of himself. His pride would be his weakness.

"You may speak, but do not let your words repeat."

"I had her rescue almost complete." Kafziel's words dripped with sorrow, as he built on the plan he had conceived when Uriel had run with the girl. It was a good plan, too. He also thought his attempt at a rhyme couldn't hurt. It would surely curry favor with this one, who spoke only in patterns of repeated sounds.

"Rescue?" This time Elemiah didn't bother to make his one-word question rhyme. The response was filled with his disgust and was a clear indication he'd seen through Kafziel's pandering.

"Yes. From Uriel." Kafziel turned his face away from the Seraph, drooping in sorrowful exhaustion, but his lips carried a smile. He was certain now that Elemiah was hooked. He had only to reel him in.

Yet, the Seraph's next words lashed the air, and they burned into Kafziel. "Gadreel told of your betrayal, Dog Kafziel. Your penchant for twisting blame is known too well."

Malak growled at the Seraph's reference, but the furred familiar sat still. Even so, its eyes glowed a little brighter, the yellow orbs becoming ever more ominous.

Kafziel tried to sink even closer to the ground, but he was already against the soil. He moaned instead, his sound one of wronged Samaritanship. It cried that there was no way he could be faulted in this.

He pleaded his case in whispers.

"The girl Uriel has stolen—" Let that get out to Gabriel! "—is mixed-blood, half-brother, half-human." He put his hand up to still the protests he anticipated, and rightly so. It was forbidden by the Strictures, and thought fully impossible by many. He continued, his words stronger, "You know full well what that means. If the brothers were to find out, she would be torn apart by their pent-up desires."

It was true, too, not that he cared. He had only begun the process of life, taking his full payment from the enjoyment those initial moments of pleasure had provided him. He didn't know his daughter, didn't consider her to be so in the filial sense, by any means. She was simply a single step in a long series of intertwined events, and the desired end was whatever power he could gain. She offered him much, so for that reason alone, she was still very important to him. For the opportunity to achieve the power he desired, he would claim all manner of devotion, even love, to the girl.

"I only offered her protection, Elemiah. I learned of her presence just days ago. The brother who parented her surely does not even know." He had known of her much longer, but his actual moment of physical contact was what the Chamber of Deeds would show. "When Uriel was cast down, out of kindness, I offered him shelter and food. The girl was with me, sleeping." His voice choked with mock emotion. "Uriel claimed he smelled her—" entirely probable, what with the cinnamon and frankincense "—and searched the premises. He claimed her for his own, even fought me for her. I tried to protect her. I truly did." He sniffled, his pain heartfelt, or so he hoped it appeared to Elemiah. They could check the mine. The signs of a battle were everywhere.

He continued, "He has run with her, Elemiah. They could be anywhere by now. I fear for her life." He forced actual tears from his eyes. "When Uriel satisfies himself with her, if she is still alive, he is sure to offer her to others in the Unity, at a price, of course. If you know where Gabriel is, you must call him down, from the Unity, if necessary—" His familiar was right here. Without doubt, Gabriel was already close by, one of the seven who had slashed pain right through his body. "—but Uriel must be stopped, no matter the cost."

"Your story rings true; such we have been told. It is a repeat of the past, when Jeqon was too bold." The great Sword was plucked from the ground, and the desert sky returned. It seemed to subtly shift over their heads, the darkness of the night flowing in hue from a charcoal drenched with blue to ebony that instantly deepened into the richest violet. It was as if more time had passed than just the few moments of spoken words between two brothers on opposing sides of a great rift in principles. An hour, perhaps. Half a day. With the shift in the sky, perhaps more. Even the smells in the air indicated it could well be a different night altogether.

The soil under their feet even seemed less alive, as if the Sword had given it a consciousness of its own, one that was now dissipated. It had, too, for with the touch of the Sword upon the soil, Elemiah had perused the events of the past hours. The Sword could read the story of the shifting molecules, for each minute particle carried the record of recent events much as sound travels through water. The actions of humans and brothers upon Earth had been recorded, and Elemiah had sensed much that matched Kafziel's story.

Of course, the events revealed to him were more the

semblance of a tale rather than crystal images of reality, but a fight had been clear, and a human—one who was half-human, anyway—had been taken without her consent. Other things had been sensed, also, but the readings by the Sword were notoriously vagarious, often used to substantiate, but rarely clear enough to determine a series of events by the reading of the Sword alone.

With a great snap as of a flag unfurled in a stiff breeze, Elemiah's wings were spread wide. His brilliance once more flooded the desert, bringing the storied glory of the heavens to this desolate place. In that moment, it was as if the shining presence of a host of Heavenly beings had been called upon to visit this remote locale to bring about a new season of miracles.

With the Seraph's eyes closed, Kafziel knew what was going on. This was no season of miracles. Kafziel couldn't hear a word spoken, either aloud or in his head, but Elemiah was without doubt in deep conversation with Gabriel.

If he intended to run, now would be the time. Nevertheless, that would be foolishness. He had this brother eating out of his hand, sopping up his lies like sweet suet, and if Elemiah believed, then soon, all those who had come down with him would be in one accord.

He laughed to himself, although he made sure it was most certainly not seen on his face. Still, now he would have Gabriel, the *Archangel*, working for him, against his own treasured Uriel, by the great and holy Unity! How sweet was that? Gabriel working to complete Kafziel's own nefarious ends!

He looked up at the Seraph standing over him with his wings spread wide, and he chuckled. Trickery, and at this level, was doubly sweet!

Angioletta Bacciarelli, Daughter of Kafziel

Angioletta yanked her hand free from the stranger's skin, her heart pounding with anticipation. Anticipation for what, she wasn't exactly certain. Surely not sex! Indeed, this man was naked, but he was also severely injured. Blood, a strange

180

reddish substance laced with yellow, still leaked from his wounds, ones that were self-inflicted, it seemed.

Still, her body desired *something* from this vanilla flavored man.

Turning, she sat on the floor, her muscles quivering, her eyes barely able to focus. She lifted her hand to stare at her palm, a small amount of the man's blood smeared across its heel. She reached and touched the not-quite-red fluid she had seen leaking from his arm to find it thick, yes, like blood, but with an oily texture. Each time she touched the substance on her hand, she tingled once again, with just a hint of that earlier vanilla scent . . . no, taste. Yes, it had been a scent earlier, but now that she'd touched him, she knew it was definitely a taste. Yet, she hadn't tasted anything. The sensation of vanilla was one she *felt* right through her skin.

She wondered if he was possibly sick, if she could catch something from him. Maybe the gravel underneath his skin had caused a reaction, and the yellow was specialized pus she'd never seen.

She turned her head to look at the man in the tub. His chest rose and fell, if barely. His skin, where it was undamaged, was oddly, impossibly smooth—flawless—as if he'd only recently been born, but that wasn't possible. He was clearly a man in every way conceivable, although his hands covered *that* part of his body from her direct observation. He was heavily muscled, nearing stockiness, with a head full of jet-black hair, curly, of all things, and the reddest full lips. His cheekbones slashed high across his face, reaching almost to his temples.

If she had to guess, she would think this man Native American. There was no hint of facial hair, other than that light dusting of down all adults wore. Full-blooded Native Americans didn't grow facial hair, but that was a rarity in the 21st century. So many of the bloodlines had been polluted with European interbreeding that it would be very unusual for this man to fulfill that very specific genetic niche.

He was quite beautiful, though. Although most men hated that term, it was the only one she could use to describe him. Handsome? Not in the rough-hewn American sense. Feminine?

Not by any measure. Exotic? Perhaps, perhaps. Beautiful, to her, gave the most accurate description possible.

Even so, as beautiful as he was, he would certainly die if she didn't get up off this floor and provide him some assistance. Reaching to the towel she had used on his shoulder, she made to wipe her palm clean. Then, impulsively, she brought her hand to her mouth and reached her tongue to the reddish blood smeared across the skin. She never hesitated, although she normally would have been repulsed at the thought of licking another person's blood. It was the smell, the *feel* of vanilla that had overtaken her senses. It prompted her actions in a way she never would have considered under any other circumstance.

When her tongue brushed against the heel of her hand, it was like electric heat inside her mouth, no, not *like*, it was the slicing of fusion incandescence into the core of her being, the crashing of a thousand waves on a thousand shores, a million births of a million children with their deaths all rolled into one; it was her own birth and rebirth happening a thousand times, and it was the taste of vanilla against her tongue.

She gasped with the sensations that surged through her body, the overwhelming need, and the release of something inside that she couldn't define. She felt it in the pit of her stomach and in the tips of her fingers. Her brain seemed to swell in her skull, and then it became normal again.

No, not quite normal. Better than normal, although she didn't know how she knew that.

She drew in a deep, ragged breath, her skin tingling, her eyes immediately clear. She knew what she must do. There was no doubt now, no waffling, and certainly no hesitation.

Standing, she stepped from the bathroom, knowing she must find food for this man. In the bedroom she stepped to the small table filled with snacks. Picking the tray up, she carried it to the bathroom, then considered what she held. It wasn't enough, surely, although how she knew was unclear to her. Besides, this man could not consume solids. Liquids. She must have liquids, and ones that were packed with calories. Juices, sodas, energy drinks. Yes, that would do.

Setting the tray on the opened suitcase stand, she touched

the pants that had been roughly thrown there. A sense of dismay, one that slowly faded to remorse—for not being able to help in some fashion, she supposed—washed across her. She couldn't imagine this man removing this item of clothing, then climbing in the tub to cut himself.

She knelt and reached to the man's face, his angelic, perfect, beautiful face. She placed her hand to his cheek, running her thumb along the highpoint of his cheekbone, letting the taste of vanilla wash her senses. She could feel life there, for his chest was rising and falling, and that meant air was traveling through his respiratory system. He moved beneath her hand with each breath he drew and each lungful of air he released. He seemed no worse than when she'd entered the room, although he seemed no better. Surely he would live long enough for her to find food.

Pulling her hand away, she noticed she had already developed a sort of resistance to this man's vanilla magnetism. She smiled. It had overwhelmed her when she'd first touched him, and this second time it had simply been an intensely pleasurable experience. Perhaps it was something that would again grow in intensity after an extended abstinence.

Stepping into the room, she looked around, reminded what she wore. Pajamas. That wouldn't do. And money. She had none. She took a deep breath. This was still doable. She had to simply step outside, and she would come up with a way to get food, even if she had to beg for it. After all, she had always shown a talent for getting things done, making people see things her way, convincing those who were filled with doubt. It was what made her shine as a teacher. She could wave her hands, and the children saw the lessons. The math was simply there in their heads, sentences forming themselves right in front of their eyes, the maps they drew perfect because her students said they could *see* where everything went. She knew because her students told her so, and so did their parents, arriving for conferences in droves, sharing what their children told them about the way they learned in Ms. Bacciarelli's class.

Stepping to the door, she grasped the handle firmly, and with a twist, she swung it wide. Expecting to see a busy street, neon signs, and buildings filling the sidewalks, she let out a gasp. Before her stretched empty blacktop, and where it ended rose the blackness of night, with little more than stars for icing. She shivered with the emptiness of it all. She couldn't stretch money that wasn't there when there were no people to help her.

Still, this place was not silent. There were insect noises, and somewhere a television blared. She even recognized the voices of Lucille Ball and Desi Arnaz. She smiled at that. When she'd left the convent, the family with whom she'd stayed had lived for that decades-old comedy show.

Breaking into her awareness, the noise that caught her attention most of all came from the roof. Something, or *someone*, was up there, and while she didn't know exactly what was going on, she needed help.

Stepping away from the building, she saw cars around the corner, so she knew she and the man in the tub weren't totally alone, but she hadn't really expected they were. This was probably out in the desert, possibly near a highway. This could be New Mexico, or perhaps Arizona. She sniffed the air. She didn't smell any juniper. That meant Arizona, for sure. New Mexico had juniper.

She turned and looked up, noticing the flat roof on the motel. Just behind a low parapet that ran all along the front wall, she could see a blond head of hair. He—she?—was looking down, very intent on some repetitive activity. Surely this person wasn't effecting repairs on the roof at night.

"Can you help me?" She was gratified to see the head look up. She was surprised to see it was the face of a boy, one certainly not over fifteen. The expression on his face morphed through surprise, then panic quickly took hold. He ducked out of sight for a moment, then she noticed his head and shoulders bobbing in and out of sight. If she didn't know better, she would think he was putting his clothing on. Was there a pool on the roof? It didn't look as if there was room, but it was certainly possible.

When she saw him running down the roof away from her without responding to her plea, she called to him again. "Please, don't run. I need your help." It was her most convincing tone of voice, the one that always seemed to break through even her most sullen students' shells.

She was gratified to see him stop and look at her.

"Yes? What do you need?" His voice cracked on the last word. It was that reedy contralto that often happened when teenage boys had only recently taken their first steps toward manhood. Now she knew he could not be over fifteen. Maybe fourteen at best, hoping for fifteen.

"I need your help. I have an—" and she paused, thinking how to phrase her request to a fourteen-year-old. "My, um, friend is a diabetic, and he needs food quickly. Do you know where I can get some fruit drinks, or better, energy drinks? It's urgent."

"Are you staying here at the motel?"

"Yes, I am. My name is Ms. Bacciarelli. I teach middle school, sixth and seventh grades. What's your name?" Asking his name wasn't part of her "talent." That was just common courtesy. It would create a bond, if he chose to tell her.

"Bobby. I'm in ninth grade. That's high school."

She smiled. His grade level was important to him. Tick off another box for fourteen.

"What's your last name, Bobby?"

"Dalton. Bobby Dalton."

He still hadn't come down from the roof, and she couldn't get the nourishment the injured man so desperately needed until he did.

"I'm Angioletta, Bobby." Telling him her first name would help him see her as a friend.

"Are you Sicilian? From your last name, I mean."

She was relieved he was still talking, at least. She didn't know the true effects of her inborn "talent," that Bobby was responding to her "Suggestions." She simply had a "knack" for drawing out the most reticent children, and she always had.

"Italian." Her response was warm and inviting. "I was born there, not far from Rome. I came to America as a teenager. Is there a pool on the roof?"

He turned and looked behind him as if he might actually find one. "No." His voice was hesitant, and in his adolescent tenor, it sounded vaguely guilty. "Why?"

"Oh, it's just that it looked like you were getting dressed a moment ago."

Then, it dawned on her. He probably had been getting dressed, and that made her smile. Teenage boys were the same everywhere, whether in Italy or America.

"If you'll come down and help me, I won't tell anyone you were up there. I promise, Bobby. I didn't see anything, really. It's too dark out here." He would want to believe that badly, and he would help her. He'd be afraid she'd tell if he didn't.

True to her expectations, he leaped the parapet, landing on the motel's porch overhang. Finding the porch supports, he knelt and grabbed the edge of the guttering, swinging his legs down and wrapping them around a metal pole. A quick drop, and he stood in front of her.

She could see the fourteen clearly, then. He was slightly shorter than she was, gangly for his size, and his face still bore the indistinct softness of childhood. His shoulders were wide, and although he had a slim waist, he moved with muscular assuredness. His clothing told her she had assessed his rooftop activities correctly, too. His shirt was tucked in the front—on one side—but hanging out in the back. His jeans were snapped, but very blue boxers protruded through the fly. She motioned with her hand and turned away, giving him time to fix the problem.

"I'm sorry," he said, his jeans unsnapping, then after a moment, a zipper sounding. "I, um, left my pants up there earlier." He cleared his throat, then a final snap of metal told her he was finished.

Turning, she saw his face was now brilliantly red beneath his shock of blond hair, and she fought to keep a smile from her face. It wouldn't do to embarrass him just when she had him ready to do her bidding.

She reached and took his arm. "Please, Bobby. Where can I get some food? Energy drinks, perhaps? Fruit juice would work, too." She motioned toward her room. "My friend—"

"Is he hurt?"

"His diabetes. Please, Bobby." She wove desperation into

186

her plea. It was a partial lie, but she didn't know the whole truth. The desperation part was certainly honest, and whatever it took to save that man was worth it, even lies.

The boy smiled, charmed, and he became charming in turn. "I've got some at home. I play baseball, pitcher on my church's team, and I've got bottles and bottles of power drinks. I need them when I'm practicing. I live just over the hill. I can run get you some."

"Would you?" She smiled at him. "Snack cakes, Bobby. Do you have any of those?"

"Sure, Angi ... Ms. Bacciarelli." That was his fourteen coming out. "I'll be right back."

He took off in a tear, and Angioletta noticed his feet. He'd been so busy putting his pants back on that he'd forgotten to tie his shoes. She hoped he didn't fall and hurt himself. If he did, he might choose not to bring the food, and the man in her room needed it desperately.

She turned to walk back inside the motel. It would be a while before the boy returned, and the gravel in that shoulder wasn't going to just fall out. If the man in that tub thought removing it was important enough to risk his life, then it was probably important enough for her to complete the job. She had held the knife in the tub already and was sure he wouldn't be too embarrassed at her seeing him naked. Besides, he undoubtedly would be passed out the entire time, and if it bothered her, she could simply drape him with a towel.

She left the door cracked when she stepped inside. It was important that the boy know just where to come. The man lay just as she'd left him, and thankfully, his chest still moved with life. His shoulder continued to ooze, too, and for that, she made a face.

Kindhearted soul that she was, Angioletta reached for a clean towel, unfolded it, and laid it across his lap. She didn't notice that in addition to his more intimate bodily area, she also covered a smooth stomach that bore no signs of something that was very familiar to all humans, a navel. If not for the very distracting damage to his shoulder, she might not have missed that.

Then, kneeling, she reached beside him and felt around for the knife. Its condition shocked her. It was broken and filthy. Rinsing it thoroughly in the sink, she knelt at his side, and she pressed on his arm, just where the stones were buried inside.

She could still feel the vanilla through her fingertips, but it was manageable. She didn't even think to find that unusual, that she wasn't overcome with pleasure. Instead, she laid the tip of the blade beside one of the stones and pressed, breaking the skin. Viscous red and yellow blood oozed out. She pushed on the stone, sliding it sideways, until it popped free. She grabbed it as it came out, setting it carefully on the side of the tub.

"One down," she whispered. "A whole bunch to go." Then she pressed the knife to the skin one more time.

Bobby Dalton, Motel Rat

Bobby was exhausted when he arrived home, and his thin tee shirt was soaked with sweat. When he burst through the door, his mother was waiting up on him, and the expression on her face wasn't pleasant at all.

"Bobby, what's this?"

That's all she said, all she had to say. What she tossed out on the coffee table told the rest. It stopped him in his tracks. Several months before, he and his good friend Austen had been prowling through the trash rooms at the motel. They weren't really rooms, but metal buildings out back that were used to store the trash until pickup day. Out in the desert, the big trucks didn't come by except every other Tuesday, and both boys knew Nigel boxed up stuff that was left in the rooms. If no one called, it went out on the truck.

Bobby'd filched the key from the front desk, and he and Austen had prowled through all the boxes of stuff. They hit the jackpot that day. Bobby found a tee shirt from a concert in San Bernardino, although neither one of them recognized the name of the group. It was cool, anyway, even if it did have a bleach mark on one sleeve, and the concert date was from five years before. Austen wanted it, but Bobby said he'd wear it someday and claimed it for his own.

There'd been some women's underthings, and they'd held them up, laughing and throwing them at each other before stuffing them back in the box. Neither one of them wanted any of that.

The next box was gold.

Austen picked it up to move it, and it was deceptively heavy. When he turned to take it out the door, it slipped from his grasp, and it split open on the floor. Maybe twenty magazines had tumbled out, some falling open to glossy pages showing women doing things the boys had never imagined any woman doing.

They'd split the stash fifty-fifty, agreeing to share the glossies after a week, or if Austen went home before then, perhaps in a month. Austen carried his in the broken box, holding it tightly under his arm, as if someone might see him and take them away. Bobby had wrapped his in the shirt with the bleach stain.

Now he was caught out, for there they were, strewn across the coffee table. Somehow they didn't look quite so much like gold spread out in front of his mother. He blanched, and he had nothing to say.

"Well, Bobby? I go in there to change your sheets, and look what I find sticking out between the mattresses! Filth! Then, I searched and found even more. How can you bring those nasty women into my house?" She went to the kitchen and snatched the trash can from under the sink, and with a swoop of an arm, all the magazines were swept inside.

He gasped, immediately calculating the best time of the night to retrieve the ones that were his favorites. Then, to his horror, she took the skillet from the stove and poured hot grease on the lot of them. Tears welled up in his eyes.

"There you go, Bobby Dalton. That nice Rikkianne has been telling me about you over at that motel she manages. I never believed a word, thinking of you all those years attending Sunday school, then crawling in my bed at night, snuggling with your teddy bear. Never did I imagine you snuggling with this filth!" She stuffed the can back under the sink, pointing to

189

his room. "Up, mister, and don't you come down until the sun comes up. I am so ashamed of you."

"But, Mom," he started, needing to explain about the woman who had asked for his help. She was from Italy, and her skin glowed. If he didn't go back, her friend might die.

His mother had no patience with him, though, and not a word he said was heard. Then, when he shut his bedroom door, she called through, "And there had better be no sneaking out tonight, young man. Tomorrow, I'll decide your punishment."

He crawled into bed, still dressed, and he hugged his pillow. It was a long time before he finally fell asleep.

Chapter 14

Fire Fighters, Engine No. 4

Laughter filled the bar.

From out in the street, the plate glass windows glowed in the early evening dusk, and those who hadn't gotten away from work early enough to avoid the evening rush were still wending their way down the city streets, certain that anywhere else, any location off the sidewalk and away from the hustle-bustle, was a better place to be.

Looking in through the windows, it would seem they were right. Polished woods glowed softly, oiled by a generation and more of hands and arms, friends gathered to toast special events or just while away the hours until their spouses gave up and went to bed without them.

When the doors opened, a patron entering, or less often, guilty feet exiting, music could be heard, and it carried a beat that drove the blood, or at other times spoke to the lonely heart. The smiles on the faces told of friends and acquaintances enjoyed, or lovers missed.

Still, it was laughter, and for passersby moving quickly down the sidewalk, the sounds through the glass were cheerful and welcoming, tempting them to enter and join in. Many times people did, slipping through the doors, the companionship inside either holding them warmly, or the lack of it summarily spitting them back out.

Separated from the sidewalk crowd, past gleaming brass foot rails and next to a large jukebox, a booth was wedged into a corner that was more private than most. It couldn't be seen from the street, and it was rarely offered to any but the regulars. To get to this booth, one had to navigate a series of obstacles designed to catch the casual visitor.

The first was the bistro tables to the right of the front door, those elevated gathering spots for individuals who wanted to be seen. The tables, small and round, with two to four barstools spaced tightly together for intimate conversation, were often crowded. They were filled with the after-work crowd, those who had stopped in on the way to their car, people who still had a hot meal waiting for them at home. Greetings would be called out, of course, and hands would reach out as one walked by, smiling and asking about the quality of the day.

There was more to the bar than just the bistro crowd, though. The serious drinkers planted their boots deeper in the depths of the building, resting them on the brass foot rails that ran along the massive bar, the real one, polishing their designer denims on the padded leather stools that twisted permanently at its altar. They sat hunched over, their laughter for those few who sat at their side. Upon their arrival they would joke with the bartenders, throwing out filthy ones if males were serving, or provocative ones for the females. It was all in humor, though, for the bar was tall and deep, and the tenders were out of easy reach.

These merrymakers had to be traversed, too. Early in the evening, they would be slapped on the back, faces would turn, and hands might be offered. A drink might be suggested, paid for, too. As dusk stole over the city, the voices would begin to slur, and the jokes would turn mean. Arrive after dark, and the backs best be left alone.

Beyond the brass rails and the boots, and the weary jeans glued to leather, the clink of glittering glassware added its own music to the bar. The song of the crystal tumblers was for those who arrived early at the brass rails, for they sometimes caught a glimpse of its beauty. When the bar was still quiet in those early hours, the jukebox songs muted by lack of interest, and the voices few, then the music filtered out to them. The dishwasher opened, and racks of glasses rattled their way inside. Steam whisked the lipstick away, sanitized the smell of alcohol from each surface, and then was gone. The glasses danced free, rubbing shoulders and chattering merrily to one another, the dishwashers' hands noisily shifting the musicians from drying rack to shelving, the singing going on all the while.

Later, though, when the bar filled, the song was buried underneath the laughter, or overshadowed by the jukebox. Only those who dared the deepest depths of the building heard it then. This night, the booth that was for the regular patrons was crowded, and it was full of laughter. The jukebox warbled Elvis, and Santana, and the Stones. It was a night for merriment.

These men were bonded, and it was a glue that was stronger than most. Their laughter was sincere, for they actually liked one another, knew each other's wives, and had been at church events honoring each other's nieces and nephews. They had also saved each other's backsides, some more than once. These men were more like brothers than friends, and brotherly laughter was the kind that bounced back and forth across the table.

A local newspaper was splashed in front of them, the sections stacked unevenly alongside their drinks. Damp circles littered its surface. Several shot glasses rested upside down on the paper, the newsprint good for catching the liquid remains that had been left inside. Many of the glasses had been there a while. An empty tumbler or two were off to the side.

One corner of the paper had grown wet, and when an errant elbow brushed against it, it gave way.

An arm reached out and jabbed at a picture right in the center of the newspaper, tapping it several times, rattling the glasses next to it. Those glasses didn't sing, though. Those songs were for the ones that were shiny and clean.

"For an angel to look like that? Ho, ho! You have got to be kidding." It was Sam, and three of the shot glasses were his.

"No angel looks like that. Why, my old grams has a better angel hanging above her toilet." The picture in the paper looked like it had been copied from a Christmas card, with a bright light shining from Heaven and everything. It showed a voluptuous woman in a flowing gown, her long hair thick and curly, and her wings folded at her back.

Gunnar's freckled hand slapped him on the shoulder. "That why you always went to Grams' house to do your business? Stand there in front of that angel, and it helps get the juices flowing?" He laughed, and it came out rough. It was the alcohol, and when the firemen had been at the booth for a while, the jokes could get bawdy.

Samuel laughed also, his own sense of humor just as rough. "Naw, Gunnar. Just needed a place you couldn't watch." He leaned back in the booth, and he moved his hand up and down at his crotch several times, an intense look on his face.

"You always were horny, from the time we were in junior high. Get a room." Gunnar's arm reached back in and moved the three shot glasses, turning the paper to get a better look at the picture. "Who spilled these beans?" He glanced accusingly at Alonso.

Alonso, his face red with drink, raised both hands. "No beans spilled here. Rosita, I say, 'Shush!'" He put a finger dramatically to his mouth, pursing his lips for effect. "I only tell Lucita, besides Rosita. She is the baby's mother. What could I do?" He smiled comically, reaching to pick up a glass tankard of beer, the foam mostly gone already.

"You're the culprit!" Samuel pointed, a broad grin on his face. Alonso was the old man in the group, the senior team member on Engine No. 4, and all the "youngsters" looked up to him as a mentor. They loved him, also, as well as his wife, Rosita. They also loved her cooking, but that was a given. Rosita's cooking was responsible for her husband's waistline, and that would someday prove true for the other three men, if they had their continued say in the matter.

"Me?" Alonso shrugged, and he quickly dodged, as Samuel's arm reached past the reticent Rodrigo to prod Alonso on the chest. "I am no culprit. I never cooked a think in my life.

194

I am just Alonso."

"A thing," Rodrigo muttered. "Not a think. Besides, there was no angel." He was as drunk as the rest, but he didn't like this discussion. He *knew* Alonso had stepped into the flames to rescue the child, just as every man at this table did. Yet, just as clearly as he remembered Alonso's heroic actions, it *felt* like something else in his heart. He *felt* like Alonso had never stepped inside that house, and he *felt* like an angel had exited through that front door, handing that baby to her godfather before disappearing back into the flames.

He did smile when Samuel tore the angel from the paper, flying it through the air. His flying angel hit Alonso's partially empty glass and knocked it into his lap, causing a scramble as he tried to get out of the way.

When he was finished, Gunnar reached for the newspaper angel. He looked at it, holding it in one hand, while he downed the last of his drink with the other. Then, grinning mischievously at the others around the table, he folded it in quarters and put it to his lips, kissing it noisily. Samuel grabbed for it, calling it his angel, but Gunnar laughed, holding it out of his reach.

"She's mine, Sam. I'm going to make sure she has a good time tonight, too."

"Good time?" Alonso sniggered. "She is an angel, my friend."

Gunnar winked, and he undid his belt. Then, dramatically, he slipped the folded angel into his pants, leaving it right in his crotch. Samuel's eyes grew large, and he hooted with laughter when he saw what his friend was doing.

"That's going to be some happy angel, Gunnar." Samuel slapped the table, causing the glasses to jump.

Alonso shook his head. "Thank my stars Rosita doesn't see this."

Rodrigo had a more practical comment. "You are nuts, Gunnar. I always knew it but couldn't prove it."

Gunnar reattached his belt, sitting up and grinning. "That's gonna be the happiest angel in heaven tonight. She's right where every angel in the world wants to be. Lucky her."

Just then the waitress came up and set a new round on the

table. When Gunnar ducked his head and turned bright red, she giggled.

"You're cute. Are you all alone tonight?" She pushed gently on Gunnar's shoulder, winking at the others, and grinning.

Sam reached and jabbed his other shoulder. "Naw, he's got a date, already. She's a real angel."

The men at the table burst into laughter, and even Rodrigo joined in. It was entirely too funny, and in spite of the fact the poor waitress didn't understand, she joined in also.

Kinky Kinkerson, Reporter

The phone beside Kinky's bed jangled loudly, the sound rough and unfamiliar. His hand grabbed it, not entirely awake, knocking the base of the device to the floor, causing even more disruption. His sleepy voice cursed roughly before he laid his head back and pressed the receiver to his ear.

"Kinkerson here. What?" He reached and rubbed his forehead, thoroughly irritated. He'd turned his cell down where it would barely ring, preferring a gentle reentry into the world of the waking, not this jarring headache. After all that lightning the previous night, he'd hoped to get a full eight, but it didn't seem it would be the case.

"Donovan pulled it out, Kinky. We got our two angel stories in. Right on the second section, first page."

"Stories?" He sat up, rubbing his eyes, recognizing Julian's voice. As he put his feet to the floor, he stepped on the phone he'd knocked off seconds earlier. "My lands!" He added a few other choice words, also, blistering the phone receiver in the process.

"Kinky? Everything okay?"

"This phone's trying to kill me, that's all. I have a cell, Julian. Could you use it sometime?" He stepped to the mirror, turning on the light, and blinking in the glare. "How'd you get this number, anyway?" He flipped the water on, splashing his face, fighting the tether that kept the phone on the floor attached to his ear.

"GPS, remember? You set it up on my computer so I could track your travels. Helps you keep track of your expenses for your travel account. I got the name of the motel and phoned the office. Anyway, I did call your cell. You didn't answer."

He glanced at the bedside table to see it was indeed blinking with a missed call notice. "Sorry. I guess I was exhausted. Now, what's this about angels?"

Julian laughed. "That fire? Then the old man you gave a ride to? You called me, remember? The paper picked it up. Ran it in the late edition. Of course, I had to get them a picture of a real angel. I cut one out of an old Christmas card and faxed it over. It didn't quite fit the story, but it was the best I could do."

"That I do remember. Sorry, Julian. Thanks for jogging my memory. I cannot get my brain going here. At least my contribution helped you out, and I'm glad to know that. Gotcha a by-line finally."

"Got *us* a by-line. I threw your name in, too."

Julian paused, and waiting, Kinky sat back down, the bed squeaking noisily.

"C'mon, Kinky. Aren't you going to say thanks for that?"

"Thanks, Julian. Now, about my car." When he'd gone out to move his car during the storm, during which it never rained a drop, the battery was dead. He needed a repair or a rental.

"Working on it. It'll be morning before I know, though. We're already picking up the cost of your room. You could just wait for a few days, you know, being paid to relax." The grin could be heard even over the line.

"Podunk, Julian. Nothing to do here except sit and watch the grass grow. What ever happens in Phoenix? Nothing." He lay back, looking at the light over the sink. He wished he'd turned it out, now, 'cause it wasn't going out on its own. He also thought Julian didn't seem appropriately upset about his car troubles.

"I saved you a copy of the story. Thought you might like it. I'll leave it on your desk where you can find it."

Over the line, Kinky could hear what was obviously a thick newspaper slapped to a desk, smacking dully.

"Oh!" Julian's voice was suddenly excited. "I nearly forgot. Something new for you to chew on. Remember that Jupiter mission that took off a few days back?"

"Io, right?' He'd been following it in L.A. but had lost track here without access to top-tier cable channels.

"I've been on my NASA feed, and they've had some unusual EMP activity up there. Angel activity, you think?" He chuckled.

Kinky snorted. "C'mon. Angels in space? Get real."

"Just thought we might find heaven up there. After all, if we found angels, we've gotta look for heaven somewhere." He obviously found his take on the concept very amusing.

Kinky didn't bother to respond.

"Kinky? It was a joke. Sorry." There was a long pause with only silence for an answer. Julian cleared his throat before speaking again. "Kinky?"

"Yeah, thanks, Julian. Sorry I was short earlier. I wasn't awake. I'm still not. How about we talk in the morning?"

"Sure. Later. Enjoy the big city."

"Sure, Julian." Kinky reached to end the call, then realized this phone didn't have an off switch. It had to be hung up. He twisted to the bedside table, only to remember that the base unit was on the floor, right where he'd stepped on it.

He lay back, a few choice words on his lips, but he didn't say any of them. Instead, he sat up once again, knowing he would have had to do this anyway. After all, the lights were still on, and there was no way he was falling back asleep with that bulb glaring in his eyes.

The room finally dark and the phone back in its proper resting spot, he leaned against the pillow, his eyes wide in the darkness. He knew it'd be a while before he found sleep again, now that he'd been awakened. That was just as well, because he thought about what Julian had told him. He'd gotten the picture he'd faxed to the paper from a Christmas card. A *Christmas* card!

How much of a riot was that?

Angioletta Bacciarelli, Daughter of Kafziel

Angioletta couldn't imagine how this poor man had managed to get so much gravel buried underneath his skin. She must have pulled twenty pieces out, and that was besides what he'd already managed to remove himself.

After an hour or so, her arms beginning to tire enough that it surprised her, she glanced toward the outside door, wondering where the boy had gotten to. Surely he wouldn't abandon her. When she got up to check, before she could make it to the door, she felt her stomach twist into a knot. Grabbing the side of the sink, she doubled over with a fire that sent stabbing jolts of pain throughout her body. Something wrenched her brain, flooding agony inside of her head, and she fell to the floor, unable to maintain her balance.

"No," she whispered hoarsely. "Surely I cannot have contracted what he has. Dear God, no." The yellow fluid in his blood had seemed too strange to be normal, and unexpectedly, the memory of vanilla surged through her consciousness. She had *licked* it off her *hand*, for heaven's sake.

Reaching for the doorframe, she pulled herself erect, her head swimming, with her sense of up and down totally distorted. The bed, the one nearest her, swam before her eyes. The farthest one she could no longer see. She turned toward the bathroom, the man lying there, and he blurred into a bizarre surrealist painting that meant nothing at all. Her stomach rose into her throat, and she knew she would vomit bile if she remained on her feet.

Her legs twisting to jelly underneath her, she stumbled to the bed, the world spinning around her, and only her closed eyes brought it to a stop.

Yet, even so, her torment didn't really cease, for as her hands twitched, and her eyelids jumped back and forth, her thoughts lived on. Lightning flashed through her sky, and the beating of wings tore her breath from her chest. She floated in blackness, surrounded by brilliant points of light, and she was

199

cold, colder than she'd ever been growing up in her mothers' convent. Drawing her arms and legs in, she shivered, and tears ran down her face. She was frightened, and she was awed with the beauty of all that was around her. It was a scene on a grand scale, wider in scope than anything she'd ever imagined.

She didn't want to be there at all.

Interlude 11

In the motel room where Angioletta's body lay, still and pale, the light continued to burn over the bathroom sink, bleeding its illumination across the woman on the bed. Not far away, lying in the tub underneath a humming electric heater, Uriel breathed shallowly, his shoulder still oozing his yellow tinted blood, the life inside hanging on tenaciously, his injured body's resources dangerously low. One arm jerked, and his leg shifted. A frown crossed his face, although he was unaware of it.

It had grown exceedingly hot in the room, and the warmth stirred small reserves of energy that hadn't yet been tapped, ones the cold had kept in reserve deep in his body, small remnants of fatty tissue snuggled next to his heart, plus some subcutaneous padding that normally smoothed out the muscle that lay just beneath the skin. If he was lucky, it might prove to be just enough.

In that moment of warmth, he groaned in his porcelain sarcophagus. One hand grabbed the side, and his eyes flickered open, barely. The room swam before him, the walls blurring, his memory of where he was deeply buried within the damage that had been done to his shoulder. All his reasoning was gone, or at least pushed aside, for what little strength the heat had coerced his cells to release could not be spared for coherent thought. He knew only need . . . hunger.

Unable to distinguish between the wall and the floor, his hands grabbed wildly. Pulling himself over the edge of the tub, he fell to the floor, his legs tangled in the towel that had covered him, and his arm disrupting the balance of the luggage rack against the wall. It came over, hitting sharply against his head.

It was the noisy clanging of the tray from the luggage rack that gave him momentary focus, the packages of food hitting his face, the tray skittering off across the floor. Frantically brushing the debris away, his hand broke open several of the packages, one a bag of chips, the salty, fried smell triggering a wild frenzy in which he twisted to his side, cramming the chips savagely into his mouth. Rolling his head to lick those that had scattered, he slipped on the smeared blood from his shoulder, hitting his head sharply. Then, his internal reserves depleted, he slumped to the floor, his lifeblood painted across the porcelain surface of the tub and onto the tiles below.

The food packages, as well as the scattered provisions from the broken containers, lay around him, a testament to his body's will to survive, holding on to the elusive prize of life.

Chapter 15

Eustorgio Ricci, Monsignor

Monsignor Ricci followed as Bishop Carnaly walked solemnly through the old convent, a wide sash pulling his robes snugly around his waist. It was cold in the building, but then it had never been considered an especially comfortable place to serve out one's vocation. It was the call of God that was important, not one's physical surroundings. The monsignor accepted that readily, and it was for that very same reason he had never bothered to venture beyond the borders of his own beloved Italy.

Ricci watched the bishop reach one hand to a rough stone wall, one that had stood for more than two centuries, and he brushed the whitewashed surface, turning to the monsignor at his side and smiling.

"What a wonderful environment in which to grow! And you say the girl was here for sixteen years, and the Church never knew?" Bishop Carnaly looked away, his eyes roving to the top of the tall corridor, the windows there letting in the afternoon rays of a sun that generously gave its warmth outside, but that barely penetrated the cold stone interior of the forbidding structure. Farther down was an expanse of windows at eye level, but they provided little light here.

The bishop's comment had been phrased in the most politically correct manner possible, but to the good Monsignor Ricci, it was a rebuke of the highest order. Clearly the good bishop didn't believe such a thing possible, although the girl who had grown up within these very walls was already pro-claimed a Servant of God.

Witnesses from within the convent had been called, the very sisters who had raised the child, as well as the family with whom she'd lived afterwards—although it had taken a special dispensation from the Holy Father to allow them the anonymity of having their names stricken from the Records. They were a good family with a good reputation, and although poor by the Church's standards, they knew they'd taken a bastard child into their home. They hadn't wanted the deed proclaimed to their friends and neighbors.

There were others, too, although those who had regularly come in and out of the convent, those not of the sisterhood, were not to have seen Angioletta growing up. Still, a girl with glowing skin walking by a window during the middle of night was bound to be seen once or twice in sixteen years. The stories had been whispered in the village, and the tale grew of a Bride of Christ and an Immaculate Conception. It must be, whispers proclaimed, for no man was allowed to enter the convent, at least not the areas where the sisters were cloistered.

In the years since being sent away, she had become the substance of myth. Other, newer sisters had come, picking up on parts of the tale. Bedtime stories had been told in the town, and the monsignor had traveled between the two. It only took careful observation before things had begun to fall in place.

It was he, Monsignor Ricci, who had contacted the postulator to open the investigation. After all, no one had heard from the girl in nearly ten years, and as far as anyone had been able to determine, for eight of that, she'd been gone from Italy. Having been unable to contact the child for nearly a decade, it was certainly possible she was deceased, and what a blessing it would be to have one from the convent declared a saint!

Now the monsignor had begun to regret his decision. The

sisters had been reluctant, also, at first, then the excitement had begun to build. The interviews had progressed slowly, but soon the sisterhood cloistered inside the walls had been pressed into receiving the members of the tribunal. The accounts had astounded even the monsignor, tales of an angelic aura, a goodness to be unsurpassed, and a magic touch in dealing with other people—or in getting her way, some whispered with a wink. Of course, no one had used the word magic.

All in all, it had been an auspicious beginning.

Bishop Carnaly didn't sway so simply, though, and his reputation preceded him. His feet were firmly grounded in the holy soil of Italy, and young monsignors did not so easily find saints in out-of-the-way convents.

"Monsignor?" The bishop turned once again to Ricci, a pleasant and conversational smile on his face. "Wouldn't you say so, Father? A wonderful environment?" He nodded his head as if the answer was already known to him, and he simply needed the priest to acknowledge the statement's validity.

"Yes, Your Excellency. Such a place would be most beneficial in the molding of one's soul. However, I believe the child was already gone before I received my assignment to this parish." He tucked his hands behind his back, emulating the formal stance of the bishop in an attempt to seem very business-like and official. He was much younger, after all, and he was very aware Bishop Carnaly had been the lone holdout when Ricci's previous bishop had recommended this current assign-ment. He was determined to make every attempt to rectify Carnaly's poor opinion of him.

The bishop stepped into a cell with a spindly chair. The rush seat was flattened and tattered on one side. He placed a hand on the back and shook it to see if it was sturdy. It wobbled a small amount, and he grunted. After a short time of consideration, he chuckled.

"Nelle botti piccine ci sta il vino buono," the bishop murmured.

The monsignor smiled, somehow eased for a moment. He knew the bishop's meaning. *In the small barrels you find the good wine.* Such idioms were the staple of conversation in Italy, and even the clergy were prone to them in private. To use them was to be Italian.

Still, Carnaly's good will controlled the canonization process.

"Is there a problem, Bishop?" The monsignor made to step to his side, but there was no room. The small bed consumed the rest of the space.

"No." Carnaly looked up at the small window in the wall overhead, his hand still on the chair. His heavy robes pulled at him, forcing him to move in a ponderous fashion, almost a doll on a swivel base. "Such a small space. Such a small child. Good can come in very small packages, eh? I just wish to sit where she might have sat. You say this might have been her cell?"

Ricci pursed his lips. He hadn't said that, hadn't even suggested it, just that she'd been undocumented in the convent, and no one knew where she had slept or how she had come to be among the sisters. Still, to call the bishop on such a small matter would be a severe breach of hierarchal etiquette. And, for all Ricci had been able to ascertain, this could have been her actual cell. It was just that no one knew for sure, at least that they would admit to.

"This was," he paused, debating on how best to continue, "is, rather, a cell in general use by the sisters of the convent. It is very possible," a poor word choice, and he selected a better one, "very *probable* that she was in this room at some point." He was beginning to perspire, for this was taking a toll on his constitution.

"This very room." Carnaly looked at a small crucifix hanging high on one wall before turning back to Ricci, and he smiled with satisfaction. "You say all the sisters are away today? There is no one to verify this room as that of our newest Servant of God?" His next words were whispered so softly Ricci barely caught them. "Or to deny it?"

Ricci bowed his head respectfully. "All are on sabbatical to Rome. The convent is completely emptied for your inspection." It would have to be. After all, the sisters here were cloistered, meaning they could not easily interact with the bishop. It had taken a special dispensation just to get them to Rome. The sabbatical had been to give the bishop total access to the convent.

"A few moments, Father?" Carnaly's request was quiet and introspective. His attention was already on the room and not his guide. "To be this close to a miracle opens up something inside the soul, don't you think?"

"As you wish. I'll be waiting outside." Ricci backed into the corridor, pulling the rough wooden door to. He wasn't sure if the bishop's closing comment had been facetious or not. He closed his eyes for a moment and groaned inside. If he had to wager, he'd go with facetious.

As the door closed, he heard the weary creak of old wood, and he knew the bishop had finally sat in the old chair. He shook his head, wondering if their Servant of God had actually used that particular cell at any point.

He stepped down a bit to where a series of open arches were filled with the most exquisite leaded glass, a special gift from a patron in answer to prayers undertaken long ago by the sisterhood. This had originally been a long esplanade, the flagstone floor open to the elements. Many years later it had been covered for the nuns' protection in inclement weather, with only the wind left for them to endure. Finally, the windows had taken all that away.

They were old, though, and several were cracked. When they caught the sun each morning, the light fractured through the corridor, bleeding the colors of the rainbow into the sisters' cells, and it was truly glorious. Now, though, with afternoon gathering over the surrounding mountains, it was simply glass, for the view outside was nothing more than a grass courtyard from decades before that had been cultivated into an herb garden.

The monsignor traced the leading with his eyes. It was mostly clear, although many of the small pieces were beveled, and the occasional patterned section could be seen obscuring what lay on the other side. A large, intricate baroque cross was in the middle of the center arch far above his head, but it was what was closer down that held his interest.

There was a small wooden manger, or at least glass meant

to resemble a wooden manger. The pieces that made up the legs were beveled, looking much like the wood they portrayed, and that of the straw was striated in a way that could have been the actual grassy material. A child was inside. Male or female, the monsignor couldn't tell. In the cut glass, it could be either, but he guessed it was intended to be male. The Christ child.

It was what hovered just overhead that made his heart beat faster, for the glass was cut in such a way that it seemed to glow, and the pieces just around the angelic figure rippled in exactly the way light might shimmer when seen through a certain type of prismatic lens. The wings were spread wide, great, feathered appendages enormously larger than the man they carried through the air.

This . . . angel, and he knew it was, had a head full of curly hair and wore only a loose cloth wrapped around his loins. It was beautiful, so beautiful the monsignor wanted to cry. Despite his rush of emotions, that wasn't the most amazing thing in the glass.

Just below, there was another figure. Another angel, he guessed. This was the one that made him wonder about the one with the wings. This second angel walked upon the ground. Literally. Oh, in the glass, a strip of patterned pieces stood for soil, the manger handily resting its four glass legs there. Still, the glaziers had been masterful in their work, because when the monsignor stood in the middle of the corridor and looked out, the line of the ground in the glass matched up perfectly with a hill that rose in the distance on the other side of the convent's far wall.

The angel on the ground glowed just like the one in the sky, but it had no wings at all. It was clearly intended to be an angel, though, with the same curly hair, and the wrappings around its loins. It could be a mistake, he reasoned, a lapse either in the window's design or manufacture. Still, the rest was planned so masterfully, that he could hardly believe that.

He turned, placing his back to the window. Other things weighed on his mind besides the angels in the glass. For the second step toward canonization of this Servant of God, a miracle was required, and there was one particular set of circumstances he hadn't yet shared with the good bishop. And he hoped he never had to.

The nuns claimed to each be the mother of the child, admitting the birth to no one in particular. The sanctity of the cloistered nuns was well documented, and there was no doubt there. Who could question the word of a sister, one who was also the Bride of Christ? Surely the girl's birth without the intervention of a man was the blessed miracle that would convince the Holy Father.

That wasn't what bothered him.

It was the whispers the monsignor had heard through closed doors, and as he walked outside the walls at night, words the sisters thought private, unheard, ones he dared not repeat to a soul, that gave him chills. It was an angel, come to the convent on a cold, winter's night, its wings ablaze with light. Then those wings were gone, the angel becoming a man, his angelic aura telling his birthright even then.

Much later, he had listened to a whispered story through a closed door, a confession, he supposed, from a nun who claimed the child as her own, telling her own version of the Heavenly Being who had fathered her child.

Monsignor Ricci turned to the glass again, the two angels his only concern. They seemed to grow out of the glass at him, until they were all he could see. This glass window, weathered with age, was why he believed that story from behind that old, wooden door. Who in her right mind would invent such a tale?

That was also the very reason he had claimed the Servant of God's miracle to be that of a virgin birth. Did it really matter whether the saint, if she ever reached that level, was of virgin birth or fathered by an angel? Would either be more miraculous? Not to Monsignor Ricci's eyes. He'd had to choose, and he knew that the diocesan tribunal, one of the very first steps in the process, would have thrown out his petition summarily, if he'd claimed an angel as a progenitor in this case.

If the girl he'd come to know as Angioletta truly deserved to be canonized, it was up to her supporters to see that she got every chance at sainthood. And if she didn't deserve the honor, it would certainly fall apart in the Congregation of the Causes of the Saints. If not there, then there were even more levels in which the undeserving could be shunted aside, from the nine who would give their vote, to the cardinals and bishops who would examine the Positio.

Even if she sailed through those obstacles, that would only bring her to the title of Blessed. Yet another miracle would be needed to raise her to Saint, and Ricci was sure he hadn't come up with that, yet. He was certainly working on it, though.

A creaking sounded from down the hall, and he turned to see the bishop entering the corridor. He paused, his gray head bowed, and it was clear he had been thinking much. Bishop Carnaly had a great reputation for thinking things through, or as the Church would say, for finding the Mind of God. He was truly a tower of strength in the Church, and the old bishop's decisions were rarely challenged. That often irritated Monsignor Ricci, as in when Carnaly's "Mind of God" had nearly kept him from his appointment to this parish.

Ricci started that way, the corridor darkening as he left the window behind. He considered asking the bishop if he wished to view the window, telling him about the angels there in order to gauge his reaction to the possibility of winged angels turning into non-winged ones. When he drew closer, the monsignor quickly changed his mind, for the bishop snapped his fingers briskly and spoke with an abrupt tone of voice.

"Monsignor, I wish to be taken to the office of the mother superior. My things are already there, I believe. I wish a work table and warmth. You may lead the way."

Ricci's heart fell. He had been so hopeful, so sure that this second step had already reached fruition, and that only one additional step was required before canonization. He hoped the failure was not due to an omission on his part, no matter how well intentioned. If keeping quiet about the girl's angelic parentage had served to sidetrack her from her rightful place in the Church, then he had cursed himself and should surely resign his post at the first viable opportunity.

Just before they turned the corner, leaving the corridor behind, Ricci glanced behind them to the light coming through the magnificent leaded glass windows far down the corridor. He thought of the manger and the two angels, one with wings and another without. Unexpectedly, a verse from the scriptures flashed through his mind, one from somewhere in Hebrews.

Do not forget to entertain strangers, for by so doing some people have entertained angels without knowing it.

He turned and walked forward once again, but he smiled at the intimations in that verse. The sisters here, cloistered, had certainly entertained a stranger, and even brought her up from birth, if the stories were to be believed. They had not forgotten the Word of the Lord, and the Master in Heaven had not forgotten them. The child had returned their love as abundantly as it had been given.

At that point, he knew it didn't matter what the bishop's decision was. The important thing was the good hearts of the sisters, and they were good hearts. God would remember their deed of charity in His Glory, and the girl they'd helped raise in secret would someday be at their side, wherever that might be.

Bobby Dalton, Motel Rat

Bobby crawled from his bed, the sun glaring through the uncovered window. He'd broken the blind while crawling out one night, and his mother had told him replacing it wasn't on her list of high priority items.

It was also hot in his room. That meant the electricity was off once again.

Sometime during the night a bright light somewhere across the desert had awakened him. It was gone now, or at least he couldn't see it. Duh, he told himself. The sun was up.

He picked up his clock, and the display was blank. No electricity. Duh, again.

Scratching an armpit, he skipped down the stairs. He grabbed a soda, still cold, thank goodness, and he took a quick look under the sink, hoping some of the magazines were salvageable.

It was all a greasy mess.

With a sigh he headed outside, only to hear tapping from

his mother's window.

"Bobby! Check the breaker box. I know you're up. I see you out there."

He sighed, and that was when he caught the glint on the horizon. He glanced up at his bedroom window, then out to the light in the desert. It could be Exxon putting in a new well. They did that sometimes, drilled in the desert. They'd have a whopper of an electric bill, unless they were sucking free power straight out of the line. It was a pretty bright light.

He jumped when the air conditioner compressor clicked on with a whir. His mother called through the glass, "Thanks, Bobby."

He grinned. He hadn't done anything. He lifted the drink to his mouth, when his mother called once more.

"Bobby, there's no picture. I want you up on the roof to adjust the antenna. Now, young man."

He groaned. "Mom! Can't it wait for a few minutes?"

"Roof, young man. You have no idea how busy you're going to be today. Do you understand me?"

"Yes, Mother."

It was later, on the roof, that he remembered leaving his favorite socks at the motel. He also seemed to remember a woman . . . Ms, um, Bacci— The name slipped away, and he shook the odd thought from his head. His socks, though. He'd have to go back for those.

Then he heard an eagle's cry split the sky, and almost immediately, the howl of a wolf followed it. A chill ran down his back. Something somewhere was very wrong, but he couldn't think what it was.

He tightened two screws and adjusted the antenna, and he headed down the ladder, just in time to hear his mother's voice once more.

"Bob—by! I'm not calling you again!"

Rikkianne Kristofferson, Asst. Motel Manager

"Nigel, remember that airplane crash?" Rikkianne's hair

was a deep auburn, so deep it was sometimes mistaken for black. It was in sharp contrast to her fair, northern skin. Once a rich ginger, as she had gotten older, her hair had grown darker and darker, courtesy of the local drugstore. Now it was mail-order, of course, living so far out, but no matter. She just made to order it far enough in advance so her roots didn't show too awful much.

"Plane crash? What the devil you talking about?" Nigel looked up from the TV. "Glad the set's working again. Channel's still hit or miss, though." Lifting his remote, he aimed it at the television.

They'd been hit or miss most of the day.

"Are you listening to me, Nigel?" She came and sat beside him, his arm, strong and smooth, next to her age-spotted one. Her fingers rested on his forearm, and the nails were bright red. She'd done them special today.

"You get the news 'bout the crash up on the Broady's set? Don't see how it could be working if ours twern't." He grimaced when he saw his favorite sports program, and the closing credits were already scrolling the screen. "Missed it again! Which of them channels did you see the crash on?"

"No channel. Not seen no channels on all day. You should know that, you running to all the rooms to keep people adjusted. You know yet why they keep blinking off?"

"Electramagnet storm. That's what they called it back in vo-ag." Fifteen years ago in high school, he'd been in a farm program, he'd once told her. One of his classes had been on proper maintenance of milkers, and he'd had to learn electrical terms during that semester.

"Weren't no clouds out today. Electra . . . electra—what'd you call them?"

"Electramagnet, like electric and magnet. Just slide them words together, and it's one word. The sunshine messes up the electricity, I think, and nothing works."

"Well, that Bobby Dalton still works. I guess he don't need electricity. His momma's had him ferrying all over her place. I called to tell her I'm sure he was up on the roof again last night, doing whatever he does up there with them pants of his off, and she didn't even hear me. Poor woman too busy yelling at him to try moving the antenna again, that she was missing her favorite show. No wonder he turned out the way he did, poor child."

"Found socks up there again today. Fresh ones." His comment was thrown out absently, his attention on the TV. "Seems that gravel'd hurt his feet or something. Me, I'd keep my shoes on up there. Always do."

She grinned. "He *was* up there. I knew it, that Bobby Dalton. How much them cameras cost, Nigel?" She snickered. "I know boys, that's for sure."

"Let him alone. The boy's a good kid, even if he don't keep his hand outta his pants. Remember him helping move my chair? I never would'a done it by myself." He grinned when a newscaster came on the set. "Look. The news. What was it you wanted to know 'bout?"

"That plane crash in the desert. That man said him and his wife crashed in the desert, falling on our roof. You didn't forget that." She slapped his arm lightly, just enough to indulge her irritation.

Pulling away, he mumbled, "Don't see no news on a plane crash, not nowhere. Maybe they got it cleaned up, already."

She snorted in irritation. "Why, that couple was in 13A. I showed 'em the room myself." She had already forgotten the part about the incident on the roof, though. As far as she was concerned, that had never happened. The couple had been dropped off in a cab, or perhaps by the local sheriff. They had arrived *somehow,* for they couldn't have driven to the motel, not with their plane crumpled and abandoned somewhere out in the lonely desert.

Nigel Platis, Motel Manager

Nigel reached to put his arm around Rikkianne, laughing at her silliness. Uriel's Suggestion had done its work, and he knew there was no one in 13A. He'd checked on that room just that morning, closing the door after him. It had been as empty as the day was hot, even if he'd never actually stepped inside. He

213

thought he did. In fact, he *remembered* it, the bed smoothly made, the bathroom empty, the toilet lid wrapped with a sanitary paper tab. There was even a stack of freshly folded towels on the rack by the sink. He had closed the door after he stepped outside, pulling it gently to, even if he'd never stepped inside at all.

He changed channels and laughed at the comedy program that came on, one from decades ago. A couple lived in a New York apartment, and their friends had just come to visit. Apparently, there was some misunderstanding between the woman and her husband, for she put her hands on her hips, and she yelled out his name, "Ric—ky!"

Nigel and Rikkianne laughed, for this was their favorite show of all, and it was one of the few that their set brought in clearly. It didn't matter that all the actors had died years before, or that it was in black and white. It was uproariously funny, and with enough laughter between them, soon there was no one in room 13A at all.

Eustorgio Ricci, Monsignor

Monsignor Ricci dutifully milked a cup of steaming decaf from the espresso machine just in front of him. The nuns who wandered these corridors, their lives given in service to God, might vow lives of poverty, but the bishop had no such qualms. His retinue carried his espresso machine everywhere he went, setting it up when they dropped him off, and retrieving it when he was whisked away.

Across the room, Bishop Carnaly clicked open his polished leather briefcase, and the lid snapped wide. Reaching inside, he grasped a stack of documents with both hands and transferred them to the tabletop.

When Ricci stepped to the table, the small white cup in his hands, he was overwhelmed to see the official-looking documents spread across its surface. His hands shook as he set the cup down, but he dared not turn away. It seemed it might still be possible, in spite of the bishop's earlier brusqueness, that some good would come of his visit today. He could only hope and pray.

Bishop Carnaly reached for the cup and took a sip, putting it down and closing his eyes for a moment. Then he sighed and chuckled. "Not quite the same without the worldly stimulants inside, is it, Father? Still, it brings back the memories, and it does warm the body as it runs down the throat."

Ricci didn't drink coffee, but he nodded and made an agreeable sound. He tried not to smile as the bishop loosened the sash at his waist, and his stomach grew a good six inches. He wondered that the man hadn't moved even more carefully, what with the sash being so tightly bound. How did he ever manage to bend his body to sit in that chair back in the nun's cell? He also knew his thoughts were unkind, and he attempted to banish them from his mind.

In spite of his charitable motives, he was thwarted when the bishop noisily passed a substantial amount of intestinal gas. At that, Ricci had to turn away. He grabbed the cup in the process, quickly walking back to the espresso machine.

"Monsignor Ricci, I do believe I still have coffee in my cup."

"A fresh one, Bishop. I'll have it to you shortly." The bishop's words had been called out in dismay, but the good priest couldn't take them seriously after what he'd just heard. For that very reason, he had to take long enough to get the smile off his face. He milked the machine once again, trusting it would fill the cup yet another time. When he turned, his face was contrite, just as it should be.

"Ah, thank you, Father. You are certainly kindhearted. I won't keep you in suspense any longer." The bishop picked up the cup, gripping it tightly this time, as he reached to thumb through several of the documents. "Yes, everything is in place. I thought you might like to see it all, since you fought so hard to win this second stage in your girl's canonization." He glanced at Ricci and held up a warning hand. "No, she hasn't been canonized. You don't have a Saint Angioletta just yet, but you have managed another hurdle. Your miracle has been validated, and both your decrees have now been promulgated by the Holy

215

Father, both for her heroic virtues and the miracle of her birth."

Although he had hoped, Ricci was dumbstruck. "But, Bishop. Upon leaving Blessed Angioletta's cell, you were so solemn. I was certain your efforts were to let me down easily." It felt good to call her Blessed, though. Blessed Angioletta. All the sisters would be proud.

"Not to worry, my boy." The bishop's manner of speech was suddenly familiar with Ricci, uncommonly so. "Sitting in the same chair our Blessed Angioletta used as her own, seeing the bed where she took her slumber, with my eyes resting upon the walls where hers once rested, I was overwhelmed with the magnitude of the presence of one of God's saints." At Ricci's sudden wide-eyed look, the bishop laughed. "It seems you have even me convinced, Ricci. I do believe this girl will be fully canonized before the year is out. We have just a few more hurdles to overcome, and I intend to help you over each one."

The bishop leaned over the paperwork he'd brought, and he pulled out one folder in particular. It had a polished leather cover, and on it was embossed Angioletta's name. When he opened it, there was a list of information still needed.

"All that?" Ricci frowned. "I thought I only needed to validate one more miracle."

Carnaly sighed. "There's one minor detail that appears to have been overlooked, my boy. It seems her proof of death is entirely circumstantial. Somehow, it has remained unnoticed that there is no official death certificate on file in Rome." He shook his head. "I've made some inquiries, and the diocese seems to have tracked an Angiola Bacciarelli out of the country nearly a decade ago. Perhaps she could be our very own Angioletta." He smiled.

Ricci had been so overjoyed just a moment ago. Now his steam fled from him, and he felt physically deflated. He'd never really researched out if she actually had a death certificate on file. He'd just assumed. All his well-intentioned endeavors might fall apart after all, and it would be his fault.

It didn't occur to him that Angiola Bacciarelli was, by the sisters' own words, the daughter of an angel, and where angels abounded, mysterious things were sure to take place. Suggestions were powerful tools, even when wielded unconsciously. More simply, things just seemed to smooth the way when an angel was involved.

The monsignor asked dejectedly, sure that all was lost, "What does that mean?"

Bishop Carnaly beamed. "Why, my boy! It means we have to go to America."

Chapter 16

Gadreel, Deliverer of Destruction

Trust was not part of Gadreel's nature. He believed in motivation. Given enough reason to perform a specific task, anyone could be coerced into cooperation. Take away the motivation, and betrayal was the logical end.

He stood on a mountaintop within the Unity of Being, unaware of the beauty all around him. Off in the distance, other mountain peaks boldly extended craggy fingers of stone that were not exactly stone through layers of clouds that were not really clouds. Even the ground he stood upon was not solid in the corporeal sense.

But then the entire Unity was out of phase with this particular universe, and nothing in the Unity was quite what it seemed.

Gadreel's golden curls were thick and fell down the back of his neck. His limbs were long, his fingers delicate, and he wore feet almost too beautiful to press against the dust of the ground, with their long toes wrapped around the rocky crag.

As always in the Unity, he wore nothing except his wings and the bodily hair that filled his armpits and groin, blending his gentleman's parts into a chaste bulge between his legs.

He brooded, his brows pulled tightly together, his wings spread wide and held high. They caught the swirling ether that tore up the side of the mountain, rippling along his wings' edges. There were no feathers attached to these wings, for those were reserved for the brothers' rather more burdensome corporeal bodies on Earth. Instead, these wings carried a lightness of substance, one that glittered in the Unity's light; the substance of dragonfly wings, breathtakingly translucent, although not quite transparent.

As he had been since arriving in this incarnation, Gadreel was beautiful. If Lucifer was once known as the Illuminator of Light, Gadreel could have been his twin. Seen apart, they could be mistaken one for another, outstandingly beautiful even among the striking looks displayed by the brothers of the Unity. Seen together, perhaps Gadreel would have paled in contrast, but the differences would have been in carriage and charm, not in physical form.

That old comparison held no interest for him, though. His appearance was as it should be. Other things were not, and that included the two hangers-on who hovered at his side, for he was not alone.

"Nabu." Gadreel turned, and his dark glance singled out the excessively short Recorder of Deeds. He and the brother at his side were perhaps the two smallest "angels" in the entire Unity. When their great interdimensional ship had shifted onto this plane, the brothers had shifted with it, their bodies taking on the form they would carry while in this sphere of existence, and somehow, in the transition, these two had been left short. Literally. Gadreel knew they played dangerous games involving intrigue and the twisting of others' fates for their own enjoyment. They did additional, viler things, too, although those only happened among the shadows.

"Yes, Great Gadreel. What do you wish?" The small brother used the old, respectful term of address with the leader of the Rebellion, careful in all he said and did.

"You have proof of that which I sent you to find. A daughter has been born." Gadreel had been given hints of illicit progeny, and Nabu had been sent to do some research. The small brother's words of subservience pleased him, for they spoke of manners and rank.

"Such is as you have said." The diminutive brother dipped his head in acknowledgement.

"You are certain." Gadreel pursed his lips. This news had consumed him ever since the two brothers had arrived. He felt himself burn with anticipation.

Nabu's face, at first solemn, became excessively animated with impending excitement. His words tumbled from his lips. "We have viewed the Records, and there is no doubt."

"What have you learned?" Gadreel held out a hand as if reaching for tangible information, presenting a truly angelic posture.

"We have viewed the child, and she is certainly all that a half-brother must be." Nabu inclined his head slightly, not quite in a bow. His wings were also opened wide, and they quivered with the mighty updrafts of ether against the side of the mountain. His expression was hopeful, even as he fought to remain steady.

"She's not a giant." That was Lipika, Nabu's companion, and the words came out sourly. His features were dark and brooding, even morose, and his wings were very small, much smaller than Nabu's. He had learned to fly with them, against all manner of difficulty, and he was enjoying the stiff breeze, if he could be said to enjoy anything at all. He'd been a giant of a winged horse in the Unity's previous incarnation. His current body didn't suit his mental image of himself, and it hadn't for many thousands of Earth's years.

"Explain." Gadreel, irritated, opened his wings wide, increasing his presence before the two Recorders of Deeds. He made his face to glower, if beauty of such outstanding quality could truly be made to glower.

"About giants?" Lipika scoffed.

"Fool! The child! The *daughter*." Gadreel's words tore at the idiocy of the question.

"We do not have the actual moment of conception, of course." Nabu shifted topics instantly and skillfully, but he turned to glare at Lipika.

"Then, there is no proof? If not, why do you consume my time?" The rebuke thundered, and in Gadreel's anger, his wings lifted him from the ground. He didn't want aberrant surmises from inconclusive guesses. Within the Unity, lightning could not fly from his eyes, but he made sure they flashed his fury, anyway.

He was satisfied to see Nabu and Lipika appropriately cowed.

"Kafziel was most devious." Nabu's words were whispered, his ducked head showing his subservience. "There is a window of opportunity when the Chamber of Deeds cannot see the actions of a brother." He kept his head bowed.

In fact, Gadreel did know of such a window. It was an ominous sign. No earthbound brother had access to such knowledge.

Lipika murmured, "He has hidden his misdeeds well."

"Your evidence is circumstantial, then." Gadreel's face turned dark, for he needed the proof to be firm and without flaw.

Before the two diminutive brothers could respond, a subsonic boom shook the ether, causing Nabu to cover his ears, quickly followed by Lipika.

Gadreel caught an unnerving and very visible wave of extremely low-pitched sound moving purposefully through the ether that made up the Unity's skies. He watched as it uncoiled long and deliberate fingers, a wave of cascading molecules flinging themselves forward in slow motion. What functioned as gravity in the Unity began to loosen its hold on the three brothers.

Gadreel understood immediately. The massive engines of the brothers' great dimension-traveling vessel, ancient beyond counting, were being attacked again, surely the counter-revolution's attempts to sabotage his efforts to maintain stability in the Unity.

"Now, Nabu," he growled. "I soon will have other matters to absorb my attentions."

Then the ground under his feet shook, an earthquake in the Unity, as the ship's great engines took control once again.

Gadreel considered the current turn of events. The attack proved once again the need for his leadership. The brothers were restless, and a female who was the daughter of a brother would be a temptation none could resist. Anyone who knew of her would give anything in exchange for the chance to relieve eons of pent-up tension.

This whole series of events carried the seeds of an ominous disaster in the making.

He motioned sharply to the Recorder of Deeds, and with the touch of Nabu's hands upon his portable viewer, the proofs were offered, the words and events spilled in jumps and starts, until Gadreel exclaimed he'd heard enough. He had seen the flight through the night, the female, and enough additional deeds that the matter could not be denied.

"There is no doubt. You have done well." He turned, churning at Kafziel's arrogance, as he dismissed the two Recorders of Deeds, wanting the fools gone from his sight. "There are ways to bring even the betrayer Kafziel under control."

The beauty that was Gadreel's alone darkened, and in that moment, perched on his lonely pinnacle, no one would think him angelic any longer.

Nabu and Lipika, 2nd Order Recorders of Deeds

The Recorders weren't finished, for they had an agenda of their own. They had brought the news, but their motives had not been pure.

"Glorious Gadreel." It was Lipika this time, and he timorously cleared his throat. He held a grudge against the sons of women—or their daughters, to be more specific. He had attended Jeqon's long-ago party, but the daughters of men had laughed at his diminutive stature. He'd never gotten over the humiliation. Nabu had made him swear to be the one to broach their proposal to the leader of the Rebellion, and in spite of his misgivings, Lipika had agreed.

"Lipika, I have never heard you speak first." Gadreel flung his accusation bitingly. "What is this you wish to say?"

"Gabriel will fail you, Most Holy One." His reverent terms of respect were to stroke Gadreel's pride. "The six are his loyal companions, and they will stand by his side, following him, only." He paused, his head humbly bowed.

"Oh? What would you have me do, loyal Lipika, to gain this success that Gabriel cannot give?"

"There are the Four Familiars. You know of them. They have great power. Unleash them, and the Circle of Brothers will be broken." He and Nabu had agreed that such would be successful. Privately, the Circle of Brothers was unimportant. Nabu and Lipika wished the Pets to be unleashed upon the daughters of men.

"The Triune Mind's Pets?" Gadreel rested against his spire, and his faced reassumed the beauty that was his due. Clearly, he was intrigued. He twirled the fingers on one hand, revealing his thought process in motion. "Perhaps you are right. Perhaps Gabriel's troupe should be scattered to the winds, for their strength as a team will be greater than any power I can command. Release the Pets, and it will be done, too, for even the greatest of the brothers accompanying Gabriel has no hope against the Familiars of the Triune Mind."

"As you wish, so shall it be, Holy One." Nabu bowed low as he spoke his words. He glanced at Lipika, and they gloated in satisfaction.

Then, the beautiful, winged brother sighed. "There is a slight difficulty, though. The familiars were Encapsulated in the Primary Forces Chamber even before the Triune Mind. They will not wish to claim us as their master."

The two Recorders already had that worked out. All Gadreel had to do was gain the Familiars' trust, and they would pursue endlessly for him, going where he sent them, and doing as he commanded.

"With proof, they will see that we wish to restore the Triune Mind to the Seat of Power." Nabu smiled.

"Proof?" Gadreel glanced away with contempt. "There had better be no proof. There are no such plans, and you know it."

"Ah, a master can find proof where none other can, even if such never comes to fruition."

Nabu touched a spot in the ether, and from the portable viewer he'd brought with him from the Chamber of Deeds, a shimmering of light coalesced into an image from the Deeds of Man. The small brother's hand moved, a series of carefully pieced together images flickered past, and Gadreel laughed.

"I'd always thought you to be of less skill than Chitar, but it seems I am mistaken. This is masterful." He smiled, and his wings quivered. "I am very pleased."

"They will believe?" Lipika's sour voice growled the question, but without doubt. The images had been manipulated skillfully. In addition, he had seen the wings quiver, and he knew Gadreel would offer rewards beyond measure.

Such was more than any brother deserved, but it was exactly what Lipika and Nabu thought their due.

Both were overcome with satisfaction.

Gadreel, Deliverer of Destruction

Gadreel reached and touched both the diminutive brothers. With no more than a ripple of his thoughts, the ether within the Unity bent, and the mountaintop stood empty. Then, almost as quickly, space in a distant location also bent, and invisible in the blackness between the stars, Gadreel stood, his impossible feet resting on impossible floors anchored by equally impossible Energy Nodes. He was not alone. The *essence* of Gadreel had brought with him the *essence* of two additional brothers, ones who were most skilled at reading the Deeds of Man. Their demonstration had clearly shown that. With them, unseen but very tangible to their insubstantial hands, they carried the viewer from the mountaintop, one that contained selected Records from the Deeds of Man. Perhaps to see the events that had transpired upon Earth would be just the thing to garner the Pets' cooperation.

Gadreel pressed against the wall that made up the Primary Forces Chamber, and the energy barrier flexed. With a motion of his head, demanding his two minions join him, he stepped through. When Nabu and Lipika made no move to follow, the energy barrier flexed again, and something that could be considered an arm, if it had been corporeal, burst through, grabbed what could well be the collars of two very nervous essences, and with no further ado, they were also pulled unceremoniously into the interior of the Primary Forces Chamber.

Calm settled once more across that vast stretch of space surrounding the Primary Forces Chamber. It was as if the eternal night had never been disturbed.

Interlude 12

Yet, on one very small spacecraft, small by the Unity's standards, anyway, and en route to Io, a human astronaut happened to glance at a specific readout that normally registered an external energy sensor's measurements. The display was on an overhead panel, to the right and out of the way. Any increase in energy that was outside the parameters of the programmed safety margins would elicit a warning message and, if necessary, implement emergency safety procedures.

Even now the signal hadn't spiked quite high enough or lasted quite long enough to trigger the warning message, although either of the two scenarios could. The designers of the craft knew that one or the other of those situations could be a precursor that additional, worse effects were on the way. It wasn't especially important for the astronauts to keep an eye on it, for it was monitored hundreds of times a second by one of the ship's many computers. It was more of an unwelcome anomaly, one that wouldn't go away.

"Odd, Jim. There's that energy spike again." A puzzled expression crossed Chet's face.

Jim held a container of pudding in his hand. He glanced at Chet, then back to his spoon, moving it very carefully. "This is what, the fifth time, or the sixth?" He put the spoon in his mouth and closed his lips around it slowly, careful not to let any escape.

"Sixth that I've seen. I don't know how many I've missed. Probably twice that amount."

"Think it's a problem?"

Chet laughed, turning his chair away from the readout. "Nah. If it was, the computer'd tell us, wouldn't it?"

"Got that right." Jim grinned, still watching his pudding cup.

"Got any more of that?" Chet set a pen sailing through the air, and it bumped the cup, nearly knocking it from his partner's hand.

Jim fumbled a moment, several choice words escaping his lips. Once the cup was secure again, he let out a sharp laugh, flipping his spoon right back at Chet. Chet dodged before he realized it had been licked clean and wasn't dangerous.

"About twenty cases. Five flavors. What's your poison?"

"Banana. Yellow, fresh, sun-ripened banana. With the peel on. Can you do that?"

"Sure can. Catch." Jim flipped him a small plastic tub, and on the outside was a picture just like Chet had described. "That do?"

Chet snorted, then he winked with a grin. "Sure. Why not?" He reached for the spoon Jim had flicked his way, and seeing it was relatively clean, he wiped it on his sleeve. Then he popped the top on the pudding and slipped the spoon inside.

"And that readout?" Jim nodded at the overhead.

"If there are little green men this far out in space, I don't want to know, not until after I finish my banana, anyway."

Not once did he look back at the display overhead.

Elemiah, Six-Winged Seraph

Elemiah stood tall, towering over Kafziel's prone form still supine on the desert floor. In their time together, the Sword of Power had pierced the soil at Kafziel's side, remaining for a full turning of this world on its axis, and been lifted once more.

More had gone on than was visible to the eye.

The light from the Sword had known neither minute nor hour, night nor day, once it had pierced the ground at Kafziel's side. It was the turning of the clock, and the changing of the seasons. Within its power were the rising of the sun and the setting of the same. Time had slipped around the great Sword of Power, for within that enveloping field, the hands of the clock moved sometimes with the gentle tick of the passing seconds, and at other times becoming a rushing gale, leaving minutes or days or months at a time behind, whether forward or backward, at Elemiah's command.

This day the Sword had remained in the soil, searching for its answers, drawing the ghosts of past events into the mind of the Seraph, and it had taken a full twenty-four hours. Those within its confining sphere knew only that time passed, although they didn't know the quantity. The Sword took the time it needed, and it did so without regard to the hours that passed in the external realm.

If someone on the outside had attempted to locate the source of the brilliance tearing across the desert floor, they could have searched until their eyes were burned blind from the light of its Power, for their feet would always carry them past the source of the light, no matter the compasses they might hold, or the straight line they might walk.

Within its protective boundaries, a tribunal of three had been held, and judgment had been passed. If Kafziel had been found guilty, the Seraph Elemiah had the power and the authority to dispatch him on the spot, his corporeal existence dissolved with the end of his essence—his soul, humans would have called it.

Such was not the case, though. The Watcher's tale had been judged faithful to the Record, as Elemiah knew it, and Uriel had been found lacking.

It was with a sad heart that Elemiah reported his findings. He knew Gabriel's sentiments, as well as the reason the Archangel had flung himself to Earth. It was for love, even though Uriel had chosen the wrong side in a battle that never should have happened. Gabriel had come to rescue Uriel, to preserve hope in a future union once their imprisonment in this dimension was cast aside, and their genders could be two yet again.

Still, Elemiah was a Seraph, and his Mandate, his duty, was to protect. Uriel had stepped outside the boundaries of Righteousness, had broken his Mandate, and was stealing another's Destiny for his own. Those who would take innocent life and use it for their own ends must be brought to justice.

Hence, the search for justice was now turned toward Uriel. He must be found and the mixed-blood female saved at any cost. To facilitate those ends, Kafziel was to be accepted into the fold as one of the Circle of Brothers.

Kafziel, Emissary of Solitude and Tears

Kafziel saw the events that took place under the auspices of Elemiah's Sword of Power differently. He had brought *Gabriel* into the fold, but it was his fold, not that of the Circle of Brothers. It was also his agenda, although for a time he'd let the Archangel think it was his own.

It wasn't, though. Kafziel didn't care about Uriel or the girl. No, they were simply stepping stones to something greater. He wanted power, he wanted to share it with no one, and he intended to keep it as long as he could hold it tightly within his grasp.

He would be successful, too, if he could get away from Elemiah.

Bobby Dalton, Motel Rat

Bobby pulled his thin tee shirt from his body, releasing it only to have it fall against his chest once more. It was hot, and he'd been up on the roof half a dozen times since morning. Not once had he managed to adjust the antenna to his mother's satisfaction. He'd also raked the gravel in the drive and washed every one of the windows in the house. He'd earned the sweat in his shirt, and it had bled into his jeans. There were salt stains around the waist. He was glad the sun was finally down.

He flipped on the shower. Kicking his shoes off, he undid his pants and let them fall to his feet. His shirt came off in a smooth motion. With a quick step, he was under the cool spray.

It was when he'd finished washing his hair and was scrubbing under his armpits that his memory was triggered. He'd been on the roof of the motel, and the woman had called to him. He'd intended to run away. Instead, he'd offered to help, and he only now remembered why.

Dropping the soap, he grabbed a towel and flew from the bathroom directly to his window. He laughed with excitement, pumping a fist into the air. It was still there, the light. It was the one that had awakened him the night before, the one he'd seen from the yard, then again on the roof that day. If it still shone, then everything was okay.

It was with horror that he saw it wink out right before his eyes. Deep inside, he was certain that if he didn't immediately fulfill his promise from twenty-four hours before, something very, very bad would happen, and he'd be the cause.

Opening his bottom drawer to grab a fresh pair of jeans, he pulled them on. It was speed that counted now, for someone's life was in his hands. Grabbing a shirt, he yanked it over his head as he took the stairs two at a time.

The drinks were in the garage with his exercise gear. He grabbed a box under his arm, and he was gone, his shoes on the dirt stirring up a dusty trail.

Nothing could slow him down now. He had a life to save, even if he didn't know exactly whose it was.

Chapter 17

Interlude 13

Angioletta lay, still sprawled on the bed where she'd fallen the night before. It was dark once again. She had lain in the same position the day through, unaware of the sun that had beat against the curtain, Nigel climbing over the roof, or the Sword of Elemiah taking a portion of the desert for its own.

Her breathing was now even, and her color was good. Where her body created shadow, there was the glow to her skin that she accepted as normal. Even in sleep—or perhaps especially in sleep—she was beautiful, but then, she had always been beautiful.

The light over the sink still washed the room with a gentle radiance, and the air was incredibly hot. The heater in the bathroom labored with liquid heat, and there was no one to turn it down.

If Uriel were awake, he would be grateful for that, but he lay sprawled on his stomach on the tiles, surrounded by the food he so desperately needed. His shoulder no longer seeped, although it was still open and raw. It had bled all the fluids it could spare, and his body had no resources to create more. It was all it could do to keep his heart in motion and air moving in and out of his chest. It couldn't do that for much longer.

Bobby hadn't come. For that, one person in that room might die while the other still lived. That was the price one paid for making a fourteen-year-old the pivot pin of a life-or-death situation.

It wasn't that Bobby was undependable, although that often went hand-in-hand with being fourteen. At that fresh age, there were so many things about life that could steal a boy's attention away, causing promises and good intentions to be pushed aside, for at fourteen, Bobby's days weren't his own. They belonged to his friends, his school, and the managers of the motel next door. More importantly, his time belonged to his mother, as well as his father when he was in from off the road.

It was also that "angels" were easily forgotten, for that was the way of angels, known as brothers to those in the Unity. One saw an angel, and one's attention just slipped around that angel. He was forgotten as soon he was out of sight, unless he wished to be remembered.

Even though Uriel had been inside the motel room, and Bobby hadn't met him, the brother's presence had been all around Angioletta. That alone made the memory of the beautiful woman slippery. Also, she was only half-human. She had asked Bobby for help, but she hadn't known how to make her request lodge in his thoughts. Simple things had been able to pull Bobby's attention away from his promise.

For that reason, one of the best of the brothers of the Unity might very well meet his end this night.

Angioletta Bacciarelli, Daughter of Kafziel

On the bed, lying where she had fallen, Angioletta's eyes twitched. Then, with a quick inhalation of air, her arms jerked, and her eyelids flew wide.

There was no hesitation in her thoughts. Newly—and strangely—refreshed, she recalled immediately where she was, and she remembered the man in the bathtub. In one swift motion, she rolled over and sat up on the bed. Her heart beating swiftly, she leaped to the bathroom door, and her face fell in dismay. He was sprawled amidst smears of blood on the floor. Dropping to one knee, she reached for his neck to see if he still lived. His skin was so cold, and she was unsure if there was any life left in his ravaged body.

Food. He had to have food, and it was strewn all about him. She saw the remains of the chips, opened and scattered across the floor. There were so many left she could tell he hadn't eaten but a few.

Bobby! How long had it been? Hours? The boy had promised!

At a faint scuffling noise from behind her, she turned to see the outside door was closed. It had been opened earlier; she'd left it that way for him. Had he already come to tell them he wouldn't be able to help, then left after shutting the door? How could she have missed that?

Rushing to the door and throwing it open, hoping she might still catch him, she was bowled down by the boy. She was surprised he was wearing clothes she didn't recognize, although she was certain he had run for help only minutes before. He fell into the room, and the box of power drinks he carried tumbled from under his arm, scattering all over the floor.

"I'm so sorry," he sobbed, and tears burst down his face. "I couldn't get the door open. My mom found my magazines, and she was mad, and then the TV wouldn't work all day, and I even had to rake the drive." He grabbed for the drinks, his words telling of emotions running high in the frantic way of a fourteen-year-old who was afraid he had left an important promise undone. "I can't believe it's been a whole day. I'm so sorry."

"A day?" Angioletta frowned. "It's still dark outside. You left minutes ago." The door was still open, and she could see into the night. It was the puzzled expression on Bobby's face that told her it might be otherwise, that and the fact he was wearing completely different clothes. He sported a new sunburn, too.

She put her hand to her mouth. "I felt ill, and I crawled to the bed. Has it really been a whole day?"

Bobby nodded, and then his eyes wandered to the partial view of the man he could see for the first time through the bathroom door. He blanched at the gore trailing down the side of the tub.

Angioletta was a teacher, and she'd seen students come to school when they shouldn't. She knew the signs of an impending eruption and how to minimize the damage. The trick was to contain it, to keep the debris as localized as possible.

To that effect, she grabbed the bathroom trash can, and holding it in front of Bobby's face, she pushed his head down. Once his body began to convulse, she stood, leaving the trusty can in his capable hands. He'd know what to do, and his body's reaction would be good for him. It would shock him into accepting what he'd seen. He'd no longer compare the scene he'd witnessed to the unmarred world from outside the motel room. Rather, he'd judge it against his own horrific display of frailty.

Reaching for the bottles the boy had brought, she looked at one, glad to see it was chock full of calories and a dozen other body-enhancing chemicals. She reached to him, now sitting with the can between his legs, and she smiled.

"Thank you, Bobby. This is perfect."

"Is he, the man in there, is he dead?" His eyes flicked to the scene inside the bathroom and quickly back to Angioletta's face. He whispered, "Is it my fault?"

That caught her by surprise. If it was anyone's fault, it was hers. She shouldn't have licked the blood from her hand. To his credit, this boy had followed through on his promise to help, no matter that other people had apparently fought him all the way. She smiled and reached to his shoulder.

"No, none of this is your fault. That man will be just fine, and all because of this." She held the bottle of energy drink at face level, her expression confident and bright.

She hoped she wasn't giving him false hope. While she was always cold, that man in there had been freezing, and that couldn't bode well for him. Still, where there was hope, there was the possibility of success.

She grasped his hand. "Come on. I need your help. We have

to get him to drink some of this."

She set the trash can aside and stood, pulling him to his feet. His face was damp, and she reached to touch his forehead.

"Are you feeling well?" She didn't need two people on her hands sick, dying, or both.

"It's just really hot in here. Doesn't the air work?"

She looked around, realizing the bathroom heater was running, and that for the first time in a very long time, she felt really warm. Her dreams the past few days didn't count. They had been nightmares she had no wish to live again. This was warmth, real and comfortable. And, for some reason, just as she knew the man on the bathroom floor desperately needed high-energy fluids, she knew the heat had to stay on.

She smiled, reaching to the floor to pick up several more of the small bottles. "Yeah, they're giving us a discount on the room because of that. Can you stand it for a few minutes? Because, I really could use your help." She would need to turn the man on the floor, shifting him to his back. She was certain he would be heavy.

"Yes, ma'am. What do you need me to do?" Bobby immediately squatted to the energy drinks, scooping up all he could reach. "Here." He stood, holding them out.

"Set those on the counter and come in here. I need to sit this man up. He's fallen out of the tub, and I can't get him to drink any of this in his current position. Do you think you can help me do that?" She knelt, putting her hand to the man's face. Even this ill, he looked so very beautiful. Except for his destroyed shoulder and the blood smeared all over his skin, he could be lying down for an afternoon nap. Then she saw his shoulders shift just a fraction, and she knew he'd just taken a breath. Galvanized, she turned to Bobby.

"Now, Bobby. Help me turn him. He's alive. We must get him food." She motioned him in, reaching to toss him a towel. "To keep your hands clean," she said, remembering what the blood had done to her. She pointed that he should step between the man and the tub. There was barely room for the teenager's slender body, and she knew she would never fit, not and have room to bend and pick him up.

Before lifting him, the boy looked up to catch her eyes, and he paused, watching her intently. He started to speak and stopped, looking away, anywhere but at the man on the floor. Then he whispered, "You weren't sure, were you?"

"I'm sure, now." She felt tears in her eyes. Just moments ago she hadn't been certain at all. "Now. Lift him."

As he did, she rolled him her way, quickly grabbing for the towel at his waist, hoping for the boy's sake to keep the man modest. Bobby never looked; instead, his eyes riveted hers.

"He's your husband, isn't he? Was he in a fight? I mean, if he robbed a bank, I wouldn't tell. Maybe he's been shot by the police. Birdshot might tear up a man's shoulder like that. The police would explain why you didn't take him to a hospital. I wouldn't want anyone to know, either. You said your name is Ms. Bacciarelli. Is he Mr. Bacciarelli?"

"Sure, Bobby. He can be Mr. Bacciarelli. I just need him to drink this right now. If he doesn't, we can both be sure his name won't matter. He won't need a second drink, either." She already had a container of the power drink open, and she held it to Uriel's lips as she spoke.

Bobby frowned. "But, I don't mind if he uses them all. I've got more at home." When she glanced at him, looking hard for a moment, he said quietly, "Oh. I understand."

The drink did go down, or at least into the man's mouth. Then he coughed once, not strongly, but enough to tell them he might be swallowing it. Angioletta motioned for another bottle, and Bobby reached for one of the ones she had carried in. Handing it to her, he stepped to the counter to bring her more.

As he turned back to her, Uriel's shoulder began to change. Earlier it had been just a mass of butchered meat. Now, the skin began to heal faster and faster, sealing the wound, then forming into brand-new skin. Within a minute, the shoulder was like new, as if it had never been injured.

Angioletta glanced at the boy to find his mouth agape. She hardly felt less amazed. She reached to touch the place where the damage had been. There were only some bumps under the skin, as if he had marbles wedged just beneath the surface. She knew what they were: the stones she hadn't had time to remove.

Finally, after a few moments, the man coughed again, harder, and shifted his position on the floor. He drew in a deep breath then released it. His eyelids flickered, and finally they opened wide. He stared at the ceiling for a moment, and he glanced at Bobby. Eventually he found Angioletta's face.

"Angioletta."

He had called her by name, and she immediately sat hard on the floor, nearly knocking Bobby down.

Uriel smiled. "It's warm in here. Thanks. I'm glad you found a friend to help." His eyes moved to Bobby's face and then back to hers. "I'm hungry. Do you have any food?"

It was Bobby's turn to collapse, sitting hard on the floor right beside Angioletta. He reached to his side and picked up an unopened package of cheese crackers, handing them to the man.

Uriel took them and looked at the plastic wrapping, then he handed them back to Bobby. "Will you open these for me?"

Bobby took them, but as he opened the plastic, he began to giggle, and uncontrollable tears ran down his face. "I just watched a man's bloody shoulder heal itself like magic, and now he needs help opening a package of cheese crackers. Cheese crackers! How funny is that?"

He seemed unable to stop the laughter.

After several minutes, Angioletta also began to chuckle, and then she started to laugh. Dear God, she thought, what is this man who's come into my life? She couldn't answer that question, though, so she had to let it go, and the laughter was the answer to that.

Gadreel, Deliverer of Destruction

Light glared within the Primary Forces Chamber, and Gadreel could see nothing. Without warning, a screech of righteous anger lashed the brilliance, and he felt himself crushed. Then, in an instant, he was blasted across the vast distances of time and space. It seemed the attack would shear the molecular bonds that held his essence within his body. It was from one of the many-winged familiars imprisoned by him long ago, and he knew the taste of real fear. He had a corporeal body within the Primary Forces Chamber, even if it was only the substantiality of another dimension. In this place and in this time, he could very well die.

"Spare me, creature. I mean you no harm." He fell to one knee, pleading. He meant the Familiars no good, either. Still, for the measure of freedom he intended to offer, they should feel grateful toward him.

As his body returned to him unharmed, the fear crystalized into determination, and he looked around, now irritated to find he was alone. The two who recorded the Deeds of Man should be at his side.

"Gadreel." A voice reverberating with power called for his attention. The naming was filled with the acid of hatred and the erupting bile of wrongs yet to be righted.

"My two companions," he threw out as a diversion, for he remembered that voice, its very sound at one time shattering the stars in the heavens. It could shatter him, if it wished.

"We return them."

With a tumultuous swirling of the brilliance at his side, Nabu and Lipika fell heavily at his feet. He yanked them erect, and at the touch of his hands on their skin, he knew they were terrified.

"Thank you for my companions' return. Your kindness is supreme." That should surely placate the Familiars. He cuffed his two cohorts when they didn't bow low enough, forcing their heads lower.

"You come to tease us, to mock our misfortune?"

The words were the thunder of a thousand storms, and their anger was fearsome. Gadreel felt the inside of his body turn wrong side out, and with a twisting of the fabric of reality, he was shattered into a thousand pieces. He had only thought he was afraid before. Only when the words stopped did he realize he was still whole.

"We have news." That was Nabu, and his words were interjected quickly. His voice was bright with his announcement, but his proclamation ended with a squeak, telling the extent of his fright.

"News?" The voice blasted its anger, and a great pressure forced Gadreel to fall against the wall of the Chamber. Inexplicably, he didn't go through. He immediately understood. He was being held.

"Gadreel, I'm choking." That was Nabu, and the words were whispered with great effort. Lipika said nothing at all.

Gadreel's own chest was being squeezed, and he could barely breathe. He did have to breathe in the Primary Forces Chamber, for within its Energy Nodes, he was as real as any brother on the surface of Earth, if in a slightly different dimension. He was not held by the speaker, though. The pressure was all around them, while the voice came from farther away, or maybe it was just that the pressure affected his hearing in a most unusual manner. He was certain another of the four creatures had come to torment them.

"The Triune Mind." Nabu's voice was all squeak this time. "A chance for his escape."

That was a blatant lie, but the Familiars didn't need to know that.

"Escape?" The voice scraped salt against raw skin, then the suffocating tightness was gone. The next words were gentler. "The Triune Mind might be freed?"

"Answer," hissed Gadreel. He reached to cuff Nabu. "Now!"

"Not exactly freed."

The Recorder's squeak was still there, but he had answered. Gadreel was grateful for his phrasing, that he didn't guarantee freedom for the Mind. The Familiar would soon see through such an obvious ruse.

"Not freed?" The salt was back, and the voice slashed it across the three who had dared to enter the Chamber. Then with more force, the words were repeated, and they vibrated the reality surrounding them. "Not freed?"

"Change the subject, and quickly," Gadreel growled.

"A situation has arisen." Nabu threw out the words. "On Earth."

With a jabbing suddenness, the screech tore through the brightness once more, and the sound was hard and angry. "You speak of Earth." The salt had turned to coarse sandpaper. "All this we have suffered is Earth. We do not wish to hear of *Earth*."

Lipika growled under his breath, his own irritation and generally bad disposition making him careless. "This is all about Earth. Grow up."

It was not a particularly wise thing to do.

The four creatures that had sat at the four corners of the Seat of Power, singing their praises to the Triune Mind since the Beginnings of Time, were clearly incensed at the small brother's callousness. They showed it in their reaction to his words, for this day they *responded*.

Great flashes of fusion lightning smote the air, and the very brightness around the brothers exploded. The air sang with screeches of fury, as the brothers uselessly covered their ears. They were slammed to the ground, trampled, and thrown far from each other. The great voice blasted their bodies, until they were sure they would live no longer. Life was stripped from their souls, their essences ground from inside their bodies, until they were nothing but chaff on the wind. The Unity was destroyed, and all they had worked for during more eons than this galaxy had cycled around its axis was as dust between the stars.

Then the torture was gone, and all was as it had been. Dust and snow and cloud and mist filled the space within the Primary Forces Chamber. All was white, and the Hand of Peace brushed the pain away.

"Nobility. It is you." Gadreel spoke his words carefully. He couldn't see his two diminutive companions. He couldn't sense them, either, and he feared for them. Still, his head was bowed respectfully, for he knew that to do otherwise was to die. Those in the Unity knew neither birth nor death, but he and his two companions were not currently in the Unity. They were in the Primary Forces Chamber, and death was a very real possibility.

A rumbling filled the fog, and it was the purring of a great animal, one that ruled what it wished to rule. The sound vibrated Gadreel's innermost being, and in spite of its deadly power, he felt comforted. An earlier *voice* had ripped him molecule from molecule. This was a gentle voice, and it was indeed a voice, a very real voice, and it told of power and intent, as well as restraint. Gadreel knew this voice, and it was the one he had come to find. It was the one that could moderate the wild and vicious responses of the other three.

"It is nobler to listen without response, than to respond without listening. Such have we been reminded." This time the words simply communicated. The salt was gone, as were the violently surging emotions. Gadreel suspected the anger had only been pushed aside. He would need to tread carefully, for he didn't want to suffer its backwash again. He needed to send it another direction.

"Wisdom." Gadreel called this final being's name. Nobility had calmed his emotions, and in the purring, his true voice had been revealed. It was Wisdom he would be able to reason with. "Are Strength and Swiftness tamed?" He trusted none of them. They were the Mind's Pets, after all.

"Tamed, Gadreel. *We*," and four voices chimed in with that corporate word, the rumble, the screech, and a quick tightening across Gadreel's chest adding a deep timbre to the first voice's declaration, "wish to know the possibilities you offer us. Tell us of *Earth*," and the voices chimed again, this time with overtones of sadness and despair, "and what we have need of there. For if there is a *chance we can free the Triune Mind*," chimed as one, "then we must exercise self-control in all things."

"My two friends are missing." Gadreel offered his statement in the barest of a whisper, and it was only a suggestion. He knew these four would tolerate no commands. "They carry the message you wish to hear." He was well aware these four creatures held all the keys in this place, and there was only control in this calmness. He had been offered neither love nor forgiveness, and he would not be indulged if he asked for either.

All around him the brilliance surged and swirled, and a screech filled with contempt lashed the air. Then, unceremoniously, out of the mist, Nabu and Lipika fell once again at his feet. They climbed up, brushing off their arms and legs, but this time, Gadreel could see them fine, and they had bright red welts on their shoulders, as if they had been carried, and not gently, either.

The purring began again, yet it was not the same. It increased in volume rapidly until it was a command, a call to all who could hear that it would be patient no longer. It was a frightening sound, building into a roaring vibrato filled with ferocity, and Gadreel could smell the fear in the two small brothers at his side. It was a well-earned fear, too, for these familiars had been wronged many eons ago, and their vengeance, when it came, would be a righteous one.

"Nobility wishes your timely cooperation." Wisdom's words were polite but terse, ones that would brook no additional nonsense. "Speak. Now is your offered opportunity. What is this message? It is suggested you not keep us waiting longer."

"Nabu," Gadreel started calmly, although he felt extreme anxiety rising inside, "show the tale."

Nabu nodded, unable to speak. That in itself was unusual. With a quivering finger, the pint-sized brother touched the space in front of where he stood, and out of the mist rippled an image. With his other hand, he pinched Lipika's ear, prompting him to narrate.

The brooding brother growled, then spat his words. "Earth has corrupted our race."

The images showed people—and brothers—involved in various activities. A brother in the form of a Ladon was there, the snake creature offering a human female an apple. Another scene showed a winged brother with his heel on the Ladon's head, the snake creature writhing in pain. Many images of brothers interacting with humans flashed by, faster and faster, including those of Jeqon's long-ago party with the daughters of men, the graphic scenes showing aroused brothers flailing against tender corporeal flesh, expressions of ecstasy on their faces. Nabu stopped at one especially revealing scene, where Jeqon's own face was the one within the throes of passion.

"*A traitor beyond measure.*" Four voices chimed the words, and they expressed the Triune Mind's own, remembered displeasure. "*He was branded for the deed.*"

"Your master took Earth as his own, gathering the humans under his wing." The images began to move once again, showing revelations of wonder and beauty, a winged brother staying the hand of a man called Abraham—the winged one was Zadkiel—preventing him from killing his own son, and yet another brother—Gabriel, himself, of course—hovering above a manger, showering blessings upon a child as he showed the Wise Men the way.

"You show us this, yet we do not understand why."

"Now one called Uriel wishes to undo all your master worked to accomplish. He returns to the old way, claiming one from Earth as his own."

The scenes stilled once again, and Uriel could be seen in flight, Angioletta within his arms. Lipika conveniently failed to point out how she glowed like a brother, or just how Uriel could be touching a human at all. After the first hour of a brother's presence on Earth, such was an impossibility.

"*Uriel.*" The four voices became harsh and discordant, word, rumble, and screech mixed as one, and it revealed the measure of their anger. Their control was slipping. "*We know of Uriel, the Bearer of Destiny. He carries much power. Now he works against the Master—*"

The words were cut off as a furious screech rang out, holding for minutes, then blasting forth over and over. It was Swiftness expressing great displeasure, unable to maintain control any longer. There came also a deep rumble in the mist, the purring of a command given, and Swiftness's voice was stilled.

"It is worse." Gadreel motioned to Nabu to go to the next set of scenes, the final ones that would take the four creatures to the edge, and hopefully create weapons of them that would be at his beck and call.

This time Gabriel could be seen, and he was on the face of Earth. It was night, but the image was clear. Also, in a rapid series of scenes, the Orator of the Oath, the Healer, the Standard Bearer, the brother Jeremiel, and twin Seraphim were shown.

"*The Archangel Gabriel,*" chimed the four six-winged creatures. "*He is the Master's choice brother. Why is he shown to us?*"

"The great Archangel has joined Uriel, abetting his plans, and his band of supporters carries the combined strength of the

Unity," Gadreel whispered, his voice expressing the heartfelt sadness of one who could bear no more sorrow. "Your master's dreams are cast down if they are not stopped. Earth will be laid waste, and no humans will survive."

"We remember one such from before, the one known to us as Lucifer. He was the Master's first love, the Illuminator of Light, and his wings were six." There was a pause, and the voices continued, a new determination heard. *"Our Master must be freed."* The combined voices spoke together at first, then their voices grew louder and more discordant as they continued, *"His hand will crush the infidels."*

They were once again *responding*, and that was exactly what Gadreel had hoped for. Now, he had to direct their rising anger.

"He will be freed, er, escape, if we can only stop this travesty. I have Uriel isolated, and his destruction is assured. My dilemma is this, I cannot also fight Gabriel and his band. Can I depend on you?" He hoped they believed he knew of Uriel's whereabouts, because he knew no such thing. Either way, in their anger, the Four Familiars wouldn't question. Their rage would drive them, and they would be blinded to all else.

Lightning flashed, and the rending sounds of claws, talons, and incisors tore the Primary Forces Chamber. The four voices had spoken their cries individually, and yet, they once again spoke as one.

"The Archangel and his companions are ours. Do as you will with the Bearer of Destiny. Our Master will be avenged."

Gadreel shivered at those words. He knew their anger could as easily be turned against him, for he was the one who had tricked both them and the Triune Mind into captivity. Still, he had what he wanted, and that was all that mattered just then. He reached above his head and clapped twice. The eight Energy Nodes that had kept the Primary Forces Chamber in position for eons winked out, their usefulness over. In that instant the Primary Forces Chamber was no more, and he and the two incorporeal brothers at his side were standing in the blackness of space once again.

There was a vast and brutal disturbance in the substance of

243

corporeal reality as the four living creatures, finally unleashed, whipped their newly unrestrained power against the fabric of space and time. They needed no lightning to travel to the small planet circling its nearby corporeal sun. These creatures, the Pets of the Triune Mind, traveled in their own way, ripping and bending both the emptiness between the stars, as well as the alignments of the nearby worlds, uncaring of the damage they caused.

Their power was such that as the Pets flung themselves earthward, a comet swinging around the other side of the sun had its vastly elliptical orbit shifted just enough out of alignment that when it approached Earth again in 170 years it would surprise scientists who would find their calculations several months off. More immediately, on one side of Earth, the rising moon unaccountably brightened, creating one of the most romantic evenings in the history of one specific country, one that nine months later would record an unprecedented, never before matched rise in infant births.

Gadreel was pleased, and he reached and pulled Nabu and Lipika to him. He wrapped his arms around them, holding their heads nestled neatly within his armpits, and he hooted with more pleasure than he had felt in a very long time.

Of course, none of that actually happened, the hugging and the heads in the arms, for the three brothers were incorporeal. It was the *idea* of doing it that counted, for to those standing invisible in the blackness of space, the idea alone made it real, and in the most embarrassingly humiliating way possible.

Interlude 14

The alarms in the spacecraft wailed their distress, and the two dozing astronauts were instantly awake. Jim blinked rapidly several times, pressing his eyes shut hard before opening them a final time. In the cabin's dimness, he glanced along the overhead console for the source of the distress call. Except for the readouts on the console and some muted cabin lighting, it was dark. The computer continually monitored the men's physical activities, and when they seemed to be resting or asleep, it automatically lowered the ambient light level. It would remain low until they manually turned it up.

Above his partner's head, a number blinked a brilliant red.

"Chet." Jim touched the man's arm and pointed.

Looking up from his computer screen, one showing readings from the outside of the craft, Chet rubbed a hand roughly across the side of his face, pushing a forgotten book reader from his lap, letting it float where it would in the cabin. He reached to tap the blinking readout. It was way off the chart and wasn't going down. Then, as he watched, it spiked even higher, and then inexplicably slid quickly back down the scale to reveal the normal numbers the ship's computer recognized as acceptable. The alarm continued to sound, though.

"Io or bust," Chet murmured underneath his breath. He reached to the console just in front of him, lifted a clear cover, and touched a flashing switch. The cabin was immediately silent except for the nearly inaudible whirr of a small fan that constantly circulated the cabin's air. After a moment, a small *chink* told him his reader had made contact somewhere within the cabin.

"Not bust, Chet." Jim was at his keyboard, touching his screens and rapidly bringing up various displays, then brushing them away just as quickly, watching them roll off to the side. All seemed normal. His eyes still scanned the information written across his features, the light from the screen making a computer display of his skin, and he whispered absently, "Never, never bust."

"We should call Houston, you think?"

"They'll call us. They'll have this as soon as our signal can get it to them. But, yeah. We should call, let them know we're awake, paying attention." He chuckled as he tapped a switch several times, raising the lighting level. "Even if we weren't."

"They know we have to sleep sometime. That's why they build in the alarms. Keeps us hopping." Chet was really coming awake, and his sense of humor, sometimes rather dry, was stirring.

Jim smiled. "Don't want to hop. Seems they gave us a mini-gym back in our quarters. I'll sit back and pedal my way to fitness, thank you very much."

"Still, a hop or two wouldn't hurt, says the NASA medtech. And the good engineers listen well, designing the loudest alarms they can convince someone to manufacture. Zowie! We get a wakeup call."

Laughing this time, Jim questioned, "You want to make the call, or should I?"

Chet winked, then slipped an earpiece over his ear and placed one end inside. "I want to whisper provocative, sexy words to the engineers who so sweetly woke me from my nap." He reached to a switch on the console and held his finger above it. "Tell them what they can do with their little alarms." He grinned wickedly.

Jim stood and slapped him on the shoulder, shaking his head back and forth. "I'll be in my bunk, Chet. Enjoy your little chat with Houston. You can replay the juicy parts for me in about eight hours." He pushed himself away, already working his shirt over his head. There was no sense in wearing protective gear inside the cabin of the ship. This was their home, and they would live in it as such during their entire trip.

By the time he'd traversed the tunnel to the living module, he was down to his boxers, the rest of the items left floating along the way. He slipped his long legs into the bunk, and touching a switch, the straps built into the unit tightened just enough to hold him gently in place.

The clothing left strewn along the corridor was another reason Jim and Chet had been picked as a team for this mission. When he came along later, Chet would simply kick the items into the chemical scrubbers, where they would be dry-cleaned and ready for wearing once again. Jim would do the same for him when Chet had a lazy moment. It was what made them a team, and a good one at that.

Chapter 18

Jeri Franklin, Newly Single

Jeri Franklin (Geraldine to those who knew her from her old life) cruised along in her car, occasionally glancing up at the stars. She liked to watch them when she was on the road at night. The babies, not really babies anymore, were asleep in the back, and an old Elvis tune moaned softly on the radio. The dash lights glowed softly, just enough that when she looked in the rearview, she could see her babies' faces, one on each end of the seat. They were snuggled, their feet together in the middle, and their heads on opposite ends of the bench, pillowed on their hands.

She rode with her seat all the way back, letting the cruise maintain the speed, her legs up under her. The vent blew the cool desert air across her face. The big old car liked to overheat under the scorching sun. That was why she drove at night and spent the days in a motel. She could sleep then, letting the kids play in the pool. That worried her sometimes, but they could both swim, and she always told Dakota to watch for his sister.

Something out in front of the car caught her eye, something in the sky. It was . . . strange. The stars were there, and then they weren't, and then they were back, like they had *shifted* to a different place in the heavens. She took a deep breath and shook her head. She must be tired tonight, and she didn't like to drive tired, not with the kids in back.

She tried to remember the last gas station she'd seen. Open, anyway. She squinted down the dark highway, hoping to see a light. She could do that, get gas. She still had plenty of money from her share of the house. A motel wouldn't hurt, either. Rest. She slept, but she never got enough rest, not with the divorce and Dakota's blank looks and Little Chrissy's odd bedtime songs.

Then the sky shifted again, and this time she was paying attention. The night just *bent*. Then the stars moved, and they disappeared for a moment before coming right back.

Her stomach shifted, also, just like it used to years ago. She hadn't done any grass in years, not since before the kids were born. The first she knew she was pregnant—that was Dakota— she'd told Zack not to bring it to the house ever again. She wasn't going to mess up her kids just for a good time. This felt like she'd been on bad grass.

Puke was what she needed to do, to stop and empty her stomach. It might wake the kids, though, Dakota especially. He woke if she turned the blinker on, the *snap, snap* of the flashing light enough to shatter his delicate sleep. She'd see his eyes open in the mirror, just looking, but he'd never move a muscle. That unnerved her sometimes, as if he wasn't really there, as if his body lay in the seat of the car, but the real Dakota, the one inside, had taken off somewhere and was never coming back again.

Looking up, she saw the stars shift two more times, twice in quick succession, and before she could turn away, her car coughed, shook, and settled into a roughness that made her truly sick to her stomach.

"God, no," she whispered. "You can't break down now."

With a spit and a rattle from somewhere between the firewall and the front bumper of the big old beast, the dash lights went dead, and the car began to coast. The steering became stiff. Using both hands, she forced the wheel sideways just before the car ground to a stop, getting it at least off the road.

She hurried to get the door open, damaging the side of her shoe in the process, but she was now truly sick. Kneeling beside the car, she felt her stomach release what she'd eaten that evening. When her body was done, she spit to take the tang of stomach acid from her mouth, although she knew she'd continue to taste it for quite some time.

"Mom?" A voice called to her from the back seat. "Are we there?"

Standing, she looked around. "Somewhere, Dakota. I'll be right back, baby." Oops. She let that one through. He didn't like to be called baby anymore. She tried to be careful, although sometimes she still slipped. "I want to walk to the top of this hill to see what's on the other side."

"Okay, Mom. I'll wait right here with Little Chrissy."

Sure, baby, she thought. You do that. There wasn't any place else to go, anyway, not with a dead car. She was relieved he hadn't complained about being called baby.

She closed the door carefully, not wanting to wake her baby girl. Glancing through the glass, she paused for a moment to watch her daughter. She might be seven, but she would always be a little girl to her. Baby. Her daughter didn't mind the pet name.

Looking up into the sky, she shivered as she began the walk to the top of the hill. Somehow, she couldn't get over the feeling that whatever she'd seen up there had killed her car. She'd seen it four times, too. She'd counted. Four times. She wrapped her arms around herself, a chill running down her spine. This was as bad as it could get. At least that was the hope she clung to. She had to cling to something, and on this night, she couldn't find much to cling to at all.

Kinky Kinkerson, Reporter

"I'm sorry for just dropping in, but I need a car. Local for a few days." Kinky rubbed his hand across his face, tired and irritated at the cost of the cab he could see driving away with his money. It'd had to come out of his pocket, and all on the off chance he could get a car on such short notice. The car would be out of his pocket, too, and that irritated him even more.

Now he thought he should have called first. Cab fare back? That was the cost of a good lunch. He set his valise on the floor and attempted to smile at the young man just in from the back room.

"Yes, sir. We have one ready right now." The night clerk with the rental car company label on his jacket smiled cheerfully, digging around behind the desk before tossing a set of keys up in the air, catching them skillfully as they fell. He looked to be barely out of high school with a face so smooth he'd probably never touched it with a razor. Then, with a clank, he slapped the keys on the counter, deftly reaching to slip a form from a hidden shelf to lay beside them. "Bet you're glad we're open until two. That's A.M. by the way."

"Should I prepare myself?" Kinky smiled with difficulty. He was picturing the cost of this car on his credit card statement. No matter the financial hit, he could not just sit in that room. He slid the paperwork around to look at it, then quickly put his signature in all the proper places. He chuckled sourly. "Without a reservation, I can't expect much."

The fresh face looked at him and grinned. "In fact, sir, we have a dozen ready. I've put you down for an SUV, if you want one. It won't cost you any more. This is our slowest month of the year. No one comes to the desert in summer. Try winter, and you'll have to have one reserved three weeks in advance." He nodded knowingly.

"An SUV, huh?" Kinky shook his head in disbelief.

"I guess the gas mileage bothers you. That's the same for a lot of people." The boy turned the paper around, and picked up a pen.

"Hey! Wait up, now. You sold me when you said 'S,' kid, especially if my new SUV goes for the same price as a compact." Before the kid could mark any changes, Kinky's hand dropped onto the form. "I get to play the big spender while here in Phoenix, and all for the compact price." He kinda liked that idea, bang for his buck and all.

He could tell already. Just the mention of an SUV, and his

mood was improved. What did that say about him?

The clerk grinned, tearing off the back sheet of each page. He stapled them and set them next to the keys. "I've put the insurance on it for you, too. Helps keep unexpected costs under control. Is that okay?"

What the clerk didn't say was that the insurance charges for the SUV were more than for the compact. That was where the real money was made, because the cars rarely came back damaged. It was a full hundred percent profit.

"For a free upgrade? Hey, I don't mind that at all. What model are you giving me?"

"Expedition. The biggest they make."

"Is that an American truck, or . . . that big Toyota?"

The clerk laughed. "Ford, sir. You'll like it. I've got plenty of time, so if you don't mind, I'll step outside with you to show you the ins and outs, just so you don't have any problems." He clicked his monitor off and stepped around the counter, grabbing the keys. "Let me help you with your things."

"I only have this case." Kinky picked up his copy of the paperwork, and he reached for the piece of worn leather luggage at his feet. It was small, carrying toiletries and one compact change of clothes. Just in case, he always told everyone. "Everything else is at my motel. I think I can figure out how to get an SUV started, and I'm sure you're busy."

"Not at all, sir. You've been my only customer all evening."

Kinky chuckled to see plaid shorts and black socks below the boy's jacket and tie, even though the night had begun to cool. This was Phoenix, and it was summer. He was pleased to have lucked into an SUV, especially if it had to be out of his own pocket. He loved to get good deals on the cheap. Who-ee, but he loved that.

Jeri Franklin, Newly Single

Jeri approached the top of the hill, and she was surprised to realize how really dark it was. Turning back the way she'd come, she tried to find the car and couldn't. She shivered, thinking of her kids all alone in the dark, nothing but the blackness to keep them company. And the night was dark. Creepily dark.

She closed her eyes for a moment, trying to imagine the road she was on underneath the brightness of a sunlit day. She couldn't. She usually had at least the moon up, or the interior lights running in the car, or maybe even a streetlight coming up as her little family slid along the road, then trailing off behind her as the car carried them along. Tonight, with the car totally dead out in the middle of the desert, there was nothing. Well, starlight, but that hardly counted. You couldn't see anything except shadows using starlight alone.

A slight breeze brushed her face, and in the distance she heard an eagle's cry. Frowning for a moment, she tried to remember what she'd seen on *Animal Planet* the week before. They'd stopped at a place with cable, and she and the kids had stayed up half the morning, snuggled in bed, just watching the shows. It seemed eagles hunted in the day, something about telescopic vision, so the cry must be something else. It chilled her just the same.

Slipping her hands in her pockets, she felt a package of crackers. It was one of those from a salad bar, the little plastic-wrapped kind with two crackers inside. She blinked her eyes, the sudden burning of unwelcome tears tearing at her. Earlier, Little Chrissy had said she was hungry, and Jeri had told her all the crackers were gone. She'd thought they were, too, and now she'd found a package in her pocket.

For no good reason, she felt like a bad mother, letting her daughter go to sleep hungry, leaving her and her big brother stranded and all alone in the dark on a desert highway, not managing to hang onto the life they'd once had. It just didn't seem fair, and in that instant, she wanted very much to run back to the car, pick up her kids, and tell them she loved them very much.

She couldn't, though. Oh, she could, but it wouldn't help the present situation. The fact was that they were perfectly safe, or so she hoped, and help was not going to come find them. In the relatively cool desert night, they would both be okay. They wouldn't dehydrate in the dark. If she went back and waited until morning to try for help, the heat would be a killer. This was her only choice.

Standing tall, she faced forward and stepped ahead, ignoring the telltale rasping of her damaged shoe against her ankle. Topping the rise, she looked around, surprised to see a light far down the highway. At first she thought it might be a distant car, one traveling right at her. Then she realized what she was looking at. It wasn't just a light. It was help in the form of a blue square with a giant red six in the middle.

At that precise moment, a distant wolf sent its mournful wail into the night sky, and Jeri didn't feel quite so safe after all. Wolves eat meat, and she was meat. At least her kids were inside the car, and with the power off, they wouldn't be able to roll the windows down.

Gritting her teeth, she walked faster. Goose bumps had gathered over her skin, and she had no love at all for goose bumps, not in any way, shape, or form.

Malak, Wolf

In the deep of the desert night, the tribunal was concluded, and Malak growled. Something was wrong. The air quivered with tension, a tautness that only a wolf of supernatural ability could sense. Malak wanted to run. He remained still, as only the Seraph could release those under his dominion. Until then, they could only wait.

Elemiah seemed to feel it, too. He glanced at Kafziel, still on the ground, and nodded at Malak, who continued to guard the wayward brother. At Malak's side stood the great bald eagle that was Gabriel's familiar, and Elemiah nodded a second time, smiling with approval when the eagle let out an unholy screech.

Then fire leaped from Elemiah's eyes, the brilliance dancing across the space where he stood. He raised his Sword before him, and shards of glittering effervescence leaped from its surface into the gathered gloom, before exploding into the night.

Malak growled as Kafziel quaked under the Sword's on-slaught. In the presence of Elemiah's release of power, even the great bald eagle involuntarily hopped back a step, its feathered wings opening with a snap, counterbalancing the solid muscular bulk that made up the core of its body. The sound that issued from its beak was a profane ratcheting crescendo analogous to the hiss of a tortured snake. It was a noise only a familiar from the Unity could twist from inside that creature's primitive avian throat.

Malak dropped a furred chest to the ground, reeling under the Seraph's rush of surging strength. There was a clear hierarchy of abilities—and sometimes gifts—within the Unity, and the line of demarcation was often sharp and unforgiving. When bounds were overstepped, the backlash could be fantastically swift and equally harsh, even among allies.

Malak didn't want to know the pain of Elemiah's backlash.

Eons ago the Lost One of Light had made that mistake, one of grasping at a rung of power that was not his due. He had been banned from the Unity and forced to take his supporters with him, living his days upon corporeal Earth.

No other had dared since, until Gadreel. Then it had been trickery and trickery alone that had won the battle.

"Draw nigh, my companions of the night." The words were draped in Elemiah's lilting rhyme. "It seems that others deign to arrive, ones who wish to fight." The Seraph called boldly into the dark, his voice shredding the air and forcing the very night-time to cower and hide. He lowered the Sword slightly, although he still held it in both hands. His six wings moved tentatively as if he searched for something he recognized within the darkness.

Malak's snout lifted slightly, feeling the presence of something familiar, hoping to find Uriel. The wolf had sensed his presence earlier, had *felt* him, then sniffing again, accepted that there was no longer any scent of Uriel in the air. His thoughts could be felt, though, even as his presence could not. That meant he was out there. Somewhere.

Uriel. The whine, not quite Uriel's name, escaped Malak's canine throat, as its thoughts cast about for its master. In the darkness, the night breeze rippled the tips of the wolf's fur, the very movement telling the animal more than anyone could understand. The rush of the air through the darkness created a dance that was its own, one that was directed by Earth itself. The shape of the desert floor was a legato melody with fluid articulation, while the cacti and other desert plants added the allegro ripple of a xylophone, one with resonating tubes for a deeper, richer sound. A distant arroyo might be the thrum of a kettledrum, while the sub-melodies of the small animals on the desert floor and the birds overhead created a harmonious interplay that told the wolf of every living creature within a reasonable distance.

Malak loved the wind.

It wasn't just the song of the wind that had the wolf's attention. There was something else there, something not in the wind. It was part of Uriel, and to Malak, it screamed *Urgency.* At least it had been urgency, and was still, perhaps, but less so. It had morphed into hunger, and yet, the tendrils of tattered urgency still spread out into the night air like beckoning fingers. They were interwoven into the air. They drew Malak, and strongly, too.

Its wolf throat whined, a sound that was high-pitched and plaintive. Its brow furrowed between its two yellow eyes, and the animal's long face pleaded with Elemiah. It needed to be released, to be allowed to go to Uriel, but it couldn't take its leave until permission had been granted. Its whine spoke its wish to go *now*.

Without further warning the stars overhead shifted, blinked, and were back again. A chill permeated the air, and flashes of electrical discharges leaped between objects. Malak's whine grew louder, and the animal flattened its body to the ground. The eagle hopped several times, screeching, equally disturbed.

At Malak's side, Kafziel truly fell flat. From his supine and subservient posture, it was plain he knew something big had arrived, and it carried a terrible strength with it.

The great Sword of Power once again thrust high into the air, its brilliance flinging the darkness aside. The Seraph's wings shifted as if readying for flight.

Then, unexpectedly, Elemiah staggered, his six feathered wings catching his fall, their surfaces whipping the air for support. He whirled in a great circle, the Sword slicing through the air, leaving bruised molecules of nitrogen and oxygen in its wake.

"From out of the darkness, such as you must come." The Seraph's words furiously probed the night, lashing out at his attacker. "Even so, from such an abomination, I refuse to run."

Malak let out a howl, one matched only by the eagle's shriek of fury.

"When attacked by my Sword, only the devious need to hide. During my coming victory, I will take the greatest pride." The tip of Elemiah's Sword moved instantly from cardinal point to cardinal point, as he again vented his defiance against the unseen intruder.

A bellow of fury was the Seraph's only answer.

Then, as if an earthquake shattered the Arizona desert, the ground shook. Great, cloven hooves tore the soil asunder, and in a brilliant flash of very visible horns and enormous panting nostrils, Elemiah was again hit, and this time he was flung into the air. His Sword flew from his hand, the light of its power flashing through the darkness in a prismatic display of luminescence as it twirled through the night sky. Before it could reach the ground, the Seraph's swiftly beating wings danced a duet with the air, and his arm flashed the Sword's brilliance once again. His skill in fighting was aloft, and he continued to remain airborne as he twisted this way, then that, his powerful body moving almost faster than the eye could follow. His Sword became a blinding blur of light, warding off another impending attack.

Malak froze, understanding more than some might think. The wolf already knew the one that had appeared, this quickness in the dark, this one named Strength; the wolf had sensed it as soon as the stars above had announced its presence. Even as Malak had awaited the Seraph's permission to leave, the desert's song had changed, adding a discordant counter-melody in an undisguised basso vibrato. It was one of the Four, and it couldn't be fought, not with just one Seraph, two familiars, and a wayward brother who would be dead soon enough if found alone with the wolf once again.

The wolf's teeth revealed themselves in a building growl. Out of the blinding blaze of fury that Elemiah had become, his Sword finally pointed at the animal, frozen for the briefest instant of time, and the Seraph was equally still for that short span, hovering, with only the tips of his six wings in motion, and the world around him seeming to freeze into a slow-motion parody of itself.

"Go, Familiar. In spite of our differences, you have helped me here. Now to Uriel, you must draw near. He has become my foe, although I release you to him. It sorrows me that it must be in battle when we meet again." He turned, and the Sword pointed at the eagle. "You are with me, and to Gabriel we fly. Evil this night is afoot, and it draws ever nigh."

Then the world crashed in upon them once again, and the Seraph leaped for the heavens. In an amazing display of luminous acrobatics, he began to spin, a brilliant drill of light piercing the darkness. The sudden burst of power ripped at the edges of those things nearest his location, leaving their sub-atomic structures stressed to the breaking point. It was to Earth's good fortune that Elemiah flew like lightning. Before the corporeal atoms of the planet could dissolve their bonds completely, he was gone, his Sword held before him, pointing his way in the dark.

The bald eagle screeched, and its oversized body shot after the Seraph, a missile in the darkness, its feathered wings tearing at the sky.

Malak immediately turned to the brother still sprawled on the ground, an opportunity unveiled once again. A long, furred jaw snapped, and the growl from earlier was back. It no longer pleaded, though. This was a threat that remembered a metal pole and the pain that had nearly been its death. Its body dropped, and the stalk began, saliva moistening oversized incisors.

Kafziel leaped into a crouch as he tensed his muscles for flight. He slapped his hands together, and his wings appeared in a rolling flash of light.

257

Malak saw the motion for what it was, and the furred familiar growled once again. Then, with speed that was no more than a blur, the wolf uncoiled powerful muscles and leapt.

Kafziel was faster, though, if only by a margin. He left Malak howling, as he tore into the night sky, with only a few feathers remaining to float from the grip of the wolf's bloodied claws.

Malak howled in frustrated fury. Death, its canine voice screamed. Death to the one who must die.

Kafziel, Emissary of Solitude and Tears

Kafziel breathed a sigh of relief, unaware for the moment of the cold surrounding hm. The damage the wolf had done was minor. His wings would repair themselves easily enough as long as he had the reserves of energy available to supply the healing process.

He scanned the horizon as he flew. Something had attacked the Seraph, the Guardian of the Tree of Life, and the brother had taken the blow, even releasing the Sword of Power for a moment before grasping it once again in an inhumanly fast maneuver. Of course, the Seraph was not human, and so his quickness didn't surprise Kafziel. Something making it through the Seraph's awareness did.

Few things were more powerful than a Seraph, and he considered what might have horns, cloven feet, and the body of an ox. Nothing, he knew, except for one of the four Pets the Triune Mind had kept at the Seat of Power. None of them could be on Earth, because they were all Encapsulated in the Primary Forces Chamber, and no one would release them under any circumstance. No one would dare. It would mean the end of the world, either that or of the brothers.

It had to have been something else he saw.

Whatever it was, it was very, very powerful. Even the Seraph had turned tail and run.

Malak, Wolf

Malak nuzzled the ground where Kafziel had lain, the triggers in its brain strong and sharp, forcing responses truly canine in nature.

Eventually, Malak was satisfied, its need fulfilled, and a sensitive nose made its way back into the air. A day and more had passed since the last pheromones had faded from Uriel's passing, but Malak was a wolf. The need to track with its nose was paramount.

Then something new was found in the air . . . not Uriel . . . but definitely human. Malak turned, its canine brain decoding, deciding. Then, with the sudden determination of confidence, four padded paws trotted into the desert, a furred snout pointed into the air, not even bothering to sniff the ground. The olfactants hovered just above the soil, drifting, carried by the breeze, and they contained the smell of loss, of sorrow, and of desperation.

It wasn't really those feelings Malak smelled. It was the smell of alarm pheromones, acrid smells produced by the sweat glands, odors that even disguised by cologne or perfume were still obvious to the sensitive canine nose. When the wolf smelled those aromas, it felt the emotions behind them. After all, Malak was Uriel's familiar. Uriel was the Bearer of Destiny, leading men to their rightful roles on the face of the planet Earth. How could Malak, Uriel's second, his *familiar,* be any different? The familiar had found a human, one who needed help. She—and the pheromones were clearly female—was desperate, too.

Soon, the powerful animal loped across the desert floor, the singing of the wind in its fur a fortissimo drumming that drove it forward at a presto pace.

Jeri Franklin, Newly Single

How far could the sign be? Jeri turned to look behind her, searching for the shadow that had been the hill where she'd first seen the blue light. From the hill she'd been able to be both places at the same time. Her kids had been within her reach, if only visibly, and the motel was just down the road. Now all she had was the darkness behind her and the blue sign that seemed no closer, although she knew it must be.

Dakota would be afraid, although he wouldn't show it. He'd stare into the darkness outside the window, and his breath would trickle from his nose, shallow and even. Only when it was gone would he allow another in. He was nothing if not in control. If his sister woke, he'd pat her on the leg and tell her everything was all right, lying to her if need be. He'd appear to be strong, but his strength was the fear that he was unlovable, that Zack hadn't left her, but had left him. He would be afraid, though. She knew, because when the lonely nights came to an end, the nights where he asked about Zack, and he pulled away from her, she would smell it on him, the way a puppy smells when attacked by a much larger dog.

She didn't dare worry about Little Chrissy. If she did, she'd run back to the car, and she'd hold her until the sun rose. Then, before help came, it would grow hot, hot, hot. She was doing the right thing, walking, leaving her children in the middle of the night on a deserted desert road. She knew she was, but she didn't feel it inside.

She closed her eyes and leaned her head back to face the sky. Maybe the tears would remain inside this time. She was so tired of crying, even when she knew it did no good. Still, it was better to cry here than around other people. If she cried here, then it wasn't like she'd actually cried at all. It could be over and done with, forgotten like it had never happened.

She blinked again, pushing it all away, and for a time her eyes felt safe from the flood. Wiping her nose with a paper napkin from yesterday's restaurant, she looked to the blue sign, the one with the red six, and she laughed at herself. Maybe she needed more of Dakota's strength, even if she knew it must be served with an equal dose of fear.

Pausing to reach to her ankle, the blister she had expected now bothering her, she heard a sound somewhere off the road: a stone overturned, perhaps; the soft brush of something against bare dirt; a breath taken in the darkness, one that was not hers.

Standing slowly, her heart filling her throat, she turned her head both ways, peering, hoping beyond hope that the desert was as empty as she needed it to be. If something was there, she couldn't outrun it, although she would sure try. To die here, though, leaving her children stranded, never knowing what had happened to her, was more than she could take, and she drew in a ragged breath, stifling it immediately.

Something brushed her leg gently, and she froze, thinking how she had pictured running, even if it was hopeless. Now her body was locked in fear, and she couldn't even breathe. The darkness closed in on her, and the night that had earlier seemed cool and almost refreshing gripped her, humid and clammy. Somewhere in the back of her mind, she knew the change was the result of her fear, but it didn't make it any less real.

Her arm jerked as a tongue licked her hand, then a furry head forced itself between her arm and hip. She looked down to see a dark shape at her side, a large dog, she guessed. It was with a giddy relief that she realized she hadn't been attacked. When the animal leaned against her, she tentatively touched its fur, surprised to find it thick and coarse. It seemed to tingle with electricity, and she noticed the tips of the fur as they sparkled with crackling static where she stroked it. She felt the snap of the charges as they leaped to her hand, but somehow, the strange yet ordinary feel of the static electricity was comforting, something she was used to in a small way.

"Good dog," she murmured. Her hand rubbed along the reassuring neck. The animal took one step forward and stopped as if waiting. She once more touched the coarse fur along the nape of its neck, unsure. In that moment she hoped this animal didn't just brush against her side, then disappear into the night. She had been horribly frightened just moments ago, and relief had begun to seep through her veins when it hadn't attacked.

With an unexpected determination she couldn't understand, she wanted this creature at her side. Somehow it was as if she would be unharmed as long as the two of them were together, that this animal had come along for her exactly when she'd needed it.

Turning to look behind her for a moment, knowing she couldn't see her car, and yet unable to keep from trying, she felt the wolf against her leg once again, pressing gently, as if demanding her attention. Her hand stroked it, then she felt it move a step forward and stop.

Suddenly giddy again, the adrenalin in her system overloading her brain, she giggled. "Okay, big boy. You want to walk, then we'll walk." Once she stepped forward, she felt the animal move ahead once more, slowly pacing four furred legs to the stride of her two human ones.

Malak, Wolf

Malak could smell the remains of the woman's fear, had not intended to cause it, but knew as well there had been no way to prevent it. All it could do now was reassure her. The wolf could also smell the presence of other humans beneath her fear, ones who carried a similarity to this one's smell, the way a litter of pups might carry the smell of their mother. Two others were there. They couldn't be felt in the song the wind ruffled along the wolf's fur, but they were definitely in the woman's smell.

There was one other thing. The connection between a familiar and its master was always there, stretched tenuously thin when the distance was great, but increasingly tangible when reunion was imminent. Uriel was just ahead. Malak could tell.

They walked forward, the wolf and the woman, and just behind them, ever so gently, the horizon soon began to lighten. It offered plenty of light for Malak, although it wouldn't be

262

enough for Jeri to see for some time. Soon enough, though, dawn was coming.

It would be a new day, a fresh chance to grab whatever opportunities came their way.

Eustorgio Ricci, Monsignor

The monsignor dropped his wallet and change into a small bucket and stepped into the airport scanner. The lights overhead were bright, hurting his tired eyes. One thing he hadn't expected was for Heathrow to be so crowded. During the transfer between stations, he'd thought for a time he'd lost the good bishop somewhere on the underground. With some small degree of trepidation, he'd waited, hoping, finally relieved to see His Excellency step off the very next train.

It seemed to him it would be rather more logical to build an entire airport in one location, although the British just couldn't seem to get the hang of that. They stuck the terminals wherever they felt like—all over the city, it seemed—and wasn't that just like the British? "La madre degli idioti è sempre incinta," he muttered under his breath. *The mother of idiots is always pregnant.* Then, catching himself, he looked around to see if anyone had heard him, chagrined at his carelessness. The security guard glanced up, giving him a quick smile when he noticed the clerical collar, and went back to his job. Clearly, Italian wasn't his first language.

"Father Ricci," the bishop called from the far side of the security barrier, as the monsignor stepped from the scanner, reaching for his things from the bucket. "Do not move away too far just yet."

Ricci waved and pointed to a chair, sitting down to wait. Apparently the good bishop had an undisclosed artificial knee, and the scanners hadn't liked it. He'd had to remove his shoes and submit to a full body search. The British had no respect for Roman Catholic clergy when it came to their airport security, it seemed.

This trip had become a comedy of errors and omissions. In Rome the paperwork they'd stopped to pick up hadn't been ready, the clerk responsible having forgotten all about the request, even though it was right on top of the stack. "Meglio tardi che mai," he'd shrugged. *Better late than never.* Then he'd realized the bishop was with Ricci, and he'd quickly changed his tune. Even so, just to have forgotten such an important request, and from Bishop Carnaly!

"How does a thing like a death certificate get overlooked, Bishop?" They were on the plane, having just disembarked Italy, and Ricci had quizzed the older man. He knew the part he'd played in the lapse, not really having searched the records thoroughly himself, and instead assuming it must be there. Even so, he was certain there was more to it than just that. It was almost as if he'd *forgotten* to look for the record, even though it was of vital importance. His eyes had slipped over that requirement, and not just once, but every time he'd gone over the forms. For those in Rome to do the same, though. How unusual was that?

"Il pessimo vicino è il parente piu stretto." Bishop Carnaly had shrugged and smiled. *The worst neighbor is the closest relation.* He'd continued, elaborating in English, "Our girl is a family member of the Church, or rather *was,* we hope," and he had smiled, for if she were still alive, then she couldn't be canonized. "Who wishes to be a good neighbor to a close relation? It is too easy to overlook those who live in your own household, thinking they cannot be important. Even in the Scriptures, it says the Christ was not respected in his hometown."

Still, it didn't quite make sense that there were no records of her leaving the country, of residency abroad, or anything else to identify her. In addition, there was no actual birth certificate to identify the girl legally. There were not even any school records. She had been tutored by the sisters for her first decade and a half. All the two clerics had to go on was a story from America mentioning the name.

Another troublesome facet of this little jewel of a search

was that everyone who had known her had described her as she was when just a girl. They were looking for a woman, as she would be an adult now.

A man touched the priest on his shoulder as the security guards began inspecting the insides of the bishop's shoes. Father Ricci glanced up, not surprised. It wasn't unusual to have an adherent approach him for religious or even nonreligious reasons.

"Yes?" He smiled, standing. "What may I do for you?" He glanced back at Bishop Carnaly to see him still occupied with his pat down. Satisfied, he turned back to the stranger.

"Monsignor Ricci. You travel from Rome, do you not?" The question was clearly no more than to open the conversation.

"Of course. With Bishop Carnaly. You can see him just through the scanners." Ricci nodded that direction.

The man didn't look, and what he said next surprised the monsignor.

"Yes. I needed to speak with you alone, and that is why your belt did not set off the scanner." He glanced with unusual golden eyes at Ricci's waist, and that was when the priest remembered. He'd picked up one in Rome, a cloth one with a substantial metal buckle. It was new, and he'd forgotten to remove it for security. It should have set it off.

"My belt? You must work here, then. Thank you. I don't remember seeing you at the scanning machine, though." Father Ricci usually had a good memory for faces, and it disturbed him to have forgotten so quickly.

"I am here only temporarily." The stranger said the words in a rush, as if to speak slowly might reveal their lack of truth. "Quickly, listen. I have information for you."

"Certainly. You must understand, when my associate arrives, I must leave. I do apologize, but it must be that way." Ricci wasn't sure he liked the tone of this man's assumptions, but he could certainly spare him a few moments, at least until the bishop got through the line.

The man motioned with one hand, and the bishop's scanner

went off again. Ricci looked over, surprised to see that he wasn't even near it. Then a hand-held wand chirped, and it was lying on the table. When Carnaly shot Ricci a desperate glance, the priest simply shrugged, calling, "Dai nemici mi guardo io, dagli amici mi guardi Iddio!" He whispered to the man at his side, motioning to the English workers in the airport, "With friends like these, who needs enemies? Nothing works in this country, not even the scanning equipment."

The man simply reached in his pocket and pulled out an envelope. "Your flight to America. You will find the one you seek in the desert. Arizona. Phoenix. Here are tickets for once you arrive in New York. You will have two hours. Then the flight will leave. These are in your names. You must save her." The man's instructions were short and choppy to the point of terseness, and he suddenly seemed in a hurry to leave. "Your friend comes. I must go." He stepped away, moving quickly around a corner.

Ricci walked after him, rounding the corner to find a dead end with a bank of windows covering one wall. There was a sudden flash of light through the glass, the sun reflecting off an airplane, the monsignor guessed. Stepping forward, he looked outside to see no airplane, and no cause for the light. He shrugged, the man perhaps being a Mystery from God, one of his angels, possibly.

Looking at the envelope in his hand, he turned back to the airport and his waiting companion, thinking how it was the middle of the day here, and that meant it'd be the middle of the night in Arizona. He hoped it was dawn before they arrived.

Ricci's acceptance of the envelope and his lack of concerns about a complete stranger handing him tickets in the middle of a crowded airport should have set off alarms in his brain. He should have been more curious as to why he accepted the unusual tickets so easily. That wasn't like the good monsignor. However, that was the way of the brothers, better known as angels for those of the human inclination.

Ricci had turned from the window just a bit too quickly. If he'd been watching carefully, he might have seen something off in the sky, something not quite human that would have given him a clue.

But then it might not have mattered. After all, a brother who doesn't wish to be seen isn't seen at all, at least not by human eyes.

Chapter 19

Kinky Kinkerson, Reporter

Kinky reached through the SUV's window to shake, pleased. He had wheels, now. Everyone back in Albuquerque should see him like this.

The young clerk called to him before letting his hand go.

"Mr. Kinkerson, be sure to turn on your headlights before you drive away." He touched one of the stalks on the steering wheel. "There. Just twist it. All the way will set it to automatic. You'll never have to touch it again the whole time you have the truck."

"Automatic lights." Kinky clicked the inside of his cheek with his tongue. "Thanks, kid."

"Thank *you*, Mr. Kinkerson. If you need help for anything, even directions, just touch that button above the rearview mirror. It's a phone, and it'll call up directions or anything else you need. Oh, and you have a full tank of gas. It's in your rental agreement that you can bring it back empty, if you want." There was a fifty percent surcharge for the convenience, but the boy didn't mention that. "I hope we can do business again, some-day."

Kinky nodded, touching a switch, and letting the window

close him in. He pressed his foot to the brake and slipped the transmission into gear. As massive as it was, the big vehicle surged forward with a silkiness that belied its connotation as a work horse.

Once on the road, he decided he wasn't ready to head back to the motel only to watch more TV. He wanted to get his new toy out on the highway for a few hours, er, miles. He reached to rub his hand across the dash, and his thumb triggered the stereo display. Surprised at the noise, but pleased anyway, he reached out a hand and touched the screen. With just a tap, he had it search for a strong signal, and it found an oldies station. *Hotel California* warbled out, and he laughed. Oh, to be rich and live like this all the time: leather, a good stereo, and an SUV with less than 10K on the clock.

He thought about changing the station after *Hotel* drew to a close and a news announcer came on, but he was enjoying the ride, and he left the controls alone. The announcer's voice was soft and melodious, with a sing-song quality, pleasing in that late night radio way, and Kinky's drive was simply too pleasant to do anything except enjoy.

"This is Kool-Radio 94.5 FM, bringing you the latest in Good Times and Golden Oldies. 100 percent music, 100 percent of the time, 57 minutes out of every hour."

Not quite 100 percent, Kinky thought with a grin. But he was in the world of media also, and 57 minutes out of an hour was pretty close. He settled into his seat as the announcer went on.

"For all you sci-fi junkies out there, there's been a rash of UFO sightings in the past hour. Just north of town, a small RV was hit by something big, and we don't mean a meteorite. The sheriff is on the way now, we're told, but for those of you out on the road, be careful. No one wants to be carried off to Mars to-night, not and miss another 57 minutes of solid music.

"On a more serious note, our friends at Kitt Peak have sent out a warning for the general Phoenix metro, including areas to the north and west. Electromagnetic activity seems to be abun-dant tonight. If you have any electronics attached directly to outside wiring, you may want to consider unplugging for a few

hours. By morning, we should be fine.

"With all the UFO and electromagnetic activity, does it seem like New Mexico is bleeding over into Arizona? I thought Roswell had dibs on the crazy stuff."

A soft chuckle came over the airwaves, and Kinky grinned. He liked this announcer.

"For tonight's weather, clear and steady temperatures with occasionally gusty breezes. Life is good in Phoenix at Kool-Radio 94.5 FM.

"Now, here's a little Michael from back before he was white."

As the music started up, building slowly at first, Kinky noticed the stars overhead suddenly change, looking funny, and then a moment later, they were normal again. He shrugged, sure it was simply distortion somewhere in the SUV's glass. After all, this was a truck he'd never driven before, and it was bound to have peculiarities.

Then his eyes caught something big, an animal, perhaps, with a long tail and a big shiny mane glittering around its neck. It ran right in front of his truck, clearly illuminated by the glare of his headlights. The oddest thing, though, was that he knew it was there, but as soon as his eyes locked on it, they just seemed to slide sideways, and the thing disappeared. Not ran out of the range of his lights. Disappeared, like it was there, and then it wasn't.

Unnerved, he hit the brakes, which at that particular moment was probably the very worst thing he could have done. Rolling down the driver's window for a better look, he glanced out to see a giant bovine barreling directly toward his door, its massive head down, and its cloven feet tearing up the desert floor. Immediately, he felt his eyes do the same as before. His glance simply slipped sideways, and the beast was gone from view.

He thought of Paul Bunyan and Babe, his blue ox.

He barely had time to wonder if he was going crazy when the horns of that invisible Ox slammed into his door. His rented truck jerked violently, and with a horrendous grinding of tortured steel, the door's hinges released their grip on that superfluous piece of painted metal, allowing the Ox to toss it roughly aside.

The force of the attack rocked the SUV violently. It had been hit dead center by a massive creature far larger than any normal ox had ever been. The animal was also amazingly quick on its feet, and before the truck could completely settle on its wheels, the door had been thrown away, and the horns caught the SUV again, this time just under the door threshold.

The creature was no longer invisible, and Kinky's eyes grew wide. The animal's head at his side was the size of a washing machine, and even in the dark, its eyes glowed with a frightening light.

With a rippling of massive shoulder muscles, it jerked its head up. The Ox lifted Kinky and his truck off the ground, and then vaulted the SUV high into the air. At the same time the enormous animal let out a bellow that rendered the peace of the desert nonexistent.

Interlude 15

Finally, with the obstruction in its path cleared, the "Familiar" known as Strength began to run once again, its massive hooves tearing into the fragile desert soil, determined to exact revenge on the one who had chosen to undo what the Triune Mind had long ago tried to build on this one small world. The enemy had been found, for Barakiel's Sword called the Circle of Brothers.

Behind the Ox, far off the road, the SUV hit the ground with an explosive sound, sending dust billowing everywhere. It rocked violently several times, the momentum of its flight through the air expending itself before it stilled. It lay on its side, one door missing, the top crushed, and all its lights still on. Kinky's leather bag had been thrown into the distance. Inside the remains of the SUV, a pleasant voice could be heard.

"Good evening. Our sensors show you have been in an accident. If you are conscious, please push the button above the rearview mirror. If no response is received, an ambulance will

271

be dispatched within three minutes."

Then the radio came back up, and Michael Jackson's *Thriller* continued to pound its beat into the darkness of the night. There was no one in the truck to hear.

Minutes later, far across the desert floor, the Ox finally came breast-to-breast with his intended prey. Immediately, a battle raged, one that centered on Barakiel's brightly shining Sword aimed high into the air as a beacon.

This was no mistaken confrontation with an unwary Seraph, two misplaced familiars, and one immoral brother. Rather, the Ox had found a rather more substantial group of brothers to challenge.

Gabriel rose to take command, his wings thrashing the air, his voice thundering commands to each of his comrades. As the fighting battered the desert around Barakiel, the Seraph's Sword of Power remained stretched ever heavenward, its light flaring into the desert sky, banishing darkness for those who dared look its direction.

Strength slammed into the halo of light surrounding the Seraph and quickly found the Seraph's overwhelming strength to be impenetrable. Indeed, the Power of the Sword washed over the Seraph, encasing him in a glowing sleeve of energy, protecting him from all attacks, keeping him safe for as long as he held it aloft.

Yet, let it fall, whether in aid to a brother, or in weary exhaustion, and the Sword would become simply a weapon, powerful in the hands of a Seraph, but just that. A weapon.

Barakiel could not afford to let the Sword fall, not even to join in the malodorous mêlée that had been slashed upon them. And his strong arm was needed, for not all of the Circle of Brothers were close enough to enjoin the fray.

Raphael had arrived on Earth farthest away from Barakiel's raised Sword, and the great distance he must travel couldn't be helped. He sent his regrets, encouraging his brothers to be strong, and that he would join the battle when he could.

The second Seraph, Elemiah, was also detained. Not only had he been roughly accosted by the Ox, but he had encountered an earthbound brother, one who had provided him with astounding information, shifting Uriel from the Betrayed to the Betrayer. The news tortured Gabriel, even as he battled the Familiars of the Triune Mind.

Three other brothers, those near to Barakiel, fought at the Archangel's side. The intensely dark Jeremiel understood the crushing news of Uriel's betrayal, and he knew the ragged gash it left in the Archangel's heart. Jeremiel's Mandate was to find strength in brokenness, and he hoped for an opportunity to turn Uriel's betrayal around, crafting what was perceived as a weakness into a mighty upwelling of supremacy that would be so powerful the Archangel would not know how he still carried it inside. Gabriel's full participation in this battle was paramount, too, for without the Archangel, there was no victory.

Hizkiel, with his cinnamon skin and legs like tree trunks, fought at their side. He flew shoulder-to-shoulder with the slender, fair-skinned Kasbeel. Their wings whipped the air, their bodies arching as a pair, a parried blow by one equaling an attack by the other. Their movements were grace and artistry, dancing with a speed to rival that of the Seraph's, if only he were able to join the fray.

Although he didn't fight, Barakiel's duties trumped those of his fellow warriors, even as the skirmish raged around him. Too brilliant to look upon with his six wings and his Sword of Power, he held high the standard, calling the final two into play, with a third to join them if Kafziel could be convinced to fight for the cause of good. Barakiel's mission on this night was not to join the contest, but to be the encouragement for those who must fight. He must stay strong, so the others could be victorious.

Encased in his cocoon of power, the Seraph watched over a scene of destruction that raged the breadth of the desert. Three of the Triune Mind's Four Familiars—Swiftness excepted— also had the six wings of the Seraphim, and they were covered with eyes that could see forwards and backwards at the same time. They were quicker than the gleam of silver, and they only had one limitation, their blind one-sidedness, their inability to think within a fight, to see what outcomes might evolve if tactics changed, and to be able to give up a small conquest in order to be the victor at the end of a larger one. The Four Familiars who had once sat at the feet of the Triune Mind only knew to *respond*.

One of the Four Familiars—and only one—held his anger in check. Nobility wore the guise of a lion, but while his corporeal body had assumed the shape of the king of beasts, no one would mistake that mighty steed for any lion ever birthed on Earth. He waged war as well, but it was his nature to war fairly. Fair was relative, though, for Nobility's legs were logs of the toughest oak, and his mane was the fire of the sun. The brothers of the Unity trembled in his presence. When that majestic feline roared, esteemed brothers of the greatest valor fell faint in their tracks.

The strength of the Ox was in that very lack of nobility. The massive beast charged and destroyed, taking possession of what he would, and none dared stand in his way.

The Eagle's swiftness showed the most amazing trait of the Four. When angered, the oversized bird could be in one location, and then in another, with no perceptible pause in between. Massive talons could slash the eyes of one victim, and at the next moment, be miles away, the great beak tearing at the limbs of another.

A Man who was more than a man brought wisdom into the mix. This Man was taller and broader than the largest human. His arms were as thick as any brother's waist, and his hands could crush a foe's skull in a single pulse of pressure. His truest strength was in his insight, and in moments of calm, he could speak with the wisdom of the great sages of Earth's past and present. It was when he was aroused that he became the thunder upon the hills, and all creation cowered, fearing for its existence.

This dark night, Eagle's claws slashed brothers' wings, shearing feathers and flesh. Tall, angelic bodies fell, crushed, only salvaged by their rapid healing capabilities. Incisors tore legs, snapping tendons and flaying muscle. Mighty hands crushed ribs and wings, flinging decimated brothers far afield.

It would be no easy victory for the Four from the Seat of Power, though, for the fight was more than evenly matched.

Their strength and power was dulled by the blind rage that ruled their every move. For where Strength charged in blindly, his massive muscles creating a battering ram, Hizkiel feinted, relying on plans long practiced as Gabriel's aide during battle. In Hizkiel's feint, Strength could not change direction quickly enough, and his blows danced wild.

Strength eventually began to tire.

When Nobility leaped at Kasbeel, his incisors extended, the brother used avarice against the Lion, uncaring whether he played fairly or not. Kasbeel used whatever ploy was at hand, sometimes a jagged rock slammed against an eye, more often a dimensional interface into a previous incarnation, one larger, meaner, or quicker than the Lion. The shape-shifting drained Kasbeel's internal energy reserves, but the brother's form flickered so rapidly that Nobility never knew what he was fighting from minute to minute, and he became wearied and confused.

Nobility was bound to fairness, and it kept him in check.

Jeremiel and Gabriel together braved Wisdom and Swiftness. Wisdom's failing was to become angered, and in that rising fury, his strength of mind faded against the blood red rage splashed all around him. His arm missed as often as it connected, mislaid more and more the angrier he grew. Even Swiftness with all his skill could not bolster the debilitating fatigue brought about by Wisdom's anger.

Still, Gabriel's leadership burned less brightly than it could, and Jeremiel knew the cause. The news about Uriel had sapped his strength, for without love, there is no purpose.

Enveloped in the cacophony of the battle, there were small moments of sanity and quiet, and Jeremiel nudged the Archangel in quick whispers and small suggestions, reminding him of Uriel's long-ago love. It had transcended genders, incarnations, and the test of time. Redemption was available to everyone, Jeremiel whispered, and Uriel was not lost. He simply had to be found. Love once known could be revived, as long as someone still cared.

Gabriel's heart was strengthened, and his powers flowed freely. The stars overhead quivered against his might, and his cries shredded the very air their corporeal bodies breathed.

Had Raphael the Healer arrived sooner, Gabriel's strength might have been enough. Raphael's touch would have provided renewal for any injury, and each injured brother could have rejoined the battle almost as soon as he was down. However, the Familiars wreaked so much havoc upon the brothers' ever more fragile corporeal bodies, that their healings began to slow as their energy reserves failed them. As one by one they collapsed to rise no more, the Familiars gleefully cast the brothers' winnowed husks to the four winds of the world, leaving the lives inside flickering to fade away until they were no more.

Even as they achieved a measure of success, the Familiars felt constrained to pursue a mission still unfulfilled. They must find the rest of the Seven with a Common Cause. Their goal was decimation. They *must* locate them, for once they had completed their mission, the Triune Mind would be released. Gadreel had promised it would be so.

Yet, when the four were cast far away, the Seraph remained, and with his Sword, he was invincible. Remaining in his position was the wisest thing he did, for his Sword was only a safeguard while held high over his head. Once lowered and joined in battle, he faced the very real possibility of defeat. It was not a risk worth indulging, for still there were two more brothers on the way. The path must be marked, no matter the cost. The four companions of the Circle of Brothers, those who had been cast to the winds, could be recovered, nursed to health, and the battle rejoined. If all were taken down, there was no hope.

Despite the Sword's power, the Four Familiars did try to barrage Barakiel's inpenetrable stronghold. Even with all they'd done, their fury was not spent. After much fruitless charging, shrieking, and otherwise useless antics, the Four listened to a slowly calming Wisdom and decided it was a better choice to hunt for the ones they could maim and destroy, rather than spend themselves against this one who would not break his stance and fight fairly.

Only when they were gone did Barakiel lower his sword in

weariness, letting it drop to hang at his side. The blade's light dimmed as he sank into misery, aware of what he'd allowed to happen. In the crush of his despair, his face was visible for the first time in many centuries: the redness of his skin, as if freckled wildly with no place left untouched, and red hair the color of flame, the ends at jarringly discordant angles. Barakiel was strikingly beautiful, as were all the brothers, and yet his beauty was a fact of which he was unaware. He was simply Barakiel, and at this moment, he had let his companions down.

Even Gabriel, gone!

Weakened in his despair, he eventually dropped into a crouch, then to his knees, one hand on the Sword, its tip buried in the soil. Only the glow of his atmospheric corporeal disharmony lit the night. His thoughts were those of misery, and he had more than enough to share.

Raphael, Angel of Healing

That was the broken Seraph Raphael and Elemiah found, a brother and a twin, the surrounding desert blanched with the fury of beings so powerful that Earth had never seen the like. An eagle—Gabriel's familiar—let out an alarmed shriek, and it settled to the ground near Barakiel. It hopped several times, its wings outspread, before finally coming to a restless standstill.

"My errand took too long." Raphael murmured his self-abasement. He had been to garner help, albeit of the human kind. Now, he wished he hadn't lingered. Who could have predicted this, though?

"Brother." Elemiah called to Barakiel.

Raphael knew the sound of that voice, and he heard the sorrow it held. He watched as Elemiah knelt at his twin's side, and for the first time in recorded history, the mighty Seraph laid his Sword at his feet, releasing it from his touch. His brilliance faded to the normal glow carried by all brothers, and in appearance, he and his twin were one.

"Look at me, my closest friend. Those who were defeated have not come to an end."

"I have failed, Brother." Barakiel looked up, his faded light revealing the brokenness etched upon his features.

Raphael knew the truth. This was not Barakiel's failure. It was his. He glanced away, the shame washing over him. He could have saved the day, if only he had come when he could.

"Gabriel's trusted familiar is still our companion." Elemiah nodded towards the eagle. "Where one walks beside us, the other will soon do so again."

"I would that it were so." Barakiel still didn't stand, the tip of his Sword buried in the soil, his light dimmed to the gray of desperation.

"I see your Sword touches ground." Elemiah rose, noticeably exuberant, and pointing to where the tip of his twin's weapon touched dirt. He paused expectantly, his couplet remaining incomplete, the power of his words charging the air around them.

"And should it not?" Barakiel's expression remained downcast.

"It should, and it does, if we wish for our friends to be found." His couplet now complete, Elemiah gleefully went on. "With our Swords, we can read what has transpired. One Sword carries strength, two stir creation's fires. Yours and mine at the same time, and our misplaced brothers we may find."

"I begin to see where your words lead, my Brother. Our Swords shall be one!" There was new life in Barakiel's countenance, and he stood, grabbing the hilt of his sword.

Raphael smiled, his hope renewed. The Twins were again as one, doing what they did best. They were working in tandem, and that was much of their strength.

With equal excitement, Elemiah snatched his Sword from where it lay on the ground, and he dramatically lifted it high over his head. With a powerful two-handed thrust, he buried it deep in the soil, the blade just shy of brushing Barakiel's.

As he held the hilt of his Sword with both hands, Elemiah's brilliance returned, slowly at first, then with a rush of magnificence that scoured the desert. With little more than a momentary pause, he placed his glowing hand on his brother's, uniting the two Swords with his touch, and immediately, Barakiel flashed with his own unequaled brilliance, causing Raphael to bow his head. They had become a single entity, their power doubled and more.

Even Gabriel's familiar squawked and turned, unable to face the Seraphim's overpowering flood of blinding power.

Raphael watched as the soil visibly rippled, and dust rose from underneath the Seraphim's feet, moving out in concentric circles, faster and faster. A low rumble accompanied the disturbance of dust, the soil itself crying its melodic question to each molecule positioned along the way.

"You are brilliant, my brother." Barakiel laughed. "If they touch soil anywhere on this planet, we will know."

Of course, those four whom they had just lost would be the only brothers they could touch, for anyone who had been on Earth any length of time would have shifted out of phase with the Seraphim's Swords. Also, anyone not touching the ground would be as good as invisible, for the Swords of Power could not read into concrete and wood. Metal was an unknown. The Swords' tips had never been sunk into that heat-fired substance, for its use in building human structures was a relatively recent occurrence on Earth.

When the Twins finally pulled the Swords from the ground, they exulted, crouching and parrying in mock swordplay. Just once the blades touched, and a towering spray of sparks sizzled far into the sky, fireworks of an unearthly kind.

"You have their locations?" Raphael wished it so, for then he could travel to find them. His white hair and long fingers flickered with sparks of excitement, a glittering showcase of miniature fireworks of his own. The sparks he exuded were part of his Healing Mandate, and each white feather on his wings dripped with its own dollop of brilliant light.

Barakiel laughed. "No, not *have*. The images from the Swords are ghosts, only."

"But you used both. I saw the soil move. The Swords are the mightiest power sources in the Unity. How can they not show the locations of our four brothers who have been so cruelly cast aside?" They were amazing engines of power, indeed, for they produced energy in dizzying amounts. It was their uses as weapons that concerned them now.

"To indicate the distance, it works. Now to find them, we must search." Obviously, that was Elemiah.

"Where? Tell me, and I am gone." Raphael's wings were already in motion, and he lifted a few inches from the ground. He wished to be away, to provide healing for those who had been lost.

"Farther than you know." Elemiah grabbed the Healer's arm, pulling him back to Earth. "To the corners of the continent we must go."

"They were carried there? So quickly?"

"Not carried." For a time Barakiel's face fell with the memory. Misery rang from his voice as he wailed, "Thrown!"

"Impossible!" Yet, Raphael didn't consider wings that appeared at the clap of his hands impossible, or even living in a great vessel that no human could see to be so incredible. Impossible in this case was simply what he could not comprehend.

"Not impossible, and you know it."

"Then who has done such a thing?" Raphael could imagine no one, or at least no one who was free. "Only the Triune Mind and his Familiars are capable of such a feat. They are Encapsulated to a one."

"It seems not anymore."

Before Barakiel could be questioned about his cryptic remark, two feet landed heavily on the ground at their side. It was Kafziel, gasping and wheezing, and he immediately clapped his wings away with a flash of light, although one that paled in comparison to that of the Seraphim's Swords.

"You didn't wait on me." He gasped several more times before catching his breath. "Do you always fly like bats out of the depths of hell?" Then he noticed the destruction strewn across the desert floor around them. He turned and searched the damage as far as he could see. "What do you think happened here?"

"It seems the Pets have been released."

All the brothers knew of them as the Mind's Pets, and that

one word spoke eons of information.

"Holy Triune Mind!" Not even Kafziel was ignorant of what that meant. They had several thousand years of pent-up anger to expel. "Who do you think they're after?"

"Us, it would appear."

At Barakiel's words, Kafziel paled and started to back away. Raphael nodded to Elemiah, for that brother had no patience with the Watcher.

"Not so fast, Brother." Elemiah reached to grab his arm. "Now we work together. We struck a deal, one which cannot be unsealed." He released the arm, and Kafziel stayed put.

"At your bidding," the white-haired Healer mused, "we chase Uriel. At someone else's bidding, the Pets attack us. Would you know the reason why?"

Kafziel looked sharply uneasy, and he hesitated before blurting in a jumbled way, "Just a few miles back as the crow flies is an overturned truck beside the road. The headlights are still on, and that means the driver might still live. I thought you might be interested, Raphael."

With a sudden leap, the Seraphim, along with Raphael and the eagle, exploded towards the sky.

Kafziel, Emissary of Solitude and Tears

Kafziel's distraction had worked. He wouldn't have to answer Raphael's question anytime soon.

Despite his brilliant evasion, he would need to join him, if he wanted his sudden concern to be convincing. Raising his hands, he clapped them together, and in a flash of reduced brilliance, his wings appeared on his shoulders. He flapped them tiredly, all out of energy. When that wasn't enough to lift him from the ground, he bent his knees and leaped the slightest amount, pumping his wings a little more strongly. He finally got himself aloft, and he slowly made his way after the other three and Gabriel's familiar.

Rikkianne Kristofferson, Asst. Motel Manager

"Nigel!" Rikkianne grabbed his knee and shook it, pulling her robe tightly around her waist. Shaking her head to clear her thoughts, she stood by his chair, picked up the remote, and turned the TV off. This late it was all static, anyway. At least he'd gotten them fixed, every TV in every room, if what happened could be called fixed. He hadn't even been on the roof when they started working again; it was more that they had all flickered onto the correct channels all by themselves. He couldn't explain it, and she didn't care.

Now, they had someone up front.

"Huh?" He jumped when the static faded. He blinked his eyes several times, clearing the sleep away. "Morning, already?"

"Someone ringing at the desk. You sleep. I'm already up." She pulled her robe tighter, unwilling to get dressed at this hour. It was too much to ask, when it was almost dawn.

"Bobby, maybe? His momma called about him. Seems he didn't come home when he should. Wanted me to check on the roof." He yawned.

Rikkianne looked at him, her heart filled with love. He was a sight to behold, with his hair sticking up in the back, and sleep in the corner of his eyes. He even cared about Bobby. She never had any kids of her own, and the boy was likely the closest she'd ever get at her age. She knew she picked on him, but that was how she showed him she loved him.

At least that's the way she thought of it.

She sighed. "I done talked to Mrs. Dalton, too. I told her, I find him, I'd send him right home. Don't think Bobby'd ring the front bell, though." She stood for a moment, her hand on the back of his chair, then the bell rang again. "I'm going up, Nigel."

He patted her hand. "Okay, baby. I might close my eyes for one second. Then I'll be up to help you out." He shifted in his chair, but his lids were already shut.

"Sure, Nigel." She didn't mind. After all, she loved him more than she had ever loved anyone before.

When she opened the back door to the office, she was surprised to see a pretty little woman outside the front glass door with a big dog at her side. The surprise was that she didn't see a car in the parking lot. Most people at night pulled up in the spaces right beside the door. She could see their cars there. If she could see their cars, it made her feel safer.

Even so, this woman didn't *feel* dangerous. Be that as it may, that was a mighty big dog. Wolf big, or maybe even bigger. The dog seemed to be pushing frantic, too. It was sniffing around, its snout pointing this way, then that. It never left the woman's side, though, like it was her bodyguard. Lucky for the woman, for Rikkianne knew there were things in the desert that needed a good meal from time to time. They didn't usually bother people, but sometimes they did.

Reaching the door, she called out through the glass, "Hey, honey! Need a room?" She took a long time looking through her ring of keys, waiting on the woman's reply. If her voice was off, slurred or something like, she wouldn't open the door at all. She didn't need any druggies in the motel at night.

"Oh, I'm so glad you're here." Jeri held up a wad of bills, pressing them to the glass. "Yes, a room, but my car broke down a mile or two out, and my kids are in it. Do you think you can take me to get them?" She smiled with a look that spoke of pleading.

Seeing the money, Rikkianne found the correct key immediately, and she had the door opened in a flash. "Come in, honey. You got kids? Stranded out there? Oh, you must be sicker'n a dog." When the woman stepped in, she was surprised to see the dog, a wolf indeed, she realized, dart in at the same time, immediately sniffing everything in the room. "Honey, gotta get your dog to stay outside."

Jeri's eyes were red, and her voice was shaky, quickly crawling upwards in pitch as she spoke. "The dog's not mine. We sort of adopted each other out on the road. I'm Jeri. If I pay for the room now, can I get that ride to pick them up? Please? My kids?"

Rikkianne couldn't miss the desperation in her voice, and she went and put her arm across the woman's shoulder. "Sweetie, you got you a ride. Just let me step back and tell my man. That lazy no-good'un can watch the desk for long as we need. Okay, honey? That be okay?" She stepped back to the front door. "Jeri, honey, I gotta ask you to step outside, though, so's I can lock the door. I'll pull the truck around. Then we'll head on out. Take your dog along, too." Then she paused and smiled. "I'm Rikkianne, by the way."

Jeri Franklin, Newly Single

When Jeri stepped outside, the wolf was immediately at her side. She had urgently needed the animal's company out in the dark, and she had appreciated the companionship, but she'd also cringed when it pushed inside the motel lobby with her. She couldn't let it keep her from a room. She was grateful the lady inside hadn't been upset at her, but then the animal had squeezed out the door as soon as it had seen her leaving.

Oh, how she had hated to admit she'd left her children out in the desert! What if this woman made her feel bad for leaving them locked in a car in the middle of the night?

When Rikkianne drove up in Nigel's old truck, she called to Jeri to climb on inside. It was no surprise to feel the truck shake as the wolf jumped in the back.

"Jeri, honey, that animal cain't stay in your room with you. I need you to know that right up front. Nigel won't go for it." She revved the engine, and the truck jumped when she let out the clutch.

Jeri leaned her head back, and tears of relief began to flow down her face. She just needed her children, and she knew without a doubt they were frightened to death out there all alone in the middle of the desert. How could she have done that to them? How, how, how?

Chapter 20

Interlude 16

Reinhardt Kinkerson was alive, although to look at him, no one would have guessed.

In the violent tumbling that broke his cannonball SUV's flight, his body had twisted viciously against his seat's restraints. His shoulder had cracked, and he had felt that. Then, when the violence of the first impact had ripped the seat restraint's bolts from the floor, he was thrown out of the vehicle as it rolled. On the way out, the steering wheel caught his chest, cracking three ribs, and forcing one of them deep into his right lung. He vaulted into the windshield while still in mid-air, and his cheekbone was shattered. As he hit the ground, one arm twisted up under his chest, snapping his forearm like a twig. He hadn't felt that. He was already unconscious.

The only real signs that he lived were the blood that still seeped from his mouth and a very slight rise and fall of his chest. He was twisted beyond what any normal body could take, and the filth of the desert soil, stirred by the crash, had settled to coat his skin and clothing with a brown sameness. Even one of his shoes had been ripped from his feet.

His SUV was easy to find. The truck's blazing lights were a

beacon to those who searched. Finding the man would be harder. The darkness blanketed him as securely as if he were inside a well.

The eagle was the one that saw him first, its cry piercing the darkness. When the others arrived, the creature was at Kinky's side with its wings out, hopping from side to side in desperation. The familiar could see, as the others soon would, that this man was holding to life by an exceedingly tenuous thread.

Raphael, Angel of Healing

Raphael was the next to land, with his white-feathered wings slowing his descent, and the touch of his feet on the ground as gentle as a leaf falling to Earth. His wings brushed the air twice, giving him time to balance before drawing to his side. Then, with a clap of his hands, light flashed, its brilliance washing across the destruction, and the brother stood as a man.

He dropped immediately at Kinky's side. From the twisted body, it was clear a great deal of damage had been done. If he were dead, he'd remain that way, no matter what the Healer tried to do. At least he wasn't in a state to feel pain. Raphael appreciated that small blessing. Then he caught the rise and fall of his chest, and hope surged within. His eyes drew out the extent of the damage in the crushed flesh and twisted limbs, not wishing his "help" to be the cause of additional pain.

He glanced up as the two Seraphim came down, also lightly, although at a good distance. Their Swords provided illumination, and the intensity of their brilliance could well blind the injured human when he woke. It made no difference that he was currently unconscious. Raphael's Mandate was that of Healing, and if any breath remained, this injured man would live again.

Such was the magnitude of Raphael's gift.

The Angel of Healing's first task was to check for a heartbeat. He had to be sure. He reached a hand down, his fingers long and slender, and he touched Kinky's neck up under his collar, keeping the fabric of the man's shirt between his "angel"

286

skin and that of the human. At the touch of the Healer's hand, Kinky moaned, and Raphael knew it for what it was, the sound more an involuntary response to the touch rather than an indication of discomfort at the pressure on his neck. He surveyed the twisted arm indicating broken bones and the blood at the mouth that told of a pierced lung. The shallow breathing suggested shock, and that meant this man's body was shutting down as he lay on the ground.

He must first be prepared for his healing, though. To rush this was to cause as much damage as the healing repaired. He breathed deeply, for this would draw from his own resources. He had a greater reservoir than his brothers, for his Mandate was to heal, but he still felt the most dramatic healings severely. He was ready, though. His Mandate demanded this of him.

For this injured man, a great miracle was about to happen.

Interlude 17

For all Raphael's impending touch of healing, the events playing themselves out in the desert night would have appeared quite ordinary had anyone been watching, and to a degree, it was. For, at that very moment, kneeling at the injured man's side, the Healer was no more than one man prepared to offer assistance to another. He had no wings, the Seraphim were unseen—as far as human eyes were concerned—and there was a tangled truck off to the side. A terrible accident had nearly taken a man's life, and a kind soul was willing to help.

Yet, looked at from a Biblical point of view, the picture was quite different, for this moment in time was washed with the essence of Biblical lore, and any child brought up in Sunday school would have recognized the story in a moment. Here was an injured traveler by the side of the road, beat up and left for dead. A man, perfect in physical form, with the inner glow of goodness spilling from his face, knelt at his side, his hand extended to help. Off to the side, two shining angels waited, poised to offer assistance. If the injured man could not be helped, they were also prepared to transport him to Heaven,

287

cradling him in their arms.

To those who might have looked closer, there was even more. In the small bits of shadows, they would have seen several things as odd. The first would be that Raphael wore no clothing as of yet. He was tall, golden-skinned, with a thick mane of curly white hair, and he was as naked as the day he was born. That was perfectly normal in the Unity, for clothing there was as odd as nudity on Earth. On Earth? It was not so normal, especially not in Arizona.

Another oddity would be the Seraphim, their violently brilliant light, their appearance less that of persons, and more of a twin arc laser, the lumens too great for the human eye to absorb, that was if the observer could focus on them at all. Men might look at the place where the Seraphim stood, and they might notice something visually slippery about that particular location. They wouldn't see the Seraphim, though. Their eyes would continually slide to the side, and if they didn't let it go, soon the luminance they couldn't quite see would begin to burn the back of their retinas. It would be painful for them, but the Seraphim would triumph, and soon the people native to this world would forget that there had been something there, something that they *hadn't* seen, something they didn't even know they had forgotten.

They would have a splitting headache, though.

The eagle would have been more recognizable to the human race, for its like had been part of this world's ecosystems as far back as humans had memories of their world. The size of the bird would have amazed them, but they would have explained that by the use of words such as perspective, angle, and illusion. Then, a naturalist might be called, so that this new breed of bird could be observed, studied, and classified.

In reality, none of that mattered, because this night, only Kinky was there to see, and Kinky wasn't watching at all. The brothers had nothing to worry about when it came to being observed, as if they ever worried where humans were concerned. It was more the likes of Familiars from the Seat of Power that concerned them, that and one particular brother who seemed to be always in the thick of whatever disturbance was at hand but conveniently out of the line of fire when the battles started. That was Kafziel, and in the darkness of the desert night, he finally made his belated appearance once again.

Raphael, Angel of Healing

Raphael glared at Kafziel as he lumbered in, his landing clumsy and noisy. The brother was obviously tiring, but why, Raphael didn't know. The Healer could help him, if he wished, but Kafziel was not infirm. He was just stupid, and there was no healing for that, at least not that the Healer was willing to provide.

"Kafziel," he called. "I could use your help."

Raphael watched the errant brother kneel, his wings arched high over his shoulders. The image looked very much as many a marble angel might, one carved from stone and presiding over a grave, kneeling with tears for the dead. That would not be Kafziel, though. He was the Watcher over the Deaths of Kings, but he wasn't one to shed unwarranted tears. Raphael considered that he was simply posturing, and the Healer had no patience with his theatrics.

Raphael called again, harsher, "Kafziel! Since when did you receive the Mandate of Laziness? Get your ugly wings over here!"

Even as Kafziel stood, weariness in his every motion, Raphael was struck by how beautiful—handsome, to the humans of this world—he really was. His slender face; his rampant head of hair. His features were finely drawn, and there was no imperfection in his skin. Not even Kafziel's wings were ugly. It was his actions that lacked in appearance, his deceptiveness that kept the brother from being desirable.

He could still be helpful, though, and that was what Raphael demanded.

"I must lay this man out, make sure his arms and legs are straightened. Help me lift him." When Kafziel gave no indication he intended to do so, Raphael threw barbed accusations at him. "You flew over this man, leaving him, willing him to die unattended. You are the most despicable brother I know. I should withdraw your essence from within your very body."

"Try it, Healer. Draw my energies to give to this man. I dare you." Kafziel's words were bold, but the fear that Raphael might make good on his threat hovered in his eyes.

"Not this night. Help me roll him over." Raphael blazed for a moment, then with a conscious effort, he pushed his emotions to a safer place. He released the shoulder, and together they got Kinky to his back. "His arm." He indicated it as he reached to inspect the damage that had been done to the face.

"Um, Rapha-*el*." Kafziel had appeared cowed for a moment, but that was not his natural state. Arrogance fit him much more closely, and it exuded from him like grain mash through a colander—distasteful and twice as disgusting. "What a-*bout* his arm? Am I to just admire it?"

Raphael glared. "I intend to heal it. Please straighten it, Brother. Can you do that, or are you too pretty and too proud?"

Kafziel snorted. "You claimed my wings were ugly. Now I'm pretty?" He smiled, vamping a bit, his manner filled with an arrogance that baited the healer for spite. "You really think so?"

"Dear Unity! I despise brothers like you, and I always have." It was Raphael's suspicion that Kafziel had more to do with this than he wished to share. It rankled him, giving rise to a greater loss of self control than he wished to show. Even that rasped against his good nature, and he knew Kafziel's continued presence for what it was, an irritation beyond endurance. He focused his words carefully. "Lay it straight so the bone can knit properly. Place his hand just there." He reached and touched a location near Kinky's waist.

Kafziel did as he was asked, but he callously spit out, "You don't even know this person. If you would just let him die, it would be a natural ending to a life he probably hasn't enjoyed living. That's why I flew on by earlier. I wanted him to go peacefully, instead of prolonging his agony."

At Kafziel's unfeeling, cruel comments, the eagle screeched, its wings opening wide, and several carefully timed flaps carrying it into the air and forward a bit before settling back down.

Raphael laughed. "It seems someone else shares my opinion of you. Now, step back, Brother. I have a healing to perform." He reached and placed a hand on Kinky's chest. "Fade, if you will. You wear your wings, yet. This man should not see you here."

With no further to-do, Raphael's hand started to glow brightly, until all of him matched. Next, the man on the ground began to shine with his own aura, and it was clear his body was beginning to mend.

The miracle of healing had begun.

Kafziel, Emissary of Solitude and Tears

Kafziel glanced at the Seraphim, then back at Raphael, and he chuckled sourly. "You, Raphael, wear nothing at all. You are no longer in the Unity. Perhaps this man should not see *you* here."

He did fade, though, as Raphael had requested, desiring Kinky's eyes to slip around him, not quite seeing his presence. True to character, he did it in his own time, after watching the injured man's body rapidly mend, the damage to the skin repairing itself, the areas where bones had been broken smoothing into something akin to perfection. Even Kinky's face, twisted with the impact on the windshield, shifted slightly, the bones rearranging themselves, and kitting properly in the process. Just at the end, Kinky jerked, his chest dancing in the direction of Raphael's hand, and he gasped, sucking in a great draught of air. His eyes flew wide, and he looked around frantically.

Kafziel waited, first as Kinky found the Healer's face, then as his eyes were drawn his direction. He flung his curls back from his face, and he thrust his wings out, showing himself to be the greatest, most glorious angel of all time. Then, with no warning, he gave a clap of his hands; light flooded the scene; and he felt the weight of his wings disappear, leaving him only a man, albeit beautiful and glowing, unclothed except for a wrap at his loins.

Immediately afterwards, Kafziel "suggested" that Kinky's

eyes slide sideways, and he disappeared completely. All that would be left was a sort of oddness in the darkness, a fuzziness, a hard-to-grasp place in the night, one where the reporter's eyes would refuse to rest.

There, Raphael. Enjoy that!

Kafziel smiled, very pleased with himself.

Raphael, Angel of Healing

Raphael didn't catch Kafziel's shenanigan, but he did see Kinky's response. His eyes opened wide, the whites showing; and his breathing came in great gasps.

He was a man in sensory overload.

"Did you see that?" Kinky glanced at Raphael, and his hand pointed. "That, that angel?"

Raphael was furious. He could see Kafziel just fine, and he shot him a look of pure irritation.

Kafziel shrugged.

Before Raphael could berate him for his insolence, his attention was grabbed once more by the man on the ground.

"Were you in the accident, too?"

"Me?" Raphael smiled. "Part of your automobile accident?"

"Well, I must have hit someone, and your clothes have been torn completely off." Kinky struggled to sit, and he inspected the tattered rags covering his own limbs. He muttered to Raphael, "How are you not dead?"

Raphael glanced down, groaning in despair. He'd been careless, letting this man's healing override all other concerns. To humans, clothing was paramount over all else.

He could fudge his answers, though.

"Yes," Raphael began, smiling warmly at the man. "There has been an accident, and I could not avoid being part of it." It was a half-truth, but at least it was for the right reason. "When I can, I will dress. My apologies. I thought checking on you more important."

"I do appreciate that, and don't kid yourself otherwise. It's just . . . you wouldn't believe it." Kinky shook his head sideways, his eyes still dazed. "I saw an angel, wings and all." He laughed. "I felt I died, and right before I reached the Pearly Gates, I got pulled back to Earth, just as I had a vision of Heaven. That must have been my angel, carrying me back to Earth. Whew! What a ride!"

"An angel, huh." Raphael looked to Kafziel to find a smirk of arrogance on his face. *Fool!* A true angel would bring kindness and benevolence. Kafziel knew nothing of the sort.

Kinky paused, reaching to run a hand through his hair, and pulling it back from his forehead. He chuckled as if embarrassed at all the trouble he'd caused. "I feel fine, now. I must have gotten a real bonk to the old noggin. Scrambled my brain for a bit."

"Come. You must stand." Raphael stood, his body's glow thankfully diminished with the healing he'd performed. If this man observed him glowing in the dark, he'd claim a second angel wandering the desert. That wouldn't do at all. Raphael reached a hand to grasp the man's forearm. The newspaperman's long-sleeved shirt would allow them to touch.

"Thank you. I'm ready to get out of here. I was out for a drive, and zowie! I'm a dusty dummy." He chuckled. "Now if I can find my keys."

"Your vehicle is damaged beyond repair, I'm afraid. Come, walk with me. We'll find something along this road, even if it's only the upcoming morning."

He also knew the two Seraphim, Gabriel's familiar, and hopefully Kafziel would be along also, although he was the only one this man would see. He glared at Kafziel, and his eyes narrowed. That brother was a deceitful one, doing as requested, but always with his own agenda stirred into the mix. He wasn't to be trusted.

Kinky waved his hand off, climbing up from the ground on his own. Before they could move very far, a siren, distant yet, called to them across the desert floor. On the horizon the faintest crack of light split the night into soil and sky, reaching from the north to the south, announcing that the coming morning was on the way. It was as if a great eye was lifting a heavy lid, and sleep had been washed away.

"You hear that siren? Was that you called 9-1-1? Beats me where you carry your phone, though!" Kinky grinned, clasping Raphael on the bare skin of his shoulder, only to have his hand slip right off, causing him to stumble. He laughed. "I guess I missed there. Maybe my eyes got bonked, too, either that, or my aim's off."

Raphael knew differently. Human skin couldn't touch "angel" skin. He put his hand on Kinky's neck, grasping him firmly just below his collar, and he laughed.

"You should see your truck. If your aim's a little off, you can be sure no one will care. You're alive, and that's what's important."

"Well, it looks like our First Responders will be disappointed to see that I'm up and at 'em. They'll have made a wasted trip. Thanks for calling, though. I could have died back there. You just never know when the end's going to come, do you? I sure lucked out this time. Good God, I feel alive!"

"You're welcome, but I didn't call." That someone had actually done so had him puzzled. Who would have notified the authorities? Not Kafziel, for certain. He went on to explain, "Sorry. All I did was stop by to see if you needed help. I'm glad to know you're fine."

Kafziel, off to the side, was making impatient gestures, telling him he needed to wrap up his interactions with this stranger. Raphael shook his head in rebuttal and looked away, noticing the Seraphim as well as Gabriel's second, the Archangel's familiar, were no longer in sight.

"Hey, there's my bag." Kinky walked around a clump of cacti, grabbing the handle of a small leather case lying upside down in the dirt. He shook it off, turning to Raphael with a grin. "I always carry an extra suit of clothes in this. Just in case, you know. Glad to see this survived. Fifteen hundred from Bergdorf's. That's New York, you know. It takes a licking and keeps on ticking. Timex, but still, you get the picture."

"Clothes, you say? Perhaps, if you don't mind—" About that time, Raphael heard a voice whisper in his ear. "Food, Brother. I cannot wait any longer." Then, the sound of wings brushed his hearing, and he turned to see Kafziel soaring into the sky.

Kinky looked around, a puzzled look on his face. "That was the oddest gust of wind just then. Did you feel it? Oh, and by the way, my name is Kinkerson. Reinhardt Kinkerson. All my friends call me Kinky." Then he laughed. "If you're going to be wearing my pants, I guess you get to call me Kinky, too."

He opened the bag and pulled out a tightly bound roll of clothing fastened with a leather belt. Tossing it at Raphael, he called, "Hope you're a whitie-tightie kind of man, 'cause that's all I've got." He turned, looking at the slowly brightening sky, giving Raphael a chance to pull on the clothes. "Never quite pictured another man in my whities, but somehow, this one morning, it seems all right with me. God, I feel good!" He drew in a deep mouthful of fresh, clean desert air, holding it for a moment before letting it go. "I've never felt so good in my life!"

Raphael grinned as he pulled a pair of lightweight slacks up over his new "whitie-tighties." He wasn't really an underwear man at all, at least not while in the Unity. That aside, he was certainly grateful for the clothes.

Pulling on his new shirt, one touting a brightly flowered Hawaiian pattern, he looked down at his feet. Kinky must have short legs, he figured, because at least four inches of his ankles showed between the hem of the pants and his ankles. They were doable, though. His crotch was covered, and that was the important thing, for humans, at least.

A fire truck pulled over a slight rise, its lights glaring. The siren wailed one last time and cycled down with an extended, mournful note, hiccupping once at the end. Immediately afterward, an ambulance flew up behind it, and two paramedics tumbled out.

"Good Lord!" The first one grabbed a black bag, his feet kicking up brown desert dust. "Someone was driving that?" He pointed to the overturned SUV, then looked at Kinky and Raphael for confirmation.

The firemen were unloading also, checking the scene, making sure the vehicle was safe for the paramedics.

"Don't see no one," one of them called. "Must have been

thrown free. Got a whole door missing here."

"Did you find the driver?" That was the second paramedic, and he looked at the two oddly dressed men, one in filthy, torn clothing, and the other wearing pants that clearly didn't fit him well.

Kinky slapped his chest, sending dust flying. "You're looking at him! Not a scratch anywhere."

The paramedic stepped up to him. "Sir, you've got blood all over your face. You've been scratched somewhere, even if you can't feel it." He reached to touch Kinky's face, only to find undamaged skin underneath the blood. He frowned. "Sir, was someone else riding with you?" He glanced at Raphael, who was obviously free of injuries. His clothes were even clean.

Kinky backed away, throwing his arms in the air, reveling in the clear early-morning air. He turned in a circle, his face to the sky, his eyes closed. Laughing, he called out, "Just me, and I'm alive! Take that, death!" He punched a fist into the sky, hooting with enthusiasm.

Raphael grinned at the man he'd saved. Times like this were when he appreciated his Mandate. People like Kinky made it worth all the effort.

An eagle's cry split the air. None of the humans looked up. Eagles were a natural part of the desert. Raphael knew that this one wasn't, though. The sound was Gabriel's familiar, and it called for its master.

That bothered him. He didn't know where everyone else had gone. There would be no mental communication with Kafziel, and the Seraphim were not responding. He accepted that he was with Kinky for the time being. Everything else would have to take care of itself. As one of this world's holy books so rightly stated, there were a time and season for everything, and now was for Kinky.

Distracting him, Kinky slapped him on the back, the new shirt keeping his hand from slipping away. "Daydreaming? Come on. We're being offered a ride back to town. I didn't get your name, by the way." He grinned at the brother, his enjoyment of life bubbling out uncontrollably.

"Raphael."

"Like the angel in the Bible?"

"Just like the angel in your holy book. If you wish, all my friends call me Ralph." No one had before, but he needed this man to trust him.

"Sure." Kinky paused, then the "Suggestion" took hold, and his face relaxed. "Sure! Ralph! How are you doing, Ralph?" He slapped Raphael's back once again.

However, a Suggestion was just that, a suggestion. To erase casual encounters, they worked fine. Kinky's experience had not been casual at all. He had been dead, or so close that it wouldn't have made any difference, not if the Angel of Healing hadn't shown up. He had been given new life, and his first vision upon awakening had been of a beautiful and majestic angel. That had been no casual experience, and it wouldn't be so easily wiped away.

It was gone from his thoughts for the moment, though, and the ride back into town was very long. When Kinky suggested a place to eat breakfast together, Raphael readily agreed. He was hungry, not having eaten at all, and the healing had taken much from him. He'd have agreed to eat road kill, if it had been available.

There was one thing he asked Kinky about on the ride to town. Did he know any place to purchase long johns?

Kinky roared with laughter. "This is the desert, and it's high summer, the hottest week on record. What a hoot! You and I are going to get along just fine. I have an extra bed in my motel room. Do you need a place to stay?"

Raphael realized what he'd done. He'd made a human friend, although he wasn't sure about the wisdom in that. Setting that aside, he relented, smiling. "Sure, Kinky. Can I impose on you for some boxers, though? I seem to be all out of money, and I'll have to depend on you."

Kinky wiped his eyes as his laughter died away. "Sure, kid. You stopped to check on me while you were naked as a jaybird. You didn't even take time to get dressed. You thought you were saving my life, and I appreciate that a lot. Sure, I'll buy you all the underwear you need."

The paramedics looked at each other, a knowing look in

their eyes.

Raphael saw the look, and he didn't care. It made him want to protect Reinhardt Kinkerson, and that's what having a Mandate was all about.

Kafziel, Emissary of Solitude and Tears

Kafziel cursed, his words thrown at the sky and the air and Earth and Uriel and Gabriel. He had fled Raphael, and now he was entangled in the clothesline from which he had intended to steal clothes.

He had already tried to "slip" from the offending entrapment. He was too exhausted. Removing his wings had taken the last of his resources. Now, it was nearly dawn. With as much energy as he could command, he pulled until he snapped free of the line, landing roughly on the ground and covered in women's undergarments. Standing, he threw off Uriel's borrowed wrapping, tossing it over a fence, and he searched through the remaining items hanging around him. They were all women's things, and he gritted his teeth. He would choose the one house in Phoenix with only women's clothes out to dry.

He did locate a pair of shorts, cuffed and very petite. Slipping them on, he grimaced as he zipped the fly. The crotch was not made to accommodate his male anatomy. He twisted his body to settle into the confines of the shorts, deciding he could manage for a few hours.

All the tops were rather diaphanous, though, with bright flower print patterns. Several were low cut, and most made liberal allowances for breasts, ones that he didn't have. Then he came across one that was more of a tent, with large pockets and a contrasting collar. It had a name sewn on it, but it buttoned all the way up, had half sleeves, and was a solid color. He snatched it from the line and slipped his arms inside. When he buttoned it, he was relieved to find it came nearly to the hem of the shorts. He didn't want to make a spectacle of himself. All he wanted was food.

When he stepped into the street, the glare of headlights

assaulted him.

"Rush hour," he muttered. There had been cars when he'd flown in, but the number had increased threefold in the twenty minutes he'd taken to get dressed. Still, the rush of drivers might work in his favor. The more people, the less likely he was to be noticed.

Seeing cars pulling into a parking lot on the corner, he glanced at the sign over the door. ALL YOU CAN EAT. BREAKFAST UNTIL 11:00 AM. He felt his stomach knot with hunger, and relief flooded him. The brightly lighted parking lot was a plus, too. The natural glow of his skin wouldn't show.

Opening the door, an older woman with a red beehive called to him, "Come on in, honey. You must be new." She winked at him. "Employees use the back door, though. You might remember that next time." She laid down her pencil and pad of paper, and she walked toward him. Closer, her eyes glanced at his shirt, and she peered back at his face. "Um, you don't look much like Bridgette, honey. She sick again?"

"Bridgette?" He frowned. She had called him . . . *Bridgette*?

"Sure, honey. The name on your smock. Are you filling in today? I hope so, because that girl's late almost every other Friday, if she gets here at all. By the way, you have the most beautiful hair. You clock in at the back. Maylene'll take care of you. Just tell her you've already talked to Momma. Everybody calls me that." She pointed to a door he could just see. "Through the kitchen. You can't miss it. Oh, and with those legs, she'll want to loan you a pair of pants. For a looker like you, short-shorts are a no-no while on duty. Too many traveling salesmen got the wandering fingers, if you get my message."

Kafziel bit back his irritation at the woman's mistaken assumptions. Food must take precedence over everything else, and he didn't dare let his temper shatter this opportunity. He modulated his words carefully, one at a time. "I'm sorry. I haven't eaten breakfast, yet. Do you think I could get something before I clock in?" He smiled, pushing a Suggestion her way.

Momma frowned for a fraction of a second, then her brow smoothed. "Sure, honey. Just don't punch the clock until you do. Breakfast is on your time. Tell Maylene to put it on

299

Bridgette's tab. Oh," she smiled, "you've got something going with that sultry voice. You're going to bring in some tips today, hon."

The waitress chuckled and winked as she walked away. Kafziel shrugged it off. He now had breakfast on his plate, or at least as soon as he talked to Maylene, and then the day would be his. His daughter was still out there in Uriel's grasp, and he didn't know just how, but he intended to get her back.

Chapter 21

Bobby Dalton, Motel Rat

Bobby stirred awake, squeezing his eyes shut against the light from around the curtain. He moved his tongue in his mouth, aware of the thickness of his saliva. He needed to brush his teeth.

He rolled onto his back, still in his clothes. It was hot. The electric must be off again. Then he remembered where he was. His mom was going to be *so* angry.

He sat up on his elbows, and he glanced around. Angioletta —Ms. Bacciarelli—was next to him. He searched for the man from the bathtub. He turned to the next bed to see the linens all crumpled, kicked aside, and the man lying face down.

Unlike Ms. Bacciarelli, this man wore nothing at all, and Bobby jerked his eyes away. He'd never seen a naked man before.

Still. He was drawn to him, a man who was alive when he should be dead. That made him a magnet Bobby couldn't resist.

He tried to look without being obvious.

The man's head was on the pillow, with his face turned Bobby's direction. Dark, curly hair tumbled from his scalp, and his far arm was up above his head. The closer one was stretched out, his hand cupped as if he were about to grasp something. Underneath the skin, the arms were thick with muscles.

That got Bobby to thinking. Maybe the man was a hunter, and he used a bow instead of a gun. Some hunters did. If he were a bank robber, it would have to be a gun, though. The idea of pointing an arrow at someone, saying, Stick 'em up! struck the boy as funny, and he grinned.

The man's back was massive. *Bodybuilder*, Bobby decided. Someone would have to lift weights to have a back like that. His waist wasn't fat at all, though, and that surprised him. People he knew who were that solid in the upper body—his wrestling teacher at his junior high last year—usually had a thick waist. Not this man.

His eyes uncomfortably skipped the man's buttocks and dropped to his legs. One knee pointed toward Bobby, and the other leg reached for the foot of the bed. There was no doubt this man could run and jump better than anyone he knew.

Then the man's head shifted, his face working through several mysterious expressions, and Bobby's eyes jerked away once again, embarrassed. At fourteen, everything embarrassed him, even admiration for a man he'd seen grow new skin right before his eyes.

Gently, he crawled from the bed. When the woman stirred, he froze, waiting for her to settle, then he gently stepped to the man's side. He had to see that shoulder. Last night Bobby had gone for more snacks and drinks, telling them he knew how to get into the storeroom where they were kept. When he'd come back, the man had already been in bed and had eaten everything that had been on the floor. Bobby had dumped his new stash on his bed, unwrapping one item after another, while the man consumed it all.

He leaned in and studied the skin he'd watched grow the previous night. Except for those bumps that still covered part of his arm, it was as smooth as a girl's.

The man made a sound, and Bobby studied his face. In art the previous semester, the class had studied angel paintings from old times. The angels had looked just like this man, with his black hair and light skin.

Impulsively, Bobby reached to touch the man's shoulder. His palm slipped across the newly grown skin, as if there was an unseen barrier separating them, and he lost his balance. He yelped as he fell on the bed, right on the man.

Faster than he could imagine, the man twisted and wrapped his arms around him, his hands under Bobby's armpits, holding the boy's chest to his own and leaving Bobby's legs dangling off the bed. Face to face, green eyes bored into Bobby. He was so scared that he was certain he'd wet himself if this man held him any longer.

"I'm sorry," he squeaked. "Please? I didn't mean anything. I just wanted to touch your shoulder."

"Could you?" The words were clipped.

"Could I what?" Bobby was all confusion by then.

"Could you touch my shoulder?" Uriel's voice was softer this time.

"No?" His answer was a question, but he knew with a flash of desperation that he should have gone to the toilet as soon as he got up. "Can I go to the bathroom now?"

"I thought not."

"Please, sir. I can't hold it much longer."

"First, you are how old?" Uriel pursed his lips. "Tell me that."

"Fourteen, sir." Bobby frowned. This man smelled different. Cake. No, *vanilla*. That made him grin in spite of his need to get away.

"Fourteen is funny?"

"You smell like cake. Please, I have to pee." He struggled, but when he tried to grab the man's arms to force them off, he couldn't.

Uriel laughed, making him struggle harder. Their exposed skin finally made contact, and the shock of electric fire forced them apart. Uriel threw his hands wide, calling out a curse.

"What'd you do to me?" Bobby yelped, curling up on the bed in pain.

"I didn't do it. You did, when you touched me. Sorry kid. I'm untouchable." Uriel readjusted his position on the bed and wrapped both arms under his head. "That hurt like hell for me, too. You're the one who brought me the food last night, aren't you?"

Bobby nodded.

"Good for you. You have a helpful spirit, and I like you. I'm Uriel. Your name?"

"Uriel? Isn't that like one of the angels in the Bible? Do people actually call you that?"

Uriel laughed. "Either that or you can shorten it to U. Uri, maybe. I'm not picky. Your name?"

"Um . . ." Bobby glanced at Angioletta, her eyes still closed. "Can you pull your sheet up? You're, um, not wearing anything. That's, um, creepy."

Uriel laughed again. "Sure, kid. I apologize. I didn't think about it." He grasped the top of the sheet with a foot and kicked it in the air. Grabbing it, he pulled it to just below his waist.

"You said untouchable. Are you from India? We studied that in school, that no one can touch certain people, or they're contaminated." He noticed Uriel's midsection, and he immediately jumped up from the bed. "You don't have a belly button. Were you in an accident or something? Does it feel weird?"

Uriel winked. "Want to touch it to see?"

Bobby shook his head no.

Uriel hiked the sheet a bit higher, and he grinned. "Birth defect. Sit, boy. You know, that'll be your name, if you don't tell me your real one."

"What will?'

"Boy. Do you want everyone to call you Boy?"

"I'm Bobby. My best friend's name is Austen." He glanced once more at Uriel's waist, then his eyes slipped away, the anomaly fading from his thoughts.

"Austen's a good name." Uriel looked up at the ceiling as if considering what to say next. Then he looked directly at Bobby. "I like Bobby better. It's a good name, too. Have you ever heard of President Kennedy?"

"Sure." He sat on the bed, crossing his legs under him, his interest piqued. "We studied him in school. He was killed, um, assassinated, in, um, Dallas, I think. Texas. Dallas, Texas." He grinned, pleased to know the answer.

"His brother was killed, too. He was going to be President, some thought. He wasn't afraid, though, even after the President was killed. He followed his heart; he had a destiny, and he never hesitated. His name was Robert Kennedy."

"I've heard of him."

"He was a good man. The best. He died for what he believed in. Everyone called him Bobby. You could do with a worse name, you know. Glad to meet you, Bobby." Uriel held out his hand as if to shake. Bobby looked at it warily, then tentatively held out his own. Just before he touched it, Uriel yanked his back. "You trust people, too. That's a good quality. Let's not shake, though. Might be painful."

Bobby frowned. "But, just a moment ago, I fell on you, and you grabbed me and wouldn't let me loose. If we can't touch, how—"

Uriel slapped his hand on Bobby's leg, and he squeezed until the boy yelped. He released his hold, patting the leg twice. "Fabric. Fabric insulates the skin just enough to let us touch." He glanced away, changing the topic. "You saw me last night, didn't you? In the tub?"

"On the floor. I thought you were dead." Bobby blew out a sharp breath, looking away for a moment. That had scared him, and he was frightened all over again.

"You saw me get better, too, didn't you?"

Bobby nodded.

"I'm special, you know. Can you and I share a secret?"

"I'm not supposed to share secrets with strangers." Bobby glanced at Angioletta and back to Uriel. "My school counselor says secrets with strangers mean somebody wants to hurt us."

"Right-o. However, I'm Uriel, Uri to my friends, and you're Bobby." He held out his hand once again. "You saved my life, right? How can we be better friends than that?"

Bobby reached his hand out, nearly shaking this time, then he grinned. They both yanked their hands away at the same time, laughing. Uriel immediately put his finger to his lips.

"Don't wake the lady. My secret? Keep it between us?"

Bobby nodded. "Sure. Cross my heart, hope to die."

"No one has to die." Uriel winked. "Especially not you. The

fact is, I'm an angel."

"C'mon. Be serious. That's not a secret. That's not even real. There are no angels." Bobby grinned at the joke. He'd expected a real secret.

"Look at me, Bobby." Uriel's face was suddenly very intent. "Watch me closely, and don't be frightened."

"Sure." Bobby continued to grin. Then, to his surprise, something happened to the man on the bed, and he simply wasn't there anymore. Unable to stop himself, he felt his eyes slide to the side, and when he tried to look back where Uriel lay, they didn't want to focus there, as if that spot were fuzzy. It wasn't fuzzy, though. The pillow was fluffed, and the sheets were flat, even the one the man had pulled up for modesty. It was stretched smoothly across the mattress, with no one underneath at all.

Bobby jumped off the bed, his eyes opened wide, and he felt them immediately begin to burn with impending tears. He swallowed hard. He'd just been talking to someone there, and now it was an empty bed. He turned to the mirror and rubbed his eyes with his hands. Behind him, a voice called.

"Bobby. Look at me."

He turned, and the man, Uriel, was back in his bed, the sheet pulled to his waist, just like he was before.

"You were gone! I saw it," he squeaked. "How, um, did you go somewhere?"

Uriel held his hand up. "Shush. Our friend is still asleep. I didn't go anywhere. Are my pants still in the bathroom?"

Bobby glanced in and nodded.

"Good. Close your eyes if you don't want to see me get dressed."

Bobby started to look away, then he hesitated and frowned. He realized he didn't mind watching. The man moved with fluidity and grace, although Bobby didn't think in those terms. This man was like a marble sculpture, and the thing was, the sculpture was walking across the floor wearing flesh and blood.

In that moment, he understood something that many adults would have had trouble getting their minds around. Uriel's skin fit him better than any clothing ever could. That was when he started to believe. When Uriel walked to the bathroom, and instead of using the door, walked right through the wall with the barest of a shimmering flicker, it only iced the cake. He walked back out through the door, wearing his pants, to find Bobby grinning and shaking his head side to side.

"What will Austen say when I tell him I saved an angel's life? This is so cool."

Uriel laughed.

Bobby put a finger to his lips. "Shush, Uri. Ms. Bacciarelli's still asleep."

Eustorgio Ricci, Monsignor

Father Ricci stepped from the plane, followed by Bishop Carnaly. The morning heat in Arizona was already brutal, and the sun, even at this gentle time of day, ate into their black clothing with needles of fire.

"Quel che non ammazza, ingrassa." *What won't kill you will feed you.* Carnaly looked into the sky. "It was never this hot in Rome. Never. Tell me again, Father, why are we in Arizona, of all places? This seems to me the Devil's Armpit."

Ricci laughed, feeling the heat just as much as the bishop. "You said it, albeit in Italian. If this doesn't kill us, it feeds us, perhaps makes us stronger. Do you not wish to be stronger, Bishop?"

"I wish to see trees. Two back-to-back flights. Has it been twenty hours, Father?"

"Longer, I think. We are here because this is Phoenix, the start of our quest." Ricci didn't say that his message from the Holy Angel had been to rescue Angioletta, not find evidence of her death. Remembering the intensity of the angel's words, he was concerned that if they didn't complete their rescue, they would, indeed, find a quite dead martyr. It was a quandary he hesitated to consider, yet he knew he must.

"You have my espresso machine? I feared it would be left in New York. We were in such a rush to transfer that I also thought I would arrive without my cassock." The bishop shivered, even though sweat already beaded his face. He turned to Ricci. "It is Gaggia. The espresso machine. Top of the line. It goes everywhere with me."

When the bishop looked away, Ricci shook his head. He knew the machine went everywhere with him. On this trip, Ricci had hand carried it the entire way. He also knew it was not top of the line. Still, at eight kilos, it was as far up the line as he wanted to haul around.

"It's in my carry on, Your Excellency." That should calm his fears. The grand title wouldn't hurt, either. A little tweaking of the bishop's ego, and he was less likely to complain about the small things. Not a lot less likely, just less likely.

"How shall we proceed first, Father? We must have a plan."

The bishop had requested an American contingent meet them at the airport, and if they had stayed in New York, they would have been accommodated. To their dismay, when Ricci had insisted they immediately flee for the Great Southwest Desert, the contingent had mysteriously dissipated. They were told without kindness that it would not reappear in the desert, so expect to travel alone. It seemed their unexpected change in itinerary had irritated the American Church.

So, it was Ricci's own fault that his toiletries were in the belly of the airplane, and he had wrestled the bishop's Gaggia into and out of the overhead bins. If he couldn't brush his teeth tonight or had to re-wear his underclothing, it would be no one's fault except his own.

He looked around, and he sighed. "First, we should proceed to the airport terminal building. It surely has air conditioning."

"And the reason they deposited us here on the runway, my good servant?"

Ricci hated being called a good servant. He sighed once again before speaking. "Construction, Bishop. Such is the way of a prosperous democracy, such as America." There were big machines parked next to various parts of the building, but none seemed to be in motion.

"Yet, in construction, nothing is convenient."

They were at the terminal and were relieved when a stranger smiled at them, holding the door for them. "Mi

Padres." The dark eyes bowed themselves as the two Italian clergy passed.

Carnaly and Ricci nodded as they entered.

"Roma non è stata costruita in un giorno." *Rome wasn't built in a day.* Ricci whispered the words in the freshly silent and very cool terminal building. One wall was draped with temporary plastic sheeting, and the material stirred with the air pouring from a massive overhead grille.

Carnaly chuckled. "It would seem that just like Rome, America is not built in a day, either, especially this terminal." He walked to a water fountain and bent to take a sip of water.

"Bishop!" Ricci called to him urgently. "I have a cup in my things. To drink directly from the fountain may be unsanitary."

Carnaly waved him away. "Il bicchiere della staffa," or literally, *The wineglass of the stirrup.* It was an unusual phrase out of context, and he chuckled, elaborating with the American version of the Italian idiom. "One for the road will kill no one. Besides, this is America, the Land of the Free, the Home of the Brave. The water is very safe in America. You can drink it anywhere."

"Yes, Your Excellency."

"Refresh yourself, Father. I have set the example." He motioned to the fountain. "It is too hot outside to do otherwise."

Ricci cringed, but he also bent over and took a sip. He was surprised to discover it was very cold, and he found it very hard to break away. When he did, Bishop Carnaly had a smile on his face, and his eyes crinkled in mirth.

"So, my example is not to be dismissed too easily, I see. If this search for your Angioletta Bacciarelli is to be successful, then we must be on very familial terms. Is it a deal, Father?" He reached an uncharacteristically bare hand to his associate. "We are not in Italy, after all. What is it they say here? Paesi che vai, usanze che trovi."

"Close, Your Excellency. I believe the Americans phrase it, When in Rome, do as the Romans do." The actual saying had been more along the line of, *The countries you visit; the customs you find,* but any Italian understood what it meant. He reached and grabbed the bishop's hand, and he grinned.

Before releasing the grasp, Carnaly pursed his lips and winked. "Then we shall need to make the saying our own. I say, When in America, do as the Americans do." He released the hand and looked at his own. "I believe that is the first time you and I have ever actually touched skin to skin. It was quite refreshing."

"Quite so, Your Excellency. There's the automobile rental counter. We'll need transportation." Ricci nodded his head the correct direction.

"Ah, there are no private drivers? Father, this will not work. I do not hold a driver's license." With that small flaw in his morning, Bishop Carnaly seemed uncharacteristically flustered.

Ricci smiled, pulling a document from his pocket. "I have an International Driving License. I've checked. It's valid in Arizona, as long we do not register any children in the public school system. We'll rent a car and drive ourselves." He smiled proudly. He had worked this out before leaving Heathrow.

"So, we have no children, and we are to do as the Americans do. Are we in agreement?" Carnaly turned to him, a twinkle in his eyes.

"Si." Ricci wasn't really sure what he and the bishop were in agreement on. Still. This was more like the Bishop, to let the problem of the driver's license fade as quickly as it had arisen. He was used to underlings taking care of the small matters that made life so distressing. Oh, well. As the bishop was his superior, it was his job to be the underling. He supposed he liked it that way as well as any other.

"What is that American sports car General Motors makes? The Concorde?" The bishop's face perked up expectantly.

"No, Your Excellency. The Concorde is a French built aeroplane. The American sports car you reference is perhaps the Corvette."

Carnaly smiled and motioned with his hand. "Excellent! Bring my espresso machine along. I wish to explore Arizona in an American Corvette." He walked off without turning to see if Ricci followed.

"Chi lascia la strada vecchia per la nuova sa quel che lascia, ma non sa quel che trova!" Ricci's comment was muttered very

310

softly. If it had been spoken in English, it might have gone very much like, Better the devil you know than the devil you don't. Back in Italy, he had only thought he knew the good Bishop Carnaly. Released of his Italian mores, he was turning out to be quite a normal man. Of course, Ricci would give him some time before he decided whether he liked the new man. Who could tell? They might just become friends after all.

As if!

Finally, he found he could laugh at the day, for the idea of Carnaly and himself as best of friends was amusing, indeed.

Angioletta Bacciarelli, Daughter of Kafziel

Angioletta jerked awake, immediately freezing, and remained very still. She remembered losing a day, and now she had slept through yet another night. At least she thought it had been just one additional night. Extended amounts of sleep usually left her groggy, but that wasn't how she felt now. She felt unusual, different, yes, but not groggy. She felt *scoured* on the inside. She didn't hurt, just felt . . . cleaner. It was like her cells had been purified, her blood run through one of those hospital machines that filter out all the impurities, and pumped back inside again.

She also remembered the man from the tub—*Uriel*, he had told her last night—asking Bobby to turn the heat up as far as it would go. The room didn't feel all that warm to her, though, and she wondered if the boy had done as asked.

Her eyes caught the men on the other bed. Men. In some cultures, both would be seen as that. Not in America, though. The *man* lay covered to his waist, and the *boy*—for he wasn't truly a man—sat on the bed beside him. They seemed to have developed quite a rapport with one another. The boy was smiling, and on one occasion they reached to shake, jerking their hands apart before touching, laughing in some inside joke.

When Uriel stood to head into the bathroom for his clothes was when she realized the magically healed arm wasn't the half of how unusual this man was. He walked to the wall, not

311

slowing down at all, and then his body shimmered, and he was gone. The shock froze her heart in her chest, and her fingers dug into the bedspread, grasping for the solid feel of reality. Men, *people*, don't just disappear. Then, moments later, he walked through the bathroom door with his pants on, exciting the boy to no end.

She closed her eyes for a moment, then when she opened them again, Uriel had his arm across the boy's shoulders, whispering something to him. The boy nodded, and the two did a hand sign of some sort, a "fist bump," she believed it was called, although the hands were supposed to actually bump, and theirs never did. Something new, she thought, remembering her students from the previous year. Anyone who used the preceding year's latest and edgiest social terms was automatically dated, a cast off has-been who should "get with the times." Even those terms were probably archaic to anyone fourteen.

Then the boy stepped to the bathroom, closing the door. After a moment she heard the toilet flush, and he slipped back into the room.

Well, she was not fourteen, and she needed that bathroom. Sitting up, she used her hands to work her hair back from her face, smiling when Uriel called to her.

"Angioletta." He walked across the unmade bed he'd slept in and sat by her side. "You must have many questions. After my, um, recovery last night, we had little time to speak." He reached a hand to touch her face, and withdrew it at the last moment. "You look well this morning."

"Ha!" She threw out her thoughts on that matter into the room. She did it with a smile, though, for this man was still vanilla, and he made her feel good.

"Ha?" He looked puzzled. "You are beautiful, and any man would say so." He glanced at Bobby for confirmation. "Do you agree, Bobby?"

The boy just grinned and nodded.

"Then, it's done." Uriel looked back at Angioletta. "You must accept it with whole-hearted enthusiasm."

He looked very serious, and she laughed, glancing at the

boy and back at Uriel. "I can see you finally have your pants on. Did you find them in the bathroom without any problem?" She could just see Bobby covering his mouth and tittering.

She glanced toward the curtained window for a moment. The question about his pants wasn't the one on her mind. What she really wanted to ask was whether she had really seen him walk through that wall. *Uriel, can you shimmer for me just once? Oh, and there's a wall, there. Please walk through it as you do so.* It sounded so silly just to think it.

He didn't seem to notice, though. Instead, he fought a smile.

"Yes. Bobby thought I was, um, what was it, Bobby? Creepy. I thought it was time to let 'creepy' go by the wayside. Now, I am mostly uncreepy. Would you say so, Bobby?" Uriel's eyes never left her face.

Angioletta relented, and she smiled at Bobby, winking.

The boy stammered out, "Not creepy. I never meant that. It's just that you being, um, knowing your, um, was right there by my side." He ducked his head, coughing out the words. "What if I—" clearing his throat "—*touched* it by accident?"

"Can't happen, can it, Bobby? Impossible. I am untouchable. Are you worried now?"

"No, sir!" He barked the words out, grinning from ear to ear. "Besides, Uri, you have your pants on."

"Uri?" Angioletta looked at Uriel with a puzzled expression. "I have to call you Uriel, and the boy is offered Uri?"

There was another wink sent Bobby's way. They were interrupted by a scratching on the door, and Bobby looked at Uriel.

"Do you want me to, um, open the door?" He hooked a thumb the direction of the door, taking a quick glance. "If it's Nigel or Rikkianne, I can ask them to come back later."

"Nigel? Rikkianne?" Angioletta looked at him. "Your parents?" Surely not. He wouldn't call them by their first names. "You . . . did you stay the night here, Bobby?" She couldn't seem to recall that he had ever left. When she woke, she'd just assumed that he'd gone home and returned.

"I fell asleep and forgot to leave. Nigel and Rikkianne run

the motel. They're friends of mine." He put his hand on the knob. "Uri?"

The scratching came again, and at a motion of Uriel's hand, he turned the knob. When he did, the door exploded, knocking the boy down, and an oversized gray canine barreled through.

In one leap, Malak hit the first bed and bounded past it onto Uriel. As the bare-chested brother wrapped his arms around the animal, greeting the wolf enthusiastically, Angioletta covered her head with her arms and jumped up to stand by Bobby.

"Cool," Bobby breathed. "A wolf!"

They turned to see a boy walk into the room, one about nine years old. As they watched, his eyes turned red, and tears began to run down his face.

Angioletta rushed toward him and knelt by his side.

"What's wrong, young man?" She reached to brush one especially large tear away. She worked with children. She knew distress when she saw it.

His mother was the one who answered, though. Jeri stepped through the door with Little Chrissy's hand in hers, and she reached to push her hair back from her face. She glanced outside, the brightness in sharp contrast to the dim interior.

"Ma'am, my son's name is Dakota. He'll be okay. It's been a long night, and the dog just found us. We thought it was lost, and my son hoped no one wanted it." She turned, facing outside, and she pressed her lips together. Drawing a deep breath, her voice was tight when she spoke. She didn't look back into the room. "We couldn't keep him, anyway. Come, Dakota. The dog's found his owner. It's time to go."

"Mister, is he really yours?" The boy's voice had the clear and open sound of a child still far from puberty, one that hadn't yet become clearly male or female. "He's your dog, right?"

Uriel sat up, his arms still around Malak's neck. The wolf had rolled on its back, and its tongue toyed with Uriel's skin. He brushed the animal's fur and motioned for the boy to come closer.

"Did you pet him?" Uriel smiled. "His name's Malak, and he enjoys having his throat rubbed, at least by friends." He leaned close and whispered, "Anyone else would lose a finger, but he won't bite you. Put your hand here. He might lick you on the face if you're not careful, though." Just then, the animal rolled over and caught the boy with its front legs, and its pink tongue lolled across Dakota's face. There were sparkles of static electricity, as if rubbing against winter carpet, and the boy laughed, pulling away.

"Mom, he likes me!" He threw his arms around Malak, burying his face in the animal's gray fur.

It was no surprise for him to be able to hug the familiar. The boy could touch the animal just fine, as long as he didn't try to hug him too tightly. The familiars that made it to Earth were, by their very natures, less focused, and therefore marginally less corporeally substantive than the brothers. It was the equivalent of a brother being at the top of a skyscraper, or better, on a mountaintop.

Malak's fur helped, too.

"Dakota!" Jeri's words were sharp. "The dog is home. It's time to go."

"It's fine with me if they play. Also, I find I like anyone who appreciates time with Malak." Uriel reached and roughly tugged the wolf's fur.

This time the mother's words were softer. "Say good-bye, Dakota. These people have things to do." She frowned, turning to Angioletta. "Have you told the manager your air is broken? I'm sure they have other rooms you can take."

Before she could answer, Malak leaped to the floor, spinning in a series of circles, pretending to nip at Dakota each time as its canine mouth passed by. The boy danced with laughter. Then the wolf dashed outside, with the boy running after it.

Little Chrissy reached to touch Malak as the wolf rushed by, laughing at the flashing sparkles of electricity that ran along the animal's fur, and taking out after it and her brother.

Jeri gasped. "They can't be allowed out alone."

Bobby laughed. "I live just over the hill. They're safe outside. Trust me." Then he darted to the door. "I'll go watch them, if you want."

At a motion of Uriel's hand, he was gone, whooping

through the morning. Then Uriel turned to Angioletta, motioning toward the bathroom. "Yours, m'lady."

She couldn't help but smile, but she did need the facilities, and with no hesitation, she made a mad dash that direction, wishing she, too, could bypass the door.

That was how badly she needed to go.

Interlude 18

Malak enjoyed the outside play, too. After all, the animal wasn't just a familiar to Uriel. It was also very much a wolf, an animal with all the genetic precursors to the canine responses that had come together to make dogs the best friends Man had ever had. Of course, no Earth-wolf would have played with human children the same as Malak did, but while the familiar was a wolf, it was much more. Now that it knew Uriel had been found, relief had flooded its canine body. Various chemicals had engorged connectors in its wolf brain, and for now, all was right with the world.

It was later that the rest of the story would come out. Uriel now had enemies on this planet, and not all of them came in the form of a brother named Kafziel.

Chapter 22

Gabriel, First Chief of the Brothers

Gabriel tried to rise, only to fall back down. He hurt. Oh, he hurt more than all the humans in creation.

His wings were in tatters about him, and his left leg had been ravaged. When he tried to open his eyes, he could see out of only one. The other was awash with something wet and sticky. In addition, he was as cold as he had ever been in his entire life, and it had been a long one.

Reaching a hand slowly to his face, he felt of it, cringing when it came away wet with blood. He remembered the cause of that. Images of Swiftness swam at him, his own time sense slowing down the avian's fantastic speed and the tearing strokes of its talons as they shredded his skin in multiple places. His energy reserves were gone by then, and no healing at all had occurred. Instead, he had fallen, leaving his comrades to destruction.

That hurt Gabriel as much as his own injuries. He was the Citadel of Justice and Power. The Angel of *Power!* Where had his power been when his companions needed it? They had come to Earth to support him, and he had failed them miserably.

Hearing the rattle of metal against metal, he looked around

as best he could with only one eye, the bleeding obscuring the other, as he attempted to place himself. It was dark, except for a jagged hole in the roof overhead. Brilliant sky teased through the opening. The ends of broken boards formed the perimeter, their splintered edges telling of something crashing through very recently. Around him he saw shelves filled with a wide variety of mechanisms, some manually operated, and others with cords and power switches. They weren't weapons, although some could certainly be used for battle.

Then the clanking stopped, and one wall of his prison was thrown wide, two doors opening as one. Glaring light flooded through, the rays of a bright sun slapping against his face. The warmth was minimal, and he regretted that, but it was sunshine, nonetheless.

"What is this dog's breath that has stolen my livelihood from me?" The words were more than spoken into Gabriel's small haven. They were bellowed, and the force of them could have peeled the hair from a lemming's tongue.

In the brilliance against which the intruder stood, Gabriel could only see that the man was tall and very broad shouldered. His face was darkened, and his features were unreadable. Behind him stood numerous other men about his same size.

The man was not conversing in English. That wasn't usually a problem for Gabriel, as all languages on Earth were as one to him. He was as fluent in Icelandic as he was in Ancient Egyptian. However, this was a butchered mix. Still, it had enough passable German in it that he could probably make himself understood if he spoke a simple phrase.

"Es tut mir leid!" *I am sorry.* He waved his hand, although he wasn't sure if the man could see him in the darkness.

"You are a man? A man did this, tore a hole in my roof? You are sorry for stealing my tools? I make my life with these tools, and you can take them just because you wish?" He turned to the men at his back. "It is a man, and he is sorry."

A voice rang out, "He will think sorry. Make him come out. Is it Larsen? If so, he's a bigger fool than even my wife thinks!" Laughter from several men accompanied the gibe.

"It's not Larsen. He is drunk at my sister's wedding. It is

why I did not go." The man called his response to his audience, moving his hand suggestively for emphasis. Gabriel watched tiredly as the man turned back to the darkness. "You. I have been offended. Name yourself."

"Gabriel. Ich habe nichts genommen." *I have taken nothing.* Hopefully, the man got his meaning. He was too exhausted to come up with a better sentence, or to put up any resistance, no matter what they did to him.

"Ich bin nicht so dumm," *I am not so dumb,* the man muttered, "that I will not find out for myself." He jiggled a switch, and nothing happened. Then he reached to several shelves, picking up one or two things, and moving a few others around. Finally, he stepped back, satisfied and muttering, "Es ist alles hier." He turned, calling to those outside. "It is all here. He has stolen nothing."

"Make him come out, then. Your roof. He must replace it. Your things, they will ruin. What will you do then? It's not fair to your family, not at all." There were several voices of agreement, and the man turned to Gabriel.

"Stand and come out. We wish to see who has done this."

The words were curt, but the yelling was gone. Still, Gabriel had tried to stand, and he could not.

"Ich kann nicht." *I cannot.* Could the man understand that?

"Have you received injuries, then? The door was locked, and you must have fallen to the floor." The man paused in consternation. "I saw no ladder. How did you get on my roof?"

Gabriel waved his hand in the air, motioning toward the hole, his weary brain offering the man German he hoped he understood. "Ich wurde geworfen." *I was thrown.* "Helfen Sie mir bitte!" *Please help me.*

The man turned and called humorously, "He cannot come out. He was thrown through my roof. We must provide help."

Several other men darkened the doorway. As a group they crowded inside.

Gabriel took a deep breath and steeled himself. He didn't even have the strength to remove his wings. Unity help him when they saw those.

Kinky Kinkerson, Reporter

"No, you're not listening to *me*, Julian. I'm telling you. I was there." Kinky looked out the window. It was nearing eleven, and Ralph was just outside. When the ambulance had dropped them off at the motel, his car had been sitting in the parking lot. When he'd called, they'd given him a cock-and-bull story about how it wasn't just the solenoid that was fried. His car had terminal old age. It seemed *everything* was fried. They said cars all over the city were having the same problem, and his was just one more. It was mostly older ones, they suggested, ones with cracked wiring. They didn't have room to store it until the parts came in, but the motel did. Yeah, they'd send a tow for it when they could work it in. Would he like to consider trading it? They had a shipment of new sedans just arrived the previous evening.

Now, Ralph was messing around under the hood. With that white hair, his too-short pants, and his oh-God-too-beautiful-to-be-true face, he looked like a crazy person out there fiddling away under the hood. What could he possibly know about cars? He'd simply said he had a way with things. If Kinky would like, he could try a "laying on of hands," and he had winked. He was a religious nut, probably, but what the heck? The car was dead, anyway.

There was more to it, though. Kinky had sat with the man in the ambulance, with all those glowing little lights all over the place. Ralph's side of the ambulance had been a little brighter than Kinky's. He'd noticed that after a while, and he'd puzzled it in his mind. He was a newspaperman, after all, and work out the facts behind the story was what he did for a living.

It was when Ralph climbed out, and the ambulance door shadowed his face, that Kinky remembered the angel he'd thought he'd seen when he first came to out in the desert. Ralph's face had glowed just for that moment until he moved back into the light. The angel had glowed like that. *Aura*. That angel out there had sure glowed with an aura, only not like the ones in all the pictures he'd seen of angels. The auras he'd seen on Christmas cards and in paintings were just around the faces. That angel's aura had been all over, from head to toe, even around its wings.

Julian interrupted his thoughts, spitting something disparaging to him over the line, and he was getting on Kinky's last nerve.

"Don't you tell me about my brain, Julian, and no, I don't need to visit the emergency room. You can't imagine how wonderful I feel. I don't know, but I think this man had something to do with it."

He paused, opening the door and yelling out, "It's hopeless, Ralph. Let it die an honorable death."

The man just waved and smiled, leaning back under the hood, as Kinky closed the door again. It was already at least ninety out there. Arizona!

"He's under the hood, Julian, just tinkering on my car, and I swear, if I wasn't already sure I'm attracted to skirts, I'd swear I could fall in love with that man. He's that beautiful. People don't come like that. Do you even remember that old drunk I told you about? The one that talked and talked about that angel he saw?" The voice on the other end must have been uncooperative, because Kinky snorted in derision. "I have not been drinking. I rented a car, a truck, actually, and something blew it up in the desert. I told you that already."

He paused, watching Raphael for a moment, giving Julian time to talk. Rather, it was more that Julian insisted on talking. Kinky grinned. Turning back into the room, he continued, "I thought something came at me, but I'm not sure, now. Maybe a wild animal. It felt like a land mine, like I drove up on it, and *bloowie,* I was upside down hundreds of feet away. Well," he chuckled, remembering, "the truck was. I was thrown out. The door had puncture marks in it. The firemen said it looked like it had been ripped off." Julian spoke again, causing Kinky to laugh. "I tell you, Julian. Not a scratch. Even those backaches I get are gone. Not a twinge."

Suddenly, something from outside caught his attention. A car engine coughed to life, roared roughly, and then settled into a loud, spitting whine. Then, before he could get the curtain open, the noise immediately quieted into an even purr. As Kinky pulled the curtain, he could see Ralph shutting the hood. Looking up, he saw Kinky and waved, his face breaking into a smile.

"My heavens, Julian! He's fixed the car, and he didn't even use any tools." Kinky paused for a moment, then he barked back into the receiver, "I know because I don't have any with me. I'll call you later." He hung up as Raphael reached the door.

"We've got transportation now. Do you know of someplace around here that sells clothes?" Raphael lifted one leg and slapped his ankle. "I'm a little short. Food, too, if you don't mind. The donuts were great, but something more substantial would be helpful. Protein. This body could use some of that. It metabolizes better."

Kinky wasn't certain, though. "You think we can trust the car? The mechanic said it was toast. What if it breaks again? I'm not sure the rental place will give me another one."

"I told you," and Raphael held up his hands, "I have a way, a healing touch, so to speak. I guess you could say it's my Mandate. I don't know how I do it, just that it happens. Do you have a full tank of gas in your car?"

"Um, do you need me to take you somewhere in particular?" The request for protein had already slipped from his brain. Being around a brother was like that.

"Nah! It's just that it's running out there, and I'd hate to hike to the station. My horse done died out in the desert." Raphael spoke with a twang, hiking up his pants in a passable imitation of a nonchalant Arizona cowboy.

Then he winked and grinned.

Interlude 19

With Raphael's quip, Kinky forgot all the questions he wanted to ask, like, how *exactly* did he repair that car, and why *exactly* did he happen to be out in the desert, and explain *please* just why he had no clothes on when he knelt to check on him. Please, Ralph, answer those important questions.

The questions that popped into his mind instead were, What size pants do you wear, and how many sausages will it take to fill you up?

He didn't realize he'd just reacted to a "Suggestion," because those were the questions Raphael needed Kinky to ask.

They were the only ones he was prepared to answer.

Fire Fighters, Engine No. 4

"Hey, Alonso! Guess who I've got on the line." Sam held up the phone so it could be seen across the room. It was cordless, and it had an old-fashioned metal antenna sticking out of the top. The battery was kept updated on a regular basis, though, and there had been no reason to purchase a new one.

"If it is Rosita, I will come and tell her I love her. Otherwise, I am eating breakfast." He cut a bite of pancakes and stuffed them in his mouth. Licking his bottom lip, he winked at Sam, shooting him a thumbs up.

Sam jumped across the back of the couch, an old, comfortable leather one, and he threw himself into a chair beside his coworker. Pulling Alonso's plate over, he grabbed the fork from his hand and stabbed a bite of the pancakes, stuffing them into his mouth. Talking around the food, he handed the phone to Alonso.

"It's Willie." He swallowed and speared another bite. "From Phoenix."

"Willie?" Alonso frowned. "Not Rosita?"

Across the room, Gunnar pulled his baseball cap off, looked at it, and turned it around backwards before tugging it back on. "Your brother-in-law," he called out. "That's almost Rosita." He had a puzzle out, and he picked up a piece, studying it carefully. With a satisfied smile, he reached to the table and pushed it into place.

"Ah! That Willie." Alonso didn't seem very interested.

"Just take it, *Al*." Sam grinned, fully aware that the

323

shortened form of his name would irritate his friend. "I'm finishing your 'cakes." He slapped the phone into his friend's hand.

Alonso looked at it suspiciously for a moment, then he whispered to Sam, "Did you mute it? I do not want to hurt Willie's feelings." His face was filled with exaggerated sorrow, but it was clear he didn't mean it.

Gunnar called, "Willie doesn't have any feelings. You know that, Alonso. Otherwise, he wouldn't have given you his sister for a wife. Just talk to him."

"That you would know," Alonso called. "You have no feelings for Alonso. I think Willie be a better choice to talk than you. Willie?" He pressed the receiver to his ear. "All my friends are crazy. Will you be uncrazy?" He looked up and winked.

After a few moments he hung up the phone and set it down carefully. He pursed his lips, holding his hands around the base of the handset, looking at it.

"How's Willie?" Gunnar called. "Sat on another cactus lately?"

Sam laughed. That was the time Rosita went to stay with her brother for two weeks. His backside was bandaged, and he hadn't even been able to sit on the toilet without assistance.

Alonso blew out a long-held breath. "Remember, I said I told Rosita about the angel?"

"And got it in the paper?" Sam grinned.

"Rosita did not tell the paper." Alonso pulled the rest of his pancakes back, grabbing the fork, too. "She only told her brother in Phoenix."

"Willie, right?" Gunnar glanced up, smirking. Willie was Rosita's only brother. She had five sisters, but only Willie for a brother.

"Willie." Alonso pursed his lips. "Willie says a truck blew up in the desert during the night."

"Christ!" Sam sat back, shaking his head. "Was the man torched? I've been to one of those."

"Do not let my Rosita hear you say the name of the Christ in vain. She will make you attend Mass two weeks in a row if you do." Alonso shook his fork at the younger man.

Sam threw his head back and laughed. "She'd do it, too. Okay, I'll watch my mouth."

From across the room, Gunnar called, "Forget Sam's mouth. What about the man in the truck?"

From a side door, Rodrigo walked in, his shirt unbuttoned, and his hair askew. He rubbed one eye sleepily. "What truck? I didn't hear the alarm. Are we going out?"

"Willie's truck." Gunnar stood, throwing himself on the sofa, his feet immediately stretched out on the coffee table. "Somebody got torched."

"Did they live?" Rodrigo was at the refrigerator by then, and he grabbed a bottle of milk.

"Well, Alonso?" Sam reached and punched his arm. "How bad was it?"

"I know I went in that house and rescued little Angelina." His words were a whisper, barely more than a murmur. "But, I am also remembering an angel. In my heart, no one can tell me otherwise."

"The truck? Willie?" Sam prodded, looking at the other two men. This wasn't normally like Alonso.

"No one was injured." Alonso pressed his lips together, his brows frowning.

"That's good, huh?" Rodrigo took a swig of the milk, snapping the lid back on when he was finished.

"The truck was blown 200 feet away. One door was ripped off."

"Jesus! How'd the driver survive?" Realizing what he'd said, Sam apologized. "Oh, sorry, Alonso."

Gunnar barked, "Apologize to Jesus, you idiot. You know Alonso doesn't like those names used like that."

"O-kay." He looked up at the ceiling. "Sorry, Jesus. I'll be better." Then he grinned at Gunnar. "Happy?"

Getting up, Gunnar pulled out a chair and sat at the table. "What else did Willie say?"

"There were two men. One should have been dead, Willie said. His clothes were all torn, and he had blood all over. Filthy, Willie said. He wasn't even scratched, even where there was blood on his head. The other man was tall with white hair and golden skin. He was clean, even if his clothes didn't fit. Beautiful, Willie said. That was Willie's word. The tall man was beautiful. Like an angel, he said. Just like an angel."

"Jeez, that's creepy." Sam shuddered.

Gunnar slapped his arm, pointing to Alonso.

Sam looked at the ceiling. "Sorry, again. I didn't mean it."

Rodrigo just rolled his eyes. He'd made it to the puzzle table by then, and he slipped a piece into its proper place.

Gunnar called out, "That wasn't the red one, was it? I've been looking for where that one goes for days."

"Now you don't have to look anymore. I'm going to shower."

Gunnar made a face and slouched in his chair. He muttered, "I wanted to put the red piece in, and now I can't. Rodrigo never likes to work the puzzles, and he just did it for me. Rodrigo, of all people!"

Sam just laughed.

Interlude 20

It was day in the Unity, and across the distances, there was no darkness to be found.

Yet, that was not exactly correct. There was no nighttime to be found. When the Triune Mind had sat upon the Seat of Power, there had been no darkness of any kind. Power and light had surged from his being, and the Unity had been gloriously warm and brilliant beyond imagining. The streets had even glittered as if made of gold.

During past eons, at each transition, the Unity of Being had morphed as it changed dimensions, remaking itself to the needs of its inhabitants. It was an essential part of the original design, and it had worked so well, the inhabitants had ceased to question it long ago. Of course, it was now thousands of years since the last known metamorphosis, but that didn't change the beauty of the process.

That very lack of change might prove to be the Unity's downfall.

Now, the temperatures were only tolerable, and it was freezing everywhere outside of the great ship. In secret places where few dared venture, the shadows of darkness had finally found a home. Those who disliked pain dared not venture there.

Most of the brothers avoided the places of shadows, keeping instead to the light. And of the rest? There were those that found the shadows good, for they enjoyed the wicked life they led.

Jeqon, Chief of the Fallen

Jeqon raised a fancy pastry to his lips, biting off a small nibble. "Um," he murmured, looking off his balcony into the distance. "Manna, I believe humans call it. It be a perfect name for a perfect food."

His home—a mansion of grand proportions to anyone used to spending time on Earth—was dolled to the nines, for he had visitors due at any time. The party meister was used to entertaining in a grand style. To share his fabulosity was part of the fun.

These were special guests, too. Jeqon had a plan, and today was when the wheels began to turn.

A deep bell shattered the peace. The sound carried over the inlaid marble and polished wood, reverberating into the buttressed ceiling soaring far overhead, and ringing against the glittering stained-glass panels rising high into the eaves. Dazzling light sparkled through the space, splayed across the interior surfaces.

The space was large and open to accommodate the vast wingspread of a multitude of brothers. After all, this was the home of the party meister.

No medieval stone mason or glass artist would have failed to notice the similarities between Jeqon's home and a medieval cathedral. Indeed, Jeqon's "mansion" had been the template for many a grand cathedral. Were the materials really the stone and wood of Earth? Of course not. This was the Unity. But, to a brother in the Unity, no difference could be seen or felt. It appeared exactly the same.

"Jeqon!"

A voice echoed across the vastness. In the distance he found his invited guests. He laughed, calling to them, "My friends! Zadkiel! Asbeel! My balcony awaits! The breezes are refreshing!"

"You have food ready, I see, and are already indulging. How like you!" That was Asbeel, nearly Jeqon's equal in social acumen. He chortled as he waved.

Jeqon laughed, motioning his guests outside, the wide doorways in the Unity always ready to accommodate the brothers' winged selves. The two visiting brothers' wings carried them elegantly across the generous expanses.

"Brothers." Jeqon stood regally, letting his wings open themselves a bit, the uplift of the ether causing them to strain against the wind. This was the reason for the balcony. At any time he could leap and be free to fly anywhere he wished to go—in the Unity, of course. On this day he was careful. Open them too far, and the lack of gravity would carry him aloft. Such a thing would be rude when he was the one who had invited these guests to his private abode.

He tucked his wings, just in case.

A bright spark appeared at his side, and he shooed it away. He couldn't play, and his small familiar would simply have to under-stand. It scuttled off, its only response a disappointed squeak.

"The Unity be especially beautiful today. See the far mountains? Their color be exquisite. Also, off to our right be many of the homes of the cherubim." Jeqon smiled and held out a plate of the manna. He was pleased to see each brother take a square. Off in the distance, numerous celestial towers thrust skyward, their slenderness making them too fragile to be believed. A handful of them glittered with glass windows to rival Jeqon's own. Several cherubim could be seen flying amongst them, their wings sparkling in the light.

Jeqon didn't show the brothers the view from his other windows. A few decades before, or perhaps it had been a century or so, several of the brothers had devised a way to capture the seconds of those brothers who had adopted them. Penned up, they had been starved and tortured until they had desired nothing more than to be free. Then they had been forced to fight for their freedom in mock battles in makeshift arenas. Many had died. When the seconds' masters had discovered their whereabouts, an attempt had been made to free their treasured familiars. A great battle had ensued, and numerous celestial towers were now no more than ragged stumps lifting their broken fingers into the sky.

Gadreel's conquest of the Triune Mind was having its consequences. Hidden from view, none of that could be seen from Jeqon's favored balcony.

"It is not often one stands on the private balcony of the party meister himself. The views are certainly among the best in this part of the Unity, and it's worth my time to admire them. Thank you, Jeqon, for your invitation." Asbeel walked to the rail, spreading his wings wide, their white luminescence contrasting with Jeqon's black. He held on as the ether buffeted him.

Zadkiel was more pragmatic. "So, Jeqon. You have need of us? Earlier, we came looking for Gabriel, and you wasted our time. What could you possibly want now?"

"Jeremiel came to see little Jeqon." Their host pulled his wings in, their enormous size towering over his head. Smiling, teasing, he pushed the tray of manna Zadkiel's direction. "Please, have another bite to eat. It would please Jeqon so very much." He pushed the tray a third time with a wink. "It be manna. Very good."

"You know he used to be called Raziel." Asbeel paraded his knowledge.

"Who? Jeremiel?" Jeqon shrugged and snickered. "Raziel, if you wish him to be. Still, he be Jeremiel to me."

"Why would he come to see you?" Zadkiel frowned. "He isn't a partygoer. He only presides over those awaiting entrance back into the Unity."

"Not for ages, Zadkiel. Remember Ramiel?" Asbeel whispered his words to the ether, shuddering.

"Well," and Jeqon began to spiral to the heart of his plans, as he rubbed his arm slowly and seductively. Over the recent eons, he had learned to take pride in his darker color, and he enjoyed touching his skin. It was so *different*. But that was neither here nor there. The plan was about to fall into place. "It seem Jeremiel be on vacation with Gabriel. A whole bunch of them partied down to Earth, and no one even thought to ask poor Jeqon. I be just an old shoe, left to kick my own dust."

"Oh, Zadkiel!" Asbeel turned, instantly ecstatic. "A party! On Earth! This is just my forte, even better than my latest trip to Io. If they've all gone down, can we? I know all the best places. New York, Paris, Rome! Of course, I hear Toronto's pretty swell these days, and Hong Kong. We must go there."

"Oh, did you hear what you said, Brother? *Swell*! You be picking up my anachronisms. I do love you! Let's all go together!" Jeqon began jumping up and down, determined to appear enthusiastic, and in reality, he was. His enthusiasm had an ulterior motive, nevertheless, one that needed a way out of the Unity. One overweeningly enthusiastic jump took him right off the balcony. Instinctively, he flipped his wings out, catching the breeze, and he tacked his way back in. He held out a hand, and Zadkiel took it, pulling him down to the floor.

"Calm down, Jeqon. If you must, come with us to Io, instead. We can surf the vents, and there aren't any humans to get in our way." That was from Zadkiel, always the practical one. "I suppose that's why you called us here. If it is, it'll be some time. We have other business to attend to."

"Almost no humans, Zadkiel. Remember those men in that little ship? They're headed to Io, and Gadreel doesn't even care." Asbeel had a pout on his face. "We asked him for help, and you said he wouldn't give it to us."

Jeqon smiled. This was too good to be believed, meshing perfectly with the ace he had up his sleeve. Not only did he need these brothers down on Earth, he intended to go with them.

He turned to take another pastry in his hand, and he looked out over the Unity as if disinterested in it all. He arched one black eyebrow, glancing at his two guests as he spoke, "Uriel be already on Earth."

330

It was a tease of the most provocative kind.

He dropped his brows in an uncaring expression as he turned away, biting into the manna pastry with a nonchalant tilt to his head. Then he held up one hand and started counting, laying his fingers down as he called names. "And Kasbeel, and Hizkiel, and Barakiel, and Elemiah." He looked over, one finger still standing, and he whispered with a sigh, "And Raphael." He slowly folded the final finger down.

Then he broke into a manic grin. "Can we please go? Since the Mind banned poor Jeqon from Earth, poor Jeqon's not been even one little time. This be my only chance." He reached and twirled one of his tightly twisted stalks of hair. "Please, for Jeqon?"

Zadkiel frowned a second time, deeper this go-round. "You are a rotten brother. Why did you drag us through all this? You could have spit out what you wanted as soon as we arrived."

"Would you have said yes?" Jeqon smiled, and then, when there was no answer, he continued, "Ah, not even for Jeqon. I must tease you into it. And it worked, did it not? I be packed and all ready." He reached behind a flying buttress and pulled out a small case. "Fresh clothes. Earth be so . . . *sweaty*." The bag was rather bulky for a change of clothes, but neither Zadkiel nor Asbeel seemed to notice.

Zadkiel reminded him harshly, "You know that only your body is affected by the atmospheric corporeal disharmony. Any clothing you take will be useless. We all have to find human attire when we arrive." He snorted in disgust. "Has it truly been so long since you've visited Earth?"

"Longer. But then," and Jeqon preened as he patted the bag coquettishly, "when something be needed, what can one do, even if one needs eight of them?"

"Eight what?" Zadkiel frowned, reaching for the bag, only to have Jeqon yank it out of his reach.

"No worries!" Jeqon patted his bag once again, then adjusted a long strap over his shoulder. "I be all ready, now."

"Me, too." Asbeel had his face turned into the ether, and his wingtips fluttered in the building breeze, showing his anticipation. "Rio awaits!"

Opening their wings wide, the three brothers let the ether lift them skyward. Asbeel did flips and turns, once starting a spin, wrapping his wings tighter and tighter about his torso, until he spun like a top. Jeqon had his own set of games, but they involved something more akin to drunken boxing than actual flying.

Zadkiel called, "Fools! Can we go, now? I want to thin the ether and start our journey. Gadreel has claimed entirely too much power, and it's now common knowledge that the four Pets of the Triune Mine are released, and not to work on behalf of the Mind. No, they are on Earth for mayhem and destruction. Uriel and his Mandate of Destiny must be rescued."

Jeqon sighed and relented. "Off to the drummer," he cried, and with a twist of their energies, Zadkiel winked out first. Asbeel soon followed, with Jeqon taking longer, his bag creating balance issues.

However they managed it, the three were gone, leaving the Unity behind. Then, as quickly, the blackness of space around the Seat of Power bent in three different locations, and three essences appeared. Each was invisible, of course, although Jeqon's voice came through loudly and clearly.

"Oh, boys! Look! It be the Seat of Power. I wonder, would anyone know if I had just a teeny little Seat time? I be so tired, I must find some place to rest these weary little feet."

"You have no feet here, Jeqon." Zadkiel's words laid his foolishness bare.

"Oh, oh! It be the idea of my feet that needs propped up and cooled down. Why, if I don't take a load off, I might not even make it down to Earth."

"Take a load off. Twentieth Century idiom, meaning to rest for a moment." That was Asbeel, showing off his store of arcane Earth facts. "Still, that's not a good idea, Jeqon, not on the Seat."

Jeqon laughed, and it was bright and carefree. "I be good. You two be sweet and do Jeqon a good turn today. Call us transport. Then Traverse, we will. I simply require a small moment."

"Not on the Seat, Jeqon."

"I be a fool, but not a big fool. Just call."

Zadkiel clapped his hands—hands that were not really there, of course—and a glowing ball of light appeared, coming to hover at his side. He clapped twice more, and as quickly there were three balls, one for each of the brothers.

With a slight shift of his unseen fingers, the balls darkened on one side, preparing for Traversing the blackness of space, thrusting the three brothers past Earth's ion layer, and down to the world below.

"Ready?" Zadkiel called to his companions, only to find Jeqon resting on the Seat of Power. "Why must you do such a thing, fool?" Then he snorted harshly. "You still have that bag? It's useless on Earth, you know."

"Perhaps not." For a moment, Jeqon let his incorporeal essence fill the throne-like space, as if he were a god. "Besides, we be leaving, and I wish it." After a relished and very satisfying pause, the dark-skinned brother rose and stepped nonchalantly to one of the energy orbs. He was unamused by Zadkiel's boorishness. Posturing on the Seat was just a moment offered and a chance taken. What could it hurt?

Without warning, behind the Seat of Power, the darkness of space twisted angrily, causing the surrounding stars to blink out for a moment. This was no simple arrival into the nothingness of space. This was clearly retribution for whoever had impinged the sanctity of the Seat of Power.

The initial concussion made their lightships shimmer.

"Ramiel!" Asbeel squealed his dismay into the darkness.

"Zadkiel, now!" Jeqon hissed his plea, suddenly fearful; all his coquettish behavior was gone. "You must do this. Send us without delay."

With a frenzied jerk, Zadkiel clapped his hands over his head, and the balls of light shattered, fragmenting into the darkness, and finally coalescing once again. Where the three brothers had stood, only the lightships remained, building a charge, readying to streak violently toward Earth.

Ramiel, Herald of Hope

"Who has violated my authority?"

Ramiel's voice crackled with electricity as his essence exploded into the frigid cold of space, and small detonations of inanimate matter flickered in the distant reaches of the heavens, the result of out-of-phase energy discharge gone wild. It was anger, and righteous anger, the worst kind. His imperative split the darkness, sparking across the distant Earth and creating a wave of electrical stars from power lines stretched tautly across the night sky.

Ramiel was furious.

"No one may sit in the chair except me!"

And Gadreel, of course. He was all powerful, now that the Mind was trapped. Despite his assertation, it was clear someone else had been here, as three glowing spheres hovered in the darkness.

Even so, he knew he could not open them now, and whoever was inside would have to eventually return. There was opportunity yet to catch the violators, and time spent on Earth was worse than anything he could do to those in the ships.

He clapped his hands, not waiting for the glowing balls of light to build up adequate power. With his command, they were gone. He was pleased to see them streak toward Earth.

"Good riddance to bad rubbish," he muttered.

Then, space bent, and he, also, was gone.

Chapter 23

Pablo Esposito, Meteorite Hunter

The barefoot boy, roughly dressed and cocoa-skinned, slapped the burro on its hindquarters, urging it on. A meteorite had fallen in the mountains, and he was on his way to retrieve it.

"Se mueven más rápido, te engañe," the boy's voice prodded. *Move faster, you fool.* If the animal didn't move more quickly than its present speed, they would not get to the meteorite and back to the village before nightfall.

The animal was a dusty color, as much from the billows of dry soil it stirred with each step, as from the pigmentation of its hair. Its ears drooped, too, a sign of its extreme weariness. Pablo slapped the animal's rump with a long stick, hoping to get its attention. Understandably, the thick hide had long ago grown callused with the beatings, and the old burro no longer noticed. Its tail simply swished as if it could send the switch packing as easily as an obnoxious horsefly. The day would end when the day ended, and there would be light once again when the sun decided to greet the morning. No amount of prodding or hurrying would change that.

The boy had dressed for the heat of a Baja day. He had

considered that a blessing early that morning. It had been hot in the lowlands as he pulled on the thin cotton pants he also wore as his underclothing on cold days. Over his chest, he had donned a long, sleeveless shirt. Also, there was a cord he used to tie his pants, one that thankfully added little weight to his attire, even when he had to wrap it around his waist twice. He had felt unencumbered, except for his knife fastened around his neck. He always took his knife to the mountains. He had learned that lesson from his father.

Now, he was chilly. He had not learned that lesson so well. They had traveled high into the interior, searching, and trees surrounded them. A breeze had picked up, whipping the thin cloth around his body and legs. He should have worn his outer pants, not just his underclothing, because the wind had no trouble finding its way through the loose weave. He regretted he had on nothing more underneath. Even his man parts were cold.

The cord around the burro's neck was also bothersome, as it was heavy and coarse, and holding it, the boy could not wrap his arms around himself for warmth. He cursed the burro for being so slow, for if it simply walked more quickly, they could have reached their destination and surely made it halfway down by now. Warily, he only used curse words that were ones a boy was supposed to know. He dared not use the ones his big brother threw about carelessly. His mama would swat him if she heard, and she would hear his words, even here on the mountain, from the trees themselves, if she wished to ask. Not even they would be brave enough to tell her no.

He breathed a sigh of relief when they finally reached the ridge his father had pointed out to him, the one that lined up with Picacho del Diablo. It was there they had seen the meteorite hit, and the norteamericano scientists would pay much for it if Pablo could find it first, before anyone else did.

When the burro hesitated at some heavy roots, refusing to step over, he slapped its rump again. "Mover, Burro!" When that brought no results, he wrapped the rough cord around his hand and stepped over the roots himself, ready to pull the animal after him. He was the boss, not that cantankerous donkey.

When he did was when he found what he had come for. It was not a meteorite, at least not one of the iron variety. This meteorite had legs like tree trunks, cinnamon-colored skin, and dark hair gracing a face that even Pablo recognized as astoundingly beautiful.

That was not what amazed him most, though, for all around this meteorite was a widely splayed pair of wings, sections of which were missing, and the body was twisted horribly in the middle. Blood, a viscous red liquid mixed with an unusual yellow fluid, covered parts of the creature. The boy was certain that even were this creature to be alive—and he doubted that— no body twisted like that could ever be made to walk again.

He looked up at the sky with tears in his eyes, and it was clear blue with a few wispy clouds. There was no storm on the horizon, neither had there been one when the meteor had flashed through the sky early that morning.

The boy murmured, "Santo de Dios." How much did God have to hate one of his angels to cast him to Earth to die?

Him. God had cast *him* down from Heaven. Pablo knew this angel was a man, because he had nothing at all on, and his man parts were much larger than Pablo's. He also knew he could not leave this angel here on the ridge, not if there was even a chance he was alive. It had taken him the better part of a day just to get here. It would get very cold at night, and this man, er, angel would certainly die.

Pablo was practical, though, and a smart boy. It was the reason his father had entrusted him with the burro. Any other boy would have stopped by the side of the road to play in a stream, but not Pablo. Pablo had held the burro's cord, and when he found the angel, he hadn't run away.

Wrapping the burro's cord around a tree branch, he stepped gingerly to the angel, being very careful not to walk on the tattered wings. He was certain the angel would be able to feel it if he did, and he didn't want to hurt the angel. Not Pablo. If the angel woke, he wanted to be able to say, "*I did not step on your wings. I was very careful, indeed.*" Truly, his mother might even ask when he returned if he was careful with the angel. He would proudly tell her he did not step on the angel's wings, and it would be the truth.

The angel was the brother Hizkiel, He Who Guards the Gate of the North Wind, and he would have been glad to offer his gratitude to Pablo for his care, but his body was quite incapacitated just then. As Pablo had first suspected, the Chief Aide to Gabriel might truly have been dead, except for the stand of trees into which he fell. It also helped that he was at a much higher altitude than the general elevation of Arizona, and on this high, Baja ridge, he was not solidly corporeal. In fact, if Pablo had looked carefully, he would have seen the faint outlines of broken tree branches through the remains of his wings. Another benefit of this high altitude was the limited effects of the sub-atomic polarization fields that prevented brothers and humans from touching. If Hizkiel had landed at a location much lower in altitude, the boy would not have been able to offer the angel much assistance at all. He would not have been able to touch him.

As it was, Pablo didn't know how to check to see if the angel was alive or dead except to put his hand in front of his nose, so he squatted beside his shoulders and reached out. The boy held his hand next to Hizkiel's nostrils, his heart beating more quickly when he felt the pressure of expelled air.

He had to find a way to rescue his angel.

Glancing around, he found two long branches that had fallen to the ground. Pulling out the small cord that held his knife, he cut off the smallest twigs, laying them on the ground out of the way. Then he laid the two long ones beside the angel. He didn't think the injured being could ride atop the burro, not with his body twisted in the way it was. If he could build a travois, the burro could pull the angel down the mountain.

There were two problems with his travois, though. He needed a cord to tie the branches together, and he also needed something to make a sling in between. Reaching to the cord around his burro's neck, he took a deep breath, considering. Only a boy not as responsible as Pablo would use the burro's cord. The burro might run away.

There was another way, though.

He reached to his waist and untied the cord that held his

thin pants snug. Holding it up, he evaluated it, and decided it would work if he cut it in half, one part for each end of his makeshift travois. Then, he reached to the burro's small pack and pulled out the cloth he had brought to wrap the meteorite. Shaking it out, he sighed. It was very small for an angel with very big wings.

His heart pounding, he dropped his pants, glad his shirt covered him below his man parts. As he cut the fabric, splitting it into one wide piece, he shook his head at his mama's reaction. She would hit him on the back of his head for ruining a perfectly good pair of pants. "*Mama*," he would explain. "*Is a pair of pants more important than one of God's angels?*" He smiled at that thought. She would have no answer, and he would be smarter than his mama.

His travois prepared, he tied it to the burro, and he knelt beside the angel to push him onto it. Holding his meteorite cloth to the bloodiest parts and using his bare hand on the other, he leaned in and pushed, rolling Hizkiel onto the makeshift sled, the brother's body landing face down with a sickly thump.

Pablo pulled his bare hand away, surprised. He wiped it on his shirt. It stung, like the sparks that had jumped when he touched a balloon at his cousin's party, except worse. After that, moving the wings to pile them on the sled with the angel, he was careful only to touch them with the cloth. His hand didn't hurt, then.

Pablo knew the trip down the mountain would be a rough one for his angel, but there was no other choice. He had to be taken to the village somehow. At least he wasn't awake, and he wouldn't feel the bumps and rocks. Pablo regretted that the angel's man parts were on the bottom side where they would drag against the ground, but maybe he would forgive Pablo. After all, he had been very careful, and he had not stepped on the angel's wings at all, not even one time.

The boy grabbed the burro's cord, and he called, "Tirar con fuerza, Burro." *Pull hard, Burro.*

Lucky Pablo. He had found an angel, and everyone would be so proud of him. He could not wait to get home.

Rikkianne Kristofferson, Asst. Motel Manager

Rikkianne stepped into the managers' rooms she shared with Nigel. She put a small towel to her neck. The day was already blistering outside, and it was barely started.

Setting aside the vacuum she'd carried in, she checked the thermostat. She sighed when she saw it was cool enough indoors. It was her. She was so overheated from just that walk that she wanted to climb in the freezer and chill for a while.

"Rikkianne?"

The door opened, and she turned. Nigel's voice was sharper than she liked, and she wondered what had got his goat.

"I'm here, Nigel. No need to yell." She stepped to the little kitchenette and ran a glass of water, downing most of it before turning around. When she lowered it, he was standing watching her. "Yes?"

"That lady you picked up last night. You told her no dog? I seen her with a dog this morning. Two kids, too. You told her them stay outside?"

She laughed, and then she straightened her face as quickly as she could, waving her hand at him to show she meant no offense. "There for a bit, I thought you meant the kids to stay out. It just fell in my head, *Outside, kiddies. Dog gets the second bed.*"

"Be serious, Rikkianne. I cleaned up dog urine before. It stank up that room for weeks. Cain't get nothing to take out that smell, just time and air. Time and air don't make this place no money."

"I told her, Nigel. You seen it this morning, I take." She set the glass in the sink. She could wish for a dishwasher, but none of the rooms had one of those. So, she washed by hand, but not too often.

"Said it, didn't I? Out playing with that fool Bobby Dalton, along with two little kids. I'm mad at that Bobby Dalton, too."

"Over what for, Nigel?"

"Ever day he's here, sun up to sun down. Sometimes he even brings that fool friend of his. Austen, I think. And that other boy."

"Little T?" Rikkianne knew he thought of Bobby as his own, he was around so much. She wondered what the irritation was. "So? You want me to call his momma and tell him he's not welcome?"

"Naw. You know better. It's that, well, just that," and finally, he spit it out, "he cain't come over to help with the antennas yesterday, but he can sure make it over to play with that fool dog and those kids. They don't let him prowl the motel, rummage through the things left behind, and swim in the pool for nothing. I even swam with him one night. Remember, Rikkianne?"

That told Rikkianne he knew about the filched keys, and she fought to keep a smile from her face. She remembered the swim. Nigel had been on his happy cloud for two days.

Then his arms wrapped around her waist, and he reached to kiss her up beside her neck, just where he liked to nuzzle her when it was the middle of the night, and he was about to finish his business inside of her.

"I'm just ventin' my steam, Rikkianne. Forgive me?" He kissed her several more times, heading down her shoulder, until he grabbed her arm playfully in his mouth, shaking it gently. "Rrrrr."

She turned, laughing. "What'd you do that for?"

He looked up, his head still held low. "I'm that dog. Rrrrr." He took her arm in his mouth again.

She slapped him away. "You want me to go check on the dog?"

"Naw. Like I said. I was just ventin'. I can do it. Might even go play with that boy and that dog myself. I just might like that dog better'n Bobby. You never know." He laughed and headed back to the door. Stopping at the thermostat, he peered at it, then reached to adjust it. Looking at her, he grinned. "Cain't let it get too warm in here. Won't stay cool in the heat if we do." Then he was gone out the door.

341

Two of the Familiars of the Triune Mind

A Man stood in a fire-blackened room, although he was hardly a man. To his credit, anyone who happened to see him, catching just a glimpse of his shape as he walked past one of the openings in the burned-out shell of a house, they might think an investigator had finally been sent to delve into the mysterious fire, the one that had nearly taken the life of an innocent little baby and her parents.

Except for the six wings, of course.

They would be more suspicious about the other presence in the taped-off structure. That mysterious shape walked with four legs the size of logs, alongside the Man at times, then moving away, prowling upstairs—what was left of the upstairs—before rejoining the Man once again. The paws attached to those legs were massive, and the brilliance of a flaming mane lighted its way, bright even against the morning sun. Occasionally, a massive lip curled, and a rumble that spoke of earthquakes, tornados, and the deepest bowels of the earth rumbled out.

"Quiet, Nobility." Wisdom came up behind the Familiar, placing his own human-shaped hand on that outsized lion's head, gently working the blazing mane, its brilliance to him no more than a gentle flicker that spoke of eons spent together at the foot of the Triune Mind's Seat of Power. "Our quarry will reveal itself. We must simply sift the clues, then make sure we are in the right place when it does."

That was Wisdom's role as one of the Four Familiars of the Triune Mind. He could see past the moment of emotion, finding the path that would lead to the earnestly desired end, or at least he could do that sometimes, when he wasn't *responding.* He wasn't responding now. He was thinking, and he needed Nobility to think, also.

Nobility growled, looked at Wisdom, and waited. He had found something upstairs, and the Man at his side would be wise to follow him. Nobility *wanted* to respond, wanted to be out tearing and slashing, righting the wrong the Rebellion had forced upon his master. Still, Wisdom said otherwise, and Nobility knew of restraint, of warring within rules, of civility. It was all that made existence palpable, and without it, life would dissolve into a morass of despicable duplicity. For that reason, Nobility usually listened when Wisdom spoke.

Now, Wisdom was the one who needed to pay attention. Nobility's voice rumbled again.

Wisdom knelt at his friend's side, his arm over his shoulders. "Yes, Nobility? It's clear you've found something. Shall we go see?"

It was in the bedroom where they gathered. There, just over a collapsed crib, one wall *felt* interesting. Wisdom placed his hand on the wall and listened to the vibrations of the scorched molecules inside, for all molecules sang, all the time, even ones that had been blasted with an unnatural flame. Neutrons; electrons; protons. They were never still, and if one knew how to listen very carefully, their song could be deciphered.

This wall told the story of a brother gently brushing by, entering the wall, each corporeal molecule of the brother's body sliding next to, around, and past those making up the wall, with incalculable numbers of living molecules teasing them hundreds of billions of times, exciting the wall, and finally leaving the molecules in the wall alone once again, wishing for more. Then, a short time later, another brother came through, roughly and with anger, his molecules slamming into those in the wall, going on by anyway, the molecules left quivering with exhaustion. Each brother had left a signature, one that Wisdom could read, if he listened very carefully.

"Kafziel came through first." Wisdom turned to Nobility, and he smiled when a growl rumbled from the great cat's throat. All the Unity knew of Kafziel. Even having been sequestered for so many ages didn't hide his reputation from the Four Familiars. Wisdom's hand remained on the wall, the molecules inside telling him also of the second person who had passed through. The molecules sang their dance, revealing their secrets, and he knew.

"Uriel followed."

The Man's face tensed as he said the name. This was the one Gadreel had revealed to them. For a moment, all was calm, the silence pregnant with building anger, then a roar broke the stillness, and black dust shifted loose from the charred beams overhead. It floated down in the early morning light, its corporeal substance littering the corporeal air that filled the burned-out hulk of the home.

Wisdom knelt at Nobility's side, looking into his golden eyes. "We promised this brother to Gadreel. He is not ours to claim. Be patient, my friend. Revenge will be ours, and our Master will be freed. We must wait for Swiftness and Strength. I have called for them, already." He stood and stepped to the window. Glancing at the beams overhead, he frowned at the falling dust. Effortlessly, he flicked his six wings out, beating the air, and driving the motes away. He felt no need to be covered with the filth of this world.

Nobility stepped beside him, a low grumble emanating from his throat, and he nuzzled Wisdom. The Man looked down and chuckled. "I know you're sorry, and I accept your apology. I still dislike the dust, though."

Nobility's reply this time was a purr that any cat owner would have recognized as unqualified contentment.

Wisdom's eye was caught by a small boy playing with a ball in his front yard across the street. The child glanced up, something at the burned house across the road catching his attention, a movement in the shadows, perhaps, or a rumble of sound that didn't seem quite right. Wisdom expected the boy couldn't have said what it was that got his attention, but he dropped his ball and peered at the house. It was just the same as it had been the morning before, the gaping opening that had been the double front doors, underneath high gables that seemed so out of place in a New Mexico subdivision. The roof was burned away now, and only parts of the gables remained, but in the charred timbers, the boy surely remembered the house that had stood there only days before.

Wisdom passed the boy a suggestion. The shadows that were there weren't seen at all. Instead, his eyes would be forced away. He wouldn't know that they had *shifted*, just that when he looked for one of the shadows in an otherwise empty window, only to find himself looking somewhere else, he would forget what he'd been looking for in the first place.

The rumbling, too. Perhaps the rest of the house would fall today. Buildings did that. Wisdom caught something from the boy, his class studying the World Trade Center attack; the airplanes that had hit the buildings; and then without warning, the Twin Towers tumbling to the ground. He impressed that the house that had burned might be the same. If he watched carefully enough, right before his eyes, the whole building might fall flat to the ground, and he would be the only one to see.

For, wasn't it true the boy had seen nothing at all, there was no one in the burned house, no conversation had ever taken place, and no hand had felt that blackened, excited wall? And, even if it were true, a simple Suggestion had been all that was needed to make it all go away.

Eventually, the boy's mother called him in, telling him he had to put on sunscreen if he wanted to remain outside any longer. Wisdom imagined she would force him to follow her to the kitchen for a glass of water, and before it was gone, his thoughts would already be on the cartoons that danced on the television in the den. The only thing left of his interest in the shadows and rumbles would be the ball on the front walk. It might sit and watch for him, but alas, it would tell nothing at all.

When the child didn't return, he turned to Nobility, resting his hand on that blazing mane.

"Our Master loves these people. We must take care in our pursuit of our prey."

Nobility rumbled his reply. He agreed, but he also knew that no matter how nobly one fought for one's cause, sometimes the innocent suffered.

"I know, friend." Wisdom sighed. "We must give our best effort."

He also undertood it wasn't Nobility he had to worry about. It was Strength and Swiftness who must be contained, and that was a task almost beyond doing, if it could be done at all.

The Other Two Familiars of the Triune Mind

An ear-splitting screech rent the morning. Feathers triple the size of any ever worn by any normal eagle rippled in the wind, catching the shifts in the breeze, telling the bird which muscle group to tighten and which to release. Swiftness was unaware of that, though. All he knew was the smell of the brothers of the Unity, and it permeated the exterior of the old mine out in the desert where he and Strength now gathered.

Swiftness felt another, too. A half-breed had been in the space.

Far below, his massive feet touching soil, a great bellowing from Strength's oversized chest caused the very dust of the ground to shake, forcing tendrils of murkiness to rise into the clear morning air. Cloven hooves the size of dinner plates stamped the ground, and great muscled shoulders lifted into the air, pounding downward as one, driving those hooves against the soil. The rocks in the ground shook in fear, for with Strength on the loose, not one place on Earth was safe.

Swiftness screeched again. *Inside, Strength! You must make clear the way! Nothing may prevent us from entering!* His feathered wings tore at the sky, uncaring of the heat or the sun. Swiftness was *alive,* and he could be here and there and back again in an instant, and none could get in his way. He was the snap of the lightning in the storm and the fear of death in the night. He was the sound that came from far away, and the instant attack that followed. He was unmatched in his skills, and all should quaver with fear, for he was on wing.

None on this puny globe were safe.

In reality, there was no need to clear the way into the old mine. All the Familiars needed to do was wish themselves in, or as close as "wish" could come to what the brothers of the Unity and their familiars could do. Solid walls were no obstacle to them.

Strength and Swiftness were *responding*, however, and

346

Wisdom was not there to moderate their behavior. They would do as they willed. What they willed just then was to force their way inside.

Strength's massive horns splintered the door through which Uriel had not been allowed to enter, and the way to the interior of the mine was laid bare. When he reared in frustration, his horns scraped the lofty ceiling. As he turned to search, his hooves crushed tables and chairs. The veined mirror from the wall reflected him in all his furor and corporeal majesty for only an instant before shattering into a thousand glittering shards, tumbling like fractured ice over the cavern floor. When he bellowed his disappointment, Swiftness joined him, his scream of fury eclipsing that of his companion.

It was when the smelter was torn asunder that the sounds quieted for a time. The smoked meats hanging in reserve provided quite a respite for their hunger, as both the Ox and the Eagle fed, stoking their fuel reserves for encounters to come.

They had nearly consumed the stores when both stopped and raised their heads. Their frantic, emotional *response* had been dulled by their stomachs, and the call was one they could not help but hear. It was Wisdom, and they were commanded to attend.

With the summons understood, Strength snorted his acquiescence, his massive tree legs stamping the rock floor of the cave. Swiftness screamed that he would follow. In a rumble of feet and feathers, the mine was behind them, its destruction as forgotten as yesterday's sun.

Not surprisingly, they did create quite the unintended spectacle when they left the mine, for damaging the smelter also broke loose the gas pipes that fueled the old furnace. The entire time they fed, natural gas was filling the mine's interior, and the ensuing results were only a matter of how quickly it reached a suitable combustion source.

The explosion happened about twenty minutes later. The cracking of subterranean rock extended to Phoenix and Tucson. The resulting shuddering of the earth was felt as far north as the Navaho Nation, and as far east as the Zuni lands in New Mexico. The earthquake registered on seismographs from

347

California to Central Colorado, and the reports were picked up by every local television station within driving distance.

By the time the reporters arrived, the flames that had licked out of the mouth of the cave, stretching half a mile into the sky, were gone. The interior of the mine was decimated, and there were no signs it had been occupied anytime within the past half century. It was simply another odd occurrence that happened during that extremely hot summer week, and other than a fifteen-second television news blurb and three lines on the fourth page of the second section of one local newspaper, it received no real coverage at all.

Chapter 24

Thomas Keaton, Airline Pilot

The pilot of the commercial aircraft frowned as a warning light began flashing on his console. Thomas Keaton had been flying for decades, and he hadn't earned all his gray hair just to lose his pension for want of a well-maintained craft. There had been that little air pocket a bit ago, just that little bump that had surprised them. The weather indicators had suggested nothing out of the ordinary. Clear sailing and all that. He hadn't even warned the passengers to buckle up, because there had been nothing to warn them of. Then, *whump!*

Still, it had been nothing to suggest any reason the craft would be losing air pressure. As far as anyone knew, only 16B had found any reason to complain, and she had been taking a drink out of a soda can. Some of it had spilled onto her collar. The flight attendant had remedied that with some soda water, though.

Now, this.

"Odd." He called his concerns aloud. "Air pressure in the cabin is off. We seem to be bleeding somewhere."

He looked over at his co-pilot, Bob Gotthardt. They were a pair. They flew together frequently, and the idiot flight controllers, those clueless nerds stuck in their ivory towers, had started this thing about calling them Jim-Bob, as if they were one person with a split personality. Not Thomas-Bob, but Jim-Bob. They couldn't even get his name right. *"Hey, Jim-Bob! Am I speaking to Jim or Bob today?"* Still, they vacationed together at least twice a year, their wives, Mary and Alice, at their sides. When their kids were small, the trips had trailed quite an entourage, both of suitcases and toys. Now, it was just the four of them.

"Do you think we should consider switching to manual backup?" Bob didn't even look up as he asked the question. His hands were already flying over the instrumentation, running syschecks, attempting to isolate the cause, although there was a hint of a smile on his face. The system for maintaining cabin pressure was fully automatic, even protected by a second, redundant system. It was unheard of for it to fail.

The flight engineer chuckled. "Come on, guys. It's just a few numbers." Connor Haskins was a pup compared to the grays in the front seats, and his retirement was a lifetime away. "Besides, have you heard any alarms, yet? The 737 has a good safety record, and this 800 is one of the best birds in the industry. Everyone knows Boeing makes a good product. Back-up systems will pick up the air pressure difference."

Bob glanced at Thomas, shaking his head, then he motioned with a thumb to the kid in back. "Probably believes in Santa, too, flying reindeer, trumpet-blowing angels, and everything."

Connor crumpled a piece of paper and tossed it forward. "Angels, especially. I've got one in Miami and another in St. Petersburg."

"Wings?" Thomas chuckled, picturing the type of angel Connor would have. Not the chaste type, for sure.

"If you want. It's not the wings that keep me interested, though. It's the rather more human anatomy that tweaks my interest." He cupped his hands at his chest, suggestively chuckling. "Va-boom!"

Bob removed his 'phones, and he made to stand, leaning to whisper to Thomas in a stage voice, "I'll be glad when the kid gets through puberty." He glanced at Connor and winked. Then, louder, "I think I'll walk the deck, comfort the passengers, perhaps do a bit of a visual check. I get chills when I think of Aloha 243, half the cabin gone, and that one flight attendant sucked right out. I remember seeing pictures of that. Stress cracks are not allowed on this flight."

"Hey!" Connor grinned. "That was decades ago. Look." He tapped one of his displays. "Pressure's still under 8,000 feet. I bet not one bag of chips has exploded."

"That's it, kid. Keep a positive attitude." Bob slapped him on the shoulder, slipped his cap on his head, and exited the cockpit, heading into the cabin.

"Getting long in the tooth." Connor gave Thomas a conspiratorial wink, indicating Bob, and turned back to his displays.

"243 was a Boeing, kid. Did you know that? And twenty years is not that long in the airline industry."

Thomas Keaton whispered it softly, though. He had no desire to step on Connor's youthful and very inexperienced toes.

Bob Gotthardt, Co-Pilot

In the passenger cabin, Bob charmed everyone he came in contact with. He was an experienced hand at working the passengers, and he moved expertly down the aisle through the First Class section. Several of the passengers were pillowed, blankets pulled up around their necks. He winked at one little boy whose face glowed with a hand-held video game, turning to see a blue-haired creature zipping along the screen, catching gold coins. As he walked, from time to time, he glanced around the cabin, just keeping an eye out for any joints or seams that seemed out of alignment.

He greeted one of the flight attendants, Forrest Lampathakis, slipping past him in the aisle, answering his questioning look with a whisper, "That air pocket from earlier. Just checking on things." The attendant nodded and moved past.

At Row 16, he made a point to speak to the passenger in Seat B, one of the few actually awake. She was middle-aged and very attractive. He wondered why she wasn't in First Class. She looked like she could afford it. She showed him her collar and laughed, gushing about how helpful the attendant had been. He was relieved there would be no snafu about that little incident. Still, in glances, while he spoke to her, he searched the side of the cabin next to her seat, making sure Row 16 was not the site of the air pressure problem. It was a limited recline row, and the exits were just behind it. If there was a weak place in the body of the airliner, it wouldn't surprise him for it to be around one of the exit doors.

He found nothing, though. He continued on, letting his eyes rove the ceiling, his smile coming alive when he noticed people watching him, occasionally stopping to make a comment or tell a short joke. One little girl had her teddy bear, one with a pink ribbon, and she asked him if he wanted to hold it. He patted its head and told her he was sure it would rather have a hug from her.

Moving back a bit, in the more crowded section of the cabin, people were squeezed in, some uncomfortably, in more seats than Bob thought any aircraft company ought to be allowed to pack into a fuselage this small. Still, the company had to pay the bills, and his paycheck was one of those bills. He had no room to complain. He was also somewhat reassured to reach the back of the cabin and to have found no signs of damage. The only things back there were the galley stretching across the width of the cabin and several passenger restrooms. Perhaps the pressure drop was nothing more than a door seal that had become damaged, or . . . and his face lit with an epiphany of understanding. He grinned. A misaligned toilet seal. He was certain that's what the cause must be.

"Shayanne," he said quietly to another of the flight attendants. He'd flown with Shayanne Grazzini for years. She was beautiful, with an exotic cast to her face. He reached to her arm to pull her to the galley, away from the passenger seats.

"Bob," she said, putting her hand on her chin. "You sure seem awfully happy at nothing much in particular. What can I do for you?" She winked.

"Well, I think I just answered my own question." He

motioned for her to come closer, and her eyes twinkled.

"Bob? Here? Everyone can see us." She licked her bottom lip, as if preparing for a kiss.

"Is anyone in the lavatory?" He glanced to see if he could tell whether the signs showed it they were occupied or not.

"Bob!" Her callout of his name was very demure, but she giggled. "I'll check." She grabbed his hand, laughing and covering her mouth with her palm.

Just before they reached the lavatory door, Forrest bumped into her and whispered in her ear, "Careful, babe. I'm getting a cup of ice for the lady in 16B. She's all wound up after talking to Bob, here. He just charms everyone."

She grinned. "He's sure charmed me, Forrest."

Bob grabbed Forrest's arm. "Can the ice wait a moment? I want you to come see this. Shayanne and I are headed to the lavatory—"

She laughed coyly. "Bob! A threesome?"

"Bob?" Forrest put his hands on his hips. "Um, does Alice know?"

Bob frowned. "Alice? I should think not. She's at home, probably getting ready to go on her church mission's getaway. How would Alice know?"

"Well, perhaps she should." He frowned. "I think I'll just take that ice up."

Bob looked back and forth between the two, then he snorted. "You two think I want to go in there for a little hanky panky? God, no! The cabin's got a pressure leak." He glared at Forrest. "I think one of the lavatories might be the culprit. I can go by myself, if you'd rather." He turned his glare to Shayanne, whispering, "Shame on you."

She sniffled, her face falling. "You're such a prude, Bob. Do you know that? I thought for a minute you really liked me." She reached to wipe one finger carefully against the edge of her eye. Then she laughed. She was a flight attendant, and a pleasant smile, one believably real and honest, was part of the job. "Okay, men. Let's go in the john."

"But . . . no hanky panky, right?" Forrest had a wary look in his eyes. When an answer wasn't imminent, he repeated his question, "Right?"

"No, Forrest. It's all about the hole in the lavatory. I'm thinking a toilet is stuck open, and it's venting outside somehow. Nothing else."

The first lavatory seemed just fine. The light came on, the water in the sink flowed into the drain, and even the air vent pumped out cool air.

"No leaks," Shayanne murmured. "Shall we check the other?" She looked at Bob, and just behind, Forrest shrugged and rolled his eyes. She grinned, pushing on Bob's shoulder to get him to back out. There really wasn't room in the small space for two, much less three.

The other lavatory was on the opposite side of the cabin. Bob reached it first, and he froze at the door, looking back at the other two. He motioned for them to hurry up. When they drew closer, they could hear air whistling around the frame. Bob had his hand on the joint between the door and wall, running it around the perimeter.

"This is it." He pressed his lips together, not entirely glad to have found this particular something. There was quite a bit of air movement, too. He placed his hand on the latch, and Shayanne immediately covered it with hers, effectively freezing his motions.

Forrest frowned, but she shut him up with her eyes.

"Are you sure, Bob? I mean," and she glanced around the cabin at all the safe and secure people, most of them sleeping, just the occasional TV flashing its images from the back of individual headrests, "that's a lot of air. What if . . . it makes the cabin decompress? Could we just tape it? We do have duct tape."

Bob pulled her hand from his and lifted it to his lips, where he kissed it. He looked her in the eyes and smiled, effectively disarming her concerns.

"You charmer." She glanced away to the passengers, then laughed once again. "Look at them. We have a made-for-TV drama going on back here, and they sleep through it. Okay, you fool. Open it, and let's see what we find."

The door didn't want to open, but when it did, the outrush

of air increased tenfold. It was loud, too. A hole had been ripped in the ceiling of the lavatory, one punched from the outside in, leaving the skin of the aircraft pressed down against the toilet space. A section of the lavatory ceiling was missing altogether, and several jagged pieces of metal pierced the remainder. Still, the actual opening visible in the fuselage was hardly wide enough for a person's arm, much less what had fallen through.

Bob, Shayanne, and Forrest saw none of that, though. Lying on the floor of the lavatory was a man, well, perhaps something resembling a man, a thing with the genitals of a man, and it had a gash in its leg that ran from just below the knee all the way up and into its groin. It looked like its member had been sliced, too, and Shayanne turned away when she saw that. She whispered for Bob and Forrest not to tell her unless it was good news.

They hadn't even noticed the possible amputation, though. What had their attention was what was beneath the man. Splayed out across the small space and up the walls were what could only be identified as wings, goodness-to-real feathered wings like angels wore. They were tattered—shredded—and loose feathers littered the small room. Still, angel wings. They could be—must be—as long as they weren't some sort of crazy hang glider setup that had gone awry and gotten tangled up with their aircraft.

When they reached for the man, he felt very cold, and his skin was rather tenuous, almost as if they could touch it and yet couldn't, either. The sensation was strange, as if he wasn't quite there. His skin was also unnaturally smooth, as if the man-creature was a baby born yesterday, although they all knew that wasn't possible. They did notice there was no belly button, and when he saw that, Bob glanced at Forrest. The flight attendant had seen it, also. Their eyes locked, and for a moment, it was as if their knowledge of what was possible and what wasn't turned inside out.

Still, it was a man—or creature—that needed their help, and their training kicked into action. Bob felt for a pulse at the base of the throat, and with a sigh of relief, he called, "We've got a live one. Shayanne, get some blankets to cover him with, and we need to get him out into the aisle. Then, this lavatory needs closed up and secured. Sealed, if possible."

With several blankets and much struggling between Bob and Forrest, the slender, creamy-skinned brother with his tousled head of dark, curly hair was dragged to the aisle behind the last row of seats. The remains of his wings were carefully gathered at his side, and for the passengers' benefit, he was covered as best as possible to look like a normal person, albeit one who was ill and seriously in need of medical attention.

"Look at that face," Shayanne whispered when they were finished. "Even with all those injuries, that's as beautiful a face as God ever gave anyone. I'd be a mess if I had my leg nearly cut off." Then, she murmured even quieter, "Was he, um, *cut* badly? His, um, personal parts? Do I even want to know?"

"It was all there, Shayanne." Bob stood at the lavatory door, the air ruffling his uniform, looking up at the hole in the ceiling, and he answered her absently. He looked to the man—he guessed it was a man—on the cabin floor. He was Mick Jagger slender, but not even the Mick could have slithered through that hole. How had this man gotten in that lavatory? Certainly not from the inside.

Kasbeel was lucky the liner was cruising at well over 30,000 feet. At that elevation, he had hardly been corporeal enough for the fuselage of the aircraft to stop him. When he hit, his arms and legs had been forced through the metal of the aircraft just fine, the weakness of the atmospheric disharmony enabling his molecules to shift around the stationary ones that made up the bulk of the aircraft. Only the core of his body had built up enough solidity to damage the outer fuselage shell. That was why the hole was so small.

The most dramatic damage to Kasbeel's body had been caused after he had passed through the external skin of the plane. The atmosphere had immediately increased, causing a sudden, regrettable solidification of the brother's physical structure, from wingtips to armpits. The interior finish materials of the plane had caused much of the injuries he exhibited, and all in the last few seconds of his tumultuous flight through the sky.

356

The flight team didn't really know what to do with him. Other than staunching the flow of not-quite-red blood from the gash running down his leg, they thought it best to let him lie quietly and to keep him warm.

The warm part was certainly what he needed. Even more, he needed food, and as much as could be forced down his throat. His body could heal itself, and completely, too, in a matter of minutes. All he needed was the fuel to do so. Yet, if the flight crew had seen that happen, it would certainly have tipped their credulity past the breaking point.

Back in the cockpit, the lavatory secured with Shayanne's duct tape, Bob closed the door gently. He stood for a moment, gathering his wits. Connor looked up with a quick grin.

"Hey, Bob! I told you this plane would take care of itself. The cabin pressure's leveled out, and all the numbers are fine."

Bob simply moved forward and dropped into his seat, reaching for his headphones, and holding them out in one hand. Thomas looked at him, his expression puzzled.

"Bob? Something unusual back there?"

"You won't believe me when I tell you." He fastened his headphones on. Then, he turned to Connor. "I found one of your angels, kid, only you won't want to take this one to bed with you."

Finally, picturing that, he began to smile. Something about all this *was* funny, after all.

Kinky Kinkerson, Reporter

"You could have driven, you know. I don't mind, and I do have insurance that covers anyone I let behind the wheel."

Kinky looked at the beautiful man sitting beside him, his ill-fitting pants comically exposing his lower legs, and his long fingers tapping his legs. He was surprised when his passenger reached to the air conditioner controls and turned it completely off.

"Why'd you turn the thing off? If you're cold, you could just turn the fan down."

Raphael tapped his knees a few moments, then he reached to the glass at his side. "Do you mind if I roll this down? This button here. It'll do that, won't it?" He turned to his benefactor, if Kinky could be called that, since it was Raphael who had saved Kinky's life.

Raphael smiled, and throw-it-out-the-window if Kinky didn't think he was turning queer right there in his own car. All this man did was suggest something, and Kinky's mind just went with it, like this was a woman, and she had him by the nuts. Only, this was no woman. Kinky'd seen otherwise out on the desert.

"Sure. Why not? It's only at least ninety out there. Who needs air conditioning?" He laughed and reached to his side, rolling all four windows down at the same time.

"Thank you. Look." Raphael pointed to a sign far down the road. "There. A place to eat." It said, ALL YOU CAN EAT. BREAKFAST UNTIL 11:00 AM. "I need food. Sausages and eggs. Bacon, maybe. Ham, if they have it." His tone indicated he also needed the all he could eat part, because it would be a lot.

Kinky started to say sure, but before he could get the word out, something crashed into his windshield, something black that was there for a moment, splintering the glass into a million spider webs, and was gone before he even knew what it was.

In a surprising change of demeanor, Raphael yelled, "Stop!" Then, without waiting, he threw open the door and flung himself from the car, startling Kinky more than ever. Kinky slammed on the brakes, throwing everything in the back seat into the floorboard and himself against the seat restraints.

"Ralph!" He yelled the man's name out the opened door, and he looked in his rearview mirror to see Raphael standing in the street, helping a naked black man to his feet. "My God," he whispered. "I just hit a man. Where did he come from?" Just then, he remembered his rented SUV, and for some reason, his hands began to shake. He reached and flipped off the ignition right there in the street. He didn't care if he was in anyone's way.

He'd nearly just killed a man, one he hadn't even seen in

the street. His heart raced in his chest, and his vision narrowed to just two thoughts.

Where did that man come from? and, *My, God, I really did; I just nearly killed a man.*

For understandable reasons, that hit entirely too close to home.

Raphael, Angel of Healing

Raphael dropped at the black brother's side, grabbing his face and turning it his direction. He laughed. "By all that makes up the Unity, it is you, you devil. What are you doing down here, and on the windshield of my car?"

Jeqon winked. "No wings, Raphael. I be dumping 'em just before I landed. You be proud of me?" He rubbed his backside. "Rough landing, though. Got your attention, did I?" His face brightened with his revelation.

"That, you did. I can't believe you're such a fool. This is a city street, and you're as naked as the day the Unity started its voyage ages ago. Stand. We're headed for breakfast. And, it seems, to get you some clothes."

"Don't need none. Look-it over there." He pointed across the street. "Got some buds be helping me out. They find a clothesline. Left me, telling ol' Jeqon to make sure you didn't get away. I did good?"

Raphael stood, looking for Jeqon's "buds." There were no wings and no naked men, and he had to search for a moment. Then, in his head, he heard, *"The sidewalk bench."*

There, sure enough, were two men, one in painter's overalls without a shirt underneath, slender and pale, with his feet in oversized athletic shoes. The other wore a pair of well-worn denims, the pockets frayed, and he had on a brightly colored tee. Hemp flip-flops dangled from his feet; and around his forehead, his sandy hair was pulled back and wrapped in a bandanna. Between them was a small roll of fabric, something that Raphael assumed were additional pilfered clothes from someone's clothesline.

"Get in the car, Jeqon."

Raphael nodded to the two men on the bench, and they waved. He already knew who they were. As soon as the one had spoken to him, their images had jumped into his thoughts. No, it wasn't the images of the two on the bench; it was their images from the Unity. He pictured the one in the painter's overalls, Zadkiel, in his most famous pose, staying the hand of an ancient Hebrew chieftain who had mistakenly tried to kill his son to prove his worth to a demanding god. The second, Asbeel, in his tee and hemp sandals, came to him as a rather pompous dignitary, one who had managed to rise high in the Unity hierarchy, mostly by keeping the right brothers happy. Both were more than welcome, although he had no idea why they were on Earth. It wasn't a vacation spot for most of the brothers.

"For Jeqon." Asbeel held up the rolled bundle, calling out loudly. "Can we come too, Raphael?" He kept his voice light and cheerful.

Zadkiel stood, his painter's clothes and bare shoulders giving him a bohemian flair. With an irritated look on his face, he slapped Asbeel's shoulder. "Of course we're going with them. Just climb in like you know what you're doing."

"Like I know?" Asbeel frowned. "What does that mean, Zadkiel? *Like* I know?"

Raphael smiled. He heard every word, although understood would be more accurate. Their thoughts were in his head as soon as they spoke them, for they were in resonance together.

By that time, they had reached the car, and Zadkiel grabbed the handle, swinging the door wide. He yanked the clothes from Asbeel's hand and tossed them to the other side of the seat. Roughly, he forced his friend down after them.

"Hey!" Asbeel slapped his hand away.

"Don't 'hey' me. Just get in." Then he dropped in also, his feet stepping over the items Kinky's quick stop had thrown to the floor.

About that time, the opposite door opened, and a third person was shoved brusquely into the back seat. Then the doors slammed on both sides, and Raphael fell into the front seat.

"I'm so sorry, Kinky. These guys back there," and he

pointed over his shoulder, "tend to just drop in like that. I never know when they'll show up."

"On my windshield?" By his glazed expression, he was in a bit of an information overload.

"Oh." Raphael reached to touch the glass. "That. I'm not sure I can fix that. I'll try later, though." He shrugged, then turned to the back seat. "Jeqon? Got your clothes on? Breakfast is just down the street." He pointed to the ALL YOU CAN EAT sign.

"Jeqon can do," came from the back of the vehicle. The rustle of cloth and a shaking of the car told those in the front seat he was doing as asked.

"Okay, Kinky." Raphael patted him on the shoulder. "You can go, now. We're all set." His hunger had started to gnaw at him, and he didn't want to be slowed down again.

"Who are these people, Ralph?" Kinky looked sideways at him. "These are friends, you said?"

A snicker came from the back seat. "Ralph? We are your friends, right?"

"Let me introduce you." Raphael turned and slapped the seatback, frowning at the black brother. "This is *Jeqon*, Asbeel, and Zadkiel. You'll like Asbeel and Zadkiel. Jeqon? I'll let you make up your own mind about him. At least you know what his naked backside looks like, although that's probably more than you ever wanted to see."

"That's . . . um, okay. After all, I did hit him." Kinky reached to turn the key, and he put the car in drive. "Sorry, guy, um, Jeqon." He finally looked into the mirror, and an expression of relief crossed his face when he found that the man was fully clothed.

Raphael interrupted, "This may seem no more than semantics to you, Kinky, but in all actuality, Jeqon ran into you. Trust me. You didn't run into him." At a thought, any brother could allow a car to pass directly through him, never feeling any pain or causing any damage. Doing so drained the energy reserves all brothers carried, but injuries? There would be none. Raphael knew beyond doubt Jeqon had fallen into the windshield on purpose.

He was relieved to pull into the parking lot. The smell of food was in the air, and human hunger pangs had kicked in, severely, even in such a radically different body. It was when he stepped inside that he got a surprise he certainly hadn't expected.

A very pretty greeter stood just inside the door. Her face was turned as she laughed charmingly at another employee. As she turned to him, Kinky glanced at the name stitched onto her uniform and smiled.

Raphael had already recognized the waitress, and he knew she . . . he, rather . . . was not the Bridgett stitched on the front of the smock.

"Good morning, sir. Five, today?" The waitress asked the question absently, and her voice was low and sultry. She laughed again with the woman she'd been speaking to when they walked in. "That's what I heard, Maylene. Isn't that a hoot and a half?"

"Yes, Bridgette. Five," Kinky replied. He grinned at Ralph, nodding to the girl with a wink.

"Oh, I'm not really Bridgette. I'm just wearing, um, *well.*" The voice went silent. "If it isn't Raphael."

Raphael snorted his reply, pushing building anger aside for a time. "And Jeqon and Zadkiel and Asbeel. Oh, and Kafziel, this is my good friend, Kinky. If you can't stick around to fight the Four Familiars, helping your *brothers* out, then at least you can feed us a good breakfast."

Asbeel leaned in to whisper to Raphael, "Kafziel turned into a woman? How did that happen?"

Kafziel glowered, while Jeqon laughed. From the puzzled expression on his face, Kinky didn't understand what was going on at all—naturally—and Zadkiel had to step back outside as he fought to keep his laughter under control.

"What did I say?" Asbeel turned to peer at those around him. When he got no answer, he asked again, "What did I say?"

Raphael slapped Asbeel upside the back of the head. How stupid could anyone get?

He felt a moment of remorse at his critical thought, realizing it was probably no more than hunger that had stripped his patience from him. He knew one thing, he was hungry enough to slap a hundred brothers on the back of the head.

Then, just to feel better, he slapped Asbeel again.

"Hey!" Asbeel reached to rub his head.

"And there's more where that came from." Somehow, that made Raphael feel much better.

Chapter 25

Grandy Grosvenor, Fishing Boat Captain

The heavy trawler surged through the waves, white spray washing the gunwales, with men's feet sliding sideways, as their hands reached to grab for support on whatever was within reach. To wash overboard was to inconvenience the rest of the crew in a best case scenario, and to risk death in a worst case one.

They were on their third week out, and even in summer, the Bering Sea could be a wild woman to make love to, no matter how appealing her charms. The sun had been up for a couple hours, but it was still darker outside than the inside of a cathouse. It was the cloud cover that caused that, and Grandy Grosvenor grabbed the crucifix he wore at his neck as he cursed the storm. If someone went over in this gale, it would be a long, hard ordeal to pull him aboard, if they could find him at all.

He looked down from the pilothouse as Whippet Vosburgh slapped the winch switch with his gloved hand. The man was burly, just the kind a seasoned captain wanted on his fishing boat. He was also quick on his feet, and he rarely fell down. Grandy would give up a dozen greenhorns for one Whippet, and he was pretty sure Whippet would help him throw the greenhorns over the side if push came to shove.

As he watched, Whippet slapped the switch again. Then he reached behind the box and wiggled something. Grandy could just hear the whine of the winch as it jerked, then began pulling the net in.

Ranier Holland ran over to him, whacking him on the back, and they exchanged a knuckle bump. Then the vessel shuddered, and a new wave came crashing onboard. When the water cleared, Whippet stood in the same spot, and Ranier was flat of his back, spitting water and trying to stand.

Grandy looked away. Like he said, he'd give up a dozen greenhorns for one Whippet.

Then, with a quick motion, Whippet killed the winch, and all four of the crew on deck ran to hang out over the net. Ranier leaned, pointing, and Whippet grabbed his collar to pull him back inboard. The other two, Bonzo Greenewalt and Woody Humelsine, grabbed the net by hand, pulling themselves up on it, prompting Grandy to grab the mike, sending his voice booming out into the dismal morning that brooded outside his windows.

"Did I sign on only idiots on this trip? Get back aboard! You two fall off, and I've got a problem. This vessel can't fish with only two crew." He slapped the 'phone away. He'd fished with Bonzo and Woody before. They weren't Whippet, but they certainly weren't stupid. What were they thinking, climbing out on the net?

It was only moments before he understood, though. The two men on the nets motioned to Whippet, and he grabbed Ranier's shoulder, calling something into his ear. The greenhorn opened a locker and pulled out a tarp, tossing it to Whippet, who then lobbed it to the men on the net.

Grandy couldn't really see what they were doing, not until the two men on the net started back aboard. They had something wrapped in the tarp, and it was pretty clear it was human, at least from Grandy's viewpoint. Dear God, he thought, we've pulled up someone from one of the other trawlers. I wonder who it is, whose wife'll get the bad news this trip out, that her man'll never be coming home again. With a deep breath, he sighed. At least they had the body, and that was more than most sea widows got.

He watched his crew haul the body—God, please don't let it be a woman—back where it could no longer be seen, and for that he breathed easier. Then the pilothouse door slammed open, and sea spray whipped inside. Grandy turned to see Ranier leaning inside, both arms hanging on the doorframe, a stupid grin on his face.

Grandy shouted, "Close the door, Ranier!"

The man jumped inside, slamming the door, the stupid grin still plastered across his too-young mug. He bounced with excitement.

"What, Ranier? I've got a trawler to run." Grandy whipped his chair away, looking out over his unmanned deck.

"Did ya' see? Christ! It's the real thing!" The greenhorn just grinned as if that said it all. "I said they could put it in my bunk."

Grandy slapped the console, and he spun around to gape at the fool standing in the wheelhouse with him. "A dead body in your bunk? Where is the brain you were born with?" He stood and rapped on Ranier's forehead. "God, I knew it. It's empty as the day you were born. We have a hold, Ranier. Bag the body, and put it on ice with the fish."

"No, Grandy. You don't understand. It's not dead. It's an angel. A real-to-God angel, with wings, feathers, and all."

The stupid grin was still there, and Grandy wanted to slap it away. Even a greenhorn knew there were no such things as angels. Still, he turned and set the autopilot, and he followed Ranier down to the crew quarters. His stomach turned over when he got there, because in Ranier's bunk lay a man, one with wings pushed up around his body. His flesh was horrendously ripped in numerous places, although there was little blood. The wet and the cold of the sea would have taken care of that, anyway. Even pale and waterlogged, his face had a brooding expression of power, one that Grandy wouldn't want to mess with, not under any circumstances. He reached and crossed himself, pulling his crucifix out of his shirt and kissing it respectfully. If this were really an angel, then they'd made the

366

catch of a lifetime. He grinned, and he looked at his crew.

"Good fishing, men. We caught a whopper this time."

Whippet pursed his mouth, then spoke thoughtfully, "I wonder if we ought'n to throw this back."

"Throw it back?"

That was Woody. He was nearly as bad as Ranier tonight.

"Yeah." Bonzo. He didn't speak often, but when he did, it was always to the point. "You think whatever did this to him's still looking? Maybe it wants to find him again."

A quiet spread over the room, one broken only by the sound of the sea outside. Then the captain kissed his crucifix again and spoke into the silence.

"And if it does, what will the Holy Father say if we don't offer what help we can?"

No one had a reply to that.

Angioletta Bacciarelli, Daughter of Kafziel

"Angioletta." She held out her hand, pleased when the other woman reached to shake.

"Jeri. Geraldine, really, but I grew up with that, and it always sounded so old to me. The minute I hit junior high, I forbade any of my friends to use it." She turned to face Angioletta, a weak smile attempting to show the humor of it all, but her eyes were red. "I'm sorry about saying what I did about it not being safe out there. How else could it be? Nothing's out there. What could they do to get hurt?"

She leaned her head against the doorframe and peered back into the sunshine. Just past the pavement, Bobby had fallen on several wiry tufts of grass that passed for lawn, wrestling with the wolf. The animal leaped at him, growling frightfully, nipping at his face, only to have the teenager spring to his feet and throw his arms around its neck, his laughter carrying into the motel room. The animal's fur seemed to sparkle with fireflies wherever it was touched, a million miniature prickles of static explosions. Dakota and Little Chrissy laughed in the high-pitched way of prepubescent children, their hands reaching to be part of the game, just wanting to touch the marauding mound of fascinating fur.

"You love them, don't you?" Angioletta stepped to Jeri's side, and she rubbed her arms. It felt so good in the room, although it was chilly at the door. She would adjust, though. She always had. After all, she'd been cold as long as she could remember.

"More than life itself. Is that really a wolf? I mean, wolves are dangerous, aren't they?" Jeri turned to glance at Angioletta, her eyes flicking to the man on the bed, and back outside again.

Behind them, Uriel could be heard as the bed creaked, and after only moments, his voice whispered at their backs, "That wolf is a very old friend of mine. Malak is more like me than he's different. I wouldn't hurt your children, and neither would he."

"Those yellow eyes." Jeri shivered.

Stepping past the woman, his bare shoulders rippling a musculature that spoke of his ability to fly through Earth's dense atmosphere, Uriel touched his forehead, and gave a hint of a bow. "Ladies, I think I'll go play with my dog." He winked. "Those children out there might enjoy seeing some of the tricks he can do." Then he was gone, his legs straining his Nomex, his torso glistening underneath the sun. About halfway across the parking lot, he turned, rubbing his arms and calling back, "Chilly out here. A bit, anyway."

For a moment, a smile glowed on his face, and then his back was all the women could see. Finally running, within moments he crashed into the wolf, although the impact didn't seem unexpected. Malak turned and leaped for him just as Uriel got to his side.

"You'd almost think the wolf . . . the dog knew he was coming. I didn't hear him call." Jeri pulled her blouse from her chest, the heat outside combined with that from the room having made her clothes sticky. "I guess men and their pets are like that, you know, able to read each other's minds." She paused for a moment, watching Uriel invite her two children to pet the animal. She shuddered when its pink tongue licked their faces. They giggled and pushed its face away, as if the tongue's touch tickled.

Angioletta saw it, and she smiled when she saw the visible effort on Jeri's part to set her reservations aside. What surprised her was that she *had* heard Uriel call to the wolf. *"Die, Second."* Laughter had laced the words. Now, with Jeri's comment, she wasn't so sure. Had she heard him speak, or had she simply known somehow that he had?

"He's your husband?" Jeri glanced at Angioletta, and she nodded her head toward the activities being played out across the lot. "The man out there?"

"A friend." That's what she'd told Bobby the night before . . . no, the night before that. A friend. She'd also later suggested he could be her husband. Yet, she didn't really know him, or how she'd come to be here with him. He seemed kind and considerate, though, and he'd been very gentle with Jeri's son. Now, he was out playing with the neighborhood kids and his dog. He seemed to be a very good man doing very normal things.

"Your friend smells nice, if I'm not being too forward. Something sweet. You know, that flavoring for cakes. He's beautiful, too." Jeri paused, frowning. "I apologize. That came out wrong. Handsome, I should say, except he really is beautiful." She laughed before she caught herself and apologized again. "I'm sorry. It's not like I'm interested or anything. It must be his cologne. He must have put something on."

"Vanilla," Angioletta whispered, watching Uriel tumbling with his wolf on the scraggly lawn. She remembered how she had barely been able to pull her hand away from his skin.

Outside, Uriel picked up a stick and threw it far into the desert; farther than she had ever seen a stick thrown before. The dog . . . the *wolf* was gone after it like lightning, faster even, if possible. The smaller children cheered, and Bobby simply stood with his hands on his hips, his mouth opened wide with amazement.

"That's it. Vanilla. I cannot believe that slipped my mind." Jeri laughed in an embarrassed sort of way. It was the angel, the "brother" in Uriel that had caused her forgetfulness. She couldn't know that, though. "Whatever he uses, it smells very alluring."

Angioletta smiled. She watched him playing, and what she thought was a little different. Maybe he's not so normal after all. No, that man who heals up perfectly in a matter of moments, and who smells like vanilla, is not normal at all.

She knew she'd come to a decision of sorts, although just what that decision was, she couldn't have verbalized. In her mind, she was beginning to believe she liked "not normal" very much indeed. That warmed her as the heat blowing from the room's air vents never would.

Eustorgio Ricci, Monsignor

Monsignor Ricci glanced at the external temperature reading on the dash of the American Corvette, dismayed to see it was nearing 100 degrees Fahrenheit. He was equally distressed that the bishop refused to let him run the air conditioning.

The staid bishop, a man who had never ventured an unholy action in his life, threw the remains of his unfinished sausage and egg breakfast sandwich through the open roof of the convertible and into the sky. "Let the birds of the air feast upon this gift from the Holy See." He turned to watch it splatter on the road behind them, and he laughed in exultation.

"Bishop!" Ricci's reprimand was unexpectedly sharp, much more so than he ever intended. To simply throw food out of the car was beyond anything he had ever expected of the highly esteemed man at his side. In Italy, Ricci had been frightened of him. Now it seemed he was frightened of what he might do to embarrass him!

"You take issue with me, Monsignor?" The bishop cast an impish grin his way.

"A buon intenditor poche parole, Bishop Carnaly." *A word to the wise.* Ricci pursed his lips as he continued. "We are in a foreign country, Your Excellency. Our example is the Christ we show to the world. How would the Holy See view your gift if he were really here?" He put in the clutch and shifted the sports car into sixth gear, pleased in spite of the bishop's actions when the

370

massive engine settled to a gentle purr. He was very conscious of how it compared to his own Cinque Cento, the ancient Fiat 500 he drove back in Italy. His little "peanut" was quite dependable, but it was nothing like this powerful machine.

"Del male non fare e paura non avere." The bishop leaned his head back in the morning sun and grinned. "The sun on my face is wonderful, and God above sees my heart."

"Is that why you say to 'do no *evil* and have no fear'? You think God sees your heart and knows your intentions are clean?" He repeated a direct translation of the bishop's idiomatic expression with stress on one particular word, wishing the bishop to hear the evil part. He felt he needed to make its meaning perfectly clear. "How is casting your uneaten bread and meat onto the road doing no evil?"

A reddish and black sign on a pole appeared in front of them, and Ricci pointed as they passed. It showed a car with trash coming out of the windows. He glanced at the bishop as he spoke the words written at the bottom. "Don't trash Arizona." Arizona was actually just the letters A and Z, but it was clear it meant the state they were in.

The bishop laughed, holding up his paper wrapper. "I have thrown no trash out, my boy. Some wild animal will clean that from the road before the next car drives by." He motioned before and behind them. What he claimed was undoubtedly true. There were no other cars out on the road. They had it all to themselves. Behind them, several birds had already started to hover over the highway. "Besides, have you forgotten, already? When in the United States, do as the Americans do."

He was right, too. It was obvious many Americans ignored the warning signs, preferring to keep their automobiles clean rather than their country.

"Still," Ricci muttered. "The Holy See would not approve."

"The Holy See is not here, and it seems the Church has abandoned us to our own devices. We must prove or disprove whether this Angioletta came to America or not, and then we must find out if she still lives. Now, though, we must find ourselves a room. I have traveled all night in these clothes, and I wish to have a shower."

"Then we must turn around and drive back into Phoenix. I've seen nothing since entering on this highway." He was wrong about the *nothing*, though, because just then they passed a behemoth of an old car, broken down on the side of the road. He remarked, "I suppose your meal couldn't be too great an offense against Arizona. Americans dispose of their cars along the roadways. Now, if we can just find a trasferimento, so I can reverse our direction, then we will return to Phoenix and a room, hopefully air conditioned." He smiled as he pushed the clutch in and downshifted one gear in order to slow the powerful Corvette down.

"No need, my son. God has accepted my gift from the Holy See. Either that or the Father appreciates that the birds have accepted the gift from His Holiness. In any case, it seems we have our motel just ahead." Indeed, just at the edge of visibility, a blue sign with a large red number plunked in the middle advertised its wares: sleep, bathing, and cool, air conditioned floor space. "I am sure they even have double rooms. And if not, then the Holy See might be willing to give an extra dispensation for the extravagance of a second room, don't you think?"

Before he could answer, three sharp reports split the sky overhead. The noise was deafening. For the briefest of moments, Ricci pulled his foot from the gas pedal, wondering if he'd damaged the car by driving it too fast. His own peanut never would have achieved this great a speed, and if he'd ever tried it, it would have died an oily death, he was sure. This had seemed so effortless, though.

He quickly realized the real cause when the bishop looked back towards Phoenix and pointed up. Glancing into a sky that remained clear and brilliantly blue, the remnants of three bolts of lightning streaked through the heavens, one strangely dark, and the other two pale in color.

Carnaly murmured, "The Finger of God points to Phoenix, it would seem. Three times together. The Holy Book says in the End Times, there will be Signs and Wonders. I wonder if that's a Sign we should follow?"

Ricci remained silent, having just downshifted to slow for the motel's entrance. In any case, he didn't think the bishop truly wanted an answer. Besides, the exhaust of the machine now rumbled throbbing basso notes, its power obvious even when driven carefully, and to speak would be to spoil the moment.

"Sometimes I think I should have done that, Ricci." Carnaly pointed to a shirtless man playing with his dog and three children off to one side of the motel.

The priest glanced over. The front door was just ahead, and he pulled into an empty spot before he asked, "What, Bishop?"

"Gotten married."

High-pitched laughter rang from a little girl playing with the dog, and an older boy, one in his middle teens, clapped his hands together. He called to the animal, *"Malak! Here!"* The boy's voice already had the reedy beginnings of a man's, and the rough-looking dog changed directions in mid-stride, roughly nuzzling the boy when he threw an arm across its back. The man with them grabbed the dog around the neck, pulling it over to the younger boy. Sitting, the dog rolled over to place its head in the child's lap.

"Married, sir? Why?" Now parked, Ricci shifted the car into reverse and touched the button for the top to close. In only seconds it had shut itself, and with a gentle touch of another switch, the windows slid upwards to seal them in.

The bishop looked in his lap at hands that were covered with wrinkled skin. "Children, Ricci. You do not see it yet, but I am old, and what is there left but the children? Oh, I have no regrets, but if I were to claim just one, it would be the children I never had."

"You should have no regrets, Excellency. You have lived a holy life, and many people look up to you." Ricci had noticed the old part, though. He felt it wise not to mention that. He reached to open the console, and he pulled his wallet out.

"Still," the bishop said, pausing, and then his face brightened. "The sun is very warm in Arizona, do you not think? It is not making my clothing any fresher. Shall we go in and see if we need to request an extra room?"

Ricci laughed. "I'll carry the espresso machine. We may require it very soon."

"When the room is ours. It will rest in the automobile nicely until then." The older man smiled. "I appreciate your thoughtfulness."

When they stepped inside, there was a surprise for them. On the back wall of the lobby were the remains of an all-you-can-eat breakfast buffet, mostly rolls and sweets, but next to it was a beverage counter. Sitting right there was an espresso machine just like the one Monsignor Ricci had lugged halfway across the world.

"Oh," the bishop exclaimed. "I do believe I've found a kindred spirit in this world." He turned to his companion. "Do you see, Ricci? Perhaps we will even find the end to our search in this very location." He rubbed his hands together excitedly and walked forward to see if the machine was ready to supply refreshment.

Ricci moved to where a sign read, *Ring for Service. Please Be Patient.* He pushed it once, didn't hear anything, and then shrugged, knowing it probably rang in a distant part of the building. That was not so very unlike what one might find when visiting Vatican City, and it seemed reasonable here. After all, the bell was not to call him to the counter. He was already here. The bell was for whoever needed to hear it. It was to call them to attend to their business. He must allow them the time to do so.

He turned to Bishop Carnaly. "Our pursuit has sent us to Phoenix, Bishop. This is not Phoenix. I do not think our solution will be so convenient."

"Chi trova un amico, trova un tesoro." *He who finds a friend, finds a treasure.* "If we show God's kindness to the people here, perhaps our desired treasure will be revealed. Stranger things have happened in Heaven and on Earth. Such is the Hand of God." Then, preoccupied with his espresso endeavors, he waved one hand to suggest the monsignor leave him in peace for a time.

Ricci laughed, but he did so quietly. The saying was one he had heard all his life. It seemed the good bishop was enjoyably distracted by the espresso machine, and that kept him from having any original thoughts in his head.

On the other hand, perhaps Bishop Carnaly needed to be distracted in order for God to put new thoughts in his head. What did the esteemed Man of God know of friends? Nothing that Ricci could see.

Somewhere in the back, a door opened, and Ricci turned to the counter. A woman walked up, older, although he wasn't one to judge harshly. He thought perhaps she'd once been very pretty. Somewhere she had left that behind, and now she just looked heat worn, much as a grandmother from his own southern Italy.

"What can I do for you, sir?" She tucked her hair behind her ears, smiling, then let the pleasantry fall away, as if the heat of the day had already pulled her down. Before Ricci could answer, a phone rang, and she held up a finger to ask him to give her a moment. "Yes. This is Rikkianne." She paused, then began to speak again. "No, Mrs. Dalton. Bobby ain't been up here that I know of since night before last. But if you say he's been gone since yesterday, Nigel might know. Be glad to ask." She hung up the phone, turning back to her guest. "My apologies. Momma of a local boy. Does odd jobs for us sometimes. The boy, not his momma." She laughed, and she held it longer than the earlier smile.

The monsignor smiled in return. "A room, possibly two. We can do with one room if it has two beds." He patted his pockets for his wallet, then remembered it was already in his hands. He glanced at the bishop to see if he'd seen that, relieved that he was still working on operating the espresso machine. "Nice espresso." When the woman looked perplexed, he clarified, "The coffee maker on the counter."

She nodded. "Salesman left that there here a few months back. Wanted us to give it a try, he said, and he'd be back. He ain't been back, and we ain't never paid for it. Use it if you please."

"You seem to have a rather pleasant family staying here. We saw them outside playing with their dog." He smiled again, understanding that small pleasantries could go a long way in brightening this woman's morning, especially if the day had already taken its toll on her. She looked like she needed a

375

moment of cheer, too. "Are they staying with you long?"

"Lady and two little kids?" She was already pulling keys and laying them on the counter.

He shook his head. "There was a man and his dog with three children, one about fifteen."

She looked up, catching his eye, and he thought he caught a twinkle there. Now he was certain she'd been pretty when she was younger. He could see it in her expression.

"Let me get you fixed up, then I gotta call Mrs. Dalton back. That boy you spoke of, he's Bobby, or my name ain't Rikkianne. He's fourteen, and don't you be telling him otherwise, 'cause he got a big enough head already. It's all I can do to keep him off the danged roof at night."

"Off the roof?" That seemed a bit unusual, and he chuckled. "Why should he be on the roof?"

"He's fourteen's what does it. Least that's what Nigel says. Here your keys. You can see the room number there. Go right once you're out the door, then right again. Pool's open 'til ten, but it's mighty hot during the day. You might want to wait 'til the sun goes down. Oh, and don't turn the air below 68, 'cause it'll freeze up."

"Thank you. We'll stay out of the pool until dark, and we promise to keep the air above 68." Grinning, he picked up the keys and paperwork, then he turned, calling, "Bishop?"

Rikkianne had already picked up the phone, and when Ricci glanced at her, she paused in her dialing. "You folks religious?" When he nodded, she said, "I seen your clothes. That black in the desert. We don't discriminate against nobody. You feel as welcome here as anybody. You can even use the pool. Don't let nobody tell you no different."

She nodded, then paused, her eyes still on him, but holding the phone to her ear.

Ricci motioned to the bishop and turned to her. "Yes, certainly." She nodded her head again in acknowledgement and began to speak into the receiver.

Outside, they climbed in the car. "Family's gone." Ricci nodded their direction, the information a minor point in a trip that had become a very long one. Then he drove to the opposite side of the motel, pulling up to the room shown on their keys.

"One room or two?" The bishop smiled pleasantly.

"She had a double." Ricci held out the keys.

"Good. I will enjoy your company."

It was as well, Ricci thought. He was going to get it, whether he wanted it or not. When the two men stepped through the door, it was cool inside the room. Ricci was immeasurably glad, because the day outside had already grown very hot, indeed.

Chapter 26

It was the Texas Hill Country, and a small boy floated alone in a large pool.

"Look, Momma!"

She was in the house with the sliding door cracked just enough to hear, and she glanced outside, searching. The boy was about seven, and he had his arms wrapped about a foam pool noodle. His hair was slicked back against his head, and in the sparkling water, loose red trunks fluttered around his waist. The sun twisted and sparkled on the bottom of the pool, and to protect his eyes, he wore deeply tinted goggles.

The family lived in the hills above Austin, and the pool in their backyard offered a clear view of the southern sky. In the fall and spring, birds could be seen on their migratory routes, and occasionally each fall they were lucky enough to get the Monarch butterflies directly overhead on their annual trip to Mexico.

Now, for the first time, it was a view of a space launch that had been offered to them, and the boy called again, "Momma! You have to come and see." One arm splashed the water in his excitement, sending droplets flinging through the air. His summer science camp classes had studied NASA and the space shuttle just the week before, and now there was a rocket like they'd read about flying overhead.

"Scooter?" His mother, Shauna Hipplewhite, stepped outside, her hair pulled back into a loose knot at the nape of her neck. Her face was young, and her skin smooth, telling of beauty regimens that surely were in line with the cost of her large suburban home. It was only in her hands that it could be seen that she was closer to forty than thirty. Even so, she was attractive and had been a good catch for a college professor. Her grandmother's money hadn't hurt, either.

"See, Momma?" He pointed overhead to two brilliant lights traveling across the sky. "A spaceship." He looked up to find them for her, then turned his goggled eyes back to his mother, waiting on her exclamation of surprise and pleasure.

She held up a hand to shadow her eyes, making a point not to squint, and she searched. Then, she gestured, "There it is. It's very bright. I thought it'd move faster." Years ago, her husband had organized a university field trip to Florida to observe a launch. He frequently spoke of wanting to repeat that exciting week, and only the school trustees' tight fists had kept him away. Yet, there had been no recent mention in their household about either an upcoming launch or landing, whether private or government.

The boy expressed no doubt, though. He pointed close to the horizon. "It was right there when I first saw it. That's when I called for you. See? It's traveled all the way across the sky."

She sighed, then tempered it with a smile. "We'll have to tell your father about it when he gets in later. He'll be so sorry to have missed it."

"Can I tell my teacher? We watched a movie about it last week." He was already kicking his feet in the water by then, sending up bright droplets of individual rainbows, the lights overhead slowly disappearing off his radar.

"I don't see why not. I'll tell you something, Scooter. I'll go write this on your Life Calendar, and then you'll always remember the day you saw an actual space launch."

"Will you come out and play with me afterwards?"

"I'll be glad to come outside. I'll sit under the umbrella and read a magazine. Would you like me to bring you some lemonade when I do?" She wouldn't swim in the sun, although she would never dream of telling her son why. Several of the scars just at her hairline didn't tan well, and too much sun made them stand out.

"Hurry, Momma." The boy's voice was excited once again, and his noodle danced in the water. "Put a cherry in mine. Please?"

However, she was already headed into the house. She would, though, because Scooter always asked for a cherry. He wouldn't drink them any other way.

Barakiel and Elemiah, Six-Winged Seraphim

High in the sky, Barakiel's Sword of Power flashed with brilliance, even against the intensity of the summer Texas sun. At his side, Elemiah's own Sword was hardly less bright, but he was the Protector, while Barakiel was the Lightning of God. The word "God" was, of course, the human term for the brother known as the Triune Mind. The words were sometimes less important than the meanings, and when the Seraphim communicated without words, as they did more often than not, the meanings were all that came through in their brilliant gestalts of understanding. They didn't say "God" or "Triune Mind." They simply sent the image they wished to convey.

They moved more rapidly than an aircraft could fly, unless that aircraft was supersonic. Even then, should such a race ever occur, it would be a close contest to see who might come out the victor. With the turbulence of the atmosphere swirling around him, Elemiah turned to his twin as they passed over the unnoticed boy in the pool far below.

"Together with mine, your Sword of Power hit the sand. Did it suggest where our four brothers would land?" His Sword had told of condition. It was Barakiel's Sword that would suggest location.

Barakiel's six wings tore at the atmosphere, carrying him

and his brother away from Arizona. His Sword extended as far forward as he could reach, its tip aglow, the air parting around it. It made it easier on the Seraph as he cut through the atmosphere, because wind resistance was wind resistance, a brother of the Unity or no.

"To the East and the West and the North and the South." His words rang out, for he spoke them with his mouth as well as his thoughts. He also added drama to his revelation, using only the cardinal directions, for his Sword had spoken to him more specifically of northeast, southwest, northwest, and southeast. Such were the four corners of this continent, and the Four had thrown their enemies as far as they could, even unto the ends of the earth, clear to the borders of the sea.

How vital was the Seraphim's search for the four defeated brothers? The likelihood of their being killed was slight. In their weakened condition, a direct impact upon landing might do enough damage. The more serious possibility was that they would not be found, thereby not being able to provide nutrients for themselves, causing their bodies to eventually expire. The prolonged suffering they would endure would be the cruelest portion of that undignified end, for they would remain alive for an extended time, unable to move or call to others, as their corporeal bodies slowly exhausted every possible source of energy they could pull from their scant fat reserves. It would be a long "starvation," although it would be more about the lack of healing than the hunger involved.

"I am with you, Brother, wherever you go. No place is too distant to pursue a common foe." Elemiah's wings thundered ahead, giving him the lead.

Both Seraphim had traveled to Earth for one sole purpose, to support Gabriel. Now Gabriel needed them, and they would search for him to the ends of the earth, no matter the time and energy it took.

They were filled with confidence they would indeed find him, as well as the other three brothers, sensing them when they got closer. Their voices, although now too weak to hear and understand, would soon call to their rescuers, even if their bodies were decimated to insensibility. The inner essence always spoke, even when it could only whisper. The Seraphim were unsurpassed in reading those whispers, and for that reason, they had known they were the ones who must make the quest.

The young boy's space craft streaked across the sky, although in reality it was two "angels" on a mission to rescue their companions.

The Four Familiars of the Triune Mind

Vases on shelves rocked, and plates in cabinets clattered. On that Friday morning, many of the homes were empty, for it was the end of the workweek. In those that were occupied, eyes glanced up and brows furrowed. Those who had once lived in earthquake-riddled California, having come to New Mexico to escape such nonsense, were instantly terrified.

While Albuquerque was not known for its earthquakes, it was in an area that was definitely ripe for them. As far back as the Great San Francisco Quake of 1906, well-documented tremors had rocked the New Mexico countryside. In late 1906, about seven months after the quake in California, the most serious earthquake ever recorded in the state hit eastern New Mexico. Then again in the 1930s, a series of serious quakes shook the area for as many as five days.

However, vases rocking and dishes clattering? No one living in Albuquerque, except the oldest of old-timers, remembered that ever happening. Curtains were pulled back, and doors were opened, looking to see if anything appeared amiss outside. Other than a quickly passing shadow that could have been an airplane, and a blurriness in the middle of the street that could have been dust rising from the quake, all looked normal. Then, with the dishes quieting, and the vases once again resting staid upon their shelves, curtains fell back into place, and doors once again shut out the rising heat. The danger was past.

The danger had certainly passed, but it wasn't gone. The Four Familiars of the Triune Mind were somewhat different from the brothers and their seconds while they roamed Earth. The brothers could access their wings at will, banishing them just as easily. Normal familiars had no wings at all, unless the forms of the creatures they assumed wore them. In contrast, three of the Triune Mind's Four Familiars carried their six-winged appendages at all times, for they were of a different nature than either the brothers or their familiars. While at times their wings might appear to remain unseen, it was simply an illusion, a "Suggestion" that created that impression. Only Swiftness carried the simpler two wings upon his Eagle body, and they came as part of what he was. He wished no "Suggestions" to make them disappear.

Like the seconds, the Four Familiars were creatures of who they were. The Ox was an ox, even if he was known as Strength. The Lion retained the nature of a lion, even as Nobility. The Eagle thought like an eagle, even as Swiftness's mighty wings streaked through the sky. The Man was always a man, even though he carried Wisdom as his name. For that reason, the winged Ox ran the streets of Albuquerque rather than traversed its skies. His tree trunk legs shook the surrounding homes, even as his wish to fade kept others' eyes from watching him as he ran by.

Swiftness had no such compunctions. He took to wing, visible to all, slowing his flight to the speed of Strength's run, which was still quicker than any normal Earth-creature could move. Traveling from Kafziel's mine to the streets of Albuquerque had taken them little time, for they had little time to spare. Wisdom demanded their presence, and at his call, they would gather.

Part of the burned-out house did come down that day, and although it had already taken severe damage from the fire, no one would be able to say just what caused the structure to completely fail. The boards were burned, but not entirely through. Those that had been were already pulled down by the firemen. The rest were expected to stand until an investigation could be done. No one was seen entering or exiting the damaged structure, for Strength had wanted to remain unseen. Despite his intentions, when entering the burned-out structure, his invisi-bility didn't stop his massive body from slamming into charred beams and weakened timbers. Neither did it keep vital support beams from turning loose of their stanchions and crashing to the ground. As they did, Wisdom and Nobility removed themselves from the destruction, shifting their molecules to ease through the wall that both Kafziel and Uriel had earlier passed so easily through. Once outside, their wings carried them gently to the ground, while Swiftness screeched far overhead, and Strength played out his inelegant games inside the remains of the charred structure.

Once finished, Wisdom demanded him to his side. "The Record is now destroyed, and you were wrong for that. However, my memory is good. Kafziel was here." He paused as the Ox bellowed his fury at the name of such an infidel. "Uriel passed by next." This time there was more than anger. There was hate, and Strength strained to be away. Where he would go, he couldn't have said. He was simply *responding*. It was Wisdom who restrained him. "Uriel is not ours to claim. Yet, to know his presence may be to find the three who remain. We will search for Uriel." His final words were spoken strongly, a call to battle.

As the Ox bellowed in rage, and the Lion matched the sound in volume, dust from the remaining beams still standing in the blackened husk behind them vibrated in worshipful fear and rose into the air. The Eagle overhead screamed his agreement, and even the Man yelled his own victory call. Four had been removed from the fight, and now only three remained. Uriel would lead them to their foes.

Interlude 22

Across the street from the burned-out hulk, something made the boy look out the window. Perhaps it was the ball he'd forgotten earlier, or maybe he was just bored of the television. It also could have been the sonic resonance set off by four overpowering voices in unanimous chorus, chanting a victory song. Whatever it was, just as he pulled the curtain back, he saw the final walls of the house across the street tumble inward, with black dust flinging itself skyward.

The house had fallen, and of all the people in the city, only he knew. It was his secret, and he would keep it for as long as he could.

As he wandered back to the den, he didn't even tell his mother. If he told, it wouldn't be a secret, would it? He just plopped in front of the television with a mysterious grin on his face, and he didn't even try to wipe it away.

Kafziel, Emissary of Solitude and Tears

Kafziel's hand flashed out, and his fingers grabbed the front of Asbeel's brightly colored tee. Insults had been bandied, and anger boiled in the Emissary's chest. He would make this one bleed with unholy pain, if he thought he could escape afterward. Then, he remembered the part these foul brothers played in his plan, and he reined his anger in.

Even so, he couldn't stop the fire that flashed from his eyes, and there was nothing feminine about his expression of hatred. He hissed his words into Asbeel's face.

"I would take you for a woman, my brother, and make you do a woman's duty for a night of pretend pleasure."

"Kaz—" Asbeel grabbed the hand, calling the brother by a shortened, familiar name, holding his eyes wide with surprise. Whether it was feigned or real was unclear.

"Not a word, *Ash*." Kafziel leaned in as he snarled, his lip curled into a sneer, and he pulled Asbeel nose-to-nose, spitting his next words with contempt. "I would take you now, except the Strictures would censure me roundly."

The Strictures hadn't stopped him a quarter century ago. He felt the remembered sweetness of that day flood his thoughts, blinding him to all that was around him. He had fallen on Angioletta's mother, and the intensity of the act still haunted him with unresolvable desire.

"He didn't realize who you were, brother Kafziel." Raphael leaned in, pushing the two apart, as he chided him. "Have you looked in a mirror? You are the most beautiful of all the angels—" the human word for the brothers "—and you are

385

definitely wearing female clothing."

"Beautiful?" Kafziel liked the sound of that, and he felt his face smooth. "I am, aren't I?"

Raphael laughed, and it visibly broke what was left of the tension. "How can you think those who know you would not find you most desirable, either as a man or a woman? That's all Asbeel meant, that you would be beautiful even as a woman. Right, Asbeel?"

Asbeel took the time to adjust his shirt at his neck, and then he looked down to grab the front of his pants and shake them out before answering. He finally looked up with a smile, and he ran his fingers through his hair, pushing his thick mane back from his face.

"Sure, Kafziel. I haven't seen you in your corporeal form in quite some time. You do shape up quite nicely. *Ve*-ry pretty, if I do say so. Even Helen of Troy was less beautiful than you are today."

"You thought Helen was beautiful, did you?" Kafziel preened. The comment about Helen of Troy was masterful and well placed, for Helen had indeed been Kafziel in drag. It had been his first real attempt at performing his duty in corporeal form, that of Watcher over the Deaths of Kings. The king of Troy had died, after all, and Kafziel had been right in the midst of it all, watching. He had also been part of the cause, some had later suggested, to his delight.

"Absolutely." Asbeel winked and gave Kafziel a mock punch to the shoulder.

"I can certainly do a mean female, can't I?" Kafziel raised a hand to his hair, giggling in a falsetto soprano. He nodded to Asbeel, willing to accept the glossy compliment, albeit one that had been given in its crassest form. It was the words that mattered to him, not the sincerity of the giver, although he would not admit to that.

"So, Kaz, why are you here working in a restaurant, and as a woman, not to state it too finely?" Zadkiel tossed in his question carelessly, his words sharp, picking up on the shortened form of the brother's name. He reached out and rubbed a hand across the name sewn into the other brother's smock. "And . . .

386

as Bridgette?"

Kafziel snorted. He was lucky to have this. At least there were no longer any short-shorts to complicate the matter. He now wore Maylene's extra pair of pants, ones made up of loose cotton twill that didn't quite reach to his feet.

He had on flip-flops below that, and he felt he was quite presentable.

"Kaz?" Zadkiel looked at him, waiting on an answer with wicked amusement on his face. "Bridgette?"

"Do you see what's all around us? Food! Do you know how hungry I was out there when you abandoned me? I could hardly fly. As a new employee, I had to promise to work the morning for the food I ate. They had never seen anyone consume so much." He was proud of that, and he threw his shoulders back. "I guessed I could stay until lunch. And besides, did you see Maylene? Hubba!"

"Unity!" The word was near to a curse. "You can't touch her, Kafziel. What's the point?"

"Maybe I could, given the right circumstances!" Some of the old Kafziel spilled out of the genial waitress's uniform. "You, Jeqon. You know." He pointed a finger, nearly jabbing the black brother in the chest. "Don't you, *Brother*?"

"That be a banana peel so very slippery." Jeqon moved his arms and shoulders in a wave that started in one hand, traveled across his shoulders, and down to the other hand. He grinned and rocked his head side to side. "Let it be swept away, for it be time for *Bridgette* to be showing us our seats. You be the beauty today all brothers wish for, and I would not dream to tarnish that for my own gain." He did a soft-shoe over to Maylene, something that resembled an old-fashioned dance called the moonwalk, and he bowed low. "Got me a dollar; got me a date; can you please show me to a plate?" He looked up and grinned, his black skin gleaming underneath the fluorescent lights. The whites of his eyes glowed in their recesses, and Maylene appeared charmed.

His Suggestion didn't hurt, either.

"I've got 'em, Kaz." She waved to Kafziel. "I heard that and think it's kinda cute. You should use it instead of your other name. When you go full time, I'll stitch it on your smock. Come on, men, and we'll get you a table." She motioned, unknowingly charmed by the smell of vanilla that had permeated the restaurant's foyer. She didn't realize that these men were even more strongly attracted to the cinnamon, frankincense and myrrh she exuded.

Kafziel was glad to see them gone. They were putrefied piles of excrement, and he had need of none of them.

Kinky Kinkerson, Reporter

"Ralph, you mean that waitress back there is a man? In drag?" Kinky reached and clapped Raphael on the shoulder. The thought he'd felt attracted to the waitress even for a minute made him feel dirty.

"Jeqon's the one to worry about, Kinky," Raphael reassured him. He laughed when he saw the reporter's horrified face. "Remember who Jeqon is?"

"From my windshield? Is he, you know, um, sweet, too? He sure seems that way." He didn't say what else he felt. Maybe all Ralph's friends were.

Raphael grinned. "Just crazy as a loon. That's Jeqon to a 'T.' But sweet? Not on your life."

Kinky was relieved to hear that, but he did sit on the outside next to Raphael. He was the one man in this group he trusted, even if he didn't know just why.

Raphael, Angel of Healing

When Kafziel brought them their food was when the fireworks sparked again. Raphael grabbed his wrist as he leaned forward to place a plate on the table, and his golden eyes fixed on his brother's dark ones. The mood over the table seemed to visibly thicken. Something passed in the air between them, an electric charge that made the air crackle. Kinky's breath drew in sharply, and he sat back in his chair. Even Jeqon's animated chatter drew to a halt.

"You know why we're here. We search for Uriel." Raphael's words were terse and low.

Kafziel's hand dipped slowly, forcing Raphael to let him lower the plate to the table. It clattered as it landed unevenly.

"The Betrayer is gone. I search for him, also." Fury danced in Kafziel's eyes. His words were hissed with vehemence, and whatever passed in the air between them grew thicker. Sparks exploded where their skin touched.

"Betrayer?" Asbeel growled. "Wrong label, Kafziel. Betrayed. Uriel was betrayed, and you know by whom." He looked at Jeqon, then turned to Zadkiel expectantly. "We all know, don't we?"

"I know nothing." Jeqon put his hand on the table, his fingertips down, making an elegantly splayed spider that displayed his beautiful black fingers. Then, about the time the silence became unbearable, he twirled his fingers, reached to the plate Kafziel had just placed in front of Raphael, and snatched a sausage. "Hmm," he exclaimed. "Better'n crawfish'n mustard."

"Put that down, Jeqon. What is this about a betrayer?" Zadkiel laughed accusingly. "Prove your false accusation, Kafziel. The truth I heard is somewhat different."

Kafziel snorted, arching one eyebrow and revealing his elevated levels of disdain. "There can be no doubt of who has betrayed whom. The Sword of Power has spoken the truth. The Seraph Elemiah was with me, as were Malak and Gabriel's second, in eagle form. Their witness cannot be doubted. Are my words not truth, Raphael?" He glared, daggers flashing, as he twisted his arm, but he couldn't pull it free.

Raphael knew the hated truth in the earthbound brother's words. He had heard Elemiah's sending. What grated at him was that it seemed grossly out of character for the Uriel he remembered. Before he could retort, another stole the stage.

"Ha!" Zadkiel snorted, slapping a hand to the table and sending the plate chattering. Fury boiled in his eyes. "Your lips drip lies like honey from a hive. You wish us to believe that one of the Seraphim honored you with as much as the time of day?

389

Speak of something that rings of truth, false brother."

"The Sword was driven into the ground, and the images it drew were read by the Seraph. There was no doubt, and Raphael shared in the truth." Kafziel drove his words home, his voice laced with sharp spikes. He turned to the Healer, pausing a moment to glance at his wrist, and he made a noise with his mouth, his lips sneering, daring him to claim otherwise. Then, he spat, "Release me, Raphael."

"The Sword hints. The Seraph interprets. Sometimes what is revealed is what is suggested by others." Jeqon butted in, his comment once more seemingly offhand, although he rarely did anything carelessly. All his catchphrases and colloquialisms were gone from his short speech, causing the other brothers, as well as Kinky, to turn his direction. They saw the black brother running his finger around one of his twisted tufts of hair. "I mean, no one was with Elemiah, other than you. Correct, Kafziel? Well, except for two familiars, and we can't ask them, can we?" Then he grinned impishly, his manner reverting to type. "What be our arguments for? I be so hungry, a horse be not enough. I chilled my beer nuts while coming down. Sweetie," he reached to tap Kafziel's wrist, "Make mine a double. Double ham, double bacon. I be hungry, baby, and without food, I can't get it up at all." He glanced around to see a couple at another table frowning at him. He laughed, calling, his hand high in the air and waving gleefully to them, "My traveling case, sweetie. I can't get my traveling case up. It weighs a ton."

He had broken the ice among the group, at least on the surface. In addition, he had cast doubt on Kafziel, as well as on Uriel's evident betrayal of everything the Unity's counter rebellion stood for.

The black brother's words also sliced into Raphael's heart. He had heard Elemiah's cry in the desert, and he had cursed Uriel for his betrayal. He had believed in Kafziel, counting him if not as a friend, then an ally for the time he needed his help. Now, all that was clouded, and the party meister seemed to be smarter than he appeared.

Zadkiel, Envoy of Freedom, Benevolence, and Mercy

Zadkiel harbored no such doubts. He'd been convinced from the beginning that Uriel had been pulled unwittingly into an earthly cesspool not of his own making. For Uriel, the Bearer of Destiny, to truly turn to the side of evil? It went against his grain.

Even his participation in the Rebellion had simply reflected his torment at losing his greatest love, Gabriel. Now he had to be saved. Without him, everything was surely lost.

Chapter 27

Kinky Kinkerson, Reporter

Kinky felt it first in his gut, the vibration as if from an earthquake rumbling deep within the earth's crust. He looked out the front of the restaurant, the plate glass wall showing cars lined up in the bright morning sun. All seemed normal.

Then, his world blew apart.

As if in a slow-motion scene displayed in full color, one normally viewed on a high definition cinema screen, with full, digitally enhanced surround sound, the back wall of the restaurant began to bend inward. The sounds of cracking boards and shattering masonry seemed surreal at first, pulling his eyes that direction. When the first fissures appeared in the wall, and the row of tables directly against it toppled sideways, flinging their plates and patrons inward, the first screams started.

This was the real thing, and Kinky flashed back to a vision of Babe the Blue Ox coming at him as he sat in his truck, although what he'd seen that night paled in comparison to what was happening in the room where he found himself now.

Interlude 23

One woman in a business suit with a slender attaché at her side lunged for her black leather case as it flew under an adjoining table, and that probably saved her life. As she jerked from her seat, an enormous hoof attached to a tree trunk of a leg shattered her chair into a dozen pieces. Great horns tore through the suspended ceiling tiles, flinging the lightweight boards across the rest of the diners. The timbers holding up the tar and gravel roof snapped under unyielding pressure as Strength shook his mighty head, his horns breaking through to the sky.

A deep-throated feline roar caused those diners farther away to cover their ears, although later they'd swear they'd heard only the rending of boards and steel beams.

It seemed the world had come to an end, as the diner was sliced neatly in two. No one remaining inside expected to survive, even though none were sure exactly why their world was crashing in around them.

Except the brothers. They saw the cause immediately.

The Four Familiars of the Triune Mind

The sun lanced like a spear through the newly created skylight, illuminating the broken edges littering the decimated remains of the shattered wall. Riding the glowing sunbeams into the interior of the restaurant, a great, feathered Eagle screeched his fury, coming to rest directly in front of Raphael. With his beak, he snatched up several of the sausages on one of the plates, and holding a feathered head high, gulped them down in a quick snap.

"Our fight is with Raphael, only." A great voice rumbled, shaking the building, and an enormous front window that had cracked in the first impact shifted in its frame. With a slow release of rubber and caulking, the massive panel fell to the sidewalk, explosively shattering, sending sparkling fragments onto the hoods of cars all along the first row of spaces next to the restaurant's front wall.

"Fight?" Zadkiel barked back the word. "What is the justification you bring for initiating this *fight* with Raphael?"

"Will the Healer leave with us willingly?" Those words were Wisdom's. "We have no desire to involve the humans still in this room, but we do not intend to let this one escape."

"Ralph? Do you think we should, um, get out of here?" Kinky placed his hand on Raphael's shoulder, attempting to pull him from his seat. Traces of dismay and an even greater dose of real fear were in his voice. "This, um, earthquake might take the rest of the building down, and we'd be safer outside. There might be aftershocks."

It was clear Kinky had heard nothing, nor had he seen the Four Familiars. Only the brothers saw them as they were. Everyone else's eyes simply slipped away from them, seeing the tumbling tables and the fallen diners. Now, those who were not trapped in the rubble were scrambling to get outside, if they hadn't already done so. Several men struggled to get collapsed tables off other patrons, helping them to safety as they did.

Not being seen did nothing to stem the magnitude of the Four Familiars' power, however, and although the humans had seen only the results of a natural disaster, with a twitch of muscular legs or the brush of talons, people could die.

Strength shifted his oxen legs, and a table on the other side of the room toppled over. Outside, a woman's voice wailed, "An aftershock! I'm from California, and aftershocks always come. We'll all die." She didn't notice that only this one building had been affected by the destruction. Her car was covered with broken glass, her breakfast had been ruined, and all she saw was an earthquake.

"What do you wish with our brother?" Zadkiel stood and spoke into the dusty fingers of sunbeams falling through the ceiling. His words were directed to the Familiars. There was iron in his voice, and it spoke of his protection for Raphael, who remained stoically at his side, stone-faced and silent.

A rumble rose from a leonine throat. It seemed all reason had not yet been stolen from the Four Familiars. Nobility's voice spoke of decency and consideration for the humans still within the building. It also told of impatience with those who would get in the way, warning that no interference would be allowed.

The Eagle simply screamed his wish for those not involved to remove themselves. Leave the fight to those who must battle for victory.

Steam blew from the Oxen's nostrils, and a giant hoof stamped the floor, shaking the sections of the ceiling that had not yet fallen.

"Ralph?" Kinky looked confused.

Raphael simply held up his hand for him to be patient. His eyes never left the space that to Kinky's eyes held only dust motes and sunshine.

"Why do you not seek Uriel?" Raphael spoke calmly, a sure sign of his power. "I remember Elemiah's message, and in addition, I am sure there are many things of which I am unaware. Uriel is at the core, of that I am convinced. Everything revolves around that one brother, both good and bad."

Nobility's voice roared, and his six wings rippled with power. Sparks flew from the electrical outlets around the walls, and three fluorescent lights still burning by the front door suddenly exploded, showering glass across the floor, through the broken window, and onto the sidewalk out front. The brothers understood Nobility's words, for they were painted into their thoughts just as clearly as those that had been spoken by Wisdom.

"Our Master must be freed. Gadreel has promised his freedom, if we but bring the Circle of Brothers to its knees. Uriel is his and his alone to tame, and him we may not touch." Nobility's sending was infused with his Dictate for Rules of Engagement, as well as those of Respect in Warfare.

"Yet, you battle with Gabriel and his followers." Raphael's voice, no longer calm, had turned molten, and he demanded answers. "What have you against us? We also pursue Uriel. Why do we not band together in a Common Cause?"

Wisdom answered in words filled with eons of anger, and as he spoke, his three companions joined him in a multilayered, discordant chorus, their whispered agreements ripping into the brothers' minds with sibilant overtones.

"We battle against the Betrayer. Gabriel has joined forces with Uriel, seeking to lay waste to Earth, and our master will be displeased. Those who have joined with Gabriel have joined with Uriel, and all must be destroyed. The Triune Mind must be freed!"

The Four Familiars had drawn closer as they spoke, and it was clearly only a matter of moments before the battle was engaged.

Electricity, like rain, filled the air.

Zadkiel, Envoy of Freedom, Benevolence, and Mercy

Zadkiel knew it was time to intervene. He had come to Earth with one agenda, Uriel's defense. He trusted his two companions would support him now that it was time to show his colors.

He regretted the humans still present, but regardless, his position had to be proclaimed.

He could now trust Raphael, for he had seen his face when Jeqon had spoken. His belief in Uriel's alleged betrayal was shaken, and for that reason, he would no longer condone Kafziel's accusation against the Bearer of Destiny as a foe.

He had also observed Kafziel making yet another getaway when the Four Familiars had made themselves known. That had guilt written all over it.

Against the Four Familiars, he knew he and his brothers had little chance. Even so, the battle had come to them with furor and determination, and it would not be easily dissuaded.

The human Raphael had claimed for a companion would have to understand.

Zadkiel leaped to stand on the table, his feet kicking the breakfast dishes aside, and with a clap of his hands, a brilliant flash of energy roiled across the interior of the restaurant. Making himself larger than life, he threw his wings wide, opening them for maximum effect. His Mandate was Freedom,

Benevolence, and Mercy. His was the power to stay the hand of the destroyer, and that he would do. Light flashed from his eyes, and power rippled across his skin. His wings crackled and popped with static electricity, and his voice thundered with the assurance of thousands of lives saved in the course of the Unity's sojourn in this dimension.

"Uriel is innocent! Take your battle elsewhere, for Kafziel is the one you seek. Look around you. He has departed without your awareness. Are you all fools? Do you believe the lies you are told? Will Gadreel really release the Triune Mind? You who are the best of the Unity, who carry the Triune Mind's heart, who are the strength and the nobility and the swiftness and the wisdom of the ages, you must see the lies you've been told. Your enemy is not Uriel and Gabriel and Raphael. Your enemy is the ones who have lied to you."

"*You are the one who tells lies!*" The discordant words were screeched, roared, thundered, and yelled into the brothers' minds, and had the voices been spoken aloud, the very walls that still remained around them would have crumbled into dust. The Four Familiars were *responding*, and all reason was now gone. "*The Master will be freed!*"

A flood of gathering power shimmered around the room, seen in the blue electricity crawling across the ceiling and down the walls. Fresh screams could be heard from outside, and dust began to boil from the floor.

Kinky fell from his chair at the sight of Zadkiel's wings, muttering, "Good god! It's a battle between good and evil, and I don't even know which side I've picked for my friends."

Raphael shifted to place himself between the human and the familiars.

"You will not take the one from this table," Zadkiel's words thundered. He stood firm, his wings shadowing all those sitting with him, his warning clear, and it was one he knew he could back up—at least for a time. His opponents knew it, too. This was his Mandated strength, and he would exercise it against all comers to protect Uriel, as well as any who would aid in providing a defense against his attackers.

"*You will not stop us!*" The discordant voices thundered, the sibilant chorus frightening in its intensity, and the Four began to move in a coordinated attack.

Jeqon was faster, though. He had moves that no one could match, and as he leaped from his seat, he threw himself at Nobility, clapping his hands over his head as he did so. With a flash of incandescent light, he crashed into the Lion, his wings already in full form, yelling for the others to join him. Even as he moved, he called, "Flee, Raphael! You must be at Uriel's side to warn him. Join me, brothers, to aid in his escape."

In a flurry of blinding flashes, each brother in the restaurant took to wing, their Mandates revealing their assumed powers. Jeqon already had Nobility in his grasp, and Zadkiel flung himself at Wisdom, his strength at wrestling him to the ground nearly the equal of the Familiar's. Asbeel danced a wall of confusion around Strength, distracting him from his goal.

Swiftness, in Eagle form, became entangled in the fray, his talons lashing, and his beak snapping at whoever he could reach. Still, the Eagle's strength was his speed, not his cunning and maneuverability in small spaces. He was at a clear disadvantage in the fight.

With a clap, Raphael took on the aspects of an angel, also. His brilliantly white wings towered over his head, and light dripped from each feather like jewels. He seemed to grow at first, his stance building him into something larger than life, then he knelt at Kinky's side. He reached a hand, a glowing hand, to Kinky's face, brushing away the fear he saw there. "As you suspect, this is indeed good against evil. You have helped me greatly. If I get a chance, I will return the favor."

Then, standing in the sun, the swirling dust motes creating the illusion of what humans might well proclaim as the proverbial Biblical Light from Heaven, Raphael lifted his head to the sky. His wings snapped opened wide, and with a leap, he was through the opening that had been torn in the roof, his wings ferrying him with incredible speed far into the blue sky.

Swiftness screamed his frustration at being unable to follow, but there were three brothers in his way.

In a moment of mental clarity, Strength tore through a wall, freeing himself from the repeated attacks. With a bellow, he looked around, only to find Raphael gone. His brain was too blinded by the moment to figure it out, though, and with another bellow, he plunged back into the restaurant to rejoin the fray.

It was the scream of fire trucks that brought the Four Familiars to their senses. Their quarry was long gone, and to fight against those with whom they had no quarrel was to pursue a dead end. Gathering together, unseen to anyone except the remaining three brothers, Wisdom's voice rang out, shaking loose what dust still remained on the timbers that formed the fractured skeleton of the broken building. He was the first to beat the sky with his six wings, searching for a departed Raphael.

Yet, the healer's trail had been decimated by the roughness of the battle, and it was long gone. Screaming their fury, the Four exited into the sky, chasing what shadows they could.

Kinky Kinkerson, Reporter

Kinky lay on the floor, having scooted off to the side to avoid the decimation. The battle had dazed him, for the sight of winged creatures—angels!—fighting against nothing at all, as well as parts of the building exploding for no apparent cause, strained his belief beyond all comprehension.

Then, unexpectedly coming to a rest, the three men . . . no, angels, Kinky corrected himself, ones whom he had so recently picked up off the street, stood, drew their wings to their sides, and clapped their hands over their heads. A blinding light rippled past, and they were men again. They did carry injuries, but by the time they got to Kinky's side, their wounds had healed, and the only evidence of their "angelness" was the tattered shirts on their backs.

Even that didn't stand out as exceptionally odd, because the rest of the establishment was tattered as well.

Willie Dominguez, Rosita's Brother

When the firemen rushed inside, they were amazed to find four men still alive inside the destroyed restaurant. The building that had made up the eating establishment was now a hollow shell, and only the portion that fronted the street retained a semblance of what it had been. It looked more as if a bomb had gone off than anything else.

Still, those who had made it safely outside had seen it all, and they gave their stories. Something blew up the back of the building first, then repeated concussions took down the rest of the structure. It was a terrorist attack, a gas line explosion, or perhaps a well-placed bomb. One woman, older, claimed it was the Hand of God, that she had seen the Angel of Death exiting the scene after the decimation had ceased. One fireman, Willie Dominguez, patted her on the shoulder gently, reassuring her that no one had died that they could tell. He also winked at his partner. They had heard of the angel several days before in Albuquerque. His sister, Rosita, had told him. Then, just that morning, he had called Alonso about that crazy truck that blew up. That tall man with the white hair had been an angel if there ever was one. No wings, sure, but didn't the Holy Scriptures say that sometimes angels didn't have wings? Now, this old woman with her story of an angel? It seemed as if all the Southwest was going to be one big Heaven before too long, with its own set of resident spirits.

Willie laughed. It was clear to him what had happened. The owner of this restaurant had gotten behind in his bills. He had needed to cash in on the insurance money. How, otherwise, could anyone explain that the building was totally demolished, and not a single soul had even gotten injured?

If Willie had been paying attention, he might have noticed one of the men headed out the front door looked a lot like a blood-covered accident victim from a wreck that had taken out an SUV not too long ago. But then, after Raphael's touch of healing, he might not have recognized him at all.

Kinky Kinkerson, Reporter

A number of the cars had already brushed off the glass from their hoods and pulled away from the parking lot before the police arrived. One of those was Kinky's. He had three strangers with him in the car. He didn't know them, except for the time they had spent together in the restaurant, but he wasn't about to let them get away. Kinky was nothing if not a shrewd newspaperman. He knew what he'd seen, and although he didn't quite believe it, and was quite willing to discount it all to stage magic or hysteria at the slightest opportunity, he couldn't erase the images from his mind. He had the story of the century, and it was sitting right there in his car with him. These men were headed back to his motel, and if he had to rent them rooms of their own and pay for it out of his own pocket, this was too good to let get away.

Interlude 24

The brothers riding with him were shrewd, also. With most of those who had been at the restaurant, the images of the fight and the ensuing decimation could be Suggested away, but that didn't work with images that were burned into one's brain. Kinky had known Raphael, and well enough to call him by the familial Ralph. When one finds a friend is an "angel," then sometimes that knowledge cannot be so easily Suggested away.

The brothers were communicating silently, well aware that they now had to find a way to work Kinky into their plans. One thought passed between them time and again.

God, or rather, Triune Mind help them!

Chapter 28

Angioletta Bacciarelli, Daughter of Kafziel

"The manager came by." Angioletta pressed the knife into Uriel's arm, cringing when blood leaked from the wound. It was not a lot, though, or at least not as much as she had imagined it would be.

"Hurry," he whispered. He was seated on the lip of the tub, and she stood at his side. It was clear he controlled the pain by sheer will. "It'll heal quickly and have to be cut again, if you don't remove the stone immediately."

Outside, a dog barked, but it was less a bark than a huff. Unmistakably, it was Malak. The animal and the teenager were roughhousing.

Uriel sucked in a sharp breath as she pressed with the knife again. "Unity, but that hurts!"

"You're such a baby." She smiled, but not where he could see, and she pressed another stone from underneath his skin. It popped out, clattering to the bathroom floor. "Your dog must remain outside."

"My dog?" He panted with the repeated pain, his eyes watering. "Outside? Malak?"

"The motel manager said so." Her students had taught her a

thing or two. If she could divert his attention, the pain would be less.

"He did? Ouch! Or was it the woman?" He gasped when the edge of the blade pressed against his skin once more.

"How does your arm heal so fast? As soon as I cut the skin, it's already started to close once again." That should also distract his attention, but she really was curious. She had seen his mutilated shoulder heal, and she had thought she must have imagined it, that the damage had been less than she remembered, that perhaps it had been just the blood smeared across his skin that had looked so horrible. Now, she knew better. His skin was doing it all over again. Repairs that would take anyone else's skin half a day to close, and a week or more to disappear, were healed over in half a minute.

"It's just who I am. *Unity!*"

She had pressed the knife into his skin once again, and she tutted at him.

"Are we almost done?" He gasped as she put her finger against another stone, and it clattered irritatingly to the floor.

"You survived." She slapped him lightly on the back, the last stone gone. "I suspect you could have survived much more with less moaning, if you had wanted." She enjoyed touching him, though, even if it was only to cause him pain. He still felt like vanilla, and yes, she knew how that sounded, even to herself. No one could *feel* like vanilla, yet this man did.

"I need a shirt," he murmured, walking into the main room, rubbing his hands over his shoulder.

"And I need something besides pajamas," she shot back, though more to interact with him than anything else. "It seems we're in the same boat. Do you have a car?" How had that question not occurred to her earlier? "Money? Do you have that? Then, I have one more question." She stepped in front of him, reaching to place a hand on his chest. "This is an important one, too."

He grabbed her wrist, removing her hand from his skin.

"Please." He paused then spoke more softly. "Be careful about touching me. It's, um, well, distracting."

"You didn't mind when I was popping those rocks from your arm." She leaned back against the door, crossing her arms over her chest. "Why now, all of a sudden, the hands-off act?"

She could see it in his face, though. There was something there, and it centered on her. She laughed lightly to dispel the tension she felt building, for she was very attracted to this man, and, she hoped, she had seen reciprocation in his actions.

"Stop that." He looked at her and frowned. "I need a shirt, that's all. And yes, you probably need something else to wear. We'll need to leave soon."

"That brings me back to my original question. I don't know how I got here, and I don't know how the damage on that arm of yours happened. Can we get some of those answers along with our new clothes?"

He paused, looking at her. "Could we get some clothes, first? Shoes, and more food? Your surgical endeavors have given me back my appetite."

She frowned. "You're not *explaining* anything, though. Why do you evade my simple questions? They're not hard. I rescued you from a train wreck, Angioletta. A giant dragon was about to eat you, Angioletta. The world would have come to an end, if I hadn't carried you away into the sky, and this just happens to be where we landed, Angioletta." She paused, her arms still folded, and she pulled away from the door, crossing to the bed to sit. "Just those answers would be nice, if rather fanciful."

He turned as she walked past. Then he walked to the window and pulled the curtain partially open.

"You are safe here, at least for a time. Know that much with certainty, if you cannot know all the rest." He glanced to her, and she kept her eyes trained on him. "I have not harmed you, and I will not do so."

"That's not much of an answer." Her tone was softer. She knew he wouldn't come clean, and to offend him would serve no purpose. "What is it you cannot say to me? How terrible is it?"

He turned back to the window. "We need clothes, first. Food, too. Then soon we must leave. My familiar will go with us, for he and I are one. We must ready ourselves."

She stood, watching his silence, silent herself, for a moment puzzled. His familiar? Not his wolf? That seemed odd. Yet, she knew who he meant, and she let it go. More important things were at hand.

"I'll ask Jeri." She looked around the room, then back to the vanilla man. "Perhaps she can loan me something suitable. Maybe someone will have something you can wear, also. I'll see what I can do." People often did things like that for her, just because she asked. It had always been that way.

Then, just because she needed to, she placed her hand on his shoulder. She felt him stiffen, and she quickly pulled her hand away. "I'm sorry, Uriel." His response was a knife nicking her heart.

"Clothes, Angioletta. We must think that far." He was very still and quiet, and he didn't turn to her.

"Sure. Clothes and food. I can do that." Careful to avoid touching him again, she stepped to the door and outside, gently shutting it behind her.

Uriel, Bearer of Destiny

As Uriel watched Angioletta walk away, he reached and placed his hand where hers had rested on his shoulder. He whispered, "You have nothing to be sorry for, Angioletta. You've done nothing wrong." Then he closed his eyes, wishing his body would let him alone. Not turning and grabbing her had been one of the most difficult moments of his long life. It wasn't fair he should want this woman so much. She was not his and could never be.

He knew that in his head. Even so, cinnamon, frankincense, and myrrh spoke to a very different part of the body, one over which even the Bearer of Destiny had very little control.

405

He suspected the next few days wouldn't get much better.

Rikkianne Kristofferson, Asst. Motel Manager

"There's a truck stop down on 10, a ways back town direction. Tonopah's the place. You can buy clothes there, I'm pretty sure." Rikkianne frowned at Bobby, although he'd done nothing but stand quietly as Angioletta had asked her question. "That young mother gonna take you?" She nodded at Jeri sitting out in her car. The windows were down, and both her kids were with her.

Just before lunch, Nigel had gone out and fiddled with the engine, replacing something called a solenoid. It had fired right up afterwards. Strangest thing, he said when he returned. How'd he know to even check that? It was like someone was over his shoulder pointing out what was wrong. He'd driven it back in, saying he'd walk out later to get the truck. He didn't mind.

"She loaned me this, too." Angioletta touched the sleeve of a simple cotton top. The shorts and sandals were of a contrasting color. "She's a sweetheart."

Surprising herself, Rikkianne reached in her pocket and pulled out her coin purse. Slipping out two twenties, she pressed them into the young woman's hand.

"It ain't much, but it'll get you a start. You cain't start with nothing, can you?" She turned to the teenager standing at her side. "You, Bobby. I'm gonna call your momma. You think she don't worry about you? But 'til then, you go with this woman. You know where the Travel Center is. There's a Subway there, too." She reached into her coin purse again, pulling out another twenty. "Here. That man of yours surely must get hungry, too. Cain't starve our men, can we?" Her face grew stern. "Bobby Dalton, that ain't for you to eat up, neither. You hear me?" The boy just nodded with a grin and was gone.

As she watched them drive away, Rikkianne wondered why she'd done that, given that stranger so much money. She didn't feel bad about it, no, not at all. It had felt so right. It was just unusual, though, like someone had suggested she do it, and she had just *wanted* to.

She began to hum a little tune as she walked along the shallow porch that fronted the motel rooms. She swished with her broom, knocking unwelcome sand back into the parking lot. Sand that was on the porch got tracked into the rooms, and what was in the rooms got sucked into her vacuum cleaner. She had to move it out here or in there, and this seemed the better option, even if was already hotter'n hot out on the sidewalk. Still, a job's gotta be done when a job's gotta be done.

She didn't consider that it had been an unusual couple days at the desert motel, even though it had. On regular days, people always came and went, and money was usually tight. This morning felt different, though, and the afternoon was building up the same. All in all, she'd given away sixty dollars, and still, she was unaccountably pleased with herself. Even the heat couldn't take that away from her.

Interlude 25

Rikkianne's little tune wafted across the parking lot, and out in the sun, resting under a small bush, Malak's yellow eyes watched her, keeping an eye out for its master. The big wolf was nothing if not faithful. Uriel had been found, and he wouldn't be allowed to get away again.

Eustorgio Ricci, Monsignor

Monsignor Ricci pushed the clutch in, pumped the accelerator, and with a push of a button, the massive engine that powered the sports car roared into life. The interior of the car, surprisingly quiet before, vibrated with a deep-throated rumble, causing the bishop to cover his ears. Surprised at the sound, Ricci jerked his right foot back, only to breathe relief when the roar instantly quieted to a low burble. He looked with embarrassment at the bishop sitting next to him, his face warming. He was supposed to be the master at cars, and that had been an unexpected boondoggle. He still didn't know just exactly what he'd done wrong.

Carnaly did, though.

"What was that, my boy?" The bishop fought a grin. "You do have a license, I believe. Otherwise, we would not have this wonderful American automobile at our disposal. Did you receive your license by default, or did you actually have to learn the skill, first?" His words chided the younger man in a teasing vein.

"Your Excellency, it's the way I start my peanut all the time." He had his hands in the air, afraid to touch anything, and his eyes searched the dashboard displays for any indications of aberrant warnings.

"Surely there are no faulty American cars for us to wrestle with here in this wonderful country." The response contained traces of laughter.

"No, Bishop. Um, I mean, I do not know if the car is faulty. The attendant drove it up. It was already started, and all I had to do was release the handbrake and put it in gear. It didn't roar like that. Should I turn it off in case it explodes or catches on fire?"

The good bishop chuckled. "I know your peanut. It is very old, and it has something under the hood called a carburetor. No new cars built anywhere in the world have those any longer. Fuel injection is the wave of the future, Ricci, and it has been for some years. Welcome to the modern world." He waved his hand over his head. "I would like some fresh air. Make this top reveal the sky. It is so wide open here in this desert landscape, and I wish to enjoy it."

Ricci's hand paused on the top's power switch, and he looked longingly at the readout for the air conditioner. It showed nearly a hundred for the outside temperature, and in the short time the car had been running, the inside temperature had dropped blissfully close to the seventy-two shown as the target goal.

"Ricci? The top?" The bishop peered down the row of rooms and out into the empty lot.

Theirs was the only car on this side of the motel. An older

sedan, one that looked vaguely familiar, was pulling out onto the highway, heading back toward Phoenix, but there was no other activity to be seen. Even the occasional desert plants seemed rather forlorn. An exceptionally large dog could be seen off under a low shrub, its spidery shade not much protection from the sun.

"I'm sorry, Bishop. I was watching the air conditioner's temperature gauge, and I got distracted." He looked over to see if the older man noticed his hint. Sadly, Carnaly simply motioned with his fingers for the top to be gone. "As you wish, Bishop."

As the top lowered, and the sun bleached the interior of the car, Bishop Carnaly touched the dash, and the air conditioner whispered to a halt. "Monsignor Ricci? I had thought we were to be informal here in this great land so far from home. Are we to already return to our inbred Church formalities? It would seem a waste to have such freedom only this once in our lifetimes and not experience its joyous blossoming.

"After all, what does The Word say to us? Unto every time there is a season, whether to be born, to die, or to enjoy the world the Father has made. In the same book, it tells us that there is nothing better for man than to be happy. Ecclesiastes, I believe."

The monsignor unhappily nodded in agreement. For him, there was not quite enough distance from Italy to the sunshine of the Great Southwest for his religious formality, all associated with Bishop Carnaly, to have developed more than a thin veneer of real friendship. A prick had been all that was needed for the old formality to boil back through.

"My sunglasses, Your Excellency. I left them in the room. My apologies. Do you mind if I return to get them?" Ricci's hand reached to shade his eyes, and he turned to look out over the parking lot. Just for a moment, he wished he was not here with the bishop. He'd been very comfortable with his little life back in Italy where no one had teased him about his driving abilities—and it was not well over a hundred degrees, even if that was in Fahrenheit.

The bishop reached an arm out and turned the engine off,

his arm beneath his black shirt pale in the brilliance of the Arizona sun. He returned his hand to his lap before speaking.

"My son, I forget that you see me as an icon of the Church, and in reality, I am simply an old man who has received too many accolades in my lifetime, not all of them deserved. I chided you in the spirit of teasing, and you took me as a fault-finding perfectionist. For too long, I have walked the straight paths of the Church, for I started at far too young an age. In the mother superior's chambers, when I realized what we must do, I had thought to cast all that off for a few simple weeks or months of normalcy in a land where I would not be seen as one to whom all underlings must convey immeasurable respect.

"In the Church, we have fathers and mothers and sons and daughters, all of whom are related to us only through Christ. Why should we not have other relations, too? During our sojourn here, I would choose to be more as an uncle to you."

Ricci frowned, squinting against the overhead glare. "Uncle?" He needed his glasses, not an uncle, and he felt the beginnings of perspiration under his clothing, not all of which was due to the sun overhead.

Carnaly laughed, obviously accepting Ricci's question as an acceptance of his proposal. "That's it, my boy. You may call me uncle for this trip, if you wish. I will even demand it, if I may. Of course, back in Italy, doing so would be greatly frowned upon, but then, this does not seem to be Italy, does it, *Nephew?*"

Ricci studied the dashboard for a moment, and he turned to the bishop. "May I get my glasses, *Uncle?*" His final word was tentative, though, as he quickly glanced at Carnaly and away again. The word "uncle" spoken to a Holy One of the Church felt hardly less blasphemous than using the bishop's given name as a familial term of address.

"Of course, *Nephew.*" He clasped his hand around Ricci's forearm warmly, then gave him a gentle shove toward the door. "Go. I grow hungry. As you have informed me, the snack machines here have been unaccountably emptied, and we must find alternate resources. In Phoenix, if we must."

As Ricci stood, climbing out of the car, Rikkianne's gently whistled melody caught his attention. He hopped around the front of the car, glancing at Carnaly and holding up one finger to let him know to be patient.

He tested his memory. "Rikkianne?"

"Yes?" She looked up, smiling.

She seemed prettier than before. Happier, maybe. Content, perhaps? He didn't know. She could probably give him directions, though.

"The bish . . . my uncle and I wish to find something to eat. The snack machines were empty, and we thought there might be a place nearby. Something plain will be fine. We are lowly clergy, and our tastes are simple." He paused for a moment, glancing back at the bishop, before he went on. "We do not require full service dining. A simple shop will do, if only it has a table at which to sit indoors."

She glanced at him, her eyes shifting to the car the bishop sat in. "I sent them back there—" pointing with her thumb toward the highway where the other car had recently pulled out in the direction of Phoenix "—down to the truck stop. Got a Subway there. Gas, too. That car probably takes a lot. Of gas, I mean. You got gas? Not many stations out here."

Ricci glanced at Carnaly, not sure if the bishop would want to travel so far. If that was their only option, it would have to do. He turned back to Rikkianne. "The subway goes into Phoenix? There will be restaurants in Phoenix, I suppose, so that would do. Can you recommend one for us to try?"

Her eyes had begun to twinkle. "You don't got Subways where you live, I don't guess. Sandwich shops. You know that one guy that was real fat and ate there for a long time, getting all skinny? Well, anyway, he turned up mostly skinny, but that was better than he was. You ain't never really been to one?"

He chuckled. "Jared. Sure. We have Subways in Italy. That will do. Thank you. How do I find it?"

"That's 10, there. Follow it that way to Tonopah—" pointing left "—and the sign sticks up real high. On the right. Come to Phoenix, you know you missed it." She looked hard at the car. "You ain't got no top to that car? Looks expensive. Seems it would have a top."

411

It was his turn to be amused. "It does, but my *uncle* likes the wide open spaces. Thank you for the help." He ran back and climbed into the car. "Subway sandwiches are down at something called a truck stop. That way." He pointed, putting the clutch in and restarting the car. This time he left the gas alone.

"Good job, *Nephew*. Both with the car and finding us resources in this desert environment." Carnaly grinned. "I like sandwiches for a late lunch. Not all the time, of course, but with my favorite *nephew*, I expect I will enjoy them just fine."

Rikkianne waved the car over as Ricci pulled forward. "You seen that car that just left?" At a nod from the bishop, she continued, "You see it there, you know you got to the right place. They just asked the same thing you did."

Carnaly waved his thanks as they pulled away, and he smiled at the sound of the woman's whistled melody as it returned. Pulling past, the dog raised a furry snout to follow them, its yellow eyes slitted against the glare of the sun.

Carnaly remarked to his companion, "Such a helpful woman. We are blessed to have been led to such a wonderful motel, my dear nephew."

"Yes, my uncle," Ricci replied, still ill at ease with the awkward familiarity. He knew the bishop's use of the word was not to be helped, though. Then, before he could stop himself, with a bit of a sour laugh, he let slip, "My *dear* uncle."

About then, the car had begun to growl loudly, and he wasn't sure if the bishop heard him or not. He prayed not. He pressed the clutch in, set the shifter into a higher gear, and the roar quieted down.

"Yes, my boy, I do believe we shall find our Angioletta soon." The bishop nodded his assurance as he reached to the dash, and finding the controls to the radio, he tapped it on. He scanned through several stations, preoccupied for a moment. When Elvis blared out, he turned it down for a moment to look at Ricci. "This is wonderful. Any sort of music we wish to enjoy, it seems to be here. So many stations, and we can pick just what we want. What is it called, good nephew?"

Good nephew? Ricci winced. Apparently, the bishop had

412

better hearing than he thought. "XM Radio. Satellite. Feel free to choose what you like. The agent said we have it with the rental." Then he grimaced. He'd been distracted, and he'd forgotten to return for his sunglasses. He'd manage, though. He could squint if he had to.

"I like Elvis." The bishop had his eyes closed, with the wind buffeting his face. "His mother was once very religious, you know. He grew up in a protestant church, although I don't recall he ever made a public profession of faith in the Christ."

"Oh?" Ricci wasn't that much into secular singers, especially not ones who had been dead more years than he had been alive.

"Assemblies of God, I believe the sect is called. It's an American denomination, although I do seem to recall it has grown quite large worldwide. It's sometimes interesting how quickly these newer sects can spread."

The bishop reached an arm and turned the sound back up. Just over the warbling of the music, he called, "I did this once as a boy."

"What is that, Bis . . . er, Uncle?" Ricci held his breath, hoping the bishop didn't notice his slip.

"Elvis on the radio, and the wind in my hair. Even the heat doesn't feel as bad as it did earlier. It has more the texture of a black-velvet Mississippi night, when the air brings just enough cooling to comfort, and the crickets and the bullfrogs lull the senses to sleep."

Ricci shook his head. Heaven alone knew where the good bishop came up with some of the thoughts in his head. This was a bright Arizona summer day, and they were rumbling along in a Corvette built for two, heading for an unfamiliar truck stop somewhere along I-10. Elvis might remind Carnaly of sultry nights and cooling breezes, but Ricci's eyes kept glancing at the outside temperature display. It also displayed the interior temperature, because, as the monsignor was uncomfortably aware, with the top down, both were exactly the same.

413

Bobby Dalton, Motel Rat

"Hey, Little T. Wha'cha doing out here?"

Bobby jumped out of the car, and he clapped an arm around his friend's neck, rubbing his knuckles on the top of the smaller boy's head. He'd gotten the nickname from Tommy's mom, from when she called him Mr. T. "Couldn't find a Subway in the big city? Huh?"

"You don't know?" Tommy Pinkston looked younger than Bobby, although he was nearly as tall. He wore his hair to his shoulders, neatly combed. He looked at the bigger boy with worship in his eyes, and he grinned. "My mom said she called yours."

"Nobody told me. Did Austen come with you?" He waved at Tommy's mother. "Hey, Mrs. P. I've got your rug rat here." He laughed the way an older brother would when harassing a younger sibling.

"I talked to your mother, Bobby." Mrs. Pinkston joined them, her eyes on the crew climbing out of the old machine. "She said she called the motel, and someone named Rikkianne told her you were headed to Subway. We could meet you here. I see your car is pretty full, though." There were two women and two small children getting out of the car Bobby had ridden out in.

"I haven't talked to Mom today."

"Well, Little T's staying with you for a month. I can take him all the way out, if I need to, and you can ride with us, if you want. Who are your friends?" Mrs. Pinkston smiled, waving at the women as she headed across the sidewalk. Reaching the door, Mrs. Pinkston held it, letting the others enter ahead of her.

Bobby grinned, still holding Tommy underneath his arm, as he pointed with his free hand. "The first lady is Jeri. Those are her kids, um, Dakota and Little Chrissy, I think." He huffed when his captive almost pulled away, but he grabbed Tommy by the shirt and tugged him back, putting him into a choke hold once again, knuckling his head yet another time.

"The other lady?" She reached to ruffle her son's hair with a smile, pulling her hand back when he screeched in dismay.

"The other one is Ms. Bacciarelli, um, Angioletta." Bobby barely got that out, as Tommy decided at that time to punch him in the stomach, running inside the door and laughing. He jerked the door shut and turned from inside, pointing back at the older boy, and making a face at having fooled him.

"I'm sorry Austen couldn't come." Mrs. Pinkston reached to move a strand of hair from her forehead, tucking it alongside her temple. She glanced to Tommy, narrowing her eyes at his rowdy antics. "If Mr. T there doesn't behave, I'm come get him, if I have to. I know I can trust you to keep him in line, can't I, Bobby?"

"Sure, Mrs. P." They were inside the restaurant by then.

"Bobby! Who you gonna call? Tommy!" The taunt came just outside Bobby's reach, and he grinned wickedly.

Bobby waved at Tommy's mother. "Sorry." Then, he was gone, calling, "Come here, rat!" He lunged, and when Tommy was close enough, he grabbed him around the waist and flipped upside down. Two dimes and a few pennies fell from one pocket. "Your mom says you're mine, and Austen's not here to keep score. I'm going to have fun. By the way, I want a large soda." Then, he carelessly dropped him, sending him sprawling on the floor.

Tommy scrambled up, scooping up the coins, and he straightened his clothing. "Sure, I'll get it. I don't have enough money, though."

Bobby laughed. Ms. Bacciarelli did. This was going to be the coolest summer ever!

Chapter 29

Jeri Franklin, Newly Single

"He's yours, then, the boy?"

Jeri's question was to Tommy's mother, but she couldn't get the woman who'd ridden out with her off her mind. Angioletta hardly knew her, and yet she'd done more for her in the last ten minutes than Zack had done in the last six months.

Jeri had chosen the cheapest meat available, then the smallest bread she thought would feed her three. They could drink water, and that would stretch her limited funds. Yet, when she'd reached for her pocketbook to pay, Angioletta had touched her sleeve with two twenties already out. She had also placed three cups on Jeri's tray, pointing to the drink machines off to the side. When she hesitated, Angioletta had simply handed the bills to the cashier and gently pushed her pocketbook out of sight.

"Dakota and Chrissy will enjoy the sodas. It's my treat."

Jeri hadn't even been able to reply. There was a lump in her throat, and her eyes had burned with impending tears. This woman doing this, and her children. She saw them as grown up, calling them Dakota and Chrissy, not Little Chrissy.

Later, at the fountain, she'd managed a whispered thank you, and was made to feel better when Angioletta whispered back, "You deserve something nice. I enjoyed doing that for you. I appreciate you letting me."

Now, there was a bond that had been formed, the kind that makes women sisters of a kind, with help offered and help returned, for sisters do that for each other.

Jeri smiled as she waited for an answer to her question about ownership of the long-haired boy.

His mother laughed. "Tommy, the one who desperately needs a haircut? He's twelve. I have him and his older sister. You know how it is." She winked at Jeri. "Sometimes they need a break from one another."

"Sometimes," Jeri repeated, looking away, thinking of her two children left alone in the car the night before. Her kids needed their father, and that wasn't something they were likely to get anytime soon. Then she laughed and was embarrassed that she did. "Sometimes, I'm the one who needs a break." She was surprised she said that, and she was even more surprised to realize she meant it. It was nice to be here at this table, and for her kids to be someplace else. "They're okay, do you think?"

Mrs. Pinkston nodded. "Tommy and Bobby'll take good care of them." They had scarfed down a few quick bites, then off they had run to spend some of Tommy's money on video games. "That Bobby's a good kid. I've known his family for a long time, and I've never seen him be anything but perfect. I'd trust my son with him any day." She chuckled. "In fact, that's exactly what I'm doing right now. He's going out there to stay with him for the month."

"A month?" Jeri had meant it about needing a break, but she couldn't imagine a month without Dakota.

"I'm just like you." Mrs. Pinkston smiled, placing her hand on Jeri's arm. "Don't tell Tommy, but sometimes I can use a little break, too."

All three women laughed.

Angioletta Bacciarelli, Daughter of Kafziel

"Are you driving Bobby all the way out?" Angioletta smiled at Tommy's mother. "I heard you ask earlier about his mother. I wondered if there was some confusion."

She hadn't exactly *heard* that. They had been on opposite sides of the glass when the question had been asked. Still, she knew it had been asked, and she thought nothing of having heard it, whether it was her skill at reading lips, or just that she picked up on people's conversations, spoken or unspoken, better than most. It was a useful skill that had served her well in her middle school classroom.

"I was to call her when I got here. I assumed she had already set up a ride. I didn't know he'd be with a big group. Minor confusion, that's all." She picked up her drink, taking a sip, and she toyed with her sandwich. "It's no problem to take him the rest of the way out."

"Jeri, could we squeeze him in your car?" Angioletta turned to Tommy's mother, explaining, "We're staying at the motel just over from Bobby's house. If there's room, we could certainly save both you and Bobby's mother a trip."

"Oh, you must be crowded, already. That would be too much to ask." Her eyes pleaded, though.

"Does he have much luggage?" Angioletta knew boys his age usually didn't. Like most teens, he'd probably packed only as much as his mother had forced him to.

"He has a backpack. I made him put in two changes of clothes." She looked hopeful. "Do you really have room?"

"Will he mind holding his backpack in his lap?" Jeri smiled apologetically. "My trunk is full. My children and I are moving, you see. West. We're headed possibly as far as California."

"Jeri . . . California!" Angioletta's eyes brightened, and she reached and touched the other woman's arm. She drew in a deep breath and repeated, "California," the name having a special, although not quite understood meaning for her.

"You've been there?" Jeri smiled tentatively. "Is it nice?"

418

"I don't know, really." Angioletta let a chuckle escape. She didn't know why she'd reacted as she did. California made her think of Los Angeles, for some reason.

Then, unable to remember why, she let it go, turning her attention back to the matter at hand. She never considered that she'd "forgotten" all about her home in that huge West Coast city. What with the drugs Kafziel had fed her, a portion of his "Suggestions" had indeed taken hold.

As far as Tommy and Bobby, she'd seen the boys together, and she was certain the younger one worshipped the older boy.

She chuckled, widening her eyes once again, "If the boys complain about being crowded, I'll suggest that Tommy sit in Bobby's lap to make room for the backpack. In comparison, I doubt holding it will be any bother at all." She grinned at Tommy's mother.

"In Bobby's lap?" Mrs. Pinkston looked momentarily concerned. Then, Angioletta's "Suggestion" took control, and she smiled. "As long as Tommy's with such an excellent young companion, he'll be well taken care of, and I'll have nothing to worry about. Bobby won't let me down. He never has before, has he?"

She smiled, and she reached for her drink once more.

Eustorgio Ricci, Monsignor

"Surely we must have passed the Subway by now." Monsignor Ricci held his hand over his eyes and peered down the highway.

"There. That must be it!" The bishop pointed to the side of the road. There was a row of canopies forming a zone of moderate shade, and he could see the yellow of a Subway sign. "Interesting. Pizza Hut. There we could clearly purchase pizza. Is it Italian style, do you think? What is Taco Bell? Food, I suppose, a taco served in a bell of some sort. We have all sorts of choices, I see."

"Would you like to try one of those instead of Subway, Excellency?" When Carnaly turned to him with a frown, Ricci

419

quickly amended his terminology. "Uncle. Meglio tardi che mai." *Better late than never.* He grinned drunkenly, embarrassed at the imagined silent rebuke. He must make a point to remember.

"Better, Nephew. Now, do not miss our turn. I'll be famished soon, if I do not eat of this good American food." He held his hand high, the sun glittering off an amethyst ring he always wore, and his fingers motioned them the correct direction.

"So, is there a desire to try either the *Pizza Hut* or the *Taco Bell?*" Ricci tried again, emphasizing the names of the two food places. *Uncle* had not clarified whether he wished to change destinations or not, and he had mentioned both those locations. Ricci might be doing the driving, but his "uncle" held the purse strings.

"We set out for sandwiches, and to sandwiches we have come. My questions earlier were rhetorical, only. I did not desire an answer, or menus, either. I only desire sustenance. Subway, my boy."

As he pulled in the Subway entrance, Ricci glanced at the bishop, thinking, *My boy?* That, at least, hadn't changed, uncle or no. It didn't matter. The bishop was his superior, not his friend, and Ricci would respect his wishes, even it if meant casting Church dogma to the wind, or at least minor portions of it. He could always confess when he returned home. He was bound to find someone who would listen.

Holding the shop door as the bishop entered, Ricci experienced the first wisps of refrigerated air as an enticement beyond measure, and he closed his eyes in pleasure. Then, stepping inside the entrance, additional coolness to compare to an Italian winter in the Alps wrapped him in relief.

When he opened his eyes, his portly companion was already studying the menu. Glancing around, he saw what one might see in any Subway, even those in Italy. People were sitting with sandwiches on their small tables, and paper cups were filled with iced drinks. One or two people had their sandwiches at their mouths, taking generous bites. One of the diners had started his sandwich in the middle, while another clearly aimed for the end. Others were simply visiting, their laughter or quiet words carrying through the cooled space.

Of course, there were more of the working variety of people in the shop than families or professionals, but Ricci understood that they were at a *truck* stop, and so that was to be expected. The term truck stop had begun to make sense to him.

He did see several familial groups, one with small children, and one nun in a distant corner. He smiled at that, wondering if she traveled alone. It was unusual, if she did. Then his eyes caught three women together, all young, one especially beautiful. Her skin had a radiance that seemed to glow. Although he had chosen Christ as his intended, his body could still feel the tug of a beautiful woman. He just didn't have to allow himself to give in to it. This one, though, didn't appeal simply to his earthly flesh. There was something else there, something otherworldly that drew him; as if speaking to her, in some way, would be approaching one of the Holy Mediators to the Christ, Himself, perhaps even a Holy Angel.

He shook his head. Taking a deep breath, he felt a measure of mortification wash over him, for he had given carnal attention to one of God's creations, when her only flaw was to be gifted with exceptional beauty. He must surely be overheated to think such thoughts. If coming to America was to be the cause of such feelings in his breast, he wished he'd never proposed this vile canonization, that he had simply let the girl who had grown up in the little convent he serviced fade away, except in the memories of the sisters who had raised her. That would have been the better choice, and then he would still be in Italy driving his little peanut back and forth across his parish, and no one would care if he pumped the gas each and every time he started it.

His internal monologue was interrupted when the door behind burst open, and several small bodies ran past him one at a time. The fourth was older than the first three. One could have been male or female, he wasn't absolutely certain. The shoulders had widened, but the child's hips were still slim, and the hair could have been long for a boy or short for a girl. All four were bursting with excitement, and it made the monsignor smile when they wound up at the table with the three women.

421

Looking away, he stepped beside Bishop Carnaly to peruse the menu.

He shouldn't have dismissed the children's greetings to the women so quickly, though, for the older boy, the one with a man's build but without a man's height, clearly called the beautiful young woman with the glowing skin by name.

Interlude 26

"Ms. Bacciarelli," Bobby panted in excitement, "You should see the arcade room. They have the best video games, ever. Thank you for letting me come."

Tommy wedged his own comments in. "Yeah, I beat Bobby at The Fast and the Furious. Twice!" He could barely stand still, and he pulled his hair back from his face with both of his hands.

"Dakota, how did you do?" Angioletta reached to draw the nine-year-old forward. "Did these big guys let you play?"

He just grinned, and Bobby answered for him, "He did NASCAR Arcade, and he came in second. I can hardly do that."

"Chrissy?"

"I played all the games with my daddy, every one." Her words were sincere, and her voice and face were bright, causing Angioletta to glance at Jeri, only to see her frown and look away for a moment before forcing a smile and giving her daughter a hug.

With a sigh, Tommy's mother stood, telling her son the most recent plans, and sending him with Bobby to move his backpack to the other car. She wished Jeri and Angioletta the best, telling them she would be stopping by the ladies' room on the way out, and did they need anything before she left?

Angioletta asked her if Tommy would mind if they stepped into a nearby store, and his mother laughed. He was hers, now, and she could do whatever she wanted.

She hugged Tommy outside, giving him a kiss on the cheek, and she shook Bobby's hand. Once in her car, the brakes flashed, and she was gone, headed back to Phoenix.

Bobby and Tommy ogled the sleek sports car that had

appeared in the parking lot, just sitting in the sun with the top down. Then, abruptly, Bobby grabbed the younger boy around the neck once more to rub his knuckles against his head before letting him go.

Monsignor Ricci missed all that. By that time, he and the bishop had ordered, and they were thoroughly occupied in watching their sandwiches being constructed. The employee's actions were practiced and sure, and the men's mouths salivated with the expectation of a familiar meal in this far-away country.

In good time, Ricci mentioned his amusing anecdote about the three women and the four children, but by then, they were already gone, and all that was left was the men's meal to enjoy. It had been a long time since they'd eaten real food, and they took their time, as any good Men of God should.

Bobby Dalton, Motel Rat

"I get the door!" Bobby pushed Tommy aside, laughing, and he yanked the back door open. With Little T around, he was the big guy, and he intended to make the most of it.

"Chrissy, you sit up here." Even Jeri had already adopted her daughter's shortened name. "Dakota, you'll be in the back with the older boys. Bobby, Tommy, put the backpack in the floor and slide the clothes Angioletta bought in the window. Also, don't squash the sandwich we're taking back." She held the sack over the seat.

"I won't, but T-man might. I can put the clothes here." Bobby laughed as they piled in, pushing Tommy aside to make room for the sacks at Dakota's feet. He dumped the backpack in Tommy's lap. When he got everything settled, he grinned.

Up front, Angioletta buckled the small girl into the center of the seat before snapping her own belt in place.

Bobby glanced out the window as Carnaly and Ricci walked out, and he pointed out the two priests to Tommy. Just then Jeri took off, and as the car passed the front door, he watched the skinny one point to their car. However, they were already past before the fat one shifted his bulk to look their way.

Turning around, he saw them climb inside the Corvette. He couldn't imagine two fancy-dressed priests driving a cool car like that.

Then, it passed them on the way back to the motel, the men's hair flying in the wind. He pointed, and he and Tommy laughed. There wasn't much that was funnier than two priests in a convertible with their hair flying in the wind.

Still, they were soon gone, and Bobby and Tommy were right next to each other. It didn't take long for roughhousing to start up once again. He grabbed Tommy's knee and squeezed as hard as he could. The younger boy yelped with a jerk, immediately attempting to squirm away.

"I'll help you, Tommy." Dakota's nine-year-old voice was bright and filled with excitement. He pulled on Bobby's hand, and Bobby convulsed into a spasm, yelling ow, ow, ow, ow, as his hand released Tommy's knee and found Dakota's neck.

"Traitor, traitor, traitor," Bobby laughed, and the three boys were soon wrapped in a knot of flailing arms, heads, and legs. "I should have beaten you at NASCAR, just to make you feel bad."

"You couldn't have." Dakota laughed, his voice high-pitched and hysterical. "I was too good. I would have beaten you no matter what."

The backseat melted into a flurry of laughter, with Bobby at the center of all the commotion.

Angioletta Bacciarelli, Daughter of Kafziel

"I'm sorry, Jeri. They should know better." Bobby had been a wonderful help with Uriel, but this was junior high behavior to the core.

When Angioletta turned to quiet the ruckus, Jeri caught her eye. She tapped the rearview mirror.

"Do you see Dakota's face? It lit up like a Christmas tree when the other boys started in. It's the first spark of life I've seen in him since Zack abandoned us, and if all it takes is letting three boys have a go in my back seat, then I want it to continue. Let them play, please. Dakota needs this."

"If you're sure."

"Please. I'm very sure." She patted her daughter on the knee. "It's Chrissy I don't know how to help, but perhaps something will come along. If so, then maybe Arizona is as far as I need to travel."

Angioletta glanced at Jeri, seeing moisture glistening in her eyes. She faced forward, unable to imagine how badly she must hurt inside, but satisfied with what was happening in the backseat. She had wished for this woman's son to find a friend in the older two boys. She was very pleased to find he had done so.

What she didn't realize was that she had Suggested it, even though she had no idea just what that was. She only knew that when students in her classroom were having difficulties with each other, she could wish for them to resolve their differences, and it simply happened. She'd harbored little doubt that Dakota would find the answer to his loneliness in Bobby and Tommy. She had wished for it, after all.

Now, if she could find a way to help Little Chrissy. She smiled as she glanced down at the girl sitting next to her. She hadn't even responded to the ruckus in the backseat, as if she were in a world of her own. Somehow, Angioletta hoped she could find a way out. In fact, she wished it so, and she had no doubt it would happen, as soon as something came along to bring it to fruition.

425

Chapter 30

Eustorgio Ricci, Monsignor

Monsignor Ricci triggered the top of the car to close, and he turned off the ignition. "Shall we go inside, *Uncle?*" Without a pause, for the interior of the small car heated quickly, he pulled the door lever and stepped outside.

He stood, making sure not to close the door until the bishop also exited. In the glare of the day, just to be outside, even standing in the sun, was better than being in an oven.

Glancing across the broad horizon, his eyes caught something that one rarely saw in Italy. The dirt on the ground radiated so much heat that the rising air distorted the light waves, creating the illusion of water.

When he looked up, he was especially surprised to see the same effect building in several places in the sky, and most unusually, directly over the motel. That was to be expected, he assured himself. He was certain the roof of the building also got extremely hot in the midday sun.

It was the thought of air conditioning that pulled his attention away. Pushing the locking button on his key fob, he stepped forward and opened the motel room door for his companion.

Even though Ricci had been surprised at the amount of heat distortion outside, that feeling paled in comparison to the surprise he felt when he stepped inside and flipped on the lights. Sitting in one of the room's chairs was a face he recognized.

"You—" He nearly choked. It was the man from the airport in London. Back at Heathrow, he had disappeared quite conveniently, leaving Ricci puzzled but surprisingly willing to accept his proffered help.

Suddenly, it seemed peculiar that neither Ricci nor the bishop had questioned such help. Now, he was back again.

"Nephew, we seem to have company." The bishop didn't seem concerned to find a man sitting in their locked motel room. Instead, he walked to the bathroom and took a washcloth from a stack, unfolded it, and patted his forehead. "Have we met, sir?"

The man sat quietly, his clothes crisp and fresh, and his golden skin clear and youthful. His hair was a brilliant white, his fingers were long, and his eyes spoke of the fabled Streets of Gold, their depth and purity mesmerizing.

"In a manner of speaking. Your companion will remember me." He glanced at Ricci and nodded. "My time is short, though, and my message is urgent. Angiola, the woman for whom you seek. She is here."

"Angioletta?" Ricci recognized his own voice asking the question and was surprised he'd spoken. He stepped forward, confused on one hand, and excited on the other. "Tell us how you know this."

"If you wish. You have been with her, and yet you did not know her. She is alive, and her protection is paramount."

"Alive?" Bishop Carnaly asked that question, and this time there was doubt in his voice. "You are sure? We have come to canonize the girl, not rescue her."

"She is very much alive," the golden-eyed man drily remarked.

The bishop turned to Ricci with a pinched mouth, his words matter of fact. "We have seen our girl, and she is not yet ours. At least we are in this together. Mal comune, mezzo gaudio." *Trouble shared is trouble halved.*

427

"Yes, Uncle." Ricci nodded his head respectfully. He was somehow certain he would share far more than half of whatever problems came their way.

The bishop turned back to the stranger, becoming somewhat less congenial. "Explain yourself, sir. Are you a messenger from God? Or, is this a test of our Faith? I tell you, sir, that Monsignor Ricci and I have come to this country in the best of faith—" the word was used differently this time "—and only wish to carry out our mission. Are you here to help us or hinder us?"

"Your mission may yet be resolved, if canonization is your goal. Even so, the girl's life is more important than the Church's Litany of the Saints. She lives, and I had hoped you would spirit her away. Now, that time may have come and gone." Even with the urgency of his words, the man's manner was calm and collected.

"So, she's in danger?" Ricci picked up on that. "What do you expect us to do?" He glanced at the bishop, and seeing a frown at his offer of help, he turned back to the oddly calm man sitting in their room.

The man pressed his fingers together, and he pursed his lips as if considering. Then he glanced at the bishop and back to Ricci. He spoke, choosing his words slowly and carefully. "Perhaps nothing. The time for help is surely past, and I have another to warn. Protect yourselves, for destruction arrives from the hills. I will help, if I am able, but such may not be possible. I now regret calling you into this battle, one in which none may be counted the victor."

"There is to be a battle?" The bishop glanced from the man to Ricci.

The visitor stood. "I must go. What means of protection you choose to take is up to you. Just do it quickly."

A sudden crack of sound jarred the glass in the windows, and the bishop and Ricci both turned to listen. "Surely there can be no immediacy so prevalent that the danger is already here." Bishop Carnaly turned to question the man who had so surprisingly entered their day, only to find him gone. "Ricci? Our friend has taken his leave."

428

Ricci turned, and when he saw that he and the bishop were alone, he remembered the feeling he had felt back at Heathrow.

"He's not just a friend, Bishop. That man is an angel of the Most High God. It was from him I received our tickets to Phoenix." Then he remembered the woman from Subway. She had fairly glowed, and he had thought her angelic. He smiled, certain he knew who Angioletta really was. "We must return to Subway, Your Excellency. I know who we're looking for. I saw her there."

Just then, an explosion worthy of an airliner collision tore the calm of the room apart. Almost immediately, something came vaulting through the window, ripping the curtains from the wall. It landed on the first bed, bounced once, then tumbled to the floor, stopping at Ricci's feet. It was a wheel from a car, and it stood on end for a moment, before falling to its side. There on the rim was the image of two crossed flags, one that could have come from only one possible car.

"Our American Corvette?" Carnaly questioned.

"I do believe so, Your Excellency."

"Oh, dear. Il bene del matrimonio dura tre die - il male dura fino a la morte." *The good of the marriage lasts three days - and the bad lasts 'til death.* "It seems our marriage—" their vacation to America "—wishes to go sour. This could get bad."

"Only until death, Your Excellency. Only until then." Ricci chuckled. Almost immediately, his expression widened to a full blown smile. In the heat of the ensuing events, the bishop hadn't bothered to correct the honorifics he had used over the past five minutes.

"You did purchase the insurance on the car, Ricci?"

The younger man nodded. "Of course, Bishop."

"Good," Carnaly said. "I would hate to have to ask the Holy See for a special dispensation to forgive that particular lack of prescience." Then he grinned. "Are you up for this, my son?"

"For what, Bishop?"

"To get our hands dirty. Nothing this exciting has happened to me since I joined the Church as a child."

Ricci wilted inside. What had he gotten himself into? His attempts to get the girl canonized had only been a simple suggestion. He never considered that it might have been a Suggestion. Then, he was only human, and where brothers were concerned, humans only knew what they needed to know. Suggestions always seemed the right thing to do, even if they were, indeed, someone else's ideas altogether.

Just then, another crash rocked the room, and looking through the broken window, they saw the car they'd so recently driven to the truck stop had finally come to rest, apparently falling from the sky back into the space where it had been parked. Dust billowed from underneath.

"What shall we do now, my good Ricci?" The bishop walked to his side, peering through the tattered curtains and shattered glass.

"Run?"

The bishop chuckled. "Well, we certainly cannot drive. Our car is missing a wheel."

It was missing much more than a wheel, but Ricci left his thought unsaid. Even the bishop could see that.

Raphael, Angel of Healing

"Uriel!" Raphael had entered the brother's room, and he stepped to his side, grasping his leg and shaking it. "Uriel! No wonder I cannot call to you. Why do you sleep? A battle is imminent, a fight we can no longer avoid."

Uriel shook his head as he blinked his eyes into focus. "Raphael? Your presence is unexpected. You are mistaken, I do not sleep. I've had injuries, and I have not had enough food to replace my needs. I rest and wait." He pushed his hair away from his face, his eyes glancing around. "Where is Kafziel?"

"With his tail tucked between his legs." *And probably hiding safely out of harm's way.* "Can you stand easily?"

Uriel pulled himself to a sitting position. The strained expression on his face told how it tired him, though, for his energy reserves had gone to heal the cuttings on his shoulder. "Angioletta. She hasn't returned. I must go for her."

He threw his legs off the bed, leaning forward to stand, only to stumble against the brother who stood at his side.

Raphael grasped him, wrapping him in his arms. He held his hands against Uriel's face, and he felt them warm with the transfer of strength, healer-to-brother, a type of renewal that was his alone to give. The glow that had surrounded him when Kinky was healed didn't light the room, for no true healing occurred. Not surprisingly, Uriel's appearance did immediately improve. It was good that it did, too, for about that time, an explosion rocked the building. Taking a deep breath, Raphael helped Uriel to sit.

"Feeling better, Brother?"

"Some." Uriel coughed. "Actually, a lot. Thanks. Tell me, was that Kafziel just now?"

Raphael laughed. "Tail tucked, remember? No, it is not Kafziel. It is worse, and we must leave now. The attack has already begun." He didn't say that he was the target, not Uriel. Yet, Uriel would eventually become the target, and this was one brother who must survive this upcoming conflagration. He walked to the window, glancing up to the sky. His expression didn't improve at what he saw. The air roiled, and it was not pretty. "Uriel?" He turned. "May we take our leave?"

"I cannot. I await Angioletta's return. I have only recently rescued her. You would not believe what Kafziel has done, Raphael. This is one human who must be protected at all costs."

"Angioletta, your human," who was by some accounts more than human. Raphael's golden eyes watched the brother at his side, his eyes speaking what his voice could not. *You are one brother who must be protected at all costs. Do you even remember, Uriel? What do you remember, my brother?* He didn't say those things, though. Instead, he asked, "Can you fly?"

Uriel stood, flexing his powerful chest muscles. "Of course, I can. Understand, Angioletta is not here, yet."

"She is soon to arrive. I have provided what warning I could for her safety. Others will provide for her, if they can. Will you fly with me now?"

Raphael hoped he could convince him, for he was deeply concerned. He knew what he'd seen in the sky overhead. The

431

Four Familiars had found him.

Unexpectedly, or perhaps it was expected, at least by Raphael, the building shuddered—another explosion—and dust filtered from new cracks in the ceiling.

Raphael stepped to his brother and grabbed his arm. "Now, Uriel. Great destruction is here, and we are at the center of it."

Raphael was at the center of it, anyway. Still, Uriel's safety was at stake here, if not from the Familiars, then from the Circle of Brothers. Raphael couldn't trust anyone else to know and understand Uriel's importance. This girl? Saving her was of the utmost importance. Uriel? Even greater. The girl must be risked. It was a calculated assessment he knew he had to make.

Even so, Uriel didn't make it easy.

"I will not fly now, Raphael, not without Angioletta. I have promised my protection, and I will not allow her harm. If I leave, I have lost her. I will not lose her simply because you wish me to run from an enemy I do not know. It is Kafziel, is it not? Has he brought reinforcements? I stole the girl from him. She is his daughter."

"That cannot be so." Raphael turned away to hide his incredulity, his breath stilled in the shock of such horrific news, and he shuddered. Even the destruction hovering at their door was put aside for a moment of time. This he had truly not wanted to believe, and for Kafziel to be the father? He wanted to doubt, and still, in that moment of enlightenment, he knew the truth of it. Such was the knowledge he had of Kafziel, and such was what he knew of Uriel. One was all lies, and the other all truth. Uriel must know this for certain, or he wouldn't speak such defamation so boldly.

"You are not unaware of Kafziel's history. What do you think, my brother?" Uriel's tone was sour.

Without turning, Raphael hissed tersely, "You know this to be certain. I hear it in your voice. Do you know how?"

Another shockwave rocked the building, and this one seemed closer. A voice could be heard yelling outside, and the sound was of uncontrolled terror. There was a short howl, as of a wolf in the night, then a great gray bundle of muscle and fur burst at full speed through the unyielding solidity of the wall, its body flickering briefly, then instantly coming to rest at Uriel's side.

"Your second." Raphael was not surprised to see the animal come directly through the wall. It was something all familiars could do. It was something he had also done, both in the first room to warn the clergy, as well as in this one.

Uriel nodded, reaching to grasp Malak's fur. "He watches for my ward."

"She is your ward, now, is she?" He turned to Uriel, watching his face, looking for lies. There were none.

"In practice, if not in fact."

Yet again, an explosion rocked the building, and the tinkle of shattering glass could be heard. A car alarm sounded, and it refused to end.

"We must go, Brother." Raphael had grown desperate. He threw out a wild card he didn't wish to play. "Gabriel is on Earth." He saw sudden anticipation flood Uriel's body, his face lighting up as it had not since rising from the bed.

"For me?" Uriel fought a smile, only to have it break across his face. His eyes leaped to the door as if he expected the Archangel to come striding through. "Angioletta will be saved."

The Healer dreaded what he would reveal next. Uriel would be staked in the heart. "He leads five brothers against you." *I was one, Uriel.* He didn't say that, though. He couldn't. It crushed him as it was to see all hope drain from Uriel's body, to see his face pale against the shadows within the room.

"Against me? What have I done wrong? I have rescued a human—" half-human, anyway "—from certain living death, and I've done it at peril of my own pain and suffering. The Deeds of Man will collaborate that. Chitar and Gupat will be able to search out the truth—"

"The Deeds have been searched, and they have been twisted." Raphael was in near despair. They must run! "Will you flee with me, now?"

"But what of Gabriel? His love for me may have faded, but to pursue me, to lead others in the chase? Does he hate me so?"

"Uriel. We must go." Another explosion rocked the building, and more car alarms followed. Something sizzled loudly, as if a high powered electric circuit was shorting out.

Uriel stepped toward the window. "If Gabriel is here, then I need to see him with my own eyes, to *know*. If it is true, then to at least see the brother I have loved more than any other is the last true thing I will ever know, because the rest of my existence will be a lie. To live without Gabriel, truly without my one love, is to wish for death, and death is something I cannot have. I will be forced to exist, knowing I do not want life."

"He isn't here." Raphael took Uriel's shoulder in his grasp, stopping him from looking out. He was giving the brother at his side partial truths, and he loathed that. And yet, the full truth would serve no purpose today.

"Then he is not in this that is happening?" Renewed hope brightened Uriel's eyes.

"He is part of it." He dared not share too much. Uriel could not know that this particular battle was all about Raphael. He must think this was about him, also.

"Where is he, Raphael? On Earth, you said. You must tell me."

"Yes, but not here. He searches for you but has not found you. He will." Raphael detested the words that escaped his lips. It was driving a second stake into this brother's heart, then twisting it just to make him bleed. He also knew that wherever Gabriel was, it might be some time before he returned. There was no telling how badly injured he was, or whether he would be given any help. It could be mere hours before he returned, or it could be months. The same was true of the other three of the Circle that Barakiel had watched be defeated.

Yet, there was truth in his words, too. The Archangel Gabriel was not the Citadel of Justice and Power for nothing. When he was convinced of an injustice—and he *was* convinced Uriel was guilty—there was no end to which he would not go to bring that brother to task for his misdeeds. Gabriel would pursue Uriel, and without Uriel's Mandate of Destiny, the Rebellion would endure. It must not be allowed to happen.

"I will not lose her, Raphael." Uriel sat on the bed. "She knows I am here. She will return."

Raphael groaned with despair.

Uriel, Bearer of Destiny

Uriel ducked his head, resting it in his hands. Images flashed through his mind. Angioletta had touched his shoulder and removed the gravel. He had growled his complaints, and she had found him humorous. She thought he had seen little of that, but she had been transparent to him. She had no mental privacy screen in place, and although the Strictures forbade the invasion of another's thoughts, much had leaked through before he'd been able to catch himself. Then, she had placed her hand on his chest, and his body had cried out for her.

Now, Gabriel was here, and Gabriel hated him so greatly that he *hunted* him like a *criminal*.

Angioletta cared for him. She had touched his chest, and she had wanted him to touch her in return.

In that moment, he knew he would wait for her until this desert motel was ground to dust, and there was nothing that would change his mind.

Malak, Wolf

Malak sensed Uriel's strength of purpose, and the animal detected his resistance to Raphael's entreaties. The wolf looked at Raphael with yellow eyes and growled. The familiar would make sure Uriel's wishes were honored, for they were one. And if not, there were teeth that could make one regret trying. No one wanted to be Malak's enemy, not a second time, anyway.

Angioletta Bacciarelli, Daughter of Kafziel

"What is it, Jeri?" Angioletta, preoccupied in a fruitless attempt to interact with Chrissy, looked at Jeri, puzzled to see dismay on her face.

"My God, Angioletta." She hit the brakes, slowing her old

car. She pointed the direction of the motel, ignoring the boys in the back, still wrestling, calling gibes, pinching, and grabbing at arms and legs.

Angioletta called for them to quiet down, and when they did, they saw it, too.

Ahead of them, the air above the motel roiled with dust and the shimmer of afternoon heat. It shimmered with something else, too, although it was hard to tell just what.

Angioletta started to exclaim that there was an enormous Eagle overhead, and perhaps a winged Lion . . . as well as an Ox . . . with wings. She immediately shut those words away. She had learned long ago not to tell of some things she could see, for if they appeared too unusual, then she was surely the only one who saw them. These were indistinct, anyway, more the ghost of those things, the way dust and heat distortion can give shape to something that may or may not be there. They were probably nothing more than her imagination.

The damage to the motel was not. The far side had been destroyed. The front wall was only partially standing in places, and it was clear the roof was missing in many others. A sports car, surely not the one that had passed them earlier, was smashed, and as they watched, the main entrance doors blew out into the parking lot. The building was being systematically searched and destroyed. By what or whom they couldn't tell, and Angioletta refused to let her eyes speak the cause. There was surely no substance to what she'd seen.

Somewhere in there was Uriel, though. The end of the building and the room they'd taken were still undamaged, and he would surely be inside. How she could help, she didn't know, but she must try. Yet, indecision gripped her, and her mind seemed frozen.

"Cool," came from behind her, and she turned to see Bobby's face looking over the back of her seat. "This is like a scene from a movie or something."

"Bobby," she cried, grabbing his arm. "Uriel's in there. I've got food, clothes . . ." Her voice trailed off, her eyes going wide with understanding.

She remembered how weak he'd been earlier, then with

food, he'd recovered. He'd spoken about his hunger again just before she'd left, but all the food in the room had been gone. What if he couldn't get out?

"Do you see Malak or Uriel anywhere, Bobby?"

"I don't think so, Ms. Bacciarelli." His eyes were glued to the increasing damage. One of the motel's doors to the right of the main office blew out, and a piece of furniture came flying through the roof.

"Can you get us closer, Jeri?" Angioletta didn't know this man, not really, but she knew there was something very important he hadn't told her. She also knew she trusted him. He had rebuffed her unwanted touch, yes, but now he was in danger. She was convinced of that.

"Are you sure? The children. Surely your man has escaped. He must have run, already."

"Please, Jeri. Just a little ways. I must make certain." She pleaded, not realizing the strength of her Suggestion, only knowing her desperation.

Jeri breathed hard. "The parking lot. I can pull up there, but you must get out quickly. I'm scared. My children, you understand."

"Thank you, Jeri. Yes, your children. I teach teenagers, and I understand how much one can care about them." She was giddy with relief, and as soon as they reached the lot, she turned to Bobby. "You job is to watch over everyone in this car." Then, she threw open the door and ran.

She slammed against the door of their room, now truly frightened at the sounds of the building as it exploded around her. She beat on it with her fist, glancing around to see if there was anyone who could help, relieved at least to see Nigel and Rikkianne off to the edge of the parking lot with a number of other people. Included were the two clergy she had seen at the truck stop, and that surprised her. How did they arrive so quickly? Before she could call to them, the door fell open beneath her, and she tumbled into the room.

In that singular moment of impending rescue, the room detonated around her, shattering in a whirlwind of bricks, boards, and wildly pirouetting insulation. She felt something

437

impact the back of her head, and her world faded from around her.

Jeri Franklin, Newly Single

Jeri sat in the car, at first certain her new friend would be successful in getting in and out before the rest of the building was destroyed. Her temporary confidence was fractured when the door through which Angioletta fell was torn off its hinges and landed in the parking lot, she was gripped with foreboding, and tears flooded down her face.

Bobby and Tommy sat mesmerized, while the two smallest children were wide-eyed with shock, Chrissy holding her mother's hand in her lap, and Dakota leaning over the seat with his arms around her neck.

Jeri motioned for her son to climb up front with her, and they all held hands together.

"Nothing good can come of this. Nothing at all." She whispered her words to no one.

She couldn't even drive away. All she could do was sit where she was and watch it happen. Oh, God, she had to sit and watch it all happen, watch everyone die.

Tears soaked her face, and her breath wouldn't come. She had never seen anything so horrible in her entire life.

Chapter 31

Uriel, Bearer of Destiny

Malak turned to Uriel with a high-pitched whine.

"What, boy?" He reached to rub him behind one ear, giving what comfort he could. "We must be patient. We wait."

When Angioletta's hand began to hit the motel room door, Raphael barked, "It's her, Uriel. She wants in. Can we leave now?"

Uriel leaped to his feet, stumbling for the door. He refused to brush her thoughts, but the feel of her desperation was clear. There was no doubt it was her on the other side of that metal barrier.

He turned before opening the door. His brother had not seemed to be the friend he needed. He had brought sour news, and he had tried to get him to leave Angioletta behind. Now, he needed to be gone.

"Leave, Raphael. You have done enough damage. You should not be here." New levels of anger coursed through his body, for he was now convinced there was more to Raphael's presence than the Healer's words had told.

In that moment, something loud detonated somewhere near, and the room shook, with great cracks appearing in the walls. A portion of the ceiling shifted, and the crack that had been there all along flexed violently, sending waves of dust floating down into the room.

Raphael covered his eyes, brushing the dust away. "You need me, Uriel. This will never be over until your innocence is proved."

"The Deeds of Man can prove it. What has been twisted can be untwisted. You know that." His hand rested on the doorknob. "I do not need your help. Not the sort you've provided today. You've tried to get me to leave my charge behind, and that cannot be forgiven."

Deep in his heart, he also doubted that Gabriel was doing as Raphael had said. Gabriel loved him, still. He must, mustn't he? He had come to the Seat to wish him well.

"Uriel, do not drive me away. I am here only to help you. I am not just your brother. I am also your friend."

"Go, Raphael." He spat the words as he turned and yanked the door open, and when he did, Angioletta fell headlong into the room.

In that same moment, a concussion of unbelievable force ratcheted the four walls of the room apart, lifting the plaster-board overhead and blowing the door into the parking lot. In the first moments of the devastation, a beam tore loose from the ceiling and came crashing down, hitting Angioletta firmly on the head, tearing the skin away. Blood flew onto Uriel's body. She hit heavily on the floor, lifeless.

Uriel cursed Raphael, for this was surely from him. However, before he could deride the Healer with his bitter words, berating him for his interference, the storm tearing the motel brick from brick concussed again, and debris started to fly.

Without a second thought, he did the only thing he knew to do, the very thing he had done with the baby not so many nights before when he had first arrived on Earth. He threw his hands together, and in a great explosion of light, one that roiled across the devastated room, filling every nook and cranny, and driving every dark shadow away, he knelt over her, drawing his wings around them both, and creating a protective space where she could be injured no further. As the room erupted around them, his wings were battered by the continued assault of falling timbers, insulation, and roofing materials. His was the small space that provided for the continuance of life in this nightmare of destruction.

The falling debris eventually began to settle, and all was quiet. Uriel felt Malak nuzzle his side, and he realized the wolf had been with them all the time, enduring the assault of the crumbling building. He looked for Raphael, aware that the sun now reached easily into the interior of the room.

Glancing at Malak, he questioned, *Raphael?* Malak sent an image back, and in the image, Raphael took to wing as the room exploded, flying directly at the sun. Following him were four creatures that Uriel found difficult to believe. The Four Familiars had been Encapsulated since before the Triune Mind. They could not be loose upon the face of Earth.

Malak was certain, though, and Uriel called to Raphael. He didn't find him, although whether that was because the brother was preoccupied or had simply shut him out altogether, he couldn't tell. In that moment of Malak's vision, he realized without doubt what the Healer had done for him, leading his attackers away. Raphael had spoken the truth, and Uriel had rebuffed his offer of help and friendship.

"I am sorry, Raphael. I was wrong. If you should return, I would welcome you." He cried his words to the dust-filled sky. He would, too. Now, he had to get out of this mess, and he had to get help for Angioletta. He had watched her collapse, and now he feared the worst for her.

With careful fingers, he reached and brushed the blood from her forehead, surprised that the injury was no worse than it was. He had seen the board strike her. Blood had sprayed everywhere, for he still wore its evidence upon his skin and clothes.

If only the Healer had stayed.

Standing, he shook his wings to clear them of rubble, then with a nod of his head, he reached his hands high in the air and clapped them away, washing the broken room with brilliant light once again. Gasping with the suddenness of unexpected

441

weakness, he felt the decimated levels of energy his body still suffered. Kneeling, he carefully picked up Angioletta's limp form, ferrying her gently through the remains of their room and into the fullness of the bright, Arizona summer sun.

Even away from the room, there was no safe place to walk. Everywhere he stepped, pieces of the building were strewn about. To the left, far across the pavement, were two priests and the couple who managed the motel. Others stood in small clusters, but he recognized none of them. To the right was the car that held the people he knew.

With tears growing in his eyes, he walked that way. They knew Angioletta, had interacted with her, had loved her as he did. How could they not? Surely they would want to help. Someone would have to. She needed help he couldn't offer, and he needed to eat. He must have food soon, or he wouldn't be able to move at all.

Finally, he fell into an open door, sending Tommy flying into Bobby's lap to give him room.

"Where do I go?" Jeri turned and looked at Angioletta, with shock on her face. "Is she dead?"

"I do not know." He was too exhausted to think.

"Where do I go?" She repeated her question.

"Away." He knew no more than that. He also suspected his attackers would return when they realized they chased Raphael and not him. With words that were no more than ragged gasps, he whispered, "Just drive. There is nothing for us here. Did you bring food?"

"Here, Uri." Bobby grabbed the Subway sack from the floor, and he held it to him. "Clothes, too. We got those." He began to dig, when Uriel held up a hand.

"Just the food. Thanks, Bobby. Can you unwrap it for me?"

"Sure, Uri. I can do that." He grabbed for the sack from Subway, dumping everything inside into the car, and out of the torrent, he lifted a wrapped sandwich. "For you."

"For me." *And not for Angioletta, ever again.* Uriel wanted to cry, and he had no strength left for additional tears.

442

Bobby Dalton, Motel Rat

Bobby understood everything. When everyone else had been crying and looking at all the stuff that was happening, he'd been watching the room. He didn't think Uri could be hurt, no matter what happened. After all, he'd already walked through a wall once that morning. After the door blew away, he saw the bright flash, and sure enough, there was an angel right there in the room with Ms. Bacciarelli, kneeling over her and keeping her safe. Then, when it was all over, he had watched the angel—Uri!—stand, and he'd done something that had caused another bright flash. When he'd walked out with Ms. Bacciarelli, the wings were gone. That was about as cool as the wall thing, if not more so.

Then he noticed Malak outside, running alongside the car. "Your wolf, Uri." He reached to get the man's attention, but Uriel nodded before he could touch him.

"I've spoken with him, Bobby." He held the sandwich Bobby had offered, but his attention was on Angioletta. "He will wait on me to return, if I can."

Bobby smiled. Spoken with him? He could kinda figure that out without too much difficulty. After the wall thing and the wing thing, it didn't seem too weird at all.

Tommy Pinkston, Otherwise Known as Little T

Tommy was now scrunched half on Bobby's lap, but his thoughts were elsewhere. He'd seen something completely different than Bobby. He hadn't known to keep his eyes trained on the empty doorway, and so he hadn't seen Uriel's wings. He'd been looking at all the boards and insulation and furniture flying through the air, and in the midst of it all, he'd seen a very familiar sight, one that was a near duplicate of one he'd once seen in a picture on his Sunday school class wall.

There, rising above the maelstrom that used to be a motel,

had been a winged person with brilliantly white wings, flying away into the sky. He knew what it was. An angel.

Overcome with emotion and insight into what had happened, he glanced at the woman sitting with them in the back seat. The angel he'd seen might be her angel, like she'd really died, and she'd flown to Heaven. That gave him the chills, that she might be really dead.

He glanced back out the window, but the car was moving already, and he could no longer see the remains of the motel. He looked at Bobby, who was grinning, and at the man he didn't know, who was eating hungrily. He closed his eyes at the blood on the woman's head, and he felt his stomach spin.

Food and blood didn't mix for Tommy, not at all.

Zadkiel, Envoy of Freedom, Benevolence, and Mercy

Zadkiel tried to rest, but there was a commotion both inside and outside that was getting on his nerves.

Jeqon had found a radio, and although it was only a small clock combination, he'd hooked it up to an extension cord. He was outside the motel room, his black skin exposed to the waist, soaking up the sun, with the music blaring for all to hear.

Inside, locked away in the bathroom, Asbeel had found that the motel complex ran one large tank for its hot water supply, one that served the entire campus. Laughing, he had collected all the soaps he could find, the shampoos, too, and he was in the shower, singing at the top of his lungs.

There was yet a third thing, though, and Zadkiel didn't like what he was hearing. He was on one of the beds in Kinky's room, resting with his eyes closed, and Kinky was on the phone.

"You don't know the half of this, Julian."

Zadkiel opened one eye to see Kinky as he walked the floor, glancing at the closed bathroom door, then stopping by the window to pull the curtain aside. The man peered at Jeqon a moment, shaking his head. He let his eyes flick around the motel room and held his hand shielding the mouthpiece, whispering, "Wings, Julian. Real, feathered wings. I know it sounds like I'm back off the wagon, but I'm dry as a bone. I know what I saw. You can check the newsfeeds for Phoenix. No, I don't know the name of the street. I wasn't running for my life, checking out the street signs along the way. I was just running. You'll know it, though. It's gone now. I mean, gone." He paused before barking back, "Not the street. It's still there. The building's gone. Hey, I've even got a broken window in my car."

Zadkiel heard him pause, listening, then Kinky snarled, "No, the broken window's not from the restaurant damage. One of the angels fell on my car. Right out of the sky, only I didn't know he was an angel, then. I just thought he was a man who fell out of the sky." Another pause, then, "C'mon, Julian. You gotta believe me. People do fall out of the sky, sometimes. You heard about that kid Back East, just sixteen, stowing away in that airliner wheel well. Fell right out into a neighborhood street. He was run over twice by drivers before they knew what it was."

After a few minutes at the window, looking out, silent, with the phone to his ear, Kinky muttered, "Yeah, and you should see my windshield. You'd think my imagination. Yeah, yeah, Julian." He turned his phone off and dropped it into his pocket, glancing back at Zadkiel, glaring. Then, he sat on the second bed.

As he did so, the bathroom door opened, and out walked Asbeel. A fog of moisture billowed out with him, and his skin steamed in the coolness of the room. His sandy hair was plastered down his neck, and he had a thick towel in his hand, rubbing water from his face.

"Ash," Zadkiel groaned, using a nickname he knew the status-conscious brother hated. "It's more than just you and me in here." When Asbeel shot him arrows with his eyes, Zadkiel jerked his head Kinky's direction. "Pay attention, Ash." That should rile him, make him notice who else was around. He was *naked*, for Unity's sake!

A noise outside got Zadkiel's attention—everyone's, in fact. A familiar voice was hooting and yelling. Then, something beat against the glass, demanding the attention of those inside.

"It be Raphael!" There was a pause, and the voice returned, breathless, "The Triune Mind's Pets, too. They be chasing Raphael."

Zadkiel glanced at Asbeel, then at Kinky. Both the brothers knew what this meant. Back at the restaurant, they had been glad just to walk away alive after the attack had ended. If Raphael now drew the Four Familiars away, the chase was still on. There was no question but what they would follow.

There was one other thing that made them the logical choice to be Raphael's backup. They weren't the ones being targeted by the Four. They could harass, fall back, regroup, and come at the enemy again, for if the Four pursued Raphael only, they would never intentionally turn to attack the other three brothers. Zadkiel, Asbeel, and Jeqon would be as flies on a water buffalo's back, once swept aside, then quickly forgotten. The flies always returned, though, as would they.

They must leave immediately if they were to provide help, and that presented a special dilemma. To exit with no delay, they must also deploy their wings. How much could this human be allowed to see?

Zadkiel suspected they had little choice in the matter.

Kinky Kinkerson, Reporter

Kinky froze. At first a voice had yelled through the window, then almost quicker than he could blink, a man had begun to coalesce inside the motel room, only it was in the form of one body part at a time. First, his shoulder and arm came through, his hand still clasped in a fist, the one he had used to beat on the window. Then, Kinky could see half his chest, and next the outline of his head became visible, his tightly twisted knobs of hair standing out. Finally, his face appeared, filled with a look of urgency, reflecting whatever had him riled.

He was clearly off balance, though, for once his upper half was inside the motel room, there was an interminable pause. A look of surprise replaced the urgency, and knocking a small table aside, then sending a lamp skittering across the floor, the rest of the black brother came tumbling through. He looked around, only to find the two brothers and Kinky watching him.

"Oops," was the first word out of his mouth.

It was an appropriate one, too. Humans should not be privy to such stunts, and already, Kinky had proven resistant to easy Suggestions. His mind had bonded too closely with Raphael. Unusual brotherly antics wouldn't be easily Suggested away where Kinky was involved.

When Kinky turned, he saw Zadkiel on his feet, and with a clap of his hands, a great flash of light flooded the room. When it faded, there was a loud whoosh, and great feathered wings opened wide at his back.

"Jeqon," he called. "Asbeel. There can be no delay. Your wings. Quickly. They cannot be allowed to escape."

Asbeel was equally quick to transform. His was the Mandate to Lead, even if it was in name only. His appearance was majestic, even as his long, sandy hair twisted in wet tendrils around his face and shoulders. His muscular body glistened with water droplets from head to toe, and he fairly glowed with power and strength. His wings filled one side of the room, and the majesty of his presence seemed to draw the air from Kinky's lungs.

Jeqon grabbed the towel Asbeel had carelessly dropped, and he threw it into the brother's arms. "Beauty be in the eyes of the beholder, Asbeel. Not so much of your beauty do the humans wish to behold. Gird yourself," and he sniggered at his joke.

Kinky stumbled back and sat heavily on the extra bed as Zadkiel flexed his wings, sending a rush of air across the room.

"You are joining us, Jeqon?" Zadkiel barked the question, again flexing his wings. Doing so involved his entire upper torso, and it showed the strength that was hidden in his slender, corporeal form. "We need your help, for whatever happens today, there will not be a repeat of the incident at the restaurant."

When Kinky turned his direction, Asbeel had his loins girded, and Jeqon's black wings arose at his back, unfurled and as majestic as those that had already joined the other brothers.

Kinky hadn't spoken a word, and at this point, he didn't

447

know if he could. It was all he could do to keep his bowels from loosening themselves where he sat.

Zadkiel, Envoy of Freedom, Benevolence, and Mercy

Zadkiel paused, and he looked toward the lone human in the room. He realized he was again frightened. Kneeling, he reached a hand toward Kinky, with his opened palm extended. He ducked his head a moment, his eyes closed in quick consideration, and he unknowingly presented the perfect image of every angel ever seen. Then, his head lifted, and he smiled.

The moment was radiant with the beatific fluorescence of his corporeal body. His spoken words were a bit more mundane, though.

"Sorry, Kinky. You can't go with us."

Zadkiel did attempt to impress a Suggestion on the man. *Stay here. Keep off the phone.* He had no idea if it would work, but it was the best he could do under the circumstances and time frame he had to work with.

Then, with a leap, all three brothers cast themselves toward the ceiling, their wings in motion, and with the barest of shimmers, they were gone.

Kinky Kinkerson, Reporter

Kinky ran to the window to see if they were in the sky, and sure enough, there they were, three winged angels, moving so fast his eyes could barely keep up.

"Julian," he whispered. "You have got to hear about this." He reached into his pocket and withdrew his phone. He even opened it and began to dial the number. For some reason, though, before he was finished, he closed it and let it fall back into his pocket. Julian wouldn't be interested. It would be like the story about his car. Julian would just laugh, telling Kinky to get a real life that he didn't have to invent like it was an overblown, pseudo-interesting fantasy.

When he turned, he picked up his car keys, then tossed them back down. Where was there to go, anyway? He would be better to turn on the television and see if he could find out anything about the restaurant that had blown up earlier that morning.

It would all come back to him later, because he was emotionally invested. For now, he was content to lie on the bed and let the television entertain him. That was what Zadkiel's Suggestion had been all about, anyway, and all-in-all, it worked just the way he intended.

Barakiel and Elemiah, Six-Winged Seraphim

The damaged airliner had landed by the time the two Seraphim reached Florida. That was where Kasbeel had impacted, and so that was where their senses took them. Entering the craft, they found the decimated lavatory, and it became clear just where their brother had lain. They considered their options for a time, then Elemiah spoke.

"Here he lay, this brother of ours. In our hands are Swords of Power." His eyes followed the Sword he held as he twirled it elaborately in the enclosed space, its light making a trail that seemed to burn a path in the very air. Any other brother would have been said to be showing off. Perhaps he was, to some degree, or maybe it was his way of teasing Barakiel into cooperation.

"And that means, Brother?" Barakiel's eyes flashed with his question. Elemiah's power, that melodious, mesmerizing rhyme, had no effect on him. He wanted this spelled out before he made any commitment to cooperation. The urgency to find Kasbeel was strong, and it was obvious he was no longer in this aircraft.

"Perhaps to tell the tale, this plane will do as well." Elemiah smiled. Metal might indeed do the trick. It had never been tried.

"Ah!" Barakiel understood the intent behind those words. "It does not hurt to make the attempt."

Without another sound between them, they raised their

Swords and slammed the tips into the floor of the cabin. Instantly, all around them recent events leaped into action, the clock turning in a backwards motion, greatly speeded up, as the proceedings of the day unraveled themselves. The metal structure of the stricken craft retained the tale better than soil and trees and rocks ever had. A medical team was on the airplane, then Kasbeel was lying on the floor at their feet. In a flash, the crew of the airliner was gathered at the lavatory door, and moments later, a thud shook the aircraft. Finally, the Seraphim knew they had reached the part where their brother had landed.

Shifting their Swords, and wishing it so, time began to run forward again. It jerked along in snatches, slowing for moments as the brothers checked the progression of events, then speeding up again. Finally, they reached the part where the medical team entered the craft.

"Oh, my God! Will you look at this? What are these things attached to this man's back? And they say he fell into the plane from the outside? I'm glad this is Mercy Hospital's problem, and not ours. No one will believe this if we tell them."

"I've got my cell. I can take a picture."

"You nuts? You want to lose your job just for a picture, in this economy?"

That was all they needed to hear. Yanking their Swords from the floor of the cabin, they leaped and were gone. They knew exactly where to go, too, for as the name of Mercy Hospital was spoken, the image that was revealed through the power of their Swords had painted the building, as well as its location, in their thoughts.

Kasbeel was found in Mercy Hospital, right there on the Atlantic Coast of Florida, overlooking the sparkling sea. He had been wrapped in protective coverings, and weakened, given intravenous nourishment by nurses wearing rubber gloves, for no one had doubted that the badly injured man was in need of sustenance. Within that nourishment were certain tranquilizers, for it was the hospital's duty to provide the utmost in care. For one as badly damaged as Kasbeel, that meant he must not feel the pain of his injuries at all.

No one had taken the time to notice the sudden and dramatic healing that began minutes after the IVs began to pump their nourishing fluids into the injured brother's body. Standing over the patient's bed would be a useless waste of their time, for the doctors and nurses knew the injuries they'd seen were severe, and it would take such dramatic wounds months to heal. The nurses sequestered in their stations could check the patient's progress on their machines.

They also knew that as soon as the specialists arrived, he would be wheeled into surgery. Then, of course, there were government agencies en route, also. A man with wings? What sort of aberrant mad scientist had been performing experiments on this poor soul? For that reason, he had been locked away where no one could see.

That, of course, didn't stop the two Seraphim. They faded their bodies, letting their corporeal selves become no more than the whisper of the froth on the ocean far below, their wings the brush of salt air on dry cheeks, and their Suggestions the very actions nearby humans had thought to do anyway. That was as it always was, and before long, Kasbeel was revived, and three brothers flew through the sky. Raphael called to them. He was being pursued. Who could come to help?

Two Seraphim and one freshly restored brother could. The Circle of Brothers was being reinstated. Now, if only Gabriel could be found, for he was the key to their success.

One way or another, they must deal with the Four Familiars, then Uriel. The Betrayer must be located and returned to the Unity. What would be done with him then was no more than speculation. However, there was a Primary Forces Chamber, and also a Secondary Forces Chamber. Who was to say but what there might someday be a Tertiary Forces Chamber?

That chilled the Seraphim's hearts, but then Uriel had made his own bed, and he would have to lie in it, no matter how dreadful it might be. He had stolen another's Destiny, and there was no crime greater, not to the Circle of Brothers, and certainly not to Gabriel. Uriel must be punished, and he would be. Gabriel would see to that, and no one doubted it at all.

Three Additional Injured Brothers

Other rescues were also made that day, involving events that were just as miraculous—or fantastic, depending upon one's choice of words—although not for all the brothers.

Hizkiel made it back to Pablo's village, pulled behind the burro, riding on Pablo's underclothes. The boy's family took him to the local church, begging the priest to allow him sanctuary inside. The angel was laid out on the altar, and his wounds were sponged clean. Then, a kind-hearted village girl began to spoon a spicy soup into his mouth. Right before their eyes, he began to change. Hizkiel's arms and legs miraculously started to heal, and his body began to glow. Soon, he started to move, and as the villagers backed away, he sat up and stood to his feet, his wings ragged and broken at his back. Raising his hands, and clapping them once, light flashed, filling the small sanctuary before rolling out into the streets, and he was left a man, although he was a man who pulsed with power. Then, he clapped them together again, and grand wings, now in perfect condition, expanded high into the interior of the humble church. The people were convinced their ministrations to the one they had found injured had been ministrations to a Messenger of God, and with his healing, their prayers had been placed before the Throne of The Most High. When the great wings flapped, the religious villagers dropped to their faces, prostrating themselves before the unpredictable awesomeness of God.

When they lifted their heads, Hizkiel was gone, yet no one had seen him exit the building. From that day on, Friday would be a Holy Day in the village, and each person would take a sip of that same spicy soup, for that was what had brought the angel back to life.

The boy who had found Hizkiel would grow up to be the village priest, and he would always tell the tale of how he had rescued an Angel of God. What he wouldn't tell was that it was also the reason he never again wore underwear under his priestly garments. The Messenger from God had required his, and to ever again clothe himself in underwear would be to insult the most Holy of Heavenly Creatures.

The only people who ever knew that secret were the little boys who hid under the village bridge. They would laugh when the priest walked overhead, and they would never tell anyone just why. It was their secret, and a secret must always be kept, for if it was told, it was a secret no longer.

Far across the continent, while Hizkiel was impressing impoverished Mexican villagers, Jeremiel lay in a bunk on a ship that rocked in a raging sea. It would be a week or more before that trawler could return to shore. The crew did their best to keep their angel warm, covering him with blankets. They dribbled water down his throat, and sitting by his side, Grandy said what prayers he knew. Still, water wasn't what Jeremiel needed, and his injuries continued unabated. There would be no miraculous rescue for that brother, for he could not rescue himself. He must have help, and although good-hearted, no one on board knew how to give him what he needed.

In the windblown wilds of Newfoundland, Gabriel was luckier. The isolated colony of immigrants, originally Franks, Saxons, Swabians, and Bavarians, with their half-remembered German, was pragmatic and quick to assess a situation. As with their German forebears, they saw the benefit in having a Heavenly being under their control, and so they quickly bundled Gabriel to the town jail. He was locked into a cell, and the townspeople were called in to see what great thing had come to them. This being, this *angel*, some thought to call it, would be at their beck and call, for they would command it, and never again would their town be ravaged by weather or deed.

The jail had a back wall, though, and in that wall was a small window. It was kept open in the summer months, and as it was barred, no one thought to watch it. Who could possibly escape through such a small opening?

It wasn't escape one half-German, half-French townsman had on his mind. His mixed heritage had been a bane held over his head since the day he was born. He had learned to feel for those who were ground under the townspeople's roughly shod feet. While his neighbors guarded the front, he slipped a loaf of bread and a sausage through that open window. It was the least he could do for one in the same position he had felt himself in many times over the years.

No one saw Gabriel as he took to the skies over Newfoundland. Even unseen, they all heard the scream of an eagle, one that was louder, richer, and more frightening than any eagle they had ever heard before. Many people hurried their dogs inside that afternoon, and several families refused to let their children out to play, even though the sun still shone brightly in the sky.

Only one man heard that sound and felt reassured. Gabriel did that for him, for it was only justice that one man should feel peace about what he'd done. As a reward for his act of kindness, the half-German townsman would never again feel less than an equal among his neighbors.

Would they view him any differently? Only they would be able to say. It was what was in his heart that counted, and from that day forward, he moved ahead in his life, becoming a successful and respected businessman in that isolated and insular community. Gabriel had wished it so, and one should never doubt the power of a Suggestion when it was made by a brother of the Unity of Being.

Chapter 32

Gadreel, Deliverer of Destruction

Gadreel stood in the Chamber of Deeds, and his anger vibrated across the emptiness of space. When he twitched, the three brothers with him jumped, and when he spoke, they cowed their heads, afraid his fury would be aimed at them.

It was, too, for they were within his reach. In fact, he barely restrained from reaching to them and snapping their necks. He was livid with rage, for he was in the Chamber of Deeds, and in the displayed images that showed all the Events recorded in the Deeds of Man, the failure of the Four Familiars now consumed him.

He slapped at Nabu, and the essence of the pint-sized brother squeaked with distress.

"Oh, Great Gadreel, Wonder of the Unity and Supreme Ruler of All." The small brother called him by all the old names. "The Records mislead, Holy Eminence. The battles that have been fought have been but precursors to the final decimation of the Circle of Brothers."

"You were to guard the Seat!" Gadreel lashed at Ramiel, and the force of his words leaped across the darkness, causing a minor "earthquake" on the moon. It was picked up by a seismometer that had been planted on Earth's satellite just hours before by a private exploration company, bringing cheers and rejoicing from their team in Omaha. There was no longer any doubt in their minds that the moon was seismically active.

"Now, three more have Traversed, and those three are not in support of the Pets." Gadreel's anger trumpeted the words, daring any dissention from the three brothers at his side.

The viewer of the Deeds of Man had shown such: Nobility in Jeqon's grasp as the restaurant fell around them; Zadkiel wrestling Wisdom to the ground; and Asbeel dancing a wall of confusion around Strength. It was a battle that had been closely matched, and if the entire Circle had been there, Gadreel wondered who would have triumphed. He suspected he knew, and the battle would not have gone in his favor.

"Smacks of Lucifer's rebellion. That didn't go so well, either." The words escaped Lipika's lips in a muted mutter, although the lips were ones that weren't really there. The words actually escaped his thoughts, but they came across as a mutter, still.

It was good he didn't speak his deeper feelings. It was no secret that the two smallest members of the Unity had claimed no side as theirs during the early days of the Rebellion. There were some who whispered that they had waited to see which way the Rebellion would go, that Lipika and Nabu had gone so far as to brag that it was the game that was important, and the balance of power had been stable far too long.

"Lipika," Nabu squeaked. "Do not voice such thoughts!"

It was too late. Lipika's words goaded Gadreel's ire, and he whipped around, the stars in the distance trembling when faced with the blast of his anger.

"Three of the four brothers the Pets took down are revived. Gabriel flies, as do Hizkiel and Kasbeel. It is only by good fortune that Jeremiel still lies in a stupor." For Gadreel, that was a major boon. Jeremiel was one with great power, one who could redeem brokenness, finding Strength in what others deemed worthless. If he rejoined the battle, Gadreel's odds would be sorely bruised.

"There is Michael, still."

456

Ramiel's voice was smooth and soothing, so very reasonable, and for a moment, Gadreel felt a surge of hope. If there was one brother who could swing the balance in this conflict, it was indeed Michael. He had much power, enough, in fact, to shift the balance in their favor, no matter the odds.

Then the hope faded, and reality reasserted itself. He turned, the molten steel of barely controlled fury flowing from his lips. "Dear Ramiel. Trusted cohort and confidant. One who handles the Keys to the Unity. My Second in Command." Each phrase was clearly separated, and that added an ominous tone to the words. "Do you know Michael? If so, tell me of his history. Did he join in our Rebellion, offering his services when required, risking his station within the Triune Mind's antiquated bureaucracy? Think, Ramiel. Rather, it seems that many eons before, Michael helped oust the Illuminator of Light, casting Lucifer and one-third of the brothers from the Unity. Michael was first loved by the Triune Mind, and he is surely one of his followers, still."

"The Record," Nabu whispered. "He will be convinced, as were the Four Familiars. Shall I invite him to visit the Chamber of Deeds? All will be well, Great Gadreel. You will rule forever."

"And if not, then Nabu and I will have a new master," Lipika muttered. "It is of no importance to a small brother."

Gadreel paused for a time, glaring at the Recorder of Deeds. It wasn't Lipika on his mind as he pondered, and he did ponder for a very long time. Time to the brothers outside the Unity was not as time to the humans at their feet on the blue and green world below. It was written that a thousand years was as a day, and a day was as a thousand years. Gadreel pondered for a very long time, and it was no time at all.

Then, in a moment of inspiration, he burst into heated action, a plan erupting in his mind, more sure of himself than he had ever been before.

"I will personally join the battle gathering below. I am the leader of the Unity, and all power is mine. If I am present, then the Four Familiars cannot fail. There will be defeat, but it will not be mine!"

That was more like him. He was the Deceiver, the one who had shown the Deeds of Death to men. Loki, he had been called in one religion, and Yama in another. One West African group had named him Eshu, and the Greeks had labeled him Prometheus. His was the power to do as he wished, and no one could stand in his way.

In his greed, he forgot how he had garnered his power in the Unity. It had not been by strength or ability. It had been by cunning and trickery. Lies and deceit were how he had trapped the Four Familiars and the Triune Mind, not through skill and wisdom. He should have remembered that.

Instead, he moved his hand in the blackness, and a great, blazing ball of light appeared. The light crackled, and tendrils flashed into the cold of space, clawing the emptiness they tried to grasp as their prize. Then, with a jerk of his arm, the ball of light shattered, and when it returned to its own, his presence was gone. With an explosive detonation, it launched itself, heading straight toward Earth.

Interlude 27

Lightning would strike that small world soon, and it would bring a storm of another kind. Good against evil had been unleashed, although it was unclear whether the humans who dwelt there would recognize the good as truly good, or the evil as truly evil. For, in the greater mural of the Universe, that eternal painting that traces the lives of races as they echo through untold dimensions, many of the beings that had once walked the stars were already forgotten, and others were still on the rise. Yet, in all the colors that swirled through the Universe, the good that was found was often not that good, and the evil was often not that evil.

Even so, this day lies had been told, and facts had been twisted. Faith in close companions had been sorely tried, and new alliances had been made. Good had been compromised, and evil now abounded.

People would suffer, both of the brother kind and the

human kind. Yet, that was also the way of war. No one was immune from the travails of battle, and the innocent often suffered the most. When one who has done no wrong takes the brunt of the conflict, whether that injury has been inflicted by the side who claims the right, or the one proclaimed as wrong, can the damage ever be made whole again? What if that innocent is a child? Can the parent's heart be unbroken again? And what of the victor? Can anyone be called a victor, when for some, eyes are forever sightless, and the flesh grown cold?

For war was coming. God help Earth, if He could, because the Unity could not. Perhaps *would* not might be a better choice of words. In the coming darkness, some people might find there was no god at all, for what god would tear apart the very world he had created? What god would kill his creation, just to satisfy his need for power?

When the lightning that carried Gadreel's lightship finished Traversing the blackness of space, the Leader of the Unity was flung into the corporeal world of air and dirt and water and weather. He yelled in exultation, and it was a victory cry. He intended to win, and damn the poor souls who got in his way.

Mildura Airport, Victoria, Australia

Banks of warning lights lit up the weather station at Mildura Airport in Victoria, Australia. A startled meteorologist leaped to his feet, surprised. This was normally a slow time of night.

"Take a squizz at this," Jerry Duncan called to his co-worker, staring at the board. The only thing coming in should have been the routine weather input. This was a shift for napping or perhaps catching up on the latest novel one hadn't been able to finish at home. It was the reason he'd agreed to it. More than one meteorologist had completed a college course during the wee hours of the Victoria morning.

"Spit the dummy," his workmate, Charlie Milton, spewed, venting frustration as he entered the room. He leaped to flip switches to get the unexpected input zeroed in. His eyes glared as he barked, "Jerry, always trigger these switches as soon as the lights came on. You don't know Christmas from Bourke Street, you know? Something's happened somewhere, and someone will want to know to the nearest waypoint. My god, you can't expect me to do it all."

"Well, tall poppies are we all! I can't remember everything."

"Yeah, that's you all around, ready with a funny, unwilling to take the blame for something that's surely not your fault."

Just then, more lights flashed, ones that had stayed quiet the first time.

"Fair suck of the sav! Think the sun's gone nova or something?" Charlie muttered under his breath. "It could be. This seems big."

Jerry laughed. "That'd be a great furphy." *A false rumor.* "Let that out, and by Chrissy, not even the postie will feel safe on the streets."

Charlie growled, "You don't really care about the postman, or his safety on the streets, because you never get Christmas cards."

"Right, Mate. I never give them, either. I only like to give the old fella a good time under the glow of the lights on me tree."

That was a bit crude, as the "fella" referenced an intimate part of the male anatomy.

Before Charlie could retort, the door opened. A loud, slightly slurred voice called out, "Thought I'd lob in. Brought you mates a roadie from the milk shop." Richie Lonergan, the third man on duty that night, opened a brown paper sack and took out two longneck bottles. "Up for one? Mate's rate."

"Holy doolie!" Jerry called, excited laughter lacing his words. "Reckon, Richie! Don't mind the occasional, even if it is just from the corner takeaway."

"Then it's all yours." Richie held one of the bottles his direction.

Grabbing the bottle, Jerry grinned. "I'm as dry as a dead dingo's donger. It'll be my shout next time." He pulled out two twenties and stuffed them in a glass jar off to the side, his share for the next run for beer.

Charlie frowned, though. "You go off your face—" *get drunk* "—and I'll have your freckle on the dirt. We'll see you make a quid, then."

Jerry just grabbed the second bottle and threw it his direction, calling, "Give it a burl, Charlie. Don't be a piker." He turned to the new guy with a grin. "Good onya, Richie. This piss'll last me a minute or two." He popped the top and took a good long draught.

Then, the board went blank, and in a moment of silence, all three men watched the readouts. That shouldn't happen, especially when a whole bevy of new information was flooding the memory banks.

"It's gone walkabout. Lost. All of it." In a burst of motion, Charlie frantically reached and flipped a few switches, his face turning red before stepping away in defeat. "It's not coming back, and I'm not certain I got a fix on it."

Jerry casually stepped to the console, and he pushed several buttons. "She right." *It'll be fine.* Then, small fans underneath the console began to whir, indicating returning life, and buttons began to glow, slowly increasing in brightness. "There's the ridgy-didge, just like the first time. We got it back. No drama." He laughed, swirling his bottle to make sure there was still liquid inside.

All the lights were indeed up, but it was just the recorded input that had come in the first time the console had gone off. An indicator light at the top of the board said so.

"I'll be stuffed!" Charlie glanced over the board. He grinned, reaching up to make some adjustments. "Got a source trace running now. You did this? Which switches?"

"You stoked, huh?" Jerry took another swig. "I'm no whacker, no matter what anyone says. I rigged that up just in case. When it crashes, just flip these here, A, B, and C. Easy. Now, where's it from?"

"Looks like it belongs to our rellies up in U.S. of A. Colorado, sure. Think we should flick this on up to NASA? Give 'em the drum?" Charlie dropped back in his chair, and he grinned.

461

Jerry reached and tapped several keys on a computer keyboard, and it sang a little song to them. He polished off the rest of his beer and set the bottle down hard. That done, he turned and winked.

"Figjam. Already done. Now, Richie, night's young. How 'bout another coldie? There's that bottle shop around the corner. Maybe that milk bar you were at before. How 'bout it?" He held out the jar with the two twenties.

Richie grabbed them and was gone.

Jerry turned to Charlie and chuckled. "Richie's a bloody good bloke, that's deadset."

Charlie snorted, but he grinned. "Don't make me crack a fat. I go for the sheilas."

"That's London to a brick." He shook his head in amusement, as he reached and tripped switches A, B, and C back to their original positions, resetting the safety on the console.

What he didn't say was, *Didn't they all?*

NASA Mission Control, Houston

"Chet, are you up there? This is Houston. Um, you remember Skinny from Burbank? Skinny Bednarz? Um, well, this is me."

The voice was tentative, as well it should be. Skinny was not the regular guy to contact the spacecraft. Alarms had gone off all over the earthside complex, and everyone who was anyone was trying to pin the problem down. Someone had to make the call. It seemed something akin to a nuclear blast had materialized somewhere over Colorado, yet no one could find any concrete evidence of fallout anywhere. Then it had seemed to angle directly toward Arizona. The country had just gone to DEFCON 3. Who knew what might come next?

"Well, Chet, and you too, Jim," Skinny continued. "Something's happened here, but nobody knows just what, yet. Even the Aussies know. They called us, you know. I don't guess they thought our systems were up and running. We got it covered, though, so don't you worry none. You're safe up there out of

462

harm's way. Well, that's all, Chet. You, too, Jim. Call us when you get a chance."

They didn't even get more than the first line of the message. Gadreel's "explosion" that was picked up by Mildura Airport in Victoria had ripped the fabric of spacetime, and while it would heal, for several hours, all communications with the spacecraft would be sucked through to another dimension.

Gadreel, Deliverer of Destruction

If Gadreel had been paying attention, he might have even seen that rip in spacetime as a possible way to escape the Unity's captivity in this corporeal universe. Then maybe not, as he was very angry, and angry people never pay attention to what they should. To his credit, he was very, very angry, so it couldn't be his fault that he hadn't paid attention. No, not at all.

He should have, though. Others did.

Kafziel, Emissary of Solitude and Tears

A tree, dead for years now, hung from a rocky cliff face. Far below, a rough bed of jagged stones littered the bottom of the distant canyon floor. Off to one side, a river surged, its whitewater surface churned by unseen boulders buried somewhere beneath the froth.

Kafziel's feet dangled beneath him, and there was only open space between him and the canyon floor. He fumed. He was stranded, and he didn't like it much at all.

He yanked his shoulder sideways hoping to untangle his left wing. The old tree's leafless branches were like iron, rigid and unbending. His wings were not, and when he was rudely blasted from the sky by Gadreel's entrance onto this world, the branches had captured him, and now he hung by one pierced wing.

Each time he moved, he cried out. Pain lanced his body, sending fire along his nerves, and he cursed every corporeal

463

atom in his being. It wasn't as if his body wasn't healing, and rapidly, too. The problem, his wing was impaled. Each of his movements tore the wound again even as it tried to repair itself with the dead branches still in place.

He looked down. Even if he could tear himself loose, he would fall into that; it would likely be only a slower way to die.

He had known who it was the minute the concussion tore the air from the sky. Gadreel always liked to make an entrance, and this time was no exception. Kafziel had been on Earth a very long time, and that meant his degree of resonance with the Unity had deviated severely. In addition, the Deceiver had literally dropped in right on top of him, his explosive *Traversing* culminating at almost the exact point in space that Kafziel happened to be.

Well, Kafziel wasn't there any longer, and now Gadreel was gone, ignoring him—or more likely, not even noticing him. When a brother drops in directly on top of another brother, he should at least make his apologies. That, as much as anything, infuriated him.

"Gadreel!" he screamed at the sky, shaking one fist in the air. "Why have you come down here? Do not interfere in my plans. I've worked too hard for too many eons to achieve this one small victory. Leave me be."

He knew the brother he called couldn't hear his spoken voice, and they were too far out of phase to sense each other's thoughts. Anyway, his words carried little real truth. It had only been a quarter of one of this world's centuries, and in the overall scheme of things, that wasn't long at all. It was a drop in the bucket of time.

Now, he had more immediate matters to resolve. He would eventually have to release his wings and let himself fall down the face of the cliff. That entailed some risk, for he might very well catch one of numerous rocky outcrops on the way down, injuring himself more before he could stop his fall. Still, he could not untangle himself, and he could not climb up.

A black cloud hovered around him, and in his eyes, everything that had happened to him was someone else's fault. He never considered that he bore the brunt of the responsibility.

No, that could never be true, not in his way of seeing things. He was in pain. He was suffering needlessly, and it was everyone else who was to blame. It always was, and it always would be, no matter how deeply he dug his own hole.

Inside Jeri's Car

The motel was gone, and for the injured and dying in the old car, Bobby offered the only sense of normalcy he knew.

Home, and he pointed the way.

Jeri drove. The devastated mother was in the first stages of shock, and she blindly followed Bobby's finger. He might live just over the hill, Bobby tried to explain, but to drive it was a very long way. The road twisted past dry washes and along numerous arroyos.

"Just point," Uriel whispered.

Little Chrissy hummed a tune, talking to herself from time to time, occasionally mentioning her daddy. She had retreated into her own world, tuning out the disaster that had enveloped her family. Her hands acted out some series of events only she could see unfolding in her private world.

Dakota was frozen in his seat. His father had left him, and he had withdrawn into his inner, lonely sanctum a long time ago, not daring to let anyone join him. Only in the past few hours had he taken the initiative to reach back into the real world, the one of people and life and laughter. His wall had been thrown up once more.

In the back seat, two boys, friends, sat on one side of the car, terrified, although they felt the need to parade their bravery and fortitude. The younger of the two watched the unfamiliar man holding the sandwich, but he also kept his eyes on the woman. He had seen the woman's head, the blood, the damage, and he had been nauseated. He had also seen more: horrific injuries repaired amazingly fast, with only red smears of blood as evidence, leaving the boy doubting his eyes.

No one in Jeri's car trusted their ears or eyes at that point. That made perfect sense, because the world as they knew it had just shifted out from under their feet.

Bobby Dalton, Motel Rat

Bobby's attention was drawn outside the car window. The air roiled. With what, he didn't know. The sun still shone, and the sky was blue. It looked like high-speed images of a thunderstorm, where the clouds banked higher and higher, growing darker and darker, rolling over one another as if they were at war with the very sky, itself.

All at once he was chilled, and he knew why. In a sudden epiphany of understanding, he recognized why today was different from every other one that had come before. He went to Sunday school, and he knew his Bible lessons. Armageddon, complete with angels and explosions and signs in the heavens, had come to the Arizona desert. His Sunday school lessons were coming to life right here, right in front of his eyes, and he would see it all.

He didn't want to see it all. He didn't want to see any of it.

There was one other thing that worried at him above all else. What about Uri's wolf? What would Malak do without Uri? How would Malak survive Armageddon? Dogs, even ones that were labeled wolves, needed to be taken care of, didn't they? Especially a wolf that had become his friend.

He grew up a bit sitting there in that car. Perhaps no one else around him could have told the difference, but the real measure of a man has little to do with the deepness of a boy's voice or the hair on his legs. All those tell of is whether his body is forcing him along that long road that will soon leave childhood behind.

True maturity happens on the inside.

Chapter 33

The Four Familiars of the Triune Mind

The sky crackled, and it grew dark along the edges. The sun hanging overhead shimmered against the coming storm. There was a tang of ozone in the air, and the hair of small mammals across the desert popped with electric firecrackers in the rising breeze. Those who had the sense of a desert tortoise found shelter, because the gathering omens spoke of great power building in a place that should never be made to suffer such an atrocity.

The building energies were a result of the Familiars' urge to *respond:* bold, brash, and angrily planned. They had drawn their strength unto them in anticipation of a great conflagration, the immediacy of *now* driving their efforts. Even Wisdom had been unable to implement a wiser plan. Fury had burned his vision red, and he had not been able to see past *action*.

Off in the distance, towering columns of thickening dust rose inexplicably into the summer sky, and they twisted and coiled as if alive, dancing with otherworldly steps that seemed to writhe from the ground as a cobra is drawn from its lair by the snake charmer's flute. Those dust columns were never meant to be watched too closely, for they were but the byproducts of ancient engines that were gearing for an assault upon other equally ancient engines, powers and harbingers of death that were not from this dimension.

As the malevolent energies churned and spit, the rumble of an earthquake belched from deep within the ground. It skulked forth and threw violent arms across the desert floor. In the dissected landscape, little more than cacti felt the initial shivering of the ground, for the small creatures had already run far away for safety. Even so, the soil shuddered, and cracks in the dirt appeared. Pillars of dust billowed skyward.

Far overhead, so high in the sky that the curve of the earth could be seen, and at a distance so great that the sky turned a beautiful cerulean bordered by a midnight blue at its farthest edges, lightning crackled, even though at this thin layer of the atmosphere, the sound didn't carry well, and it was more of a snap, crackle, and pop. It was beautiful, though, just as is the lionfish or the Portuguese man-o-war. Reach out to touch, though, no matter how gingerly, and the pain of that contact comes crashing back along tender flesh, the searing of surprised nerves lashing the body's sensory system with waves of agony. Touch too long or too hard, and death will come to call, anxious to claim another soul's essence as its due.

Against this magnificent drama, otherworldly creatures had already started to gather. Feathered wings tore at the blistered sky, and mighty hooves stamped the soil. Strengths were being bargained for, traded to the highest bidder, and great bolts of energy danced across the heavens.

The fate of a world was being decided this day. It might cause no immediate change in governments, and blasts of turbulent energy might not roll across the planet's surface, wiping all life away. But make no bones, where good and evil were concerned, this shift in power would nudge the world this way or that, and with the nudging would come the change. It might be fifty years or even a hundred before it became an unstoppable avalanche, but it would, for the world goes the way its leaders lead, and this world's leaders were susceptible to Suggestions, as were the people under their care.

On the horizon, the sky seemed to shift degrees of corporeality, blinking out of existence and back again, and as it did, vast quantities of corporeal electrons were ripped from equally vast quantities of corporeal atoms. Great harvesting engines absorbed the trapped energy, sending it into the reaches of the sky as bolts of otherworldly lightning. Where the surrounding mountains thrust skyward from the land, fingers of harnessed and tormented electrons, stripped bare and screaming in pain, began to jump violently from their highest reaches into the boiling heavens. The dust columns drew this electricity unto themselves, building a storehouse of reserves that the Familiars hoped would eventually be a match for all that the Circle of Brothers could throw at them.

Still, for all the power gathering, it was no more than a temporary capacitor built of desperation, one meant to be used quickly in the time of need. In one mighty conflagration, Gadreel and the Four Familiars intended to squash the opposition, taking from this world that which was their due, without the intention to return anything of value at all.

Across the desert, the lightning increased fourfold, for the time of war approached. A line would soon be drawn in the desert sand, and there would be no turning back.

The Circle of Brothers

Another type of power, one intended for good instead of evil, intended to counter that of the Pets, also erupted across the surface of the desert.

A great bolt of horizontal, incandescent energy split the landscape, reaching from one side of the desert to the other, traveling inches above the dissected soil. It sizzled, breaking apart the very molecules of the air.

Each end was anchored by a Sword of Power.

The Circle of Brothers knew the Familiars' building strength must be dispersed, sent back from whence it came, else they would be overcome. New methods of warfare must be implemented to best the Pets. A wild and untried plan had been concocted, one that had never been attempted before.

It worked, or all was lost.

469

Elemiah held his Sword of Power before him, its horizontal surface dancing with the brilliance of its unlimited Power, and his mandated Authority billowed from it. It was he who traced the line in the air just above the desert's floor. Many miles away, Barakiel's Sword mirrored that of his twin's, creating an elemental feedback loop to Elemiah's Sword. They held their positions as the Power built, until it vibrated the very mountains themselves. With confidence, they would shatter the gathering storm building over their heads, for only they could.

Then, as one, they slammed the tips of their Swords into the ground, breaking the feedback loop, and shattering the energy across the desert floor. It crackled fiercely across the surface of the soil, popping and snapping, its electric fingers wrapping around cactus and creosote, hill and dry wash. When it found holes in the ground, it flung itself downward, searching for what it could find. It dipped into pockets of natural gas, and even an oil well or two. As each reservoir of flammable material was engaged, the soil above erupted violently, and flames washed the sky. Yet, the Swords' energy was not slowed, and it continued to fling itself outwards, leaving churning dust and charred plants in its wake.

When the Seraphim's wash of elemental energy reached the boiling clouds of energy in the sky, making contact with their coiling columns of dust, the light crackled up each insubstantial leg, unrestrained, in a bold and otherworldly dance that wove a tapestry of terrible beauty in the sky. In a final assault against the audacity of the Pets' power reserve, it lanced into the ever-darker cloud, sending blue tendrils of rising lightning forking out, sizzling, popping, and crackling through the gloom. Small explosions began to light up the sky, igniting the energy that had been gathered there. With a series of rapid, staccato booms, the explosions multiplied throughout the rising storm until they could no longer be told apart.

The culminating blast was so great that an enormous hole was sloughed into the desert floor, flinging tons of dirt and debris far into the sky, and creating a mushroom cloud that was visible as far away as Las Vegas, had anyone in that busy city been watching that day. The Four Familiars inside were tossed like kittens in a tornado, their flight out of their control, and they tumbled into the desert sky.

The line had been drawn. The battle was now engaged.

Gadreel, Deliverer of Destruction

Gadreel came upon the scene just in time to witness the shockwave, and he immediately saw the situation as it was. The Four Familiars were engaged in straightforward attack mode, and in doing so, they had suffered miserably, for they were best at seek and destroy. This type of static warfare was as foreign to them as corporeality was to most of the brothers in the Unity. Without direction, they would regroup and fail over and over. That was not what he needed. He needed Uriel under his control. To have Uriel in his grasp was to manage Gabriel, allowing him to divert the most pressing danger to the Rebellion.

Yet nothing was under his control, for before him, as far as he could see, the desert roiled. This had become an open sore of unacceptable proportions.

"Wisdom!" Gadreel's voice was the slicing of an ax though the tenderest sapling flesh, and it was cruel in its downward stroke, uncaring of the damage it did. His wings beat the air as he called his minion to his side. His feet would not be allowed to touch the soil of this world as long as his enemy was at large.

"Swiftness!" He flung the new word from him with vehemence; and with the force of his call, the two cacti closest to him split down the middle. Even his mental sendings carried power that could maim and destroy.

He was satisfied. Those were the two he needed first. Wisdom would accept his direction, and Swiftness would deliver the message. The final two would be so driven that their fury-fueled brains would hear nothing except their own screams for victory, no matter how elusive it had become.

Swiftness arrived first, his dust-covered wings beating the air to slow his passage. His talons clutched empty sky, and a gash across his chest healed as Gadreel watched.

471

So, Gadreel considered. *There has been damage. Already my team suffers.* Then, breathing hard, Wisdom was also at his side.

Before Gadreel could speak, though, a third pair of wings, white and dripping crystals of light, snapped to an abrupt stop in front of him, and the two Familiars hovering in the air at his command immediately tensed for engagement.

It was Raphael; it seemed the quarry had come to them.

With a screech of fury, Swiftness's beak snapped in anticipation, and one leg slashed the air in the Healer's direction. The Angel of Healing moved a bit farther back, but there was no fear on his face. Off in the dirtied sky, more brothers could be seen arriving. Kasbeel's wings were held high as an announcement of his presence, their feathered surfaces dominating the sky, and Hizkiel's tree trunk legs, ones prepared to stomp the head of the opposition, told of the victory that would soon be his.

Swiftness twisted his feathered head and screamed his challenges.

"Ha!" Raphael laughed lightly and with pointed accusations. "It *was* you, Gadreel. I should have known. Do you have your leash prepared? You will need it soon." He motioned to the Pets at his side. "These are your *weapons*? You maintain your power by *these*? You have no control over the Four. They will control you. You have done yourself a disservice, and you know it well, Great Prince."

He poked fun, and Gadreel felt the words burn. When the Familiars made to surge forward, he clinched his fist to signal them to hold.

"*You promised him to us. Our Master has yet to be avenged.*" Twin voices screamed in a cacophony of defiance, with Swiftness' screech telling the truth of his fury. From across the desert, faint agreement sounded from the other two Familiars.

"You will have your prey. Bide your time." Gadreel turned to Raphael with iron in his words. "Uriel. I must have him. The girl is yours, if you wish to keep her. This is your chance to save her and protect all the other humans on this world. All I

472

want is the Bearer of Destiny. Release him to me, Raphael." As he spoke the Healer's name, he also sent an image of Raphael with his hand outstretched, and from that hand, healing flowed forth. He mentally recognized the brother's Mandate, hoping to coerce his cooperation.

"I have not seen Uriel. If that brother is your target, I hope to Unity that I do not." Light erupted like exploding diamonds from Raphael's wings, and power flashed from his eyes. His words may have been spoken with precision and clarity, but it was clear each one carried the power of an anger that would not be bound by something as foolish as Gadreel and his wild card Pets. "Go, Gadreel. Leash your Pets and return to the Unity. If you do not, you will have no defense against the upcoming storm."

Gadreel felt his own anger boil inside. He was not one to be taken lightly, and to have such words thrown in his face was unforgivable. He had borne the burden of the Unity when the Triune Mind had fallen, and he would shoulder this attack on his pride. He took the challenge as it was offered, in fury and with hot blood. If Raphael were so ill advised as to threaten him, then he would face the wrath of the Four Familiars, for they would do Gadreel's will.

"Wisdom. Swiftness. I release you." Gadreel's voice thundered, and the dust of the ground far beneath their feet vibrated with the force of his words. "Raphael is yours, and if he should die, I have no regrets."

With a shifting shimmer, one almost too quick to see, where Raphael hovered existed a Colchian dragon, a creature from a long ago dimension that had at one time been the incarnation of the brothers. On this world, it had been seen to guard the Golden Fleece, and for that job, it had been an appropriate choice. It never slept, never rested, and never lowered its vigilance. In addition, it was huge, with a great crest around its head and three deadly tongues.

It was by the power of the Swords that Raphael's transformation was possible, for the energies to maintain such an incarnation were immeasurable. Luckily, the Swords' reservoirs were deep, and their reserves had never been breached.

The Colchian's tongues sliced the air, and a hiss of power spewed vengefully from the animal's mouth. The dragon drew back its legs, and with a movement so swift it could barely be said to not have instantly been in one place and then another, its front claws slashed the face of Wisdom. Then, it was gone, hurtling into the sky.

Wisdom screamed in fury, and his six wings flung him in pursuit, yet his speed was just that of a much-loved Pet. The dragon outmatched him with distance to spare. Swiftness screeched his anger, opening his wings wide to join Wisdom in pursuit.

Gadreel yelled after the retreating Healer, "You are a fool, Raphael! Shifting forms will burn your energy so quickly you will fall in defeat, vanquished in battle. Face me fairly, and you will have a chance." He thought not, but it would be a fairer fight, at least for the Four Familiars. "Take other forms, and you will be crushed beyond measure!"

His final words blasted across the crater that had consumed the desert floor. Leaving Gadreel's words flat, Raphael was long gone, and there was no one to hear.

A Great Conflagration Begins

In his haste—or carelessness, some might say—to gain control of the escalating situation on Earth, Gadreel had listened to the promptings of Nabu and Lipika, and he had unleashed the most powerful threat the Unity knew, short of the Four Horsemen of the Apocalypse. Those four deadly forces might have been able to hold back the plans being put in place by the Circle of Brothers. Those known as the bringers of Conquest, War, Famine, and Death—the Four Horsemen—just might have been able to stem the rising tide, but they were still in the Unity, and no one had dared call them forth. Besides, theirs was of a more long-term sort of investment, and Gadreel had needed something a little more immediate.

Raphael's counterplan was audacious, and indeed had a high chance of failure. The "angelic" abilities of the corporeal brothers of the Unity consumed a prodigious quantity of energy. When fading, flying, or passing through solid objects, their bodies had to be refueled often. Just the calling up of wings could drain an already weakened brother to near collapse. To assume and maintain the corporeal identities of past incarnations from previous dimensions was difficult at best, and to do so while battling a viciously vindictive enemy was surely suicide. The plan of attack against the Four Familiars would require even more energy.

The Swords of Power would be put to the test this day, for they would be the untried energy source to fuel a great war between opponents with the ability to destroy entire worlds. It had never been done before, and only the Triune Mind knew if the Seraphim could stand the strain. If the battle went on too long, they might fail, and all chances for success would collapse with them.

It's true that even the most foolhardy of battle plans are risky only in comparison to the desired results, as well as the cost of failure if the plans don't succeed. The cost of failure this day was more than worth the risk to the Circle of Brothers, for to fail was to lose the opportunity to restore the rightful leadership to the Unity of Being. Only when the Triune Mind was rightfully returned to the Seat of Power would the Unity return to some semblance of order. Then and only then would there be any real progress made on breaking free of this corporeal dimension.

That was worth all the risk in the world.

Once Raphael had broken rank, the other brothers took leave of their corporeal forms to pull from whatever incarnation best suited their needs in warfare. Whether they desired quickness or strength or deadly weaponry, they shifted as needed, having access to vast reservoirs of forms. The Unity had been through many dimensions and many incarnations, and all were theirs to command.

To their disadvantage, the Four Familiars, the Triune Mind's Pets, were just that, pets, treasured Familiars of the Triune Mind. Their forms had been set by the very act of becoming corporeal. They could not change those shapes at will, not as the brothers could. If Raphael's plan worked, that would be their undoing.

When Hizkiel was forced to fend off Strength's marauding attack, he dodged, sending the Pet barreling past in a roiling cloud of dust. When the powerful Ox turned, Hizkiel was nowhere to be seen. In his place stood a Golem, an unnaturally muscled creature Jewish folklore claimed was created from inanimate matter. Muscles strained from the Golem's neck, and its arms and legs were the trunks of the largest trees, wielding the phenomenal strength from long-ago legend. With a sweep of its hand, Strength was thrown from his feet, and he knew the taste of this world's dust in his mouth.

Watching from far above, the Eagle known as Swiftness saw the change from brother to Golem. He also saw the Ox's body hit the dirt, stirring the dry, desert soil. When Swiftness cried his annoyance, sweeping to Strength's aid, he found not a Golem, but a horrible monster with four eyes. Once adapted to a water environment, the ancient Greeks had named this particular incarnation Scylla. With six long necks equipped with grisly heads, each of which contained three rows of snapping teeth, there was much to be feared. In addition to its four eyes, the body consisted of twelve tentacle-like legs, with six dog heads ringing the waist. There was no nemesis the Scylla hesitated to combat, whether originated of this earthly world, or of the bizarre creatures from another.

The Scylla—still Hizkiel, of course—flashed razor teeth, and each tentacled leg leaped to grab at the Eagle. Within moments, the two were entangled, for the Scylla was a fitting match for the Eagle known as Swiftness. They soon accepted that one must relent for the two to go free, but Hizkiel intended to hold on, slashing and maiming, until the battle was done.

What tipped the scales was when Strength rejoined the fight, skewering the Scylla's body with his horns. Hizkiel hadn't seen him coming, and he was impaled on the mighty beast. With a roar, the immense Ox tossed his head, and threw them both aside. Swiftness was set free, and he flew with the wind to find temporary respite for recovery. Yet, when Strength turned once again to face this most unusual foe, the Golem had returned, all injuries healed in the shifting, and for the Ox, the inanimate creature was a match he could not beat. He bellowed his rage as a massive arm slammed into his head, and he tasted dirt once again.

When Swiftness leaped for the sky and his perceived refuge, suddenly Zadkiel was there, although no one who knew him would have recognized the brother as such. Instead, the colorful plumage of the Phoenix flashed in the sky. The creature was known for its immortality, but when freshly reborn, it also knew incredible strength and a ferocious nature. Its beak tore at one of the Eagle's wings, and as the Familiar turned, the Phoenix changed, becoming an even deadlier creature. A Lernaean Hydra was poised for battle. With a serpent-like body and nine poisonous heads, its very breath brought death to whoever happened in its way. Right then, Swiftness was the foe, and the Hydra spit its anger, lashing out with its tail. Swiftness finally knew fear, for there was no defense against the breath of the Hydra. Zadkiel had made a wise choice, and he exulted when the Pet fled in terror.

The conflict had only just begun, helter-skelter, and dust still roiled in the sky. Lightning filled the air with the crackle of ozone, fangs were bared, and there would be no release until one side tasted defeat. The enormous crater that had resulted from the Seraphim's explosive display of power was filled with strange thumps and roars, and with each sound, massive quantities of dust flooded the sky.

Nobility was still fresh, for he had wished to maintain his dignity, only engaging in the fairest of conflicts. However, when viewing Strength's mauling and Swiftness's terror, his own voice roared from his throat. Immediately, another brother's attention was turned his way.

Jeqon reached the Lion first, and he matched the Pet and did him one better. Drawing on the shape of the ancient Gryphon, the brother took on the body of a lion, giving him Nobility's strength and quickness. As a Gryphon, he also had the tearing beak of an eagle, and slamming hard into the Pet, he tore at his underside, wetting his beak until it ran red. Then, as quickly, he was the winged Harpy, the stealer of food, and he snatched a bite from the Lion's soft underbelly, swallowing the bloody flesh whole. Immediately, in another swift change, one for no other purpose than to torment Nobility, Jeqon transformed into a creature long ago called Argos, a primordial giant with one hundred eyes. He held the Pet down, and he stared him in the face, as if he intended him to die.

"I see you, Nobility." Triumphantly, Jeqon laughed. His words danced like water droplets across a hot summer sky. "Get it? I be a hundred eyes. How be it I can miss a big brute like you?"

Again, with no warning, he changed once more, becoming the Mother of Ants, an ant-eating serpent the ancient Greeks of this world had called Amphisbaena. He was fearsome, with heads at both ends, and his laughter was doubled, with both of his faces scorning the Lion's weakness. With a twist of his body, he disappeared into the dust, and Nobility was left alone.

As the battle raged, for hours and days to the participants' subjective sense of time, and for minutes only to the outside world, the Seraphim controlled their Swords of Power, and they sent strength and renewal to the brothers when they were in need. Such had never been done before, but this day, much was tried that had never been done before. Such was the way progress in the Skills of Battle was made, and this day, much progress was required.

Others fought, also. Asbeel, unlike his nature, was the hideous Gorgon, with hair of living, venomous snakes. His hands were brass, and sharp fangs filled his mouth. He and Wisdom battled alone, and the injuries were many. With a great blow of a fist, the Familiar sent the Gorgon tumbling. Dust obscured the downed brother, and Wisdom exulted. Sadly, Wisdom was one, and Asbeel was many. Out of the cloud of dust, the enraged Gorgon reemerged, and Wisdom was reengaged once again. Asbeel fought with his hands, and each snake on his head fought for him, also. It seemed a shame for the fight to be so unfair, but winning the battle was what it was all about, and Asbeel desperately wanted to win.

Kasbeel was less sure of his desire to win, though. He had once tried to learn the True Name of the Triune Mind, and it was something that had been denied him. He still wished that information. If Gadreel and his Four Familiars were defeated, he might lose his chance forever. For that reason, he took the guise of Gaea, with limbs of sticks, a bodice of grass, and budding branches for his hair. He was hideous in appearance, and that made him fearsome. Best of all, the guise was simple to maintain, and he had no intention of fighting. He had something else in mind, and his business was to watch the fray and determine when he needed to step in. He'd already done what he could, revealing Uriel's location to Gadreel. When it was time, he would make his presence known, helping out where it would benefit himself most. Until then, in the background was the only place he wanted to be.

Gabriel was the only one of the brothers who kept his true corporeal shape. He flew high over the conflict, his presence there for all to see, his familiar at his side, the eagle occasionally darting into the maelstrom, only to be recalled by the Archangel's command. Gabriel was the one who spoke the directions to his companions, both those of the Circle as well as the three who had joined them. He choreographed, and they performed. Admirably, he would have said. Supernaturally, human witnesses might have intoned. Whichever, Gabriel knew the stakes. This battle stood in the way of his true goal, and that was to punish the Betrayer. Uriel must be found, and he must be made to pay.

The Archangel would have done well to remember what love truly is. To ride that razor edge of emotion is to risk both elation as well as pain. The razor has two sides, and to maintain that love is to remain on the sharp edge for all time. To slide one way is to slip into obsession. The other way, one finds hate. Either direction is only a razor's edge from truth, and if one falls down the side—either side—the razor edge of love slices the heart all the way through.

Gabriel also would have been wise to consider what was happening all around him, for the events taking place as he watched suggested he was already on a downward tumble. Gadreel had been very convincing, and that razor edge was very narrow. Perhaps it was no surprise that in the heat of the moment, Gabriel had teetered right off. He would know the pain, though. True love, when it is cast aside, is always the love that cuts most deeply. It cuts the heart right out, and once that is done, how can it ever be made whole again?

Chapter 34

Uriel, Bearer of Destiny

The sky was in turmoil. As seen from Jeri's car, impossible flashes of lightning leaped from nothingness to nothingness, crackling in brilliant bursts that were more crystal blue and transparent red than lightning white. The air roiled in unreal shapes, twisting this way, then that, as if the very heavens were sentient. Each time those inside the car thought it had finally come to an end, another burst of lightning exploded, and they jumped, certain it was closer than ever before.

Uriel's eyes saw more. He observed the great streams of light lancing out from the Swords of Power. There were glimpses of brothers who had once been his friends and supporters flashing in and out of the maelstrom, an arm held out with visible power surging forth, a tangled wing that had not yet healed, or the quick movement of limbs leaping back into the fray. It was with distress that Raphael was not seen, for Uriel was convinced he had only the one friend left, although he harbored doubts Raphael would claim him as such. At the motel, he had cursed him, sending him packing. Even so, the Healer had led Uriel's attackers away, allowing him to rescue Angioletta. That must count for something.

He turned to the woman at his side. With the food he'd eaten, he felt somewhat renewed, although pure meat would have been better. The bread was less efficient to metabolize, and it took enormous quantities of it.

Angioletta no longer seemed lifeless, although she hadn't come to. Her head had healed, and surprisingly fast. That was totally unexpected. Still, she breathed, and if life entered and exited her chest, there was every reason to hope.

His eyes lifted to see the new boy looking at him. He allowed himself to brush the boy's mind just enough to learn his name. This was a desperate time, and the boy was clearly frightened.

"Tommy, I'm Uri. I'm a friend of Bobby's." The older boy turned toward him. There was new understanding in those eyes, and Uriel caught it immediately.

"Bobby knows you?" Tommy turned to his friend, doubt in his words.

"Sure, I do." Bobby looked down at his hand and flexed it into an easy fist, pausing for a moment before opening it again. "I know Uri."

"For very long?" The little boy that had taken Tommy's place begged for reassurance.

"Long enough to know that you can trust him with anything. He won't let you down."

Uriel held Angioletta, though, and he looked at her face. It seemed he had become quite good at letting people down. He'd stolen this woman from her father, and now she lay poised on the ragged precipice of death. How was that for being trustworthy? All it took was a chance meeting with the Bearer of Destiny, and that became your day to die. He knew it was self-pity speaking, but his thoughts also carried an element of truth. Who else under his care would traverse the teetering edge of their own demise this day?

As the boys talked, Bobby telling of Malak and finding Uriel on the bathroom floor and staying the night in the motel room—everything except the wings, oh, and walking through the wall, Uriel noticed—he held the woman he had failed to help. At one point, he glanced into the mirror, only to catch

Jeri's bewildered eyes looking back at him. He dropped his gaze to Angioletta, wishing Raphael were here. He would know how to heal her. He would reach to her, and his thoughts would instantly know why she didn't wake. Then his touch would bring her back to life.

He could no longer do this alone, not if people had to die. He felt his eyes burn with helplessness, but he didn't raise his hand to rub the fire away. If he did, his tears might fall, and he couldn't bear that, either.

Perhaps he should have done exactly that. Many tales of old revealed the power found in the tears of angels, and who knew but what Uriel's tears might have been just the help he needed to offer. He didn't cry them, though, and for that reason, he would never know.

Gadreel, Deliverer of Destruction

The battle had not gone well for Gadreel, for Gabriel fought with vigilance against all comers. Gabriel's tactics—Jeqon's, really—had been brash to the point of deceitfulness, for who could war against the incarnations that he and his Circle of Brothers were bringing forth? Unless something tipped the scales, the Four Familiars would soon find themselves facing defeat. Gabriel must be distracted, and it must be cruel and total.

Gadreel drew from his deepest and most despicable trough of slops. His thoughts delved into realms he never should have broached, but in that moment, he became certain just what to do.

"Familiars," he cried. "Pay heed to my command. I need Swiftness, for we are at a crossroads. Either we win, or we lose, and now is the time to decide."

Within moments, the great bird was at his side. He had been bloodied and healed more times than he could remember, and even as he hovered in front of the brother who had called him, great rents in his body closed as if they never were.

"I release Uriel to you, Swiftness. That one brother is the

true enemy of your master. Take him, and do with him as you will."

Swiftness screamed in exultation.

Gadreel understood what his decision meant. He would never be able to control Gabriel, but he could still make his enemy pay, and in the most cuttingly cruel way possible. He knew the mighty Citadel of Justice and Power still cared about Uriel, even if those feelings had been submerged beneath trickery. To hurt Uriel, and even kill him, if the Familiar could be persuaded to do so, would be a victory of the sweetest kind.

With a quick push of his thoughts, Swiftness knew instantly of Uriel's whereabouts. He was near the edge of the conflagration, running in fear. That was something Gadreel also pushed across, Uriel's fear and his guilt and his intention to keep the Triune Mind sequestered forever.

Swiftness ripped the air with his talons, and a scream of hatred filled the sky. Gadreel didn't have to endure it long, though, for with no hesitation, the giant bird leaped into the sky, and he was gone.

Gadreel smiled. Not under his control? The great Familiar had been all too easy to manipulate. He had been able to do it once before, trick the Four into the Power Nodes, and then it had been so simple to pull the Triune Mind inside, also. They had been so trusting. They were still trusting, and because of that, everything he wished to happen would come to pass just as he willed. After all, he was the leader of the Unity, wasn't he? There was no one more powerful or with a greater mind in the entire Universe, and he hoped the Triune Mind read his every thought.

"No one," he spat harshly. "No one at all."

His words were empty, though, for there was no one to hear. But then, he was the only one who needed to hear the words, because he was the only one who cared.

An Angel Weeps for an Innocent

Something hit the roof of the car hard, and electricity

crackled around the outside of the vehicle. Jeri screamed, letting go of the wheel.

Just as quickly, the engine died. Her foot stomped the gas, and she cried in a panic, "Not again! It won't go. It's dead!" She grabbed for her children, tucking Chrissy under her arm, and squeezing Dakota's shoulder with her hand.

Immediately, the car was buffeted, as if by great wings, and the back window exploded. A great claw sporting enormous talons thrust through the opening and grabbed Uriel by the shoulder. The broad-shouldered brother screamed in pain as he was torn from the vehicle.

In an instant of comprehension, even though he couldn't see what had grabbed Uriel, Bobby flew from his seat, past Tommy, and reached over the unconscious Angioletta. He grasped the man's legs, and he refused to let his "angel" go.

Still, there are times when intent, or even maturity, is not enough. The great Eagle known as Swiftness was too strong for the boy. When Swiftness wished to take something someone else had, the Eagle simply took it, and there was no question about that. A strong back and strong arms wouldn't hold what the Eagle wished to own.

In the destruction, the bird didn't really want to own Uriel. He wished something far more deadly. Evisceration. The hated brother was far too difficult to take adequate revenge upon inside the car, and for that reason, he must be removed.

Yanking the weakened brother from the window of the vehicle, dragging him roughly over shattered shards of broken glass, and lifting him into the air, Swiftness shook his prize violently, attempting to damage him enough that he couldn't flee. Then, he violently cast the brother down on the deck lid of the car, screaming his satisfaction. With a thrust of his wings, he barreled into the sky. He was a bird of prey, after all, and his actions would have been clear to any handler. The massive creature would turn, and with all his strength, he would impale the brother with his talons. Then, disemboweling him, he would feast upon the corporeal flesh, and the nourishment would renew the creature's strength. It had been the way of raptors throughout the span of history.

485

After that, the Eagle would follow another agenda, one more specific to the Pets of the Triune Mind. The battle with the rest of the Pets would be rejoined, and victory for the Mind would be won.

When Uriel hit the car, Bobby saw him land on his back, and the weight of his falling body crushed the metal deck lid. He reached out of the window and grabbed Uriel by the arm, intending to help him back inside. Physical contact was made only for an instant. Then, because of the sub-atomic polarization fields that prevented their skin from touching, his hand was painfully flung away. That quick touch was all that was needed, because for that brief moment, his eyes were opened. He no longer saw just the roiling sky and the lightning. He took in everything Uriel had seen. Directly overhead, a giant Eagle, larger than any eagle he had ever known, tore through the sky directly at the car, aiming for the injured man lying exposed and helpless on the deck lid. Bobby understood instantly that this was Uriel's death knell, that the winged creature intended for him to die. That could not be allowed to happen.

Bobby flung himself from the car to protect Uriel from the coming decimation. Where human skin touched angel flesh, Bobby's arms burned with fire, and he danced with the touch, the electric intensity lancing through his body.

"You're safe now, Uri." Bobby's voice shook with the convoluted convulsions contorting his body. For a moment, his eyes looked into Uriel's, and he smiled.

Uriel knew better though, and throwing his arms about the teen, in a singular motion, he clapped his hands together hard. With a blinding flash, instantly his wings were at his side. His instinct was to wrap the boy inside to provide some measure of protection.

He was not quick enough. There was a valid reason for the Eagle's name. The Familiar had been in no hurry when Uriel had lain exposed for the attack, and the animal had been pleased to take time to anticipate savoring the brother's impending disembowelment and death. Now, another was in the way, and rage flooded the bird's perceptions. Swiftness would not be denied his rightful revenge.

The enormous, deadly talons, aiming for the brother underneath, slammed into the boy, the great daggers of death slicing through Bobby's back as they reached for Uriel, for the touch of incorporeal flesh turned corporeal, to know the warm sensations of quivering tissue as the hated brother died within his clutches.

Instead, Bobby shuddered and fell against Uriel, no longer aware of the pain of his human flesh pressed against that of an "angel." As his brain shut down the pain receptors in his body, refusing to channel the screams of his tortured nerves any longer, he relaxed in the clutches of his angel.

As the Eagle's talons dug deep, tearing through flesh, and struggling for the brother they sought, the touch of human blood burned the animal's feet with a fire the creature had never felt before, and it angered him. Swiftness screamed his rage, jerking his talons from Bobby's body, their scissor edges covered with blood that this time dripped truly red.

Then, he was gone.

Belatedly, Uriel's wings engulfed Bobby's body. He could feel the boy's blood seeping across his skin, the electric fire of its living matter burning his own. Life oozed from the boy's wounds. Yet, he had no power to heal such injuries. That Mandate was Raphael's alone.

"Why, Bobby?" He reached to brush the blond hair from a face that would never know another day of sunshine. He felt the death rattle from the boy's chest, and he felt unwelcome tears blur his eyes. He could barely speak. "You've just begun to live. Why did you risk yourself for me?"

Blood had begun to leak from the boy's mouth. His lips attempted to move, but it was his thoughts Uriel understood.

"You couldn't save yourself, Uri. Someone had to. Now you can save everyone else."

Then, his body stiffened, and with one last release of warmed breath, the pain of angel skin pressed against living flesh faded. That was when Uriel knew the boy was truly gone.

There was little time to feel sorry for either Bobby or himself, for a voice wailed from inside the car, and it was in the most horrendous agony possible.

"Dakota! Dakota, baby, you've got blood running from

your head! Somebody, please help!"

When Uriel tried to rise, he fell back to the metal surface of the car. He'd known he had no resources for bringing about his wings, and yet there had been no other choice. Now, with Bobby's mutilated body holding him down, he couldn't even stand. He could do nothing except turn his head to look inside the car.

When he did, there were Tommy's eyes, and they looked back at him. Uriel closed his own and pushed all thoughts away.

All except one.

Who else would have to die this day? Who, indeed?

Chapter 35

Angioletta Bacciarelli, Daughter of Kafziel

Time was nonexistent in Angioletta's world. She smiled, but it was a dream smile, one that was larger than any real smile could be, and one that lasted longer than any smile could last. She was warm, and the sky was bright, and there were angels flying all around. It seemed her mothers had been right after all. Heaven was a real place where people went when they died. She knew. She was there.

She stood on a mountaintop, and she breathed in the clear, refreshing air. She realized it didn't smell like the air she was used to, in fact didn't even *feel* like the air she was used to. It was lighter, almost as if she were breathing in nothing at all. Her body felt weightless, also, as if she could step off her mountaintop and simply float away, as if she would be kept aloft by the wind, her feet never touching the ground.

Turning, she saw a great city in the distance, although it was too grand to be any city that might be found upon Earth. Slender towers soared into the sky, and filigreed walkways entwined among them. Great arching buttresses attached the towers to the sides of the mountains as well as to adjoining towers. The wide avenues wending along the bases of the needles thrusting into the sky glittered in the brilliance of the day, much as gold glitters in the sunlight.

Everywhere were muted pastels of purple and mauve, teal and chartreuse. The salmons of Italy and the brick reds of England were softened and washed across the landscape. The intense blues of the French Riviera and the sandy browns of the Sahara were the watercolors of the sky and the thrusting mountain peaks. The greens of the Amazon were a Pointillist accompaniment, filling in the transitions from one color to the next. Over it all, a snow of effervescent clouds swirled with the barest of brushstrokes against an unlimited sky.

All the details that Angioletta took in were beautiful, but each item of beauty in itself was not unknown to her. She had seen them on Earth, for otherwise, how could she compare this beauty to anything at all? If she traveled to England or France or the steamy jungles of Brazil, she would find the same images that stretched forth from her feet. There was something else that truly told her this was real. The angels. From each and every walkway, angels lifted in flight, their wings catching the light, as they banked and soared, at times coming to rest on some impossible fairy bridge, only to fling themselves forth once again, snapping open enormous wings to control their fantasies of flight.

With one hand, she brushed the skin of her arm. When she touched her chest was when she first looked at her own body. Glancing down, she saw the rise of two naked breasts, the skin golden, their sharp points dark and pronounced. That surprised her, because they weren't the breasts she remembered. Hers were much fuller, and her skin was not golden at all. Reaching to explore, she touched her stomach, and without needing to reach farther, she knew she wore nothing at all. She was surprised to realize that it didn't bother her. She stood on a mountaintop in a place so beautiful she could hardly imagine it as real, and she wore not a thread of clothing. Yet, it seemed that this was simply the way it should be, the way it should have been her entire life.

All the amazing wonders she had seen paled in the next moment, though, for the wind swiftly picked up. She felt herself buffeted, and she instinctively moved to wrap her arms around herself. In that motion, something else appeared at the edges of her vision, and startled at first, she quickly smiled at the unexpected revelation.

This was Heaven, was it not? And who was to say that in Heaven, even lowly Angioletta should not have wings? They were weightless, and rather than being covered with feathers, they seemed to sparkle in the day's light. Opening them wide, just for the joy of doing so, the wind caught them and lifted her aloft.

She was flying, and it was effortless. It took no conscious thought at all, as if she had been born to do this.

In actuality, she had. Her father was a brother of the Unity, if one that was in rather ill regard at the present. That made her half what she could possibly become. The other half of her Destiny had been found in a motel room on the bathroom floor. She had reached to touch the shoulder of an injured man, and then she had been drawn to touch her tongue to the blood on her hand.

She was a child of the Unity, with every possibility offered to all the brothers who had come to this dimension so many eons before. That ingestion of "angel" blood had been the key to gifting her body with the final half of her legacy. Her birthright was being fulfilled as she slept in the back seat of Jeri's car. That was as it should be, for she had been rescued by the Bearer of Destiny, had helped that very same brother back from the brink of destruction, and then she had been held in his arms as she had been bought near to her own death.

No one else's blood could have transformed that poor little infant from decades before, born to an unsuspecting nun, and raised out of view of the world, to flower into what she was intended to become. Only Uriel's lifeblood would do that for her. For, just as Raphael's Mandate was to Heal, and Jeremiel's was to give Strength to the broken, each of the brothers could perform only the tasks to which they were assigned. Uriel's body, his *blood*, carried something that no one else's in the Unity offered: the path to one's Destiny. Everything about Uriel was about finding the Destiny that each human deserved.

491

Somehow it seemed fitting for it to also apply to one who was half-human and half-brother.

Now, all Angioletta had to do was pursue her Destiny. It was out there. It awaited her. It would also be grand and glorious, a Destiny only she could fulfill. However, that was for another day. Right then she slept, unaware that Uriel lay at her back, and Bobby was held in his arms, the life gone from his young body. She only knew that she floated upon the Winds of Heaven, and that there was no place more glorious to be.

She was an angel, even if it was only in her dreams.

Interlude 28

"Get that Viper off the ground!"

The aircraft referred to was the F-16, an Air Force jet with an incredibly successful track record, but one that resembled an attack fighter from a popular movie. That was the reason for the vicious nickname. A better one might be Pilot Killer. It was the only jet aircraft with enough muscle in its engines to force it straight upwards, to lift it so high, and so quickly, that as the atmosphere thinned, the pilot could no longer maintain consciousness.

Still, no matter how powerful the aircraft and no matter its assured place as an amazing American Air Force jet, the commander wanted it in the air more quickly than was humanly possible.

"I want that craft at angels fifteen—" *fifteen thousand feet* "—before another quake registers in that godforsaken wilderness." To the base commander, Arizona was a wilderness, too, one that should have had no earthquakes or registered any EMP activity. Unexpectedly, for the past hour, it had been decimated with both. The commander wanted to know just what was out there, and if it had a foreign insignia pasted on its skin, he wanted it blown out of the sky.

"Wants us there and back, three down and locked, before we even know what's on the radar," the pilot muttered. Wisely, he made sure his words missed his microphone. It wouldn't do for comments like that to make it back to his CO. His hide would be toast without question, if that happened. What he said over the radio was, "Got my speed slacks on, and I'm off to spank that fighter puke up there, no matter the pucker factor." He grinned at that. The guys in the tower would know exactly what he meant.

The response came back with equal vigor, although not from the CO. "Grab your pole, you spud, you. We finally got you spooled up and ready. Also, thought you might like to know we got you some playmates on your wingtips. Plumbers need not apply." The voice chuckled at that. Plumbers were inept pilots, and there were none of those stationed at their base. Only the best of the best would do for the Air Force. They even had a motto that summed it up nicely. Lead, Follow, or Get Out of the Way.

The pilot grinned, although he knew he couldn't be seen. "I'll have that puke padlocked and in a smoking hole before you can make a combat dump. NFOD on this baby." NFOD. *No fear of death*. If he were back in an outdated aluminum cloud, the F-14, he'd have to think twice about such a bravado remark.

"Get me a judy, and I'll be pleased." *Judy*, radio confirmation that the enemy was in sight. Clearly, he wanted to know that *something* was up there. All their instruments kept going crazy, and then nothing showed up at all.

"Will do. This Viper here might make a few Indian night noises, but she'll jink around and bring me home. You can count on it."

"Just keep your head on a swivel. We've no idea what this thing is. We want you back and dirty ASAP."

"My fangs are out."

"Check six." *Be careful*.

With those final two words, the turbines flared, and the aircraft leaped forward. The pilot was glad to be in this particular plane. He'd flown the F-14 with its hydraulic systems, and he appreciated the F-16. Give him an electric jet any day. He was confident that no matter what he flew, it would do what was required of it, and that was to get the job done.

That was all that mattered, and the pilot would make sure

he got this job completed, no matter the cost to whoever got in his way.

Ramiel, Herald of Hope

Ramiel hovered in the Chamber of Deeds, images of Earth flickering before him, and he was alone. He was indeed the proverbial Angel of Hope—for reasons long forgotten—but he also guided those who died back to heaven. Well, at least he guided the brothers back to the Unity. He had no idea if dead humans went to any sort of heaven. His job was to judge whether the exiled brothers had redeemed themselves, garnering enough experiences to be allowed back inside. Those experiences would then be assimilated into the Corporate Memory, enabling many to experience the Pleasures of New Knowledge. In a society as ancient as that of the Unity, a constant infusion of new information was paramount.

When he had seen the battle unleashed, his brothers flickering from incarnation to incarnation, he knew that Gadreel's chances for ultimate success were poor. The Four Familiars were outmatched in that sort of fray.

Touching one of the images, he searched for the Seraphim. To his dismay, he found their Swords feeding the energy needs of the brothers. How clever! How detestable! How quickly the Four would fall! There was no recourse against such unlimited power.

He shifted nonexistent fingers on his nonexistent hands, and a glowing ball of light appeared. All he had to do was fling it, and the brother he wished to retrieve would be snatched from the planet's surface, his corporeal bonds shattered into incorporeality. The lightship would summon him back to the Unity, where his deeds would be judged for all to see. All he had to do was pull in a few key players . . . and then let the rest of the participants see whether this travesty of a battle went the way they hoped!

Nevertheless, he wanted to be on the winning side. If Gadreel proved himself to be incompetent, perhaps it was time for new blood to ascend to the Chair. Ramiel's sort of blood, not to be too greedy.

For that reason, he watched and waited, trusting in his own machinations. After all, he had to give Kafziel a chance. What good was an alliance, if it was not allowed to mature to fruition?

Now he could only hope that the events played out in his favor, because what transpired on that blue and green ball would be remembered forever, and there was no way to remove what had been placed within the safekeeping of the Collective Memory. For all the eons of the future, it would be there, and time would judge the brothers over and again.

Time would also judge Ramiel, but he didn't consider that.

An Angel's Tears Continue to Fall

Uriel's tears of remorse blurred his vision, their salty flavor finding its way to his mouth, a bitter taste for the brother to swallow. "Tommy," he called. "Can you help me with Bobby?"

"There's broken glass everywhere." The boy's eyes were red, and his voice shook.

"It will be difficult, so take great care." Uriel reached his hands to his face and brushed his eyes clear. He couldn't let his presence endanger these innocent humans any longer. They were dying in his arms.

When he grasped Bobby to roll him aside, the remains of Uriel's tears mixed with the blood of an innocent who had died needlessly, and Bobby's Destiny changed. Whether he wished it or not, Uriel *did* change Destiny, and unwittingly, the damp touch of his hands started that process once again.

Incredibly, from the front, Bobby's body appeared nearly undamaged. His features were smooth and serene, as if he simply rested for a few moments, his eyes taking in the unusual conflagration in the skies. Yet, when Uriel lifted his hand from the boy's chest, a bloody print remained as damning evidence of the truth, its screaming accusation staining his shirt.

"Has my friend awakened?" Uriel inquired. Angioletta's

495

face seemed brighter, although blood still smeared her head. He hated that an outlaw now protected her, a fugitive from the brothers of the Unity.

"I-I don't know. I haven't seen her open her eyes."

Uriel rolled heavily off the car. Brushing his fingers against Bobby's face for the last time, he opened the car door and knelt at Angioletta's side. "Angioletta, you must come awake. Can you hear me?"

"Sir? Can you help my son? I can't stop the bleeding." Jeri wailed her distress over the seat. "Please, sir."

Uriel stood, and with a clap and a flash of blinding light, his wings were gone. His body sagged against the car with a new level of physical decimation. The top of the vehicle was crushed against the window frame, and it was the third try before the front door came loose. Glass had pierced the boy's scalp, and he sat with dazed eyes. Uriel looked to Jeri, dismayed at the blank look in her eyes. He pulled the glass free in one quick movement, taking the cloth from her hand and covering the injury, pressing down tightly.

"Hold that, as long it takes the bleeding to stop."

"I don't know what to do." Her eyes were dazed.

"You have a daughter, also." He pressed a Suggestion her way, hoping it would take. "Your daughter needs you."

"She needs me. My daughter?" She stared vacantly.

Uriel had reached the end of his tether. He had nothing else to give. His was the Mandate of Destiny, and yet, here in this desert landscape, he couldn't even find his own. He was as lost as these humans.

To even breathe was an effort almost beyond compare.

"Uriel?" Angioletta. She sounded disoriented. "Are we stopped on the side of the road?"

"You have awakened. Thank the Unity. Yes, we are on the side of the road." He reached to motion Tommy's hand forward. "The wound, Tommy. Help Jeri. Press it tightly."

He stood, asking Angioletta, "Can you move?"

"I think so." Her words were stronger.

"Tommy," Uriel asked, touching the boy on the shoulder. "How far to Bobby's house?" He couldn't abandon these people, but he could no longer care for them. They must find a level of safety he could not offer.

"Down this road and over that rise. I could walk it, if you need me to—"

"Uriel, look at the sky," Angioletta interrupted. Her voice trembled. "There are things up there. What are they?"

"You see that?" He masked his surprise with difficulty. "Just what do you see?"

"A flying lion . . . with six wings. Other creatures, also. I dreamed I was in heaven, and I've awakened to hell."

Two of the creatures, closer than Uriel would have liked, tore into each other. Electricity crackled around the car. Uriel knew it for what it was, the rage of his brethren and the thrash of otherworldly energies bringing destruction to Earth.

"Bobby?" Angioletta's voice twisted with panic, and her words jumped in pitch. "Where's Bobby? He was with us earlier."

"Angioletta—" Uriel's stomach churned. He dreaded telling her.

"Oh, Dakota!" She turned to Uriel. "What did we hit?"

He steeled himself and spoke gently. "Something hit *us*. Bobby took the brunt of it."

"Took the brunt? What does that mean?"

Tommy let out in a gush, "He's dead. Something killed him."

"I'm sorry, Angioletta. He's gone."

"No, he cannot be." Tears flooded her eyes. "Uriel, how can Bobby be dead?"

Together they managed to get Bobby into the car, laying his inert body in the back seat. As soon as he was settled, a new sound caused them to look skyward. Three F-16s thundered overhead, and the vibration of their passing shook several fragments of glass from the back window, the pieces tinkling as they fell onto the window ledge.

"Over the hill, you say?" Uriel was relieved when Tommy nodded.

"And down that road."

"What kind of planes were those, Tommy?"

The boy searched for the jets. The sky was clear; they had gone already, their speed driving them fast and hard. "F-16s, maybe, from the sound."

"They were fast, weren't they?" *Focus, Tommy. Run.* "Can you lead everyone to Bobby's house?"

"What about Bobby?"

"Bobby will be fine here. We can come back for him later."

As the living began moving away from the car, Jeri with her daughter, and Tommy's protective arm around Dakota, Angioletta helped Uriel stand, although to say stand was to overstate Uriel's abilities. Rather, he leaned against her, and their forward motion was more of a broken stumble than a run toward safety. Before they were across the road, the drone of the planes returned. This time the dusty thump of gunfire strafed the desert floor, heading straight for Jeri's car. With surgical precision, it pierced the passenger's door, shattered the windshield, and continued on into the driver's door. Another line of strafing danced across the deck lid, piercing the fuel tank, and leaving gasoline leaking across the road. Flames whipped up, racing across the surface of the liquid, and the top of the asphalt began to burn.

"Run," Uriel yelled to Jeri and the kids, his words breaking off into choked coughing. The young mother took off, Chrissy's hand in hers, but when Tommy hesitated, Uriel pointed and yelled again, "Go! Dakota needs you to run." The boys took off after Jeri, running through the desert scrub, and with any luck, Uriel hoped, straight toward Bobby's house.

It wasn't Jeri and the kids who were in danger. It was him, and of course, whoever was with him. "Go, Angioletta. You can make it to safety without me." He had reached the point where he had to give up watching out for her welfare, for there was no way he could protect this woman. Perhaps it was time to consider his end, or if he lived, his capture and punishment, even if he was innocent of whatever crime he was believed to have committed.

"You are a fool if you think I'm leaving you here. It's dangerous out in the open, and I don't think you'd get very far on your own. We're heading for that wash over there." She pointed a short distance off the side of the road. "Can you make it that far?"

"Perhaps," he groaned. "With your help."

When they finally dropped into the shadow of the wash, they were at least out of the sun, and it was distinctly cooler. The sound of the airplanes was less, too. She turned to him, and she rubbed her hand over her face, sighing dramatically.

"I bought you that shirt you wanted. I think I dropped it back on the road. What chance do you think I have of retrieving it?" She paused, and her eyes were red. "I used Rikkianne's money to buy it. Do you think she'll be angry? Bobby picked it out." Tears began to run down her face. Then, with surprising forwardness, she stroked her hand along his chest. "Your vanilla. It's hardly there anymore."

He didn't answer, for he could no longer move. He needed food. That and the fact that a human boy who had claimed him as a friend had died in his arms. He'd seen the leaking gasoline running from underneath the car. If the car burst into flames, the body would be burned beyond recognition, and the ultimate tragedy would be made worse.

Uriel sank even further into despair.

The stroke of Angioletta's hand brought to roost the most searing devastation that he knew would ever come his way. He closed his eyes in abject self-pity. His reason for life had left him, for Gabriel would never stroke his chest in that way ever again. Uriel knew of the taste of vanilla. It was the feel, smell, and taste of a brother's skin, no matter the dimension they were in. In that touch of Angioletta's hand down his chest, he knew the truth as he had refused to truly face it before.

Gabriel was his no more.

It felt as if his heart had been cut out, and how was he to live ever again? He squeezed his lids tightly and wished the world away.

Angioletta Bacciarelli, Daughter of Kafziel

Angioletta rested her head against Uriel's shoulder and

breathed in his smell. Even with the turmoil raging all about them, this was where she wanted to be, next to this man. She remembered an old children's verse telling what girls were made of. She decided it needed to be rewritten. Vanilla is spice and that's nice, because that's what Uriel's made of.

She smiled. She knew this moment couldn't last, for there was a battle of some kind going on just over their heads. She had these few minutes, and sometimes that was all the world gave, just what a person had in his or her grasp at the present moment. To reach out and take it, holding it tightly for that brief period of time, was all one could do.

Interlude 29

"Don't tell me that was no tank." The pilot of the F-16 yelled into his microphone. "I'm not sending my plane back to the taxpayers just because you hear some music playing. I had him painted."

"C'mon. You were cherubs two—" *two hundred feet* "—and you could see it was a car. You think it's just going to go away when you fire, and you can gaff off the residue? Remember, you buy the farm, I buy the farm. Don't be a hinge-head. You want word to get around that you lost the bubble, taking out a disabled car?"

The pilot knew he'd seen what he'd seen. That had been a tank down there, and it was aiming at his F-16. There was no way he wasn't taking it out. Still, he didn't want any trouble, and his wingman had a good point.

"Thought we were jumping into a furball up there." He chuckled, diverting the conversation. Like dogfights of old, too many aerial combatants could create plausible confusion. Then he laughed, making at least an attempt at joviality. "Did you ever see so many bogeys on the screen? And not a one of them was really there."

"Not in my life. Anyway, whatever you saw, it's gone now, and nothing valuable's been taken out."

It seemed that Gadreel's Suggestion to the pilot had worked

just fine. The only thing was that it had come about five minutes too late. Except for Bobby, the car was empty when the pilot fired his guns at the enemy tank that wasn't really there. That hadn't done Gadreel any good. In spite of his last-ditch, desperate attempt to punish Gabriel, his quarry had still gotten away.

Chapter 36

Elemiah, Six-Winged Seraph

Elemiah's Sword of Power slammed into the ground at his feet, its tip driving deep into the desert soil. He had withdrawn from the battle, abandoning the remaining brothers to fight alone.

It had been a desperate choice of necessity.

Light billowed out from the Sword's point of impact in a ball of energy that quickly engulfed the Seraph, Jeri's car, and the unburned gasoline that dripped from the car's ruptured fuel tank. There, it formed an impenetrable wall, separating the real world outside from the Sword's miniature world inside. Just beyond its edges, flames curled and leapt with fervor along the top of the road.

However, they could not get inside.

Within that glowing sphere, time became malleable, for the Sword knew neither minute nor hour, night nor day. It controlled the turning of the clock and shifted the changing of the seasons. It manipulated the rising of the sun and the setting of the same. *Time* was what was needed within that pulsing orb, for the boy inside had been touched by Destiny's tears. Even so, the tears needed *time* to do their work. Without the intervention of Elemiah's Sword, that time would never be there, and Destiny would soon ripple a new pattern once again.

The mighty Seraph had seen what Uriel had not, although *sensed* was perhaps the more accurate word. In the instant of Uriel's touch against the shredded skin on Bobby's back, the fabric of Destiny had *twisted*, and each participant in this great game, one that impacted the future of this world in the most dramatic way possible, had felt it. Whether they recognized its importance or not was another matter. It was as if the existence in which they lived, for the briefest of instants, had become slippery, and the next moment, things were put right again, although, in some indefinable way, they were not exactly the same. That had been Uriel's touch, and even the Seraph's Sword had slipped in his hand during that one, brief moment. He had known instantly, though, for he held the Sword of Power, and through it, he understood many things.

The thing Elemiah had felt most strongly was the assurance that the tears of the Bearer of Destiny would continue to heal the child, even though life had fled the body. It was an old story told often in this world's holy books. One of the most widely read was that of the man called Lazarus. Then there was the account of the religious leader Jairus, and his dead daughter. Both bodies had lain without life for days before their breath had been renewed. Yet another example was the Shunammite's son. A religious prophet who went by the name of Elisha had stretched himself out upon the child, and life was given back to him.

How? By Destiny's tears.

The brothers of the Unity took whatever guise best suited the duties they must perform on this world, whether it be under the pretense of a human prophet, a healer, or an angel. The humans saw only what was Suggested to them, and because of that, such events were considered miraculous. They weren't. They were, instead, simply the result of what the brothers of the Unity of Being were capable of doing.

Outside of Elemiah's protective field of Power, time slipped past with barely a whisper, the linear seconds following one after another, the barest touch of their breath pressing against that glowing orb, then recognizing that there was to be no entrance allowed. Conversely, inside that pulsing ball, time didn't move in a linear, uniform fashion at all. It was held and twisted into what the Seraph wished it to be.

The rippling gunfire from the Air Force jet had shredded insulation from various wires, and the brush of metal against metal had thrown sparks where sparks should never be allowed. Under the dashboard, flames already licked the wiring from their leads, and when the dripping gasoline finally seeped under the engine, it would ignite with a vehemence that would make itself known for many miles. Elemiah had done what he could within the sphere, pinching the time around the flames to mere seconds every hour, and slowing the leakage of gasoline, until it seemed not to drip at all. Without keeping his sword planted in the soil for all time, he couldn't prevent the explosion. All he could do was manipulate its moment of ignition.

At the same time, around Bobby, time was a rushing river, and his flesh repaired itself with incredible rapidity as the enzymes in Uriel's tears spread like wildfire throughout his bodily fluids. Once his heart restarted, and his youthful lungs drew in that first sudden draught of air, he would need to be prepared to run. The car would explode, and it would be mere moments after Elemiah withdrew his Sword from the ground.

During his sojourn at Bobby's side, if the Seraph had thought there was a human god in the heavens above this corporeal planet, he would have prayed to it. He held the crux of Destiny in his hands—in his Sword, not to put too fine a point on it—and not even a Seraph took that duty lightly.

His efforts to help Bobby also impacted the outcome of the raging battle just outside his sphere of influence, and not for the better. He had abandoned his post to come to Bobby's aid. Without his Sword, the Circle's energies would soon fail. No brother could maintain the dimensional interface required to fight the Four Familiars without constant renewal. That had been his and Barakiel's job. It was possible that he could save this boy, and in the doing, lose the battle.

He would simply have to be successful at both, for neither was something he was willing to let go. He had once guarded the Tree of Life, and its sanctity had never been breached. He would do this, too. Destiny would be preserved, and the battle would also be won. Such was the strength of a Seraph, and especially the strength of the one known as Elemiah.

He spoke words of encouragement, "Hurry, Bobby, your body to heal. Then you must run with the greatest of zeal."

It was the closest to a prayer the Seraph knew how to pray, but he meant it with all his heart. The boy would have to run, and there must be no slowing down. He must live. Elemiah had felt it in the shifting fabric of Destiny, and that was no small thing.

A Great Conflagration Reaches a Resolution

Jeqon, that eternal party meister, was the one who finally ended the terror that reigned over Arizona's skies.

Subjectively, the battle raged for weeks. Those in combat had limbs and wings slashed, and they healed themselves over and over. The brothers were empowered by the Seraphim's twin Swords, then finally Barakiel's Sword alone kept them renewed. Only by wearing the Four Familiars down could the Circle hope to win the conflict. They couldn't kill the Four, and in fact didn't wish to try. They were the Triune Mind's companions, and the battle was being waged under false pretenses. At least Raphael and the three who had joined him knew that. The others wouldn't listen to such reason, even if they were told. They had been convinced, and sometimes righteous anger was the most stubborn kind.

To observers on the outside, the lightning storm was simple. It built in strength for a time, raged for an hour or two, and then the skies began to clear. Contrary, what made it dissipate was strictly Jeqon's doing.

When the Sword wielded by Elemiah was removed from the equation, the brothers' energy immediately began to suffer. Barakiel did what he could, his power lancing through the dust-laden air, but for one Sword to maintain what had required two was an impossible task. When Asbeel's Gorgon began to falter, and Wisdom threw the brother to the ground, was when Jeqon tossed caution to the wind.

"Barakiel," he called into the maelstrom. "All your power must be mine." He could no longer maintain his own dimensional interface adequately, and his Amphisbaena began to flicker. Still, the response he expected didn't come, and he watched Hizkiel's Golem fall to the desert floor, Swiftness slashing his back with a scream of victory.

"Barakiel," Jeqon repeated, this time stronger, his two heads calling as one. "I am prepared. You must trust me. We fail otherwise." His dancing speech was gone. This Jeqon was the true one, the brother who was master of all he wished to perform in life. The jokester was his ruse, his disguise. It was how he wished to be known. He was much more, though.

This time his cry was successful, and he felt the brilliance of the Sword's power surround him. Its energy swelled inside his Amphisbaena body, his two mouths crying out with excitement. The end was here, and the Four would fall. It was written, as it was impossible for them to resist the onslaught of the one Jeqon would become.

Such a long time ago that few of the brothers bothered to recall, the Unity had shifted into a dimension that had lost the ability to link tenuous atoms to other equally tenuous atoms. The result was that the Unity and its inhabitants had swelled to enormous physical proportions, each inhabitant of the Unity stretching as tall as the stars, and the Unity expanding to contain them all. Only their own physical makeup, their internal electrical bonds, had kept them from expanding forever.

No one had accessed that particular dimensional interface since that time. The power drain was simply too much. To keep that interface in place would require the entire energy output of one of the most powerful ancient engines known to the Unity.

A Sword of Power.

It had never been done before, but Jeqon knew he had no other choice. He would become the Typhon. His human half would tower to the stars, and the viper coils of his lower body would encircle the earth. His hands would reach as far as the West was from the East, and a hundred dragon heads would inhabit each.

Then, with a release of unparalleled energy that drove the air from the sky and tore the soil from the ground, the accumulated power of the Sword transformed Jeqon's body in one mighty thrust heavenward. The atmosphere shrieked past him as his body lunged into the sky, and he knew what it was like to be taller than the stars in space. He was massive, and he could rule all things. He was the god the humans claimed to worship. Not even the Triune Mind could speak in his presence, for he was greater than the Unity. With a voice that was too deep for human ears to hear, he laughed in exultation. He *was* God, for he could pluck the stars from the sky and place them back again.

It was one of the side effects of the dimensional interface. The incarnation could absorb the wearer, for its reality was total as long as it was worn.

Unwelcome, a voice tickled his consciousness, one so small, it seemed as if it was not even there. He started to brush it aside, then it came again, stronger. He paused, and he listened.

"Jeqon. Remember your name. Remember your Mandate. Remember the Sword of Power. Remember that we battle. Remember, Jeqon."

He roared his frustration, and on Earth, chandeliers shook in the great halls of power, and dust from cracking walls showered freshly cleaned sideboards. To be God was what he deserved. To be pulled away was cruel. Yet, he had listened, and with that half-step, his cooperation was assured.

With his hand, the one that reached into the West, Jeqon stretched toward Earth and gathered the Four Familiars. They struggled, but his new skin was thick, and there was nothing they could do to him. After all, his hands were filled with the heads of dragons, and they were a hundred times the size of any of the Familiars. Then, with his hand that reached into the East, he opened his incorporeal bag, the one Zadkiel had teased him to leave behind. With the tongues of the dragons that made up his hundred fingers, he pulled his special prizes from inside.

Eight Energy Nodes rested on the caressing tongues of eight hissing dragons. Red saliva dripped from each, and with a swift motion, the great Typhon that Jeqon had become spewed the Nodes from the mouths of the dragons into the blackness of space. A Tertiary Forces Chamber winked into being, created out of nothingness, and it hung invisible in the blackness between the worlds. His other hand threw the Four Familiars after the Nodes, and in a superheated flash of light, one that roiled through the blackness of space, painting an invisible wall of energy throughout the solar system and battering the very ozone layer that protected Earth, the Four Familiars were Encapsulated once again.

With no warning, the power of Barakiel's energizing Sword was gone, and Jeqon was God no more. In that moment, he was once again a simple, dark-skinned man, and even his wings were nonexistent. With the Power from the Sword gone, he didn't have the reserves to bring them back. It didn't make matters any better that he had been hovering a full two stories above the ground when he had taken command of Barakiel's Power. Unable to halt his fall, he dropped heavily twenty feet directly onto the dirt, his shoulder taking the brunt of the impact.

"Who-ee, baby! That be the pain I intend to forget. Barakiel, brother, did you so need to just *turn it off?* My wings be fine for flying to the ground. Floaties be not part of my package."

Still, he could stand, and he did so, brushing soil from his body. All in all, his black skin seemed just fine. Still, in all the interfaces he'd slipped through, it seemed his clothes had gotten lost once again. He was now nothing more than a black brother standing naked in the wilderness, and there was nothing he could do about that.

"Elemiah?" Jeqon called loudly for the second Seraph. "You be dead, Elemiah? AWOL, maybe?"

He grinned at the cleverness in his words. He turned to see

Gabriel coming down at his side, and he reached to grab his arm.

"Oh, Gabe, honey. Such a marvelous party you throw. Invite me next time, too." Then, his exhaustion overtook him, and he collapsed to the ground, dead to the world.

He would live, though. The brothers of the Unity usually did.

Gadreel, Deliverer of Destruction

Gadreel screamed his frustration as his plans evaporated before his eyes. When he had seen the mighty Typhon begin to form, he'd known the Circle of Brothers had grown desperate. They were plying frantic measures, and that meant they were out of options. Then, the Typhon that was Jeqon had pulled the Energy Nodes from some incorporeal location, and that was when he first wailed his anger.

When his voice quieted, and he was still once again, he was startled to hear a voice at his side.

"Is it all out of your system, now?"

He turned to see Gaea at his side. "What do you want, Mother Nature?" He spoke her more modern name. "Who are you, anyway?"

Gaea shifted, and Kasbeel stood at his side. The brother had a look of amusement on his face. He laughed before speaking. "The Four are once again imprisoned. Do you wish to also be Encapsulated? I fear this bunch can do whatever they wish. They have already removed your greatest weapon from the equation." He paused expectantly. "I can get you back into the Unity."

"Is there a price I must pay?" Gadreel knew his options were gone. He hoped, because Kasbeel had helped him once already and asked for nothing in return. Perhaps he wouldn't require too heavy a price this time.

Kasbeel chuckled. "Just remain in power. Oh, and one other thing." He paused for effect, and then he grinned. "If you should ever come across the True Name of the Triune Mind,

509

please get in touch with me."

Gadreel breathed easier. That was a simple request to dance around. He would never know that, and so he would never have to settle this debt. He nodded, and in that moment, a great ball of light crashed into him, shattering his corporeal form into a hundred glittering shards of matter. They began to shimmer and twinkle, then one at a time, they faded into nothingness. By then, the lightship that had come for him had Traversed well on its way back to the inky depths of space, leaving only Kasbeel to see.

Kasbeel, Orator of the Oath Shown to the Holy Ones

Kasbeel turned back to the remains of the battle, its evidence strewn over the tortured Arizona desert. He couldn't be bothered to watch Gadreel's lightship streak heavenward. He had other things on his mind. If he had the True Name of the Triune Mind, he could control the Unity. He had only to speak that name, and all creation would bow before him.

Just to imagine it made him smile.

The Triune Mind, True Leader of the Unity

The Triune Mind felt the screams of his Four Familiars as they were cast once again into captivity. With his Three Glorious Faces, he demanded his prison walls to fall. Yet, even with all the power at his command, the walls were stronger.

Belief in others, and hope for reconciliation, had trapped him here. Lucifer had played him for a fool, pretending contrite remorse, and the Mind had believed his words to be true. Only later, when his twisted machinations had revealed themselves, and the Mind had called for his Familiars, did he find that they had been Encapsulated before him.

It was too late by then. Still, he had battered at the boundaries for thousands of Earth's years. There were now cracks through which he could sense what was happening on the outside, and where a crack could be made, that crack could be made larger.

Through his Familiars' eyes, the Mind had watched the battle with the brothers. He had seen the deception, and he had wanted to cry, "No! Do not battle against those with whom you war. You fight for the wrong side." Yet, it was all he could do to maintain that one small element of contact, for his strength was now pulled in two directions.

When Gadreel had exploded upon Earth, his anger had made his entrance brutal, shattering the sub-atomic cohesion of space and time itself. The rip had pulsed with sensations of old dimensions from many eons ago. It was the feel of life, of escape, of the chance to lead the Unity home. A way home had been opened. The door could not be allowed to close.

Then Jeqon had morphed into the mighty Typhon, and the sound of his voice had shaken the world itself. It had also shaken the Secondary Forces Chamber. The crack that the Triune Mind had forced open shifted, enlarged, and then it stabilized once again.

He was offered an impossible choice, and it wasn't really a choice at all. The crack was not enough to allow for his escape. Achingly, it was just adequate for the Mind to reach out and stabilize the hole Gadreel had torn in space.

He couldn't break free, but he could hold onto that chance for his people to escape. He could never let it close, no matter what it cost. By each of his Three Glorious Faces, the first of the Planner, giving him the ability to plot their course through the intricacies of dimensional interspace, the second of the Rememberer, for it was through the Triune Mind that the Corporate Memory was maintained while slipping from one dimension to another, and the third face of the Executor, that personality with the ability to grasp the intricacies of space and time, and twist them to do his will, he would give his all to hold that rent in space open.

Without it, the Unity was stuck in this dimension for all

time.

Elemiah, Six-Winged Seraph

An hour had passed, or maybe a bit more, outside of Elemiah's sphere of energy. For those who could see it, the surface of the ball glowed and pulsed, like snakes of light writhing across its surface. Blue-white in appearance, it seemed a miniature translucent sun, although one that cut deeply into the soil, claiming a bite of Earth within its circle of protection. Only the vaguest outlines of . . . *something* could be seen within the sphere.

Time had not been allowed entrance into that glowing ball. So, for the moment, outside of the sphere, the flames that had charred the roadway now burned low, the surface oils already consumed, for the gasoline that had fueled its incendiary burst was long since seared away.

Just inside, a battered car waited, the deck lid crushed and the sheet metal pierced with a line of holes. There were few windows left in the tortured machine. Those on the side had been down when the car had unexpectedly died, and both the front and back windscreens were now completely gone. The doors stood open, left that way as the occupants had fled for safety.

Inside the car, the remains of the shattered glass littered the front seat. Under the dash, the glow of otherworldly flames illuminated the floorboard, the ghostly movement barely perceptible in the Seraph's frozen sphere.

In the back seat Bobby lay face up. Only in that specific spot did time fly forward at a greater than normal speed. The enzymes affecting his recovery were the same ones that had begun a slow but inexorable change in Angioletta's body, and if days were needed, then days were what the Seraph would give.

As Bobby's youthful skin knitted back together, organs that had been ripped from their moorings were made new again. His face smoothed, and slack muscles began to twitch. Hours passed—for Bobby's body, anyway—and then days. Angioletta had taken that much time. Bobby's needs were no less.

Then, electricity jolted the fist-sized muscle within his chest, its white-hot fingers forcing his heart into life, before releasing it to begin working on its own. His blood pulsed into action, forcing color back into his skin and warmth into his limbs. He inhaled a massive quantity of air, his muscles tensing, as his body arched upward from the seat. Then, his eyes opened, and the brilliance of Elemiah's protective capsule assaulted him.

One hand grabbing the back of the seat, he pulled himself up to look outside. A man wrapped in a brilliance so bright it could only be flames stood majestically outside the car door. There were wings at his back—wings!—and it seemed to Bobby he could see three on each side. Six wings! The man's hands were wrapped around the grip of a glowing long sword that was almost as tall as he was. One hand brushed the pommel, and the other rested against the cross guard. Its point was buried in the ground, covering much of the central ridge, and what could be seen of the weapon pulsed with power. It was clearly what made everything around him glow. The man's head was bowed as if in prayer.

Then he looked past the man, the *angel*, he told himself, to the walls of energy that encased his small world. He could see nothing at all outside except the vague outlines of small bushes and several large cacti. He made to climb from the car, and only then did he notice his shirt and the handprint there. Tugging at it to see it better, he was surprised when the entire shirt came off in his hands, the back tattered and smeared with the remains of someone's blood. Whose blood? His? Surely not. He felt just fine. In fact, he felt better than fine, just very hungry. Reaching a hand to his back, he felt of the skin there, and there was nothing that was not as it should be. Still, he couldn't wear the shirt he held in his hands, and he threw it to the floor.

That was when he noticed the flames glowing under the dash, and he became aware of the smell of gasoline. It was also when he heard a voice speak directly into his head.

"Time is of the essence, young man. Before I release my Sword, you must have a plan. There are flames, for you have

513

seen them glow. When I remove my Sword from the ground, quickly you must go."

Surprisingly, Bobby had no questions about the unusual directive he was given. He certainly didn't understand the reasons for what he'd been told, but the words the man, the *angel* spoke were clearly just what he must do. When the Sword lifted from the ground, he would run as if his life depended on it. He had heard, no, *sensed* that in the man's words. They had carried an urgency that gripped him inside with fear . . . but again, not with fear. It was not fear at all. It was with determination.

He knew without a doubt he must run as if his life depended on it, for he knew it did. He had things to do, things that were bigger than what he'd spent too many nights doing on the motel roof. He had a purpose in life, a *destiny*. He shook his head at that, wondering at the new word. It had leaped into his thoughts unbidden. Destiny? He had a destiny? Yet, the feeling inside was there, and he knew he would do as the angel had instructed.

Grabbing the doorframe with his hands, his torso shirtless, his jeans bent at the knees, and his shoes stepping on the gasoline covered roadway, he threw himself from the car even as the angel lifted the sword from the ground. In that moment, the world he knew returned in a rush of kaleidoscopic color, and he flung himself through the desert, heading for where he knew his house would be. He had barely gotten to the first low ridge when a massive explosion lit the sky and flung him to the ground. Turning, the car was no more than a fireball, and black smoke billowed from flames that leaped fifty feet into the sky.

His heart pounded in his chest, and adrenalin flooded his body. He had been there, *right there*, and if he hadn't run when he did, he would be dead right now. How did that man know?

He also wondered if the stranger got away in time.

Scrambling up the ridge, he looked around, just locating the peak of his house's roofline. He needed to go home and see if his mother was there. She could call 9-1-1. Heck, maybe even his father was home for a change. Sometimes his father just showed up without warning, off the road for a week or two.

Then, he remembered Tommy, and he grinned. Little T was with him for a month, and he liked Little T. There was no telling what sort of mischief they could get into, and Austen would never know. That'd serve Austen right for moving away to Phoenix and leaving him behind.

It might seem surprising how quickly Bobby's thoughts *slipped* from the unusual events of the day. To say the least, there were Suggestions and brothers at work, and besides, he was only fourteen, and at that age, the world was fresh and ripe for adventure. Who knew what good things might come his way? A car had blown up, and he had run for his life. How great was that? This might be his best summer ever.

With a laugh, he took off towards his house. It was his *destiny* to be the greatest adventurer in the world, and he wanted his friend Tommy to be part of everything he did.

"My Destiny!" He yelled the words aloud as he threw a fist into the sky, leaping into the air with the thrill of the moment. He didn't know why he'd never used that word before. It was a great one to use all the time, and as he ran, he yelled again at the top of his lungs.

"My Destiny begins today!"

It did, too, and in a way that he couldn't begin to comprehend.

Interlude 30

To the boy, Elemiah had already become a man once again, for Bobby was still human, and as a human, there was no Suggestion he could easily ignore. The Seraph's words had told him to run, and his Suggestion had told him that his help had come only from a man. Sure, he might remember someday, for being brought back to life was the most emotionally intense connection with an event that anyone could have. That meant the memory had only been put away, not forgotten. There was a big difference in the two.

What would have really made Bobby's heart pound within his chest was the part of the story he would never know. He'd seen the flames billowing into the desert sky, and he'd thought how he could have been killed when the car exploded. What he

515

didn't know was that he was already dead, and the explosion had been postponed just long enough to allow him to run for his life.

It was no accident that he'd escaped barely in time. It was no accident that he'd escaped at all. It had been part of the Seraph's plan, and rarely did a Seraph have a plan that didn't work out just as he intended. That was why the Seraphim were entrusted with the Swords of Power. That right was theirs, because they earned it, each and every time they used their Swords for good.

Chapter 37

News Reports

UNUSUAL EXPLOSION RIPS ARIZONA DESERT
By Martha Collins
The Associated Press

PHOENIX – Yesterday, a massive explosion of unknown source gouged a crater from the desert floor just west of town. A local 14-year-old boy barely escaped death as the car in which he was resting was ignited during the incident. One unnamed source suggests the car was strafed by an F-16 just before it exploded, but authorities at nearby Luke Air Force Base categorically deny any involvement in the incident.

"Spontaneous combustion," one lieutenant serving as spokesman explained to this reporter. "Yesterday was the hottest day of the summer so far, and the car was very old." He refused to explain why the remains of the car had apparent bullet holes comparable to those carried by the F-16 jet.

More than one authority now links the series of earthquakes felt yesterday with the explosion. There is some speculation that this was an underground nuclear test. At this point that is speculation only, as there is no evidence to corroborate those claims.

GOVERNMENT SURPRISED AT SEVERITY OF QUAKES
By Varahgiri Jatti
The Associated Press

MUMBAI – Despite the repeated occurrence of significant earthquakes throughout India over the past few years, and the introduction of many new government programs to monitor possible earthquake conditions, the people of Mumbai were hit hard yesterday with no warning. Three buildings in the downtown area collapsed after swaying dangerously for several minutes. One, the Broad Apartments, was subdivided into many smaller apartments, and it is feared that more than 300 people may have perished.

Reports are arriving from all over India that other cities have received comparable damage. This is the fourth severe earthquake just this year, and with no government warnings, more are sure to die. The IMD's Seismology Department reports that there was no data indicating these earthquakes would strike simultaneously all across the Indian peninsular shield region.

As aftershocks continue to pound the region, people are being encouraged to seek shelter in parks and open areas. Emergency supplies have already begun to arrive, and it is expected that in coming days, such generosity will increase one hundred fold.

Lucita, Alonso's Niece

Lucita held little Angelina and shivered.

"Rosita, you and Alonso should have been here. The walls shook, and I didn't know this place could contain so much dust inside." She smiled, but it had frightened her very much. Her home had recently burned, and they had moved into this small furnished apartment just days before. The dust the quake had shaken from the walls was not the real issue. She **didn't** want to lose her home all over again.

Rosita reached and patted her on the hand. "I have spoken to Alonso. He called my brother, Willie. He is in Phoenix, you know." She nodded as if that told it all, and her fingers reached to play with Angelina's hair. "She is most adorable. Besides, there is the insurance, and you and Cristian will be back in a warm house of your own soon. It will take a few weeks, that is all."

"I read that it was much worse in Phoenix." Lucita's words were very quiet. She **didn't** really want to know of worse. She wanted assurance that her daughter would grow up in a world that was safe and secure. She looked away, hoping Rosita would tell that story.

"Not too much worse." Rosita smiled, then clucked her tongue at the baby. "A small piece of the roof fell from the fire station. It hit Willie's truck and smashed the front."

"Oh, Rosita!" Lucita turned, dismayed. "He must he devastated." It wasn't especially the loss of the truck that concerned the young mother. It was that the news frightened her. If a piece of roof could fall in Phoenix, then what might fall in Albuquerque? How could Angelina ever be safe?

The older woman laughed. "Willie was not upset at all. His truck was insured. He will get a new one, Lucita. He was very glad he parked it right where he did. You do not need to worry about my Willie. Nothing bad ever happens to that man."

It wasn't Willie Lucita worried about. It was Angelina. She always would worry about her daughter, and that was a feeling she hoped never went away.

Chief Mabry, Albuquerque Fire Department

Chief Mabry tossed the paper onto his desk, then turned to the filing cabinets behind him. He reached and readjusted a picture frame.

Laid out on his desk, turned to the editorial page, an article was circled in red.

"Okay, Sam, Gunnar. Give me your take on that. You guys on Engine No. 4 rescued that little girl, um," and he paused, his brow twisting in thought, "and now I can't remember her name." He tapped the side of the picture frame as the silence grew.

"Alonso's goddaughter Angelina."

The chief turned. Rodrigo. He looked at the man, and then his eyes cut to Alonso. Alonso had already given him an earful, and it sounded too much like the nonsense from this Kinkerson guy. He hadn't expected Rodrigo to speak at all. He hardly ever did.

"What's that, Rodrigo?"

Gunnar removed his baseball cap and ran his fingers through his hair nervously. "I believe him, Chief." With his hat, he motioned to the opened paper. He pawed the floor, then turned to Alonso. "Right, Al? You do, too, right?"

Alonso pursed his lips. He also kept quiet. He had said his thoughts, already.

"So, that's the way it is." Chief Mabry turned and walked to the window, a new rock sitting sourly in his stomach. He watched a yellow school bus stop and turn on its blinker. Not a school day, he thought. Must be training a new driver. Then, wishing this problem gone, he whipped around, his anger exploding from him.

"Out!" He pointed with his finger. "Out, and not a word of this to anyone. Got that?" Then, just before the door swung shut, he leaped forward and caught it, yelling into the corridor, "Not another word at the picnic next month, either. You got that? Alonso?"

They were already gone, though. Sighing, he walked back into his office and slammed the door. He threw himself into his chair, the rollers carrying him backwards into the filing cabinet. It clattered, and the framed picture on the top fell over.

Catching himself, finally finding the amusement in his infantile antics, he rolled forward and turned the newspaper to where he could see it easily. He knew it by heart, and he knew of this Kinkerson. Went by Kinky, he understood, and was looked upon as a quite good newspaperman. Had a bad spell a number of years ago, alcohol, the chief seemed to remember, but any information that escaped his pen was deemed quite reliable. That was what concerned him. This Kinkerson guy had a streak of reliability that ran all the way to hell and back again.

ANGELS IN ARIZONA
By Reinhardt Kinkerson
rkinkerson@abqjournal.com

ALBUQUERQUE – There are those of us who believe in angels, and there are those of you who don't. Just for the record, I'm writing to those who do. If you don't believe, feel free to turn the page, and head to the latest report on the Lakers' game. They'd love to have you. However, if you decide to read on, you might just find that you've changed sides. Nah, you say. Angels are for Christmas and old people when they die. Angels are for priests who are too weak to survive the real life that the rest of us are forced to endure in the workaday world.

Well, I'll tell you like it happened to me. Angels do live in the real world, and here's how I know . . .

Chief Mabry continued on, but the whole story seemed too fantastic for any sane person to believe. There was something about Kinkerson's way of telling the improbable events, though, something that made it seem as if maybe . . . just possibly there was something more to this story than met the eye. Maybe it was the naked man who fell from the sky, and that restaurant. Who could fake that? The chief had eaten there once before, and he'd checked into that after talking to Alonso. It was destroyed just as Kinkerson said. Then, what about all that other stuff that'd happened over the past few days out there in Arizona?

The chief had spoken with Old Joel, too. Someone at the

Albuquerque Journal had pointed him that way, someone named Julian. Even the old man's story matched to the nittiest detail. Not one kernel was out of place.

As the chief finished the article and slid it to the side, he pursed his lips and stood. At the window he looked out once again. The bus was still out there, and apparently it was now trying to park. He could faintly hear it beeping each time it moved backwards, but it never seemed to find its mark. It was off a little bit each time, and it would pull up to try again. Someone was in training, for sure. God help the kids if they didn't get reverse figured out. That driver'd be able to get the kids to school, but to get them home? The chief grinned. Ditch, here they come!

He turned back to the paper on his desk. There was one part in Kinkerson's story that the chief just couldn't put out of his mind. He said it was Raphael who found him in the desert. Mabry had talked to Alonso's brother-in-law, Willie. What was it Willie had told him? If he hadn't seen Kinkerson walking around, by the clothes he had on, he'd have pronounced him dead, and he would have never asked to check his pulse, either.

Chief Mabry knew his angels. He'd been raised in a parochial school. Raphael was the Angel of Healing. Why else would a newspaper reporter who wore the clothes of a dead man be walking around an accident scene unharmed? Raphael had been sent to heal him, of course. Willie had even faxed him the pictures of the truck. It had been demolished, the door torn off, and the whole thing on its side, to boot. Who could have survived that?

Chief Mabry shivered as he opened a file drawer and dropped the paper inside. If word of this ever got out, he wanted nothing to do with it. He'd never be able to attend any picnics at all.

Chapter 38

Eustorgio Ricci, Monsignor

"How is this possible, Bishop? We have no proof." The bishop had proclaimed their mission a success, but even so, Monsignor Ricci was despondent at the depths of their failure.

"You saw her, my dear Ricci. There will be no doubt in Rome that our objective has been satisfied to the Holy See's satisfaction." Bishop Carnaly leaned his head back, the First Class seat in the airplane his deserved reward for having to cut his American vacation short. "My missive is already on the way, and when we arrive, the procedures for final canonization will be underway. You will have your saint."

As soon after the devastation at the motel as they could, the emissaries from Italy had made arrangements to modify their travel plans. Everything they had brought with them had been destroyed with the motel. Natural disaster, Ricci'd told the airline. They must return home at once. The day had turned into night, and then the next morning they'd been on the way to the airport with Rome as their destination.

"But, Bishop." Monsignor Ricci was not to be so easily mollified. "We have no death certificate to show the Congregation. What if the Holy Father decides against our Cause?" It was certainly possible. Five years must pass after a person's death for canonization to be approved. Without a certificate, the waiting period might be extended indefinitely. That worried him, although that was as it always was. He always worried, especially where his candidate was involved.

"A caval donato non si guarda in bocca." *Don't look a gift horse in the mouth.* Carnaly glanced at his companion. "We have been given the news we came to seek. Your candidate no longer lives. Do you think there is a death certificate on file for every saint included in the litany?"

"I suppose not, Bishop."

Carnaly closed his eyes. He said one more thing, though, just before he breathed deeply and began to softly snore. "If your angel of the Most High God may be quoted, our mission may yet be completed, if canonization is our goal. I think he was telling us exactly what we needed to hear. She was about to die, and he needed us to be there to see it. If that's not a gift horse, I don't know what is. Don't look too closely, Ricci. Just accept God's graces when they come."

Ricci sat back in his seat, and he pulled out a leather portfolio. Opening it to one particular form, he tapped with a pen several times, and then he began to write.

Final miracle by the Blessed Angioletta (Angiola) Bacciarelli: The Blessed arrived out of nowhere to provide protection to a man, enabling him to survive the total collapse of a building. Numerous witnesses were present.

Ricci didn't note that she arrived in a car and was still alive at the time of the building's collapse. He thought that was immaterial. The woman was now dead, and already being one of the Blessed, she deserved to be made a saint. After all, she had given her life for her fellow man. What could be more saintly than that?

With a sigh, he closed the portfolio, and he slipped it into his case. He leaned his head back and closed his eyes, also. He should be so heroic sometime. All he had ever done was spend a week with Bishop Carnaly. Then, just before he dozed off, a smile grew on his face. He guessed that had been pretty heroic, after all, and now they were friends, of a sort.

His favorite moment of the entire trip? After the dust from the motel had settled, the bishop had looked over the rubble in dismay. Then, he had run to where their room had been and dug frantically.

"Bishop!" Ricci had raced after him. "What is it, Bishop?"

The bishop had stood, and holding a broken piece of wallboard in his hand, called with real pain in his voice, "Ricci, my espresso machine. I believe it may have been destroyed. What will I do when it is time for my coffee?"

Ricci had turned as if to help look for it, but it was really to hide the smile on his face. All the events that had taken place around them, and the bishop's greatest concern was for his next cup of coffee. Maybe he really was human, after all.

Chet Lawry, USA *Rapide Explorer*

"Houston, this is Chet. Jim's in back asleep. We've got a problem up here."

He reached and touched several switches on the overhead, just hoping they'd magically fix themselves, but he knew better. He also knew that hope was good for the soul, and he refused to give up on that. Jim was the one who worried about everything. It was having a wife and kids that did that to him. No one at home to worry about certainly made Chet's life easier. If he died, who was there to care? Jim was his only real friend, and if they died together, then that was the best he could hope for. He intended to see that they lived, though. Nothing was better than that.

"You guys probably picked this up at home, but I thought I'd let you know what we know. We got hit by another EMP. This was a big one. You guys may have lost a few com towers like we did. Well, Jim's been outside, and he thinks we can send. He worked on getting us reception, but he thinks it's a no-go. He's going back out when he gets rested up, and he thinks he can jerry-rig us a new antenna so we can receive.

"Hey, we're on our own out here, and we know it. We'd just like to be reassured someone at home knows what happened if our lights go out for good."

Jim would, anyway. He'd said that to Chet just before heading back to sleep. Chet didn't make that distinction over the radio, though. In fact, that's why he was sending this out while his friend still slept. This message was for Jim's wife and kids. Chet thought they ought to know, just in case.

"We can't receive anything if you radio, so if you get this message, have Skinny run outside with a flashlight and shine it up in the sky." He laughed to think that Skinny was now at Mission Control. He never thought he'd make it that high. "Make sure it's a bright one. We're a long ways away. Chet out." He reached and clicked off the machine.

There was a sound behind him, and he turned to look. It was Jim, and he was rubbing a hand over one sleepy eye.

"Um, Chet? What are you doing?" Jim still looked exhausted, and he sounded even worse. He pulled himself into the cockpit, and he sat in his chair. His eyes took in the readings, and he licked his lips, thinking for a time before whispering, "Doesn't look good, does it?" Minutes passed in silence, the mood dark. This mission might not return them home. They both knew that, now.

After quite some time, Chet cleared his throat. "I sent it for Sara, Jim. She has the right to know." He looked away. Jim really loved her. Chet knew that, even if he didn't really understand it. Jim loved Sara more than anything in the world, well, maybe except for riding in a spaceship with his best friend, Chet.

"Thanks, Chet. You're a good friend, you know. I'm glad it's you up here with me." His eyes were red. "The message? I'm glad you sent it. You're right. I should have been on the radio already."

Just then the radio crackled, and an excited voice burst into the cockpit. "Hey, Chet. It's me, Skinny. I'm sorry I took so long, but they had to come find me. They said I called you last,

526

and since you asked for me by name, I should do it again. I was down emptying the trash can in the men's room, and I had to wash my hands before they'd let me on the microphone.

"We got our ears fixed, and we just got your message. Um, Jim, sorry you had to go outside. I'd be scared if'n I were you." He chuckled, and it sounded odd over the speakers. "Hope you get all fixed up before this gets to you. Houston out." There was a scuffling sound, then there was a different noise, probably of something rubbing across the microphone head. Skinny's voice sounded distant and hollow when he spoke again. "Hey, guys. How'd I do? That was cool, huh, me talking to space."

Another voice, also hollow. "That's all, Skinny. You get back and get those johns clean. You did right good."

"Um, sir? Commander? The mike's still live." Yet another voice, a female one. Then there was a click, and the cabin was silent.

Chet took the time to breathe deeply for a minute, his eyes searching the overhead displays. He was surprised to see every single one up and running perfectly, the numbers right on the money. "Jim?" Chet glanced over, and then he chuckled. Before he could speak, it grew into a laugh. "I guess someone loves us. Everything's running as normal, except that exhaust sensor. It's still a trifle cold."

Jim's face was twisted with emotion, though. "Maybe I'll get to see Sara and the kids again after all. I knew we weren't about to *crash*, for God's sake, but there have been entirely too many anomalies aboard this mission. For this one to clear up on its own is something I really needed."

Chet was surprised at his feelings, too. The spontaneous laughter. He guessed he did care after all. Maybe he did want to get home. Maybe what he needed was a Sara of his own, one who would care when potential problems arose.

Jim reached beside his seat, rumbling around for something, and finally he glanced at Chet. "Want to celebrate?" He hefted a package of banana pudding. "My treat."

Chet laughed. "Sure. Let's celebrate. We're going to live to get home, if it's the last thing we do."

Interlude 31

Just on the other side of the spacecraft's exterior metal wall, a nearly invisible hand held the antenna firmly while another nearly invisible hand attached it securely, completing its repairs. A voice that wasn't really there chuckled, and within minutes had crawled back to the ship's exhaust port, barely corporeal in the flaring exhaust. This was the only way to travel to Io. It was warm and toasty all the way. If a brother had to make a repair once and again, it was worth it, just to jump the volcanic vents on lovely, lovely Io.

Jeremiel, Presider over Souls Awaiting Resurrection

Jeremiel's wings snapped wide, the feathers at the edges catching the currents, as he braked for a landing. The desert air was clear, and the evening's heat felt good on his skin. In spite of the warmth, there were no hints of pleasantries on his brooding face. His dark stare swept the landscape, and he knew exactly what had happened in this place.

Clapping his hands together, the flash of corporeal disharmony energy transference that told of his wings disappearing washed the broken desert floor. It was broken, too, for a great crater ate into the soil, and what it had consumed was blasted into ragged piles around its perimeter. Military tape and fencing cordoned off the entire area, although that was no deterrent to a brother with wings and the ability to fade from human sight.

There was no one about anywhere, and several strips of the tape were broken. They flapped loosely in the breeze, suggesting that time had taken its toll, that their usefulness had perhaps passed, and it was time for the world to move on. Jeremiel knew just how much time had passed, too. Ten Earth-days. *Ten!* When Ranier had finally thought to dribble a spoonful of soup in the "angel's" mouth, the ship was already approaching port. That had been enough to rouse Jeremiel, and after several bowlfuls, his body had taken on a new feeling of potency, his sudden transformation surprising poor Ranier.

Jeremiel had remembered immediately what had happened, that his part in the battle with the Four Familiars had yet to be rejoined. He knew and was dismayed. Ranier told of the week and a half that had passed, and urgency had overtaken the brother's heart, demanding that he be gone from that place.

Impressing his strongest Suggestions that he be forgotten, remembered only as an oddly vague part of an unusual voyage, a visitor who was no more than the ghost of a dream, he forsook his benefactors, and on wing, he searched for his companions, those brothers he had forged an allegiance with in the Bonding of Those with a Common Goal.

To Jeremiel's chagrin, in his ten days of stupor, they had shifted just enough out of phase with him that as much as he called, there was no sense of being heard. He didn't even know if they'd survived, or whether they'd left to return to the Unity.

"Ramiel," he called into the sky. "Are you watching? Chitar. Gupat. Was the battle waged fairly?" He knew better. There was nothing fair about the Four Familiars being released upon Earth. He called again, lifting his arms into the air, his voice elevated loudly, "Is anyone up there? Or, am I all alone down here?" He turned, looking to all corners of the sky, and when he dropped his eyes, he was surprised to see someone he knew very well.

"Feel better now?" It was Kafziel, and he was neatly dressed in a cream-colored summer suit with loafers on his feet. Except for the enormous wings opened at his back, he could have stepped off a fashion show runway. His hair was swept back, and he was indeed as beautiful as his reputation called him out to be. "I have a proposition for you, Brother." He smiled, and his face carried a look that was clear and honest.

Jeremiel took that for what it was worth. In Kafziel's world, nothing was clear and honest. "You were here for this?" He motioned with his hand, its sweep indicating all the damage spread before them.

"For this?" Kafziel's eyes narrowed. Then, his face relaxed into a confident smile. "Ah, the final page in Gabriel's little story." He turned, his wings obscuring his face, and he motioned with a hand for Jeremiel to step forward and join him. When he did, the finely dressed brother smiled and motioned again, pointing out several places, all of which looked very much the same.

"There, Jeremiel. See that place? Strength had his horns broken there. And over there," he pointed a different direction, "Swiftness fell to the ground, defeated. Even Nobility and Wisdom couldn't withstand the total power of your Circle of Brothers. Gabriel was magnificent!"

"You were here, then." Jeremiel didn't trust Kafziel's words. Still, he had been accepted as an ally, if temporarily, and that meant something. At least he hoped it did.

"You cannot doubt me, my brother." Kafziel smiled convincingly, and standing there, with his hair catching the breeze and the wind ruffling his feathers, he looked the part of every angel the humans on this world had ever drawn in their holy books. "Come, you must need sustenance. I have a place I know."

Jeremiel sighed. He realized his limited options, and in that moment, he made a decision and nodded. "Our alliance is temporary, Kafziel. I promise nothing to you."

Kafziel laughed, and it was light and pleasant. "Of course not, my dear Jeremiel. I have nothing I wish from you, other than to see that you receive whatever help I can give."

Jeremiel doubted that, but what else could he do?

Chapter 39

The Litany of the Saints

"Lord, have mercy on us." At the front of the great cathedral, the words of the Litany of the Saints rang out. It was in Bishop Carnaly's voice, too.

Out in the midst of the people, Monsignor Ricci sat with a handful of the sisters from the convent. Even to have this many present had required a special dispensation of the Holy See, and those who had been allowed to come felt honored. Their voices joined in with the appropriate response.

"*Lord, have mercy on us.*"

"Christ, have mercy on us," the bishop intoned.

The response was returned, "*Christ, have mercy on us.*"

"Christ, hear us."

Dutifully returned, "*Christ, graciously hear us.*"

The names of the Godhead were called next, although they used the term Holy Trinity instead of Triune Mind. Instead of naming the Planner, the Rememberer, and the Executor, the Litany expressed the names of God as the Father, the Son, and the Holy Spirit. They were the same, though, no matter what names they were given.

After that, a very long series of names was called, one for

531

each of the saints, and after each one, the people intoned, "*Pray for us.*" When the list of names began to grow long, those sitting with Monsignor Ricci grew giddy. The Litany finally approached the one name they had come to hear. Even the priest felt a moment of anticipation, for one name among the rest was special to them. It would be spoken in the Litany for the very first time, and they were gathered to participate in its glorious introduction to all those who didn't know the story.

In the Litany of the Saints, all women who had been canonized were named in the final group. As soon as Bishop Carnaly called the name of Saint Clare, the next-to-last saint, and the people intoned their response, he paused. He certainly could not speak any words of special praise for Angiola, their newest saint, but he did what he could. He cleared his throat and glanced at the monsignor and the nuns who sat with him. Then, he smiled. After a moment, he spoke the words they waited with bated breath to hear.

"Saint Angiola."

The sisters beamed as they responded much more loudly than precisely necessary, "*Pray for us.*"

The Litany went on, moving past the list of saints, but for the sisters of the convent, from that point on, the rest of the Litany was mumbled by rote. They had heard what they came to hear, and it was more glorious than they had dreamed. They could hardly wait to return and tell sweet Angiola's other mothers just how special this moment had been. Christ had smiled on them and their little convent.

One of the sisters sitting there was brought to tears, and she couldn't repeat the rest of the responses. She was the one who had given Angioletta her new name, for she was the one who had loved her daughter enough to give her up. It had been the only way to keep her, but it hadn't stopped her from loving the child more than any other mother Angioletta had.

Malak, Wolf

The sun was down, and the Arizona desert was still and

532

quiet. A gentle breeze stirred now and again, but its cooling effects weren't really necessary. Darkness had reigned for hours, and the air had grown chilled. Under a full moon, cacti raised tall arms into the sky, and the shadowed silhouette of the distant mountains broke the line between land and sky.

West of Phoenix, just off the highway known as I-10, where the motel had once stood, only rubble remained. Insurance adjusters had come by, and they had shaken their heads, but the checks were still "in the mail." When would cleanup start? No one had any idea. When the wind breathed, scraps of paper danced to this side of the parking lot, and when they tired of being there, they danced the other direction, playing gaily along the way, biding their time until they could return.

Among them stepped four furred paws. A wolf's snout, one just slightly larger than normal, and attached to a body that seemed too big to be a regular wolf, sniffed the air. There was something there, if only it could find it. Then, sensing a trail, a remnant of a pheromone, the animal turned its yellow eyes to the west. It had found what it needed, and it knew the way to go.

Malak raised a furred head to the sky, and a small shifting of the air ruffled the tips of the canine's fur. That shifting told Malak more than all the satellite photos of man could ever show. Uriel had been found, or at least Malak now knew the direction to look. Aiming its snout at the moon, that other-worldly howl that all wolves knew so well lifting into the air, Malak called for Uriel. It was time to go to him.

Four pawed feet stirred into a patterned trot, and Malak headed westward across the desert. The familiar's master was out there somewhere. Malak would find him. They would be together again, for a brother and his second were inseparable. Not even a war instigated by the brothers of the Unity could keep them apart.

Angioletta Bacciarelli, Daughter of the Unity

Lights could be seen coming down the highway. They were

the first in a very long time. Angioletta now wore jeans and a denim top. The shirt was decorated with rhinestones, and a colorful flower was sewn onto the back. She had pink sneakers, although she didn't think she'd ever worn pink her entire life. But then, when one's clothing store was someone's backyard clothesline, one took what was available.

Uriel had on white coveralls, although they were hardly white any longer. One leg had a rip in the fabric, and in the darkness, his skin showed through. He had found a hat somewhere, and he incessantly kept it pulled down over his eyes. It had a brim all around, and it made him seem very bohemian. His mane of hair was tied at the nape of his neck, and when they were around other people, he kept it tucked out of sight in his coveralls.

They were a couple on the run. From just exactly what, she didn't know. Uriel hadn't even dared to call his wolf. There were those who might trace him if he did. Malak would have to find them on his own. The animal could. When asked, Uriel simply told her that he had faith in his second.

Angioletta hadn't understood that, either. At his side, she had come to trust this man, and she knew one thing. She would run with him to the ends of the earth. Her home? She remembered Los Angeles, but that seemed a dream she'd had long ago. She'd held a job in that dream, teaching, she recalled. She had no home, now. She had only Uriel. He had that effect on her, he and his vanilla skin.

As the lights grew closer, she jumped to the edge of the road and waved her hands up and down. She leaped away as the lights, a big-rig, barreled on past. Turning, disappointed, she watched it go on down the highway for a bit before the brake lights suddenly flashed on.

"Uriel," she called, excited. "It's stopping. We've got a ride."

"Let's go." He waved a hand, and together they ran the direction of the big truck. They went first to the driver's side and waved. When the window rolled down, Uriel called up, "How far are you going?"

"Got some stops west aways. Maybe on from there. Gets

534

lonely traveling alone. Saw your girl back there, and I thought she, um, that you two might keep me some company."

"We'd love to!" Angioletta laughed, and she felt bright and unaccountably happy. As they ran to the opposite side, she slapped Uriel on the arm. "I can't believe he's taking us along. Truckers never do that anymore."

Climbing aboard, Angioletta first, they settled in, and Uriel reached to shake hands.

"Uri. This is Angie. Man, this is the sweetest ride. You don't know how much we appreciate this." He smiled, although his hat remained low over his face.

The driver glanced at the gloved hand, and he frowned for a moment. Then, his face relaxed, and he reached to shake with a smile. "Grover. After my gramps. Glad to have you along. You going all the way?"

"As far as your rig'll take us."

As the truck with its heavy load started to move, the engine roared, accepting the changing of the gears only when the driver forced it to submit. In the near darkness of the enclosed space, Angioletta leaned into the crook of Uriel's arm, resting her back against his side. She didn't know how long this ride would last, but with Uriel at her side, she was on board until the very end.

Uriel, Bearer of Destiny

Uriel wondered when Angioletta would figure it out. The trucker never questioned why his two hitchhikers glowed wherever their skin was exposed. Uriel's Suggestion had pushed those thoughts far away before they could even be spoken, just as soon as he'd seen the massive vehicle coming down the road.

Of course, he'd had to Suggest that the driver stop in the first place, but that hadn't been so hard. Uriel was a brother of the Unity, and for brothers of the Unity, such things were very easy, indeed.

www.ingramcontent.com/pod-product-compliance
Lightning Source LLC
Chambersburg PA
CBHW071336020726
47502CB00001B/109